The Long Journey

Revised Edition

a redemption story

by

robert luis rabello

This book is a work of fiction. All of the names, characters and incidences are either a product of the author's imagination, or are used fictitiously. Any resemblance to actual events, locales or persons, living or dead, is strictly coincidental.

© 2006 by robert luis rabello. All rights reserved.

No part of this book may be reproduced, stored in a retrieval system, or transmitted by any means, electronic, mechanical, photocopying, recording or otherwise, without written permission from the author.

ISBN: 1-4196-8286-5 (softcover)
ISBN: 1-4196-8320-9 (hardcover)

Cover art by Pamala Harrison

27jewel@bellsouth.net

I would like to thank Tim Polmear for helping me understand how to lay out this book's cover.

This book is dedicated to the glory of God,
and to my sister, Leilane:

*You are the beat of my heart,
the breath of my soul*

robert luis rabello

Sardis, British Columbia
July 2006

Acknowledgments

No creative work of this magnitude comes to life in a vacuum. I am grateful for the patient and consistent help of my previewing readers.

I would like to thank my colleague, Kelly Schmalcel, whose fearless commentary sharpened my focus in the affective realm, kept me honest about my characters, and encouraged my aspiration toward excellence.

Alan Petrillo, a veteran whose knowledge of the minutiae of military life has solidified my story into something a warrior can read without suspending too much disbelief, is primarily responsible for transforming my ideas about soldiering in the Tamarian army from rough outlines into finely tuned concepts. I've appreciated the ongoing and selfless dialogue he's maintained with me concerning all aspects of my work.

To Julian Gray, whose expertise in psychology has proven invaluable as I've processed how my characters respond to the events in the narrative, I offer my sincere appreciation. Julian also has an excellent eye for grammatical and syntactic errors, which has made final proofreading and editing far easier than it would have been without his sharp analysis. Thanks also to Julian's wife, Annette, whose advice and guidance on map creation will make the story easier for every reader to follow and understand.

And finally, to Shannon Ward, who was a complete stranger to me when I approached her for assistance. I express sincere gratitude that she took time out of her busy life to assess and comment on my story. I have been affirmed and challenged by every word she's written. Thank you!

More information on the author and the milieu of Devera, including character images and full color maps, can be found by visiting the New Adventure web site:

www.newadventure.ca

The Republic of Tamaria

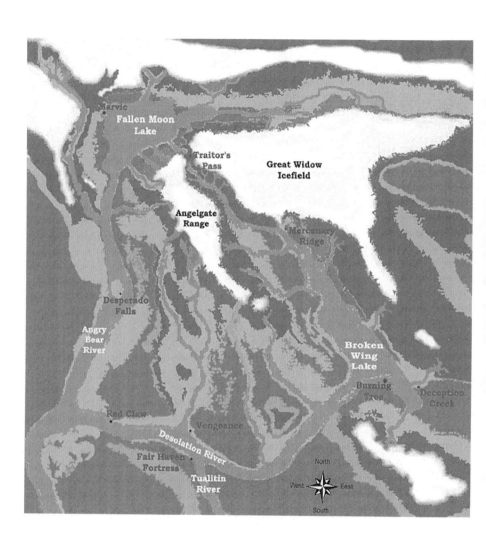

The Frontier of Northeast Kameron

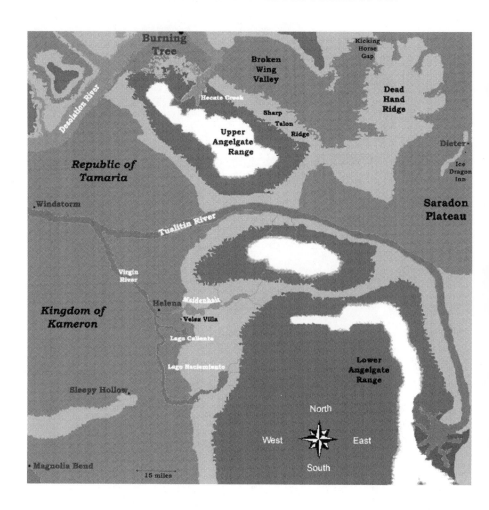

Betrayal

Kindness betrayed them. Their gentle tones of voice, expressions forever bordering on a smile, and the subtle and soft glisten of longing gazes proclaimed their compassion in a compelling manner. They did not touch in public, yet often sat close enough that only a paper leaf could pass between their shoulders. Never did they refer to one another in terms of endearment, preferring first names spoken in Southern Vulgate, a tongue native to neither, but one they both understood.

Hearing the girl's meek voice speaking the enemy's language might have aroused the rightful suspicion of many Tamarian citizens. However, the dark-haired maiden looked nothing like the fair daughters born within the high, alpine valleys, along rushing rivers or bright, glacial lakes, and because of this fact, native Tamarians extended her a measure of linguistic grace, even as their eyes narrowed and suspicions arose. Yet as long as she accompanied the young soldier of whom she'd become so fond, the common contempt reserved for tourists, exchange students, enemies and other undesirable aliens remained unspoken.

Still, people stared. Natives whispered to one another in phrases just above the hearing threshold, so that their displeasure might be accurately perceived, only to stop or avert their eyes if the pretty girl glanced away from her companion.

The young soldier sensed this ever-present tension. No action on his part could amend the low regard his countrymen held for visitors in general, and Lithians, like the girl sitting next to him, in particular. He'd learned that with time, most people set aside their initial scorn for an attitude approaching tolerance, but resolutely far from full acceptance. The girl seemed unable to merit respect.

However, most of the warriors from his former unit had grown quite fond of her, not simply because she looked lovely–for that reaction often constituted a large part of anyone's initial response–but for the civility with which she, a wealthy warlord's eldest daughter, regarded even the poorest among them. The foreign girl earned their trust with consistent benevolence and clear forgiveness over her initial mistreatment. They didn't know that she'd only been able to muster such grace by spending time in prayer. Yet her petitions to God changed nothing in other people; by praying she became changed.

The Lithian girl had proven her worth during combat. She seemed utterly fearless and never hesitated to lend medical aid to a

The Long Journey: *Betrayal*

stricken soldier, even if he'd fallen under direct enemy fire. Such bravery earned this foreign mercenary the right to wear four silver lions, coveted citations for valor worn on the left collar of her dress uniform that testified of her exploits. The medals could not explain how faith inspired her calm demeanor, but secular soldiers didn't concern themselves with the religious explanations she offered. Though they privately scoffed at her faith, every warrior wanted her nearby when the shooting started. Edgy infantrymen sought her comfort after combat, while their sergeants developed confidence that whenever she accompanied them into battle, the fight would follow in their favor.

Nonetheless, few Tamarians beyond this intimate circle of soldiers extended any kindness further than basic courtesy toward her. The bond between her and the young, grey-eyed veteran sitting at her right hand could not easily be concealed, despite their mutual effort, and the relationship itself, though it should have been lauded for its chaste and noble selflessness, inspired deep disdain instead.

Private Garrick Ravenwood, now on a civilian train taking him northward to Officer's Training School in the Tamarian capital, reflected on the latest incidents underscoring the division his culture wished to impose between him and Brenna Velez, the girl he loved.

The week after Garrick's birthday, the Tamarian Defense Force finally succeeded in pushing an invading horde from the far south–the dreaded Azgaril Northern Liberation Army–across the Tualitin River, Tamaria's southern border. After months of fierce winter combat, Garrick's unit rotated for a deserved rest to the sprawling military base adjacent to the ancient city of Burning Tree, located along the western shore of Broken Wing Lake.

Winter's fading influence lingered on a landscape where spring remained a whispered promise. Brown grasses, flattened by snowfall, lay exposed along the lakeshore. Storm-driven waves pounded the graveled beach and the resulting spray flew on the wings of wintry wind, coating three-foot thick walls with fine mist until the dull, plastered finish gleamed in even the weakest light. Naked tree limbs reached into the endless cold rain descending from an overcast sky.

Not a soul lingered on the wide avenues, nor did the crowds that casually mingled on fairer days near military monuments appear. The base lay empty, save for its skeletal staff, awaiting battle-weary warriors returning in gradually increasing numbers from the southeastern front.

The Long Journey: *Betrayal*

Thus the compound appeared graveyard silent to the young couple whose scandalous love simmered in secret.

During the long train ride around the lofty Angelgate Mountains to Burning Tree, Sergeant Harold Krebes, under whose leadership Garrick had served during the war, wrote a commendation letter concerning the young soldier to their platoon commander, First Lieutenant Oskar Kohler. This officer, awaiting final approval of a battlefield promotion, subsequently summoned Garrick into his untidy office several days after their arrival.

The lingering, musty aroma enclosed by windows shut tight against the cold didn't seem to bother Lieutenant Kohler at all. Garrick eyed the file folders littering his commander's desk, the partially eaten lunch lingering on a side table, stepped over an ammunition box filled with scented letters from Lieutenant Kohler's fiancee and stood at attention, out of custom more than respect.

"Before you get too comfortable here," the lieutenant began, "I'm recommending that you transfer out of my unit."

Garrick felt panic surge in his soul. "Why?" he queried, struggling to control the emotion evident in his response.

"Sergeant Krebes has been watching you, soldier. He sees that you're a natural leader, and I agree with his assessment. I'm sending you to OTS in Marvic."

"Thank you, sir." Garrick responded, somewhat, though not entirely, relieved. Being an officer merited better pay and prestige in an army that consistently rewarded effective leadership. Garrick, who earned a gold lion for his own combat exploits, felt grateful that he'd been found worthy of this honor.

A long silence followed, during which the lieutenant carefully considered a change in his discourse. "But, before you go, there's one more thing. I don't think you'll like hearing what I have to say, but I'm going to tell you, anyway."

Garrick constrained his worry. "I'm listening, sir."

"Take this as good advice from someone who knows how skilled a soldier you've become. Your career will never move forward as long as you maintain such cordial relations with a *foreign courtesan*."

The young soldier flushed. "Sir, how can you say that? Everyone loves Brenna! She's upheld high standards of moral conduct while serving in this unit, and you know that!"

The Long Journey: *Betrayal*

Lieutenant Kohler glanced at the young woman's file, smiling as he recalled his first encounter with her, but he did not back down. "I'm not disputing her character. I'm offering you a dose of reality, soldier. What everyone else believes about the girl is far more important than whatever it is you think. As long as the two of you cling to each other, whispering like a pair of insurgents, your career will go nowhere."

"She's not the enemy, sir. You of all people should know that by now."

"Mark my words, Ravenwood. No one cares that your little friend is still a virgin. She's a foreigner. She's Lithian, and few of us hold those people in high esteem. Listen to me and find yourself a nice, Tamarian girl. You have a bright future in this army. If you make it through OTS, you can take your pick from the best of them!"

Garrick seethed at the injustice, feeling powerless. "Your views are noted, sir," he replied, struggling to keep his voice steady and only barely managing to do so.

"Good! You'll see the light." Lieutenant Kohler returned Garrick's salute. "Pick up your ferry and train passes from my adjutant. You're dismissed."

Garrick left the office in a foul mood. The harmonic, polyphonic interchange of an ancient melody soothed his soul and drew him toward the base chapel, where he found Brenna practicing one of her favorite compositions on the pipe organ. Something in her muted delight softened his demeanor to the extent that he couldn't summon the courage to tell her everything his lieutenant had said.

An hour later, they braved the wind driven rain and scurried across the empty base to a nearly deserted wharf, arriving–cold and wet–at a closed ticket counter. A small, paddle-wheeled steamer ominously named *Queen of Deception Creek* lay silent at her berth, buffeted by the billows rolling down from the north; her double stacks remained void of any rising heat that might suggest a boiler ready to work against the waves.

The two friends sought shelter beneath a covered porch, relieved to remove their heavy packs. Brenna felt cold, and Garrick, taking pity on her, zipped his waterproof poncho together with hers and huddled close. They sat with their backs to the wind until an employee spotted them, checked their passes, and out of forced courtesy offered shelter inside the building.

The Long Journey: *Betrayal*

"Everyone has to wait until this wind dies down," the skinny man remarked, posturing to improve his view of Brenna's softer features when the young couple took off their ponchos. "No sense in trying to cross if we'll only wind up at the bottom of the lake!"

Garrick found no humor in the remark. Brenna ignored the man, settling with her handsome soldier onto a quickly vacated bench in a gloomy, stuffy room. Five other travelers–two of whom had moved away to permit the young couple room to sit–lifted their eyes, a few of them grunting a half-hearted greeting. A small boy prattled restlessly, standing on his toes to gaze outside, not understanding why he and his mother couldn't board the ferry **right now**.

A kindly old woman approached and offered the young couple a printed religious tract. Garrick knew that it outlined the supposed benefits of adhering to rigorous meditation, of respect for local spirits, of transcendent holiness attained by denial of desire. The young soldier politely, but firmly, declined. He steadfastly held to his own, eclectic and rational view, and knew that Brenna, who couldn't read the Tamarian language and devoutly believed in only one God anyway, wouldn't find a treatise on pantheistic musings particularly interesting.

Hours later, long after any discussion among the passengers had faded into languid silence, the wind and waves slackened. With black smoke belching from its twin stacks, the paddle wheeler's boiler coughed to life. The small boy pointed and jumped up and down with delight, calling his weary mother to the window, then repeating the same question he'd asked 137 times since Garrick and Brenna arrived: "Can we go now?"

At this stage in her career, the *Queen of Deception Creek* had worked the waters of Broken Wing Lake for nearly thirty years, and her battered condition attested to rough but faithful service. Crafted from fir and powered by twin, triple-expansion steam engines, she measured 150 feet from stem to stern. Fully laden, this vessel could carry as much as 200 tons of cargo, usually iron and copper scrap destined for the recycling foundries at Burning Tree, or Vengeance on the Desolation River; bauxite for the big aluminum smelters in Marvic, or seasonal fruit shipped to more distant markets linked by rail.

Garrick led Brenna up to the dining saloon, a large room with cafeteria-style services and forward-facing windows. They sat together, taking no particular notice of anyone else when a middle-aged steward approached the young couple, his face brimming with apprehension.

The Long Journey: *Betrayal*

"I'm sorry," he said to Garrick in a whisper. "We don't serve her kind in the saloon. She'll have to eat downstairs, in the cargo area."

"Then what kind do you serve?" Garrick inquired, not bothering to lower his voice.

The veneer of feigned courtesy vanished from the steward's face. "You know very well what I mean, young man," he replied in a menacing tone.

Brenna closed her eyes and muttered a brief and frustrated prayer; her words inaudible as breath streamed through drawn lips in a plea for freedom from this kind of humiliation, or at least, the grace to overlook such a callous affront. She stood and gestured for Garrick to follow, understanding the steward's intent, if not the words he uttered. "Let's go," she whispered, knowing that Garrick, who sincerely loved her, brokered little tolerance for the steward's attitude. Wisdom informed her milder response, for though the indignation of her younger friend represented high principle, Brenna realized that nothing could be gained from escalating the conflict further.

Garrick arose slowly and glared directly into the steward's eyes. He sniffed, then wrinkled his face as if inhaling something foul. "I hate the smell of your kind," he sneered. After uttering that remark, the young soldier walked away, fantasizing about how satisfying it would feel to slam his left fist into the steward's smug face. The vessel shuddered as its steam engines began turning the aged stern wheel. As they approached a staircase, Garrick turned toward Brenna and said: "I'm sorry about that."

"Sorry about what?" she replied, her dark blue eyes innocent, imploring, "You feel bad about what the rude man said, or do you regret your equally impudent response to him?"

Sometimes Garrick wondered why Brenna objected so strongly to his protection of her honor and felt mildly hurt by her rebuke. "I'm only trying to defend you," he said, suppressing a more biting remark that urged expression.

She smiled, pleased beyond words with the strength of his character. "I need you to love me, not defend me," she responded. "You know full well that I can take care of myself." Then, glancing furtively around to ensure they were not being watched, she placed her right hand behind his head, lacing her fingers through his wavy blonde hair, leaned up and planted a brief kiss on his lips.

The Long Journey: *Betrayal*

Garrick felt his wrath melt away, replaced by a surge of desire that he struggled to control. He let his fingers slide down her arm and linger for a moment on the back of her hand. "I don't know how you can stand being mistreated," he told her. "I don't know where you find strength to put up with it."

Brenna raised her eyebrows, laughing lightly. "I pray," she said. "I pray a lot!"

In truth, though she never complained, this ongoing reproach hurt Brenna badly. Raised in an affluent family where she'd always felt love and unconditional acceptance, Brenna had never endured systemic prejudice prior to arriving as a refugee in Tamaria. Exposure to unearned loathing came as a shock, at least initially.

Handsome and well-regarded Garrick moved among his own people with ease, yet ironically, his pleasant company increased her exposure to bigotry. Brenna admired his social grace and longed for him deeply, resolving to forgive any prejudicial offense his countrymen committed. Additionally, her personality preferred avoiding conflict altogether. Compounding this natural reticence, the Lithian girl aspired to protect her favored warrior from the social consequences arising whenever they encountered discrimination. Thus, she remained quick to overlook any trespass and willing to comply with every demand for segregation these Tamarian natives imposed on her.

Garrick disagreed. Long ago the Tamarians fought a lengthy, bloody war to rid themselves of oppression. They'd overthrown the brutal reign of giant kings, proclaiming liberty with their victory, yet enslaved themselves in ignorance, religious superstition and mistrust. In Garrick's mind, Tamaria would never be completely free until she buried the chains of intolerance and jingoism.

Confined to the cargo bay, where open portholes provided both a view and a means for cold air to flood the compartment, Garrick and Brenna searched for shelter. Near the bow, in front of the boiler room, they found a dry spot where sweet-smelling, recently cut hay bales from a warmer clime had been loaded for transport. Heat from the wood-fired boiler radiated into their space, inspiring the young couple to remove their winter parkas, spreading them out to dry on a nearby bale. The damp freshness of the lake, the aroma of warm hay, the familiar, comforting scent of their close proximity mingled with traces of wood smoke drifting through the open porthole, creating a safe and pleasant refuge like a secret childhood hiding place. They shared memories–he

The Long Journey: *Betrayal*

of his younger, twin siblings, and she of her three younger sisters–until they became hungry. At that point, Garrick mustered courage to brave the galley and inquire for some food.

He returned a few minutes later, finding Brenna deeply involved in her daily hair combing ritual. She always began over her right eye, very gently and slowly pulling the comb through the top of her raven locks, distributing the preserving oils from her scalp through the ends of her waist length hair with increasingly rapid strokes. Garrick loved the way light played over her tresses as she combed, the deep base color reflecting grey highlights as she separated a long braid strand with her left hand and methodically stroked the comb all the way down to its ends. He lingered quietly for a moment, watching as she moved further back behind her head, pulling a handful of hair over her shoulder. Brenna quietly murmured an old hymn while her body swayed slowly and gently in a worshipful rhythm. This ordinary act displayed docile, comforting femininity, a part of her that seemed delicate, strangely exotic, and yet familiar as daybreak.

When she paused, noting his presence and wondering why he simply stood there without saying anything, Garrick revealed his provisions. "I bought some fresh bread and cheese," he told her. "The guys in the galley had better manners than the steward. They also gave us some raisins, and a jar of apple juice."

The *Queen of Deception Creek* leisurely crossed the 25-mile distance to the far shore of Broken Wing Lake at an angle that took the vessel toward the southeast. Garrick became quiet and reached for Brenna's hand as the ferry neared the shore, an indication, she'd learned, that something troubled him.

Brenna waited for him to speak, but he didn't.

Evening approached as the ferry docked along the eastern lakeshore. Here, placid water reflected dark images of the towering, snow-clad Copperhead ridge line. One prominent peak, known locally as the Necromancer, loomed high above the tiny village where Deception Creek spread its lively, rippling waves into the glassy lake surface.

The train that should have taken Garrick and Brenna northward had already departed, forcing them to wait until early morning. Initially, Garrick seemed strangely reluctant to leave the station, but Brenna felt hemmed in and wanted to walk. In the absence of the ever-ubiquitous wind, outside air felt cool and pleasant, scented with pine oil, fragrant with wood smoke and burning incense. A few other warriors, heading

The Long Journey: *Betrayal*

home for leave, along with pilgrims traveling to the sacred Temple Elsbireth in Marvic, moved through the small town streets looking for refreshment and amusement. Native townsfolk milled about, some hawking their textiles and handmade jewelry, others gathered in small groups around scattered tables playing cards or socializing. A lamplighter worked the gas petcock and ignited a streetlight, smiling from his high perch at friends and neighbors, inquiring of their health and prosperity. Many people recognized Garrick, but the reception he received from them–while polite–seemed somewhat unfriendly.

Fiddle music wafted from a nearby tavern. Drawn there by the lively sound, Garrick and Brenna stood listening outside when a group of older, veteran soldiers walked by. One noted the young couple and tersely inquired why Garrick and his foreign companion were attired in combat uniforms.

Garrick stiffened respectfully, explaining that he was en route to Marvic for Officer Training School.

"You?" the thick-limbed master sergeant inquired, incredulously. Embroidered, cloth versions of their valor citations had caught his eye and raised personal misgivings. "You're just a boy! And she looks like she ought to be at home with mommy. What's going on?"

When Garrick related that he had fired the first shot against the invading Azgaril, the veterans laughed. As his story unfolded, however, the other soldiers grew intrigued, listening with increasing wonder. The young warrior described unfolding events in vivid detail he could not have known apart from personal experience. He revealed that Brenna had served in the medical corps of his unit, but avoided any mention of their commendations for bravery.

These older men had been deployed in the hills above Sutherlind, overlooking the great Saradon plateau. Heavy casualties had characterized the conflict in that region, and two of these soldiers remembered hearing stories about a lovely, long-haired Lithian nurse with mysterious healing power working at a firebase on Dead Hand Ridge. The fact that the very girl responsible for saving many lives actually stood before them gave further credence to Garrick's testimony, though they openly questioned how such a young-looking couple had seen action in the war.

Interested in hearing more from the young officer candidate, the older veterans invited the two friends to exchange anecdotes and enjoy a few beers in their company. Garrick shrugged. His father struggled

The Long Journey: *Betrayal*

with alcohol, and he didn't want to develop his father's problem. "I don't drink," he said, "but let's go inside. I'd like to hear your stories."

Brenna followed, smiling politely but offering no comment. As they entered the nearly empty pub, its proprietor warmly welcomed the prospect of new business. One of the soldiers bought Brenna a glass of sweet mead, which she accepted with gratitude and sipped ever so slowly, but she declined a subsequent offer to dance. Since Brenna could speak very little of their language, the men said nothing more to her.

Garrick drank apple juice mixed with soda water, even when the evening turned dark and the warriors' recollections blurred in alcoholic haze. He thrived in the spotlight of their attention, controlling the ebb and flow of storytelling with questions, quick-witted additions to the bawdy jokes each soldier exchanged, as well as anecdotes of his own. Garrick's skill in conversation ensured that the evening remained an engaging experience; he employed a charisma so natural the older men willingly followed his lead.

Very late that night, the couple bade their new friends farewell and Garrick fell into silence again. Since neither of them had enough money to pay for a place to sleep, they returned to the train station and settled on separate benches for rest, using their knapsacks as pillows. Other travelers, who had done the same, already lay fast asleep. In this quiet space, where rhythmic breathing prevailed as the dominant sound and Garrick's troubles remained unspoken, Brenna approached, knelt next to her friend and finally implored: "Garrick, please tell me what's bothering you."

The young soldier didn't answer right away, but reached for her right hand and squeezed it in affirmation. "This is my hometown," he admitted. "My family's orchard overlooks the lake, a few miles up Deception Creek. Everyone who lives here knows me, and my family has a rather unflattering reputation." The young warrior paused for a long time, thinking. "I'm worried about my brother and sister. I haven't seen them in more than three years and I wonder if they're ok."

"Also, my dad should have pruned all the trees by now. That's a big job, and this has been the second year in a row I've not been there to help him."

Brenna knew that Garrick had left his father's farm in fear and disgrace. This train station, she realized, must have been the first stop on the trip where he'd smuggled his frightened younger siblings toward safety in Marvic. His return to the town where he'd betrayed his own

The Long Journey: *Betrayal*

father likely brought vivid and unsettling memories to mind. She knew Garrick didn't touch alcohol because he'd seen Cyrus, his father, drink too much, and watched in deepening despair as the man he loved and admired steadily lost control of his life.

"I'll pray for you," she promised.

Garrick sat up. "Thank you," he replied. "But if you're gonna go through the trouble, can you remember my parents and siblings too?"

Brenna nodded, touched by the endearing vulnerability he shared only with her. "I will," she assured, though when she prayed she did so privately, because he didn't share her faith.

After this, she lay quietly on the hard bench, fingering the sacred blessing from a Lithian psalm delicately engraved upon an enchanted silver and turquoise locket. It had been given to her by her trusted friend, Woodwind. The locket opened with a whispered word, revealing her own, three-dimensional image, softly illuminated in dark blue light by an obscure charm Brenna appreciated, but didn't fully understand.

The day after her arrival at the Burning Tree compound, Woodwind's frustrating, second search for her ended. They'd talked in private and at length, mostly about their wartime experiences and respective plans, never venturing to discuss the important issue that separated the two of them. She returned the sword he'd lent to her, insisting that he take it, and asked him to deliver a letter she'd written to her parents. Woodwind gave her the enchanted locket containing her portrait, a trinket he'd carried with him for many months. The engraved blessing spoke of Allfather's protection, yet every time she considered it since their departure, these words reminded her of Woodwind.

"I will always love you," he said in farewell.

"And I remain your friend forever," she replied.

She remembered Woodwind's brave smile, but his expression revealed the bittersweet pain of unrequited love. Brenna could not bring herself to heal that hurt; yet strangely, in the darkness of the train station, she felt a pang in her heart, wondering if she would ever see him again. Brenna longed for a private place to pray. A whispered phrase welling up from within her wounded spirit among strangers would simply not suffice. She desperately needed seclusion to pray.

As dawn encroached upon the lakeside train station, a Model 12 steam locomotive rumbled slowly down the tracks. This elegant machine, one of Tamaria's "pure" steam designs, far outnumbered the newer, more efficient vapor-electric hybrid and pure electric engines

The Long Journey: *Betrayal*

working the rail lines across the nation. A pair of radial steam expanders powered this uniquely Tamarian locomotive. Each expander consisted of a compact, sleeved cartridge containing six axially configured cylinders, with a steam injection head mounted on both ends. As superheated steam worked against the double-acting pistons in each cylinder, the cartridges spun on a roller bearing cam drive, like the chambers of a revolver pistol, exerting tremendous torque directly to the drive shaft upon which they were mounted. This simple engine produced full power every thirty degrees of rotation, enabling a wide range of operating rpms and higher efficiency than traditional steam engines. In addition, the Model 12 produced a unique sound, like the purr of a giant cat, that rose and fell in tandem with engine speed.

    Great clouds of vapor filled the passengers' galley, accompanied by a deep, throaty growl as the locomotive entered the station at Deception Creek and stopped for fuel. Sleek, aquiline lines blended art and bright aluminum alloy into an aerodynamic shape eerily appealing from every angle. Its battered, sloping nose, polished by wind borne dust, shone in the glare of loading deck lights. This machine looked fast even when standing still.

    Garrick awakened as the train approached and quickly found a toilet to relieve himself. As was her early morning custom, Brenna had wandered off alone, leaving him anxious for her arrival as the car doors opened to unload and admit passengers. When the conductor announced his final call Garrick raced to the station's door, scanning the street with increasing anxiety as the train began moving down the tracks, until he saw Brenna emerge from the creek bed and run toward the station. She moved with the speed and grace of a gazelle as she leaped from the loading platform onto the moving train.

    By the time Garrick joined her, the Lithian girl had completely recovered her breath. She smiled in a shy and endearing manner, an expression frequently employed when she had some delicious secret to reveal. Brenna could tell that he'd been worried, but felt confident that her tidings would bring him needed relief. Watching his anxiety melt away at her appearance pleased the Lithian maiden beyond words.

    "Your parent's trees are pruned," she told him.

    Incredulous, Garrick inquired: "What? How did you even know where to look?"

The Long Journey: *Betrayal*

Brenna pressed her forefinger into the name tag on his uniform. "I saw this on the mailbox," she replied. "You don't have to worry anymore."

Garrick wanted to kiss her in gratitude, but didn't. Brenna's kindness touched his heart, as her benevolence often did, soothing many emotional pains and settling troubling memories. She had a way of discerning his needs and offering comfort without demanding anything in return. "Thank you," he responded, wishing he had something better to say.

The young couple drifted to the rear of a passenger car older than the sum of their respective ages. They hooked their weighty backpacks onto a stylized, spearheaded shaft that protruded from the window's aluminum shutter, then seated themselves into a pair of well-padded seats that were upholstered in worn velveteen fabric.

Passenger comfort never rose to the forefront of design criteria in most Tamarian rolling stock. Aside from soft seats, the unheated cars boasted no other amenities. The narrow center aisle fit only one adult, requiring courtesy most economy-class passengers had long since developed out of necessity.

This car carried four people who had crossed Broken Wing Lake, along with eight soldiers and a sprinkling of poor pilgrims. Garrick did not see who occupied the first class coaches and expensive sleeping berths to the rear, but the brief length of time required by the conductor to reach his section of the train suggested that it wasn't very full.

Sheer boredom and the previous evening's restlessness inspired sleep. Brenna rolled up her parka and used it as a pillow against Garrick's left shoulder, gradually lulled into a slumber by the gentle, rhythmic, side-to-side motion of the car rolling swiftly down the track. Since they occupied the last two seats and no one could see them, Garrick enjoyed the pleasant sensations of Brenna's thick, black hair brushing against his cheek, the weight of her soft body on his left arm, the warmth of her breathing on his skin. He felt content, savoring the moment. Garrick let his girl sleep in peace, reflecting on her experience among his people, wishing silently that other Tamarians could recognize her sweet, selfless temperament and value the woman as he did.

Moving at top speed, the Model 12 locomotive required three and a half hours to traverse the 144-mile length of Broken Wing Lake. The tracks departed the lakeshore and meandered into the Copperhead Foothills, passing through rolling pastureland, orchards, vineyards and long abandoned mining claims. The train crossed over a myriad of fast flowing streams, through forest groves bristling with giant cedar and redwood trees, then gradually descended toward the lake when the Copperhead ridge line again thrust its lofty, snow-clad peaks beyond the cloud cover.

Brenna awakened with hunger rumbling through her belly. The air within the train car had grown colder with every mile it traveled further north, until passenger breath began condensing on the windows. She remained quietly close to her friend, sharing his warmth, tracing the contours of his face with her eyes until they settled on the lines that formed his mouth. Her hand gently squeezed the firm swell of his upper arm and felt him draw closer. She savored his masculine scent in silence, longing secretly for more intimate contact, though never daring to articulate her desire.

Several minutes later, when the train tracks returned to a bluff overlooking the lakeshore, she sat up, cleared the moisture away from the window with her sleeve and studied the passing landscape. The waters of Broken Wing Lake marched southward, driven by the returning wind. "What am I supposed to do when we get to Marvic?" she asked. "Why did the lieutenant send me with you?"

Garrick had been worried about this from the moment he'd received orders for officer's training. "I don't know, but as of now, you're still a civilian specialist employed by the army," he replied. "Lieutenant Kohler included you in my orders because he had no reason to dismiss you, he's up for a promotion, and it might not have looked very good to request your discharge without cause. This way, he got rid of both of us and left the formal decision concerning your disposition to the base commander in Marvic, who doesn't know you at all." Garrick paused, thoughtfully. "That leaves your continuation on the army payroll at the mercy of someone who didn't witness your contribution to the war effort. But if all else fails, you have a bursary for university study that you've earned for your service."

The girl crossed her arms, continuing to stare out the window. "I can't read your language, Garrick. How does anybody expect me to learn anything?" A nagging doubt, one that would have surely broken Garrick's heart had she expressed it, persisted in Brenna's mind. Had she been fooling herself by not returning home with Woodwind?

"You'll learn," Garrick replied. "I'll be in Marvic for twelve weeks, and I'll do what I can to help you."

The Long Journey: *Betrayal*

A long silence ensued as the train labored uphill against gravity and the waxing wind. Landmarks Garrick remembered from his previous journey, such as a large ethanol facility that combined pressure and ammonia to convert pulp waste and straw into fuel feed stock, came into view as the train turned west and descended a steep incline, toward an industrial town called Mercenary Hill. Here the bright waters of the Weeping Widow River plunged into the northern shore of Broken Wing Lake. Paper mills, cold storage warehouses and an ore smelter lined the docks. Beyond these, a rail yard sprawled toward the river front.

Many massive wind machines, planted firmly on a low ridge line north of town, turned gracefully in a bitter breeze, supplementing hydroelectric power for industrial activity. Their calm, mesmerizing motion belied the brute force of freezing wind twisting through their blades. Snow and ice crusted a landscape that only approached warmth during the height of summer. For this reason, people living in this region built their homes along the lakeshore, where deep water acted as an effective thermal sink. The population here remained small and devoted to sustaining the industrial base in an area where very little agriculture, other than raising small cattle herds on the lush summer grass and imported hay from lower elevations, could be practiced.

The locomotive slowed to a stop on a siding, where it remained for nearly twenty minutes as a long southbound train passed. Cold air swirling around the aluminum passenger car swept any warmth away, until the windows became hopelessly glazed in ice. When the train finally pulled into the windswept Mercenary Hill station, Garrick and Brenna sought food at the cafeteria, only to be told by a woman in authority that Brenna had to eat either in the kitchen at the staff lunch table, or outside in the cold.

Garrick didn't voice his displeasure, heading for the staff room with the same resignation Brenna had long ago adopted. This area turned out to be a cozy, warm environment where hot bowls of soup, fresh bread and creamy, spiced tea, served by an indifferent, ageing waitress who couldn't remember how to smile, made for a hearty, satisfying meal.

Mercenary Hill served as a switching point for rail traffic. The shortest distance between the regional capital of Burning Tree and Tamaria's national capital, Marvic, cut through Traitor's Pass, in between the towering Widow Glacier and the northernmost peaks of the Angelgate Mountains. The source of the Weeping Widow River lay at the

The Long Journey: *Betrayal*

apex of a steep valley where the Great Widow Icefield slumped from jagged arêtes into a series of lakes gouged into the rock by retreating glaciers and fed by a myriad of subterranean eskers and surface streams. Glacial melt overflowed from these features and poured into the swollen river, sweeping downslope in tandem with an ever-present wind. The combined sounds of wind and water gave the stream its name.

Walking slowly with hardly a word exchanged between them, the two friends passed through the Mercenary Hill train station to a small waiting area on its northern side. There, a cogwheel rail line led up the angular valley through Traitor's Pass and down the Hangman River on the windward side of the Angelgate Mountains. The engines serving this line were purpose-built Model 12 E pusher locomotives, featuring cog drive wheels mounted on a vertical axis, with teeth engaging from the edges of the rack rail, rather than the top. Thus, the twin rotary steam engines were mounted upright on either side of the center rack rail. The locomotive cab "floated" on an adjustable air suspension to keep the boiler level as the grade increased to its maximum of nearly 50%, and the tender it pushed carried extra fuel and water for the trip.

Laughter echoed from the waiting area. An arrogant officer named Major Gretschel puffed a pipe while relating a story of his heroic logistical exploits. Nine other soldiers of various rank, most of whom remained too intent on a card game to listen, occupied benches near a window, while their comrades slumped along the outside wall reading novels, writing letters or sleeping. The twenty-odd civilians crowded into the room kept to the other side, as if repulsed by the vulgarity of their nation's warriors.

Major Gretschel stopped abruptly when he saw Brenna walk into the room, her face and figure derailing all other trains of thought. "Nice rack!" he said, admiring her. This remark inspired laughter and approving whistles from the other men.

Brenna felt the fire of many eyes settle uncomfortably upon her and self-consciously slid behind Garrick for shelter. He, however, merely smiled, stiffened respectfully, and took a big risk by responding: "I know I'm handsome and though I appreciate your admiration sir, my preferences go the other way."

Major Gretschel accepted the remark with laughter of his own. "Well said, son! Come over and join us."

The Long Journey: *Betrayal*

For the next several minutes, Brenna endured overt leering that made her feel uncomfortable. Two of the men tried unsuccessfully to engage her in conversation. Garrick handled the situation admirably, deflecting attention away from Brenna with great skill, but eventually resorting to holding the girl's hand as a signal that she belonged to him. She feigned complete ignorance of the Tamarian language, never responding to a word spoken in her direction. Brenna fully understood that touching her in public crossed a certain social threshold she and Garrick had learned to approach with great reluctance.

The tactic proved effective. Every soldier who might have thought Garrick too young to command the Lithian girl's affection witnessed her sentiments expressed in the lingering embrace and gentle caress of interlocked fingers, and ceased his thinly veiled lechery.

When the locomotive moved into position on the loading dock, a sense of anticipation rose within the assembled Tamarians. For many of them, this would be their first trip on the slow train ride up to the Traitor's Pass station, an excursion renown for its breathtaking scenery. However, with only a few hours of daylight remaining, most of their nearly eight-hour journey would take place in the dark.

A portly conductor, his face reddened by the cold, opened the door leading out to the loading platform, allowing a blast of glacial wind entrance to the stuffy room. While fresh air brought relief from stale pipe smoke, the freezing wind warned of plummeting temperatures worsened by the twin dangers of approaching night and a rapid rise in altitude.

Thirty-two passengers boarded a pair of cars, separating according to the value of their tickets. Those with more expensive seats would experience an unhindered view of the upcoming ascent from a glass-domed car at the head of the train, while the economy class passengers filed into a basic model behind them.

The Tamarian army never paid for luxury transportation when moving its enlisted soldiers around the country. Garrick, Brenna and the ten warriors who'd waited in the lobby moved rearward, along with a farmer, a businessman working in the concrete industry and two mature, white-haired nurses. Finding a spot at the rear of the cabin, Garrick and Brenna hung their backpacks on the same kind of stylized, spearheaded shutter shaft ends found on all rail cars within the Tamarian Republic. Unlike the unheated second-class coaches common to most domestic rail lines, this particular car had been fitted with condensing coils in the floor, and comforting warmth rose from below.

A clattering sound, coupled with the rhythmic shudder characteristic of cogwheels locking onto the rack rail made all forward progress sound like the endless, uphill climb of some great roller coaster. The train crawled slowly along the precipitous grade, following a path blasted to create narrow ledges above the swiftly descending Weeping Widow River. A steady purr of rotary steam power, the whine of turbo fuel pumps and the dull, consonantal chatter of conversation mingled with the restless rush of glacial wind.

As the train crossed a magnificent, concrete and steel trestle high above the river, Brenna could see the valley floor widen as it dropped all the way to Broken Wing Lake and the snow-clad foothills on its western shore. Stunted pine trees clinging to cracks in the talus gradually gave way to low grasses, lichen, rock and ice. She turned toward Garrick, noting a shadow of stubble on his chin for the first time, and smiled. Brenna unsheathed her boot knife and with a mischievous grin, feigned a move to shave her friend with it. "I can take care of that facial hair for you!" she teased.

Knowing how effortlessly her custom-made, crystalline-edged blade trimmed hair or pared through flesh and armor, Garrick recoiled. "I'll do my own shaving, Brenna. You can keep the business end of that blade far away from my face, thank you!"

Brenna pretended to pout, but a smile curling at the edges of her lovely mouth betrayed a different emotion. Sitting back on the padded bench, she pulled out a comb and began inspecting the ends of her long, dark locks as the comb's ivory teeth parted through them. Any hair shaft end that did not meet her approval, she deftly slid across the boot knife's edge, slicing off the offending split with frightening ease. "Those men don't seem interested in talking to you," she remarked.

The unconsciously adroit manner in which Brenna switched tools with a single hand unnerved Garrick initially. Though she did not flaunt her dexterity, the girl frequently performed complicated motor tasks with such agility Garrick found himself enchanted, watching. This time, when she stopped and made eye contact, as if waiting for a response he should have made already, the boy shrugged. "They're logisticians. I'm a combat soldier. I guess we don't have much in common."

The Long Journey: *Betrayal*

How much of that remark was actually true Garrick couldn't accurately determine, but Lieutenant Kohler's warning haunted him. He meditated on these thoughts as the hours passed and the train trudged uphill through the deepening gloom. While Brenna performed her personal grooming routine, he let his gaze linger on her face in the fading light, following the sweep of thick, dark hair down her ivory neck, noting the gentle pulse of life in a blue-green vein. He admired the manner in which her long locks fell and gently spread across the graceful curve of her bosom, only to tumble again to the girl's slender waist and land in her lap.

Aware of his arousal, Garrick turned away, striving to contain a strong, physical desire for the girl he loved. Brenna privately admitted feeling distressed whenever she experienced a similar yearning for him, knowing that out of respect for her chastity, Garrick always restrained his ardor. With a glance she noticed his change of posture and wistfully dreamed of the day when they could share the full measure of their mutual passion. On this occasion, as was often the case, the two friends suppressed what they really wanted to say and remained silent.

Shortly after passing one of the ubiquitous, military firebases that guarded the valley against attack by mountain giants, the train slipped into heavy fog and all outdoor visibility vanished. After climbing several hundred additional feet, the train broke free of its concealing cloud cover and appeared underneath a cold, star lit sky.

Brenna's Lithian eyes gleamed in response to the deep, ultraviolet glow filtering down from her world's lofty, spangled heavens. Ablated glaciers, reflecting light invisible to her companions, glistened brightly, magically casting shadows across a bleak, stony landscape that ascended along narrow arêtes and thrust rocky horn peaks high against the dark blue sky.

Garrick, whose human vision caught none of this, noticed an orange glow several hundred yards distant on the track ahead. He stared at it, curiously, then nudged Brenna and pointed. "What do you suppose that's all about?" he inquired, nervous tension evident in his voice.

Momentarily blinded by the orange light, Brenna squinted until her eyes adjusted and she could see flames. "It looks like a bonfire," she responded.

"That's what I thought, too." Garrick felt his heart quicken. "Major Gretschel!" he called. "We have a serious problem, sir!"

The Long Journey: *Betrayal*

The Tamarian officer, alarmed by the urgency in Garrick's voice, stood from his seat and moved back to inquire about the cause of the young soldier's anxiety. "So," the officer replied, initially annoyed that he'd been disturbed. "It looks like a fire on the tracks. This is a problem for the engineer, not us."

"Who would build a fire on a railroad track in the middle of nowhere?" Garrick inquired. "And, more importantly, why?"

"What's your worry, soldier? Fire is a natural phenomenon." The major backed away, his facial expression dismissing the blaze as irrelevant.

"Someone wants the train to stop, sir," Garrick continued, rising out of his seat. "Someone wants us to stop in the middle of the mountains, in the dark."

Major Gretschel thought for a moment, then his facial expression changed. "Giants," he realized, arriving at the grim conclusion and comprehending the reason for Garrick's concern.

The young warrior nodded nervously. "Nobody else lives here."

That remark inspired a pause and a deep breath. "Do you have any weapons?" the major inquired, profound worry now evident in his voice and agitated body language.

"Brenna carries a bow and a boot knife," the boy stated. "I turned my rifle in back at Burning Tree. What about your men?"

The major shook his head, completely rejecting any role the slender girl might play in an armed conflict. "We're all unarmed. Can you use that bow?"

"Sir, she's a far better shot than I am, and the arrows are measured to her draw length." Garrick reached for his backpack, and then Brenna's, placing them both on his seat. "Maybe we can pull these things off," he said, referring to the shafts upon which the window shutters had been mounted. As he worked to disconnect them, other soldiers followed his lead.

Garrick's warning stirred several nearby passengers. Soon, Brenna could hear many voices chattering with a tension clearly underscoring their rising sense of fear. She could have run away, knowing that her superior night vision and speed would serve well to preserve her own life. However, she loved Garrick and watching him prepare for a fight steeled her resolve. After helping him remove the window shutter and reassemble its shaft into a rudimentary spear, Brenna stood near the back wall and strung her bow.

The Long Journey: *Betrayal*

The engineer, riding in the isolation of the locomotive cabin, noticed the fire on a flat section of the track ahead and began slowing in time to halt forward progress before his engine pushed the passenger cars into the blaze. As his train came to rest, the engineer disembarked with his fireman and walked forward to inspect the tracks.

A low whistle, followed by the crash of shattered glass and the shudder of the forward observation car deepened Garrick's heartbeat to a strong pounding. Passengers screamed. Another impact rocked the train. All sense of social order disintegrated as men and women desperately sought escape through the doors and windows. The young couple found themselves pressed against the train's rear wall, unable to move.

A rapid series of smaller impacts splintered west-facing windows and thudded against the train's outer, aluminum skin. Flying shards of glass mingled with wind-driven dust and snow as sling-propelled ice bullets and atlatl darts the size of a strong man's forearm slammed into the train cars. Wintry air flooded the passenger compartment as doors and windows opened, allowing people outside. Instantly, the temperature within the economy class car plummeted dangerously.

Brenna winced, flinching as something stung her cheek. Touching it, she felt warm, sticky liquid on her fingertips and removed a sharp shard of glass from her face. The Lithian girl kissed her left index and middle fingers, then pressed them into the injured flesh, *believing* that Allfather God would give her power to heal the wound.

Garrick controlled his own sense of panic, hearing Major Gretschel repeatedly call for a calm evacuation. Strict training and battle experience suppressed fear, until the familiar, pre-combat adrenaline rush the young soldier experienced inspired focused determination for the imminent fight. As sub-freezing air flooded the cabin, he thought of the gloves, scarf and headgear packed in his knapsack. While he waited for the cabin to clear, another pair of heavy impacts slammed into the forward train car, rocking it dangerously. Garrick began counting.

The cabin finally emptied. Garrick pulled Brenna toward the door but motioned for her to stay inside and keep low. While he counted, the young soldier slid Brenna's backpack toward her and untied his own, reaching for winter gear to shield his skin from the extreme cold. Brenna followed suit, then grabbed Garrick's binoculars.

When he reached 86, Garrick heard two more large projectiles coming and felt the train rock as they slammed into the forward car.

The Long Journey: *Betrayal*

Picking up his makeshift weapon, Garrick led Brenna outside and found Major Gretschel organizing the civilians near the locomotive.

The Tamarian officer sent half a dozen women and children inside the engineer's cabin, where they would be sheltered from the cold and hidden during the upcoming battle. He arranged injured passengers, most of them suffering glass cuts or crush-related damage trying to get out of the train, into groups on the ground, allowing the two elderly nurses to perform triage. They began tending to wounds, but one of them vigorously shooed Brenna away when she offered to help.

Since the officer was busy, Garrick found a sergeant named Henkelmann while Brenna crept around the train and peered westward with Garrick's binoculars.

"It's a small group," Garrick told the sergeant. "They're firing two onagers, each of which needs a crew of four. The rate of small projectile fire suggests half a dozen others on foot. Brenna will scout them and let us know for sure."

"Ever fought giants, boy?" Sergeant Henkelmann asked in a wistful tone.

Garrick shook his head. "Not yet. But that's about to change, isn't it?"

Sergeant Henkelmann clasped Garrick by the shoulder. "Let's hope we live to fight another day. If the giants don't kill us, the cold certainly will."

Major Gretschel arrived and pulled the sergeant aside, conversing with him in low voices before he turned his attention to the soldiers and citizen volunteers waiting for his leadership. "Lightweight spear shafts are not ideal for engaging giants," he began, "but they will have to do. The engineer has a rifle onboard with one magazine, so we have seven rounds to work with." Major Gretschel pointed to a young soldier, then continued: "Private Hansen, I want your hands on that rifle. Make every shot count."

"Yes sir!" the warrior replied.

Garrick felt mildly hurt that he, the only combat veteran among them, had not been given the gun to fire, but he said nothing. In the midst of his mental meandering, Major Gretschel barked out his name.

"Yes, sir!" Garrick responded.

"You say that girl of yours can handle a bow. I want her on the left, opposite Hansen. Where is she?"

The Long Journey: *Betrayal*

Brenna suddenly appeared, as if summoned. She spoke excitedly to Garrick in vulgate, though it turned out that Major Gretschel understood her. "There are fourteen of them. They've just come over an esker about a hundred yards away."

"How do you know that?" the major inquired.

The Lithian maiden turned to face him, her bright eyes shining eerily in the deep blue, nocturnal light. "I can see them," she replied. "We need to hurry!"

Major Gretschel gave his final instructions, then ordered the fourteen soldiers and civilian volunteers into a crouching position on the western side of the idling train. By staying low, they would minimize visual contact until the giants–who could see into the infrared spectrum–came close.

At a range of less than 50 yards, the giants stopped to fire another volley with their slings, hurling ice bullets the size of softballs and frozen to granite hardness, against the train. The metallic song of yielding aluminum and the crack of fracturing glass swept over the shivering soldiers.

Private Hansen squeezed off a round, its bright flash blinding, and the deafening discharge from his big rifle echoing across the smooth, glaciated rock, reverberating from the distant arêtes as if answered by other guns far away. Though startled and alarmed, every giant remained standing. Hansen had missed.

"Hold your fire!" Major Gretschel spat, his ears ringing.

The giants paused. Brenna could see them conversing, their flattened facial features disfigured by war paint. Suddenly, the immense humanoids raised a frightful battle cry, then broke into a dead run, their long strides powerful and purposeful, their iron spearheads black against the snowy landscape.

"Steady! Steady!" Major Gretschel warned his nervous troops. "Set your weapons on my mark!"

At a distance of thirty yards, Brenna could see angry, savage facial features clearly. Menacing expressions of ill intent sprang from dark eyes widened in battle lust, while ritual scars displayed rank and skulls boasted of human warriors slain. "Allfather God," she prayed, "deliver me!" Brenna took aim and fired into the open mouth of the leading giant. More than twenty years of archery experience that melded skill, faith and the multiplied power of Brenna's recurve bow tipped the survival odds into the Tamarians' favor. Her arrow slammed into the giant's soft palate and pierced through the conduction pathway for all nervous activity.

    She would have seen his eyes roll back as the giant's legs buckled and he slid along the rocks, but the girl had already selected another target and fired her second shot. This time, her arrow struck her victim's right upper shoulder, cut through the trachea, nicked the sixth cervical vertebra and lodged in his back. The giant, seared by unending spasms of intense pain, could not breathe. He slid to his knees, tugging on the arrow shaft, coughing, choking on blood and thrashing, only to be trampled by the giant running behind him.

    "Fire!" screamed Major Gretschel, a little too late. Private Hansen, frightened and inexperienced, managed to get in a single, deadly shot that blew apart the chest of an attacking giant before ranks closed and firearms became useless.

    In unison, on Major Gretschel's command, the Tamarians rose from their crouch, planting their spear shafts to create a fearsome forest of angular steel. Left-handed Garrick, in the point position, let out a loud shout as he knocked the leading giant's weapon head aside and circled into his enemy's belly. The impact nearly forced him backward, but Garrick's grave determination prevailed and the giant's momentum didn't stop until Garrick's right shoulder slammed into his adversary's breastbone. Hot, foul-smelling breath assailed the young soldier's senses. The giant dropped his weapon and tore at Garrick's right shoulder while the young warrior drove his enemy down. Garrick stepped on his opponent's thigh and slammed the dying giant onto the rocky ground, retracting his spear and jamming it into his assailant's torso repeatedly.

    The Tamarians pressed forward, their second rank filling any gap in their triangular formation. However, their inadequate weapons, fear and inexperience put them at a serious disadvantage. Failure to fight in concert allowed the giants to wrap around the right flank and easily bat aside spearheads shifted to counter them.

    With powerful, thrusting weapon strokes the giants tore through unarmored human flesh. Deep voices screamed triumphantly when the monsters pinned hapless men against the train car. In a matter of moments, the giants killed four soldiers, including Private Hansen. Victory seemed within their grasp, elevating their murderous rage into a terrifying frenzy.

The Long Journey: *Betrayal*

Behind these combatants, three more giants emerged, carrying long, heavy poles that they pushed beneath the leading train car. Grasping the ends and heaving together, they began working to dislodge the heavy coach from the rack rail in an effort to push it over the canyon's edge.

Brenna, on the opposite side of the formation, saw nothing of this. She circled to the left and fired two more lethal shots into the rear flank of the assembled giants, drawing the attention of one humanoid who stood taller than two of her put together. Unlike the others, this one drew a gleaming sword, leaped toward the young maiden–covering almost ten feet in a single bound–and hacked at her for all he was worth.

The Lithian girl shrieked as the giant's weapon whisked past her ear, nearly slicing her in twain. Shouldering her bow, Brenna stepped toward the giant, grabbed his left boot and twirled her body to the right with well-trained grace and speed, knowing that she needed to get very close in order to stay safe. Now crouching behind her powerful enemy while he stupidly looked around his body to find her, Brenna drew her knife in one smooth motion and pulled his left leg toward her. She then jabbed her keen, ceramo-steel blade into the giant's muscle, just above his boot and cut downward, to the right, easily slicing through his leather armor, severing both tendon and muscle.

The giant screamed in agony and rage, instantly lost control of his leg and spun to the left, fruitlessly flailing at his agile opponent. Losing balance, he tumbled to the ground, broke his left wrist in the fall, and cursed the Lithian girl savagely.

Now that the massive humanoid lay on the ground, Brenna pounced onto his back, pulled on his brow ridge with all of her strength and slashed her knife across his exposed throat. Dark, arterial blood spurted from the wound. Shuddering and wheezing pitifully, the giant dropped his sword and though he gasped and trembled, Brenna knew he could no longer threaten her. She wiped her knife on the giant's back, sheathed it, then reached for the weapon he had wielded against her.

Garrick could tell that while three-man teamwork on the left side of the Tamarian formation kept the giants at bay, its right flank was falling apart. The giants shifted in that direction, and behind him he could hear screams of panic and pain. Trusting the soldier on his left, Garrick quickly reached for the sharper, heavier spear of the giant he'd slain, then arose to continue fighting.

The Long Journey: *Betrayal*

Fueled by the strange, heightened sense of power and control he'd often felt in combat, Garrick lunged to the right, thrusting his spear beneath the scapula of a giant who'd been busy killing a different soldier. When, enraged, that giant circled his strong arm to the right and deflected Garrick's blow, the young soldier passed his own spear head beneath the giant's weapon and jammed its iron tip into his opponent's jawbone, drawing blood clearly visible in the flicker of bonfire light.

The giant lashed back, thrashing his weapon to the left, nearly decapitating Garrick, who withdrew his spear and ducked beneath just in time to save his own life. Instead of killing Garrick, the heavy, iron warhead burst the skull of the man who'd been shielding the young warrior's left side. Not satisfied, the giant slashed mightily back toward the right, the sound of his terrifying strength manifest in a low whoosh that passed ever so slightly above Garrick's head. Having missed two times in a row, the savage creature growled in rage, then lifted his weapon high as if to throw it down.

Taking on this giant without any assistance on either side, Garrick shuffled his feet in a leftward arc, forcing his enemy to twist awkwardly. As the huge humanoid stepped to the right in order to square his powerful body against the young Tamarian, Garrick charged forward. His spearhead entered just below the giant's belt, parting abdominal muscle, piercing the bladder and small intestine before stopping against the giant's sacrum. Garrick thrust again, and again, and again, each time with a grunt that focused his strength on the grim task of killing a monster more than four times his weight.

With a gasp, the nine-foot humanoid managed a feeble, downward thrust that merely glanced off the parka covering Garrick's left shoulder. The giant fell backward and slowly bled to death.

Brenna spent a moment admiring the lovely longsword she'd earned in battle. A two-handed, leather-wrapped gel grip and self-repairing, crystalline edge revealed its Lithian origin. Beyond its hand-width ricasso, runes etched within its wide, central fuller consisted of a script so ancient she struggled to comprehend the words until a scream returned her attention to the ongoing fight and she glanced upward.

Sergeant Henkelmann, who had lost support on both flanks when his comrades succumbed to injury, was now locked in a desperate struggle with an attacking giant. The sergeant had his left hand crushed when the powerful humanoid's spear shaft collided with his metacarpal bones. Unable to fend off the giant's relentless assault, he fell to the

The Long Journey: *Betrayal*

ground and would surely have perished, save for Brenna's fearless intervention.

Even through her gloved hands, the blade's handle instantly and comfortably conformed to the Lithian girl's grip. It felt nearly weightless as she leaped forward and swung the sword in an overhead, right to left cross-body arc that cut through the giant's spear shaft and sent its iron head flipping backward. As the blade swept downward, to her left, Brenna's right foot followed and her back leg shuffled forward. Now facing the giant's torso, Brenna lunged ahead and thrust her new weapon through the ligament above her adversary's left leg, plunging the slender, sharp sword at a steep angle into his left kidney.

Once in this position, Brenna brought up her back foot, twisted to the right, slid her right boot to the rear and in so doing, retracted her longsword with a nimble, downward stroke that effectively disemboweled her opponent. As he fell toward her, Brenna again stepped forward with her right foot and swiftly swung the sharp sword in a front-handed arc that severed the giant's head as easily as if she'd been cutting grain.

With her bloodstained blade held aloft and her feet in a perfect stance, Brenna breathed deeply and prepared for her next attack. However, after witnessing her deadly skill with the sword, two giants melted back, neither one daring to face her.

Garrick, panting in the thin mountain air, realized he could not sustain prolonged exertion, but caught a glimpse of a familiar and far more effective weapon. Discarding the heavy spear he'd wielded, the young soldier grabbed hold of the large caliber rifle that lay next to Private Hansen's body, chambered a round and fired into the side of a giant's head.

An explosion of blood, bone, brain and encephalic fluid erupted in the aftermath of a thunderous rifle discharge. Garrick momentarily lost his hearing, but worked the weapon's bolt with well-practiced efficiency while he turned to the right and selected his next target. With only four shots remaining, each one had to be fatal.

Realizing that their attack had been swiftly and successfully defeated, the remaining giants called down curses as they dropped their weapons and leverage poles and fled back toward the esker.

Firing a big Tamarian rifle with accuracy required a degree of control that Garrick easily summoned from the depths of his consciousness. He knew the drill. Lining up his fleeing targets one by

The Long Journey: *Betrayal*

one Garrick calmly squeezed the rifle's trigger, worked its bolt action to discharge and insert a new bullet, and in doing so, ruthlessly sent each giant tumbling to the rock and ice before any could cover two dozen strides.

Major Gretschel, panting from exertion and fear, watched Garrick fire the large caliber rifle in awe. Although every Tamarian soldier had to qualify on the target range, the serene, merciless demeanor he witnessed in Garrick's shooting inspired regret that he'd not initially put that rifle into the young warrior's hands.

Having done well to avoid death and actually injure a giant in the melee, Major Gretschel also noticed that Brenna, who crouched, cringed and covered her ears while her friend fired the rifle, deserved credit for killing six giants, one of them with nothing more than a boot knife! Astonished, the Tamarian officer shook his head and muttered a curse. "Who'd have thought a waify thing like her could fight?" he mused.

When his final, fatal shot brought down the last of the fleeing giants, Garrick emptied the rifle's chamber of its spent cartridge, slung the weapon over his back and scanned the survivors for Brenna. He found her tending to Sergeant Henkelmann's hand, but still deafened by the lingering roar of rifle fire ringing in his ears, could not hear the endearing words she spoke to him.

Her face, spattered in blood, yet showing no evidence that flying glass had cut her creamy complexion, expressed kindness and concern. Brenna's bright eyes scanned Garrick's strong body for injury, and finding none, she breathed a sigh of relief. Anticipating a return to her healing duties with the wounded, Brenna smiled in surprise when Garrick pulled her supple body close. He slowly, softly kissed her lips with a gentle passion that betrayed his secret love for the Lithian girl. She requited his affection in kind, lingering within his embrace, praying to Allfather in whispered gratitude, feeling the pulse of their mingled heartbeats.

Five uninjured battle survivors witnessed this display of tenderness, but not one of them thought Garrick a traitor for consorting with a foreigner. In recognition of the young couple's bravery and combat skill, they began to applaud.

Above the Clouds

Gray, swirling fog obscured the deep chasm in which the Weeping Widow River flowed. In the freezing stillness and descending silence that followed a frenzy of combat exertion, Major Gretschel struggled to catch his breath and clear his mind. Everyone else seemed pensive, waiting on his decision, for his command to do something.

He saw that Brenna, the petite foreign mercenary, relinquished her lover's grip and turned her attention to the injured. The girl removed her gloves, opened her backpack and administered a morphine inhalant to one of the suffering men after examining his wounds. She quickly bent her head to pray, then worked to stem his blood loss, strangely kissing her knuckles repeatedly and touching the area around his injury.

A chill flashed up the officer's spine when he saw flesh instantly restored at her touch. Witnessing that inexplicable capability inspired a blend of dread and wonder, but he could not linger on the scene. Averting his eyes, Major Gretschel saw that Garrick, the young marksman, picked up a spear and systematically jammed it through the torso of every giant, grimly ensuring that none would never rise again.

Major Gretschel turned to Sergeant Henkelmann. "Take that lad and one other man. Scout the esker and make sure we don't suffer any more surprises."

After this, Major Gretschel asked the uninjured farmer and businessman to strip the giants of any valuables they carried into battle, knowing that giants considered trinkets, precious metals and gems as good luck talismans. Tamarian customs assured that anyone participating in battle should receive an equal share of all spoils. The fraction belonging to the five slain Tamarians would be sent to their respective families. This duty was considered a sacred responsibility, so Major Gretschel felt no need to monitor the distribution of booty. Each combatant, including Brenna, ended up with sixteen silver coins and a couple of poorly cut gems. The total value of this treasure exceeded that of Garrick's pay for five months.

Next, the officer turned his attention to the engineer and fireman, inquiring about the health of the track and the prospect of continuing up to Traitor's Pass.

The engineer removed his hat and swept his grimy, right hand over a sweaty, balding pate. "It doesn't look like they've tried this before," he said. "The rack is still intact, and on this slope that's the most critical thing."

Major Gretschel sighed, mildly annoyed. "What about the fire?"

"It's burned some of the cross ties and the rails might be a bit soft," the engineer responded. "We'll have to get a repair crew up here right away."

"Can the train get past the damage?" the officer asked, revealing his only concern.

"I don't think it will be a problem, but I suggest we get everyone off loaded while I drive over the rails. That way, if anything goes wrong, nobody else will get hurt." The engineer, having witnessed courage in saving his train, seemed willing to demonstrate that same spirit in risking its destruction.

"Get it done, then," Major Gretschel replied.

Giving orders and having them obeyed cleared the major's mind. He spoke to the elderly nurses and demanded that they let Brenna examine and treat civilian injuries. When one of them objected, the Tamarian officer flatly rejected her concern. "That girl is under my command," he stated in a tone of voice underscoring his authority. "She will treat these injured, and you will not impede her. Give her the most serious cases first."

The women complied, their fear of the officer's wrath overcoming prejudice and resentment. Although they remained silent, contempt filtered every expression as they watched the girl subserviently heal wounds their lesser skills could not manage. Ironically, had they seen the young Lithian mete out vengeance on the attacking giants, both women would have held her in higher regard. Because neither one witnessed her combat skill, neither one considered that the blood all over Brenna's clothing might not be her own.

Garrick followed Sergeant Henkelmann and a private named Jos Kindershields up to the esker. On its reverse slope, they found a pair of wooden onagers and a store of heavy ice balls. The sergeant sent Kindershields back to obtain a small quantity of ethanol from the drain valve of the train's fuel tank and a firebrand from the conflagration on the track, while he and Garrick examined the surrounding snow for additional evidence. When Kindershields returned, he handed Sergeant Henkelmann the burning stick. The private dumped half the ethanol he carried in a water flask onto the spool of one onager, then emptied its contents in a like manner upon the other. Sergeant Henkelmann thought

The Long Journey: *Above the Clouds*

the alcohol would accelerate combustion, but the liquid didn't vaporize well in the extreme cold. The sergeant held the firebrand steadily in place for several moments, until the fuel ignited and each war engine caught fire. Nearly invisible blue-colored flames turned bright orange and smoky as the dry wood and hemp caught fire. Once the onagers were fully engulfed, Sergeant Henkelmann discarded the burning stick and helped push the stash of ice balls close to the fire. After this, the three soldiers returned to the train.

By this time, the engineer had successfully piloted his locomotive beyond the damaged track section and most of the civilians were busy sweeping glass out of the economy class cabin. Major Gretschel ordered his soldiers to wrap their dead in blankets and load them onto the ruined, glass-domed car.

"We found at least two sets of boot prints leading west, away from the esker," Sergeant Henkelmann reported between breaths. "I'd say the odds are good that reinforcements will soon be on their way."

Major Gretschel nodded. "Then get everyone loaded up and let's get out of here."

Twenty-five survivors easily fit into the economy class car. Most of the windows had been shattered in the pre-melee ice bombardment, so the engineer turned up the heat circulating through the floor and the train trudged onward. The noise of human conversation rose above the sounds of machinery. Without windows to shield passengers from the cold, thin air, this part of the trip would prove very uncomfortable.

Garrick waited impatiently for Brenna to finish her ministrations. Many passengers sustained injuries from flying glass or crowd crush, and some–particularly the men, he noticed–basked in the exotic warmth of her attention. An old feeling of insecurity crept into his consciousness while he watched her smile, touch other people and pray over them. He became so fixated on Brenna that he missed Major Gretschel's approach.

The Tamarian officer sat in the seat to Garrick's right. "Tell me," Major Gretschel began. "Where did you ever find her?"

Garrick cleared his throat. "Last fall, on the first night of the war, my Junior Scout unit engaged the enemy just north of the border. After a brief firefight, I went to check our rear flank and found her nearly frozen to death at the bottom of a hill."

Major Gretschel grunted, half-listening. "She fights well," he said. "But what's with the kissy fingers flesh healing thing? How does she do that?" As he watched her repeat the process, a look of incredulity crossed his face.

"She believes in God, and says he fills her with power," Garrick replied. "She gives God credit for everything she does."

"What god does this?" Major Gretschel remarked. "I have never, in all my years, even heard of such sorcery!"

Garrick smirked. "Sir, she'd get upset at you for saying that," he replied. "She tells me it's all for God's glory." The young Tamarian shifted nervously in his seat, partly because he felt cold, but mostly because he knew that discussing Brenna's personal superstition did not put her into a favorable light.

"Do you believe her?" Major Gretschel inquired.

Garrick phrased his response with care. "You discern there are many natural forces in existence that even our scientists don't fully understand," he began. "Ice floats when it should sink. Ultraviolet light from the Great Eye Nebula should sterilize our world, yet it doesn't. Brenna can see well in what you and I consider darkness.

"A power I can't perceive flows through her. It fights from within her, sustains and nurtures her soul. Yet it's kind and gentle, a spirit that loves beauty and laughter. I don't understand what it is. She calls this inexplicable force Allfather God, and says that every healing act she performs is a manifestation of this one, true God."

"Hmm," the officer grunted, disapprovingly. "So why the kissing?"

Brenna had related her story to him once, so Garrick felt comfortable describing a bit of her personal history. "When you were a child and you skinned your knee, what did your mother do to offer comfort?"

Major Gretschel simpered, understanding where Garrick's story led before he finished his tale. "She kissed it and told me it was all better!"

"Yes!" Garrick replied with a nervous smile. "I think that's a universal mother response. When Brenna was a little girl, her mother did the same thing. Then one day when her mother wasn't around, one of Brenna's younger sisters fell and cut a nasty gash on her forehead. Since Brenna was the eldest child present, she wanted to comfort her little sister. So, she kissed the injury as her mother would have done and prayed that it would stop bleeding." Garrick paused. "It worked. She's been doing this ever since.

The Long Journey: *Above the Clouds*

"In our unit," he continued, "she began kissing the back of her fingers and then touching the injury because the guys were repulsed when she tried to put her lips on a wound."

When he heard this, Major Gretschel raised his eyebrows and wrinkled his nose. "And she thinks that her god honors every childish request she makes?"

The major had a way of consistently belittling other people. Garrick didn't like this, especially when Brenna became the subject of his ridicule. He'd learned, however, to temper his response in the presence of an officer, so he concealed his irritation. "The way she prays is hardly childish," Garrick began. "There's a strength in it I find hard to explain. She relates to God as if he's deeply interested in her every concern. Her faith is not a toy; it's not a crutch. Her faith is an army with heavy artillery!"

"But you don't believe in this god of hers?" the major more stated than asked, his remark intended to underscore the irrational folly of Brenna's conviction.

Garrick didn't take the bait. "Do you, sir? Can you offer a more plausible explanation for her healing skill?"

Major Gretschel scoffed, as if he'd been asked a very stupid question. "I say she's a demon. She gets her power from evil spirits."

This time Garrick shook his head. "A demon who plays hymns on the chapel organ? A demon who bleeds, grows weary, grieves over her smallest character flaw and talks to God in her sleep? A demon who weeps at the beauty before daybreak, feels hurt for being hated without cause, and recites long passages of Lithian scripture from memory? In what demonic realm does such a frail and gentle creature exist?"

Major Gretschel thought for a moment. "Well, at the very least, I'd say she sounds like a fanatic." He rolled his eyes and shook his head, daydreaming about her shapely figure, frustrated that such a girl would never fulfill his personal fantasies. "What a waste!"

"I would describe her as devout, sir. Brenna doesn't impose her religion on other people. It's a deeply personal matter for her."

"And thus, you're not swayed," the officer continued. "You won't admit having fallen under the spell of this god of hers."

"That's all the more reason to accept her explanation of the matter," Garrick countered. "She says her God does not compel belief, but rather, reveals his presence through creation and the influence of those who trust in him."

The Long Journey: *Above the Clouds*

Major Gretschel raised his eyebrows. "So you do believe in this god nonsense!"

"I didn't say that, nor did I imply such a thing," Garrick replied, defensively. "I'm an atheist, but she believes, and we all stare in wonder at the power she exhibits. I feel nothing of that drive in me, nor do I desire its influence."

"Why not?" the officer inquired. "Imagine our soldiers fighting with godlike skill! Imagine how our enemies would cower! Imagine our warriors healing their own wounds! We should seize that kind of force! Think of the good we could do in eradicating evil!"

Garrick shook his head again. "It won't work to suit our own ends. That's the paradox of it."

Major Gretschel noticed that Brenna had completed her medical rounds and was returning to her seat. "Religion is all madness and confusion!" he exclaimed. "But I'm glad that you two were on my side tonight. That was some impressive shooting, soldier."

"Thank you, sir. I was just doing my duty."

"Not giving glory to your girl's god?" Major Gretschel smirked. "How unfanatical of you!"

As the officer departed, resentment of such arrogance flashed across Garrick's face. Brenna noticed the expression but elected not to pursue the matter, knowing that if Garrick believed she'd benefit from the conversation, he'd tell her about it. The fact that he remained silent suggested many possibilities to her mind, all of them negative.

Her smile and the brightness of her eyes revealed an overflow of excitement that further endeared her soul to his. "Garrick," she whispered. "Look at my sword!"

Sitting down, Brenna unsheathed the weapon to a point just beyond the ricasso, displaying gold inlaid etching and the classic, crystalloid polymer edge that kept Lithian blades frighteningly keen. "This," she began, pointing to letters on the ricasso itself, "is the name of the metallurgist, Illian Lael, and beneath is Lael Mirror Forge, the place where this blade was cast. I've been there once. It's a light-powered factory in the deep south that hasn't made weapons for more than a hundred years!"

Darkness aboard the rail car prevented Garrick from actually seeing the letters. In her enthusiasm, Brenna forgot that he couldn't see in the deep blue light that bathed her world when the Daystar set. Further, Lithian script made absolutely no sense to Garrick. He gently reminded her of these two facts, momentarily interrupting her discourse.

"That's right," she replied, her zeal undeterred. "But let me tell you what I can see!" Brenna hurriedly described the script engraved within its finger-width fuller. "This says: 'Allfather Triumphs' in very ancient letters. Not even Woodwind's sword has this type of work in the fuller. That means this is a very old blade!"

Brenna flipped the weapon over in her curiously dextrous manner. "On the back side of the ricasso, I found my mother's family name engraved!" She reached for Garrick's hand, pulled off his glove and ran his fingers over the letters. "It says 'Ithael,' which is my mother's maiden name. That means that this particular weapon was forged for one of my ancestors!"

Garrick shuddered at the thought. "Isn't that ironic?" he exclaimed in genuine astonishment. "I wonder how it wound up here?"

Brenna smiled and replied: "Allfather is good!"

In the months following the end of Tamaria's war with the Azgaril force, details of that private army's interactions with emissaries of giant clans remained undisclosed. Brenna didn't know that the weapon she'd earned in battle had been among the museum treasures looted from her homeland when the Northern Liberation Army laid waste to her nation. An enemy embassador carried the blade northward, presenting it to a giant chieftain as a gift for his clan's cooperation in disrupting Tamarian rail traffic during the Azgaril invasion.

News of the war's end and Tamaria's triumph had not yet reached inhabitants of the Great Widow Icefield, a little more than 400 miles north of the combat zone. With winter slowing his travel homeward, that particular giant chieftain could not fulfill his treaty obligations for nearly four months. At his earliest opportunity, he'd gathered his forces to attack Tamarian rail traffic, only to meet his demise at the hand of a Lithian warlord's daughter descended from the very family that paid for his favored weapon's forging.

Brenna sheathed her sword and laid it on the floor beneath her seat. "It's getting cold," she announced, suddenly changing the subject. "Why don't you warm me up?"

The Tamarian standard issue military poncho consisted of a hooded, waterproof and insulated garment that could be unzipped and folded flat. Garrick and Brenna had learned that a pair of these garments, zipped together, effectively protected against wind and cold as long as the two of them sat very close. Since they remained in the darkness at the back of the rail car and no one else could observe them, they snuggled together to share warmth.

They sat quietly for several minutes before Brenna loosened her parka, took hold of Garrick's hand and slid it to her breast. The boy felt her soft flesh compress beneath his fingers through the fabric of her uniform and undergarments, his heart pounding in breathless wonder as Brenna's flesh responded to his touch. Their eyes met, lingering, until Garrick felt he would burst. He closed his eyes and gently moved his hand away. Garrick's young body trembled as he willed himself into control, then looked again at Brenna with a rising sense of determination that she immediately misunderstood.

"Do you love me?" she inquired, quietly.

He nodded. "Yes, I do."

"Then why did you move away?" Her voice sounded hurt.

Garrick struggled to express his thinking carefully. He let out a deep sigh, then returned his worried gaze to hers. "Because I want you, but love is not about what I want."

He did not see the flush of affliction wash over Brenna's fair complexion, believing that she accepted such self-control as further evidence of his integrity. Yet this thought did not enter her mind. Grief stricken for acting on her own desire, Brenna turned her head away. "I'm sorry," she whispered.

Her reaction surprised him, as her responses often did, leaving Garrick uncertain about what to say. He pulled his left arm out from under the poncho and very lightly turned her chin back toward him. "There's no need for you to say that," he told her, softly.

Brenna leaned her head against his shoulder, embraced him beneath the poncho and quietly began to sob. She gripped his upper arm with her right hand and circled his back with her left, holding him with surprising strength as she emptied her soul.

Garrick kissed Brenna's head and let her cry. He felt bewildered by her behavior and feared he'd made a grievous mistake, thinking that she should have better understood his love for her having experienced restraint, at a moment when he really wanted to caress her body without restriction. He did not comprehend the extent of her desire to please him, nor did he appreciate how the fervor developing within his friend's mind conflicted with her commitment to chastity.

The Long Journey: *Above the Clouds*

Brenna found no words to articulate how weary she felt of the ongoing need to be spiritually strong. The social pressures projected upon her drained emotional energy, strained her awareness and left her experiencing intense isolation. She wanted to feel loved and accepted without conditions. Gentle and handsome Garrick stirred her longing in ways she couldn't explain. He sought understanding and always regarded her respectfully.

While she appreciated and admired his consistent moderation, knowing from his obvious physical arousal that he desired intimate contact urgently and passionately, the fact that he moved away on his own recognizance smote her conscience. Her desire to share herself with him seemed utterly selfish in light of his restraint. Worse, though he did not believe in God, Garrick's moral conduct rose above the cloudy mix of contesting motivations that influenced her own behavior.

Yet, consumed by her own desire, Brenna didn't realize that Garrick struggled with the same problem. The strong, physical yearning he experienced from just looking at her or feeling her pliant body meld into his embrace, rose in ardent fervency with the memory of how pleasant her breast felt to his fingers. Pressure gave way to pain. He believed that denial of his healthy reproductive drive could not be sustained, and though he felt an incredibly strong temptation to simply have his way with the young woman, he loved her so desperately that he willingly sought a different path, one his perceptive mind warned would prove wiser in the end. Garrick thought about his words with great care while he waited patiently for his friend to settle down.

"Brenna," he began. "Please trust me."

She sniffed, but wouldn't look at him. "I do."

"I don't want to hurt you," he continued, "and I don't want to be hurt either."

Brenna nodded, fighting back tears. "I know."

"So let's be careful. Let's not rush." The boy paused, searching for words. "You're beautiful, talented and smart. You fill my life with joy and soothe every ache in my soul.

"But I can only exert so much self-control. My desire feels like a rising flood, and I long for you in ways I can't put into words. Are we ready for everything to change? Is our friendship strong and trusting enough to move beyond where we stand right now? For your own sake, think about this. For my sake, think about this."

The Long Journey: *Above the Clouds*

Brenna shut her eyes, slowly shaking her head from side to side. "Ok," she said, meekly, sniffing again. "I'm really sorry."

"Brenna," he whispered, longing to look into her eyes. "Please look at me."

Although Brenna found compassion there, she could not requite his gaze. "I don't deserve you," she replied, turning her head away.

"That's not true," Garrick responded, drawing her close again. "You don't have to be perfect to meet my approval. You can be yourself, and you'll be safe. I'm grateful that you trust me, delighted that you want to share yourself with me. But if you discard me over my respect for your virtue, I'll be crushed beyond recovery."

Brenna embraced him, vowing in her soul that she would never hurt this boy. She prayed a whispered blessing upon him, thanking Allfather God for love, even though she felt her prayer went no further than a listening ear might have heard her words.

Garrick, who did not pray nor understand much of the Lithian language, realized the purpose of Brenna's murmuring, if not the intent of her thoughts. He relished the comforting yield of Brenna's body, the texture of her fine hair against his skin, while the vigor of her grasp reassured his fearful heart that she loved him.

Despite his stated hesitancy something fundamental changed in their relationship from that moment forward, as if they'd arrived at steep, winding stairs that spiraled up above the clouds. Its apex lay shrouded in secret, but the mystery of discovery compelled them to climb with trepidation. They sat in silence, their proximity a comfort, their nearness a temptation.

A chance to end his relationship with Brenna teased at Garrick's consciousness. His military career hinged, to a large degree, on the perception superior officers developed concerning his judgment and leadership capability. Major Gretschel's disdain of Brenna's religious belief and Lieutenant Kohler's warning compelled a critical review.

Memories flooded Garrick's mind. He thought of his cousin, Gudrun, giggling in the hayloft of Uncle Werner's Saradon ranch. He remembered her responsive body writhing in delight at his touch, and his to hers, only to recall her ruthless, selfish betrayal. How easily and willingly she'd accepted his affection, then suddenly repudiated his devotion! Garrick would never forget that experience.

Brenna's benevolent soul, her unending kindnesses and sweet companionship lifted his spirit. Her efforts to seek and support his

The Long Journey: *Above the Clouds*

welfare made him feel valued. Though his fellow citizens might forever project prejudice, though his career might suffer grievous harm, Garrick preferred an uncertain future with Brenna at his side.

As the train climbed steadily upward, reaching a point where the grade exceeded 45% for a long time, the machine slowed, laboring in the bitter, thinning air. All conversation died down as the passengers focused on breathing and staying warm, until Brenna heard only the growl of the steam engines, the purring of fuel pumps and the doubts raging within her mind.

Purity, for years a bright standard held aloft in Brenna's soul, now lay trampled in the mud of her own desire. The experience left her feeling hollow. Brenna rested against Garrick's strong shoulder, conflicted between her need for solitude, for meditation and prayer, and that strange, insistent urge to abandon all virtue for the sake of elusive intimacy with a young warrior who did not even acknowledge the existence of God.

Though she tried to pray, Brenna found her words empty, meaningless platitudes recited by rote. A solitary tear traced the curve of her cheek bone, lingered on her chin, then dropped silently onto the poncho's fabric and quickly froze, a tiny mirror reflecting dark despair from which the Lithian girl saw no escape.

As the glaciers tumbled from lofty heights, compression and rapid ice flow created great ripples revealed in the night by subtle contrasts of dimly reflected light, whiter, somehow, at each strange crest, falling to deep blue in the troughs visible from the broken windows of the passing train. A nameless outlet glacier's toe pushed its terminal moraine to the edge of a deep tarn, where lofty, gloom-shrouded mountain peaks cast their shadows on its still surface. This lifeless, yet strangely beautiful cryosphere filled the ample streams that cast their bountiful, mineral-laden waters into distant, fertile valleys long ago liberated from the glacial grip from whence they'd been carved.

Among the narrowing ridge lines, scarred and scoured in the ancient contest of ice and rock, lateral moraines climbed high toward sheer arêtes whose rock faces wore thinning blankets of snow. A slender, tear shaped drumlin rose above the valley floor between two horn peaks, commanding a view of the tarns, the eskers and blue-white streams dancing among the rocks below. Crossing a thin, concrete bridge that arched over the ablated remains of a glacial toe, the Tamarian locomotive turned into the lee of the drumlin and began its final ascent.

The Long Journey: *Above the Clouds*

Traitor's Pass lay on the stoss end of this particular drumlin. Its cordwood and concrete station house, along with a modest hotel facility, shared the drumlin crown overlooking the Angelgate Divide with a military firebase. On its lee side, the drumlin showed man-made contour marks where glacial till had been graded to provide clear fields of fire, but aside from this, the facility boasted no other defensive fortifications. The uppermost grade served as a level surface for long, off-axis heliostat troughs that heated water for residents and visitors. Their mirrored surfaces could blind human eyes during the day, but now a deep blue glare overwhelmed Brenna's vision.

The Lithian girl shielded her eyes and pointed to the structure. "Why didn't they build any walls here?" she asked.

Garrick had never seen her do this before, but reasoned that all the ultraviolet light reflecting off of the surrounding snow and ice and into the heliostat mirrors must have been overpowering. Having visited Traitor's Pass on two previous occasions, he knew why the grounds lacked the formidable defenses common to most firebases. "We're too high for giants now," he replied, answering her question. "They can't breathe at this altitude. Once you get out and start walking around, you'll notice. Signs in the station warn passengers against physical exertion. You can easily get very sick, so take it easy when we stop."

Gas-powered lights burned in tall fixtures neatly arranged on the loading area, where a slight wind wafted across the platform. Garrick and Brenna unzipped and packed their ponchos, shivering while they waited for the train car to empty. They were the last to stand and exit. Shouldering their heavy backpacks, carrying the treasure they'd won during their melee with the giants, the two friends followed the rest of the passengers across an arched footbridge and into the station's air lock.

A sign welcoming visitors proudly proclaimed that Traitor's Pass was the highest elevation, continuously occupied settlement in the world. In addition, as Garrick said, the sign warned about altitude sickness and gave directions to the infirmary. The station's floors, tiled in light blue ceramic squares radiated warmth in a subtle, yet compelling way. Expensive hardwood furniture graced a lobby, behind which the ticket counter and main hotel desk had been set. Potted plants, set in clusters around the lobby perimeter, thrived indoors. Feminine statues representing liberty and equality stood on either side of the counter. A portrait of Queen Tamar mounted on a beautiful jade slab occupied a

The Long Journey: *Above the Clouds*

position of honor on the wall behind a raised dias, flanked by a pair of national flags.

Garrick felt lightheaded from the small exertion of walking over the footbridge with his backpack, and noticed that Brenna was breathing hard. She dropped her pack to the tiled floor near a wall and rested her hands on her knees with her head down. "Don't do that," he warned. "You'll get a nasty headache!"

Brenna straightened. "I feel weak," she said.

"Just sit here. It takes time for your body to adjust," Garrick responded, gently guiding her into a padded couch near the wall. "I'll get us a drink."

The Lithian girl sat, feeling her world spinning, finding her ability to recover breath strangely slow. She noticed that people had begun shedding their parkas, hats, scarves and gloves, then took hers off as well, observing bloodstains that had dried into her hair. After several minutes, the gaslights, the warm floor and the consonantal chatter of people milling about the station making further travel and lodging arrangements inspired a dull throbbing above her sinuses.

When Garrick returned, bearing a large mug with a steaming liquid, he noticed that Brenna looked pale. He sat down close to her, but without touching, and offered her a drink. "Drink this. It will help you feel better," he promised.

Brenna sipped the pungent, peppery tea. "What is it?" she questioned.

"You're not pregnant or nursing, are you?" he teased. "It's a blend of analgesic herbs used for altitude sickness that's not recommended for pregnant women and nursing mothers."

"Hmm," she mused. "You seem quite intent on preserving my virginity, so I think I'm safe."

Garrick nodded. "It also stimulates appetite. You'll need to rest, drink a lot and eat up here to avoid getting sick."

Brenna smiled weakly. She examined Garrick in the light, noting the dirt and blood crusted into his blonde hair. "A bath and clean clothes are in order," she added. "You shouldn't go to meet your new commander looking like this."

Although each of them carried training sweats and a clean dress uniform in their backpacks, their destination lay across the Fallen Moon Valley on the western side of the Angelgate Ridge. Garrick expected more than a full day of travel ahead and didn't want to soil or wrinkle his

The Long Journey: *Above the Clouds*

parade uniform. In addition, the extreme cold they'd experienced at high elevation made the use of their dress apparel impractical.

Once Brenna finished her tea, Garrick led her toward the pharmacy where he returned the mug, thanked the man on duty and searched for the spiral, bluestone staircase leading up to the hotel and military base. After ascending a single flight, the young couple found they both needed to rest in the hotel's common area before recovering enough strength and stamina to climb further.

Every building at Traitor's Pass owed its warmth to the previous summer's insolation, where very long days and a location above the clouds maximized exposure to the Daystar's energy. Chimneys of wood-framed glass over copper sheathing passively forced rising hot attic air through ducts that led down into an insulated foundation, where the thermal lag of warmed, glacial till gradually rose into the buildings as the weather turned cold. Thick, cordwood walls and shuttered windows effectively enclosed the rising warmth, creating a remarkably comfortable environment during the fall, winter and early spring. The system had been engineered so that very little fuel had to be imported.

Given that no trees survived at this lofty elevation, a single train car laden with charcoal made the uphill trek during the summer. A large gas retort supplied extra winter heat as it produced gas for lighting, while its combustion exhaust warmed metal coils beneath a greenhouse where the staff raised fresh vegetables throughout the year. The outdoor heliostat arrays ensured an ample supply of hot water and also supplemented building and greenhouse heat during the coldest winter months.

For this reason, as Garrick and Brenna labored up the long, stone stairs toward the military base, the two of them soon broke into a sweat. They stopped to rest several times at lookout platforms built for this purpose, unable to do much more than gasp for air until their bodies slowly recovered.

By the time Brenna made it up to the women's bath area, her headache had blossomed, she complained of dizziness, and Garrick genuinely worried about leaving her alone. A lovely, red-haired female soldier in training sweats who introduced herself as Mariel Hougen, offered to look after the Lithian girl so that Garrick could go and wash without worry. A different woman brought Brenna's clothing out for the laundry a few minutes later.

The Long Journey: *Above the Clouds*

After a thorough scrubbing, Garrick put on his own flannel sweatshirt and pants, then visited the laundry, where he paid to have two sets of dirty uniforms, undergarments and battle parkas washed. The clerk raised her eyebrows as she separated a small female halter from male undergarments, but didn't say anything. Garrick merely smiled, leaving a clever remark unspoken. After nearly an hour transpired, he waited for Brenna on a bench in the foyer that divided the male and female washing facilities.

Mariel Hougen came out wearing a uniform that displayed her rank as a 1st lieutenant. Garrick rose and stood at attention, but she seemed embarrassed by his deference. "You're waiting for Brenna?" she inquired.

"Yes ma'am," responded Garrick. "How do you know her name?"

The lieutenant shrugged. "I'm a linguist. I translate documents all day, so to hear Brenna speak in her native tongue is a real treat."

Garrick wondered why the Tamarian army would be interested in translating anything written in Lithian, as he'd gained the impression from Brenna that nearly all their published material had been religious in nature. He didn't broach the subject, and his clear discomfort in this area led Lieutenant Hougen to excuse herself and wish him well. "Brenna is just getting dressed," she said. "I'm sure she'll be out momentarily."

"Thank you, ma'am," the young warrior said. "I appreciate you looking after her."

Brenna emerged a few minutes later with uncombed hair, wearing her baggy training sweats and walking unsteadily. Her face seemed a little swollen, her fair complexion flushed and she was still having trouble breathing. When Garrick inquired about her headache, Brenna told him she felt better.

"We have to eat," he said.

"I'm not hungry," she replied.

"Maybe so, but you need to eat."

Brenna denied any desire for food. "I think I ought to know when I need food," she stated, growing a little annoyed at his insistence.

Garrick steadied her by holding her hands. "We haven't eaten anything for better than nine hours, you battled a band of giants and healed half the passengers during the trip up here, yet you don't think you should eat something? I know you don't feel hungry, but that's an altitude effect. Trust me. I've gone through what you're feeling right now."

She looked longingly over her shoulder, back at the bathroom.

"You need to relieve yourself?"

Brenna smiled, embarrassed. "For the third time in the last twenty minutes."

"Me too," he admitted. "That's why we have to keep drinking. Meet me back here when you're done."

Afterward, he talked Brenna into visiting the cafeteria. They'd long since missed the hot food service, so they contented themselves with cold sandwiches, shared three apples and slowly drank herbal tea in the otherwise empty mess hall. Though she tried to sustain a conversation, Brenna often found her speech drifting into her native tongue, which Garrick could not understand very well, only to realize this too late to remember what she'd said. "I'm sorry," she repeated. "I think I need to sleep."

In any place where gender divided sleeping quarters were provided by the military they normally separated for the night. Even when their unit had been engaged in battle they did not sleep together, but Brenna's unusual behavior worried Garrick to the extent that he insisted they rest in the hotel's common area, where he could observe her closely. He carried their backpacks downstairs while she clung to the handrail, navigating the stairs with a peculiar uncertainty.

The hotel's common area, a place reserved for those too poor to afford a room, lay adjacent to the stairwell and contained many flourishing, potted plants, whose foliage provided some privacy. As a courtesy, the hotel offered blankets, pillows and mats for its nonpaying guests. Armed with these amenities, Garrick set up a sleeping area near a south-facing window, a quiet place in which they found themselves completely alone.

While Brenna lay down to rest, he rummaged through her backpack to find a comb, but when he tried to unravel her hair, Brenna ordered him to stop with a degree of irritation he felt he'd not deserved. She simply didn't want to be touched. Garrick knew that Brenna always engaged in fastidious hair grooming, so her lack of interest in the combing and braiding ritual seemed out of character. By the time he'd but her comb away, the Lithian girl had fallen asleep, her long locks tangled and matted across her face, spread loosely over her shoulders and down her slender back like the under surface of a blind weaver's rug.

The Long Journey: *Above the Clouds*

She stopped breathing many times as the hours passed, only to rapidly resume again within fifteen seconds, then drift back into a shallow, normal pattern. Garrick watched her with great concern, unable to sleep. As the night passed on, Brenna awakened with an urge to empty her bladder. Whenever this happened, Garrick steadied her steps to the bathroom and visited the toilet himself.

An hour or two before dawn, Brenna began talking in her sleep, using the vowel-dominated language of her childhood in a worrisome tone of voice that stirred Garrick in every instance. When the girl awakened again, she complained of being haunted by strange, vivid dreams. On their way to the bathroom Brenna seemed frightened and confused. He heard her retching the remains of last evening's dinner and knew that she either needed medical attention, or had to get back down to lower elevation soon. Garrick plodded up to where he thought the infirmary lay, only to find a closed and locked door. By the time he came back downstairs, Brenna had fallen asleep again.

This restlessness both indicated and compounded their altitude-related sickness. By the time daybreak beckoned on the eastern horizon, Garrick had finally drifted into a deep slumber and Brenna rose for her morning prayer suffering a splitting headache. She knelt below the window and prayed through her misery, imploring God to forgive and bestow comfort. Brenna's headache grew in its intensity until it seemed she could feel the nerves in her head burning, then pain followed some obscure pathway to ignite her ethmoid sinus and raced into her right ear as if the inferno craved the dry tinder of her tender hearing.

The Great Eye Nebula, a bright and distinctive astronomical feature that graced spring and summer skies, made its first appearance of the season, just creeping over the horizon before the Daystar rose above the ice field. When Brenna saw the beautiful, blue-green disk wash away in the glare of morning light, she wept until every tear welling from within spilled from her eyes.

Lieutenant Hougen, passing near the stairwell on her way to breakfast, heard Brenna's sobbing. Mariel approached and offered her assistance, wondering whether the handsome Tamarian soldier sleeping nearby played a role in the Lithian girl's obvious misery. Brenna seemed inconsolable, so Lieutenant Hougen approached Garrick and roused him from his slumber. He didn't awaken easily.

When Garrick saw Brenna's distress, he staggered over to her. "What's wrong?" he inquired.

The Long Journey: *Above the Clouds*

Brenna embraced him tightly and wouldn't let go. She spoke between episodes of rapid, shallow breathing, but Garrick couldn't understand what she was saying. He looked at Lieutenant Hougen, whose dark brown eyes expressed worry.

"She says she's forsaken and beyond hope. Other than that, she's not making any sense," the lieutenant stated.

Garrick nodded. "It's altitude sickness. I tried the infirmary earlier, but it's closed."

"Nonsense!" the Tamarian officer spat. "It's open all night long. People get sick up here all the time!"

Garrick looked at her with incredulity. "I swear, ma'am. Last time we were awake, I went upstairs but the door was shut and locked!"

"Let's get her up there," Mariel ordered in a manner more suggestive than authoritative. "It's clear she needs a doctor."

Under normal circumstances, Garrick could have carried Brenna up the stairs with ease. When she stood, Garrick could rest his chin on the top of Brenna's head, and she possessed a far more slender build than he. However, Garrick found his strength sapped in the thin air. He could not lift Brenna for fear of either falling or dropping her, and struggled to complete the ascent under his own power.

Lieutenant Hougen put Brenna's left arm around her own shoulder, while Garrick did the same on the right side, and together, the three of them attempted the climb. They needed better than five minutes to scale a single flight of stairs, and when they arrived, Garrick discovered, to his astonishment that the infirmary entrance didn't even have a door!

After Brenna had been admitted, the Tamarians went to the outside waiting area. "I think the thin air has affected your judgment, soldier," Lieutenant Hougen teased, grasping his shoulder and letting her hand linger there a little longer than was necessary.

Garrick sat down, shaking his head. "I got sick last time I was up here, too, but I felt worse than this. I must have gone to the wrong place last night."

They chatted about how high altitude effects human physiology, sharing anecdotes from their experiences, learning a little about each other's respective backgrounds. In the midst of this pleasant conversation, a tired physician appeared. "The foreign girl is very ill," he began, speaking directly to Garrick. "I'm not entirely certain that her internal physiology is identical to yours and mine, but her symptoms lead me to believe she's exhibiting early signs of cerebral edema. We need to get her downhill right away."

"But the train doesn't leave until this afternoon. What do we do until then?"

The doctor shook his head. "I meant right away," he clarified. "She'll go down on the emergency tram. It leaves in fifteen minutes."

Because of its extreme elevation, the Traitor's Pass facility maintained a tiny cable tram leading down the Hangman River cataract to the Lonely Meadow Valley, far below. The sole purpose of this service involved transporting people with severe altitude sickness to safety. It carried a maximum of four passengers and a single nurse.

"I can't let her go alone," Garrick stated, his worry cutting an edge into his voice. "I need to get her things."

When he began to rise, the doctor stopped him with an outstretched hand. "No, son. You have to take the train. The tram will be full with your girl, a medic and two other patients. You can meet her at the Lonely Meadow Sanitarium. If she survives the trip down, I expect she'll be fully recovered in a day or two."

Stunned, Garrick slumped into his seat and rubbed his hands over his face. He thought for a moment and looked up at the doctor. "Isn't there anything else you can do?"

"She's sleeping and we have her on oxygen right now. You should've brought her to me hours ago."

The boy let out a deep sigh and shook his head. "I know," he muttered. "Can I see her?"

The doctor shook his head. "No. I want her to rest. In my judgment your presence agitates her. She settled down once you left the room."

This news hit Garrick hard. He'd developed a subconscious belief in Brenna's physical invulnerability that lay shattered in the gravity of her current condition. Initially, he wanted to deny the obvious truth, but as doctor's diagnosis sank into his mind, Garrick felt angry, blaming himself for exposing her to this kind of danger. "We should have gone the long way," he grumbled.

Wishing to distract the young solider from this line of thinking, Lieutenant Hougen offered to share breakfast. Garrick innocently agreed, under the condition that he could gather Brenna's belongings and send them downhill on the tram with her. "She'll need her cold weather gear at least," the boy said. "Otherwise she'll freeze to death."

The Long Journey: *Above the Clouds*

At the laundry, the two soldiers picked up freshly washed clothes. Lieutenant Hougen carried winter gear in for Brenna and helped her put on her parka and gloves, while Garrick changed in the men's room. The two Tamarians watched as Brenna and the other sick passengers were loaded into the aerial tram. Garrick lingered at the window until the cable car vanished downslope, fighting tears, feeling angry and impotent.

"Come on, soldier," the lieutenant called. "Let's eat breakfast."

Mariel Hougen had freckled skin and a remarkably slim figure for a Tamarian woman. In general, the daughters of the High Land appeared sturdy, strong, tall and round-faced with blonde hair and light-colored eyes. The lieutenant's hair, tied up in a bun behind her beret, reflected reddish light that glinted in her dark, smoky quartz-colored eyes. She looked exotic when contrasted with her citizen sisters.

Though Mariel, like Brenna, was much older than the young soldier, Garrick found her intelligent and interesting. But unlike Brenna–whom people frequently mistook for a teenager–Mariel looked her age. He learned that her mother came from eastern desert region south of the Saradon, where dark eyes and red hair frequently graced the features of people native to that area. Mariel's family owned land on Sharp Talon Ridge, a place famous for its apples and a location significant to him because during the war he'd battled a deathwolf in an orchard a few miles from the Hougen property.

The cafeteria bustled at the height of breakfast service. Due to their unusual mountaintop posting, the garrison stationed at Traitor's Pass ate their meals together. Officers mingled with enlisted men, their laughter and discussion growing as the food service progressed. Hot food smelled delicious and though eating felt deeply satisfying, Garrick restrained his zeal for the sake of good manners.

While eating, Garrick learned that Mariel joined the army to help pay for her education. An interest in language, particularly her mother's native dialect, availed no advantage to a farmer's daughter, even a wealthy one, but the army maintained a large corps of linguists in its espionage department. Lieutenant Hougan, who'd learned seven languages, translated documents written in Azgaril Vulgate or Parsinnian, the obscure, desert-derived tongue of her mother that was often used for message traffic, two languages of Kameron and that of the Vatherii, a people living to the north. In exchange for this service, she claimed the Tamarian army subsidized her ongoing studies. At present, she said she was traveling to the university in Marvic to work on a doctorate in linguistics, and on the way, had stopped at Traitor's Pass to relax for a few days. Her last statement raised suspicion in Garrick's mind, but he said nothing, letting her talk.

"Most of what I do is boring," she admitted. "I translate newspapers and government publications, but the army wants to know what it all really means, and that's the job of an analyst familiar with the culture."

"But enough about me," she concluded. "Tell me about you."

Garrick shrugged. "There's nothing interesting about me."

"Ah, but there is!" she countered. "You're romantically involved with an alien mercenary. In my line of work that makes you interesting."

"So, lieutenant, you're a spy now?" he queried.

She dismissed the remark. "Don't be silly. At first I wondered why a good-looking Tamarian boy would bother with some foreigner who speaks the enemy's language, but then I took a good look at her while we got her into her clothes and I know why you like her!" Mariel smiled lecherously. "Let's just say I noticed how she fills out those little running sweats of hers."

"You think that's all I care about?" he asked, blushing, desperate to change the subject. "If I took an interest in you because of your red hair, how long do you think that would sustain my attention?"

"I think that would depend on which red hair you were looking at," she replied, lowering her head, crossing her legs and provocatively leaning forward.

Garrick felt he was being outmaneuvered and needed to think fast, but he stammered uncharacteristically with his words. "Lieutenant, I know that Brenna's beautiful," he began. "But don't patronize me with that kind of simplistic talk."

Lieutenant Hougen laughed. "Yeah, right! Convince me that when she moves around, or rubs her soft parts on you that you're thinking about her goodness and character. Come on, soldier, do you think I was born yesterday?"

Although Garrick knew it was risky to reveal his irritation with an officer, he'd grown impatient with this kind of accusation. "Lieutenant, I don't appreciate you talking about her like that. What do you know about Brenna, anyway? How can you disconnect her intellect and focus on her body like she's some rack of meat in the market? I've just watched her leave here on a cart with a tube in her nose, I don't know if I'll ever see her alive again and you think my primary concern centers on how she looks when she's wearing her running sweats? Are you out of your mind?

"I've fought with this girl at my side for months. I've watched her risk her life for the guys in my unit, dragging their broken bodies to safety while the enemy shot at her. Together we've been tired, cold, hungry and terrified. I've heard her laugh; I've watched her cry. I've listened when she vents frustration because people hate her without reason.

"She prays over me, lieutenant, though I don't even believe in her God. Brenna accepts me just as I am. In the past few hours I've seen what she's like when she's deathly sick, and I don't know if I'll ever see any of those other things again." Garrick's eyes brimmed with tears, but he restrained his anger, holding back his fear and sorrow. "Don't tell me what I love about her, " he concluded. "That's for her and me alone to know."

Lieutenant Hougan felt a tide of remorse rising within her, having utterly miscalculated the depth of Garrick's dedication. She looked away, regretting her attitude, regretting her words. The linguist shook her pretty head. "Well, Mister Ravenwood, I've been out of line." She paused, searching for the right thing to say, as if words well spoken could mend her mistake. "I hope you can forgive me for misjudging you and misjudging her. She's clearly put her name on your heart, and I can honestly say she's honored to have won your devotion."

When Mariel met his gaze, she saw the eyes of a killer gradually soften. "I can forgive you, lieutenant," he said. "I can forgive you."

* * *

Brenna drifted into consciousness, vaguely aware of a pulsing sensation, a vertigo-inspired nausea wrenching at her belly. Cold and disoriented, she didn't recognize any of her surroundings, but the irresistible siren song of sleep lulled her into darkness again.

Voices faded in and out of her memory. Light and shadow flashed across her lovely face. Time drifted like the current of a languid river rolling into a serene sea. Pain swelled in her temples, remorse flooded her mind. Brenna rolled her head to the side, opened her eyes and saw a benign smile spread across the countenance of a heavyset woman.

A ravenous thirst soon gripped her throat. Brenna tried to get up, only to find that she'd been strapped to a gurney. "Water," she

The Long Journey: *Above the Clouds*

whispered, speaking the Tamarian word in the hope she'd pronounced it well enough to be understood.

The nurse gently lifted the back of Brenna's head and held a cup to her lips, watching carefully to see that the foreign girl did not choke. A moment later she removed the tube that had been taped to Brenna's nose, shut off the oxygen supply, then turned to care for someone else. Brenna remembered nothing more.

A long time later she felt a jolt and heard voices speaking Tamarian words too rapidly for her to understand. The aroma of thick, sweet, forest-scented air teased her senses. When Brenna inhaled, she felt her lungs fill, realizing that her headache had faded into memory. People moved about, three other patients vanished and Brenna was left alone until she began napping again. Suddenly, someone swirled her hospital gurney around, she felt its wheels rumble over something metallic, then glide on a hard, smooth surface.

A raindrop fell on her face from the clouds above. She saw trees bursting with the foliage of a new spring, and the glorious sensation of a pleasant, cool breeze caressing her skin. An unfamiliar landscape, dotted with blooming aspen, alder and cottonwood trees, covered in grasses sprouting delicate pink, yellow and violet blossoms, flashed across Brenna's field of vision.

The idyllic scene passed as she traveled beneath a low overhang, set with electric lights. Brenna felt the cart stop, saw a male figure wearing white open a set of double doors, then return to pulling her bed into a building that smelled of detergent and overcooked food. He led her through a long hallway then stopped at several rooms. In each instance, Brenna heard female voices protesting the sight of her, and by this time in her Tamarian experience, the Lithian girl didn't need the words translated to comprehend their intent. The attendant dutifully moved onward until finally, he stopped at a quiet room, lowered the gurney and loosened the straps across Brenna's body.

He spoke to her with a respectful tone, though she did not understand what he'd said. Brenna sat up, took off her gloves and parka, straightened her rumpled running sweats, then dropped to the warm floor while holding on to the hospital cart for support. The man silently beckoned her inside with a universally understood gesture, pointing to a bed near a window in which he apparently wished her to rest. After this, he unloaded Brenna's belongings, then disappeared with the gurney down the hall.

The Long Journey: *Above the Clouds*

The tiny room contained little in the way of furnishings. A neatly made bed equipped with white sheets and a yellow blanket lay next to a small wooden stand upon which a pitcher of water and a drinking glass awaited her attention. Next to the pitcher lay a writing pad and pen. Along the wall adjacent to the bed stood a clothing rack with wire hangers, and beside it, a simple, two-drawer bureau. A toilet, a washbasin and an elevated, freestanding shower stall with a starkly white cloth curtain completed the room furnishings.

While Brenna grew accustomed to the antiseptic odor, she rummaged through her backpack for a comb, desperate to restore her matted and disheveled hair to its normal, glistening glory. She began working the comb through her tangled locks with care, irritated with herself for neglecting this task, not remembering why she had.

Just as she completed her grooming ritual, a middle-aged woman wearing glasses and holding a clipboard strode into the room without bothering to knock. "Specialist Velez," she called in vulgate with a throaty, Tamarian accent. The woman held out a wristband. "This is your identification bracelet. You will wear it at all times and use it to pay for meals served at this facility."

"Where am I?" Brenna inquired. "What am I doing here?"

The woman put her chin down, peering over her glasses. "This is the Lonely Meadow Sanitarium," she responded in a condescending voice. "Your illness at Traitor's Pass compelled the army to transport and admit you here at great expense, one compounded by the fact that none of the other guests are willing to share a room with you. The doctor will be in for his examination shortly. I expect your stay will be brief, perhaps no more than a day, and we'll send you off to wherever people of your kind go."

Brenna overlooked the insult. "Where's Garrick?"

"I don't know who you're talking about," the woman said as she turned on her heel and headed out the door.

"What about the train?" Brenna cried. "Where do I go to meet the train?" Her words met the woman's back, but had no further impact.

Brenna shut and locked her door, drew the curtains across the window, drank a glass of water, then knelt on the hard, tile floor and prayed for nearly thirty minutes. She talked to God about the direction of her life, asked for strength, remembered her family members by name and prayed a blessing upon Garrick, who remained somewhere above the clouds. She missed him. Though she felt lonely for his companionship, after praying Brenna felt better.

A knock interrupted her meditations. Brenna opened the door to find the heavyset nurse and a tall, thin man wearing wire framed glasses waiting together in the hallway.

"Why missy! You're up!" the nurse said in vulgate. "That's good news!" Without asking to enter, the woman walked into the room and introduced Dr. Schultz to Brenna, as if she'd been a friend of the Lithian girl for a long time.

The physician, speaking through the Tamarian woman, asked Brenna a series of well-being related questions, listened to her heart and lungs through a stethoscope, then grunted and muttered a few sentences to the nurse. He walked out of the room without a farewell.

"He says that for somebody knocking at death's door a few hours ago, you've come up strong as a fish thrown back in water," the blonde-haired nurse began. "But he wants you to rest before you move on."

Brenna shook her head. "I can't. I need to be in Marvic soon."

The nurse wrinkled her face and shrugged. "Doctor's orders. You ought to relax. Put your feet up and rest a spell. Fetch some dinner if you fancy. They got someone working the grill right now. The cafeteria's just behind the lobby."

Worried that her separation from Garrick would lengthen, but not wanting to trouble this kindly woman further, Brenna sighed. "Thank you. I appreciate your help."

The nurse patted Brenna on the knee as if she were a small child. "I take care of people," she said. "That's what I do. And I don't much care what folk say about you being a foreigner and all. I pay no never mind to that sort of thing, 'specially since they told me what you done for my people. You take care, missy. I'll see you 'round."

When the nurse left, Brenna began feeling hemmed in by the small room, confined as if she'd been imprisoned. Eating seemed like a good idea, given that she'd had neither breakfast, nor lunch, and that last night's meal ended up in the multrum toilet. The girl found her cleaned halter–using the unique, Lithian garment as underwear–pulled on her boots, hid her valuables beneath the mattress and took the note pad and pen from her bedside table. Then peering out of her door, Brenna waited until the hallway lay empty before venturing out of her private space.

The Long Journey: *Above the Clouds*

Originally developed as a resort for wealthy patrons, the Lonely Meadow complex retained its distinctive luxury when sold to an investor who converted the facility into a health spa. Its rich carpet, patterned in roses, the inlaid floorboards, intricately designed crown moldings and expensive, electric lights attested to a fading, former glory.

The main building, constructed in a V shape, segregated men and women on opposite sides, with a blossoming garden and an overgrown lawn that functioned as a common area between them. Directly behind the lobby, located at the building's vertex, its renovated restaurant served as a cafeteria. Hoping to avoid the dinner crowd, Brenna headed there, sat in a chair and watched a handful of guests select food and show their wristbands at the cashier's table.

Her inability to speak more than a few Tamarian words compounded the girl's natural reticence. Brenna felt anxious enough, however, to attempt some form of communication. On the paper she'd brought, Brenna drew a mountain whose peak ascended above the clouds, a train with an arrow pointing downhill, and a V shaped building representing the sanitarium. She knew the interrogative words for "where" and "when" in the local language, having heard them spoken many times, and did her best to spell them correctly on the paper.

Selecting a tray and moving through the cafeteria line, she picked some fruit, dinner rolls, smoked fish, raw vegetables and salad, avoiding the jolly man at the grill entirely. At the cashier, she presented her wristband, then gave the elderly woman the slip of paper on which she had diagramed her questions.

The white-haired woman looked at Brenna, smiled without showing any teeth, nodded, and flipped the paper over. She drew the V shaped building, the Hangman River and a long rectangle upstream of their current location with a railroad track going into and out of the figure. The woman pointed to the word "where," then directed Brenna's attention toward the northeast. Next, the woman drew two mountains and a circle with rays that clearly represented the Daystar. She drew arrows showing the Daystar's path across the sky, with it setting behind the far mountain. She circled the setting star, then pointed to the word "when."

Brenna thanked her. The woman regarded her with an expression of sympathy, and Brenna prayed a blessing on the elderly matron when she sat down to thank Allfather for her food. She felt grateful that at least some Tamarians, though they might be strangers, extended civility to her.

Hours later, Brenna decided to defy the doctor's orders, gather her belongings and head for the train. Knowing that Garrick liked the way she looked in her form-fitting parade uniform, she washed, changed and made herself as attractive as modesty allowed. She slipped her backpack and weapons out of the window and hid them behind a shrub, then simply walked out of the entrance and around the building to the window. The Lithian girl put on her backpack, slithered into her waterproof poncho, grabbed her weapons and scurried away. No one noticed her departure.

A light rain fell. Tall grasses painted Brenna's boots and skirt with moisture as she walked through the meadow. Mist clung to the tree-clad mountainsides, moving slowly in the cool, gentle breeze, first enshrouding, then revealing, tall spruce and fir trees. Brenna felt alive and free, purposeful in her escape, rejoicing to breathe deeply and feel a familiar, youthful vigor pulsing through her veins.

The train station lay several hundred yards away, along the banks of the Hangman River. A simple, wood framed structure with an elevated platform served the modest transport and mail delivery needs of the Lonely Meadow Sanitarium and local residents. Its siding and large timbers, painted yellow and trimmed in white, showed the tender care of regular maintenance, as the date on the station's marquee boasted that it had been standing for better than one hundred years.

Brenna found a seat on the platform, glanced at the clock and waited. Nearly an hour later, she heard the distinctive growl of a Tamarian locomotive descending from above the clouds. She removed her poncho and stood on the platform, waiting.

Lieutenant Mariel Hougen noticed Brenna through the mist as the train slowed to enter the Lonely Meadow station. She turned around to rouse Garrick, who'd been sleeping in the seat behind her. "Wake up, soldier! Your damsel awaits!"

Garrick found his heart pounding. When his eyes met Brenna's longing gaze he thought he'd never seen her as beautiful as she appeared at that moment. Before the train came to a complete stop, he leaped through the opening door, ran toward Brenna's smiling face and into her outstretched arms.

Anger

High Priest Volker Pfaff rubbed his forehead, wishing the young men under his care could skip adolescence altogether and move directly from the sweet cooperation of childhood into the maturity of an adult mind set. The ageing priest often complained to his wife that hair loss resulted from raising other people's children; he cared for the spiritual welfare of boys whose problems often originated in family dynamics imprinted long before he and the Temple community had any opportunity to exert significant influence.

He'd found not a single more compelling case during his entire career than could be ascribed to the sullen young man sitting before him. Dressed in the dark grey robe that proclaimed his rank just one tier below that of Initiate Priest, this boy moved through his studies with astonishing alacrity. He demonstrated a gift for learning quickly, along with an independent spirit unafraid to question orthodoxy. Intense, and driven by smoldering rage often manifest in an ill temper and an acrid wit, this boy possessed an alarming tendency to raise nearly every conflict with anyone he did not respect beyond the threshold of violence.

As had been the case several times over the past three months, the petulant acolyte waited for Volker Pfaff to administer the appointed wrath of the Supreme Council. This responsibility, the priest often complained to his wife, put him in an adversarial relationship with a boy whom he genuinely liked. The strain showed on the priest's worried face, his tired, green eyes and the tone of a voice that preferred gentle counsel to the reprimand this boy deserved. Calloused hands ran through thinning hair as the old priest searched his soul for words he wished could remain undelivered.

The boy broke the silence. "Are you going to sit there all day?"

Volker looked at the acolyte and sighed deeply. "You do yourself harm with that tone," he said, gently. "There is no need for insolence."

Those angry, grey eyes, that piercing stare so often employed against the other priests in the classroom, other students on the practice mat, other citizens living near the Temple compound, swept across the bright, white painted walls and simple wooden furnishings that lay arranged in Volker's office. "The Council can't control me. You can't control me. Give me my punishment, I'll do my stinking penance and you can put this sorry exercise behind you again."

The Long Journey: *Anger*

"Until next time," Volker replied, "and the time after that. How long must this go on?"

"It'll go on until I'm ranked high enough to leave this pathetic place."

Volker pointed to the door, his gentle voice steady, despite the tension projected by his favored student. "You are always free to go."

The boy rolled his eyes and shook his head. "So you say," he replied. "But if I leave now I'll have no future and there's always a mountain of work waiting for me when I come back. Nobody else around here lifts a finger to help."

Volker Pfaff held up his hand to silence the diatribe. "Work takes no vacation. Why do you believe that when you disappear for days on end another must shoulder your burden? Would you appreciate a brother who did such a thing to you?"

"This is about control, not responsibility. I always get my work done, no matter how high you pile it on!"

"You have no more toil here than does anyone else your age," the high priest interrupted. "But that isn't the cause for this meeting, and of this, I am sure you are well aware."

The boy slumped in his high-backed chair, crossing his arms, staring at the religious books neatly arranged on Volker's study shelf. "Yeah, I hurt the fat kid," he muttered.

"The practice mat is no place to vent your anger," Volker continued. "We work together on skill, balance, speed, power and agility. We sharpen our combat skills. We do not seek harm to our brethren."

"Oh, come on!" the boy countered. "Dietrich flops around like a lame gerbil and cries like a waterfall. How can you expect me to avoid knocking him down?"

Volker remained unruffled. "I expect self control. That is the essence of our being in the spiritual community. We serve others because we keep our own desires in check."

Now the boy scoffed. "Oh, that's why you permit my slutty sister to go around giving blow jobs to everyone in the dorm!"

This type of exchange occurred with great frequency whenever Volker had to mete out punishment for some kind of misbehavior. Acolyte Algernon Ravenwood always tried to avoid accountability by deflecting attention onto someone else's miscreance, and though clearly disgusted by his twin sister's conduct, the boy felt no compunction about openly discussing her impropriety if doing so meant he could use her malfeasance to effectively obviate the Council's wrath.

But Volker didn't follow that path. "Kira is not under my care, nor is she the subject of our discussion. However, since you insist on addressing licentiousness, I must also elucidate that your habit of snooping on the women's bath and the self-stimulating behavior that follows will, from this moment, forever cease."

If Algernon felt shock over this revelation, he recovered quickly enough that Volker barely noticed a change in the acolyte's expression. "You can prove nothing," he replied.

"I have witnessed what you do," Volker admitted, his tone devoid of the emotion rising in his student's voice. "Priestess Sommer has repaired the orifice you drilled into the wall and set a tapestry on the other side. Regular inspections of the bath have begun to ensure that the privacy of our women remains sacrosanct."

Algernon seethed, his lips tightening. "So what's the verdict?"

"All outcomes depend upon you," Volker responded. "Neither I, nor the Council, wish to impose a punitive sanction upon you. However, as leaders in this community we assent to the incumbent responsibility of maintaining peaceful relations, not only within the walls of the Sacred Enclosure, but also beyond them."

"And you pull that off with punishment!" Algernon sneered. "How noble!"

The boy lacked courtesy, but he fully understood the tenets of *Gottslena*, the sacred set of Tamarian writings to which the Great Temple Elsbireth had been devoted. In this philosophy, an unnamed deity–a spirit humans could not comprehend–set forth the process of creation with love and great piety, then observed it from afar. The Great God, the chief of all spirits, left to humankind the responsibility of safeguarding life, maintaining justice and defending liberty. Within the context of many local spirits competing for worshipers and exerting control over limited spheres of influence, this mysterious deity encouraged all creatures to live in harmony with their appointed purpose, that it might vicariously learn the lessons experienced by every living thing. Only within a mutually edifying community that practiced self-control and meditation–so the monks believed–could they attain the nobility of mind for which they'd been destined and ordained.

Algernon used this ideology against his teachers at every opportunity, twisting the precepts presented to him as truth in a manner that exposed their folly. The need to impose order by force, in his particular case and from his view, utterly contravened a critical concept in the *Gottslena* philosophy. An individual, whose unique perspective offered lessons for the great deity, simply should not require any measure of restraint to assimilate into the community for which that person had been destined. While it would have been easy for an outsider to attribute base deviancy to Algernon's behavior, an idea promoted within *Gottslena* to explain criminality, Algernon sustained the highest academic achievement ever attained by any acolyte, and only in the past few weeks had his concupiscent sister, Kira, begun falling behind. This prevented any serious discussion of their dismissal, for the extreme self-discipline demanded of *Gottslena* study, which included mathematics, sciences, martial arts, languages, economics, history and philosophy, should have naturally overwhelmed an unsuitable candidate at an early stage.

Therefore, the Ravenwood children presented an enigma to the experienced priests, who for over three years watched them with a blend of dismay and wonder. While many Supreme Council members agonized over the mounting evidence of Algernon's violent temper, they could not prevent him from learning the combat skills intrinsic to his program of mental, spiritual and physical development. Nor could they arrive at a suitable means of restraining Kira's libido, as the girl continually exploited her considerable sensuality to shame, embarrass and control her teachers and fellow students, male and female alike.

Typically, the Council encouraged the priests who oversaw the Ravenwood siblings to up the ante with additional study and more physical work in response to the rising tide of transgression. Limiting the free time in which the two Ravenwoods could get into mischief didn't really work, as Algernon seemed to attract trouble wherever he went, and Kira found that the shameless, semi-public performance of fellatio or cunnilingus often increased the intensity of her selected lover's response.

Volker Pfaff suppressed a deep sigh, saddened that so much potential for excellence lay within a boy for whom that nobility seemed an anathema. Algernon did not know how stridently his mentor advocated for him at the Supreme Council meetings, nor did he appreciate that Volker's position eroded with each accumulated incident set before the increasingly impatient priesthood.

The Long Journey: *Anger*

"Discipline can be unpleasant," Volker stated. Then, using the weapon he'd been reluctant to wield, the priest began outlining the scope of Algernon's penance. "Though you may leave here any time you wish, as of this hour when the doors close behind you, they will forever remain closed. You will not be permitted re-entrance within the Sacred Gate. And should you elect to depart from our care, where will you go? Can you return home to your drunken father? Will the mother who forcefully evicted you draw her wayward son back into her bosom with a gentle embrace?"

Algernon's face began to pale. He slumped in his chair, eyes widened.

"This is your home now. You are my son now, and if I did not love you I would not wish to restrain your self-destructive impulses. So these are the conditions upon which your stay in this hallowed place may continue: First, you will always show deference and respect to senior priests. You will remain silent in your classes. All questions directed to your teacher must be written down and submitted with respect at the conclusion of each lesson. Second, you shall not leave these premises without my direct permission."

Volker paused, noting that Algernon's icy expression melted rapidly. When the boy said nothing in response, the High Priest continued. "Third, you will not engage in any undisciplined social behavior, which includes, but is not limited to, all physical contact with and clandestine observation of acolyte priestesses, whom you are to regard as sisters with absolute purity; unrestrained force on the practice mat and any use of secret martial knowledge against civilians within or beyond these walls. In addition, you will treat these venerated grounds with the greatest respect and refrain from inflicting damage herein. This includes mischief such as putting flour in the organ pipes, urinating in the consecrated wine and blending opiates into the meditation incense.

"You must conduct yourself in a manner worthy of the calling to which you aspire. Your labor shall always be done in a timely manner, with excellence and without lament. If you do not agree to these conditions, I must remove you from the Sacred Enclosure."

Stunned, Algernon said nothing for a long time. He straightened, swallowed and licked his dry lips. "So, that's it, then?" he asked. "I do what you say, or you kick me out."

High Priest Volker Pfaff made a steeple of his fingers and nodded, sadly. "To my dismay, it has come to this."

The Long Journey: *Anger*

Algernon paused, thoughtfully. "Then we have nothing more to discuss," he said, rising from his seat.

"There is one more thing," Volker stated. When the boy turned around, he continued. "Your elder brother has contacted us, looking for you and your sister."

"Garrick is here?" Algernon inquired, astonished. "He made it through the war?"

Volker knew the esteem in which both of the Ravenwood twins regarded their older sibling, and he'd hoped that Garrick's arrival in Marvic would inspire a higher degree of self-control. Yet the High Priest had been disappointed so many times in the past, he could not sustain confidence that Garrick's presence in town would have a lasting impact.

"He's attending Officer's Training School and will study in the city for a period of twelve weeks."

Algernon approached Volker's desk and put his hands on its lacquered surface. "Can I see him?" the boy inquired. "Please?"

Volker understood this need for connection with family, but Garrick had not come in person, he'd sent a letter from the big military base on the northern edge of town, near the wall. "He writes that his course work, training and an upcoming court appearance will preclude visiting here for several days." The High Priest removed a neatly folded letter from a right-hand drawer and offered it to Algernon.

The meek tone of Algernon's previous question vaporized like mist on a summer day. "You read my brother's letter?" the boy inquired, accusingly. "You opened something addressed to me?"

Volker shook his head serenely. "I have done no such thing, nor would I."

Algernon saw that the letter had been written to the Supreme Council, and that Garrick implied in his opening statement that he knew something of the trouble his younger siblings were capable of creating. In actual fact, Garrick asked permission to come to the Temple, in fear that his surprise arrival might be disruptive.

"Well, that's my brother," Algernon muttered. "Still sucking the tit of authority."

Volker raised his eyebrows. "Yet you respect him," he stated, somewhat surprised.

Algernon folded the letter and slid it back across the desktop. "He's my brother. No one loves me like he does. He's my blood, the beat of my heart and the breath of my soul."

The Long Journey: *Anger*

"Your devotion is well placed," Volker replied. "I will let you know when he comes to see you. That is all for now."

Algernon left Volker's office, shutting the heavy oaken door with more force than was necessary. He ignored the stern glare of Priest Willem and turned down the long, wooden-floored hallway, past the chapel nave where sacred services were underway and into the classroom annex, where remedial mathematics teaching awaited his attention.

Some nameless architect of long ago had drawn plans for the Temple building and several of its lesser structures. The Elsbireth complex, unlike most Tamarian architecture, reflected the philosophy of simple function. Therefore, its high ceilings did not feature colorful frescoes, its doors and alcoves remained unadorned, and the only nod to beauty within its hallowed space lay in seasonal tapestries hung from its walls. These often consisted of theological lessons, depicted with a great flourish in pictorial form, for the benefit of illiterates and children.

The landscaping that lay around the Temple, however, thrived in the cool, high altitude climate. Ferns and flowers arranged in flowing borders, carefully trimmed evergreen shrubbery and terraced gardens graced ornamental grasslands, permitting quiet introspection near blue and green groves of tall spruce and fir trees. Bamboo clumps, cedar lattices graced with dark delphinium, and fruit trees spreading their blossoming arms into the mist contrasted color and texture to please every lingering eye.

Near gurgling pools formed by hot mineral springs, where the River Honeywater began its descent toward the distant sea, carved lanterns stood among the mosses, guarding narrow stone bridges leading toward tiny, secluded islands that lay amidst the falling water. Iris and azalea adorned dark rock formations. Even in winter, the warmth of the Honeywater preserved plant life that could not long survive at this altitude, and provided respite for a troupe of visiting macaques that spent the coldest months in these gardens before moving back into the upland forest during the spring.

These intelligent and sociable creatures chattered incessantly in their rudimentary language, beyond the tall, multi-pane classroom windows where Algernon led a group of orphaned children in the study of basic mathematics. He liked teaching. The quick wit that inspired chagrin among the older monks served him well when fielding questions, or finding a unique way of explaining a given operation to a struggling student.

At the end of the lesson Algernon dismissed his charges and headed to the men's serving room to eat a meal of soup and bread. Prayer and meditation hour in the chapel followed this. Afterward, a science and history review at a library table occupied the evening until his candle waxed low. Later, he spent some time working through quadratic formulas until he could barely keep his eyes open.

Algernon slept in a large room on the upper floor with fifteen other candidate priests. Often his devotion to study made him the last to retire for the night, so no one found his late arrival unusual. Although he felt very tired, the distractions and trouble of the day made it hard for him to relax. Eventually, the rhythmic breathing of the other young men lulled him into sleep.

It seemed that he hadn't been in dreamland long when a soft hand and a whispered, female voice roused him. "Wake up," she urged. "Come on, wake up!"

The tall and slender young woman at his bedside sniffed, then wiped her nose on the right sleeve of her thin gown. Algernon recognized her as his mind labored into consciousness, and he hid no contempt from his tone of voice. "Astrid! What are you doing here?"

"I need to talk to you. It's important."

"Blow off, you slut! I'm sleeping!"

"Algernon," she pleaded. "I need your help! Your sister's gone!"

Something in the urgency of Astrid's voice stirred an old emotion within Algernon's soul. He didn't like Kira's proclivities, especially as they related to Astrid, who was widely rumored to be her favorite partner, but he did love his sister. The young acolyte sat up in his cot and reached for his robe and pleated overcoat. "We can't talk in here," he whispered. "Follow me."

Algernon enjoyed solitude and knew of several secret hiding places within the Temple compound. Although spring flushed the afternoon air with the lukewarm promise of coming summer, nights in Marvic still remained uncomfortably cool. His feet felt cold as he stole a stealthy, barefooted path down from the men's dormitory, through the back of the dark and silent chancel nave, and up an old, narrow staircase that spiraled into the Temple's bell tower.

This area remained deserted at night, and because it ranked low on his list of hiding places, Algernon did not hesitate to lead Astrid up the

The Long Journey: *Anger*

dim stairwell. In fact, he felt surprised that she trusted him enough to follow, for he could have overpowered her easily on a stair landing and no one would have heard her cries for help.

Astrid knew that Algernon didn't like her, and was wise enough in a worldly sense to feel uncomfortable in any isolated place with a boy well known for his violent temper. Fighting back tears, emotional vulnerable and frightened by an unexpected turn of events, her proximity to Kira's brother inspired a swelling storm of contradictory feelings that felt ready to burst from within her soul like rain from dark, heavily laden clouds. She climbed the stairs in trepidation, ready to flee if she felt threatened.

Sensing this, Algernon sat down across the landing, just below the final approach to the bell chamber. Cool air drifted down from the open shutters of the tower. The stairwell smelled of old wood, rain, incense and candle wax. "I won't hurt you," he began. "Tell me what happened to Kira."

Astrid leaned against the wall, crossing her arms in a defensive posture. "They caught her with one of your friends, you know," she said, somewhat tentatively.

"I have no friends," Algernon replied. "I can't trust anyone around here."

The young woman shivered as cold air swept through her thin, flannel gown. "Gunnar thinks you're his friend," she continued. "He made Kira swear she would never tell you about them."

Algernon shook his head. "Well next time I see her I'll tell her to bite!" he snapped, his emotions roiling angrily as he imagined Gunnar enjoying Kira's intimate pleasures. A cold stare hardened on his face.

"You don't understand her," Astrid said in Kira's defense. "It's the only way she has any control in her life. It's her way of getting back at everyone. It's her way of feeling good when everyone else in the world, including you, makes her feel bad. You have the same problem, but your methods are different."

"Don't lecture me!" he warned. "You're a lesbian slut wearing a saintly mask, crying because you have to please yourself tonight. Don't sermonize me about good behavior."

Astrid began to weep with her head in her hands, shaking and sobbing. "I love Kira!" she said. "You don't understand. You'll never understand!"

The Long Journey: *Anger*

"No!" Algernon replied. "You diddle her. She diddles you. That's not love!"

"What do you know about how I feel? Why am I even talking to you?" Astrid cried aloud, turning and heading down the stairs.

Realizing that his attitude was driving Astrid away, Algernon responded angrily. He leaped toward her, his strong hands forcefully grasping the soft flesh of her upper arms, and pinned the slim girl against the wall to prevent her escape. She struggled, but he quickly overpowered her resistance. "Astrid, listen to me," he commanded. "I admit that was a dumb thing to say, and I'm sorry. But you dragged me out of bed for this and I want to know what's going on."

Astrid's wrinkled brow expressed pain. "You're hurting me!" she exclaimed. "You promised you wouldn't hurt me!"

Algernon hadn't even thought that his grip might inflict discomfort, and the shock of Astrid's lament coursed through his mind like a high voltage current. He dropped his hands and backed away, as if they'd acted by a will of their own. "Ok," he said, cautiously. "I'm sorry. I really didn't mean to hurt you." Algernon slowly retreated to the stair across the landing, watching Astrid carefully, cursing himself for reacting rather than thinking. "I love my sister," he said, "even if I don't like what she does."

Astrid rubbed her aching arms, staring skeptically, fearful of this boy whom she had to trust, and astonished at the strength of his grasp. She waited for what seemed like a long time before speaking. "Don't ever touch me again!" she warned.

Though she waited for Algernon to respond, he held his tongue and glared at her with a dangerous, predatory look. In the quietude of that moment, he could hear the breath quivering from her lips. Algernon knew how to inspire fear.

"Priestess Dorothea called her into the office again," Astrid continued, her voice trembling. "Kira told me that if she did another thing wrong, the Council would kick her out of the Temple forever."

Algernon gave the Supreme Council credit for its evenhanded treatment of his twin sister, but didn't appreciate their ultimatum to her any more than he did the one he'd received. "They won't do it," he muttered. "Too many of them benefit from her skills . . ."

"Stop it! Damn you!" Astrid exclaimed. "I don't care if you don't like me, but she's your sister. How can you talk about her like that?"

"Yeah, she's my sister," he replied. "But she's a cheap slut."

The Long Journey: *Anger*

"And you're a violent sociopath who can't deal with authority. You come from the same sick, demented family. You're two sides of a single coin."

Astrid's angry words slapped Algernon in his most vulnerable spot and they hurt him badly. He sat in stunned silence, and though he wanted to lash out and retaliate, the truth of her accusation wounded him so deeply he could not prevent his head from falling into his hands. Shame swelled within his mind. Algernon struggled to reassert control. The stairwell remained too dark for her to see tears flooding his vision, so he let them fall, irritated that she'd found his weakness. It took him a moment to regain command over his voice, but even then, it trembled with more emotion than he wished to reveal. "Don't talk about my family like that," he said. "You have no idea what we've been through." Algernon paused, inhaled slowly, then returned to his inquiry. "What happened to Kira?"

Sniffing, Astrid slid her back down the wall and curled up on a stair. "She told me she'd been seeing this guy named Marco," the young woman began. "Kira gets a new guy every week, it seems, so I didn't pay it much mind at first. They'd meet in the garden house during prayer time. She'd do her thing for Marco, and he started paying her with opium."

Algernon grunted in disgust and let out a long, low sigh. "That's why she's been losing weight," he said. "That's why her grades have been slipping."

"It hasn't been that long," Astrid replied, defensively. "There's a lot of other stuff going on with her that you don't know about."

"So what makes you think she's run away?" Algernon inquired.

Astrid remained quiet for a moment. "Normally, she comes to me at night," the girl admitted, "when it's quiet and everyone else has fallen asleep. I was expecting her, and when she didn't come I went to her room. I found her bed made, but her stuff is gone."

Because there were fewer female students aspiring to the priesthood, and because *Gottslena* acknowledged the need for a greater degree of privacy among young women beyond menarche, every young woman living in the monastery slept in a tiny, private room. This enabled the clandestine visits between Astrid and Kira, so long as they kept quiet. However, small rooms and thin walls made it very difficult for the two girls to keep their secret for very long. Hence, Algernon heard widespread whispering about the alleged relationship between

The Long Journey: *Anger*

Astrid and his sister, though no one offered any substantive proof of their murmured accusations.

Astrid's affirmation of this physical relationship presented Algernon with a hard truth he did not want to hear. Idle talk exchanged between third parties did not carry the same weight as an outright confession. Thus, he felt confronted with the awful choice of whether or not his love for Kira, the person with whom he'd shared their mother's womb, should diminish in light of this revelation. He simply couldn't make that choice, yet he struggled to distinguish her being from behavior of which he did not approve. Further, he knew that repudiating his sister altogether would not motivate any change on her part. Their relationship, already suffering from many strains, might be irrevocably harmed if Algernon made a another mistake, and the boy worried that without his protection, Kira might experience serious mistreatment.

In reality, High Priest Volker Pfaff faced the same problem. Algernon knew the old man loved him like a son, and though the boy hid behind the facade of an uncaring disposition, Algernon understood that his misdeeds hurt the compassionate priest. On a personal level the young acolyte felt guilty about this, but the momentum of reckless behavior he'd established prevented any real remonstrance and subsequent repentance.

At this point, Astrid began to cry again. She wept uncontrollably for a long time, unrestrained in her sorrow, until she felt Algernon's hand rest gently upon her shoulder. The girl stiffened. "I said don't touch me!" the girl shrieked, shrinking back, expecting pain. When she looked at him, however, Astrid realized that Algernon's eyes expressed a glint of pity, his reaching fingers intended comfort rather than repudiation, and in his right hand, Algernon offered his overcoat for her to wear. Astrid had never seen Kira's brother exhibit any kindness before, but the words that spilled from her lips underscored the reason for her trust in him.

"There's goodness inside of you," she said, sniffing, looking at the male reflection of her lover. She accepted his coat and slid it over her shoulders. "I knew it. You're just like Kira. There's goodness deep inside."

Algernon nodded. "I know," he whispered, sighing in meek admission. "I know."

The Long Journey: *Anger*

Astrid composed herself, embarrassed and a little afraid that Algernon would use her vulnerability for public humiliation. "Swear to me you won't tell anyone about me and Kira," she demanded.

Algernon bowed his head. "Do you really think anyone believes a word I say? My whole life is a lie! Besides, everybody knows what kind of girl you are."

"Kira told me all about you," Astrid said with an accusing tone. "Don't think that you have any secrets I don't know about."

Algernon wondered what that meant. At one time, he and Kira had been close. They were the best of friends and shared every childhood joy, their greatest hopes and deepest fears; however, the sibling bond between the twins began eroding when they were first separated at the Temple. Algernon watched his sister blossom physically, witnessed a change in Kira's demeanor and heard ill talk spread within the sacred community. In revulsion he distanced himself from her, though he never felt good about doing so.

Astrid knew why Kira had changed when forced to live apart from her beloved brother. She knew many dark secrets of the female orphanage to which Algernon was not privy; horrible happenings behind closed doors in the deep, winter gloom that forever altered the perspective of girls too young and too weak to fight back. Kira turned physical victimhood into triumph in the same manner that Algernon resisted conformity, and thus the tall priestess extended pity toward the Ravenwood twins, knowing intimate mysteries that motivated their behavior.

"You weren't there to protect her from predatory people," Astrid continued, referring to a selected group of adults rumored to favor certain children. "But you judge Kira without knowing that a girl in her position is powerless without the weapon of her sex."

"Pedophiles are an abomination!" Algernon snapped, his rage rising again with frightening speed. "If you knew about this, why didn't you go to the Supreme Council?"

Astrid shook her head, this time without fear. "I did, and that's why they dismissed Priestess Alba. But think for a minute about who else is on that Council, Algernon? Why do you think Priestess Dorothea and High Priest Volker are constantly being outmaneuvered?"

The essence of many conflicts Algernon experienced with authority distilled down to control. He felt powerless to do anything, knowing that the Supreme Council's edicts carried the force of law

The Long Journey: *Anger*

within the Sacred Enclosure. He thought about this, then realized he felt too tired to develop a plan for locating his missing sister. "What do you want me to do?" he asked at length.

Astrid's face brightened. She turned toward Algernon and knelt down on the worn stair landing. "Help me find her," the girl said. "We can bring her back where she belongs."

Doing this, however, would violate the terms High Priest Volker outlined earlier. "I can't do that," Algernon admitted. "If I walk out of the Sacred Enclosure, the Council won't let me back in. I'm sure they've extended the same threat to Kira."

Astrid sank back against the wall, pulled her bony knees up to her breast and slowly shook her head. The priestess looked away, sadly. "We can't just leave her alone out there. We have to do something!"

"We do, and we will," he agreed. "But it's late now and I can't think. Go back to bed and we'll talk about this tomorrow." Algernon arose and offered Astrid his hand.

She looked at him with uncertainty, then allowed him to pull her into a standing position. "So, you'll help me?" she queried, looking at him eye to eye, an expression of hope lingering in her countenance that Algernon had not seen there before.

"I'll think of something," he promised. "We'll find Kira, somehow."

*   *   *

Yet as he arose in the predawn darkness for prayers, Algernon felt empty and exhausted. No creative resolution sprang into his mind as he ate breakfast in solitude. Though his eyes and imagination often wandered during the long, formal recitations led by senior priests in the chapel, Algernon drifted listlessly into the vaulted, rectangular nave without raising his eyes to the ceiling. He could not focus on the haunting, minor-keyed melody sung by a choir in honor of the Great God. Algernon knelt on the hard, wooden floor, his hands raised on the back of the scratched and worn bench directly before him as if praying, though he paid little heed to the ministrations and long memorized worship responses uttered by the young men around him. Rather than dreaming up some new prank to play, Algernon worried about finding Kira.

The Long Journey: *Anger*

Later, in the exercise room, where the lingering smell of sweat and the musty odor of old, padded mats used for sparring practice usually inspired daydreams of physical domination and the fearful respect of every enemy, Algernon experienced a strange mix of guilt and impotence. Flecks of dust, illuminated in the strong, early morning light, drifted in the air like long forgotten memories. He loved Kira. He couldn't abandon her.

Algernon focused mental energy on stretching, gaining control over individual muscles and deliberately relaxing them as his hands reached forward and his chest leaned precariously over his right knee. Then, with his palms held flat as if pressing on a wall, the young Tamarian slowly moved his arms outward, breathed deeply and felt the sinews within his arms protest the transition. Where he found this tension, he stopped, holding the position until the sensation faded, then roused his aching arms again until that familiar strain returned. He repeated this process until his entire range of motion felt free of all resistance. When his right leg finally wobbled from long supporting his entire weight, Algernon switched and leaned forward on his left knee, drawing stale, sweaty air deeply into his lungs while he worked the muscles in his back and shoulders.

Despite the familiar discipline of bodily awareness, Algernon consistently found his mind drifting in search of a solution to his sister's disappearance. Tamarian law considered the Ravenwood twins old enough to be responsible for their own decisions. Kira's departure from the Temple would not concern the police, unless they received evidence that she'd been taken against her will. Given Astrid's description of Kira's quarters, convincing the police that she'd been abducted seemed unlikely.

Algernon considered asking High Priest Volker to send an adult priest or priestess to search for Kira. This option required the approval of the Supreme Council, which also seemed implausible, given their recent ultimatum. Worse, doing this also might inspire the evil machinations of someone who'd already exploited Kira. Algernon envisaged an unprincipled pedophile legally apprehending his sister beyond the Temple walls, only to drag her back for further mistreatment. In thinking this, the boy felt his teeth clench and his hands wrap tightly around an imaginary neck.

Though he didn't wish to consider the option, Algernon also deliberated the concept of simply letting Kira go. She was, after all, an intelligent girl with a strong will of her own. However, Astrid's revelation of opium use inspired rejection of that idea altogether. Kira could not exercise control and good judgment if she'd become an addict. Algernon feared that Marco, the foreign lover to whom Astrid referred, could supply or withhold opium as a means to subvert Kira's free will and control her behavior.

    Algernon snapped upright, strode to a 150-pound practice bag suspended from a stout ceiling beam and slapped it forcefully with a right-footed roundhouse kick. He drove his body forward as the bag quivered from impact, beat and snatched a handful of leather with his left hand, then with breathtaking speed, retracted, then rotated his elbow out and rammed it into the yielding leather, followed by a shuffle step, and a hard left knee into the tough sand at the bag's base. Next, as his left arm extended and his thumb faced down, Algernon again smacked the bag with the palm of his left hand, grabbed another handful of leather and spun the bag around while stepping forward to generate the fury of a right-handed uppercut punch. The twisting force of his back and shoulders multiplied into a thundering blow that shuddered through the ceiling.

    From this position, Algernon lifted his right foot and quickly torqued his body to the left, so that as his right foot planted on the ground its toes faced the wall behind him. In this well practiced circular move, Algernon brought his left hand up to shield his face, his right hand firmly down to protect his crotch, while his left foot rose in a blur until his entire leg was perfectly horizontal. He snapped a kick outward and grunted loudly. The sidekick's impact resonated all the way up Algernon's spine and bent the heavy bag in half. All the force of his well-focused rage lifted the chain upon which the bag had been suspended. As it swung outward and snapped taut, the bolt holding it to the ceiling beam broke under the strain and the practice bag sailed several feet before it landed with a great crash on the floor, then rolled and bounced against the far wall. Plaster and bits of broken beam rained from the roof.

    No, he couldn't let Kira go.

    "Take it easy," a fellow acolyte warned. "Get yourself under control."

    Algernon glared at him. "Shut up!" he retorted. "Just be glad that wasn't you!" Then, he stalked away toward the shower to cool down,

The Long Journey: *Anger*

leaving the mess for later clean-up as several other monks raced toward the practice room to investigate.

Algernon ignored their commands to return and stormed through halls flooded with bright morning light, his imagination dark as an abyss. Sandaled footfalls fell on floor beams swept clean by the tireless hands, young and old. He ran his fingers along the wall tapestries, touching priceless, ancient thread out of habit that exasperated the curators of this treasure, but no thought of intentionally inflicting damage entered his mind.

Instead, Algernon's mentation meandered toward his older brother, as it often did whenever he faced a bigger problem than he alone could handle. The young acolyte concluded that his brother's devotion to the army would preclude any direct assistance. Garrick couldn't leave officer's training without destroying his own career, and thus, Algernon could not seriously consider asking for his brother's help.

He had to rescue Kira alone.

Strangely, the thought of permanently leaving the monastery inspired a twinge of brooding sadness. Algernon knew that High Priest Volker loved him, and the thought of bringing further remorse to the old man inspired tears Algernon fought fiercely not to shed. He'd gone too far with his belligerent attitude to repent of it now. No one would believe him. He had to leave.

But how?

Fear of Algernon's temper kept the other monks at a distance while he showered. After washing, the boy felt calm enough to return to the practice area with a broom, dustpan and a bin for garbage. He shouldered past a group of young men who stood around a pair of senior priests as they examined the damage.

Priest Abelard and Priest Lambret stopped their discussion when Algernon appeared. They said nothing as the boy labored to move the bag away from the mess and begin sweeping the floor.

"This is your doing?" Priest Lambret inquired, his abrasive tone flooded with contempt.

Algernon didn't stop working.

"Acolyte Ravenwood!" he called sternly. "Address me when I address you!"

Slowly, Algernon stood. "You were speaking to me? I don't recall being invited into your conversation," Algernon retorted.

"Enough insolence!" the priest demanded. "I am weary..."

The Long Journey: *Anger*

"You were speaking to Abelard when I walked in!" Algernon interrupted in a far more commanding tone of voice than the middle-aged priest could muster. "You did not use my name, you spoke to me in an accusing tone of voice, yet you expect my deference. You will get the respect you think you deserve when you begin acting in a manner worthy of it!" Then Algernon turned his back and continued sweeping.

All sound, other than the scraping of straw against the floor, drained from the room in an instant. Algernon listened while he labored, aware of the many astonished eyes lingering on his shoulders, waiting to hear a retreat that didn't come. He would not find victory on this battlefield, and feared that swift and certain retribution would come.

Algernon's long excursions beyond the Temple walls gave him a measure of confidence that escaping the Council's certain wrath was feasible. He made a mental list of everything he would need. Aside from the clothing on his back and the sandals on his feet, Algernon's personal belongings consisted of a simple bed roll, grooming tools, one set of winter clothes that included gloves, boots and a warm overcoat, and a small amount of money he'd been saving. These funds wouldn't last very long.

Food, shelter, warmth and water would comprise basic necessities. One of his favorite hiding places, a dilapidated feeding stall on a long abandoned farm, lay within a twenty-minute walk of the city walls. It would be cold during the winter, but would provide shelter from the wind and rain before next autumn arrived. As long as he wore his priestly robe, Algernon could travel on Marvic's public trolley cars without paying a fare. In the event he couldn't find work to support himself, he was entitled to take food offerings from the many shrines located along the roads leading into town. While this might not give him a great variety from which to plan his menu, at least he could avoid starvation.

In the midst of his brainstorming Algernon finished his cleaning and noticed, quite suddenly, that he stood alone in the room. Pausing at the door, he heard the sound of many footfalls approaching and his name uttered in an angry tone of voice. Algernon raced for a casement window, opened it, slithered outside, then shut it behind him.

He crouched along the wall beneath the windows and scurried to the back of the building, where a flight of stairs led from the exercise area down to the greenhouses. Here, the sacred community grew fish in

The Long Journey: *Anger*

tanks along with vegetables to supplement their diets, and flowers to sell as a fund-raising project for building maintenance and expansion.

Algernon moved through the glass enclosures, finding them very warm already. He nodded to Dmitri, the quiet, scaly-skinned monk whose highly refined combat skills set him above every other member of the Elsbireth community. Dmitri picked a strawberry from a vertical growing tube and tossed it to Algernon. "Enjoy," the older man offered.

The fruit tasted sweet. Algernon offered a smile, as Dmitri was one priest whom the boy held in honor. Then, trying not to be obvious about what he was doing, Algernon walked to the back of the greenhouse airlock, exited and scampered toward the men's dormitory.

Dmitri watched him leave. He'd long seen leadership potential in that boy, and genuinely liked him. When an agitated group of monks came into the greenhouse looking for Algernon, he tended to his plants and said nothing to them.

Although the men's dorm remained largely deserted at this time of morning, the news of Algernon's exercise room exploit had already echoed through its halls. As Algernon arrived at his room, Gunnar Vinkholdt called to him from the stairwell.

"Wait!" Gunnar said. "I need to talk to you."

Algernon barely restrained his contempt. "You have nothing to say that I need to hear."

"They're looking for you, and it sounds very serious" Gunnar replied, catching up. "You've got to get out of here."

Algernon stuffed his personal belongings into his bed roll and tied them with an old belt while looking for his overcoat. "What's it to you?" he inquired.

"I heard about Kira," the other boy admitted. "I'm really sorry."

This time Algernon muttered a curse under his breath. "Sorry that you got caught, or sorry that you exploited my sister?"

"It's not what you think, Algernon. Kira's special. She means a lot to me."

"Gunnar, if she'd meant anything you'd have kept your pants on. Your contrition is worth as much to me as Kira really means to you." Frustrated that he couldn't find his overcoat, Algernon overturned his bed.

"I'm sorry if you feel offended. I didn't mean to hurt either one of you and I feel bad that she got into so much trouble. What can I do to make it up to you?"

The Long Journey: *Anger*

Algernon slammed his bed back down. "In my eyes you've worked yourself into the bottom of a deep hole. You want to help? Stop digging!"

Gunnar felt genuinely hurt by Algernon's repudiation. "So what are you going to do? They're going to take your robe away."

This was precisely the action Algernon intended to avoid. His robe would make survival beyond the Temple walls much easier. "They have to catch me, first!" Then, exasperated and throwing up his hands, he inquired, to no one in particular: "Where is my blasted overcoat?"

"They found Astrid with it," Gunnar replied. "That's one of the reasons why they're looking for you."

"What?" Algernon asked, astonished. Then he remembered giving it to her the previous evening. "Ugh!" he muttered, clenching his fist and shutting his eyes. "It's not what they think!"

Gunnar's green eyes widened at Algernon's admission he'd been with Astrid. "I thought you didn't like her," he said. "But I guess that doesn't matter anymore. You're in big trouble and you really need to get out of here!"

At that moment, Algernon heard footfalls coming up the stairs. He cursed. "How did I ever muck this up?" Then, slipping the strap holding his belongings through the belt around his waist, Algernon dashed for a window, carefully maneuvered outside, then deftly climbed up a drainpipe to the slate roof above.

The hardest part of this escape route consisted of the transition from the roof back down to an open window above the women's cloister. He found one leading into a storage room, dried his hands as best he could, then very carefully lowered himself onto the window ledge. The storage area contained boxes and crates that looked like they hadn't been moved in decades. It smelled vaguely of mice, but nothing moved within. Algernon listened carefully at the door before opening it and peering into the hallway.

Empty and quiet, the hallway and nearby stairs provided a route for Algernon to transition unobserved. When he descended the stairs, however, he found himself on a dormitory floor where a startled priestess candidate named Gretchen confronted him.

"What are you doing here?" she asked, simultaneously surprised and annoyed.

Algernon had no time to explain, especially to a girl who likely wouldn't listen. "Help me find Astrid!" he commanded.

75

The Long Journey: *Anger*

Gretchen, who was three years older than Algernon, recalled the day when the Ravenwood twins arrived and knew enough of the Temple community's social milieu to recognize that Algernon did not like Astrid. "Get out of here!" she responded. "I'm not helping you!"

Algernon grew angry and panicked. He pinned her to the wall with his left knee, clutching her throat with one hand and covering her mouth with the other. "Don't play smug with me!" he warned. "I will kill you without thinking twice. Where **is** she?"

Gretchen's blue eyes grew wide in horror, her face reddened as she realized that Algernon fully intended to take her life if she didn't help. She nodded, desperate for air.

"If you scream," Algernon threatened. "It will be the last time you ever do so." Then he lifted his hand and loosened his grip on the girl's throat.

"Downstairs," Gretchen said, gasping, "in her room. She's in number 23."

Algernon grabbed a braid of Gretchen's hair and led her, whimpering, back up to the storage room. He took off her belt and tied her hands behind her head with her elbows pointing forward and the fabric between her teeth, shoved her into the room and shut the door, ignoring the muffled sound of her pleading.

He ran down two flights of stairs, through an empty hallway and opened the door to room 23 without knocking. Astrid sat on her bed with a pencil drawing in her lap, a mixture of fear and surprise flashing onto her face. "Where's my overcoat?" he inquired.

She pointed to a peg on the wall. "They were waiting for me," she told him. "They wanted to catch me with Kira, so they know I was with you last night."

Algernon picked up his overcoat. "Are you coming?" he inquired, wrongly assuming that she knew of his plans.

"Where?" she asked. "I'm under Discipline. I've been confined to my room for the day."

"Make up your mind," he said. "Are you coming with me to look for Kira, or are you staying here?"

Astrid needed no prodding. "I'm coming," she replied, arising. "Let me get my things."

"I don't have time," he told her. "Meet me at the garden house fifteen minutes after prayer time begins. They won't miss you."

The Long Journey: *Anger*

Algernon closed the door and raced back upstairs. He returned to the storage room and felt guilt swarm over his soul when he saw Gretchen weeping on the floor. Gently, he knelt down to speak to her, his grey-eyed glare piercing her fearful gaze. "I've never hurt you before," he said, wiping away her tears. "And I don't intend to, ever again. Please forgive me!"

Gretchen trembled, terrified as Algernon gently reached behind her head, untied her belt and pulled it out of her mouth. Her skin, reddened by contact with the fabric, felt tender. He helped her up, gave her the belt, then opened the door.

Though Gretchen's expression morphed from terror into anger, she didn't lash out at him. Algernon's violent reputation inspired so much fear among the young Temple community members, no one dared cross him. She looked into his grey eyes as the door closed, then ran downstairs to find help.

Wasting no time, Algernon raced to the window as he heard Gretchen flee and climbed back onto the roof. Retracing his steps, the acolyte squeezed himself into the attic, quietly shut the grate and waited. Threatening Gretchen had been a stupid, impulsive act and he cursed himself for endangering his mission. He couldn't let anyone find him now. Though he could hear voices searching for him in the garden around the corner, no one thought to look up.

The boy crept along the attic beams, moving toward the bell tower. Vent pipes for the multrum toilets in the inner sanctum followed a narrow service shaft at the back of the chapel nave. Once the organ began playing its morning call to worship, no one would hear him climb down the shaft, all the way to the basement where the big, rotating drums that processed human waste were located. From there, a tunnel lead out to the composting bins on the far side of the gardens.

Algernon waited, sweating in the sweltering attic, until the bells rang calling the Temple community downstairs into the sanctuary for formal worship. Once the organ prelude began, he opened the ventilation passage and worked his way down to the cool basement while music resonated powerfully through the building, dislodging dust and vibrating the multrum vent pipes. He leaped behind the rotating drums, wiped away his sweat and rested until well after the prelude's conclusion. Algernon felt vulnerable and afraid for hurting Gretchen, but he suppressed his anxiety and scurried down the tunnel.

The Long Journey: *Anger*

Once in the garden, Algernon slipped into a grove of trees and climbed high into an oak. From this perch he could view the approach to the garden house, an octahedronal, wooden-framed structure with glass windows. Its white pillars supported a roof overhang that covered a wraparound porch. From its elevated vantage point, anyone seeking solace could view the hot mineral pools, mossy islands, and tranquil flower plantings.

Algernon observed the garden house carefully, making sure it was empty, and that no one followed Astrid when she came. From this hiding place he also traced a mental path through the research plots, hidden from view of the garden house by a low stone wall, to the compost and manure piles. Through blueberry bushes and raspberry canes he knew of a path that led to a thorny blackberry thicket near the monastery wall. This was one of two main escape routes he'd used many times in the past.

He waited for what seemed like a long time, then noticed the tall, slender, blonde-haired girl scurrying alone along the gravel path. She kept glancing over her shoulder, worried that she might get caught violating the terms of her punishment, but the girl pressed onward, entered the garden house and came out a few moments later with an expression of fear and panic on her face.

Algernon climbed down and quietly called her from a juniper hedge.

Astrid approached fearfully. "Promise you won't hurt me," she demanded.

"What do you want me to say?" he replied. "I could have left without you, and I'd be in less trouble right now as a result."

When Astrid saw his face, flushed with exertion and sweat, she stopped. "Gretchen didn't deserve the brunt of your anger," she accused. "That was completely uncalled-for."

"I know," he replied, wishing he could re-live that confrontation and handle it differently. "But what do you want me to do about it now?"

The priestess followed him fearfully, asking a myriad of questions. Clearly, she hadn't given the prospect of leaving the Temple a great deal of thought, but she worried about it now. Algernon explained that he'd been preparing secret places beyond the Temple walls for many months, in the event that he needed to leave. That kind of foresight would serve him well now, but Astrid reasoned that the extensive planning she heard from Algernon indicated his longstanding intention to leave. She concluded that this explained some of his extreme behavior and boldness in dealing with adults in authority.

The boy led her along a narrow, winding maze between berry hedges toward a place along the eastern wall of the Sacred Enclosure. Here, where untrimmed blackberry thickets presented an unpleasant barrier, a section of the Honeywater flowed through a grate beneath the wall.

"If you don't want to get your things wet, you'll have to roll them up and carry them overhead to keep everything dry," he told her.

"Isn't there another way out?" she inquired, fearfully. The water swirled in languid spirals, inspiring visions of drowning as she watched.

"Only if you want to risk the front gate," he replied, lying. "I'd appreciate it if you'd not look."

Astrid complied, her heart pounding in trepidation. "It's not like you've got anything I'd be interested in seeing," she muttered under her breath.

Algernon stripped to his underwear, then waded into the warm water holding his belongings overhead. "Make sure when you come in that you keep your sandals on," he warned. "The rocks are sharp. Stay to the right when you pass under the grate. I'll keep my back to you until you're ready."

Astrid didn't know how to swim, but she found the water pleasantly warm when she entered. Because she'd grown tall and lacked Algernon's muscular control, she had to bend awkwardly in order to get beneath the grate. Astrid lost her balance in the current, slipped and ended up completely submerged. She broke through the water's surface on the outside of the grate with a sputter and a gasp, her personal items drifting downstream, totally soaked.

Hearing her distress, Algernon turned around. "Do you want me to help you?" he asked.

"No!" she snapped, reaching for her bed roll, submerged for the sake of modesty. "Just turn around!"

Algernon set his overcoat out for her and turned his back, wondering how Astrid would cope with the steep descent to the city below if she couldn't handle something as simple as wading beneath a grate. "You dumb ox!" he muttered, listening to her struggle out of the water. Since she didn't possess the shapely physique that interested him, Algernon kept his eyes focused southward to honor her privacy. For a fleeting moment, he wondered how Kira could find a weedy-

The Long Journey: *Anger*

framed young woman with stringy hair like Astrid attractive. That had to be a female thing that he wouldn't understand.

Twenty-seven hundred and forty-two feet below, the city of Marvic spread across a hilly plateau and stretched to the brink of a precipice in three directions. Beyond the city walls, a safety measure built long ago to keep people from falling off the edge, a sea of white cloud stretched into the hazy horizon. Marvic appeared to float beneath the pale sky, an island fortress in a universe all its own.

The Elsbireth monastery, built on the highest of nine peaks, commanded an excellent view of the city. Angular, blue-tiled roofing graced slender buildings oriented at angles facing south, their windows glinting in the golden morning light. Wide, tree-lined avenues that bustled with electric traction trucks, trolley cars and humanity crisscrossed the plateau. Green patches of parkland mingled with grey concrete, huddled near the Honeywater, where industrial clusters edged residential neighborhoods. White, water vapor clouds drifted in a gentle wind, rolling eastward, toward the beautiful, red marble palace complex on the far edge of town.

Dark-green Tamarian flags waved from schools and libraries. A police station stood guard near every hill. Granaries and warehouses lined the major rail routes. Rows of small shops, restaurants and pubs punctuated the street grid. Marvic's clean lines shone bright in the thin, mountain air, a city teeming with opportunity, bursting with promise.

Astrid wrung out her clothing in disgust and slipped into Algernon's overcoat. She fumbled through a bag and found a brush, which she snapped through her shoulder-length hair in quick, aggressive strokes. Then, satisfied with her readiness, she gave Algernon permission to turn around.

"Stay close to me," he admonished, giving her a bemused and almost playful glance. "I know the way down and would prefer that we arrive there together."

Thankfully, from Algernon's perspective, Astrid proved sure-footed and confident in her descent. While the Temple's main entrance boasted a beautiful, curving set of forty seven-hundred stone stairs, the route Algernon selected required far more than the forty minutes a healthy person invested in descending from the Temple gates via the staircase.

"So where do we start looking?" Astrid inquired.

The Long Journey: *Anger*

Algernon had been mulling this over already. "There are two things we need to investigate," he began. "You said Kira had this boyfriend named Marco. That's a Southern Kamerese name, so he'll probably stand out around here and people will remember a stranger's face. Did you ever see him?"

Astrid, whose artistic eye gave her an excellent memory for faces, nodded. "I can draw him once my paper dries out," she replied, chagrined at the memory of her clumsiness, hoping that her companion wouldn't tease her for being maladroit.

"That's good," Algernon replied. "But until then we need to think this through. He's a foreigner, which limits the kind of place willing to take him in. I figure that if he climbed the forty-seven hundred stairs to see Kira every day, he'd want to be close to the Temple. That means we need to look for a low-rent boarding house within a short distance of the Grand Staircase.

"And it also brings up the question of how and where they met. Did Kira say anything to you?"

Sharing whispered secrets in the evening was an activity Astrid recalled with wistful longing. "Yes," the girl admitted. "But I don't think your low-rent theory pans out. Kira said she met Marco during a student tour of the Temple grounds. She was working in the greenhouse, he lingered behind, and that's how they got acquainted. Apparently, he's a rich kid attending the university."

Algernon stopped and cursed. "Great!" he exclaimed in exasperated wonder. The University of Tamaria and its associated colleges clustered around Liberty Hill, adjacent to the Hall of Justice and the palace complex on the far eastern edge of Marvic. "It would take him better than thirty minutes to get over here riding the trolley."

"He owns his own car," Astrid admitted. "Kira told me that she wanted to be seen riding around town in a private car."

Electric automobiles, an expensive luxury, remained very rare throughout Tamaria. Most people rode public transportation out of necessity, and the vast majority of electric trucks working to move goods and material through Marvic's broad avenues were owned by companies, not individuals. This meant that Marco moved through social strata well above any in which Algernon and Astrid could claim familiarity.

"If that's the case, let's start at the university," Algernon offered. "If we can find him, he ought to know where Kira is staying. If that

The Long Journey: *Anger*

doesn't work, we can look in the opium dens." Algernon let the words drift off of his tongue as if he'd been speaking about a stranger.

Astrid worried that even if they did find Kira, she might not be willing to return to the Temple. One recent experience underscored her concern. Kira had come to Astrid's room as was her custom, but the girl seemed distant and disinterested; describing vivid, dreamlike visions and a gentle euphoria she claimed felt like an unending orgasm. Although Kira urged Astrid to share the experience, the change in Kira's behavior warned that opium use shackled its addicts with a heavy, invisible chain, and Astrid refused.

The tall Tamarian girl followed Algernon out of the industrial compound, past grey warehouses used for cold storage and onto an avenue that led toward Victory Street, Marvic's primary east-west thoroughfare. Beneath the shade of an apple tree they sat in uncomfortable silence and waited for the trolley to arrive.

People passing by offered blessings, bowing their heads while they pressed their hands together, as if in prayer. This custom, practiced by nearly everyone in the nation regardless of their religious conviction, stemmed from the fact that basic education remained the primary domain of the Temple community. People owed their literacy and numeracy to devoted priests and priestesses. Thus, despite their youth, Algernon and Astrid were treated with deference on Marvic's streets.

They boarded a trolley car and stood so that elderly passengers traveling with them could sit. As the machine glided smoothly and quietly down Victory Street, pausing at its designated stops, the commercial section of Marvic yielded to a neighborhood devoted to post secondary education, the administration of justice, and government.

The University of Tamaria stood upon Liberty Hill. White marble buildings, constructed in the classical style with colonnades and covered porticos, graced parkland grounds. Its various colleges clustered in groups according to discipline. Sciences and mathematics shared an extensive collection of stately buildings fronting the compound, where study and research, conducted under the scrutiny of a famed faculty, advanced knowledge for the benefit of all nations. Arts and language colleges occupied an area overlooking the military base on the northwest, while the departments of economics and government sprawled on the eastern edge of the campus, toward the palace complex. Physical fitness facilities, along with a sports stadium, stood on the

The Long Journey: *Anger*

northern side of Liberty Hill, hidden from view as the trolley car stopped at the university gates.

Administration, along with various dormitories and the cafeteria facility, crowned Liberty Hill. A great, broad flight of stairs led up from the street to a series of four terraces. On the first, the university chapel, a student center and a three-sided steel bell tower lifted their spires high into the sky. The second terrace contained a fountain and common area adjacent to a pair of domed libraries. A singular flag pole stood on the third level, surrounded by an assembly area paved in massive stones. A series of circular walls, cut from polished, red marble stood behind planter boxes filled with low, berry producing shrubs. Upon this wall, the full name, degree and nation of origin for every university graduate had been engraved. Many foreigners were honored here, in curious contrast to the overwhelmingly xenophobic attitude prevalent in Tamarian society.

Stone paths on each level led to various faculty offices and classroom buildings, but Algernon and Astrid headed straight toward the administration building. Algernon smiled, offering a blessing to everyone who deferred to him. Though he did not admit this to Astrid, the boy felt uncomfortable in an environment where others, older and better educated than he accorded him automatic respect.

An overweight and overworked clerk with heavy glasses peered curiously at Algernon when he inquired about a student named Marco. After several minutes of remarkably calm and persuasive discussion she found the name in her filing cabinet and directed Algernon to a certain dormitory. "Given that it's lunch time," she concluded. "You should try the student commons, first."

Algernon thanked the clerk and led Astrid to a campus directory, where they located the cafeteria. "You remember his face?" Algernon inquired.

"Yes," Astrid replied, a little bit fearfully. "Don't make a scene!" she warned.

The cafeteria building, often called the commons, occupied an area slightly below a men's dormitory. It bustled with activity as hundreds of students filed inside for lunch. Algernon pushed his way through the crowd and into the main eating area, where he began examining the faces seated at every table.

Astrid tugged on Algernon's sleeve. "Over there, in the corner!" she whispered. "That's him!"

The Long Journey: *Anger*

With a determined stride, Algernon approached the table. Four burly young men whose dark hair and heavy beards marked them as foreigners, sat with one of a slighter build. The Kamerese students, bedecked in gold chains and wearing fine clothes, ignored Algernon as he approached.

"I'm looking for Marco," he told them.

"Oh look!" said one of the muscular young men in the language of Southern Kameron. "It's a monkey boy!" Laughter erupted at the table.

Algernon glared. "Are you deaf, or stupid?" he responded, speaking Southern Kamerese without a trace of his otherwise strongly Tamarian accent.

The young man stood, revealing that he was much larger than the acolyte. "Watch it, little boy!" he warned. "What do you think you're dealing with here?"

"Failure," Algernon responded, noting that conversation at the surrounding tables had suddenly grown quiet. When the Kamerese native drew near in an effort to intimidate Algernon with his greater size and strength, the boy shook his head. "And stupidity!"

Astrid, watching this unfold, closed her eyes. "No Algernon!" she commanded. "Don't do this!"

But the Kamerese student believed he could easily deal with this impudent young Tamarian. He grabbed Algernon with both hands by the lapel of his robe and tried to lift him off the ground.

In a flash, Algernon's right foot slid backward and his hands moved from a prayer-like position, upward between his adversary's arms. With elbows extending, Algernon flicked free of the grasp and jabbed his fingers directly into the dark eyes of his much larger opponent. Before the foreign student could reach for his stricken eyes, Algernon had crossed his hands, snapped his knuckles with stunning force into the man's temples, then grabbed him by the ears. Pulling downward and raising his right leg forward at the same time, Algernon slammed his right knee into the Kamerese student's face, resulting in an instant explosion of blood that erupted into the air as the foreigner fell backward, into another man sitting at the table.

Slim and handsome Marco, witnessing this, leaped to his feet and ran. When Astrid followed him with her eyes, she saw a small, dark-haired woman racing toward the scene while students at the surrounding tables stood to get a better look at the fight.

The Long Journey: *Anger*

When one of the burly students swung a wild fist at Algernon's head, the young acolyte circle-blocked and sidestepped the blow, then swept his left foot forward and to the right. Algernon's right hand shifted outward in a grasping motion, never leaving contact with the attacking man's arm. He grabbed the offending forearm and pulled it down, while wrenching his own body violently to the right. Within this motion, Algernon twisted the palm of his left hand down with great force. His palm met an elbow in an aggravated collision. The Kamerese student's punching arm, now hyper-extended and fully exposed to Algernon's fury, snapped at the elbow and bent in the wrong direction. His ensuing scream of pain ended abruptly as Algernon spun his body further and slammed a hard, right-footed sidekick into the foreigner's right armpit.

One heartbeat later, Algernon felt a strong arm clamp around his neck from the left. Gasping, he grabbed the attacking limb with all his strength, stepped to the side and pulled down hard. The man holding him was very strong, but Algernon managed to lower his chin sufficiently to bite down on his enemy's forearm. He bit in rage, like a cornered beast, then lifted his left fist until he could see his fingers tighten across his palm, and slammed his elbow backward, into the gut of the man who held him. Then, Algernon hammered his fist down to the man's crotch, grabbed a handful of tender flesh and yanked upward.

Sudden, uncontrolled spasms of multiple muscular contractions forced the Kamerese man to relinquish his grip. In doing so he felt the Tamarian monk twist. The man could do nothing as an astonishingly powerful hook punch drilled straight into his chest. Crushed ribs yielded to the staggering blow. Dumbfounded and breathless, the muscular Kamerese student dropped to his knees, then down to the floor.

Above the din of a cheering crowd, Algernon heard the distinctive ring of a blade drawn out of its sheath. He turned toward the sound and saw a petite woman wearing a tight, Tamarian military dress uniform standing near the table, a lovely, crystal edged longsword extending dangerously from her right hand. Directly across from her, one of the Kamerese students stopped as if frozen still. He held a drawn knife and looked as if he were ready to leap.

"Put it away!" the woman warned in Azgaril Vulgate. A determined look in her eye and the steady manner in which she held the blade warned that she fully intended to use the weapon, if necessary.

The Long Journey: *Anger*

The student didn't back down. "Take it easy, little lady," he replied. "This isn't your fight."

"Make one more foolish move and you'll not make another," she responded, never taking her dark blue eyes off the man she confronted. "Put it away!"

Slowly, the student complied, backing down. He turned toward Algernon and said: "You fight like a girl!" Then, noticing a commotion at the entrance that announced the arrival of campus security he bolted for the back door.

"If that's so," Algernon panted in a retort to the fleeing figure. "What does that say about you and your pathetic friends?"

Astrid watched the petite woman sheathe her weapon and bend down to examine the three young men lying on the floor. She had a pretty, heart-shaped face and very long, dark hair. Inexplicably, one of the men cursed and pushed her away. He scooted along the floor and huddled near a table, gasping, holding his broken chest in pain.

The woman stood up and reached out with her right hand. "Algernon Ravenwood?" she asked in a demure tone, gently touching his neck. When he nodded, she continued: "You are the image of your brother. Are you hurt?"

He shook his head, strangely soothed at the sensation of her touch, unaware of the redness around his neck that otherwise would have darkened into a nasty bruise. "You know my brother?" he stammered, astonished. "Who are you?"

Just then, campus security hustled onto the scene. The senior officer, a slim former soldier with a commanding voice, demanded to know what had transpired. He ignored both Algernon and Astrid, finding a student eyewitness whose testimony painted the Kamerese in a poor light. Three other security agents attended to the badly beaten students on the floor, none extending much sympathy. In Tamaria attacking a priest, especially a much smaller and younger one, did little to elicit empathy.

In the singular moment his attention had been diverted, Algernon looked about him and discovered that the diminutive woman had vanished into the crowd.

Astrid shifted from foot to foot, nervously. "We're going to be in big trouble now!" she lamented. "I warned you, but you wouldn't listen."

The Long Journey: *Anger*

"Shut up and calm down," Algernon advised. "Keep your wits about you and when they ask what happened, tell the truth. They won't take kindly to foreigners threatening either of us."

Later as Algernon sat on the floor with Astrid, locked inside the silent, grey walls of a spare room within the security building, he reflected moodily on the events of the day. He'd managed to violate nearly every demand High Priest Volker conveyed from the Supreme Council, save for the prohibition against masturbation, and if the Temple community learned what had transpired at the university, he would certainly lose his robe.

Astrid, who always sought to avoid trouble, trembled nervously. "I don't want to criticize you all the time," she said. "But the guy in the cafeteria would have cut you open if that pretty, Lithian girl hadn't come to your rescue."

Algernon crossed his arms, unresponsive.

"You've really got to learn how to control your temper," she continued. "One day you're going to meet either someone who fights better than you do, or you'll wind up with a blade in your belly or a bullet in your back. If you keep feeding your rage like this, the ensuing violence will be your undoing."

Astrid was right, he knew, though he said nothing in reply. Following the path of anger would certainly ruin his life. Algernon knew he needed to change.

But how could he modify his own nature, and where would he begin?

Approval

A steady, measured stride set his rhythm for breathing. Increasing distance and shortening time, blending with the aching of many muscles pushed beyond strength and endurance, prolonged the pain of these early morning runs like a harbinger of greater hardship to come. Though he'd been warned before arriving of a high attrition rate, though he understood that officer training would be mentally and physically tough, Garrick found himself ill-prepared for the ordeal.

Trouble began shortly after his arrival at the Dragon's Lair Military Training Facility in Marvic, when he was called into TAC Officer Vogel's office. Recalling the experience inspired a brief rush of nausea. He'd hardly had an opportunity to shower and shave, his dress uniform needed pressing, yet he'd been ordered to face the man responsible for his training, his career, and for the next twelve weeks, his life.

"You're late!" Manfred Vogel announced. "I'm not impressed!"

"Sir! We encountered bad weather and missed our connection at Deception Creek," Garrick replied. "Then our train was attacked by giants, and after this we had a problem with altitude sickness at Traitor's Pass. That's why we were delayed."

TAC Officer Vogel, a severely handsome man with short-cropped hair and pale eyes appraised the young officer candidate with a cold, penetrating stare. "You had a problem with altitude sickness?"

Garrick suddenly found his self-confidence melting into the floor. "No sir. Specialist Velez got sick."

"Hmm," Manfred Vogel mused, turning the pages of Garrick's dossier. "You take her everywhere you go?"

"I translate for her," Garrick responded.

"Is she your wet nurse?" the TAC officer mused, raising his eyebrows. "Does she wipe your nose and wash your soiled underwear? Is she your lover, your concubine? Why are you traveling with a foreign woman on the army's tab, Private Ravenwood?"

Garrick felt a lump rising in his throat. "Lieutenant Kohler wrote the orders. I obeyed them."

"What a good boy!" TAC Officer Vogel replied, as if speaking to a small child. "I see here that she earned four silver lions for valor in combat, yet the men in your unit referred to her as *Little Sister*." He looked up from Brenna's folder and glared at Garrick. "How very cute! Tell me, what did she have to do in order to persuade your sergeant,

The Long Journey: *Approval*

better than half the men in your company, and your lieutenant to write commendations?"

The ensuing silence made Garrick feel as if he'd been thrown into a whirlpool and pulled underwater by a vortex far more powerful than he could overcome. "Sir, the conduct of Specialist Velez has been outlined in her dossier for your perusal. She did precisely what has been written about her, nothing less and nothing more."

Manfred Vogel grunted. "She did nothing more? So why is she here?"

"I can't speak for Lieutenant Kohler," Garrick replied nervously. "Perhaps he thought Colonel Weiss might find use for her medical skills."

"Perhaps Lieutenant Kohler had no more need for her skills," the TAC officer retorted in rapid response. "So he dumped his pretty, little problem on Colonel Weiss, who in turn, dumped the pretty, little problem on me. Now I'm telling you to make the pretty, little problem go away!

"I don't know what you think you're doing here, Ravenwood. I don't know why your shell-shocked lieutenant thought you worthy of this honor, but putting your personal bravery aside, I tell you that no one in this organization will think twice about turning your tender butt right around and sending you back for latrine duty where you belong.

"Nobody is going to cut you any slack just because you're fresh out of diapers. Nobody gives a pile of monkey scat that you fought make-believe monsters and that some logistician officer cabled the colonel about your track-side spat with a few, feeble giants.

"You think you've got what it takes, Ravenwood? You will work harder under my watchful eye than ten generations of your dead ancestors did scraping rocks and shoveling slop when they were slaves. You will dream for the nightmare of my control over your life to end. But when you raise your eyelids at night, I'll be there, little boy! I'll be there to remind you that you don't belong here!"

Garrick's lip quivered, his mind racing through a myriad of thoughts, but he kept himself at attention.

TAC Officer Vogel walked slowly around his desk, pacing deliberately to Garrick's left side. He peered at the blonde strands of Garrick's hair. "You must think you're a pretty boy with your long hair. You cut it! I don't want to see it again!"

"Yes sir!" Garrick responded.

As Manfred Vogel stepped around to Garrick's right side, he flicked at wrinkles on Garrick's dress uniform. "What's the matter,

The Long Journey: *Approval*

Ravenwood?" he sneered in a whisper. "Your pretty, little girlfriend can't wreck her dainty, little fingers ironing clothes for you? She must be really good at other things for you to keep her around." Then changing his voice as if addressing an infant, he taunted, "But she's not going to be here to hold your hand and kiss your owies when you fall!" Manfred returned to a serious tone abruptly. "I don't want to see her pretty, little face again!"

"Yes sir!" Garrick replied, struggling for control. He did not like **anyone** speaking badly of Brenna.

"You think you have what it takes, Ravenwood? Everyone here is older than you are. They don't beat off in the shower. They have wives and some of them have children." The TAC officer paused, as if experiencing a moment of revelation. "Or, maybe you're not so different! What's she like, Ravenwood? What's she like when you're all alone?"

Garrick remained silent, staring straight ahead, not dignifying that remark with any response.

"You think you have what it takes?" Manfred Vogel repeated. "Everyone else here has a college degree. Some of them are doctors. Some of them are lawyers. But they all know how to study. Are you smarter than they are? Let's see, where did you go to school?" Returning to his desk, the TAC officer flipped through Garrick's dossier again. "Ah yes, that noble institution of high learning, the famed public school of Deception Creek in the Southeastern District of Broken Wing Lake! You didn't even graduate . . .

"You think you can pass ten different tests in history, mathematics, language, physics and chemistry; along with battle doctrine, logistics, ordinance and personnel management with a score exceeding 80%; in addition to your 48 pre-commissioning common core tasks; in addition to 14 leadership exercises in-garrison and in the field? Are you smart enough for that, little fair-haired farm boy?"

Again, Garrick remained silent. He didn't know whether he was supposed to answer that line of questioning, or merely stand quietly and take the abuse meted out to him.

Manfred Vogel stood with akimbo arms. He leaned forward and lowered his voice. "Then, there's the physical training," he continued. "You think you're tough? Can you run three miles in less than 20 minutes? Can you foot march nine miles in three hours wearing full gear? You will run more than 150 miles in the next 12 weeks, if you last that long. Can you last that long, Ravenwood?

The Long Journey: *Approval*

"I think you'll be crying for momma, or your pretty, little girlfriend before you get through half of what's in store for you. I see bad things ahead. I know you'll struggle with the land navigation tests. You've got to do them at night too, and I bet you can't even read a map!

"Oh, and have you heard about the combat water survival training? We don't do that up here in the city where the Honeywater is nice and warm. We hike up to Hungry Valley, where the wind never stops. In Hungry Valley you'll be up to your elbows in glacier melt. You think you've been cold Ravenwood? You've never been cold until you've been to Hungry Valley!

"Now, I'm not done with all the abuse I intend to heap on your head. Spare yourself all this trouble. When you pack your bag to leave this place I will never lay eyes on your sorry butt again. You should know that one out of every three men who get sent here washes out. This is no place for little boys, Ravenwood."

Garrick shifted his eyes to look directly at TAC Officer Vogel. "You underestimate me, sir. I will not disappoint you."

Manfred Vogel returned the stare, then grunted. "We'll see about that," he replied. "Until you leave this place, every aspect of your life must meet my approval. Get your effects in order. Notify your little nursemaid that you won't be seeing her again any time soon. Class begins in 30 minutes."

And for every waking moment since that encounter, Garrick had been pushed harder than he ever dreamed. In performing most of the combat-related common core tasks, such as accurately adjusting indirect artillery fire, implementing force protection measures to avoid fratricide, and tactical communications, Garrick's battlefield experience served him well. Fortunately, his high aptitude in these skills significantly helped some of the older officer candidates, who genuinely appreciated his assistance, and his ability to explain how these concepts worked earned their respect.

In the academic realm, where his development lagged better than five years behind the next youngest warrior, Garrick found himself struggling to keep up with the heavy demands for nightly reading. Certain subjects, such as medicine and military law, required deeper analytical skills than Garrick could muster at his age. He floundered when composing written responses, especially as his work compared to the far better educated men against whom he competed for grades.

Despite considerable help from some of the older officer

The Long Journey: *Approval*

candidates, Garrick had to exert more effort in his law and medicine classes than his achievement indicated at first glance. Two assignments requiring the application of military case law in disciplinary action threatened to drag his overall score below the 80% requirement for course mastery.

"You're in way over your head, Ravenwood!" his exasperated instructor complained.

News of that event spread rapidly among the men and earned Garrick the nickname, "Overhead."

Although he thought himself fit, the persistent demands of physical training sapped Garrick's vigor. He lost weight. Three days out of every five his class engaged in the dreaded, three mile cross country run, where Garrick, who had never been a strong runner, lacked the endurance to keep up. Consistently coming in last during these distance runs also endangered his class standing. Fear of disqualification forced Garrick to work on developing greater stamina, and in doing so, he often chased an elusive runner the other warriors named *ubermadchen*, because no one could keep up with her. Yet as his own endurance improved, so did everyone else's, and thus he remained in last place during every running exercise.

He often fell asleep within moments of collapsing on his cot, only to waken with a growing sense of physical exhaustion. And as the course ground onward, TAC Officer Vogel relentlessly criticized every effort and completed task. The only time Garrick escaped his TAC officer's scrutiny occurred while he was sleeping or running. As the OTS program progressed, Garrick found the days blending into a blur of connected tasks and often longed for the solace he enjoyed in these two solitary activities.

Cool, pine-scented air drifted on a gentle, easterly breeze. Marvic mornings always carried a warning of winter, and even in high summer a light crust of silver frost often clung to north facing rocks, shrubs and grasses growing in the shadows. Garrick felt the muscle in his legs protest the onset of another climb as the cross country path turned away from the military base and entered the university research forest.

A few minutes later, as the track moved out of the trees, Marvic's wall loomed ahead. Defenders, Queen Tamar's elite palace guard, manned the parapets and walked the balustrades along the towering bluestone barrier. Hoots and hollers rose from the ramparts. The soldiers cheered, but not in solidarity with their brothers in arms.

The Long Journey: *Approval*

Garrick heard light feet falling on the path from behind, sustaining a pace far faster than he could muster. Her rhythmic breathing, timed perfectly to every second step, motivated the only smile of Garrick's day. He felt Brenna's hand pat his backside as she raced by and watched her long legs tirelessly propel her bantam body past every runner laboring up the hill ahead.

No one could catch her when she ran!

That brief exchange, the only physical contact between the two of them, inspired enough confidence for Garrick to carry on. He treasured that moment every day it happened, holding the memory of her touch close to his heart.

Brenna did not imagine the positive impact her small encouragement made in Garrick's life. She dreamed of him, longing for his company, finding that her thoughts meandered through small memories of their companionship. Each of these blurred her loneliness and modulated the minor key of her experience in Marvic. Though she complained to Mariel Hougen more than once that Lieutenant Kohler had deliberately arranged Garrick's transfer to facilitate their separation, Brenna deliberately manipulated her own schedule to coincide her fitness regimen with his.

As she passed the leading elements of Garrick's OTS group on the lengthy uphill climb, hearing them chant the term Mariel politely translated as "super girl," Brenna kept her eyes averted until she crested the hill and found herself alone.

When she and Garrick first arrived at the Dragon's Lair Training Facility, he'd been sent to quarters while she was assigned residence in a small cottage with angular roof lines, located on a grassy knoll near the Honeywater. Though flowerbeds trimmed the pathway and planter boxes graced the window ledges, her stay in the pleasant, private residence amounted to a prison sentence.

Less than an hour after settling in, Garrick knocked on her door. He'd shorn his head, and Brenna knew the outcome of her disposition from evaluating the expression on Garrick's face, before he uttered a single word. He embraced her tenderly and warned that they would not see one another again for quite some time. Though he left many things unspoken, the gentle demeanor Brenna had grown to love steeped every affectionate word he kissed into her ear.

Four days transpired before her authorization to transfer to the university came through. Colonel Weiss ordered an armed guard to

The Long Journey: *Approval*

stand at Brenna's door, supposedly for her protection. Brenna suspected that the military policeman's role had more to do with ensuring separation from Garrick than her personal safety, and long hours of lonely boredom inspired a brooding anxiety over their detachment.

During this intervening time, Lieutenant Mariel Hougen visited often and proved invaluable in navigating Brenna through the maze of procedures necessary to ensure access to her promised college bursary. In addition, a dispute arose concerning the cost of train fare and medical treatment Brenna received on her trip to Marvic. Initially, these things had been deducted from Brenna's pay, but Mariel's competent advocacy resolved the situation in the Lithian woman's favor.

While Brenna remained restricted to quarters, Mariel invested much of her own free time teaching basic grammar, syntax, and how sound / letter relationships worked in the Tamarian language. This task proved tedious, as Brenna struggled to wrap her lips and tongue around the various phonemes upon which Tamarian speech depended.

Lengthy hours in confined isolation burdened Brenna's spirit. She fell into a listless mood, vaguely dissatisfied with her situation, yet powerless to effect any change. Brenna frequently transitioned between dark despair and glimmering hope, often crying herself to sleep, only to awaken with terrible nightmares. She ate very little. The long separation from a supportive community of *believers* intensified her loneliness, and soon, Brenna's prayers became long, impassioned pleas with Allfather God, tainted by guilt that ranged from worry about her parents' disapproval to distress over her terrifying battlefield experiences

Yet the very act of expressing her grief and fear in earnest prayer melted those emotions away until gradually a sense of peace settled upon her soul. The power of Allfather's influence pervaded Brenna's reality until she found that she could simply wait, quiet and comforted, for her situation to change.

When Mariel arrived with Brenna's bursary documents in hand, the feeling of triumph she experienced when finally allowed to leave the cottage inspired laughter.

"May God be praised!" Brenna exclaimed.

Mariel scoffed, her beautiful brown eyes rolling. "It seems that I've done an inordinate amount of work for you to attribute credit to your god!"

The Long Journey: *Approval*

Reaching out to grasp her new found friend's hand, Brenna replied with a gentle, explanatory smile: "I think you're a gift from God, and I am grateful that you're here to help me."

Acknowledging that Brenna attributed every kindness to her deity's influence, Mariel gracefully accepted the Lithian woman's gratitude. "Well, if your god used me to make things easier on you, then I have a favor to ask of you in return."

Brenna nodded.

"I need a subject for my upcoming dissertation," Mariel began. "I would like to study you as an example of an adult learning my language. If you agree to help me, this kind of research will involve my assisting you with your course work and studying how you handle the demands of an academic program. You'll have a questionnaire to fill out concerning the time you devote to learning language versus actual assignment completion and study. I'll have to track your grades to see how your improving language skills correlate to academic performance.

"If you help me, this will benefit both of us. If you elect to handle your course load on your own, I'll have to ask one of the Kamerese who are attending a program up here. They don't treat their women very well and I expect they will extend little courtesy toward me, so I'd rather not work with any of them. Can I count on you?"

Brenna had believed Garrick's promise that he would help her learn the Tamarian language. Now, however, she realized that he felt overwhelmed by the OTS program and simply had no time to offer aid, a problem he did not foresee when he spoke to her on their trip to Marvic. Mariel's idea not only solved this problem, but Brenna also felt confident that a linguist brought skills into the learning process Garrick simply didn't have. "Great idea!" Brenna replied, grateful to refocus her mental energies. "When do we start?"

Mariel smiled broadly. "We can register today."

*   *   *

Later, on Liberty Hill, students lined up for the registration process snaked down the long stair in front of the administration building. Despite her expressed need to enroll in postgraduate classes, the egalitarian mentality common among Tamarians compelled Mariel to wait her turn, quite literally, at the back of the line. Though the two attractive women in uniform drew much curiosity, they conducted their

The Long Journey: *Approval*

conversation in Brenna's native tongue, which no one around them could comprehend. Aside from the obvious leering of a few ill-mannered young men, no one bothered the two women.

Mariel seemed at ease in this place. Though she didn't look like a Tamarian, the university milieu provided an accepting environment where the talented and intelligent woman thrived, despite her exotic appearance. Mariel well understood the negative bias frequently projected upon Brenna, having often felt like an outsider amid a sea of blonde-haired, light-skinned faces. Here, however, whatever racism existed remained carefully hidden, and Mariel found even more acceptance at the university than she did in the army.

In the administration office, the heavyset and overworked secretary seemed less than pleased when she saw Brenna, standing last in line, behind the counter. The sight of an armed foreigner wearing a Tamarian military parade uniform simultaneously amplified all the secretary's prejudices and shocked her sensibilities. However, she went about the registration process with perfunctory efficiency. After searching through her records, the clerk admitted that a dormitory room would not be available until late afternoon. "I'm sorry girls, but you'll have to wait," she said.

Better than an hour later, when their class selection processes had finally been completed, Brenna complained about feeling hungry. She followed Mariel down the stairs, past freshly weeded flowerbeds in full bloom and a fountain memorializing veteran graduates that sported a sign warning that its reclaimed water was unfit for human consumption. Mariel explained that the lack of potable water remained a serious problem throughout the city because the entire plateau complex upon which Marvic stood consisted of porous, volcanic rock. Heat from deep beneath the ground boiled through the water table and nearly all the surface water in the area contained high concentrations of dissolved minerals. Hence, many public facilities were irrigated by water drawn from reservoirs following three-stage sewage treatment.

A few minutes later they arrived at the commons. Here they inched forward in yet another extended line for food service, then found an unoccupied table near the back of the room. In the midst of a lunchtime conversation, Brenna suddenly dropped her fork and stared, wide-eyed at a young couple entering the room.

"What's wrong?" Mariel inquired, turning around in the hope of observing whatever it was Brenna found so obviously troubling.

The Long Journey: *Approval*

"That must be Garrick's brother!" Brenna exclaimed. "They really look alike!"

Mariel made brief eye contact with a boy who indeed appeared as a younger, slimmer version of Garrick. He was accompanied by a willowy girl who wore an ill-fitting but lavishly embroidered Temple Elsbireth overcoat. "He looks upset," Mariel observed.

Brenna watched the boy stalk to the far side of the room and stop at a table. Angry words ensued, then violence erupted and Brenna, without another thought, leaped to her feet and raced through the crowd with her sheathed longsword in hand.

Mariel followed, but could not match Brenna's agility as the smaller woman wove through the rising tide of student interest. Pushing her way through the crowd, Mariel watched in fascinated horror as the young monk left three Kamerese students blooded and badly wounded on the floor. Then she gasped as one of their companions hopped onto the luncheon table with a drawn knife in hand.

She heard, but didn't see, Brenna draw her sword. One moment later, Mariel saw the tip of Brenna's crystal edged weapon stay the attacker from his intended victim. Then, a commotion near the front of the commons distracted her attention. Mariel saw campus security men enter the commons while the knife-wielding student raced for the back door. The security team worked their way through the crowd and questioned eyewitnesses while the tall girl who accompanied Garrick's younger brother complained loudly.

In the meantime, Brenna disappeared. Mariel scanned the crowd, then slowly wandered back to the table where she'd left her food. There, she found Brenna nervously finishing a slice of buttered toast.

"Are you ok?" Mariel inquired, gently touching Brenna's shoulder.

The Lithian woman shook her head. "No," she said, trembling visibly. She swallowed a modest bite of bread before continuing. "I think I just stopped someone from murdering Garrick's little brother."

Mariel sat down, intrigued that Brenna, a combat veteran, should appear so edgy about saving a life, rather than taking one. However, given that the boy looked so much like Garrick, Mariel appreciated that Brenna's thoughts fed on emotion unrelated to fighting skill. Lieutenant Hougen refrained from judgment and extended her friend a measure of sympathy. "I imagine. But the security people will want to talk to you anyway."

The Long Journey: *Approval*

"Then maybe we should leave," Brenna advised, standing. "I don't want to cause any trouble and we can get out of here before they come looking for me."

Mariel shook her head and stayed Brenna's motion with a calm hand. "Don't run away, Brenna. You haven't done anything wrong. You have nothing to hide.

"Besides, you're the only Lithian here. You're wearing a dress uniform with silver lions on your collar, walking around in boots, with an army backpack, a bow and a longsword. How long do you expect they'd need to look before they found you?"

No sooner had she finished those words than the senior campus security officer approached the table. As a former military man, he recognized Lieutenant Hougen's rank and nodded to her before he turned his attention toward the young mercenary with the name "Velez" stitched into the fabric above her left breast.

"Miss Velez, you'll need to accompany me to the Security Office," he ordered firmly, offering his hand to help her up in the manner of a Tamarian gentleman.

Brenna's face paled as she looked at Mariel, pleading soundlessly for a translation.

"We will go together," Mariel told the security guard. "I'll translate so she can answer your questions."

Though Brenna said nothing during the walk across campus, Mariel flirted with the security officer, using a gentle, lingering touch, a mildly seductive tone of voice and a lovely smile to disarm his demeanor. The alien beauty that attracted his interest became a means to ensure that Brenna received fair treatment. As Brenna watched Mariel's manipulations at work, her regard shifted between admiration and disgust.

Mariel had learned long ago that most men remained more interested in what she looked like than what she thought. Her academic interest and high achievement worked against her in the social realm, severely limiting the pool of worthy and available mates. Even among equality-minded Tamarians, bright women with advanced degrees often found their social options restricted. Although she'd begun to believe that she simply didn't need a man for anything, Mariel felt occasional resentment toward those who remained intrigued with her fit figure, shapely legs and flaming hair, but felt threatened by her mind and lacked the confidence to engage her in intelligent discourse.

The Long Journey: *Approval*

In addition, she struggled to contain a well-hidden measure of envy toward Brenna, whom she initially considered a vacuous, foreign siren who'd stolen the attention of a worthy young man. Mariel recognized Garrick's potential and grew in her admiration of him with every conversation they shared, but no matter how hard she tried, Lieutenant Hougen could not shift his fiercely loyal interest away from the girl he loved.

Due in part to her lengthy education, Mariel understood that most measures of human intelligence remain rooted in language. As she spent time in Brenna's company, Mariel learned to appreciate the Lithian girl's thinking ability, recognizing that Brenna possessed a sharp wit–especially in her native tongue–that often remained hidden behind her shy demeanor. Brenna seemed highly skilled at fading into the background in a group setting, and therefore, her intelligence could easily be overlooked. Yet, to Mariel's delight, this reticence vanished whenever she engaged Brenna in one on one discussion, where the Lithian girl expressed genuine interest not only in Mariel's work, but in her point of view as well. These things drew Mariel into the embrace of an unexpected friendship.

For this reason, Mariel turned on every bit of charm she could muster in Brenna's defense, deflecting attention away from the act of a drawn sword toward a flash of shapely, exposed calf muscle in the slit of her own skirt. Recognizing that this technique worked astonishingly well, Mariel used the walk toward the Security Office to glean information from Lukas, the hapless public safety officer.

Just as they arrived, a deputy ran to the stairs clutching a small brick wrapped in wax paper. "You need to see this!" the deputy said, breathlessly. "I found it on the floor under the table."

Lukas opened the package, revealing a pungent, rectangular mass of brown / black gum about the length of his middle finger. He sniffed and wrinkled his nose.

Mariel saw Brenna's eyes widen. "What is it?" she inquired in Lithian.

"Opium sap," Brenna replied, her tone reflecting disgust. "It's come a long way to get here. Usually it's refined into morphine bricks, which are solid, less aromatic and easier to smuggle."

"How do you know this?" Mariel inquired.

Brenna glanced at the security officers, then back at Mariel. "Poor farmers grow poppies in the mountains of Southern Kameron,

The Long Journey: *Approval*

where it's dry. My father, who owned property just over the ridge line from the opium fields, fought many battles to keep narcotics traffic off of our land. The drug lords who processed opium gum into morphine often tried to smuggle it eastward, right through our territory."

"Well, it won't be long before the police become involved in this," Mariel responded. "You and Garrick's brother might have uncovered something very dangerous here."

The serious discussion between Lukas and his deputy confirmed Mariel's conviction. During the interview with Brenna in his office, Lukas inquired extensively about her knowledge of the Southern Kamerese drug operations, information which Brenna willingly provided. As Mariel translated, she sensed that the opium issue had arisen previously and that the scope and origin of the problem lay beyond campus security's ability to contain.

When Lukas stood to dismiss them, Brenna turned back to Mariel. "What about Algernon?" she whispered. "What will happen to him?"

When Mariel translated Brenna's concern and explained who she was in relation to Algernon and why she needed to know, Lukas glared at the Lithian woman, a sign that betrayed a host of mixed feelings. "I wonder what brought him here," the security officer replied. "We understand that he has a right to defend himself, but fighting in public indicates an underlying problem we must investigate. Further, I would like to know how the opium we found ties into his conflict with the students. We tolerate no drug abuse on campus either. How the narcotic relates to the boy simply can't be determined without talking to him. I have already sent word for his brother to ensure his safe return, and I will interview the young man myself."

After Lukas dismissed the two women he brought Astrid into his office, spoke to her for about ten minutes, then addressed Algernon. Not knowing the young monk at all, he was initially taken aback by the acolyte's abrupt manner, especially after he'd proffered the traditional Tamarian blessing on the younger man.

"I came here looking for my sister, who took off with that foreign slime swine, Marco," Algernon said. "While his friends attacked me, that porcine fop ran away like a squealing pig! That's the true story."

Lukas folded his hands and raised his eyebrows. "So you provoked them?"

The Long Journey: *Approval*

Algernon ignored the question. "I want to know what he did with my sister. She's my twin, and I have a right to make sure she hasn't been harmed. Why would he run? If he had nothing to hide, why wouldn't he talk to me? What's he afraid of? Why were his friends so quick to come to his rescue?"

"Good questions!" Lukas replied. "I'd like your help in answering them."

Algernon grunted in disgust, his grey eyes narrowing. "Marco is the key player in this sordid little episode. Find him and all the fog in this drama will vanish."

"I see. What do you know of this?" Lukas asked, pulling the opium sample out of his drawer and setting it on the desk, just beyond Algernon's reach.

When the young priest caught a whiff of the narcotic aroma, his expression morphed into something venomous and he sat back forcefully in his leather chair. "That's how he seduced my sister," Algernon admitted with clear contempt. "Marco's Kamerese opium pulled her out of the cloister." The boy leaned forward again, speaking in a menacing tone. "I'd like to know where it's lead her."

That response indicated the young monk had enough experience with opium to recognize the drug, and correlated nicely with Astrid's testimony. In this light, Lukas accepted the story as truth, though the manner in which Algernon delivered his reply wrought a refrain of worry in the security officer's mind. He paused thoughtfully. "I would like to keep you here until the police arrive so you can answer their questions. In addition, your brother is coming to ensure your safety," Lukas offered.

Algernon laughed. "Look at them, then look at me," he replied. "I don't need anybody's protection!"

"You were very nearly attacked with a knife. All of the eyewitnesses claim that the mercenary girl saved your life," Lukas countered.

"I don't even know who that *sicklian* female is," Algernon retorted, using the ugly, racist term for Lithian people common in the Tamarian language.

Lukas, suspecting on the basis of Brenna's uniform that she'd met Garrick in the army, realized that Algernon must not have seen his brother for quite some time and knew nothing about Brenna. "She's your brother's . . . girlfriend," Lucas revealed, clearly disapproving and uncomfortable with the concept.

The Long Journey: *Approval*

Algernon let the shock sink in, shook his head, then turned his attention to a tree beyond the window. "Grief!" the boy muttered. "You know, he could have picked someone of his own species! But it's his life and she's his problem. I've never seen that girl before, and I have no idea why she bothered helping me."

Someone knocked on the door. Lukas paused to invite the caller in. A very tall police officer entered, wearing a light blue uniform and holding his hat politely beneath his arm. Clean-shaven, square-jawed and broad-shouldered with neatly trimmed blonde hair, he looked like a living, breathing police recruitment poster.

Lukas greeted the policeman warmly. "Lieutenant Streng! Welcome!"

Algernon, dwarfed by the giant man, felt somewhat intimidated at the manner in which the detective seemed to occupy all of the free space remaining in the room. Listening to the banter between the two men, the young acolyte correctly assumed they'd known one another for a long time. The policeman offered a blessing to Algernon, who smiled; he steepled his fingers and nodded in response.

"This is an ominous development," the lieutenant said, occupying the chair next to Algernon when Lukas motioned for him to sit. "We've been working to crack the growing power of foreign drug lords and their influence here. We have an ongoing investigation, and I trust we can expect your complete cooperation."

Rather than looking at Lukas, the police detective directed his remark toward Algernon, who seemed initially bewildered that he needed to be in the same room to hear this discussion. "I have nothing to do with this!" Algernon exclaimed.

"Ah, but you have involved yourself already," Lieutenant Streng replied. "I have interviewed the young men who attacked you, several students who witnessed the incident in the dining commons, and I have also spoken to your girlfriend in the next room. Now, I would like to hear your side of the story."

"That woman is not my girlfriend!" Algernon retorted, defensively.

"She's wearing your overcoat," the policeman replied. "She's also very worried about your safety. Whatever you make of your relationship with her does not interest me, but I am concerned that you've become involved with a very dangerous group of people."

The Long Journey: *Approval*

Algernon slumped in his chair and slowly blinked his eyes. "So everyone says!"

"I can't emphasize this enough," the detective continued. "Foreign criminal gangs responsible for illicit drug trafficking have infested the city. We've already found several of their members guilty of murder, and they will not think twice about killing you. I would strongly recommend that you return to the Temple and leave this investigation to us."

At this revelation Algernon sat up, adrenaline rushing into his blood. "My sister has fallen into favor with one of these people," he began. "How can you tell me to run and hide when her life is in danger? How can you expect me to sleep in safety while she's under their control? If you say these people are killers, don't you have any interest in her protection? Why should I rest and let you investigate when I've already managed to find the man who lured her away?"

"Son, they will kill you," the policeman warned, solemnly. "Leave this to the professionals. I would hate to see you get hurt."

Algernon would not back down. "Where did you have to go to interview the men who attacked me? Did you find them calmly sitting here in a chair like this, waiting for you?"

"No," the detective admitted. "I spoke to them in the hospital."

"Well, I encourage you to think about that! There were three of them and only one of me, yet we're having this conversation in the comfort of an office. I'm not needing medical care! I suffered no damage worse than a bruise and a scratch!"

"Yet that mercenary girl came to your rescue," Lukas reminded him. "Otherwise, you'd now be dead."

"It's possible," Algernon admitted, "but you don't know that for certain. I'll just have to be more careful next time."

"I'm sure they'll track you down," Lieutenant Streng cautioned. "And they will come in greater numbers, or with weapons your martial skills cannot defeat."

Algernon thought for a moment. "Then what of my sister?" he inquired. "Would you recommend that I abandon her to them?"

Lieutenant Streng nearly offered to add Kira's disappearance to his investigation, but aware of Tamarian law, he stopped to think before speaking. "How much younger is your sister?" he inquired.

"She's my twin," Algernon replied. "I was born first."

The Long Journey: *Approval*

The police detective looked at Lukas, then returned his gaze to Algernon and shrugged. "If she left the Temple on her own volition, there's nothing I can do."

"Then you understand why I simply have to keep looking. I can't abandon her to a gang of hoodlums. If you won't help her, then I must."

Lieutenant Streng decided to come back to his point later on. He asked Algernon why he'd come to the university and confirmed the motive he'd previously heard in speaking to Astrid. He asked several uncomfortably pointed questions concerning Kira's interest in Marco before Algernon began resisting a direct response.

"You admitted there's nothing you can do to help me find her," Algernon accused. "If you're going to leave me to look for Kira on my own, then I have no interest in answering any more of your questions."

This reply, delivered in a less than respectful tone of voice, initially caught the police detective off guard. He recovered by deflecting the direction of their discussion. "Helping me helps you," Lieutenant Streng offered. "Your cooperation will ensure your personal safety and bring us closer to the people responsible for your sister's disappearance."

Algernon saw the policeman's eyes flick upward, to the right. *Gottslena* writings contained much advice about detecting dishonesty, and Algernon remembered that people did this in order to visualize what they wanted to say, often when they didn't want to tell the truth. "Lying to a priest will not help your cause," Algernon retorted. Rather than wasting your time with me, you ought to be searching Marco's dormitory room, interrogating his friends, impounding his car and inquiring to learn his whereabouts."

"Young man," the detective replied, "though I respect the institution you represent, I'm not seeking your approval, nor do I need your advice on how to do my job. I'm interested in your well being and preserving your life from grievous harm."

"This conversation is pointless if you won't listen to me," Algernon concluded

This remark, delivered in an irritated tone, reflected resentment rooted in frustration. Algernon interpreted the police officer's repeated concern for safety as proof that no amount of intelligent discourse could persuade the detective to reconsider any action he'd already decided to undertake. Therefore, continuing the meaningless dialogue prevented him from doing something productive. "Can I go?" he asked.

The Long Journey: *Approval*

"Your brother should be arriving any time now," Lukas remarked in a manner indicating that the interview had been completed. "He will escort you off campus during a break in his schedule late this afternoon. I would like you to remain here until then, and afterward, I do not wish to see you and your girlfriend again."

Algernon stalked back into the small, ill-furnished interrogation room, finding that Astrid had changed back into her own clothes. She sat on a bench–looking through a window along the western wall–watching small, brown birds flutter from branch to branch among the tree canopy that sheltered a ravine outside. On a table next to the bench, Algernon saw that some kindly person had left them a vegetable plate and a pitcher of water with two cups. Astrid turned her attention toward Algernon and brought a slice of cucumber up to her lips. She waited for him to speak.

"Are you ok?" he asked.

"This isn't going very well," she said softly. "Marco got away, and we're in trouble!"

Algernon shook his head and sat down next to her, his nearness gradually melding from a threat to something safer and more familiar. "That isn't true," he told her. "We're not in trouble. We've covered a lot of ground in a short time. Marco's on the run and now the police are looking for him. He'll have to divide his attention between us and the authorities. That's something he won't be able to sustain for long."

Astrid seemed unimpressed with his claim. "The detective said these people are dangerous, Algernon. He said we should go back to the Temple because the criminals will want to kill us now."

Algernon sat down and leaned against the wall, accepting a slice of cucumber that Astrid wordlessly offered to him. "It's true that we have to be careful," he admitted. "But we have many advantages in our favor."

Astrid looked directly into Algernon's fearless, grey eyes, recognizing that same spirit of fierce independence she so adored in Kira. "And what would those be?" she asked.

"To begin with, the police aren't looking for us. The criminals can't conduct their nefarious business without distraction while detectives tail them. Therefore, their energies can't be fully focused on any single activity, whether selling their narcotics, avoiding the police or seeking harm toward us. Yet all we have to do is pursue Marco relentlessly.

The Long Journey: *Approval*

"Furthermore, local people respect us because of who we are, and we'll likely get more cooperation from them than a bunch of Kamerese who don't even speak our language very well. This is our territory, our town, and our people. Marco and his gang can't possibly operate as effectively around here as we can.

"And one more thing," he said in conclusion. Have you ever met a smart criminal?"

Astrid's left eyebrow lowered while her right one raised, an expression of puzzlement. "What do you mean?"

Algernon smiled. "If these guys had real brains, do you think they'd be pushing opium?"

The expression on Astrid's face changed. "I know you're intelligent, yet you regularly and deliberately violated every edict in the Temple, even the reasonable ones. I don't think your logic holds up."

She had a very annoying habit of pointing out character flaws, but Algernon didn't let her remarks bother him this time. He took another slice of cucumber that she offered, chewing on it thoughtfully. "My motive for doing that was based on principle, not greed," he replied softly. "There's a fundamental difference in approach that distinguishes the two." A proverb came to mind in support of his position: "The heart of a man determines his step; as his mind decrees, so his will shall be done."

Astrid turned back toward the window. "That's hardly comforting," she complained. "I think you're rationalizing this to make yourself feel better. We've been sitting here for hours already. I'm hungry, and all we have to eat is a plate of vegetables they brought in.

"We now have a bunch of bloodthirsty thugs wanting to kill us, yet we've only been searching since this morning. You can't go back to the Temple, and I don't think they'd be too happy to see me right now either. We're no closer to Kira at this point than we were last night. I don't understand your optimism, Algernon." Astrid's eyes welled up with emotion, but she didn't let herself cry.

Algernon accepted the essence of her argument and rested his hand on her back. Astrid initially stiffened, but didn't ask him to move it. So, he left it there and patted her right shoulder blade, as he would have done in comforting Kira. "We'll find her," he promised. "I know we'll find her."

Astrid straightened, a signal Algernon correctly interpreted that she'd had enough of his physical contact. He moved his hand away.

The Long Journey: *Approval*

"We've come too far to go back now," he told her. "The police won't help us. We have to find Kira on our own."

"So what do we do?" she asked. "How are we going to move about when killers are looking for us?"

"We stay in plain sight," Algernon responded. "We don't ever let them find us alone. No one will move against us when there are witnesses around."

She remained skeptical. "An assassin with a high-powered rifle could hit either one of us from a thousand yards away, or we might get knifed in a crowd!"

"That takes way too much planning and prior knowledge of where we might be found at any given time. They're not that clever. You're being unreasonable!" Algernon struggled to stifle his irritation. "Come on, Astrid! You said you loved my sister!"

Astrid paused in incredulity. "That's not fair, Algernon!" she retorted. "Don't try to blackmail me!"

"I'm doing nothing of the kind," he replied, annoyed that she felt so free to constantly question the mettle of his character while restricting his freedom to return the favor. "I've given you the benefit of the doubt in this. I'm trying to understand how you can find someone of your own gender physically attractive, and I'll freely admit that I simply don't get it. But now when you seem so reluctant to put your life on the line for someone whom you claim to love, it underscores my suspicion that your attraction to Kira has more to do with your own pleasure than any concern for her welfare."

Astrid blushed and uttered an astonished grunt, looking away from Algernon while shaking her head. "This is not about Kira," she said between gritted teeth, pausing for emphasis before turning back toward him. "This is about you. That scene in the cafeteria was impulsive and reckless. Now we've got to deal with the consequences of your out-of-control behavior. Now we don't know what these people are going to do to us, nor do we know what they're going to do to her.

"You talk in grandiose terms about your devotion to Kira, but the way you behave puts her life in greater danger. So keep that sanctimonious attitude to yourself and stop judging me for the way I feel about your sister."

"How can I help but judge you about this?" he replied. "Did you think this was going to be a warm dip in the river? I recall it was you who first revealed the opium connection. Did you expect that proto-brain Marco to apologetically hand Kira over to us like he'd accidentally left her in the back of his car?

"Of course the guys we're dealing with are dangerous. Bottom feeders usually have teeth. But keep in mind that Kira's my twin, and I'm willing to do whatever it takes for her sake, even if I don't approve of what she's doing. If you aren't like-minded, you should have stayed in your room!"

Astrid shook her head and whispered to no one in particular: "How can somebody who is supposed to be so smart be so dense?" When she turned back to Algernon, Astrid spoke with strong conviction. "You are complicating everything, making the whole situation worse by escalating conflicts far beyond where they need to go!"

"What did you expect me to do?" he argued. "Those guys attacked me!"

Astrid slapped her hands on her knees. "This is exactly what I'm talking about. You think the trouble begins when it comes to blows. I'm telling you that you need to use your head and think long before the situation goes that far."

"Ugh! How can I reason with you?" he lamented.

"You can start by listening! Not just by hearing my words, Algernon, but by really listening. Think about what I say. You're not the only one with a brain, and if you had paid attention to my advice while we were in the cafeteria, you might have been able to avoid a confrontation that not only risked your life, but put Kira's in greater jeopardy as well."

Exasperated, Algernon groaned, pulled at his hair, then dragged his fingers down his face, lifting his head toward the ceiling. He knew she was right. He hated to admit that she was right, but every tenet of *Gottslena* that he'd learned supported Astrid's position. The careful exercise of judgment coupled with an attitude motivated by selflessness and nurtured by a humble demeanor all contributed toward enlightened behavior. He could no longer afford the luxury of denying that he'd too long relied upon invective, threat and violence to solve his problems. In a moment of brutal honesty, he perceived that by raging at authority, he sought to impose the very control he himself resisted. That realization brought his emotions to the surface, and Algernon broke down and wept.

Astrid watched his response with understanding, her wrath cooling. She didn't ridicule; she didn't condemn him. Instead, she reached across his back and drew him into her embrace. "It's ok," she breathed. "Let it out."

And he did.

The mild scent and soft texture of her clean hair, the pleasant, mineral oil aroma from the Honeywater lingering on her skin, unifying with the warmth of her arms soon stirred a different feeling in Algernon's mind. Unaccustomed to emotional vulnerability, he had no mechanism to screen against the strong sense of desire he felt for her at that moment. Algernon composed himself, moved away ever so slightly, then placed a very light kiss on her lips.

Astrid backed off in surprise, not returning the favor. "I'm sorry," she told him. "I've given you the wrong idea."

An expression of shock and shame flashed over Algernon's face. He turned away and closed his eyes. "No," he replied, sniffing. "Don't be sorry. I'm being stupid." Flustered and embarrassed, Algernon searched for words to assuage the situation, but found nothing in his soul that would right his wrongdoing.

So he sat in dishonored silence while Astrid slowly bit on another slice of cucumber. She glanced over without speaking, then offered him a carrot stick. Astrid sensed his wilted pride with a measure of compassion, but said nothing.

Fifteen wordless minutes passed, marked by the steady ticking of a wind-up clock hung on the plain, grey wall and the crunching sound of masticating teeth working through an occasional vegetable. The creak of the front door opening, a worried, yet familiar voice and anxious footfalls on the hardwood floor raised a sense of anticipation in the young monk's mind. Algernon smiled when the stocky figure of a sweat-stained warrior in running garb stood in the doorway.

"Are you hurt?" the soldier inquired.

He'd grown, Algernon realized, and cut his hair short. "Garrick!" he exclaimed, rising to embrace his elder sibling. "No, I'm not hurt! But am I ever glad to see you!"

"Me too!" Garrick replied, also noting that Algernon now stood taller, spoke in a deeper voice and possessed manly strength. "It's been too long, little brother! When I got the message that you were in trouble, I worried about you!"

Astrid stood, waiting for an appropriate moment. She could see the strong facial resemblance, especially in the shape of eyes and the rounded nose that wistfully reminded her of the unpleasant circumstances that had broken up this family of attractive children.

Garrick relinquished his brother, noticing the tall, slender woman near the window. She had pretty, northern features, he noticed: high cheekbones, narrow eyes and a small, almost delicate mouth. Dark blue priestly clothing disguised her figure, but the belt around her waist revealed that this woman's hips were shapelier than her breasts. He smiled at her, surprised that Algernon had picked someone older and so fine-boned as a companion.

"Garrick, meet Astrid," Algernon announced as an introduction.

Garrick put his hands together in a prayerful position and bowed his head slightly, while moving his hands from his abdomen, to his chest and face, then extending them forward and opening his palms to the sky. This blessing, according to local custom, offered his strength, soul and mind in service to her. Though he didn't ascribe to the traditional Tamarian religious philosophy, this was the way any self-respecting Tamarian addressed a priest or priestess, and she returned the greeting with a bowed head and steepled hands. "You're my brother's girl?" he inquired.

"No," Astrid responded. "I'm *Kira's* girl."

In the past she'd not been inclined to admit this to anyone, due in part to the reaction she expected from such a revelation. However, after Algernon kissed her, Astrid wanted no part in any misunderstanding. Astrid saw Garrick's astonished jaw drop and his eyes move back toward his brother, as if expecting Algernon to refute her admission.

But Algernon nodded. "Much has changed since we were last together," he said. "One day, when you have time, we'll sit down for a long talk."

Garrick, his mind reeling, found no suitable words to frame a response. More than anything, he felt shock. Leaving the pressure of the OTS program aside, the terse message from Lukas inspired brotherly concern. Now the revelation that his young sister had taken a female lover hit him like an unexpected blow. Then, regaining control over the flood of emotion rising up within his soul, he turned his eyes back to Astrid. "I hope you can forgive me," he stammered. "I would never have expected that my little sister . . ."

"Do you love her?" Astrid inquired, interrupting.

The Long Journey: *Approval*

"Of course!" Garrick replied, the immediacy of his words verifying their truth.

"That's good enough for me," she told him. I'm not asking for your approval."

Garrick sighed, trying to make sense of the news. The tables of discrimination turned, and he now faced the ugly side of his own prejudice. He resented the way people treated Brenna. How could he claim any moral high ground in that relationship when he felt so strongly repelled by the girl representing this one? He didn't like people misjudging Brenna on the basis of her appearance, yet he'd just done so with Astrid in an equally thoughtless manner. The conflict troubled him. He knew he'd have to think long and hard about this, but decided in the meantime to accept Astrid without passing judgment on her.

Lukas stopped by the doorway and leaned in. "You two are free to go," he said. "Please carefully consider my advice and return to the Temple immediately."

Garrick turned toward his brother. "It's a long way up there," he said. "I don't have a lot of time, so we'd better get going."

Algernon said nothing, shouldering his meager belongings and helping Astrid with hers. He remained silent until they'd walked out the door, down the worn concrete steps in front of the security building, and onto the stone path that led toward the university's main entrance. Their footfalls slapped on the blue rock. "I'm not going back to the Temple," he announced. "Kira's in trouble, and I need to find her."

"Hold on, I thought you were the one in trouble," Garrick replied. "The Security Department contacted me, warning that your life is at risk."

"Garrick, they're using you to make sure I leave the campus and don't come back. They really don't understand what's going on, and if they did, I would be the least of their concerns. It's Kira that we need to worry about." Algernon spoke with a measure of anxiety that Garrick had never heard from him before.

Bewildered by conflicting information and clearly out of touch with the issues faced by his siblings, Garrick's own troubles paled in comparison. "What happened to her?"

Astrid, walking on Garrick's right, explained the situation. She outlined crucial background information, allowing Garrick to grasp the motivation behind Kira's otherwise inexplicable behavior, while leaving out the intimate details of her relationship that had shocked Algernon the night before. By the time Astrid informed Garrick of the opium connection, his heart had sunk into a pit of guilt over insisting that his younger siblings leave their wretched home in favor of the Temple Elsbireth.

At a point where the west-facing hill descended steeply toward the military base, the tree-lined path led into afternoon daylight. Warm, late afternoon air, faintly carrying the scent of roses from some unseen garden, inspired perspiration on their faces. Wind rattled the aspen leaves and whispered through the pine boughs, hinting of hidden secrets. Marvic's wall slithered along the northern edge of the city, its stone spine leading, it seemed, toward the Sacred Enclosure high upon the ancient hilltop, whose white buildings shone against a clear, cloudless sky.

In the background, mountain flanks robed in forest green reached into soaring peaks, the realm of glaciers and barren rock, high alpine meadows and the last refuge for the remnant giants who dreamed of vengeance against Tamaria and its fortified capital. That distant reality remained on the fringe of consciousness, continually renewed among the city's inhabitants whenever they caught sight of Queen Tamar's crimson-clad Defenders patrolling the wall.

As the trio passed the stately Arts and Language buildings and reached the staircase leading down to the university's gates, Garrick turned to Astrid as she finished her story. "What about you?" he inquired. "Are you going back?"

She shook her head. "Not until I find Kira."

A group of strangers, a family group no doubt seeing a freshman student off to college, hustled down the stairs to meet them. These people greeted Astrid and Algernon with smiling faces and offered blessings, their hands reaching out to touch, and be touched. Garrick knew that Brenna would find this kind of attention very uncomfortable, but watched Algernon handle the recognition with feigned grace that would be apparent only to those who knew him well, while Astrid's expression overflowed with compassion. Garrick felt like a killer among saints, walking in their company.

In the midst of this social tension, Garrick mulled over what he could do. "Tell me what you need," Garrick said. "What can I do to help you?"

Algernon, respecting the difficulty of Garrick's training regimen, didn't want to trouble his brother any further, nor place a burden that

The Long Journey: *Approval*

might limit his success in officer's training. However, Algernon appreciated his brother's concern and knew that accepting a gift would honor him. "I need a good utility knife, a can opener and a lighter," he admitted. "I could really use a skillet and a length of rope, too!"

"We can go to the commissary and I can get those things for you. How are you fixed for money?"

"I have some. We don't need much," Algernon replied. "As long as we're in the city, people will take care of us."

Garrick didn't like to see his brother surviving on the good will of strangers, though if the family they'd just met provided any indication of widespread appreciation, both Algernon and Astrid would be looked after by anyone they encountered. Thinking back to his battle with the giants, Garrick imagined an idea of how he might offer more direct assistance, but withheld his intentions for the moment. Smothered in an awkward silence, the three Tamarians completed their descent and walked briskly toward the military base.

A low stone wall topped by a palisade of pointed, wrought iron demarcated the official boundary of the Dragon's Lair Military Training Facility. Though decorative in nature, this barrier remained under active patrol and the soldiers who protected the base perimeter followed standing orders to subdue and arrest anyone who attempted unauthorized entrance.

These historic grounds, following a gently undulating landscape along the North Fork of the River Honeywater, served as a training facility for the first recruits of the fledgling Tamarian army. The base, its grounds, many monuments, and the buildings sprawled across its breadth, conveyed a sense of care across many generations of soldiers who had learned the art of warfare within its gates. Though beautiful in its architecture and painstakingly landscaped, the officers who served here appreciated its utilitarian layout more than any other feature. Designed around concentric rings, with straight, radial pathways between its facilities, soldiers moved around the grounds with ease.

Garrick led his brother and Astrid into the base, then turned along a walkway leading westward, toward the commissary. A small, four wheeled electric truck ferrying supplies to the loading dock quietly passed them and stopped at the commissary entrance. Garrick groaned, knowing that the clerk inside would have to check the truck's manifest and unload before helping him with his supply requisition. He had little time to wait.

The Long Journey: *Approval*

Garrick entered the commissary airlock, waiting for his brother and Astrid to come inside before opening the second door of the vestibule. The commissary stood two stories high and featured a steeply angular, copper-colored metal roof designed to shed snow and catch rainwater; this, a common design element necessitated by the chronic lack of potable ground water within the city limits. Garrick stopped the requisition clerk in the midst of his labor. "I'll fill out the form for what I need," he told the harried young man. "When you have time, you can put it on my account for my brother."

The clerk trustingly agreed and departed. Garrick admonished Algernon and Astrid to sit down while he scurried back to quarters. "I have something else I want to give you," Garrick promised.

On his way back toward the men's barracks, Garrick noticed a higher level of activity than had been present when he left the base earlier in the day. Officer candidates, wearing full combat gear and carrying weapons, scurried away from the barracks in purposeful rhythm. He approached Greg Schmidt, a man who'd always treated Garrick with kindness, to inquire about the situation.

"Chasing the *ubermadchen* again?" the blue-eyed warrior teased, noting that Garrick remained attired in running gear. "Colonel Weiss announced a surprise deployment about an hour ago. I picked up an extra OpOrd for you," he said, fumbling through his belongings for the document. "I'll find another map and get it to you on the train."

Garrick, though grateful that Greg Schmidt consistently looked out for him, shut his eyes and muttered a curse. "When are we leaving?" he inquired.

"Twenty minutes," Greg responded. "If you're not ready to load up by then, TAC Vogel will give you a chewing out that none of us will soon forget. Better move!"

Garrick raced to a bathroom on the second floor of the barracks, where he quickly dunked himself into a cool shower to rinse off his sweat. One floor above, he changed into full battle regalia, made sure his area looked presentable, then pulled a small pouch out of his footlocker. Garrick laced his boots in haste, grabbed his knapsack, which he always kept fully prepared for immediate use, his poncho and the leather pouch, then dashed downstairs with about ten minutes to spare.

Next, Garrick raced to the armory. He discovered that he was the last of all officer candidates to sign out weapons and training ammunition. After checking his side arm and rifle quickly to ensure they

The Long Journey: *Approval*

were clean and in good working order, he dashed back to the commissary, his mind brimming with worry.

Algernon, now equipped with the supplies Garrick had bought for him, seemed startled to see his brother dressed in battle gear and carrying a big rifle. Noting that Garrick seemed distracted, Algernon regretted involving his older sibling in the search for their sister.

"This is for you," Garrick offered, handing his brother a brown pouch with a draw string laced into its opening. The bag had a faintly unpleasant, musky odor. "There's enough money inside to last you awhile."

Algernon ignored the smell and accepted the gift with gratitude as he embraced his brother. "Bless you! You are my heart and soul."

"And you are mine! Find Kira!" Garrick whispered. "Tell her I love her." Then, grasping his younger brother by the shoulders, Garrick looked him in the eye. "Be very careful out there. Write to me and tell me what happens. If you need more money, or anything else, don't be afraid to ask."

Then Garrick turned, offered the traditional gesture of blessing to Astrid, then ran off to rejoin his OTS class.

A crowd of warriors milling around the base train depot caught Garrick's attention. He arrived, out of breath, to find that TAC Officer Vogel was busy organizing the chaos of a few hundred enlisted soldiers, so Garrick nosed through the OpOrd documents until he found one entitled "Field Deployment Exercise Assignments," a list that specified the leadership roles for each of the twenty-eight surviving officer candidates in Garrick's class. Scanning through the pages, Garrick noted that the sergeants for his platoon were two men named Vidders and Ringer.

The growl of an approaching steam train heading down the spur line urged Garrick into the mass of assembled soldiers, where he queried every sergeant he could find for the whereabouts of Sergeant Vidders. Near the back of the group, he found two veteran warriors discussing some matter of trivial importance, neither of whom even noticed Garrick approaching.

"Sergeant Vidders!" Garrick called with a surprising degree of authority.

A stout, redheaded man in his early thirties turned at the sound of his name and appraised the young officer candidate with a blend of shock and dismay. He stood at attention, for it was not customary in the

The Long Journey: *Approval*

Tamarian army to salute anyone who had not yet earned his rank. "Candidate Ravenwood, I presume?" he inquired, with a note of disdain. "You're leading this exercise?"

"I am," Garrick responded. "Do you have a problem with that, sergeant?"

At the sound of Sergeant Ringer's groan, Sergeant Vidders shot his colleague a disapproving glance. The beefy-handed noncom took Garrick by the shoulder and led him away from the assembled troops. "Let's talk," he said.

Garrick's mind raced as he walked. He thought he'd successfully transitioned out of the mode where he needed to fear the wrath of a sergeant, yet he couldn't help sensing that his initial contact with a noncommissioned officer hadn't gone well. Stiffening his demeanor, Garrick inquired: "Tell me. What's on your mind, sergeant?"

Vidders, who stood half a head shorter than Garrick, looked up at the young man with an expression of concern that wrinkled his sunburned brow. "Mister Ravenwood, how old are you?"

"I'm old enough. What does that matter?"

Glancing back toward his squadron, Vidders tightened his lips. "You look younger than every buck private in the platoon, Ravenwood. How do you expect them to take orders from you?"

Garrick, who'd been thinking about this already, recalled his carefully formulated response. "Sergeant, if you follow my orders, they will too. I'm not asking you to make any special allowances for me, but I do expect you to conduct yourself in a professional manner. Can I count on your support?"

Sergeant Vidders narrowed his eyes. "Don't make us look bad out there, Ravenwood, or I'll make sure your post-op evaluation puts an end to your career."

"Just be fair, sergeant," Garrick replied. "That's all I ask."

Vidders nodded. "Alright, kid. Let's go meet your platoon."

Afterward, as the Model 15 locomotive pulled through the city, Garrick stared out the train car window, distractedly ruminating upon the events of the day. Kira, his younger sister, had been a sweet, affectionate little girl who loved to play in water pools during the summer heat. He pictured her running through the orchard toward Deception Creek, darting through apple and plum trees on stubby legs, laughing and shrieking in mock terror at the feigned threat that her older brother might pick her up and dump her into the water.

The Long Journey: *Approval*

Now, she reclined in some drug smuggler's embrace. Now, she had a girlfriend! Garrick rubbed his forehead in disgust. What happened? And what was really going on with Algernon? Though his brother had not admitted any wrongdoing, Garrick knew him to be difficult and hard to understand. Something dreadful must have occurred at the Temple if Algernon did not intend to return there.

Then, he wrestled with the issue of his own suitability for the OTS program. It seemed that while the older candidates remained helpful, few people in leadership took him seriously. The men he was supposed to command on the upcoming training exercise eyed him with whispered suspicion, yet he had to lead them in a surprise combat exercise having had no time to establish rapport. Compounding his ill-preparedness, Garrick had to review the operational orders on the train so that he had some clue about what he was supposed to be doing. TAC Officer Vogel, who stopped him on the loading platform, warned that Colonel Weiss would be observing the exercise.

"I expect a favorable impression!" Manfred Vogel warned. "We'll be watching you!"

Fortunately, TAC Vogel, busy in his organizational role, had not noticed that Garrick missed the pre-deployment announcement, and Garrick felt no compelling need to enlighten him. He'd long ago learned that some things were better left unsaid.

Heading into the unknown, carrying the added burden of serious trouble among his siblings, unable to share any of his worry and grief with a caring friend, Garrick shouldered his distress alone. The industrial heart of Marvic gave way to a commercial sector, where bank buildings reached for the sky. High rise apartment complexes clustered on the fringes of broad, well-planned avenues, where pedestrian walkways connected a myriad of accounting and investment firms, law offices, printers, high-end clothiers, restaurants and neighborhood pubs. Beyond his window, Garrick noticed the preoccupied expressions of citizens far wealthier than his family had ever been, and wondered if any of them could be moved from their disinterest to care about how he'd dedicated his life for their defense.

Those troubled thoughts faded as the train slowed at Marvic's main gate. As the train slid beneath the elaborate secondary and tertiary defenses, their interlocking steel bars casting shadows across his window in the late afternoon sun, Garrick's mind wandered toward memories of Brenna and lingered there while the locomotive descended steeply along the path of a long vanished glacier, into a westward valley.

A market garden economy flourished beyond the city walls. Greenhouses and raised vegetable beds mingled with hybrid cherry and pear orchards that extended beyond the city walls for many miles. Small, plastered straw shacks roofed in corrugated tin served the itinerant harvesters who swelled the local population in season.

Soon, the train turned northwest and followed tracks alongside the tumbling, milky waters of the Lost Maiden River. As the valley floor narrowed and began its inexorable climb toward high elevation mountain passes leading toward Vatheran in the north and the great coastal cities of Norda and Castille in the west, fields of wheat, rye and barley–green and vigorous in the rich soil and cool, mountain air–stretched into rising, rolling ranch land far in the distance. Grass blanketed hills, whose eroded folds supported hardwood groves, climbed into breathtaking ridge lines eternally burdened in ancient snow. Along the tracks, grain elevators stood in silent vigil, waiting a harvest many weeks into the future.

Greg Schmidt worked his way through the train cars, looking for Garrick. He stopped and pulled another document out of his pack. "I thought you might need this," the officer candidate said, handing Garrick a folded paper. "I picked it up when TAC Vogel wasn't looking. Platoon camp assignments are on the second page."

Garrick smiled, accepting what he knew was the promised map. "Thank you!"

As daylight and evidence of civilization gradually faded, Garrick examined the plat, studying its terrain features as he struggled against exhaustion. An excellent memory for details, well-developed visualization skills and experience with map reading gave him a feel for the area long before the laboring train turned north and stopped at a lonely outpost with a singular stone marker that read: "Hungry Valley." Someone had carefully painted "You ain't been cold 'till you been here," beneath the formal inscription in a matter that so adroitly added to the mystique of the place, no one in authority had seen fit to remove it.

The mouth of Hungry Valley, an age-old glacial washout field in the midst of an active volcanic rift, showed the ancient, lingering scars of periodic deluge. A long jumble of lichen-encrusted boulders worn smooth by water polish marked the place where a once flowing waterway long ago plunged toward far mightier rivers downstream.

The Long Journey: *Approval*

Now, active fissures ran in long lines parallel to the north - south mountain ranges on either side of the valley, and from these, a series of flood basalt scarp lines created sharp, angular ridges where living plants struggled to force their roots through cracks in the dark rock. Surrounded by gloomy peaks permanently covered in glacial ice, freezing wind roared through Hungry Valley every moment of every day. Over eons, the strange, mixed forces of ice, water, wind and molten rock created a landscape hostile to living things.

Twilight hung pink halos over the western mountains and the twin moons shone in full glory just above the eastern ridge line as Garrick shouldered his backpack and stepped off the train with his platoon in tow. Temporarily settling the men in the lee of the train depot, Garrick checked the platoon's ammunition boxes, food and medicine stores, oriented himself with the terrain, then approached his two sergeants.

"We'll march about three miles up this valley to our designated deployment area." Garrick pointed to the northwest. "There's a scarp line that looks like a big lava tube on the western side of these boulders. If we follow that, then veer east at this vertical fault line," he said, pointing to a feature on his map, "we'll strike camp below the fault to keep the men out of the wind."

Sergeant Ringer grunted, then turned toward his squadron, ordering the men to their feet. Sergeant Vidders paused for a moment, then said: "You'd better lead from the front on this one and keep a solid pace. Don't let the men think you're soft."

Garrick thanked him, put his map away, and let his memory wander back to the final exercise of his junior scout training. That night, less than seven months earlier, seemed a lifetime ago, yet the sensation of imminent danger he remembered from that experience haunted him now. Carefully pacing himself, Garrick climbed the narrow trail leading up to the valley floor while his grumbling platoon followed.

A forbidding surface strewn in sharp rock greeted Garrick's eye and a strong wind wrapped him in a cold embrace. Scattered in thin patches across the landscape he could see low grasses and stunted trees flailing toward him in the failing light. Navigating uphill, across the valley floor, Garrick found his assigned area about an hour and a half later.

He asked Sergeant Ringer to send a three-man patrol around the perimeter, then designated four places around the camp where he

The Long Journey: *Approval*

wanted mortars, the heavier guns and shoulder-fired rockets placed. Sergeant Vidders suggested a slightly different placement for the tripod mounted, multi barrel cannons in order to provide a clearer field of fire for their crews, a recommendation Garrick accepted. The soldiers hunkered down for the night, burning sticks of dry wood to keep warm in tiny, gasifying stoves that looked like glorified tin cans with an elbow on the bottom.

Less than an hour later, TAC Officer Vogel and two observers arrived in a four-wheeled electric vehicle, known as an EPT, an acronym for *Electric Personnel Transporter*. Soldiers frequently heaped verbal abuse on these machines because of their need for recharging, often referring to them as *inEPT*. Manfred Vogel inspected Garrick's camp and its defenses wordlessly, then approached the young officer candidate. "I'm sure you've read that your first objective will be to secure the Giant's Fist formation by oh-eight hundred hours. Expect resistance. The OpFor consists of a company sized unit operating anywhere within your designated zone. Questions?"

Garrick seethed. An opposing force twice as large as his own lay waiting for his platoon, on this, his first field leadership deployment. "No sir. No questions," Garrick replied, holding back the curse that ached to be uttered.

Manfred Vogel turned away, paused, then turned back. "Pay attention to Sergeant Vidders," he warned. "He's a good man."

"Yes sir!" Garrick responded, standing still. No one saluted an officer in the field.

Once TAC Vogel left Garrick and the observers behind, the young officer candidate called for Sergeant Vidders and huddled near one of the tin stoves for light and warmth. He pulled out his map, found the formation labeled "Giant's Fist," then grimaced at the distance they needed to cover.

Sergeant Dagmar Vidders, who half expected the young soldier to quit on the spot once he learned how large a task he'd been ordered to lead, stifled an expression of delight when he listened to Garrick outline a battle plan. The boy's idea defied convention, but that's precisely why Sergeant Vidders struggled to refrain from smiling.

Together, they refined Garrick's idea and informed the skeptical observers of their attack intentions. Then, Dagmar Vidders went to check on his men and explain the plan to Sergeant Ringer while Garrick crawled into his bedroll. Within two minutes, the boy had fallen asleep.

The Long Journey: *Approval*

He awoke to bitter cold some three hours before dawn, a surge of energy and purpose pulsing through his veins. Garrick relieved himself, found the sentries awake and alert in the freezing air, then roused the sergeants. Within thirty minutes, the entire platoon had eaten breakfast and assembled to hear Garrick present his plan of attack.

"A company?" one soldier asked, astonished. "We're taking on a whole company?"

"Sergeant Ringer will lead a recon team and report back to our forward deployment positions," Garrick responded. "We'll revise as necessary. OpFor may have greater numbers, but we'll have surprise. They know I'm leading this platoon, and they probably think I can't find my own backside with both hands. But they don't know any of you. Let's make their morning so unpleasant they'll never forget who we are."

The platoon advanced at 90 paces per minute, covering a full mile in slightly less than 40 minutes. Every man labored up the incline, carrying his share of the platoon's weaponry and ammunition. All of the physical training Garrick endured to this point served him well as he led the panting members of his platoon in a grueling, predawn march.

With the Great Eye Nebula blazing in the heavens, casting eerie, blue light across the landscape and the twin moons long vanished behind the western ridge line, Garrick's platoon reached their initial objective nearly three hours after departing. In the darkness they climbed a rocky bench overlooking the valley floor, where the Giant's Fist-a bizarre outcropping of hardened rope lava-rose above the broken basalt beneath. Around this formation, the white tents of the OpFor company glowed like beacons in the ultraviolet light.

Garrick set up his mortar crews, then watched Sergeant Ringer lead his recon team downslope to evaluate defensive positions. Fifteen minutes later, he came back with a breathless report. "You were right," he huffed. "Their defensive positions face into the valley, toward the south, with nothing but razor wire and piled rocks around the perimeter. They're expecting a frontal assault." The sergeant sketched the barricades and machine cannon nests on a knee board notepad with a grease pencil. Garrick nodded, readied his men and waited for the right moment to attack.

Just as a narrow band of light on the eastern horizon outlined the distant, snow-clad ridges, the rhythmic percussion of falling mortar shells punctuated the natural melody of wind sweeping across the broad valley. These air-bursting rounds simulated actual artillery with noise,

The Long Journey: *Approval*

smoke and colored chalk, shocking the encamped warriors out of their slumber. Through the smoke, attacking soldiers wearing combat gear and protective, metal screens over their faces cut through the razor wire and emerged in a rapidly advancing line, firing bursts of dye-coated rubber bullets.

The machine gun nests on the southwestern part of the camp went down quickly as observers declared their equipment damaged and crews out of action. Layered defenses crumbled as Garrick's platoon attacked from the flanks, driving down prepared firing positions in an alternating manner, carefully choreographed to prevent fratricide. Simulated grenades burst in front of the officer's tents, and amid all the noise, Sergeant Ringer heard a first lieutenant cursing loudly.

A cluster of alert OpFor soldiers established a skirmish line, keeping pressure on Garrick's attacking troops while falling back to regroup. They held their ground near the Giant's Fist while machine gunners from the eastern side of the encampment raced forward with their heavier weapons.

Garrick watched his attack bog down as superior numbers stayed his aggressive maneuver. He grabbed a nearby soldier and shouted in the man's ear to overcome the battle din. "Tell Sergeant Vidders to disengage and file left. He needs to swing around my flank and roll up the line after we've hit them with the mortars! Go!" Then, pulling another messenger aside, he wrote down the time and coordinates for his mortar crews and sent the soldier back uphill.

It took several minutes for Sergeant Vidders to get his men in position. During this time, the OpFor skirmish line strengthened and growing losses forced Garrick to order a retreat behind the prepared firing positions they'd just overrun. There, his machine cannon crews kept the opposing force at bay while the two sides exchanged heavy rifle and multi-barrel cannon fire in a stalemate. He hoped that the mortar crews, sitting in sheltered positions on the bench overlooking the valley, would observe the situation and make the necessary adjustments.

Garrick heard the artillery shells arcing overhead, then reflexively shielded his eyes as their rounds burst above the recently repositioned machine guns. Eight detonations rippled through the opposing ranks. "Forward!" he screamed. "Move! Move! Move!" The young Tamarian scrambled to his feet, leaped over the rocky barrier he'd hidden behind, and charged toward the OpFor skirmish line, his rifle spitting rubber bullets as fast as he could fire.

The Long Journey: *Approval*

Sergeant Vidders lead his squadron down the flank of the OpFor position. The coordination of the attack, coupled with the lack of friendly artillery support, collapsed the line and before the warriors converged within hand-to-hand range, the observers blew whistles to stop the action.

The combat portion of the exercise lasted less than ten minutes.

Garrick heard his men raise a victorious cry and saw the OpFor officers shaking their heads in disbelief. Breathless and overflowing with elated adrenaline, he wanted to laugh, but suddenly felt many hands pushing him forward, forcing him up the Giant's Fist. There, standing in the strong wind at the top of the rock, Garrick raised his rifle heavenward. All the soldiers in his immediate vicinity, even those among the opposing force, began chanting "Overhead!" while they applauded in approval.

Run Away

Long before the first fingers of daylight reached through narrow gaps between the weathered siding of a small feeding shed, Algernon awakened. The early morning stillness and quietude filled his heart with peace as the young monk strode through an overgrown field run wild with blossoming clover and damp with dew, to wash himself in the warmth of a nearby mineral spring. Birds began stirring during his routine prayers and stretch. Algernon planned his day listening to their song, noting that the blue-green light of the Great Eye Nebula lingered as the Daystar spread its luminescence across Superstition Mesa, a sign of the coming summer.

Astrid remained asleep in the hammock he'd made for her, the bones of her shoulders and spine outlined beneath the thin fabric of her nightgown. On their journey to this abandoned farm several days earlier, she'd expressed skepticism of his planned living quarters, but the girl did not complain when they arrived. One nice thing about Astrid, Algernon concluded, was that acetic living conditions pervaded her experience as an orphan, so she didn't find their modest accommodations uncomfortable. Suspended between posts above tiny stalls some barnyard animals had once known as a sheltered place to eat, she slept peacefully on her right side, curled into a fetal position.

Careful not to awaken her, Algernon took out the portable cook stove he'd cleverly fashioned from a pair of tin cans. The open top of the smaller can protruded through a tight hole sealed with clay in the lid of the larger one. He placed a fist full of small, dry sticks in the central burner section, then sprinkled a bit of straw on the top and started a fire using the lighter Garrick had bought for him. The simple design of this little stove belied a complex interaction of heat, air and fuel. As the straw caught fire in the open top of the central can, it drew air in from holes Algernon had punched through along the base of its perimeter. As air moved up through the fuel load, replacement air traveled down along its outer sides, supplied by holes in the lid of the larger can. As the fire grew, fresh air moving down the outside of the inner can rose in temperature on its way into the fire. Small holes along the top perimeter of the burning chamber provided secondary air for combustion. Once it started, this little stove burned very hot and produced no smoke.

The farmhouse on this homestead had long since burned down, the last of many events leading to the demise of agriculture on a marginal

The Long Journey: *Run Away*

piece of land, but its teetering, metal-roofed barn still remained standing. Along the outside of the barn, four catchment pipes led from its roof to a partially buried cistern. A hand pump, still operable despite years of neglect, produced water from a cistern with a little effort.

Though this reservoir supplied rain water that filled three large tins they'd cleaned and brought with them from the Dragon's Lair cafeteria, Algernon didn't trust the condition of the cistern and wouldn't drink unless the water had been boiled first. He'd punched two holes on the opposite sides of yet another tin can, through which he inserted a stick the diameter of his thumb and the length of his forearm. Algernon partially filled this can with water collected from the cistern, then set it to boil on top of his cook stove.

Astrid stirred as daylight poured into the feeding shed. She blinked, yawned, then carefully slid her wiry frame out of the hammock and reached for her overcoat and sandals. After a brief trip outside to relieve herself, Astrid sat close to the cook stove and warmed her hands in the fire. "You've found a way for us to survive, at least for now," she remarked. Do you think we can we sustain ourselves here?"

Algernon filled a tea cachet, dumped it into a pot he'd salvaged on a previous excursion, then arranged a rock on the dirt floor in such a way that he could use it to tip the base of the boiled water tin without touching its hot surface. He poured boiling water into the teapot, set aside the tin can, then reached for his new skillet.

"This is a pleasant place, teeming with potential" he responded. "But whoever lives here has to work with the environment, not against it. The hardwood forest on the ridge behind us shelters this property from the worst of winter winds. It can provide organic matter to build soil, as well as firewood and building material," he said, pointing to the framework and siding surrounding them.

"A greenhouse, a fish pond and raised beds will work well here, just as they do at the Temple. When the pioneering monks established Elsbireth, they had less to work with than what I've found abandoned here. The barn is full of tools, though I'm afraid it might collapse and we need the roof for water, so I haven't gone in there. I've seen an old tractor inside that might run with a little tinkering, if the batteries are any good. There's the steam shed for power, but the boiler's missing; either stolen, salvaged or sold."

Distracted for a moment, Algernon examined the curve of her cheekbones, letting his eyes drift back across the mild acne scarring her jaw to rest upon an oily, stringy lock of hair. He dismissed a silly, mental fantasy and returned to the task of making tea. "We could live here once we find Kira, but we'd have a lot of work to do before winter."

Astrid turned her eyes and stared fearlessly into his. "Is that what you really want in life, Algernon? Would you be happy?"

"No," he replied, looking away. "It's not enough. I hate being celibate. I want a wife," he explained, "one who's not afraid of me. I want a home where I can be myself, without having to conform to everyone else's expectations. Right now I don't know where my path will take me, and I really don't care what I will do. But I want independence. I want a home of my own."

Astrid's head sank. The only home she'd ever known lay within the Sacred Enclosure, a community so overflowing with devout, spiritual people that the few immoral characters living there only survived within an elaborate framework of deception and secrecy. It had not always been an ideal place, for when she hit puberty Astrid briefly attracted the unwanted, amorous attentions of Priestess Alba, but aside from this, the monastic order at Elsbireth always nurtured and educated Astrid as one of their own. She longed for community, for a sense of belonging, and worried that leaving the Temple would forever deprive her of that opportunity.

The young priestess accepted a tin cup from Algernon and breathed its herbal aroma before passing the hot liquid over her lips. Living at high elevation, where water vaporized at a lower temperature, enabled Astrid to drink without fear of burning her own flesh. "Kira told me all about your family situation and why you had to run away. She always talked how much she loves you and your brother. She told me all about your mother, and how everything changed for the worse when your father started drinking..."

Algernon's cheeks reddened and his lips drew into a tight line. "What happened with my family is not a subject I will ever discuss with you," he warned in that dangerous, menacing tone that boiled from within the hot cauldron of his soul.

"Ok," she assented, taking care not to further arouse his wrath. "But at least you have siblings. You belong to a brother who looks after you and a sister who adores you. That's more than I've ever known!"

"My sister adores me?" Algernon inquired, disbelievingly, so self absorbed that he didn't think to question Astrid about what motivated her statement.

The Long Journey: *Run Away*

The priestess nodded. "Yes. Do you think that I would have come and asked for your help had she not constantly talked about how smart you are? She knows your goodness better than anyone else. Kira told me that you two were really close before coming to Marvic, and she thought highly of you. Though she hates the way you've treated her in the last year or so, you can't convince me that she doesn't love you."

"If that's true, she had a strange way of showing it," Algernon retorted. "I'm sure that I'm the only guy in my dormitory who didn't benefit from her tawdry behavior. How did she expect me to react?"

Astrid drank deeply from her tea and moved her eyes across the roughened feeding troughs that stood on the far side of every stall. "You could have talked to her," Astrid began. When Algernon began to interrupt, she held up her hand. "I didn't say preach at, I didn't say condemn. Kira never questioned your character when you put flour in the organ pipes or made dung pies for the acolyte initiation ceremony. She didn't hold you in obvious contempt for trying to fondle Marie."

Impatient with her constant criticism and annoyed by the unpleasant memory of Marie's humiliating repudiation, Algernon gritted his teeth and struggled for self-control. "Drop it, Astrid!" he snapped. "The incident with Marie didn't happen the way you think it did."

Silence settled upon them. Astrid finished her tea as a disappointed expression lingered upon her slender face. "I wouldn't say anything if I didn't care about you."

Algernon cut a bit of potato and a few mushrooms into his skillet and shook his head. "You only care about yourself," he spat, oblivious to the fact that she could have easily leveled the same criticism at him. "You're on my back all the time!"

"It's not like I want to hurt you," she replied, putting down her cup. "I'm just trying to encourage the goodness underneath all that rage."

"Goodness?" Algernon queried. "Everyone talks that way, but everyone complains. Everyone demands perfection out of me, as if I always have to conform to lofty expectations in order to be loved and accepted. Honestly, Astrid, no one serves as a better example of this than you do!"

Astrid sighed. "You don't see what I see. I came to you because I didn't know what else to do, but from the moment I told you what was going on with Kira you've been totally decisive and full of confidence. You find a way out of situations where ordinary people feel trapped, and

The Long Journey: *Run Away*

you can do this because you don't think like everyone else. Kira's the same way, and I'll bet it's true of your brother, too!

"High Priest Volker knows that you will rise to the top of whatever task you set your mind to completing. He and some of the others have tried, with great patience, Algernon, to mold your character in a way that will make you even more effective as a leader. If the expectations of people who love you are high, it's only because they know you can soar!"

"It's a little late for that!" Algernon snapped, stirring the potato slices and mushrooms in the skillet. A pleasant aroma rose from his cooking.

"No," Astrid countered, putting her hand on his shoulder. "You're like this homestead. There's lots of potential within you. Don't give up on yourself."

Algernon shrugged her off, annoyed that she would touch him after rejecting his affection several days before, but he said nothing to her about this. "I'm not giving up on myself. I'm talking about love."

Astrid expressed surprise. "People do love you, Algernon."

"Not the ones I want to love me, and not in the way I'd like them to. You have an advantage that way, Astrid. You didn't grow up expecting people to care about you."

"You're talking about your parents and girls like Marie?"

He nodded.

"Well, I don't have any family, aside from the people in the Temple," Astrid replied, smiling wistfully. "But if it makes you feel any better, Marie wouldn't let me fondle her either!"

Algernon rolled his eyes. "You've tried?"

The hot expression of embarrassment flashed over Astrid's pale cheeks. "Maybe not as overtly as you did, but don't think I haven't thought about it. I mean, who wouldn't?" Her sheepish memory of an incident with that girl forced Astrid to look away.

For the first time since she'd been in his company, Algernon laughed. He slid the potatoes and mushrooms onto a plate for her and left them to cool, then dumped another serving of the same into his skillet to cook. Poor people in Tamaria ate using their fingers and since neither Algernon nor Astrid owned eating utensils, they ate in the manner of their nation's most wretched citizens. "Marie's the kind of girl who leaves broken hearts in her wake," he mused. "It's good to know that you and I have at least one thing in common!"

The Long Journey: *Run Away*

      *   *   *

In the quiet darkness near the antiphonal pipe array of the campus auditorium, Brenna rose from her early-morning prayer session and scurried downstairs with a smile and a hymn lingering on her lips. Though her knees hurt from long contact with the hardwood floor and her aching feet protested the rapid descent, excitement spilled across her face as she pushed through the dark, concert hall doors and quickly approached the main register of a large pipe organ. She loved music, and playing this instrument was a treat!

Perched above an elevated stage, the instrument's ivory keys reflected ultraviolet light descending from an oculus high above. Towering over the four-tiered keyboard, arranged with the largest diameter tubes flanking many columns of smaller midrange and upper pitch cylinders, more than five thousand pipes, representing the massive body of the instrument, stood in silent ranks.

With the flick of a switch, an electric air compressor purred quietly as Brenna quickly set up her principal chorus, pulling out stops to suit a meditative composition she'd long favored. With her fingers gently resting on the cool keys, Brenna began to play. As her touch coaxed tone and rhythm from the great organ, Brenna's mind drifted into a private place where the resonant interaction of melody and harmony soothed the many stresses of her soul.

Several weeks of chronic sleep deprivation weakened Brenna's mental acuity. Her normal sleeping pattern of five to six hours per night could be reduced to as little as two or three for a while, but Brenna couldn't recall a single night in the last month where she had slept soundly for more than two consecutive hours. Mistakes riddled her practice, and though she normally chided herself ruthlessly for any errors in her performance, on this morning Brenna felt too tired and too distracted to notice many of them. She played on, her mind wrestling with lingering turmoil. Her memory, alive and vivid, washed conflicts new and old onto the shore of her consciousness, spreading the flotsam of each one into an ill-defined ache that persisted beneath the pleasant veneer she projected to hide her weakening self-image.

As the months of separation from her family dragged on, Brenna drifted into a forlorn state of mind. Now, with Garrick so deeply involved in officer's training, a desperate loneliness that haunted Brenna's waking hours so pervaded her thinking, not even Mariel's patient and pleasant company could alleviate the impact of its influence. A lot of prayer and the predawn practice sessions Mariel had arranged on her behalf strengthened Brenna's ability to function without breaking down entirely.

Disturbing scenes from battlefield experiences spilled into her dreams, a dreadful monster lurking in the darkness. Having awakened from a vivid nightmare a few hours before dawn, sweating and trembling in fear, Brenna had been unable to fall asleep again.

Mariel, startled from her slumber, suspected that combat trauma lay at the root of Brenna's night terror. She turned on an electric light and sat on Brenna's bed, an increasingly familiar expression of worry etched upon her face. Lieutenant Hougen didn't know what to say that might be helpful, but filled with pity, she felt that if Brenna could express the distressing memories that stalked her sleep, the very act of bringing them into the light would help banish them forever.

Although fully qualified with a rifle and capable of being sent to the front lines, Mariel Hougen's linguistic knowledge kept her far beyond the reach of battle. "You've been dreaming about the war again," Mariel stated. "Tell me. What was it like?"

Brenna, reluctant to talk about her experience, wiped the sweat from her face and willed her trembling fingers into control. She drew her lips into a tight line and held her breath for a long time. The Lithian girl gave Mariel a hard glare and spoke in a very quiet voice. "Industrial butchery," she breathed, closing her bright eyes. "When I dream, I feel like I'm still there . . . I remember everything . . ."

Brenna stopped, her thoughts incomplete as a shiver raced through her body. Fighting back flooding tears she continued, a melancholy sorrow cracking in her voice. "They pounded us with their big guns. Hour after hour bursting shells fell like summer rain, shattering the trees, hammering the hillsides, thundering through the forest. We cowered in our holes, powerless and terrified. All I could do was pray for it to stop.

"Incoming artillery screamed overhead, our foxholes overflowed with sulfur and smoke, the stench of burning flesh, of bowels and bladders loosened, the reek of blood and vomit. I could feel concussions rattling through my bones as they fired their rounds nearer and nearer our positions. The ground shook endlessly. Dust and dirt lingered in the air. But worse, I could hear men screaming. I could hear men cursing. I could hear men weeping." She paused again, then looked back at

The Long Journey: *Run Away*

Mariel. "I still hear them. I pray for their voices to go away, but I still hear them."

Brenna returned her stare to the wall. "And when the shelling finally stopped they would come. Wave after wave they would come. Like a flood rising up to the neck, sweeping over the frozen landscape they would come. Riflemen tore their front lines apart. The rocket artillery ripped great, ragged holes in their formations, but they just kept coming. I could see their faces, blistered and burned by the cold. Their swollen feet dragged through the snow, but they kept coming. The killing went on and on."

"Garrick told me you were very brave," Mariel replied, trying to offer encouragement. "You earned those silver lions, Brenna, and from what I know of you I can understand why the men always wanted you nearby when the fighting began."

Rather than acknowledging the compliment, Brenna shook her head. "I was not brave. I've never been so afraid," she admitted. "I've never wanted to run away more than I did in those days."

"But you didn't run," Mariel reminded her. "Nobody would have blamed you for leaving. Though it wasn't your fight, you faced danger with resolute firmness in the company of men fighting for their freedom. That's the essence of valor."

Brenna swallowed hard. "I told no one how I felt, not even Garrick. The men in our platoon called me *Little Sister* and always treated me with respect. They watched carefully, waiting to see what I would do. Had they seen fear in me, it would have made them more afraid. So I couldn't run. I couldn't leave them, and I know in my heart that none of them would have left me either." As she recalled their faces, Brenna bit her lower lip and contemplated the truth of this statement in a private way. "Any one of them would have risked his life for me. So I stayed in my hole and listened to their screaming, praying for all of it to end."

Brenna paused for a long time, thinking, then shook her head and let out a sigh. "Besides, I couldn't go anywhere. The Azgaril looted my home, killed my people, burned our temples to the ground. They took everything but my family away from me." Her voice hardened as she turned back toward Mariel. "Allfather punished them for their brutality, using the winter and your men to stop them." Then pausing, Brenna shook her head. "And too often I could do nothing but watch them suffer. I held them as they bled and died."

The Long Journey: *Run Away*

"Garrick told me that you saved many who would never have survived without your help."

"Allfather works through me," Brenna admitted, lifting her head to look at the ceiling and shutting her eyes, invoking God's name as if in prayer. Then she opened them and looked back at Mariel. "But there were too many wounds beyond my skill. A severed artery bleeds like a river. How could I stop that? What could I do about a lost limb or a shattered skull? Sometimes my tears were the last things they saw. I cried because I couldn't help. I cried until I simply couldn't cry anymore." Brenna sniffed and dried her eyes.

Mariel put her arm around her friend's shoulder and squeezed her in solidarity. "You did the best you could. Your god will honor you for that."

"That's not it," Brenna replied, sniffing. "My faith isn't about me. I'm just tired of binding broken bodies. I'm sick of blood. I never want to go through another war again."

Lieutenant Hougan stood and walked over to the window, glancing into the darkness beyond. "What about Garrick?" she inquired. "He never talks about his own experience."

"The army turned him into a killer," Brenna replied, coldly.

At this, Mariel turned around, her red hair hanging in disheveled curls around her face. It caught the lamp light in a peculiarly pretty way. "Why would you expect anything different? That's what soldiers do!"

"I know, but I didn't expect him to become so good at it, so ruthless, so automatic." Brenna's voice fell as she wiped her eyes again. "Mariel, he was completely sweet and gentle when I first met him!"

The Tamarian woman pursed her lips, considering her words carefully. "He's a warrior, just as you are." The accusation, though gently delivered, stung. "I spoke to Major Gretschel," Mariel continued. "He told me you cut a giant's throat with a knife. He doesn't think highly of foreigners and scoffs at your religion, but he said that you and Garrick saved a lot of people on the train that night. Now, I also know that his attitude toward women falls short of a gentlemanly ideal, but he praised your combat skill and believes that had you two not been there, he and his unit would have been easily overpowered and everyone onboard that train slaughtered. It's not like the two of you are killers without a conscience."

"We did what we had to do," the Lithian girl retorted. Then, seeing that Mariel was not backing down, Brenna breathed deeply and

The Long Journey: *Run Away*

emptied her lungs in a slow, deliberate manner. "I love what is beautiful, what is pure. I long for joy and comfort. I dream of peace." Absent-mindedly, she pulled on a lock of hair and began running her fingers along its length. "But I will always be a warlord's daughter, and sometimes duty calls from over my shoulder. Whenever that happens, I feel compelled to string my bow and stand for what is right."

Mariel nodded. "You're a woman of faith. In this world, even those who are faithful walk in the dust with the rest of us. You've stood shoulder to shoulder with my people to resist evil. For this reason I respect you. I don't condemn you," she concluded.

"Thanks, Mariel," Brenna replied. "I don't condemn Garrick either."

"You love him?" Mariel inquired.

"Yes," Brenna responded. "He is the missing piece of my heart."

"Even though he's a killer?"

"Yes," the Lithian girl replied without hesitation. "I do."

These thoughts echoed through Brenna's mind while she played. Minor keyed harmony dissipated the emotional intensity of that experience. Music had long served her in this way. As the composition rose to its melodic, counterpointed climax, Brenna sustained the powerful resonance of the massive organ as the entire auditorium, all the way up to the oculus nearly 100 feet above her head, rang with lovely overtones until every frightening memory of combat fled from her consciousness.

* * *

An old trail, tangled in the vigorous growth of young alder and fir trees fighting for supremacy over lesser, pioneering plants whose long established roots remained unplucked by human hands, led gently downslope from the old homestead and joined with an ill-maintained, rock-strewn, dusty, rutted and gradually narrowing dirt path. Spring flowers flourished in the tree-shaded verge, and with their youthful, vigorous steps Algernon and Astrid startled small creatures unaccustomed to sharing their mostly wild domain with human beings.

After washing in the hot spring, Astrid had pulled her thin hair into a tight ponytail that accentuated her elevated cheekbones and revealed her slender neck. Anticipating a warm day, she left her overcoat behind and walked in a leggy stride that projected a decidedly unfeminine demeanor.

However, as the silky fabric of Astrid's robe pressed against her flesh, the slight sway of her rounded hips and small breasts caught Algernon's eye. Distressingly and obviously aroused, he walked faster in order to stay ahead and avoid embarrassment.

"Algernon!" she called repeatedly, struggling to keep up. "What is with you? Don't run away from me!"

"Let's just get there," he replied.

Exasperated, Astrid reached for his shoulder. "Come on! Slow down!" she urged.

Algernon's patience neared its end. He knocked her hand away as he turned around. "Don't touch me!" he warned.

Reflexively Astrid's hands moved into a defensive position. Worried that he might send a kick in her direction, Astrid flashed her gaze to his thigh then stopped short. She covered her mouth, looked up at Algernon's face, then down again in utter shock. Having never before been the object of a boy's desire, and never believing that this boy thought of her with any feeling rising above contempt, all words fled from her mind.

"Happy now?" he inquired. "It doesn't help for you to stare!"

Astrid looked away. "Why are you thinking about me like that?" she asked.

"Ugh!" Algernon groaned. "It's not like I'm thinking about anything in particular. A warm, summer day will do!" He turned around and began walking again.

Astrid followed in silence, remembering a night when Kira told her that every boy and every man suffered the same weakness. Though she didn't like sharing her girl with anyone, Astrid rationalized that Kira simply used relations with the masculine gender as a means to gain control of men and didn't apply any emotion to her girlfriend's activities.

Now the dawn of a different understanding rose upon Astrid's mind, for though she thought herself devoted to Kira, she could not deny feeling a small sense of delight and triumph to have inspired arousal in Kira's brother. This implied, however, that Kira might also experience the very same fervor in her contact with male lovers, and for the first time, Astrid felt a tinge of jealousy coloring her perception.

Kira had not only run away from her life in the Temple with a Kamerese drug dealer, Kira had also run away from *Astrid* with a

The Long Journey: *Run Away*

Kamerese boy! Such thinking fed an emergent sense of betrayal that grew until the young priestess found herself brooding moodily.

Algernon longed for release, but he didn't want to leave Astrid alone out here, and he certainly wasn't going to ask her to assist in the matter! He refocused his mental energies by moving through a hand *kata* until his ardor faded, then muttered curses upon himself. It didn't matter that she had witnessed his arousal, he reasoned, because not only were they socially isolated, *nobody* would believe her.

At least, he hoped not...

Tall, mixed forest growing on the narrow, gently ascending summit of Superstition Mesa concealed the city of Marvic from view. Though its gates stood only twenty minutes from the abandoned homestead, most of the city occupied land that lay somewhat lower in elevation. Only the sacred mountain of Elsbireth, dominating the southern skyline, rose above the towering trees.

Amid a frenzy of nesting activity songbirds fluttered in the steadily warming air, the rapid beating of their wings mingling with higher frequency insect sounds. The path turned left where it entered a steep canyon, then descended before joining the main road as a flank of the mesa slumped toward the Lost Maiden Valley.

Farmers, returning home from the early morning market in the city, smiled and waved from their buckboards and electric tractors as the young couple walked by. Leaving behind the solitude of their secret refuge on Superstition Mesa, Algernon and Astrid approached the main gate to Marvic amid a growing tide of humanity.

Most of the cities sprawling across the Deveran continent had long since overgrown or abandoned walled defenses. The spectacular demise of Shirak, the once proud capital city of Illithia, underscored the folly of erecting physical barriers against the onslaught of cannons and mortars. Even the famed citadel of Fevera in the east, whose walls were rumored to exceed 100 feet in height, had long ago taken down its gates as metropolitan sprawl spilled beyond its lofty ramparts.

Yet the fortifications surrounding the Tamarian capital did not conform to the pattern typical of more ancient cities. Marvic lay on the end of a broad, undulating promontory that, on three sides, dropped nearly a mile to Fallen Moon Valley. Hence, its wall served mostly as a safety measure to keep people from falling off the cliff, and all military defenses clustered around its west-facing entrance.

The Long Journey: *Run Away*

Four graded terraces, arranged in concentric arcs in front of the city wall, rose steeply above the Lost Maiden Valley. A layered network of steel reinforced concrete bunkers, laid out in mathematical precision to ensure that several different guns covered every approach, lay beneath an angular, outer wall. Behind this barricade, heavy rocket launchers and 4-inch howitzers maintained their silent vigil.

Though the city stood at an important commercial junction between nations to the north and west, Marvic represented a very difficult objective for any potential foe to secure. Its high elevation and the rugged topography of the region made any concerted attack by an invading force difficult to sustain. Tamaria's traditional enemy, a race of giants now banished to their distant, rocky strongholds, felt so intimidated by the formidable firepower arrayed around the city that not even the strongest of their clans ever attempted an assault against the capital.

All traffic entering and leaving Marvic split into three separate areas. Two rail lines passed through a walled corridor on the southern edge of the entrance wall. In the center, a wide avenue for vehicle traffic passed beneath three graceful arches with interlocking steel gates that could be lowered–though they never were–from the stonework above. Pedestrian traffic followed a broad, elevated stone pathway, across a bridge that turned over the road and approached the city wall after a long, southerly walk running parallel to the protected firing positions manned by Queen Tamar's elite Defenders.

Though initially intended to discourage a direct assault on the city gates, the pedestrian walkway now served as an open-air market for merchants. Awnings and display tents crowded the path boundaries on both sides. Pleasant food aromas wafted on the warm, gentle wind. A complete cross section of Tamarian society, ranging from the wealthy to the impoverished, lingered here to exchange news, hunt for bargains, beg for money, or pick up a bite of specialty food on their way into and out of town.

For Algernon and Astrid, the circuitous approach to Marvic's wall gave them an opportunity to mingle with many people. Citizens uniformly greeted them with kind regard and respect. Astrid produced two drawings she'd completed earlier, inquiring if anyone had seen either Kira or the Kamerese student, Marco.

Though discouraged when she didn't receive any news concerning her girlfriend, Astrid offered a smile, a nod and a blessing to

The Long Journey: *Run Away*

everyone who reached out to touch her hand as the young couple moved through the crowd. She followed Algernon forward, through the huge steel doors rendered in twelve relief panels that marked the city entrance, beneath a vaulted arch whose stonework towered to a peak better than 40 feet above her head.

Several Defenders, clothed in their red and gold uniforms and battle armor, but no weapons, stood on slightly raised platforms and glanced at each person entering the city. One of the soldiers stopped Algernon, offered a blessing, and asked that the young acolyte pray for his sickly mother. Moved by the humility of the warrior, Algernon agreed, though he secretly doubted doing so would do anything to improve the woman's condition. This kind of youthful cynicism pervaded much of Algernon's thinking. He didn't notice that his conversation attracted the attention of another Defender who stood on a balcony above.

Once they'd moved beyond the city gate, a newspaper headline caught Algernon's attention. It read: *"Civil Unrest in Kameron: Refugees Flee North."* He grunted, thinking that Marco and his friends represented the rats leaving a sinking ship.

As he stood, reading through the first paragraph of the story, a stranger approached Astrid, tapped on her shoulder and bowed with his hands folded together. Dressed in expensive silk and linen, leather shoes and wearing a series of braided gold chains around his well-tanned neck, the man spoke Tamarian with a trace of Kamerese accent. "I beg your pardon, holy mistress," he said. "I overheard you asking about a boy named Marco. May I please see your picture?"

Astrid smiled. "I didn't get a very good look at him," she replied, handing the middle-aged gentleman a folded paper containing her sketch.

The man produced a pair of spectacles and examined the drawing with raised eyebrows. "Ah, yes. I know this boy," he said, nodding while he put his glasses away. "He is, as you say, a favored–no, spoiled–young man!" The man smiled. "Why do you seek him?"

Algernon turned away from the paper. Not wishing to describe the situation to everyone who might happen to overhear the conversation, he switched to the Kamerese language and introduced himself. "My sister has been seen in his company."

"That is unfortunate," the man replied. "You will not find him a reasonable fellow."

The Long Journey: *Run Away*

Algernon's countenance darkened. "I was afraid of that. Do you know where I might find him?"

The man appraised Algernon with a contemplative eye. "Marco Fang attends the university here, among his other pursuits," he stated. "His uncle owns a clothing store and runs a textile import business in the garment district. He is one of my fiercest competitors."

"You didn't answer my question," Algernon replied. "Where can I find him?"

Breathing a sigh, the man's eyes narrowed. "The clothing store is not all it appears to be. He also frequents *The Bloody Bucket*. Neither one is a place for the holy."

Algernon nodded. "I expected nothing better. Thank you!"

As the young Tamarian grabbed Astrid by the sleeve and turned to depart, the Kamerese fabric dealer stopped them with an upraised hand. "I warn you," he said. "The Fang family will not hesitate to harm either of you. They have no regard for God."

"I'm not afraid," Algernon responded.

The man paused momentarily. "Perhaps not," he demurred. "But you should be."

* * *

Brenna sulked through her ecology class, distracted and bored. A musty smell of old books, the scent of waxed floors, chalk dust and the musk of sweaty, male bodies permeated the lecture hall atmosphere. She twirled her pencil around her fingers, first one way, then the other, in an exceedingly dexterous manipulation that caught the attention of an equally bored male student sitting to her right. As the elderly professor droned on, pontificating about the relationship between various elements of a given watershed, Brenna flipped through her expensive textbook, wistfully aware that she could comprehend very little of what had been printed there.

Mariel Hougen once pointed out that most human interchange involved nonverbal cues. In her military experience, Brenna developed acute sensitivity to these signals and could often determine the intent of speech directed toward her, even if some of the vocabulary rose above her level of knowledge. Nearly every Tamarian soldier who'd come to know Brenna adored her, and out of respect, each one remained careful to limit the content and scope of his language while addressing her.

The Long Journey: *Run Away*

The university milieu, however, brokered no such favor. Large, auditorium style halls with seating galleries rising above the professor's podium depersonalized the learning environment. Science faculty members never limited their erudite lectures for the benefit of any student whose linguistic proficiency did not aspire to their own. Thus, Brenna found herself among many disadvantaged foreigners–dark skinned, bearded Kamerese, round-faced, tan-complected Nordans and tall, pale Vatherii–sitting in the hot, humid rows near the top of the class. She, like her fellow immigrants, often could not comprehend what the professors were teaching.

Unlike these other students, however, Brenna did not fit into a social network that supported her studies. Though her dress uniform marked the Lithian woman as one of many military scholars studying at the university, a social stigma excluded her from sitting with native Tamarians. Other students, including Lieutenant Hougen, wore similar clothing, but none of their uniforms featured a narrow, rectangular bar of white porcelain bordered in gold trim, with a single red line bisecting its long axis; this was the combat action badge for the recent winter campaign against the Azgaril.

Small, silver lion figures, sewn neatly into her collar, testified that Brenna had been formally cited on four separate occasions for valor in combat. Battalion commanders awarded these when lower-ranking officers reached a consensus concerning an individual soldier's conduct; whereas the rarely issued Medal of Valor had to be approved by a committee of high-ranking officers and signed by Queen Tamar. Brenna's friend, Woodwind, had earned one of those in the battle at Dead Hand Ridge.

Wearing four silver lions, while not entirely unusual for warriors serving in units that had seen heavy action, underscored the foreign girl's willingness to risk her life for the sake of her comrades. These had never presented a problem in the past, as Brenna interacted with other veterans whose combat accomplishments often equaled or surpassed her own. Five such citations merited a gold lion, a decoration that adorned Garrick's collar, and Sergeant Harris–a veteran who'd served in a different platoon–boasted three!

At the university, however, her silver lions drew doubting stares. Though no one said anything directly to her, Brenna perceived hostility that served as an effective barrier against establishing friendships with the non-veteran warriors on campus. At one point, Brenna threatened to take the silver lions off, complaining that other soldiers thought her a poser. Mariel Hougen, however, warned that removing citations dishonored the memory of the men who died in battle. "Given that you're Lithian, in addition to the fact that Lieutenant Kohler didn't like you, it's impressive that he passed the recommendations along," Mariel said. "You've earned those silver lions. Don't scorn that achievement!"

Thus, the decorations remained, even though Brenna sincerely wished she could fade into the background and avoid attention. As she endured an hour of sheer boredom, half listening to the consonantal gibberish emanating from her ecology professor, the Lithian maiden fanned herself with a leaf of loose paper, squirmed in her uncomfortable chair, and decided that as long as she remained outside of military circles, she could not continue to wear her dress uniform.

Thus, when her classes were completed for the morning, Brenna lingered in her seat until the lecture hall emptied, then scurried reticently back to her dorm room. The small space presented a comfortable, quiet refuge, and Mariel's pleasant company calmed much of Brenna's socially inspired anxiety.

Lieutenant Hougen, seated at her desk with her forehead leaning against her left hand, browsed through a collection of news reports strewn about its surface. "How did it go today?" the Tamarian woman asked, keeping her focus on the paper she studied.

Brenna shut the door, set her own books down, then proceeded to wiggle out of her dress uniform. "I don't belong here," Brenna replied, "and I can't wear this thing anymore." Fumbling through her drawer, Brenna pulled out all of her clothing, including the tiny, lightweight blouse she'd worn the day she ran away from her home in Shirak.

Hearing the sound, Mariel turned. "What is that thing?" she queried.

Brenna looked at her as if she'd not been serious, then realized that Mariel had likely never been introduced to Lithian clothing before. She held out the blouse for Mariel to inspect. "It's my favorite top," Brenna said. "I put it on underneath my sweats whenever I run. It gives more support and is way more comfortable than anything you Tamarian women wear."

Mariel Hougen took the little piece of green fabric out of Brenna's hand. It had a silky texture to its thread and seemed to weigh virtually nothing. "This is a blouse?" she asked, incredulously. "It looks like something you might put on a doll!"

The Long Journey: *Run Away*

"It conforms," Brenna explained. "When you put it over your head, the fabric stretches to fit the contours of your body. They're all like that. Try it on!"

Mariel shook her head. "No thanks. I wouldn't want to wreck it."

Brenna smiled, laughing. "Oh, you won't wreck it. Try it on!"

Clearly squeamish, Mariel handed the blouse back to Brenna. "No. I want to see you in it first."

Brenna shrugged, untied her boned, lace bodice and tossed it onto the dresser. She took the little green garment, stretched it over her head and pulled it down to her waist. The silky fabric fit flawlessly, like a second skin, and seemed to hold every nuance of the Lithian girl's athletic body in an intimate embrace. Brenna stood and glanced at her reflection in the mirror hanging behind the door. "I wish my Tamarian clothes fit like this," she admitted.

Mariel looked astonished. Though she considered herself well educated and liberated from the superstitions that restrained her citizen sisters, the Tamarian woman found it hard to believe that a pious girl like Brenna would allow herself to be seen in such a form-fitting outfit. "You wore that in public? What would your father think?"

"He would think that I am the image of my mother," Brenna replied in an utterly innocent tone of voice. She turned back toward Mariel. "He adores her."

"Has he ever seen you dressed like that?"

"Of course! He had it made for me. Among my people, every maiden old enough to marry wears a blouse like this one. It represents purity. Both of my parents have always supported my virtue. Why wouldn't they want me to be seen in it?"

"If you wore that around here, you wouldn't be a virgin for long!"

Brenna shook her head. "You Tamarians!" she muttered. "I'm far safer in this outfit than I am in the silly clothes everyone else in your country expects me to wear."

Mariel dismissed Brenna's remark as naivete. "I don't think you understand what I mean," she said, rising noisily from her chair, trying to think of how she could explain the link between modesty and morality in terms that a Lithian could understand.

Brenna approached Mariel, a mischievous expression spreading over her face. "Try to take it off of me," she whispered. "Go ahead."

The Long Journey: *Run Away*

The Tamarian officer looked at Brenna with a puzzled expression. "If you're trying to seduce me, that's the lamest line I've ever heard," she replied. "Besides, I'm not into that sort of thing."

"No, that's not it," Brenna replied. "Once I've put it on, no one can remove this blouse but me. It's not like anything you've seen before. Go on, try to take it off. I won't move."

Tentatively, Mariel reached for the strap on Brenna's shoulder. With an awkward touch, she tried to get her fingers under the fabric, but found that it conformed so perfectly to Brenna's skin, Mariel couldn't get her fingernail to lift a single thread from the Lithian girl's flesh. Touching the garment was like touching her skin. An expression of wonder flashed over Mariel's face. "How does it do that?"

"It's all in the way it's made," Brenna explained. "There's a little bit of magic in our clothing, and though I'm not sure exactly how it works, it has something to do with the fact that Lithian textiles are not woven, they're hammered together in a light forge. This makes the fabric very strong. The distance between the fibers and my skin is so tiny nothing can get underneath, and it's so tough it simply won't tear. It's selectively permeable, keeping dirt out, while allowing heat and sweat from my body to pass through."

"How do you take it off?" Mariel asked.

"Like this," Brenna replied, pulling the blouse over her head just like she would a garment made of cotton. "Once I want it to come off, it does." She flipped the shirt inside out and offered it to Mariel. "Try it on."

Mariel looked worried. "I'm much taller and not as busty as you are. It won't fit."

"They're all the same size," Brenna said, reassuringly. "It will conform to you."

The Tamarian woman, who towered over Brenna, remained skeptical. While she didn't really mind wearing another woman's clothing in principle, the diaphanous quality of Brenna's garment stirred an old insecurity within her she'd rather have kept hidden. Mariel turned her back and began putting Brenna's blouse on.

Honoring Mariel's privacy, Brenna turned away and glanced at the desk, noting that the papers strewn there didn't look like school work. That piqued her curiosity, but she refrained from saying anything. Glancing backwards and noting Mariel's struggle with the halter, she smiled. "It only works on flesh," Brenna warned. "Think of it as underwear."

"I see," Mariel replied, a worried tone creeping into her voice. But when she slipped Brenna's blouse over her shoulders, the silky fabric slid over Mariel's skin and magically swept down to her waist, then seemed to lift and become utterly weightless. Mariel could not believe how it felt. She smoothed her hands across the garment in disbelief.

Brenna glanced around Mariel's shoulder and smiled in satisfaction. "That's better!" she encouraged. "You look great!"

Mariel checked herself out in the mirror, noting that the influence of gravity suddenly became inconsequential. "It's like I'm standing up to my neck in water!" she exclaimed. "It feels incredible."

Brenna nodded. "You can run and jump, do cartwheels and handstands with full, three-dimensional support. You'll never worry about spilling out of it," the Lithian girl explained. "Wearing this makes you feel like you're eight all over again."

"No," Mariel argued. "Look at me! I'm sixteen!"

"Now you understand," Brenna replied. "That top was designed for the way Allfather made a woman's body. The hateful under things women wear in Tamaria dig, bind, itch and pull in the most horrible way." Then Brenna smiled in her uniquely impish manner. "And the boys can't get their hands underneath it, either!"

Mariel turned around and reached for the fabric end pulling the top off effortlessly. She dressed quickly, feeling a twinge of regret that she had to give the garment back to Brenna. "Make that thing so nobody can see through it and I could get used to wearing a top like that in a hurry," she admitted. "Or, turn it into underwear and every woman will want one."

Brenna leaned forward and slipped the blouse back on. She willed its fabric smooth and the garment obeyed her wishes. "There won't be any more of these made any time soon," she muttered, remorsefully. "The Azgaril destroyed our light forges. They think themselves civilized, but they were centuries behind us in technology."

Lieutenant Hougen shook her head, suppressing a curt reminder that the allegedly technology-deficient Azgaril had utterly defeated Brenna's people. "If you wore that around here none of the boys would get anything done, and it's really not right to show up for class in combat fatigues or running sweats either. Don't you have anything else?"

The Long Journey: *Run Away*

Brenna slipped into her running sweats, pulling her long, dark hair from beneath the flannel garment and flipping it onto her back. "The Azgaril burned my house down," she replied. "My entire wardrobe went with it. I had a skirt that goes with that blouse, but I tore it up for bandages."

Mariel looked puzzled. "I thought you said the fabric didn't tear. How could you tear bandages from something so strong?"

"It tears if I want it to," Brenna stated, trying to remain patient with Mariel's obvious ignorance. "It does whatever I want."

"So Garrick can't get his hands under there?" Mariel inquired.

Brenna smiled but she didn't answer the question. The Lithian maiden pulled out a pouch from beneath her disorganized clothing and examined its contents. "I have some money," she said, changing the subject entirely. "Can you take me shopping?"

*   *   *

Marvic ranked high among people friendly cities because of its careful and clever municipal planning. Integrated green spaces flourished throughout the town, providing play areas for children, meeting places for teens and young adults, and repose for anyone seeking relief from the fast-paced business climate thriving within the city walls. These linear parkland areas, the walkways, and streets and alleys remained free of trash because the municipality encouraged its poor citizens and children to turn recyclable materials in for a small reward at designated, "Neighborhood Pride" centers.

Residential development followed dedicated light rail corridors running along Marvic's east-west axis, with feeder routes serving outlying areas. Vehicular and animal-drawn traffic remained restricted to certain avenues; especially ring roads and back alleys designed to move raw materials and finished goods between rail depots, manufacturing outlets and the commercial sectors of the city. Heavy trains lumbered along two main lines near the southern wall, where Marvic's major industries, particularly those related to metallurgy, textiles, grain and lumber milling, sprawled.

A pedestrian network and bicycle paths connected the major commercial centers. These vast, covered complexes featured glass roofs that collected precious rainwater and kept Marvic's citizens dry while

The Long Journey: *Run Away*

they shopped downtown during heavy winter rains. The ease of personal travel through the city served its merchants and citizens well.

Though they did not take the most direct route to their destination, Algernon and Astrid traversed the undulating city scape quickly, from its gate toward the palace complex, on the Victory Street express trolley. They disembarked near the courthouse, crossed a grassy basin named Discovery Park, past a stone coliseum known as Memorial Stadium, then climbed up Memorial Avenue until they arrived at a connecting stop.

Neither Algernon nor Astrid spoke about their plans while waiting beneath the glass transit shelter. Once the cursory greetings, traditional blessings and smiles to other citizens were dispensed, the young couple stood in silence. Algernon's mind raced through an outline of how he would go about finding his sister, and the uncertainties of the process plagued him. Not wishing to cast doubt in Astrid's mind, he kept his personal thoughts to himself.

They boarded the light rail car beyond Marvic's downtown core, with its herringbone walkways, trimmed foliage, decorous store fronts and massive shopping centers, along Paradise Avenue, a road leading into a section of the city where the irony of its name soon became evident. Decaying row houses and shabby apartment buildings sheltered many wage-worker families, whose proximity to employment in the nearby industrial zone did not prevent vagrants, prostitutes and thieves from mingling among them.

Astrid grew nervous as passengers disembarked and the neighborhood around them grew steadily more dismal. A palpable sense of despair permeated the Paradise neighborhood. Though litter free, it stank of vomit and urine. Though universal education and employment opportunities existed throughout the city, social inequities and crime remained intractable problems.

When the trolley stopped at its final destination, Algernon inquired about the specific location of the garment district, thanked the car operator, then beckoned for Astrid to follow him, unaware that he was being watched by a lone figure sitting in the shadows on a porch not far away.

"I've got a bad feeling about this place," she complained, glancing around. "It's like someone's following us."

Algernon closed his eyes, desperate to draw out what little patience for her remained in his soul. "I'm getting off this trolley right here. You can either follow me, or go back downtown and meet me at the library later on. The choice is yours." Without another word, the young monk strode to the exit and hopped down to the street.

Astrid sulked behind him, conveying her disapproval by slapping her sandals heavily on the stone pavement. She felt genuinely afraid to go downtown by herself, so she persisted in this purposeful stride, ignoring the remarks of various male residents likening her to the *strichmadchen* plying their trade nearby.

Housing units blended into the garment district. Old, weather-stained buildings adorned in decorative stone served multiple functions, with street fronts reserved for retail display of finished garments, bulk fabric sales on the next floor, followed by two or three tiers of rabbit-warren sweat shops. Hidden behind iron mesh partitions well above street level, an army of low wage workers, many of them women and illegally exploited children, toiled with scissors and sewing machines. The expansive suites on the top floors remained reserved for the offices and residences of wealthy merchants who profited from Tamaria's thriving textile trade.

Finished garments imported into the country were subject to a heavy tariff. Raw materials that could not be produced in Tamaria, however, remained exempt from taxation. Wool, the only fiber native to the region that was produced in sufficient quantity to meet local demand, mingled with cheap cotton, high quality linen and silk imported from Southern Kameron and coastal islands arriving in Marvic by train. Unloaded in the back alleys and stored in huge rooms behind the store fronts, these materials fed the industrial textile factories, whose tireless, electric looms and spindles churned out reams of quality fabric for the sweat shops. Labor-intensive garment manufacturing provided a significant portion of the overall revenue generated within the city of Marvic.

Algernon wandered through the streets, studying the store marquees. Suddenly, he stopped and turned to Astrid. "Fang Family Fine Clothiers," he read, noting that the sign sported a coiled snake. "How appropriate! That's probably where we need to start."

Astrid agreed, nervous but silent. She felt a persistent nagging that someone was following them and kept looking over her shoulder.

Expensive garments stood in racks beneath a fabric awning. High fashion women's clothing graced the window displays, where live models posed, smiled and fluttered their eyelashes at potential shoppers.

The Long Journey: *Run Away*

Incense and the sound of stringed instruments playing a gentle composition wafted from within.

Algernon had never been in a place like this before. Beautiful dresses tailored from the finest fabrics hung from dozens of circular racks. Shirts in many colors, dress pants, men's suits and coats adorned the walls, but small cards displayed prices well beyond the means of a lowly monk. Tapestries lined the back wall and rich, patterned floor rugs softened his footsteps. Running his fingers to feel the fine fabric of expensive garments, Algernon drew the attention of a well-dressed young woman who approached with a condescending smile on her face. The flowery scent of her perfume arrived a few moments later.

"Can I help you?" she asked, turning her head between Algernon and Astrid as if she sincerely intended to offer them something neither one could afford. The expression on her face changed slightly as she returned her gaze to Algernon, examining his features as if he looked familiar to her.

She was pretty–Astrid noticed–pretty in a dark-skinned, southern way. Her flawless, milk-chocolate complexion rose to form a sharp nose and angular cheekbones that melted into black eyes that beckoned beneath long, mascara-laden lashes. Soft, painted lips formed accented words uttered in a breathy, seductive tone. She wore a series of gold chains around her neck, and the cut of her suede jacket and thin, cotton blouse, while conservative for Kameron, seemed a little more daring than necessary for Tamarian sensibilities.

Astrid tried not to stare, but noticed that the southerner held no sway over Algernon. "We're looking for Marco Fang," he stated, glaring at the woman in a frightening way.

She smiled demurely, suddenly remembering that she should have bowed her head and blessed anyone who came from the Temple. Too late to recover from her social blunder and taken aback by Algernon's aggressive demeanor, the sales lady glanced toward a man standing near the back of the store.

"Do you know him?" Algernon demanded, this time with far less patience. He felt Astrid's hand rest gently upon his upper arm, a warning that he struggled not to ignore.

"Yes," she admitted. "He's my cousin. Why do you ask?"

"I think you know," the young monk replied. "Where can I find him?"

The Long Journey: *Run Away*

Nervous now, the woman's smile seemed far less practiced and her eyes shifted in a familiar fashion. "At the university, of course!"

Anger flared on Algernon's face just as a man wearing a dark, pinstriped suit approached. "Don't lie to me!" the young priest warned.

Astrid held her breath.

The man appraised the situation with far greater calm than the woman had been able to muster. He steepled his hands and bowed briefly to Algernon, though he ignored Astrid entirely. "Can I help you?" he inquired, his voice barely concealing outright contempt.

"No!" Algernon retorted. "We were just making progress with the sales lady."

She turned to the older man and spoke in Southern Kamerese. "This unwashed, barbarian flea bag in leather underwear wants to know where he can find Marco," she said, struggling to keep her tone even and silky smooth.

Algernon couldn't resist responding. "I had a bath this morning, and my underwear is cotton, not leather," he said, speaking her language far better than she did Tamarian. "And further, if good manners and modesty mark the civilized, you fail on both counts." He wanted to add: "But what else could I expect from a smelly whore like you," and likely would have, had Astrid not been increasing pressure on his upper arm.

Embarrassed, the woman rolled her eyes, excused herself and fled as quickly as her high heeled shoes permitted, disappearing behind a screen that hid the women's changing area from view.

The man, whose receding hairline and grey temples marked him as old enough to be Algernon's father, spoke in a serene tone of voice. "Why don't you come with me? I'll show you what you need to see."

It was a lie. Algernon could tell the man wanted him away from the wealthy store patrons who might think twice about returning to a place where harm had been done to a monk. Running through the scenario in his mind, Algernon considered resisting the command to follow, but also worried that if he didn't go he'd be asked to leave, and that the police might arrest him for refusing to leave private property. Desperate in his desire to save Kira from harm, Algernon knowingly put his own life in jeopardy and walked to the back door.

A long, dimly lit hall led past several doors and a staircase into a dark, smoky room that reeked of opium. Candles shrouded in dark cylinders provided meager light. The man walked in, then stopped

The Long Journey: *Run Away*

halfway across the floor, turning and gesturing with his head. Feet shuffled quickly at his unspoken command, the door closed and the sound of a handgun hammer clicking backward froze Algernon in fear. Six men surrounded him, blocking off his escape.

As Algernon's eyes adjusted to the darkness, the features of his adversaries emerged from shadows. He knew that no one would fire a gun while standing in a circle, nor would the weapon wielder do so while the well-dressed man from whom they took orders remained in the center of the room. The young acolyte searched for an exit, noting the outline of a closed warehouse door on the back wall. He felt Astrid trembling at his side.

The merchant walked up to Algernon and lashed him hard across the cheek with a leathery tool the boy had not seen. His face burned in pain, tears welled in his eyes and a gush of blood poured from his nostrils. Algernon felt adrenaline surging through his body in response and instinctively put up his hands and slid his right foot backwards to fight.

"There will be none of that here!" the man spat. He rocked on his heels, keeping his hands hidden behind his back. "The next time I see your ugly, meddling face, I will kill you," he threatened. "Do not harass my family any further."

Algernon slowly dropped his hands. "I want my sister, and nothing more," he said.

"Your sister? Who is your sister?" the man taunted. "That pneumatic, opium whore dancing girl my nephew brings around here? You admit family relations with a wanton strumpet like her? Does she serve your needs too, or is this shapeless plaything your consort?"

The man strutted toward Astrid, revealed a riding crop in his right hand and plunged it through the fold above the belt of Astrid's gown, opening it completely. He flicked the riding crop upward until it slapped against the bottom of her chin. "Hmm . . . Not much there, I'm afraid," he sneered.

Algernon felt Astrid quiver in pain, heard her bravely suppress a whimper and simply could not restrain the rage within his soul. Erupting in violent fury, the boy spun to his right, grabbed the man's wrist in a powerful, twisting, right-handed vise. Thrusting with every muscle from his legs through his shoulders and grunting in exertion, Algernon slammed the palm of his left hand into the man's upper arm. Bone snapped audibly and the Kamerese merchant screamed!

The Long Journey: *Run Away*

In less than a heartbeat, Algernon's left elbow crushed the merchant's ribs while his right hand tore the riding crop from his victim's grasp. The Tamarian boy hurled his left knee into a kidney, then twice jammed the riding crop's butt end into each of the falling man's eyes. Algernon hammered his fist off of the merchant's head then brought the riding crop up and around in a rapid, circular motion, to flail wickedly at a Kamerese crony who dared attempt to subdue him.

Voices shouted in pain and confusion. He kicked rearward and felt the full force of his focused blow bend a grown man into a crumpled heap against the far wall. Algernon spun and kicked again–low this time–and splintered the shin of someone reaching for Astrid. Allowing no one anywhere near the girl, the enraged Tamarian hooked a savage, open-handed heel-palm and subsequent grab that rent facial flesh and snapped cervical vertebrae as he hurled his bearded victim into another man rushing toward him.

Algernon wanted to hurt them. He wanted every one of them to suffer. Pure hatred poured from his soul. Venting all the angry passion he could muster, Algernon kicked and punched and lashed with unbridled fury until somebody fired a gun . . .

The noise deafened him. In the unnatural, ensuing silence, someone flung open the large warehouse door he'd seen earlier, and strong daylight flooded the room. Algernon reached for Astrid, who lay crouched and cowering on the floor. He grabbed her left arm and dragged the girl toward the open portal, desperate to escape.

*   *   *

Warm, afternoon light spoke a compelling promise of summertime. Casually strolling along the herringbone-patterned brick walkway, Mariel watched Brenna as she passed by various storefronts, noting that her Lithian friend expressed very little interest in the clothing she saw displayed there.

"I take it that you don't see anything you like?" Mariel inquired.

Brenna didn't want to disappoint Mariel, yet at the same time, nothing caught her fancy. "It's all rather . . . matronly," she complained. "After I've been married for a hundred and forty years and my grandchildren have grown up this kind of thing might have more appeal. But for now, I'm young, and I want to look young!"

The Long Journey: *Run Away*

Mariel covered her mouth and laughed, her dark eyes sparkling. "I can take you to the grandmother stores if you like," she said. "Trust me. They're far worse than this..."

Brenna resumed walking, wrinkling her nose at the spring fashion collection laid out for every shopper's perusal. "Is there anywhere else we can go?" she inquired. "Even the Vatherii don't wear dowdy clothes like these." Brenna pointed to a pair of particularly offensive pinafore dresses.

"We can go up to the garment district if you like. It's not the best neighborhood in town, but you may find something there that suits your tastes a bit better."

Brenna agreed, so they walked over to Discovery Park, up the hill to Memorial Avenue, then paid the fare for the Paradise Avenue trolley. They didn't talk very much until the light rail car stopped at the end of its line.

"You still have that boot knife of yours?" Mariel asked, growing increasingly worried as she examined their surroundings.

"Of course," Brenna replied. "I carry it with me whenever I go out. Why do you ask?"

Mariel glanced at a stairwell, then over to a covered porch. "This place is full of thugs and thieves!" she whispered.

"So do you want me to give you my knife?" Brenna inquired, the beginnings of a smile bending the corners of her mouth.

"No. I'm just thinking that you may have to defend yourself around here."

Brenna laughed. "I'm not worried. Do you really think a thief could catch me?"

"Can you outrun a bullet?" Mariel retorted.

"Can any bullet find its mark on me, apart from Allfather's will?" the Lithian maiden replied. "An entire army was shooting at me a few weeks ago, yet I'm still here. Why are you worried?"

Mariel sighed. "This area gives me the creeps, that's all."

The two women meandered through the streets in the garment district, casually browsing through the street displays, commenting to one another about the cut of a certain dress, or the quality of given fabrics. A few minutes later Brenna glanced upward and noticed a marquee sporting a familiar name. She stopped abruptly. The Lithian girl stood on her toes and scanned the store area that lay behind the smiling models in the fashion window. A familiar and powerful sensation compelled her to walk into the building.

Mariel followed bewilderedly. "Brenna! Have you seen the prices in this place?"

"Yes," the Lithian girl replied, not bothering to turn around. Brenna stopped at a certain rack and pulled a pastel-patterned summer dress down for close inspection. Double stitched seams, thick fabric, a fine weave and a trim cut drew her eye, but something else made her linger a moment longer.

It was the smell.

"Mariel?" Brenna called, speaking in Lithian so that nobody else could understand her. "Be casual about it, but put your nose to this fabric and tell me what you think."

Mariel knew that Brenna's religious beliefs bordered on the fanatical, but smelling dresses in a high-end boutique moved beyond fanatical and well into the realm of the lunatic fringe. Noting that her friend's expression had suddenly turned very serious, Mariel obliged. Her eyes widened as the scent traced its way into her memory. "It smells like that opium from the campus security office!"

"Yes, it does. I recognize the family name on the marquee. These are very dangerous people. They come from Southern Kameron, near the border with . . ."

A male scream echoed from behind the back wall. Mariel turned her head to look, then shifted back to Brenna with eyes widened in fear. "What's going on here?" she whispered. "We should call the police!"

At that moment a gunshot reverberated from the same area where the two women had heard the scream. Other customers shrieked in fright and panic spread throughout the store. Brenna felt her heart quiver as an overwhelming sense of purpose flooded her mind. She *knew* what she had to do. Grasping Mariel's arm, Brenna said: "I have to go!" then bolted for the street, turned right and sprinted away.

"Wait!" Mariel called, knowing she could never catch her fleet-footed friend. "Don't leave me here all alone!"

*   *   *

Algernon felt a strong, leathery hand reach through the light and guide him forward. For a fleeting moment his eyes met with those of a much welcome benefactor–Dmitri, the quiet monk from Elsbireth who'd offered him a strawberry in the greenhouse. Dmitri slammed the warehouse door shut and slid the shank of a padlock through its bolt to trap everyone else inside.

"She's hurt!" the older monk exclaimed. "Stop dragging her!"

Blood stained Astrid's robe below her right shoulder. She looked weak and pale, her gaze unfocused as she groaned in anguish. Foam appeared on her lips and realizing the extent of her injury, Algernon trembled fearfully. "Oh no! Astrid, what have I done?" he cried. "Stay with me!"

She tried to look at him, tried to speak, but her eyes rolled back and her head slumped. Astrid's breathing came in shallow spasms, accompanied by a gurgling sound barely audible above the shouts and pounding that came from behind the locked door.

With great gentleness, Dmitri picked up the girl. "They will come looking for you," he replied. "Let's go!"

Algernon followed, dazed, horrified and afraid. They scurried up the alley, then turned left, onto a ring road that circled back toward the main pedestrian walkway of the garment district. There, near an expanse of green belt, Astrid stopped breathing.

Dmitri paused, carefully laid the young woman down on the grass and felt her neck for a pulse. "Come on, Sister Astrid!" he encouraged. "Breathe, girl!"

But she didn't.

*   *   *

Brenna sustained a full-speed sprint, weaving through startled pedestrian traffic and hurtling over obstacles with tremendous grace and directional control. Although she didn't know where she was going, the image of a kneeling man burned into her mind. Driven by an inexplicable, familiar desire and power as she ran, the words to an ancient psalm sprang into her memory.

Buildings abruptly gave way to an area graced by parkland trees, whose leaves fluttered prettily in the afternoon wind. A draft horse stopped in its tracks–much to the dismay of its driver–stomping its great hooves on the cobbled pavement until Brenna flashed by. Then horse leaned into its load again and continued forward as if nothing had happened, leaving an astonished driver to ponder its mysterious halt while he watched a petite, long-haired girl race toward the park.

The Long Journey: *Run Away*

The vision in Brenna's mind perfectly matched the scene before her and a tremble raced through her spine. She slowed, gasping for breath as her body recovered from the long sprint. Brenna recognized Garrick's brother, but gently pushed him aside to evaluate yet another in a long list of gunshot wounds she'd seen since her arrival in Tamaria.

Dmitri carefully rinsed the foam from Astrid's blue lips using water from his own canteen. When Brenna's soft hand halted his ministrations, he yielded to her expertise and backed away.

"No! No! No!" the Lithian girl repeated, feeling for a very weak and intermittent pulse, listening for breathing. Brenna opened Astrid's mouth and gently moved her head back, checking the airway for obstructions, then turned her attention to the gunshot wound. She pulled Astrid's robe away and lifted the girl to see if the bullet had gone all the way through.

"Water need!" she commanded in her peculiarly accented way. When Dmitri handed her his canteen, Brenna quickly rinsed her hands, then cleaned the blood away from Astrid's skin. Shaking her head, Brenna placed one hand just below Astrid's neck, and the other on the girl's pale forehead. Reverting to her childhood language, Brenna closed her eyes and prayed.

Algernon felt sick! He didn't bother stifling tears that coursed down his face. As he wiped them away, the boy noted that his own hands were smeared in blood, most of which was not his own. The young acolyte cursed himself in deepening sorrow. And when he saw Garrick's girlfriend plant a kiss on her fingertips and reach forcefully into the wound, he lurched forward to stop her.

Dmitri stayed him with an outstretched hand. "Go easy, my brother," the older monk said. "The Great God is working here."

Brenna carefully explored the injury, feeling for broken blood vessels within the Tamarian girl's chest. Thankfully, the bullet had missed the aorta and traveled clean through Astrid's flesh, exiting through her back. Along with extensive tissue damage and massive blood loss, Brenna felt bits of shattered clavicle and manubrium with her fingertips, and with a little effort, managed to pluck the bone fragments out. Astrid's torn sternoclavicular ligaments would take time to heal, provided the young priestess survived the shock and trauma.

Breathing a deep sigh, Brenna kissed her bloody fingers, then reached back into the wound, working her way up toward Astrid's skin. Flesh knitted together at her touch. She laid her lips on Astrid's chest

The Long Journey: *Run Away*

and the bullet wound vanished. Even the acne on the young Tamarian's face faded away. Next, she closed Astrid's nostrils with her left hand. "For Allfather's glory . . . live!" she commanded, then placed a healing kiss on Astrid's lips and blew air into her lungs.

Astrid opened her eyes. She felt pain. She felt a tingling sensation rippling through her body. She felt Brenna's soft mouth leave her own, and looking at the lovely Lithian face, she managed a weak smile. Then she felt the overwhelming urge to cough.

Brenna helped Astrid to her knees and patted the Tamarian girl on her back while she coughed great gobs of blood out of her lungs. Then, turning to Dmitri, Brenna touched him and said: "Girl water need. Drink much need. Rest much need." Brenna retrieved and cleaned her knife, left Astrid and stood, reaching for Garrick's younger brother.

Algernon, wide eyed, retreated. "Get away from me!" he demanded. "I am not holy!"

Brenna shook her head. "God's love gift be," she said, haltingly. "Refuse not. Run away not. Let God love you." In her gentle, appealing manner, the Lithian maiden disarmed his opposition. Standing on her toes, Brenna kissed his cheek, healed his broken face and touched his broken heart.

Unexpected Visitors

With the wind at his back, Garrick crouched over his tiny cookstove fire and warmed his right hand in the hot air rising from its flame. He chewed on a bit of lunchtime sandwich, half listening to the banter of the older men eating nearby, struggling to focus on his next task with the memory of the latest after action report running through his mind.

Sergeant Vidders walked over and knelt next to his young commander. "Tough break on that last exercise, Mister Ravenwood. If it makes you feel any better, Candidate Schultz will take the brunt of the blame for that fiasco."

Garrick shook his head. "We're supposed to be on the same side," he muttered. "I don't understand what that guy is trying to prove."

"His attitude is not your problem, and everyone knows he left us high and dry. But you need to stop brooding over it. Focus on your job, Mister Ravenwood."

Garrick nodded. "I will sergeant, thank you. But what about the men?"

Sergeant Vidders leaned forward and spoke in a lowered voice. "You let me and Sergeant Ringer worry about them, son. But just between us, these guys will follow you to the Gates of Despair, if necessary. Don't fall apart now and let them down."

"Ok," Garrick responded, a smile spreading across his face. "I hope you're still saying that when we're in the water on the other side of Caldera Diablo!"

The middle-aged sergeant slapped Garrick on the shoulder. "I hope you can swim, Mister Ravenwood. That water gets very cold, really quick!"

Although Sergeant Vidder's words rang with wisdom, Garrick found it very hard to put aside the humiliation of his last combat exercise. As part of a brigade-sized task force, his platoon seized an entrenched OpFor position on Dysentery Ridge and firmly held onto the high ground for several hours, awaiting reinforcements that simply never came. Running low on ammunition, Garrick made a decision that cost him the perfect score he'd earned in Hungry Valley thus far.

Candidate Darren Schultz, a well-regarded young man from Burning Tree whose familial connections nearly assured a prominent posting at the conclusion of the officer training course, served as the

The Long Journey: *Unexpected Visitors*

company commander for that particular exercise. Darren Schultz made no effort to conceal his irritation that Garrick, whom he considered a hick from the hills, had become the rising star of the Hungry Valley maneuvers. Candidate Schultz ordered Garrick to capture and hold an untenable position without any support, deliberately–so Garrick's men claimed–destroying the platoon's astonishing record in these exercises.

Prior to the recent debacle, Garrick's platoon had soundly defeated OpFor adversaries in five separate engagements. This time, however, forsaken on Dysentery Ridge by his company commander and subsequently surrounded and outgunned, Garrick ordered his troops to dig in, then called down an artillery barrage very close to his own position in an effort to break a hole in the OpFor line and retreat.

However, the close proximity of the bombardment was ruled as potential fratricide by the observers. Initially, during the After Action Review, Garrick had been criticized for inaccurately targeting indirect fire, but once Sergeant Vidders confirmed that the young officer candidate had purposely ordered the artillery strike so close to his own position, the reviewing officers shifted their stance and Garrick received a sound scolding for failing to implement force protection doctrine.

Everyone knew he'd been abandoned and left without any other option. Even TAC Vogel acknowledged that Darren Schultz should have responded to Garrick's repeated pleas for assistance, yet the official record would forever show that Garrick had put his own platoon at risk. "Welcome to the burden of leadership," TAC Vogel had said. "Don't forget that those men have families too, and you're responsible for their lives. Don't throw them away for the sake of personal glory. Even if you survived something stupid like that, you'd have to cope with the consequences of it for the rest of your days."

On an intellectual level, Garrick wanted to follow Sergeant Ringer's advice and simply put the sorry incident out of his mind, but he couldn't. His defeat at Dysentery Ridge deflated Garrick profoundly and TAC Vogel's counsel haunted him. Was he really suited for leadership, or was his goal of becoming an officer some childish fantasy pursued by a young fool?

After Garrick stuffed the rest of his sandwich into his mouth, he dropped his left hand toward the cook stove and warmed his fingers in its heat. The lesson learned from this experience proved hard and emotionally painful. Garrick wanted to shine on the battlefield so that everyone around him would recognize that he was, in fact, worthy of

The Long Journey: *Unexpected Visitors*

officer's training. Now, however, he'd become preoccupied with the concept that he might not be.

After swallowing his last bite of sandwich Garrick put the lid on his cook stove to extinguish his fire, then asked the medics to arrange for a foot check. This daily ritual enabled Tamarian platoon commanders to evaluate how well the men were holding up and offered the opportunity for each man to spend a moment of time under the direct care of his unit officer.

Even though Garrick only wore a single, silver pip on each shoulder that indicated he hadn't yet met the requirements of a 2nd lieutenant, as acting commander he took on this responsibility. Tamarian platoons typically consisted of 28 enlisted soldiers broken into a pair of squads, each with 14 men. A total of four men per platoon operated small mortars. Each squad had its own medic and one soldier in charge of the sound-powered phone most often used to communicate with artillery units. Two soldiers carried shoulder-fired rocket launchers while two others served as the crew for a multi barreled cannon. While the six remaining soldiers waited to rotate through the heavier weapon duties, they served as light infantry. Extensive cross training and a rigorous rotation schedule required that every soldier develop and retain proficiency with every squad level weapon.

Each platoon had two, sometimes three, sergeants and one or two lieutenants, depending on the experience of the junior officer, for a full-strength total that ranged from 31 to 33 men. Everyone serving in the army, from the cooks and logisticians, the linguists, intelligence and staff officers–all the way up to the four star generals–had to maintain rifle qualification. In harmony with this egalitarian ethic, every infantryman in the field went through the daily foot checking ritual.

Once satisfied that all of his men were physically capable of sustained marching, Garrick ordered his platoon to pack up and form a line behind him. Sergeant Vidders approached and whispered into Garrick's ear. "Go to the back of the line, son. Put someone else on point from now on."

Garrick nodded. "Luther Sondheim! You will take the lead position."

"Yes, Mister Ravenwood!" the enthusiastic recruit responded.

Garrick waited as the men marched past in double file. He nodded to them as they glanced in his direction, many of them smiling,

The Long Journey: *Unexpected Visitors*

then hefted his backpack onto his shoulders and took up a position at the back of the formation.

A well-worn path along the western edge of the valley floor wound between huge, erratic boulders and over ripples scoured by powerful vortexes that lashed the deluged landscape during floods in the distant past. As the brooding, snow-covered ridge lines drew closer, converging on a narrow gap known locally as Cutthroat Pass, Hungry Valley ascended into a long, steep slope that taxed the vigor of every soldier making the climb.

Booted feet crunched on lapilli gravel and larger pyroclastic sediments. Breathing the cold, thin air and sweating beneath their uniforms and body armor from heavy exertion, talk among the men dwindled until each one fell into silence. Seeking comfort in secret, Garrick focused on memories with Brenna, shut his eyes and for a brief moment, imagined the sensation of her strong, yet yielding embrace.

He thought about what she might be doing at that moment, wondering if she missed him as much as he missed her, and if her mind ever drifted back to recall whispered words of devoted affection, the nearness and warmth they'd shared in the bitter cold, and of kisses stolen in secret. Whenever personal doubts nagged at the fringes of Garrick's consciousness, the assurance of honest love that Brenna inspired soothed those uncertainties away.

But Garrick didn't enjoy these thoughts for very long. Sergeant Ringer stopped the column near the top of the slope, ordered the soldiers down on the ground and beckoned for Garrick to come quickly. "I think they've seen us!" he rasped, pointing into the distance.

A group of thirty giants in full armor raced toward them from the east, roughly a hundred yards away. Garrick glanced through his binoculars, considered retreat toward a supporting unit for a fleeting moment, then suddenly, the determined look of a warrior hardened on the young man's face. "We'll draw them close and engage with bayonets!" he spat. Then pointing to the ancient slope of Cutthroat Pass to their left, he urged the men forward. "Secure the top of that hill before they do!" Garrick ordered. "We set up on the reverse slope and make them climb up to reach us."

"Mister Ravenwood," Luther Sondheim replied, incredulously. "All we have for ammo are rubber bullets, flash grenades and chalk mortars!"

The Long Journey: *Unexpected Visitors*

"They know that!" he replied. "That's why they're coming after us. Now, move!"

*　　　　　　　*　　　　　　　*

Brenna was not thinking about Garrick. She sat on the porch swing of Freda Bergen's house with an expression of irritation slathered across her otherwise patient and kindly face. "This is the third time he's asked the same question!" she complained.

Mariel Hougen sighed. "He doesn't believe your story," she replied. "He's looking for inconsistencies because he doesn't understand your healing power."

Brenna shook her head and dropped her face into her open hands. She said nothing for a moment, then glanced up to the roof that sheltered Freda Bergen's wrap around porch. "I'm trying to cooperate, but this is frustrating!" she exclaimed. "I've done nothing wrong here, yet I'm being interrogated like a criminal!"

Mariel appreciated Brenna's position in this situation, but also understood how difficult it was for an educated, secular man to accept information that didn't fit into his paradigm of reality. She turned back toward Lieutenant Streng, the tall, handsome police detective who leaned against the painted porch railing, adjusting his head to get a better look at Brenna's womanly features. Because her ample breasts hung on such a delicate frame, the Lithian maiden often attracted this kind of attention from men and roused the envy of other women. Mariel spoke to the detective in the Tamarian language, trying to mask her own envy. "She's annoyed that you don't believe her."

Lieutenant Streng folded his note pad and put his pencil away. "Miss Hougen, I found three bodies in the loading area of a textile store who'd been bludgeoned to death. Three foreign witnesses blame the young monk and swear that they acted against him in self-defense, but none of them will admit to firing a gun, no weapon has been recovered from the scene, and we have found neither bullet, nor casing. That same boy, who has blood all over his hands, put three foreign students from the university in the hospital not long ago. In both instances, this friend of yours just happened to show up at the right time to save the day.

"I've got a young priestess lying on a bed upstairs who looks pale as death. Her robe has a through and through hole in it and a fresh

The Long Journey: *Unexpected Visitors*

bloodstain half the size of Fallen Moon Lake, yet the doctor tells me there's no evidence of a wound anywhere on her body.

"Your friend has blood under her fingernails too. She gave me a collection of what looks like bits of shattered bone, then claims that she dug these out of a nonexistent bullet hole. After this she says that she healed this near-fatal injury to the priestess by virtue of fanatical devotion to a delusion she calls '*Allfather God*'. Now, what exactly do you think I should put in my report, Miss Hougen?"

Mariel, accustomed to dealing with assertive men in the military, remained completely unflustered. "I'm certain you're capable of writing down what she has told you, lieutenant. I have faithfully translated my friend's testimony, and the only reason you're reluctant to put it on record is because you don't like what she's trying to tell you. Now, is it your job to transcribe the eyewitness accounts, or is it your job to screen them?"

Lieutenant Streng shook his head. Having already interviewed Algernon, Astrid and the older priest named Dmitri, he found that while their stories shared a remarkable consistency, the scenario those three painted for him made no sense. The Kamerese at the clothing store seemed very nervous and reluctant to relate what had happened, citing the right of privacy in their family matters, and refused him permission to thoroughly investigate the scene. "My job is no concern of yours!" he snapped. "And I don't appreciate this kind of hostility from you."

Mariel Hougen smiled coquettishly and ran her fingers across the police investigator's cheek as she sauntered by. "No one is being hostile to you, or obstructing your investigation," she cooed. "You're simply looking for lies in a mountain of truth."

"Then what about the opium?" he inquired, turning away from Mariel and focusing his admiring attention back to Brenna. "On two separate occasions, I have linked your friend to the Kamerese opium trade. Given that her family name is Kamerese, I can't ignore that connection."

Annoyed by his obvious leering, Mariel put her hands on her hips. "Your examination seems curiously distracted, lieutenant. Perhaps you should put your eyes back into your head, pay attention to what I'm saying and focus on her testimony instead of her tits. She may have a Kamerese name, but she's got nothing to do with the drug issue."

Lieutenant Streng quickly averted his eyes and made a point of returning his notepad to a pocket inside his jacket. He regained his

The Long Journey: *Unexpected Visitors*

composure and cleared his throat. "I will record her claim that certain articles of clothing in the boutique smell of opium. You tell her I will investigate this further, and that she had better be telling me the truth! Good day, ladies." He tipped his hat politely, then turned to leave.

Mariel sniffed in haughty indignation as the police officer clomped down the wooden stairs and strode purposefully toward the wrought iron gate leading to the street beyond. She was about to say something to Brenna when Algernon came through the front door. He didn't look very happy.

"Mrs. Bergen is a little agitated right now," he said, speaking Tamarian to Mariel so that Brenna wouldn't understand. "She wasn't expecting so many visitors and wants you two off her property."

Mariel raised her eyebrows and dropped her jaw in disbelief. "First, she refused Brenna a welcome into her home, then wouldn't even serve us a glass of water, and now she wants us to leave? I thought she was the sister of the High Priest! What kind of hospitality is this?"

Algernon shrugged. "When she told High Priest Volker that we could come here for rest and safety, I don't think she was expecting a police investigation. Don't feel bad just for her sake," he said, pointing to Brenna. "Mrs. Bergen wants me to leave, too."

Dmitri opened the door and walked out. "We need to talk before you go, brother," he interrupted, putting his hand on Algernon's shoulder.

Mariel offered the traditional blessing to the two young men before turning away. Brenna did the same, but afterward stood on her toes and kissed Algernon's forehead. She said something to him in her own language, smiled sweetly, then leaped lightly down the stairs and scurried toward the street with Mariel.

Algernon let a long breath slowly escape from his lips. "They sure are lovely!" he whispered, captivated by both women in sincere admiration. "And the more time I spend in that Lithian girl's company, the more I understand why Garrick likes her."

Dmitri grunted. "Beauty fades," he reminded Algernon. "Though they all want to be noticed, a good woman is worth far more than her appearance alone. A pretty face and form give but temporary pleasure to your eye. Carry my words in your heart, brother. The strength of a woman's character and the depth of her intellect will endure long after the scythe of time has bent to collect its bitter harvest."

The Long Journey: *Unexpected Visitors*

"Maybe so," Algernon murmured. "But wouldn't you love to wake up next to one of those two, or maybe even both of them, every morning?"

This time Dmitri gave Algernon's shoulder a gentle squeeze, ignoring the inappropriate question. "I think you know what I must say to you," he began. "I took on this task because I didn't want you to perceive any malice on the part of High Priest Volker."

Algernon retreated to the porch swing with his hands in his lap, anticipating a long delayed reckoning. There would be no escaping this time, no running away. His actions had very nearly cost Astrid her life, and he felt so much remorse over her injury, the young acolyte simply could not bring himself to argue. "This whole situation has evolved far beyond what I expected," he replied. "If they'd hurt me instead of Astrid there might be some justice in all of this."

Dmitri stopped him, shaking his head. "They've tried to kill you twice, my brother. The prosecutor's office would have recommended that you face an Investigative Jury for murder had the threat against your own life not been so obvious. While you have a right to defend yourself, and though you have outstanding martial skills, violent deeds lead to death. I think you have come to realize this truth. The blood on your hands will not bring your sister back, and your reputation is suffering because of your actions today." Dmitri paused, choosing his words carefully. "Additionally, your conduct has brought disrepute to the Temple."

"I know. I know!" Algernon muttered, restraining a curse that lingered near his lips. "You've come to take my robe away!"

"I hope you understand why I must do this," Dmitri said softly. "High Priest Volker loves you and wishes you no harm."

"Yeah, right!" the younger monk spat. "I'll be as much an orphan as Astrid by the time you're done with me. I have nothing now. I may as well die!"

Dmitri remained gentle, unfazed by Algernon's impudence. "This is not so. High Priest Volker loves you as his own son. He's found a way for you to survive."

This remark piqued Algernon's interest, but he remained skeptical, disbelieving that any way existed out of his current dilemma. "Will he let me back into the Temple?"

The Long Journey: *Unexpected Visitors*

"No," Dmitri replied. "Given the ultimatum you've already received, that is no longer possible. Come inside with me and I'll explain further."

*   *   *

Breathless and teetering on the brink of sheer terror, Garrick and his platoon reached the northern summit of Cutthroat Pass. The giants running in pursuit closed to within maximum range of their atlatl-propelled darts, slings and crossbows, and the rage belching from their voices matched the violent war paint slathered upon their faces.

Garrick rested his hands on the strong shoulders of his sergeants. "Machine cannons on flanks," he began, gasping for breath. "Keep them in front of us!" He pointed directly ahead and inhaled quickly. "Wedge formation ... Hold fire until my order ..." He breathed while glancing at the giants lumbering uphill. "Aim for faces ... Make them fall backward ... When they're down, we charge!" Garrick turned toward his men. "Fix bayonets, boys! Get down! Get down!" Then, to a mortar crew he yelled: "Red flare!"

Volcanic rocks whistled overhead. Thick atlatl darts, driven hard toward their targets, whispered through the clear, cold air. Crouching behind the crest of the hill, Garrick's platoon remained safe while the giants hurled their missile weapons. Success in defending against giants involved keeping them far enough away so that their muscle-powered projectiles could not inflict harm. Killing them in hand-to-hand combat, however, required getting very close, where their great strength gave them a significant advantage.

Some of the attacking humanoids stood at nearly twice Garrick's height and weighed more than 600 pounds. Armored in leather and banded steel, they would not be seriously injured by the rubber bullets fired by Tamarian guns. But their broad, flat faces remained unprotected, as giants thought it unmanly to cover their heads in combat. Instead, they smeared themselves in ochre and blood-based war paint during violent, pre-battle rituals.

Garrick intended to use this practice against them. "Steady, men!" he called as the giants approached. Lying on the sharp gravel, Garrick pulled back the bolt action of his rifle and lined up the biggest attacker in his sights. He had only six rounds to fire.

The Long Journey: *Unexpected Visitors*

Three ranks, each containing ten of the huge humanoids stretched across a line measuring nearly forty feet in breadth. They stopped roughly ten yards from the summit of Cutthroat Pass, then brought their long pikes down. This formation presented a wicked array of sharp iron against an inexperienced platoon with only bayonets to counter the threat. All Tamarians rightfully feared giants whenever they lined up in a phalanx such as this one.

A long, silent pause ensued. Huge chests heaved in the thin air. Strong muscles flexed in eager anticipation. Large, yellowed and blackened teeth set forward in their protruding lower jaws raised the giant's upper lips into a perpetual, reptilian snarl. Human bones hung from sinews tied around their necks and hips. Matted and dirty fur adorned their powerful shoulders, and had it not been for the wind, the stench of their unwashed bodies would have invoked nausea among Garrick's men.

"You are all my slaves now!" the giant leader called.

Garrick smirked and couldn't resist a mocking reply. "You are all going to die now!" Then he turned to his men and yelled: "Fire!"

The thunder of thirty rifles and crew-serviced, multi barrel cannons obliterated all other sounds. Rubber bullet impacts rippled through the giant's ranks, shattering facial bones, destroying eyesight and forcing the huge humanoids to drop their weapons and shield their faces. Grenades sailed through the air, erupting in ear-shattering noise and thick, chalky smoke. Giants tumbled backward, into their second rank, coughing, wheezing and screaming in pain.

"Forward!" Garrick cried, ordering his men out of their protected firing positions and downslope at a disciplined, deliberate pace. The four soldiers manning multi barreled cannons turned their attention to guarding the platoon's flanks and stopped shooting. Near point blank range, Garrick gave another order to fire. Then into the smoky confusion, he sent his men–armed only with their bayonets–to battle stricken giants.

Slashing aside a lowered pike, the young Tamarian commander led the attack downhill. He thrust his long rifle forward, sending its sharp bayonet blade deep into the neck of a kneeling, blinded monster who had, only a few moments earlier, envisioned these soldiers an easy kill. Pulling backward with ruthless brutality, Garrick cut through the giant's neck, slammed the butt end of his rifle into the giant's head as it fell, then kicked it hard to clear it out of the way.

The Long Journey: *Unexpected Visitors*

Swirling smoke and the confusion of combat enveloped him. Garrick sensed his platoon's attack stall as they reached the second layer of pike points, and heard the tormented cries of his own men suffering the ferocity of the giants' counterattack. From his right, he felt the full fury of a giant's thrust slam against his armored chest, striking him so violently that the young commander felt his feet leave the ground. His body flew backward as if he'd been toy-sized and flung by an angry child.

Garrick crashed hard against the rocks and found he couldn't breathe. Panicked and vulnerable, he rolled away from a strong pike thrust, yet maintained the presence of mind to fire two more shots directly into the mouth and eye of the giant trying to kill him. As it tumbled backward, the boy staggered to his feet again. Then a wounded soldier fell into his right shoulder, pushing Garrick forward to the point where a pike very nearly found its mark on his face.

Gasping for breath, fighting fear and reacting in desperate self-defense, Garrick jammed his bayonet tip upward, deflecting the blow that otherwise would have killed him. His rifle discharged, but its rubber bullet sailed harmlessly into the afternoon sky. Cursing and slashing wickedly, Garrick knocked pike shafts aside as he lurched downhill in deep gravel, until the broad figure of a giant appeared directly in front of him. Garrick jammed his bayonet into the giant's left, inner thigh and felt a spray of warm blood wash across his neck.

The giant screamed, pounded a mighty fist onto Garrick's helmeted head and lashed at his face in violent fury. The monster beat Garrick with such force the boy rolled and reeled under the punishment of many blows. He struggled against disorientation, willed his body back under control and kept fighting, grim and determined. Talismans rattled in rhythm to grunts and groans as Garrick repeatedly rammed his bayonet into the giant's belly, across its arms and into its chest. He blocked so many hits with his rifle he felt sure it would bend, but the giant kept on fighting and Garrick refused to give in.

An incredibly strong, three-fingered hand grabbed his limbs and tore at his flesh, but could not seize him because Garrick fought back with equal savagery. Enraged, the burly creature thrashed the young commander with a broken pike shaft that bounced off Garrick's tough armor, his helmet and flesh, but no inflicted suffering persuaded the determined Tamarian soldier to yield.

The Long Journey: *Unexpected Visitors*

Garrick's own hands soon became slick with sticky blood and the rifle grip felt slippery, but he attacked relentlessly until his bayonet found and severed a major artery. Only then did the massive humanoid finally weaken. Then, grunting for all he was worth, the boy shoved the dying monster downhill.

Dizzy and reeling, Garrick heard a sword ring from its sheath and saw the flash of bright steel on the flank, three positions over to his right. With great force of will Garrick worked the bolt action of his big rifle, lined up the right ear of the blade-wielding humanoid and sent the last of his rubber bullets into its brain through that orifice.

Using his bloody rifle as a kind of shield while he stumbled beneath a row of pikes, Garrick reached for the sword. He discarded his rifle and picked up the blade just in time to use it defensively, crouching beneath the weapon and deflecting a blow that otherwise would have impaled him. An unseen, bone-crunching thrust slammed into his armored chest on the left side and Garrick dropped to his knees, but a falling Tamarian soldier took the full brunt of the follow-through attack, trading one life for another.

Garrick groaned in pain and disorientation as he gasped for air. Screams and shouts, angry curses and the clash of metal surrounded him. Something primeval drove the young man onward, an inner strength that burst from deep within his soul. Sharp steel carved the wooden pike shaft as Garrick stood erect and forced the enemy's weapon over his head. In a brutal, two-handed motion, he swung the big blade into a leftward arc that slashed across the shoulder of the giant now on the right flank, and buried its entire breadth deep into flesh like the wedge of a sharp maul splitting into a soft, pine block. The huge creature roared in agony, dropping its pike. With a fierce grunt Garrick thrust the sword between the giant's belt and armored vest, then corkscrewed the weapon into his adversary's body until its hilt met the giant's belly and he ran the powerful humanoid back into the giants' third rank.

Garrick yanked the weapon out of its grisly sheath and spun around, twirling the blade over his head with such force he clipped the left arm off of another giant and still maintained enough momentum to slam the sword into its neck on his next rotation. Cutting toward the right, he hacked into the giants' third rank, then thrashed left and mercilessly worked his way between the two rows.

Lacking the skill of an expert swordsman, Garrick's enraged strength and the ferocity of his attack nonetheless turned the tide of battle. The big blade sang as it sliced through the air, cutting every spear shaft recklessly shifted to counter it. Whenever the sword slammed into giant flesh, it hacked hunks of bloody muscle and sinew from bone. Within moments, all Garrick needed to do was walk downhill swinging the heavy weapon around his head for the nearby giants to discard their spears and run.

Garrick felt a crossbow bolt smack hard into his armored chest. He heard someone yell at him to get down as a hazy, yellow veil enveloped his vision. He dropped to his hands and knees as the giants fled. Several of the big humanoids paused about ten yards away and picked up rocks to hurl, but their efforts were quickly thwarted by the crew-served multi-barrel cannon. It wickedly spat rubber bullets in the platoon's defense until the big humanoids turned to run again.

Utterly winded and dizzy, with every nerve throbbing in pain, Garrick dragged himself leftward, out of the way of his cannon, where nausea overcame him and he vomited repeatedly. Embarrassed, but realizing that the enemy was in full retreat, he wiped his mouth and evaluated the condition of his platoon. "Don't let them get away!" he screamed, far weaker than he would have liked to have sounded. Looking for Sergeant Vidders, Garrick yelled: "Rockets! Now!"

Had any surviving giants managed to regroup at the bottom of the hill, the Tamarians would have lost their significant terrain advantage. Garrick didn't want to be stuck on top of Cutthroat Pass at nightfall, waiting to be either attacked or rescued in the event that a friendly set of eyes had actually seen his unit fire the red flare.

Rocket contrails whisked across the sky. Sergeant Ringer led a squad of men downhill to dispatch the giants knocked down by rocket fire while Sergeant Vidders secured the hilltop. The brief engagement resulted in seven slain from Garrick's platoon, with five other soldiers rendered unfit for combat, suffering from blunt trauma and puncture wounds. Although the Tamarians showed no quarter to the giants they caught, nearly a dozen of them got away.

*   *   *

Freda Bergen's house smelled of old books. Like her brother, High Priest Volker Pfaff, Mrs. Bergen loved to study and learn. During her forty years of marriage she'd collected an extensive library, and now

The Long Journey: *Unexpected Visitors*

as a widow, she had plenty of time to pore over thick tomes written in the three languages she knew how to read.

Algernon, who understood Tamarian racial prejudice, could forgive the old woman for not letting Brenna into the house. He might have forgiven her for blaming Astrid's injury on his propensity for violence. He might also have forgiven her for complaining about the arrival of Marvic's police investigator, but he simmered angrily over her complaints about High Priest Volker.

"My brother's an old fool!" she'd snapped. "I've heard about his wasted efforts on you!" she lectured Algernon when he'd first arrived. "Your ingratitude to his devotion will be your demise. Mark my words!"

So even though Freda Bergen's house contained many literary treasures that would have delighted Algernon's inquisitive mind for many hours, he felt very uncomfortable walking back into her abode.

But Dmitri seemed serene as he led the way through Mrs. Bergen's parlor and into her personal library, a rectangular room with a long, sturdy table, several chairs and a reading area set into a bay window that overlooked her ample, blossoming garden. He shut the door behind them, then sat in a leather chair and beckoned for Algernon to do the same. "Before I work through High Priest Volker's plan with you, I would like to know why you threatened Sister Gretchen in the women's dormitory."

Because Algernon respected Dmitri, he couldn't meet the older man's eyes and answer honestly. The boy slumped forward in his chair, put his face into his hands and shook his head as a flood of emotion overwhelmed his soul. "I've been thinking of no one but myself in all of this," he admitted. "I didn't intend Gretchen any harm, but in the heat of the moment I didn't know what else to do and I acted impulsively. I've been doing that a lot, lately."

"Do you wish to make this right?" Dmitri inquired.

Algernon wiped tears away from his eyes and sniffled. "I wish it had never happened."

Using one of Algernon's tactics, Dmitri pressed him. "That's not an answer to my question, nor will your stated desire change the past. Do you wish to make things right with Sister Gretchen?"

"How can I?" Algernon responded. "You know I can't go back to the Temple."

Patiently, Dmitri leaned forward. "She is upstairs, caring for Sister Astrid. Would you like to speak to her?"

The Long Journey: *Unexpected Visitors*

Shocked, Algernon sat up. When he realized that Dmitri was serious, he nodded. "Yes, I think I should."

"Remain here," Dmitri commanded. He walked out of the room, disappeared for quite some time, then returned with Gretchen, who entered with clenched fists and a determined expression chiseled onto her face. She left the door open so that she could escape, if necessary, and Dmitri waited in the other room.

"Swear that you won't hurt me!" she demanded.

Algernon shook his head meekly, finding no emotional strength to contend with her. He understood that he lacked any valid justification for his behavior on a day that already seemed like a lifetime ago. "I'm in no frame of mind to hurt anybody," he replied.

"You've killed three people with your bare hands today, Brother Algernon. I will never forget that you threatened to kill me, too." Gretchen approached with anger rising in her voice. "You threatened my life, hurt me, tied me up and left me all alone in a storage room, though I've done nothing to harm you, or your slutty sister!"

He let the insult go, but the pain of Gretchen's words stung in his heart. Algernon stood and trudged toward her with his head bowed. "I know I've taken life," he replied, meekly. "And at that moment on that day I fully intended to take yours. It's also true that I have hurt you, though you have done me no wrong." Slowly, desperate to contain his emotions, Algernon knelt in front of her, kept his head bowed and put his hands flat on the floor at her feet.

Gretchen recognized the humility of his confession and posture. Though moved with pity, she remained silent.

Algernon looked up, battling tears. "Please, forgive me!" he pleaded. "I'm very sorry, Gretchen. Find it in your heart to absolve me of all wrong toward you!" Then, moving with great deliberation, he gently dropped his face to the floor again.

Gretchen struggled not to spit at him. Part of her wanted him to feel the same humiliation she'd experienced in the dormitory. Part of her wanted to doubly repay him for the unnecessary pain he'd caused her. But he had asked to see her, he had asked to restore the relationship, and as his posture indicated, he'd been humbled beyond any indignation she'd be able to muster against him. Shaking her head, Gretchen remained true to *Gottslena* philosophy and bent to gently place her hand upon his shoulder. "Go in peace, brother," she said to him. "I forgive you."

The Long Journey: *Unexpected Visitors*

The girl turned, disappeared upstairs, and though Algernon often grimaced at the thought of how badly he'd treated her, he never saw Gretchen again.

After Gretchen's departure, Dmitri came back in with a candle, a flask of oil and a package under his arm. He put these items on Mrs. Bergen's table, paused to pray, then shut the door and glanced at the young man, gesturing him into a kneeling posture. Then, the older monk lit the candle and stood directly in front of Algernon. "I know that you love your sister and are willing to lay down your life for her. You are brave, my brother, but the burden I lay upon you now will demand greater courage and servitude. Are you ready for your final vow?"

Algernon rocked backward, eyes widened in disbelief. "Now?" he asked, meekly.

Dmitri nodded. "Raise your hands to heaven. Swear to the Great God that you will serve him always."

This moment had come unexpectedly. "I so swear," Algernon responded, lifting his eyes and hands toward the paneled ceiling.

"As the appointed servant of Volker Pfaff, High Priest of the Sacred Elsbireth Order, I now commission you in service to the Great God," Dmitri proclaimed, placing his hands on Algernon's head. "I grant you the full honor and responsibility of priesthood, in the new Holy Order of Ravenwood."

Algernon's eyes widened. An order named after him?

"Let the renewed man clothe himself for service. Remove your student's robe, and place this new raiment over your shoulders." Dmitri opened the package and produced a simple, blue robe made of coarse fabric, with a brown-colored band circling the thighs. It came with a matching overcoat, lined for warmth against the winter. When Algernon put the new robe on, Dmitri dabbed his fingers into the oil flask and touched each of Algernon's temples, then pressed hard against his forehead. "Rise, Brother Algernon!"

Astonished, Algernon didn't know what to say.

"Bless you!" Dmitri said, with the hint of a smile on his otherwise solemn face. "When you leave this place, go in service to the Great God."

"How will I know what to do?" Algernon asked.

"This will become clear to you in time," Dmitri responded, handing Algernon a book. "Study this and learn about your sister's addiction. You will have a difficult road to walk with her. For now, we need to go outside. There is one more thing I have to show you."

The Long Journey: *Unexpected Visitors*

Algernon accepted the book, a thin medical text on the symptoms and treatment of opium addiction, and quickly thumbed through a sampling of pages with widened eyes. Though he had an inkling of insight into Kira's problem, the young monk had no idea how desperate her situation had become. He thanked Dmitri and followed him out of the room.

Mrs. Bergen remained upstairs. As they walked through her spotless kitchen toward the back door, Algernon could not resist asking a question. "The man with the gun would have killed me today," he began, "but you opened the back door so I could escape. How did you know I was there?"

Stepping outside, Dmitri paused on the back porch. "We knew you were leaving the city every night because the Defenders had seen you come and go several times. One of them agreed to stop you on your way in and ask you to pray for his mother. I had been waiting in the administrative center within the wall complex for the signal that you'd arrived. The Defenders on the balcony notified me. I sent a God-fearing Kamerese merchant out to find you. He delayed your departure long enough for me to arrive in the garment district ahead of you.

"I took a direct route along the warehouse road, then waited for you near the last trolley stop. Sister Astrid kept looking my direction, as if she knew I was there, but you didn't notice me following behind when you got off the trolley and walked into Fang's boutique. When I saw you head for the back room, I knew you were in trouble. I went around the block until I found the back door, intending to go inside and come to your aid. That's when I heard the gunshot, and feared the worst."

"Thank you for helping me," Algernon responded, astonished.

Dmitri continued down the stairs and strode toward a small, wooden framed garage with badly peeling white paint. "I did not save your life. Your companion has faithfully watched over you from the moment you left the Temple. Further, I have acted on High Priest Volker's behalf throughout this situation. Ordaining you to a new priesthood was his way of subverting the will of the Supreme Council."

"Why would he do this for me?" Algernon wondered aloud. Though he remained curious about the elder monk's passing remark concerning Astrid, he didn't broach that subject.

Dmitri laughed. "Why are you so blind, brother? High Priest Volker loves you as though you were his own son. He could no sooner abandon you than he could abandon his own flesh!"

The Long Journey: *Unexpected Visitors*

Algernon shook his head. "I don't understand. He was always so hard on me!"

"No true son escapes his father's discipline," Dmitri replied. "As you reflect on his counsel, High Priest Volker's words will remain the compass by which you navigate your life. They will serve as a map when you are lost, and a light when you find yourself in darkness. He and Priestess Dorothea have high hopes for you and your sister." Dmitri placed his hand on Algernon's shoulder. "Don't disappoint them, brother."

A thousand thoughts swirled in Algernon's overwhelmed mind. Ultimately, being loved meant being loveable, and though Astrid kept telling him this was so, the young monk found this fact hard to believe. He'd always dismissed her remarks, but now, in light of Dmitri's cryptic statement, something about her role in the drama bothered him. She'd also claimed that High Priest Volker loved him, and now, confronted with irrefutable evidence of this fact, he could no longer ignore her counsel.

This revelation sunk into Algernon's consciousness as Dmitri pulled open the garage door. The older monk retreated into the darkness and reappeared walking a bicycle. "This belonged to the High Priest when he was young," Dmitri said. "Because you're living outside of town, he asked me to give it to you."

"I can't accept this!" Algernon exclaimed, astonished. "I wouldn't be able to pay for such a thing working for a year!"

Dmitri smiled. "It's a gift, just like your ordination. As long as you wear your vestments, you can take food from the shrines to feed yourself, as you've always done. That too, is a gift you cannot repay. Don't make light of charity done in God's service, my brother."

This bicycle was no ordinary machine. Its sleek, aluminum frame sported fluid pump foot pedals that propelled a rear wheel motor. This bicycle's hydraulic gearing could be infinitely varied between its lowest and highest settings by virtue of a thumb-activated lever.

The bike also featured a handlebar-mounted basket rack and a small, pull along cart mounted to the back of its frame. With these, Algernon could transport food and supplies between the city and his new home on Superstition Mesa.

It was an extraordinary gift.

The Long Journey: *Unexpected Visitors*

"There's a girl's version like it that belongs to Mrs. Bergen," Dmitri continued. "She hasn't ridden it in many years, so she's giving it to Sister Astrid once the girl is fully recovered."

"What am I supposed to say?" Algernon inquired. "How can a mere 'thank you' express my gratitude for this?" He put the medical book into the front basket, pulled the bike into an arc, then stepped over its frame and stood, silent in disbelief.

"Live your life in devotion to the Great God, brother. That will be all the thanks High Priest Volker will need. Go now," Dmitri urged. "Find your sister, and save her soul."

Algernon nodded, then pushed off and let the bike glide effortlessly down the gravel path leading to the front gate. "Thank you, Brother Dmitri!" he said in response, over his shoulder.

The older monk smiled, his mottled, scarred face expressing pure delight. "Go with the Great God, and by all means, be careful!"

*   *   *

Someone in Greg Schmidt's unit saw the red flare climb high into the windy heavens and drift lazily down the valley as it burned into embers. Greg Schmidt pulled out his field lens and examined the crest of Cutthroat Pass in the distance. "That's got to be Mister Ravenwood's platoon," he remarked. "No one else marches his men that hard."

As word spread among the warriors moving toward their next objective, all forces operating in Hungry Valley shifted into "hostile territory" operations. Candidate Greg Schmidt contacted Brigade Command via a messenger, reporting the red flare and informing them of his intention to collect live ammunition from a nearby storage depot and march to Garrick's rescue.

His actions lay within a local commander's discretion, so he didn't expect a response from them and rightfully believed that other units would follow to back him up. Nearly two hours later, Greg Schmidt and his platoon arrived at Cutthroat Pass, bringing plenty of ammunition to share with Garrick and his men. Out of concern for the bruising and swelling visible on Garrick's face, Mister Schmidt recommended that Garrick return with his platoon to Brigade Command.

"No way!" the young officer candidate countered. "We'll send the wounded back, but we're not leaving you and your men out here alone!"

The Long Journey: *Unexpected Visitors*

Greg admired Garrick for his sense of duty and appreciated his willingness to remain in action, but he questioned Garrick's wisdom. "You're tired, you're hurt, and you're covered in blood!"

"None of this blood is my own," Garrick replied. "I feel like I've been run over by a train and yes, I want to sleep, but I'm no worse off than anyone else in my platoon who can still walk. And, you'll be in far better shape having us in your ranks when the giants come back for seconds."

"You think they'll want to tangle with you again?" Greg inquired.

"Count on it. They must have been watching us and realized we didn't have real bullets. They'll be back, and in bigger numbers."

These words met fulfillment later that afternoon when another, larger group of giants arrived on the scene. This time, however, they met a battalion-strength group of fully armed and angry Tamarians. Bracketed by mortar and rocket fire, the giants walked into a hailstorm of rifle bullets that ripped into their ranks with devastating effect. None of the humanoids got close enough to throw so much as a rock, and none lived to tell the tale of that engagement.

Aware that senior commanders had already interviewed the observers who fought alongside his platoon, Garrick steeled himself before reporting to TAC Vogel at dusk. He felt dizzy and had not washed before entering the command tent, but once he stepped inside, he longed for a shower, a clean uniform and a nap.

Manfred Vogel stood behind a table alongside another, older officer whose graying hair remained neatly combed. His demeanor exuded dignity and commanded respect. An expression of dismay passed over the two officers' faces when they saw the physical evidence of Garrick's afternoon skirmish. Darkening bruises and extensive swelling proved the boy had tangled with at least one creature far bigger and stronger than he.

Garrick's eyes flashed to the small, silver hawk insignia mounted on the colonel's collar, and he stiffened. "Colonel Weiss, sir! Candidate Garrick Ravenwood reporting as ordered." He stood at attention.

In the light of a kerosene lantern, the colonel maintained a very serious demeanor, but spoke with kindness undergirding his words. "At ease, Mister Ravenwood. You look terrible, son. I understand you saw some action today."

"Yes sir," Garrick responded. "As we climbed into position on the eastern side of Cutthroat Pass, our movements were detected by a war

The Long Journey: *Unexpected Visitors*

party of giants. It's clear that they had been observing our exercises long enough to know that we were not adequately armed. I ordered my men to seize the high ground, establish defensive positions and repulse the enemy."

"With rubber bullets?" TAC Vogel more stated than asked.

"Yes," Garrick affirmed. "They underestimated us. We defeated them in the name of the Republic with rubber bullets, chalk grenades and the bayonet."

Silence dominated the tent for a moment before TAC Vogel continued. "Tell me, Mister Ravenwood, why were you so far ahead of all the other platoons on today's march?"

"It's a lesson I learned from the Winter Campaign," Garrick explained. "Early on, the Azgaril often beat us in battle because they maneuvered quickly. Once we learned to cover ground better than they could, we picked engagements that favored our forces. This gave us flexibility to adapt in an evolving tactical environment, and it worked well. I train with my men like I intend to fight with them."

Colonel Weiss nodded, understanding. He knew about the force deployment doctrine problems revealed when the Tamarian army faced the Azgaril. They'd trained to fight giants for so long, only the most creative commanders effectively transitioned to a new style of combat in time to favorably impact the war on the Saradon Plateau. Now that Tamaria faced a different kind of threat, her way of making war had to change. "Are you capable of leading your platoon through the remainder of these exercises?"

Garrick looked the colonel directly in the eye, a challenge not lightly undertaken by anyone of inferior rank. "My men are ready, sir! I will lead them, and they will follow."

"You seem quite confident of yourself, Mister Ravenwood. We thought, in light of your platoon's losses and your obvious injuries, that you might wish to return to Marvic for some well-deserved rest." Colonel Weiss made this remark in a tone of voice that expressed more concern than command.

"If we were at war today, you would expect me to carry on, sir. While I sincerely regret the loss of many fine men, I must honor the memory of their sacrifice and continue. I will stand at my post until I am unable or you see fit to remove me!"

Colonel Weiss smiled and glanced at TAC Vogel, whose expression remained blank. "There's a visitor coming tonight who would

The Long Journey: *Unexpected Visitors*

like to have a word with you. Get yourself cleaned up as best you can. Meet us here in thirty minutes!"

"Yes sir!" Garrick replied.

After the young man went back outside, Colonel Weiss turned to TAC Vogel. "This boy is the best candidate we have? He looks like he's been beaten up in a street brawl!"

"Indeed," Manfred Vogel responded. "He's taken a pounding today. But trust me, in a fight, Mister Ravenwood has no equal."

"And grown men follow him?"

"Yes, they do. We put him with our most experienced sergeants, thinking that he would benefit from their guidance. They report that he listens well, yet his intuitive grasp of how to operate on the battlefield surprises them, and he needs very little of their advice. He's planned every movement of his platoon since getting off the train as if he's had years of experience under his belt. The combat action observers who referee his platoon report that Candidate Ravenwood has established excellent rapport with his men, and most telling of all, the OpFor units complain when they have to face him."

"Why? Is he unfair?" the colonel asked, intrigued.

TAC Vogel shook his head. "Relentless and tactically clever, but fair."

"What about his judgment?"

"We've seen fewer rookie mistakes out of him than anyone else in memory. He's a born leader. If the boy survives the storm ahead, he may become one of those men celebrated in history books for centuries."

Colonel Weiss chuckled. "That's high praise, coming from you, Manfred!"

TAC Vogel didn't smile. "He's earned it, colonel. Though I didn't believe this would be the case when I first met him, I watch that boy from a distance with pride in my heart."

Garrick had no idea that his commander thought well of him. As he wandered back toward his own encampment, several other officer candidates stopped to inquire about his condition, the worry in their voices a clear indication that they'd taken a brotherly interest in his well being. Garrick, though preoccupied with a compelling desire to sleep and distracted by his own physical pain, appreciated their concern and took their encouragement as affirmation that he'd become an accepted member of their community. For the first time since his training began, Garrick felt like he really belonged among them.

The Long Journey: *Unexpected Visitors*

Sergeant Vidders had a hot washcloth waiting for Garrick when he returned to camp. "I talked to the brigade quartermaster," the sergeant explained as the boy began scrubbing the blood and dirt off of his battered flesh. "He gave me a greatcoat for you to wear over your uniform. It's *borrowed*, so be sure to get it back to me in good condition after you're done with your meeting tonight."

"Thank you, sergeant," Garrick replied, accepting the garment. "I don't even know whom I'm supposed to be seeing." He winced when the older man put a firm hand on his shoulder.

"Ah, you're a bit tender there!" Sergeant Vidders exclaimed. "Sorry, Mister Ravenwood. After watching you battle with that giant I should have known better." Then Dagmar Vidders leaned toward Garrick's ear. "Unexpected visitors on a field exercise are typically high in rank, and that's why the colonel wants you cleaned up. Be on your best behavior. I wish you well."

These words, while intended as encouragement, inspired nervous worry. In the strange limbo between an enlisted soldier and a commissioned officer–that odd state in which he and his fellow candidates existed–Garrick's dream of a military career could come to a quick and bitter end, depending on many factors he believed were beyond his control. The fate of seven soldiers who'd perished earlier that day demonstrated this chilling reality. Further, two of the officer candidates who'd come to Hungry Valley had been summarily dismissed from the program. Despite his stellar performance and the confident demeanor he displayed in public, Garrick remained anxious and felt exhausted. All he wanted to do at that moment was collapse on his bedroll and sleep.

As lengthening twilight faded into darkness, stars and bright planets gradually appeared in the black sky. When the Daystar's influence finally vanished, the twin moons arced high above the ridge lines and the blue-green glow of the Great Eye Nebula lightly painted the southern horizon. Garrick ate a hot meal with his unit, then headed back to the command tent.

Laughter resounded from inside, but abruptly stopped when Garrick asked permission to enter. Standing next to Colonel Weiss, Garrick saw a man whose shorn head and hawkish nose reminded him of Sergeant Streckert, the fallen leader of his Junior Scout troop. Two silver stars adorned this man's collar.

The Long Journey: *Unexpected Visitors*

Colonel Weiss introduced Garrick to General Leo Braun, excused himself, then he and TAC Vogel departed, leaving Garrick alone with the general. "They tell me you fight like a lion," the older man stated. "I wouldn't know that from looking at you."

Garrick didn't know what to say, but figured he should respond. "I do my duty, sir."

General Braun sat down behind the table and motioned for Garrick to pull up a chair. "They also tell me you speak Lithian."

At this, Garrick felt a hot flush of embarrassment swell up from his neck. "Sir, that information is overstated," he replied. "I've been studying the language in my spare time. I know some nouns and a verb or two. I can speak a few terms of endearment, but I wouldn't yet claim that I can sustain much of a conversation."

General Braun nodded, listening. "Tell me what you know of the Lithian people," he ordered.

Garrick paused, collecting his thoughts. "From what I understand, their culture values individual freedom and they make great effort to respect the views and decisions of their peers. They focus on consensus and relationship when dealing with others and believe that they answer directly to their God for any impropriety they may commit. Many of them are devoutly religious, even though they are well educated and have an excellent command of the sciences.

"Family relations form the basis of their society, as they do not believe in formal governance. Yet they developed a civilization that survived the Great Cataclysm and managed to fight off their enemies until last summer. We often criticize them because their ideas concerning modesty differ from our own, as Lithians consider their thinly veiled flesh an indicator of innocence rather than shame. May I inquire, sir, why you are asking this of me?"

The general pursed his lips, evaluating the battered young man sitting across from him. "I hear you have a Lithian girlfriend."

Garrick shut his eyes and sighed. "Yes, I do."

"Are you ashamed of her?"

"No sir, not at all."

"Then why the resignation?"

"Because she is not well understood among our people," Garrick explained.

General Braun pointed directly at Garrick. "That," he said, "is the reason I asked you the question."

The Long Journey: *Unexpected Visitors*

Puzzled, Garrick risked a further inquiry. "What does this have to do with me?"

"Do you understand her?" the general replied.

"Not always," Garrick admitted. "But I accept her as she is."

"That is precisely what my inquiry has to do with you, and is exactly the reason for my interest."

"I'm sorry, sir. I don't understand."

A smile spread across General Braun's face. "You will, soldier. Soon enough!"

*   *   *

Long before the earliest hint of dawn tinted the eastern skyline, Brenna roused from a restless slumber with her heart pounding and her pale skin awash in a sheen of sweat. She slipped out of bed, careful not to disturb Mariel, grabbed a towel, soap and her underwear, then took the simple peasant dress she'd bought in a consignment store the previous afternoon off of its hanger and examined it for a moment.

Barefooted, wearing a clingy undershirt that had once belonged to Garrick, she quietly crept to the communal shower and washed away the anxiety that had awakened her. No one stirred until well after she'd scrubbed away her sweat, washed her hair, put on her unflattering new outfit and returned to her room. Carefully and quietly opening the window blinds to let in ultraviolet light, Brenna glanced at her image in the full-length mirror mounted behind her door and frowned. Her parents certainly wouldn't approve seeing her dressed this way!

Brenna's early morning destination at the campus auditorium lay within the College of Arts and Language, a cluster of curvilinear, marble-faced buildings that stood a brisk five-minute walk away from the women's dormitory. Creeping down a lovely, glass-enclosed staircase, and waving to the weary Resident Assistant stationed behind the lobby desk, Brenna quietly opened the outside door and put on her new, rubber-soled Tamarian shoes while sitting in a chair on the narrow, covered porch.

Songbirds had not yet stirred. The still air smelled of sweet wisteria blossoms. Dew dampened grass reflected a myriad of bright pinpoints like a carpet of tiny, shimmering jewels. Brenna's world, flooded in blue light, glowed in a peaceful luminescence made more and more vivid each morning by the waxing Great Eye Nebula. Within a few

The Long Journey: *Unexpected Visitors*

weeks it would dominate the night sky, and its rising signaled the season when nations mobilized their armies for war.

Brenna reached the peak of Liberty Hill and paused for a moment. Looking north across a deep gorge, beyond the heights of Superstition Mesa, she gazed at the sheer, snow-clad ridge line towering in the distance. Behind these mountains lay Hungry Valley, where the boy who held her heart in tender care slept on the hard, rocky ground. Brenna closed her eyes and prayed for him, longing for the sweetness of his company, believing in her heart that he thought of her with equal yearning.

She almost wept, but fought back her tears. An ache plagued her soul; a sense of uselessness and despair pressed upon her mind. Brenna found her feet moving toward the auditorium as if they possessed a will of their own, but her thoughts lingered with Garrick in Hungry Valley, sensing vague dangers that threatened him from the shadows.

The elderly custodian, one of the few old men she'd seen in Tamaria, smiled and bade her a good day in his raspy voice, then complimented her on the new dress as his hands trembled with a set of keys. He let her in, as was his custom, then locked the door behind her.

In the apparent darkness, Brenna raced to the top of the auditorium with fleet and confident strides. Her secret place, hidden alongside the antiphonal pipe array, beckoned like an old friend. She dropped to her knees, put her face into her hands and trembled with uncontrolled weeping. Brenna prayed. All of her sorrow, the terror of her past and the anxiety about her future swirled in a storm of strong emotion expressed in beautiful, melancholy language that spilled from her lips for a very long time.

"How long must I feel this way? How long must my soul wrestle with terror and torment? How long before your strong hands deliver me? How long?"

Her prayer ended with these words. As the intensity of that experience ebbed, Brenna thought she heard a door open. She waited in silence, every movement frozen, every nerve keen, every muscle prepared for action. Once certain that she'd been mistaken, Brenna trotted downstairs and removed her shoes to practice the organ.

She hadn't been playing long when suddenly, stage lights flashed into full glory. Momentarily blinded by the surge of brightness, Brenna shielded her eyes and heard the heavy sound of booted feet trample over the lingering, melodic echoes fading from the auditorium walls.

The Long Journey: *Unexpected Visitors*

A male voice spoke Tamarian words she didn't understand. Brenna helplessly turned to face a fully armed and grim-faced Defender who focused the deadly mouth of his small caliber carbine on her as he approached. Behind him she saw three others, then turned her head at the sound of more soldiers stomping on stage to her left.

"No understand!" she pleaded meekly. "Little speak only!"

Eight of Queen Tamar's elite soldiers surrounded her. The man who initially approached dropped the business end of his rifle down. She recognized his rank as a staff sergeant but said nothing to him. He tilted his head slightly and spoke again, this time in Southern Vulgate. "Are you Specialist Brenna Velez?"

Eyes widened, Brenna nodded.

"Keep your hands visible, move slowly, and drop all of your weapons."

"I am practicing," she reminded him. "Why would I carry a weapon when I'm playing the organ?"

"Stand up!" he ordered.

When Brenna obeyed, he jerked his head toward one of the other soldiers, who handed his carbine to a companion and approached with an apologetic look on his face. "Please put your arms out and spread your legs apart. Forgive me for the indignation miss. I'm only doing my duty." The soldier firmly ran his hands down the sides of Brenna's dress, then squatted in front of her and patted down her thighs and calves with both hands. Brenna wanted to slap him, but she didn't.

He stood, tight lipped, and tipped his red beret in a sincere apology to her before retreating. "She's clean!" he announced.

"What have I done to deserve this humiliation?" she inquired.

"It's routine, Miss Velez," the sergeant told her. "Her Grace, Queen Tamar, Sovereign of the High Land, requests the pleasure of a private concert."

Brenna felt thunderstruck. "What? When?"

"Right now, miss. She's heard your music all the way from the palace every morning and asked us to secure the hall so she could hear you perform in person. We will remain on the perimeter. Her Grace, the queen, will enter through one of the back doors. Do not look at her. Do not speak to her unless she speaks to you. Do you understand?"

Brenna nodded.

The Long Journey: *Unexpected Visitors*

"Just start playing," he said. "Pretend we're not here." At his command the soldiers moved offstage, leaving Brenna alone in stunned disbelief.

She wished they'd turn the lights back off, but knew they wouldn't. Brenna adjusted the organ stops, breathed deeply, then started a slow, simple ostinato melody in a minor key. Over the top of this she gently added a haunting, chromatic chord progression, then brought in counterpoint with her left hand. She played with this for a while, improvising, before moving the ostinato into the lower register and working the counterpoint into her right hand. Several variations later she'd brought the foot pedals back into play. The organ rang in all its magnificent power, and Brenna completely lost herself in the music.

That's when she noticed movement in the mirrors above the organ register. Startled, she stopped, turned, and made eye contact with Queen Tamar.

"Don't stop on account of me," the executrix of the Tamarian Republic said, speaking Lithian with perfect diction and syntactic ease.

"Your Grace!" Brenna exclaimed, bowing her head nervously. She didn't like meeting strangers, and though her family had moved among elite and powerful social circles, Brenna had never met a national leader.

Queen Tamar stood more than six feet tall. Dressed in dark red linen with metallic silver trim, when she moved every stitch of meticulously embroidered fabric draped across her broad shoulders flowed like the rise and ebb of the tide and swished like a gentle wind through evergreen trees. Strands of bright platinum glimmered in coiffured, blonde hair that dangled with perfect curls to the nape of her slender neck. Silver rings adorned with lovely, precious stones graced her earlobes, and silver bangles tinkled prettily on her arms and ankles. Pale-skinned and grey-eyed, the queen somehow looked old and young at the same time.

Tamar could not be mistaken for an ordinary woman, as her demeanor exuded something terrible and fierce that transcended mortal character. The regal figure standing before Brenna mysteriously appeared and led exiles out of Kameron to establish the nation that bore her name. She founded this very city more than 200 years ago, and ruled from it with great nobility and wisdom. Tamaria had never known another leader.

The Long Journey: *Unexpected Visitors*

Brenna felt warm fingers lifting her chin. "You look tired, child," the queen said in Brenna's language. "Your soul troubles you."

"Yes," Brenna replied.

"Yet you are a heroine of the Republic," Tamar stated, "a brave warrior in service to my people."

"It has been my honor," said Brenna, relaxing at the queen's gentle touch.

Tamar moved away slightly. "It has also been your burden. You heal my sons and daughters, though you remain wounded."

Brenna blinked back a tear. She didn't understand how Tamar knew this, but the queen's words rang with truth. "I miss my family," she breathed. "I feel empty inside."

"Your heart is torn because you long for their company, though you have wisely chosen to flee from your home and live as my guest in the High Land. I tell you that your reunion will come, though in times of trouble and at great personal cost. Yet, had you not traveled here, the future of your loved ones would have been bleak.

"While you think yourself despised among my people, you serve to awaken their understanding, to reveal where they must grow. You do not see how a bountiful and beautiful harvest emerges from the seeds you have sown. In this place, though you struggle in your studies, you do so with the expert guidance of a caring friend. Given time, you will know success."

Tamar paused, gliding, it seemed, to Brenna's right. She sat on the organ's bench, her nearness intimate, yet not threatening, then continued speaking as if she were an old friend strangely familiar with every detail of the Lithian maiden's troubled heart.

"You love one of my sons and worry for his safety. Yet you have willingly bound yourself to his warrior's destiny, and your future to his. You fret because he does not share your faith and think yourself unworthy of him, while your heart tells you he is a gift to fill your soul with delight. He, who is utterly captivated by you, sustains noble conduct springing from steadfast love. He has shown you a gentle and selfless spirit that should assuage your doubts. Don't be afraid.

"As for your friend, who wanders the wild land of Northern Kameron, did he not reveal a worthy devotion by releasing your heart to love another? You do not hear the prayers of a lonely woman who longs for him, though she does not yet know his name. He will find the comfort he seeks in the arms of another, as you have done.

The Long Journey: *Unexpected Visitors*

"You remember the terror of battle and forget that your Keeper does not slumber amid the noise and fury. You feel guilty for surviving when others perished, yet your day to die will come, and you overlook the endowment granted by every moment your young, brave heart beats strongly. You hear the voices of the dead in your sleep and think that you should have done more to save them. Yet in their agony and fear you provided them with comfort and hope. They looked to you and faced death with renewed courage."

Tamar's face drew near, her fear-inspiring gaze muted. She gently placed her left hand on Brenna's back and spoke softly. "Why are you downcast, Lady Brenna? You are the hands of the Great God among my people. My words are the answer to your prayers. Play the organ for me now, be comforted and be healed."

*   *   *

Though her eyes overflowed with contempt, Freda Bergen allowed Algernon to enter when he knocked on her front door later that morning. "I didn't expect to see the likes of you again," she said, shutting the door behind him. "Wait here." The elderly, round-faced woman ascended her stairs with surprising ease, given her age, and returned a few moments later.

"She's working on her drawings for the police," Mrs. Bergen announced. "She asked me to send you up. Mind your manners and keep the door open!"

Algernon wiped sweat earned in an exhilarating bicycle ride from his brow and climbed to the second floor. He found an open door on the right-hand side hallway that led into a small bedroom. Astrid lay beneath a down comforter on a four-poster bed. A heap of pillows around her back supported her shoulders and neck and a new sketch pad rested on her raised knee. She looked frail, though her cheeks reflected recovery.

She wore an ill-fitting nightgown that clearly didn't belong to her. Astrid put her drawing down and smiled at Algernon. "How does it feel to be a full priest?" she inquired. "Brother Dmitri told me."

Algernon shook his head. "I didn't come up here to talk about me. I want to hear how you're doing."

The Long Journey: *Unexpected Visitors*

Astrid shrugged. "I'm feeling better," she replied. "I get a little light-headed whenever I stand up to go to the bathroom, but I'm stronger than yesterday."

"That's good! What are you working on?"

The girl handed him her sketchbook. "The police detective delivered it last evening. You can see that I haven't had a lot to do."

Algernon sat on the bed and studied her drawings. Her current, unfinished sketch showed Brenna's face, the hint of a smile lingering on her lips, an expression of pure kindness reflected in her eyes. Yet there was something of an erotic quality to the drawing that inspired Algernon to quickly flip to the first images recorded on the sketch pad.

Astrid had a remarkable ability to recreate a scene with pencil and charcoal, accurately depicting the front of Fang's Fine Clothiers down to the style of dresses worn by the live models in the boutique window displays. On another page she'd drawn him from the back, interacting with the Kamerese sales lady. Her reproduction of the woman's lovely face looked nearly photorealistic.

"Wow!" he remarked. "I didn't realize you were so good at this."

"I remember everything I see," she replied, "and I draw what I remember."

The next page showed the salesman in his expensive suit, drawn in slightly less detail. Algernon pursed his lips, seeing Astrid's preference for female figures and faces manifest in the care of her sketching. Four frames on the following page outlined their journey to the back room, and the drawing technique reversed to negative imagery, where heavy charcoal dominated the scenes. Astrid depicted the interplay between shadow and light with startling skill, carefully showing lines with the absence of a stroke.

She had drawn a pity-inspiring view of unarmed Algernon getting struck in the face with the riding crop. The next image showed the Kamerese merchant recklessly opening Astrid's robe, as if the viewer witnessed this act from her own perspective. Though she did not graphically depict the humiliation of public exposure, she certainly implied the shamefulness of that moment. This picture unsettled and angered Algernon. He knew she'd drawn it to elicit that very response in the police investigator.

Algernon now watched yesterday's drama unfold as Astrid had seen it. She drew him fighting, his limbs a blur and the Kamerese flailing from his punishment. Confusion reigned among the henchmen as their leader fell with a broken neck. One of them raised a gun toward the young priest, holding it with two hands as if steadying the weapon to fire, but the very next image showed the shooter facing the artist and pointing his handgun directly at her. In the scene after this one, Astrid had filled the frame with charcoal.

Algernon stopped, his heart pounding. He stared at Astrid with eyes brimming in horror as Dmitri's words struck home. "He didn't aim for you," the young priest realized. "He wanted to shoot me, and you deliberately stood in his way..."

Astrid nodded, trembling at the memory, and a moment later a tear traced down her cheek. "I didn't know what else to do," she sobbed. "If he killed you, I just knew Kira would be lost forever. I'm not brave like you are. I can't fight like you can. You're my only hope of saving her, Algernon. Nobody else cares about Kira. I couldn't let him kill you."

Her face reddened and her lip quivered. Algernon reached for her and they clasped in a strong embrace. Astrid cried loudly and without shame.

"I've been so wrong about you," he murmured, feeling her shiver as she wept. "I didn't want to understand how you felt about Kira. I thought I knew the truth, and I've been very quick to dismiss anything you've said. I thought you were living a lie. I thought that you were selfish and cowardly, but you've been courageous enough to confront me and force me to think. You were brave enough to stand in front of a bullet that was meant for me. I was wrong about you in every way, Astrid, and I'm sorry. I'm so sorry!"

Just then, Freda Bergen appeared in the doorway. "What is going on here?" she demanded sternly. "Young man, leave her alone and get out of my house! Now!"

Algernon let Astrid go. "It's not what you think," he replied, keeping a tight lid on his irritation. "She saved my life."

Mrs. Bergen put her hands on her hips. "Is that so? What a fool thing to do! Now, get out!" She pointed at the exit with her thumb.

Algernon rose in compliance, glaring at Mrs. Bergen in his uniquely intimidating way, though he carefully restrained the invective poised to leap from his lips. At the bedroom doorway he paused and turned back to Astrid. "I'm not the only one who was wrong," he admitted. "My sister's a fool for leaving you!"

*   *   *

The Long Journey: *Unexpected Visitors*

Snarling dogs lunged against their harnesses, baring teeth in eager anticipation of imminent freedom. Dark figures armed with small caliber rifles scurried into place, guarding exits, checking windows, climbing up the fire escapes to take strategic positions on upstairs doorways and windows. Several more appeared on the building's roof. Civilians lingered in morbid curiosity just beyond the perimeter established by Marvic's police.

Lieutenant Streng and his men were about to pay Fang's Fine Family Clothiers an unexpected visit. At his signal, the armed policemen moved forward. Screams emanated from within the boutique. Police in civilian clothes had quietly evacuated customers from the premises only moments before gunfire erupted within.

Bullets ripped through expensive clothing. Racks of beautiful women's wear toppled, trampled beneath booted feet as the police charged forward. Voices shouting in two languages accompanied the barking dogs and the terrified egress of unarmed citizens beyond the barricades, fleeing from the unfolding drama.

The gunfight, though brief, ended the lives of two young Kamerese men. Once loosed, the drug-sniffing dogs burst into frenzy, tracking all over the garments and barking excitedly. Their handlers took them deep into the building, where the dogs' keen senses revealed long tubes of opium sap hidden within fabric bolts. Weapons, including a small caliber handgun, came to light in the same search, and wedged into the outer wall of the back room one policeman discovered a bullet.

Lieutenant Streng stalked through the mess, disgust frozen on his face. He learned that upstairs, at least fourteen children slaved under the abusive reign of a foreign work supervisor. Between the narcotics, weapons and violations of child labor statutes, he could build a very strong case against the Fang family in court that would ensure long prison sentences, or worse.

The detective ordered his men to seize the company records and check the origin of the recovered guns as well as any fingerprints found upon them. As the day progressed, he learned that every weapon had been stolen. In addition, his experts matched the fingerprints on the handgun to the university records of an AWOL student named Marco Fang. A receipt for southbound train fare, dated the previous afternoon and left on top of an office desk, included charges for transporting an electric car.

The Long Journey: *Unexpected Visitors*

Investigators returning from the train station reported that the vehicle in question appeared on the manifest of a locomotive that departed for the town of Red Claw, along Tamaria's southern border, some twenty hours earlier. Nobody, however, had signed himself onto the passenger list using the Fang surname. Lieutenant Streng immediately ordered an emergency cable to alert every police station along the train's route in an effort to prevent Marco Fang from fleeing back to Kameron.

Moving into the interrogation room, the detective pointed his finger at the beautiful Kamerese woman from the boutique whose haughty eyes glared at his approach. "I will see you and your family hang for all of this!" he threatened.

*   *   *

TAC Vogel shivered in the cold, morning air. Hearing his name, he turned and expressed surprise at the sudden and unexpected appearance of Sergeant Vidders at the Battalion Command breakfast line. "What can I do for you, sergeant?"

The ruddy-faced noncom pursed his lips. "I have bad news, sir. Mister Ravenwood went to sleep last night, and we can't stir him now. The medic thinks he might have a severe concussion and recommends we evacuate him to a hospital."

TAC Vogel paused, thoughtfully. "Thank you, sergeant. Take the platoon out of rotation, put them on the first southbound train and give the men some rest. I will deal with Mister Ravenwood personally."

*   *   *

A dull ache throbbed in Garrick's head as he raised his eyelids. Afternoon daylight poured through the window of a small room. His memory melded images of this place, vague, disconnected and without context, into the strange sensation of displacement.

"Welcome back!"

That familiar voice, deeper than he remembered, seemed out of place. "Algernon?" Garrick called, turning in bed and startled to see his younger brother sitting on a stool nearby. "What are you doing here?"

"Sh!" Algernon pointed to the sleeping figure of Brenna slumped against a pillow on a padded chair in the opposite corner. A pile of books and papers lay at her feet. "The high priest got a message from your commanding officer, informing me as your next of kin that you'd been hurt," he whispered. "High Priest Volker relayed the message to Mrs. Bergen, who told Astrid. Astrid told Lieutenant Streng, who told me when I was at the police station this morning."

"What are you talking about? Where am I?" Garrick found that it hurt to move.

"You're at Liberation Memorial Hospital. Apparently, you picked a fight with some giant who whopped you something fierce, upside the head." Algernon looked at Brenna and spoke to her as if she were awake and able to understand him. "Personally, I thought my brother was smarter than that."

Garrick's mind began to clear. He sat up, feeling woozy, and reached for a glass of water. "So how did Brenna get here?" Garrick inquired.

"When I saw that you'd been beat up, I figured you needed her in a hurry. I went to the university and found her roommate, who in turn, found her. You look a lot better now that she's done her kissy thing on you."

The realization that he'd been hospitalized in the midst of his training dawned upon Garrick's clearing mind. "Oh no!" he rasped. "I'm missing the final exercise! I'm missing the Combat Water Safety Training too!" Garrick tried to raise himself out of bed and felt overwhelming pain pound through his temples.

Algernon stayed him with a firm hand. "I've already lost one sibling," he warned. "I'm in no mood to lose another. You took a bad hit, Garrick, maybe more than one, and you're lucky to be alive. Your life is more important to me than some stupid training thing that you can do later on, when you're feeling better."

Garrick slumped backward and rubbed his forehead. "How long have I been here?"

"About three days," Algernon replied. "You need rest. Brenna says your headache may persist for a while, and we need to watch you carefully."

Disappointment pressed upon Garrick's aching mind. "They're never going to take me now," he murmured. "I've blown my chance for a decent future."

The Long Journey: *Unexpected Visitors*

"What a load of compost!" Algernon retorted. "Nobody keeps you down, brother. You always rise to the top of whatever you do, so stop feeling sorry for yourself and start thinking straight."

Brenna stirred. She said something in her own language that neither Garrick nor Algernon understood, then turned away from the window and settled back to sleep. Garrick looked at her with a longing in his heart that his brother could clearly identify. Though lost in thought for a moment, Garrick willed his way back into conversation with Algernon. "What about Kira?" Garrick inquired. "What did you mean about losing one sibling already? What's happening with her?"

Algernon's expression darkened. "She's disappeared, Garrick. The police thought she might have taken a southbound train with her boyfriend, Marco, but he didn't sign the passenger list. I've been asking around in the opium dens. I checked at *The Bloody Bucket*. People are reluctant to talk, but I've heard rumors that she's been working there. I've also been told to check the flophouses where *strichmadchen* hang out, but when I follow up, she's nowhere to be found."

"Wait a minute," Garrick interrupted, overwhelmed and confused. "If she's got a boyfriend, why is she hanging out with strippers and prostitutes? Why does this Astrid girl think Kira's interested in her?"

"It's complicated," Algernon replied. "I don't really understand it, and I'm disgusted at what I've learned, but the one thing I know for certain is that Astrid loves Kira."

"Of all things!" Garrick exclaimed with a knitted brow. "How did she ever get mixed up with a girl?"

Algernon shook his head. "I don't know the details, I don't want to know the details, and I don't think you do either. Astrid told me that Kira's trouble started at the Temple. Don't get me wrong, brother, it's a holy place and a good home for the devout, but there were a few wicked people there, too.

"Certain adults took a fancy to some of the orphans under their care, and the shame of their illicit behavior created a code of silence. For years, nobody ever said or did anything to stop it. Astrid had been abused like this when she became a teenager, but when she saw the same thing happening to Kira, she intervened."

Garrick's face reddened with anger. He sat up, despite the pounding headache, to vent his rage in a whisper. "I took you two there because it was supposed to be a safe place, and now you're telling me I put you at risk among pedophiles! Whatever happened to holiness in the priesthood? Where's their morality? Exploiting children is sick!"

"Yes, it is. But getting upset about it now doesn't change what happened to Kira, and doesn't help you get better." Algernon paused to let his brother cool down before continuing. "Astrid said she went to the Supreme Council with her story and a lot of accusations flew back and forth. Certain priests and priestesses were quietly defrocked and expelled, but the damage had already been done. Astrid says that some powerful people remain on the Supreme Council who want to pretend the whole issue didn't really exist, and she thinks some of those people were part of the problem."

"So this is an ongoing thing?" Garrick inquired, seething.

"I don't really know because nothing like that ever happened to me," Algernon replied. "Astrid says Kira wanted to expose everyone involved. She started acting openly promiscuous to blow away the smokescreen of shame, and soon afterward, everyone began whispering about Kira spending the night in Astrid's bed. Kira's plan didn't work out as she hoped, but as she came to realize this, her behavior had a kind of momentum that moved her along and the whole thing spiraled out of control. By the time you came back to Marvic, the Supreme Council was ready to kick her out of the Temple."

"I don't get it. If this Astrid girl is part of Kira's problem, then why are you hanging around with her?"

"I warned you; this is complicated! Astrid's a lesbian. Whether she was born that way, or whether her experience at the Temple turned her into one I can't say, but she is what she is, and she loves Kira. I wouldn't have even known Kira disappeared if it weren't for the fact that Astrid came to me, looking for help."

"But you said Kira has a Kamerese boyfriend, and this little slut, Astrid, told me that Kira's developed an opium habit."

"Don't talk about Astrid that way!" Algernon warned, stridently, loud enough to stir Brenna once again. "She's not a bad girl."

Garrick looked puzzled. "Have you taken a shine to her?"

Algernon glanced at Brenna, who drifted peacefully back to sleep, then turned his focus toward Garrick once more. "It's not like that. She saved my life. If it weren't for Astrid, we wouldn't be talking right now." Returning his admiring eyes toward Brenna, Algernon continued. "The same is true of her." Then he sighed, shook his head and stared out of the window. "Who would have thought it? My life has been spared by my siblings' love interests on two separate occasions in less than ten days." He looked back toward Garrick with a serious, almost angry expression. "I would no sooner reject Astrid because she's a lesbian than I would reject Brenna because she's a Lithian.

"As for Kira's boyfriend, you need to understand that her relationship with this Marco character has nothing to do with love. Astrid says that Kira learned how to please men in order to control them, but Marco hooked her on opium so that he could control her."

Garrick leaned back against his pillow, amazed that his little sister acted so much like their mother. "I should have never taken you to the Temple," he muttered. "This is all my fault."

"Not true!" Algernon replied. "Dad would have killed me and Kira for burning the still if you hadn't helped us get away.

"We're all of legal age now. We control our own destinies. Some of the choices we made weren't very wise in retrospect, but we're accountable to no one but ourselves now. You were my age when you smuggled us out of Deception Creek. You did what you thought was best, and I'm telling you that the Temple Elsbireth was a far better environment for me than home ever would have been. I learned how to read and write in four languages. Math, science, philosophy, martial arts and music filled my days for nearly three years. I am defined by my experience there."

Garrick grew frustrated. "Who else knows about all of this? Algernon, the scenario that's coming out of your mouth is making me sick! What are people going to think? What are they going to say? I'm having a hard time accepting your story, and I love you and Kira!"

"That's all I'm asking you to do," Algernon interrupted. "Love me. Love Kira. Don't concern yourself with anyone else, or judge Kira for what she's done. I know the story I'm telling you must seem like a nightmare, and though it's far from over, you don't have to worry about anything. I'm going to look for Kira until I find her, and when I do, I want to bring her back among people who love her. I want her to feel like she's part of a family. I want her to feel like she has a home among us. That's what she needs, more than anything else."

Garrick grasped his brother's hand in resignation. As their strength mingled, he felt the old, familiar and comforting sense of brotherhood envelop his soul. "You've always been so determined to do what is right and create a happy ending!" Garrick said to his younger sibling. "But how are you going to find her?"

The Long Journey: *Unexpected Visitors*

Algernon sat back. "Brace yourself, brother. It gets worse," he warned. "At *The Bloody Bucket* I learned that Kira had been working in a certain back room, dancing privately for wealthy customers to support her drug habit..." Algernon's voice choked off and tears welled in his eyes. "She's no better than a whore, Garrick. I've learned from some of the *strichmadchen* that guys like Marco look for young, confused, exploitable girls." Algernon paused, sniffing. "They get them hooked on opium, then pimp the girls at places like *The Bloody Bucket*."

"But opiates reduce sexual desire," Garrick said, closing his eyes, confused, wanting to deny the truth of his brother's testimony. "How can this be?"

"You're right," Algernon replied, remembering this and other details from the medical book Dmitri had given him. "Astrid told me about that. But when the body comes down from its high and goes into withdrawal, the craving for more drug is intense. Kira will probably do anything for a fix when she's feeling that way."

"Ugh!" Garrick sighed in disgust and suppressed a rising tide of emotion. "My poor little sister! My sweet little sister! Why did she get mixed up and self-destructive like this? Doesn't she know that we love her?" Then, turning back toward his brother, Garrick inquired: "So, even if you find her, she's become an addict. What can we do about that?"

Algernon swallowed hard. He reached for a satchel and pulled out a small vial of aromatic herbs. He handed it to Garrick. "Brenna made this," he said. "She tells me that when taken as a tea, it reduces withdrawal cravings and opens up the bowel."

Garrick smelled the mix, taken aback by a strong scent that made his eyes water. "So you exchange one drug for another?"

"No," Algernon replied. "Brenna promised that this tea won't create dependence, but it will take months for Kira to fully recover. Once she starts drinking it, her body will naturally flush out the narcotic. Now, Brenna warned that the road back to normalcy for Kira will be long and hard, if I can find her, and if she's willing to give up the opium."

Garrick believed in his brother's ability to help Kira recover, knowing that the twins had been emotionally close, but he remained skeptical about the prospect of finding their sister. "Well, she can't have just disappeared! Where else have you been looking?"

"I've been to every cathouse in town," Algernon replied. "I've ridden my bike through the worst neighborhoods in this city and

The Long Journey: *Unexpected Visitors*

interviewed every thief, thug and *strichmadchen* working there. I've heard rumors of Kira, but nothing more. I've gone to all of the opium dens. I visit the morgue every day and stop by the police station twice, once in the morning, once in the evening. Kira isn't anywhere in Marvic, brother. Marco took her away and I'm sure they went to Kameron."

"Kameron?" Garrick inquired, puzzled. "There's a civil war going on down there. The whole country's a disaster. If the guy had any brains, he'd go somewhere safe, like Vengeance, or Burning Tree."

"Brenna laid out the scenario for me," Algernon explained. "She says that the Fang family has a whole network of properties and businesses in Kameron. The social unrest in that country actually makes their illicit dealings easier because the authorities are too busy putting down a rebellion to concern themselves with the narcotics trade. Brenna also told me that there's an active slave market in Kameron. Once this sewer sludge Marco guy has had his fill of Kira, I'll bet he'll sell her."

Anger swelled in Garrick's voice. "Sell our little sister? Sell our flesh and blood? Anyone who mistreats Kira better hope he doesn't fall into my gun sights!" Garrick spat. Yet as he mulled over the situation, a sense of helpless arose in his soul. "There's a full-blown civil war going on down there right now. It's not a safe place for anyone to travel, especially a pretty, drug addicted and vulnerable blonde-haired girl," he stated, deeply troubled over his little sister's predicament.

Algernon shook his head. "I know," he replied. "But I'm leaving on the train to Kameron with Astrid tomorrow. Brenna bought our tickets and told me where I need to go."

Garrick sat up again. "She did what? You're out of your mind, Algernon! Kameron is crawling with murderous criminals and wild-eyed religious zealots who fan hatred into a frenzy. There are full-scale battles going on between well-equipped armies. We've been hearing whispers for weeks that our accelerated training schedule is preparing us to secure the southern border.

Garrick's expression turned grim and he lowered his voice, as if revealing a secret. "All the officer candidates think we're going to occupy the borderlands of Northern Kameron. The army has been looking for multilingual officers because the Kamerese speak two separate dialects. Azgaril and Vatherii live in that region as well, and within the last year or so, a whole population of Lithian refugees has relocated on the border. Brenna's family is among them. I had an interview with a general who thinks I understand Lithian culture because of my relationship with her," he said, pointing at Brenna.

"You just survived one war, and now they want to send you to another?" Algernon replied, disgusted. "We just finished pushing an Azgaril army out of our own territory and now we're going to invade a sovereign nation? That doesn't make sense! Aren't we allies with them, anyway?"

"I understand it completely," Garrick responded. "We'll get sent there to support our alliance with Kameron. If we control the border, we control trade. If we control trade, it supports King Alejo in Kameron City, and whatever forces he can muster that remain loyal to him can focus on putting down the rebellion further south. But if the king loses control of trade, especially of all the grain and textiles that come up the Angry Bear River, he won't have any revenue to suppress the revolt.

"The difference between my going there and your travel arrangements is that when I go, I'll have trained, professional soldiers under my command and enough artillery support to blow Kameron City into oblivion if need be. But you're all alone, unarmed and sworn to poverty, with nothing more than a skinny lesbian girl for a companion. Algernon, think about this!"

"I'm not afraid, Garrick," the young priest replied. "These people are not that smart, and not as strong as everyone thinks. Besides, if I don't go, who will?"

"You'll be on their turf, brother," Garrick warned. Silence reigned for a moment. Then he crumpled forward and breathed a sigh into his hands, an ache in his soul matching the pounding in his head as he desperately tried to imagine a way to recover Kira without sending Algernon to Kameron on his own.

"After the war ended, I thought we'd soon be a family again," he admitted to his little brother. "I pictured us together and united. I had no idea how much trouble Kira had gotten herself into, and now I can't help at all. Poor little thing!"

Garrick looked away with bitterness rising in his soul. "Part of me wants to stop you from leaving, while another part of me wishes I could drop everything and look for her myself!" The young solider paused, resting his hand on Algernon's shoulder. "But I can't go. Maybe when I'm deployed I can help somehow, but at the moment, I have to leave her in your hands. You have to find her. You have to tell her we love her and bring her back home."

The Long Journey: *Unexpected Visitors*

"I will," the young priest replied, rising. "And don't worry about me. I know how to take care of myself. The Fang family isn't smart enough to perceive me as a serious threat, and I doubt they'll be ready to entertain unexpected visitors."

Conversations and Introductions

"She actually talked to you?" Mariel inquired, wide-eyed and incredulous, placing her hand on Brenna's left arm for emphasis.

Brenna smiled and nodded, her eyebrows raised. Then, suppressing a burst of laughter, the Lithian girl put her right hand up to her lips and pulled her textbooks a little bit closer with her left arm. She'd never seen Mariel so excited before. "Not only did she talk to me, she even mentioned you!"

Mariel paused in the midst of the walkway. Other students nudged by, oblivious to the content of a conversation occurring in a language none of them could understand. "No!" she exclaimed in mock denial. "Queen Tamar talked about me?" Then, before Brenna had a chance to respond Mariel added in a serious tone: "What did she say?"

Not wishing to cause any undue attention, Brenna pulled at Mariel's arm and urged her onward. "She said you were a caring friend, and that with your expert help I would be successful in my studies."

Mariel struggled to keep up with Brenna's renewed walking pace. "What? How does she know any of that?"

Brenna shrugged. "She talked to me about things I haven't told anyone else, not you, not even Garrick! It felt like she could look into my mind."

"Ugh! That's a scary thought!"

Brenna glanced at Mariel, and this time she laughed. "I guess that depends on what's in there, huh?"

Mariel feigned offense. "Oh, if only I could be pure, like you!" the Tamarian woman mocked.

Brenna shook her head, walking purposefully toward the College of Natural Sciences, where her midterm ecology test grades had been posted. "It was very strange, Mariel. When she put her hand on my back, I felt like I was a little girl again, snuggled against my mother, listening to her sing an old hymn. I felt like my father was holding me in his strong arms, like he did when I was small. I can't describe it any other way."

"You talked to Queen Tamar, and the experience inspired you to think about your parents?"

"I love my mom and dad," Brenna stated, finding it strange that Mariel would consider her remark unusual. Then, looking away, Brenna

The Long Journey: *Conversations and Introductions*

wrinkled her brow and tightened her lips. "She said I was going to be reunited with them, soon."

A change in Brenna's tone warned Mariel to be careful. She knew far more about this than Brenna, but Mariel hadn't found an opportunity to broach the subject. "That doesn't sound quite as positive," she remarked. "I know you love your family. Why wouldn't it be a perfectly good thing to be with them again?"

Brenna slowed her walking, thinking while she sustained her conversation. "It's hard to explain," she replied. "The whole experience seemed surreal. She looked young, but seemed old and full of wisdom. Some of the things she told me filled my soul with peace, but the way she talked about my family and my future makes me worry that some kind of trouble is brewing. And she also said it was better that I'd chosen to come here, for had I not done so, their future would have been bleak. Those were her words. She spoke about the future with confidence, as if she's in tune with Allfather's counsel."

Mariel's secular world view did not accommodate the active faith of her Lithian friend. Yet even among the most skeptical of her people, none could deny the mysterious longevity of the Tamarian queen. Although various explanations had been proposed during late night discussions among military peers in neighborhood taverns, and in cosmological debates with men and women of equal education and wit, Mariel always found the topic of Queen Tamar's appearance, wisdom and apparent immortality unsettling. Brenna's testimony added to the enigma.

"We've never known another queen in the entire history of the Republic," Mariel stated. "You think she might be a goddess of some kind?" Though curious to learn what Brenna thought, Lieutenant Hougen had a very practical explanation for Tamar's apparent clairvoyance in this instance.

Surprisingly, to Mariel at least, Brenna shook her head. "Don't be silly. Your queen knows there is only one God." Brenna scurried up the stone stairs that led to her destination. "My mother comes from a bloodline in which there has been very little intermarriage. She will outlive me, as will my grandparents, so I have no problem believing that Tamar is a type of being who can live for a long time."

Mariel raced to keep up with her smaller, more agile friend. "Then how can she know what's on your mind, Brenna? How does she

The Long Journey: *Conversations and Introductions*

know so much about me? How do you explain the fact that she can she tell you what's in your future?"

"My sister, Thea, can sometimes see the future in her dreams," Brenna replied. "It's a gift from Allfather, just like my mother can manipulate nature, polymerize water, and I can heal wounds. Maybe Queen Tamar is likewise gifted."

The College of Natural Sciences, a pentagon-shaped building with a metal, pyramidal roof, had five main entrance doors, each one labeled for a separate discipline: zoology, marine biology, ecology, human biology and botany. Brenna pulled on the south-facing brass and oak door leading to the ecology department, stepped into the airlock vestibule, then waited for Mariel enter before moving into the building.

Tile floors and bright, high-ceilinged halls echoed with many footfalls. A crowd of students pressed around a bulletin board, on which the marks for their mid term exams had been posted. Brenna stood at a distance, waiting for the crowd to thin. After most everyone else had moved on and she finally looked at her midterm grades, an expression of disappointment appeared and lingered on her face.

Mariel seemed far more optimistic. "Wow! You've improved your marks by 20% over the past three weeks!" She smiled and placed her arm around Brenna's shoulders, squeezing her in friendly solidarity. "That's impressive!"

Brenna rolled her eyes. "I'm still at the bottom of the class," she replied. "I'm not even passing . . ."

"But you have another four weeks to go, and another 20% improvement will put you well into average territory. It's unreasonable to expect more from yourself, Brenna. Learning a new language takes time and effort."

Brenna turned away from the bulletin board. "This is a beginner's class, Mariel. I'm not really learning anything I don't already understand."

Mariel remained firm. "Be patient, Brenna. You're learning a whole new language, one that differs in grammar and phonemic structure from your own. None of your mother-tongue experience applies, but you've been delightfully quick in acquiring Tamarian.

"On top of that, you haven't been sleeping properly since I first met you. The anxiety and post combat stress you've carried around naturally interferes with learning ability. Yet even without adequate sleep, you're doing remarkably well."

The Long Journey: *Conversations and Introductions*

"For the last three nights I've slept for at least five hours," Brenna replied. "That's normal for me."

Mariel shrugged. "You nap a lot during the day too, but that's not my point. Although you haven't had a nightmare since your meeting with Queen Tamar, before that you were waking up in a sweat or crying out fearfully in your sleep every night. I was beginning to wonder how you could function at all, because your constant stirring kept me awake, and I hadn't felt so tired in my whole life!

"In spite of this, over the past few weeks you've developed a functional understanding of the Tamarian language that's enabled you to hit the 40% mark in a college level course. Eight months ago you hadn't been exposed to a tongue that you can now read with a degree of fluency. That's an astonishing accomplishment, Brenna!"

"Thanks to you," the Lithian girl replied. Brenna reached out to give Mariel a hug. "I've worked hard, but I couldn't have done this without help. I'm grateful that you've been so good to me."

Mariel accepted Brenna's expression of gratitude, then released her. She pushed the airlock door open, thinking that she'd lost objectivity by building a bond of friendship over the chasm of contrasting cultures. Torn by conflicting motives and loyalties, Mariel remained silent about her actual role in Brenna's life, while hoping that her companion suspected nothing. The Tamarian linguist could not cover the truth much longer, as Brenna learned far faster than Mariel initially believed would be the case, and living in close proximity increased the likelihood that the Lithian girl would one day discover, read and understand information not intended for her eyes to see.

"There are rumblings," Mariel began, broaching the long avoided subject once the two of them stepped outside, "that the army is setting up new units for expeditionary service. I may be called back any day."

Brenna suspected, based upon Garrick's accelerated training schedule, that some imminent, important deployment motivated the rush to graduate new officers. A trace of terror crept into her voice as she spoke. "If you have to go, then I'll be left here to flounder in my studies all alone."

"It's not quite that simple," Mariel replied. "You're not the only one who's had a recent conversation with someone important. When Garrick's brother came looking for you the other day, I went down to the base to find out what had happened. I ran into Colonel Weiss, who asked me to see him in his office."

The Long Journey: *Conversations and Introductions*

"Why would he want to talk to you?" Brenna inquired, knowing that Mariel did not fall beneath the colonel's chain of command.

"The meeting was about you," Mariel replied.

Brenna stopped at the bottom of the stairs. "Me? What does he want with me?"

Mariel urged Brenna onward and lowered her voice. "This isn't classified information, but it's not something I want overheard by Kamerese students, who might understand me," she began. Mariel glanced around to ensure no one was listening to her. "You know that part of my job involves reading newspapers and government dispatches in various languages. Even though I'm here with you, I remain on the army's payroll and I have to report my findings to the Intelligence Service. While this is routine, what's going on south of our border is not.

"I can tell you with confidence that Kameron is a mess. It's a big, dysfunctional family of criminals, slave masters and bullies who've been fighting a low-level conflict with each other for decades. They thrust and parry among themselves in shifting alliances and calculated betrayals, but with the Azgaril halted at our border and looking for new lands to conquer, Kameron looks like a prize for the taking. The stakes have risen for everyone."

Brenna nodded. "My family has already experienced Kamerese corruption. This is common knowledge among my people."

"Well then, you'll understand that Kamerese citizens have been oppressed by a system that denies them opportunity. Over the years, the civilian population has swollen into a sea of rage. Since last summer, without your people in the Valley of Shirak to stop the illegal weapons trade, narcotics flow east, and guns flow west without restraint. A new conflict has arisen among warlords who seek to dominate this trade. The lure of easy money draws them in, and the Azgaril are likely complicit in its development.

"Some religious leaders in Kameron have been agitating for land reform and changes to Kamerese law that would grant greater freedom to its citizens. Most of this has been peaceful. There are a few, however, who seek political power and use the pulpit to exert influence on congregations of angry young men, whose growing discontent often swells into violence. Well-armed and organized militias have proliferated. There have been riots and outright rebellion across the country, especially in the heavily populated south, where the conflict I spoke of earlier has blossomed into a full scale civil war."

The Long Journey: *Conversations and Introductions*

"What does all of this have to do with me?" Brenna inquired.

"It has a lot to do with you," Mariel continued. "The war is moving north. Kameron cannot continue to exist without land reform. The drug trade, gunrunning and slave markets will continue unabated unless the root problems are addressed. Property rights law in that country serves the financial interests of wealthy warlords who control huge estates. One of those warlords is your father, Lynden Velez."

Brenna's tone sharpened considerably. "My father is a godly man who attends to the well being of his people! He would never become involved in narcotics, illegal weapons and the slave trade!"

Mariel put her hand on Brenna's shoulder. "I don't know him, and I'm not passing judgment. Apparently, certain members of the Kamerese ruling class believe your father has chosen the wrong side in this conflict."

Brenna felt like knocking Mariel's hand away, but instead, she simply moved backward. "You're my friend, Mariel. What's that supposed to mean?"

"It's not an accusation, Brenna!" the Tamarian woman replied. "You need to hear the whole story! King Alejo in Kameron City is under pressure to preserve the status quo. He's calling for all loyal warlords to unite with the national army and quell the rebellion."

"And you think that my father would join them?" Brenna spat, accusingly.

"No, he hasn't, and that's a problem." Mariel had expected Brenna to be upset about this, but the speed at which the Lithian girl grew angry surprised her. Mariel allowed Brenna some time to process the news while she tried to control the release of information. "King Alejo demands your father's loyalty, but Lord Velez, like many other Lithian land owners who don't have long histories in Kameron, believes in land reform. The problem is that anyone who doesn't fully support the king and his domestic policy is viewed as a traitor."

"That's ridiculous!" Brenna replied. "Treason can only be committed against the people, and if the king of Kameron can't serve his own people, then he is the traitor and should be replaced by someone who will look after them."

Mariel shook her head. "While internal Kamerese politics remain the business of the Kamerese, should their rebellion impact trade Tamaria's economy will suffer. The problems there have been ignored for so long they've led to a huge crisis, and between the two of

The Long Journey: *Conversations and Introductions*

us, I doubt that King Alejo will survive this conflict unless his mutual defense treaty allies come to his rescue."

The dawning of a dreadful understanding rose across Brenna's face. "Tamaria has a mutual defense accord with Kameron," she breathed. "And thus, if Tamaria enters the conflict, your army will be deployed against my father!"

"That's possible, but more likely with than against," Mariel replied. "It depends on how the situation pans out. There are many intrigues over which we have no control. Tamaria treads a fine line in this situation, and the army needs effective leadership. That's why General Braun has been touring the training facilities all across the country, interviewing officer candidates.

"Colonel Weiss told me that General Braun talked to Garrick before they sent him to the hospital. They've made the connection between Garrick, you, and your father, and I suspect Garrick may be selected for operations among Lithian land owners, possibly your own family, for that reason."

Brenna shut her eyes and sighed. "How dreadful! How unfair! How can they rend the loyalties of his heart like that?"

"Tamaria is a sovereign nation, Brenna. In reality, Tamaria does nothing that is not in her own self-interest, and I suspect that the money of powerful, influential investors lies at the root of all this."

Seething, Brenna quickened her pace. "Garrick won't disobey orders. I know he won't," she said. "I can't believe they'd put him in a position where he'd have to betray me!"

Mariel reached for Brenna's shoulder again. "You said that Queen Tamar's touch brought you comfort. You said she told you that your presence here prevents a bleak future for your loved ones. Do you really think she would tell you this, then order her army to destroy your family?"

Brenna stopped, her dark blue eyes searching Mariel's lovely face as if looking for answers there. "She did say that, but she didn't tell me why."

"Then she must know something that we don't," Mariel replied, lying.

Turning back toward the dormitory, Brenna began walking again. She thought for a moment before speaking, and worry crept back into her voice. "If you get called back into service and Garrick gets deployed to Kameron that will leave me here all by myself."

The Long Journey: *Conversations and Introductions*

The moment of truth arrived without further ceremony. "Not exactly. That's why Colonel Weiss wanted to talk to me," Mariel admitted. "General Braun had your file when he met with Colonel Weiss. They've considered the idea of asking you to deploy with the new expeditionary units, should they be called into action, as a liaison between us and the Lithian land owners, particularly your father."

"And betray my own family?" Brenna cried in startled wonder. "Who do they think I am?"

"You misunderstand. This isn't about pitting you against the people you love, Brenna. They're looking for your help. You've lived in both worlds. You understand us better than we understand you and your people."

Brenna's eyes burned with deep emotion. "You speak my language fluently. If they want to understand, then you help them!"

Mariel shook her head in growing frustration. "I'm a linguist, not an analyst. I can tell them what the words say, but I lack the cultural context you've been steeped in from birth. Knowing how the Lithian people will respond to our actions is critical in the careful and wise application of military power. Why are you so opposed to this, Brenna? You're a decorated war heroine. You've proven your loyalty to the cause of peace and freedom. Nobody wants you to betray anyone!"

Clearly, Mariel didn't understand. "My family lives in Kameron because we were forcefully driven out of our homeland," Brenna replied, somewhat impatiently. "The conflict in Kameron is not ours to fight, nor is it yours, yet the Republic of Tamaria is planning to send her army across the border to occupy territory that is not her own, just as the Azgaril did on the Saradon last fall. I fought with noble warriors who stood against the very oppression you're proposing to me. I watched many of them suffer as they died in my arms, and I will remember their names and faces to my grave!"

"Nobody disputes the evil of the Azgaril incursion," Mariel contended, "but there's a fundamental difference between what we've been asked to do by the legitimate government of Kameron in helping maintain order, and what the Azgaril did to us."

Brenna's mind quickly countered that argument. "A semantic one, perhaps, but little more than that. What direct interest does Tamaria have in Kameron, Mariel? Why would Tamaria want me to march with an invading force and occupy lands belonging to my own people? You tell me that King Alejo wants to put down his well-

The Long Journey: *Conversations and Introductions*

deserved rebellion with the aid of Tamarian power, and perhaps my presence among your troops would act as a deterrent to any action my warlord father and his personal army might take to prevent the occupation of his own territory. Wouldn't that be so?"

"You're looking at this the wrong way, Brenna!" Mariel replied. "Your father is a legitimate land holder. He's the type of person we'd be there to protect."

Brenna's eyes burned. "He's a warrior with his own army. He can defend himself! What's really at stake here is that Tamaria can't survive without grain and textiles from Kameron, so it's in Tamaria's interest to keep the borders open and trade flourishing. That means Tamaria would naturally seek to support King Alejo and the status quo. You admitted as much, yet this puts your nation directly at odds with my reform-minded family. It also drives a wedge between me and Garrick. How do you expect me to see this in any other light?"

"You can look at it that way," Mariel admitted. "Or you can consider what outright civil war would do to your family. You know that Lithians are not well understood. You know that some of the Kamerese will view your people as the invaders." She didn't want to remind Brenna that Lynden Velez once commanded troops that tried, unsuccessfully, to repulse the Azgaril invasion of Illithia, and Mariel believed that he would suffer the same fate against the Kamerese. "How will your father's forces defeat the rebels and the Kamerese National Army?"

Brenna bristled as she neared the dormitory stairs. "What are you really trying to say to me, Mariel? Do you expect me to blithely consent to betrayal?"

"Not at all," Mariel reassured her. "General Braun wants you serving in the army again to help prevent your family and other Lithians from being destroyed in the civil war."

Brenna turned away. "What you're saying makes no sense!"

Mariel sighed. "Brenna, please! Your father's personal army is too small to defeat the forces arrayed against him. He lacks advanced weapons, logistical support and the numbers to hold back the tide. Kameron is a nation of millions. Without Tamarian forces on his land, your father stands no chance of defending his territory."

"How do you know all of this?" Brenna asked, her passion rising again as she opened the dormitory door. "Are you a spy? Is your

The Long Journey: *Conversations and Introductions*

friendship a ruse to gain my cooperation? Is someone higher up the chain of command manipulating you? Can I trust you, Mariel?"

The Tamarian woman dropped her jaw in astonishment. "No, I'm not a spy. And it's completely absurd to think I'm being manipulated. Most of what I've said to you can be freely read in the newspaper, and further, my desire to share these things with you comes straight from my heart. I admit that at first, I envied you for so firmly turning Garrick's eye, but since I've come to know you, I've learned to honestly appreciate your character.

"I offer my friendship to you of my own volition, Brenna. I've said all of this to you as a warning because I care about what happens to you and the people you love. If I didn't, I would have remained silent and let your family suffer whatever fate may bring. As to whether or not you can trust me, that's a decision only you can make, but I'm more than a little hurt that you would question my integrity."

Brenna saw the emotion brimming in Mariel's expression and immediately regretted doubting her. The Lithian girl shut her eyes and sighed deeply. "Mariel, I'm sorry!" she said. "I'm upset about this. I've always been sensitive and maybe even irrational when it comes to the well being of my family. I know I shouldn't have been so quick to judge your intentions. Forgive me, my friend. Please!"

Though Mariel smiled and dismissed the need for any apology, she felt exposed and betrayed. Lieutenant Mariel Hougen didn't like lying to anyone, especially a friend who had a sharp wit and a long memory...

*   *   *

One advantage of the Model 17 locomotives involved the use of their electric motors as a regenerative and dynamic brake. In this mode, the steam engines idled while the battery packs received a recharge. Once the batteries were full, all electrical current was dissipated as heat to control the speed of the big locomotive's descent. With the aid of friction brakes, this system prevented gravity from dragging the heavy machines downslope at runaway speed.

The precipitous grade between Marvic and Fallen Moon Lake required Tamarian rail engineers to design and build a series of three spiral tunnels, carved out of the mountainous terrain using compressed air-powered hand and jackleg drills. This tripled the distance between

The Long Journey: *Conversations and Introductions*

Tamaria's capital and the main rail line that followed the Angry Bear River south to Kameron, but reduced the slope by 67%. These tunnels were vaulted with steel support pillars and lined with concrete to ensure smooth airflow, with bypass channels built into the rock to prevent smoke from building up in the tunnel.

"Look up there!" Algernon exclaimed to Astrid. "You can see the entrance to the tunnel we just left!"

Astrid, who'd never been on a train before, had been so excited about the prospect of traveling by rail that she'd not slept well the previous night. Though she'd nearly recovered her strength, soreness persisted in her chest and her right arm seemed a bit stiff. It hurt a little to turn around, so she didn't let her eyes linger on the sight.

Far below, Fallen Moon Lake sparkled like a beautiful, bright blue jewel, its vast breadth stretching endlessly, so it appeared, into the hazy distance. Its bountiful waters supported so many fish that crossing boats were said to slow from the friction of fish schools shoaling near its surface. Glacier gulls–huge, ill-tempered and long-legged predatory birds that stood taller than a man–spread their wings over the lake winds and scanned the waves with sharp eyes in their lonesome hunt for giant pike and catfish.

As a boy, Algernon had fished for salmonids and trout in the narrower, windswept waters of Broken Wing Lake. He'd spent many hours exploring its shoreline for the best fishing spots and knew every sheltered cove and streambed within several miles of his family's farm on Deception Creek. The milieu of his childhood home, dominated by another lake far away, now seemed equally distant and obscure.

Astrid had never eaten any fish other than the relatively tasteless ones that were raised in the Temple's greenhouse aquaculture barrels. The expanse of water she saw reaching toward the eastern horizon inspired realization that her personal world had been a very small one. She felt strangely vulnerable as the train dropped to a rocky bluff that had long ago served as the shoreline of a much larger lake.

The braking sensation ceased as the locomotive engineer applied full steam to power the purring rotaries. Many passengers crowded the economy class car, their collective conversations growing loud enough to drown out the steady growl from the train engines. Amid this din, Algernon shifted uncomfortably in his seat, nervous about posing a question that had long plagued him.

The Long Journey: *Conversations and Introductions*

"I don't want you to take offense to this, Astrid," he said. "I'm asking out of curiosity, that's all."

Astrid's green eyes grew wide. "Oh great!" she replied. "Here it comes!"

"How do you know what I'm going to say?"

"I just do. Go on! Get it over with!"

Algernon took a deep breath. "Ok, just don't get mad at me." He paused, summoning courage. "What is it with you and girls? "What is it about my sister that you find attractive?"

Astrid sighed. "That's a really stupid question."

"No, it isn't!" he retorted. "I don't get it."

She wrinkled her lips, then let out a short, determined breath that whispered from her nostrils. "First of all, why don't you tell me what you find attractive about girls?"

"Now that's a stupid question!" he smirked.

"Well, it's equally stupid to ask it of me. What do you think, Algernon?"

"Would I ask the question if I'd been able to figure this out?" he replied.

"You know, for someone who is supposed to be really smart, you sure have a tough time with something that should be very obvious!"

"What's that supposed to mean, Astrid? What we're talking about here lies beyond the realm of my personal experience."

"No, it isn't!" she insisted. "Everybody knows that you like Marie, and Kira told me all about the shower room episode. I've seen what happens when you look at me while I'm walking."

"That's not the same!" he responded. "You and Marie are girls. I'm supposed to find girls attractive. The indiscriminate nature of my sex drive proves that I'm a normal guy!"

Astrid crossed her arms. "You're wrong. It is the same," she said. "Why do you find Marie so alluring?" She didn't look at him, letting the question linger.

Algernon sighed. "I'm in love with her mind."

Hearing this, Astrid looked directly into Algernon's eyes. "Liar! Just tell the truth, Algernon. She's got beautiful tits and you'd love to fondle them. But unlike you, I've seen them gloriously uncovered, and I don't get why you think my feelings would differ from yours!"

The Long Journey: *Conversations and Introductions*

"Because that wouldn't be normal for you," Algernon replied, embarrassed and simultaneously incredulous at Astrid's audacity. "It goes against nature."

"How can you believe that?" she inquired. "Who are you to decide what is natural? I've seen the way you look at your brother's girlfriend. Is that natural, too?"

Algernon rolled his eyes toward the ceiling. "Of course! Everyone stares at her. She's stunning!"

"Would you leer at her like you do when your brother's around?"

"Don't be ridiculous!"

"So it's something you control?"

"To a point, yes!" he replied. "Relations between men and women are a complex and intricate matter. I know what I want, but I can't just caress any girl who attracts my attention, and you know that!"

"So you can control your response, right? But, can you control the attraction?"

Algernon wrinkled his forehead. "What kind of a question is that?"

"One that illustrates the folly of your reasoning," she responded. "If you can't control the attraction you feel toward your brother's girlfriend, what makes you think I'm any different?"

"You're a girl. That's what's different. You're supposed to find guys attractive!"

"And if I don't, I'm not like you; therefore, I'm not normal? What kind of logic is that, Algernon?"

"All right, if you want logic, we can go there," he offered. "In the natural world, the ultimate purpose of attraction, stimulation and copulation involves reproduction. Among all higher life forms these behaviors lead to offspring. Can you reproduce with another girl?"

Astrid shook her head. "The attraction isn't about reproduction. You don't find Marie or Brenna attractive only because it's possible to have children with them. And in Brenna's case you're dealing with a strong social taboo because she belongs to your brother. So you stifle the expression of your desire, but every time you look at her your heart beats just a little bit faster, doesn't it? You have to look away, or sit down, or do something to cover your obvious arousal. That illustrates that your sex drive has more to do with pleasure than anything else."

The Long Journey: *Conversations and Introductions*

"What nonsense!" he exclaimed, incredulously. "I'm at the peak of my sexual drive! It doesn't take much to arouse me; an erotic phrase, a pleasant memory, a warm summer day, or even you will do! If my sex drive existed only for my own pleasure, why wouldn't I simply throw a girl like Marie or Brenna on a bed and have at her? I'm bigger and stronger than either of them, right? But what kind of horrible world would that be? We only agree to sexual relations if the arrangement is mutually edifying, and ultimately in the best interest of the potential offspring. Both parties have to agree–otherwise we're talking about violence, not sex–and the process of negotiating that consent requires a great deal of care.

"If we had no drive to reproduce, the hassle of getting along with members of the opposite gender would hardly be worth the effort. Nearly every conversation I have with you underscores my point, and neither of us is trying to seduce the other person. It's far easier to get along with guys because sexual attraction doesn't complicate the relationship. Some people are celibate for that reason!"

"But even celibate people like you masturbate," she replied. "What purpose does that serve in the grand scheme of reproduction?"

Algernon blushed. He hated the fact that Astrid could so quickly corner him with his own behavior, but he moderated his anger this time. "You don't understand how a guy's reproductive system works. It's all about quantity. We're like a vast repository of genetic material that's just waiting to be expressed, and the desire we feel to do this is unbelievably urgent. It's like pressure that builds up and simply must be released. That's the main reason why guys want to get married to a woman and start a family with her. I don't go around fantasizing about members of my own gender!" he responded. "I didn't bore a hole into the men's shower room."

Astrid remained unconvinced. "True, but that still doesn't demonstrate that your kind of sex drive is normal and mine is not."

"Yes, it does!" he insisted. "Male creatures that don't become aroused until the female of the species is entering estrus, like elk, provide a perfect example. They don't have sexual relations for any purpose other than reproduction. It's about offspring, not pleasure."

"Many creatures engage in same gender pairing," she replied, dismissively. "I've seen same sex bonding among the macaques around the Temple, and they're closer to our kind than elk."

The Long Journey: *Conversations and Introductions*

"But not long-term pair bonding," Algernon countered. "You also won't ever observe homosexual behavior among the dominant members of the troupe. Their social arrangements are not as complex as ours."

"So you agree that same gender attraction exists in nature, beyond the realm of human beings?"

Algernon shook his head in disbelief. "Think about what you're saying, Astrid. You're claiming that the expression of homosexual activity among non-dominant animal pairs in a herd is an equivalent example to your relationship with my sister. If the dominant animals only select the finest specimens with which to reproduce, in order to generate offspring most likely to survive and pass on their genetic legacy, that leaves only undesirable members of the herd available for same gender pairing. Is that what you believe about yourself?"

Astrid's face reddened in anger and shame. "What a horrible thing to say!"

"Yet that's the implication. Would you feel this way about Kira if you were shaped like Marie and all the good looking guys were always paying attention to you?"

Astrid shook her head, her eyes suddenly damp. "I've always been this way!" she insisted. "I don't find boys attractive, and I don't care what you think!"

For a moment, Algernon held his breath. He felt he could have pushed her on this issue and really driven his point home, but when he saw that he'd touched a nerve within Astrid's soul, the compassion he'd developed for her after the shooting incident compelled him to stop.

"Ok, I'm sorry," he said gently. "We're not going to convince one another." Then he put his hand around her shoulder, leaned over and kissed her forehead.

Astrid stiffened and pulled away. "Leave me alone!" she demanded.

Algernon sighed and retreated to the window. It seemed that he never did anything right in Astrid's eyes.

* * *

Someone had washed Garrick's combat uniform. He found a fresh pair of underwear, a white, cotton tee shirt and clean socks on the dressing table of his tiny hospital room. The young soldier had just

The Long Journey: *Conversations and Introductions*

changed into these clean clothes and had begun lacing his boots when he saw Brenna peek around the corner.

A demure smile spread across her alluring lips, and a look of anticipation rose in her dark blue eyes. For a moment she lingered just beyond the doorway, hesitating. Then as Garrick stood and reached for her, Brenna's smile broadened and she held out her arms to embrace him. The door clicked shut, and for the first time in many weeks, they were alone.

"I've missed you!" he whispered, pulling her soft body close, breathing in the pleasant, feminine scent of her hair and skin. Garrick nuzzled her ear and gently kissed her flesh.

Brenna relaxed in his strong arms and let her head fall back, allowing unfettered access to her neck. "Hmm," she exhaled softly, standing on her toes to reach him, offering herself freely, willingly. He smelled clean. He felt strong. Brenna longed for the closeness of his body against hers, basking in the comforting assurance of his desire. As Garrick pressed against her, carefully controlling the urgency of his own response, she let him circle her neck with little kisses. Then, sensing his nearness, opened her mouth to meet his lips.

The building passion they shared remained measured and restrained, though each time they found themselves alone their physical contact lingered a little bit longer and pushed the boundaries of where their hands were permitted a little further than either had allowed before. Garrick pulled her head to his shoulder, felt her pliant body compress against his abdomen, then ran his left hand down her back, just above her waist and tickled her.

Brenna shrieked and let out an embarrassed laugh. She pulled away and retreated to the chair near the window that had been her resting place on earlier visits, eyeing him in mock suspicion. As the erotic tension dissipated, a comfortable and familiar silence settled upon them. A smile lingered on Brenna's face as she followed his movements with her gaze, admiring the way his fingers manipulated the bootlaces. The curve of his back, muscular shoulders and powerful neck gave way to short cropped hair that had grown in considerably since she last saw him.

Garrick finished tying his boots, then sat on the bed facing the window. He patted a spot next to him and beckoned for her to come near again. "Tell me all about what's happened to you," he urged.

The Long Journey: *Conversations and Introductions*

For nearly an hour they shared their stories. He listened to her outline struggles related to language and study, the intense loneliness, listlessness, despair and spiritual isolation she endured, ending with her remarkable encounter with Queen Tamar.

He related how daunting and overwhelming the Officer's Training Program had been. He described how older candidates helped him work through his academic course load and spoke of the brotherhood that developed among them. With a measure of pride he recalled his platoon's victories, its humiliation on Dysentery Ridge, and the triumph over the giants at Cutthroat Pass that had led to his hospitalization. He explained that a glimpse of her, the touch of her hand and the memory of her comfort sustained his soul whenever he felt like giving up.

She talked about her longing for togetherness, of simply having the time to be in his company. Though much of what she felt about him remained unspoken, she conveyed her affection and commitment by touch, by facial expression and proximity. When Brenna spoke of her friend Mariel, a shift in her tone told Garrick that something had gone wrong between the two women.

"I don't trust her," Garrick replied, shaking his head. "She seems devious, like she's hiding something."

Brenna rested her head against Garrick's right shoulder. "She's always liked you, and sometimes I think she resents me for absorbing so much of your interest. But I think you're judging her a bit harshly. I'm not doing well at school," she admitted. "Without Mariel's help, I'm sure it would be far worse. She wouldn't have worked so hard on my behalf if she didn't genuinely care about me."

Garrick absent-mindedly played with a strand of Brenna's hair, but said nothing.

Brenna curled her left arm around his back and drew him into an embrace with all of her strength. She remained silent for a while, then released him and reached for his hand. "I'm worried about your brother," she admitted. "I sent him to see my family in Kameron in the hope that they can help him find your sister, but Mariel says that the situation down there has become very dangerous."

Garrick rested his cheek on Brenna's head. "I've heard the rumors, and I'm worried too." Then he moved away, lifting Brenna's chin with his left hand, his grey eyes locked onto hers. "My sister Kira is in big trouble, but I can't help her right now. The only one she can

The Long Journey: *Conversations and Introductions*

count on is Algernon. He's the smartest person I know, and if anyone is bright enough to find a way to get her home, he can."

"Your brother attracts the wrong kind of attention from evil people," Brenna said. "Once he's across the border and after he leaves my family, he'll be completely on his own. I don't read your language well enough to understand the newspapers, so I didn't know how far the civil war had spread when I bought his tickets. I thought I was helping, but now I think I've made a big mistake. I'm really sorry, Garrick."

The young soldier sighed, dropping his forehead onto Brenna's shoulder. He felt her fingers run through his hair and linger lightly on his neck. "I was upset about your role in this little drama when he first told me, but I've thought about it a lot since then." Garrick lifted his head to look at Brenna again. "If they hadn't gone by train, my brother is miserly enough that he and Astrid would have ridden their bikes all the way down there. By that time Kira's trail would have grown cold. You've saved them a lot of time and energy.

"I know that on the surface it seems crazy to send my little brother into a war zone, but what else can we do, Brenna? To whom can we turn?" He gazed at her, as if looking for answers within the lines of her face. "We're a broken family. We've always moved from one crisis to the next, and this one is nothing more than a culmination of many that preceded it. I brought my siblings to the Temple to protect them from our parents, but it seems like my brother and sister have carried their childhood baggage with them..."

An expression of frustration arose and lingered on Brenna's countenance. "You hint at this kind of thing all the time, but never come right out and say why you thought bringing them to Marvic was necessary. When are you going to level with me?"

Garrick had long been reluctant to talk about his family, but the confidence Brenna's love inspired within him finally washed away all fear that she might repudiate him for telling her the truth. "Relations between my parents have never been very good," he admitted. "I was born five months after their wedding, so everyone in Deception Creek knows that I was conceived out of wedlock. Grandpa insisted that my parents marry, but aside from an intense physical attraction, my mom and dad have nothing else in common.

"My father never felt worthy of her because she came from a family who owned land and he had nothing. He tried really hard to

The Long Journey: *Conversations and Introductions*

inspire her love, but she dismissed his overtures, his affection, and did everything she could to make him feel miserable. He used to say that if he could turn the farm into a profitable operation, things would go better for us. I think he was trying to please her, trying to make her love him. She does, in her own strange way, but not the way he needs her.

"Another problem is that everyone knows my mother is a loose woman. When she became pregnant with Algernon and Kira, father grew angry and denied they were his children. All of us look like her, so he's never been sure that we are, in fact, his. A few years ago, my dad took me to the apple festival in Sutherlind with a load of fermented cider. While we were gone, mom had a rather obvious affair with a neighbor. We came back with a lot of money, but our whole world fell apart after that. Everyone began whispering, nobody would associate with us, and soon afterward my father began his battle with the bottle."

Brenna's eyes widened as she brought her hand up to cover her open mouth. "That's horrid!" she exclaimed. "I had no idea that your mother . . . ugh! I'd had no clue! Based on what you've hinted at in the past, I thought you'd run away from home because of your father's drinking problem."

"I can pile a mountain of blame on both of them," he continued, "but it all started with my mother. She's a passionate woman. She exudes a sensuality that men find attractive. She uses her love and affection as a way to control the people in her family, most especially my little brother. To offer them comfort, she nursed the twins until they were about five. But she played favorites with Kira, pushing Algernon away whenever he'd done something wrong. Now, he's clever and finds interesting ways to get into trouble, but this became her special way of punishing him, and it happened a lot. In addition to her endless screaming and crying, she'd sit on the rocking chair with her blouse undone, cuddling with Kira while she dumped all of her disapproval on Algernon. She treated him like her personal whipping boy."

"What kind of mother would behave that way?" Brenna inquired softly, looking into the courtyard beyond the window. The story Garrick told her lay so far beyond her own experience that her mind strained against disbelief, yet the picture he painted colored the background of his life in a way that explained why Garrick viewed the world as he did. She realized that his desire to choose a partner with care motivated his restraint toward her, and this elevated the stature of his character in her eyes.

The Long Journey: *Conversations and Introductions*

"Yes it was awful, and this kind of treatment made him very angry. He felt he could never do anything to please her. So now, just about every girl he meets turns into some kind of replacement for the affection our mother withheld from him."

"But his friend, Astrid, told me that Algernon was not interested in her. He apparently loves some girl named Marie at the Temple."

Garrick shook his head. "Astrid won't do. She's too skinny. Besides," he said, pausing as if reluctant to continue, "Astrid ... prefers ... relations with her own gender. She's with Algernon because she says she loves Kira."

Brenna recalled the expression in Astrid's eyes when she'd been brought back from the brink of death, and suddenly she realized the truth of Garrick's testimony. "She looked at me like you do after I'd healed her!"

"Oh no!" Garrick replied, teasingly. "Do I have to worry about losing you to a woman, now?" He then turned on her and started tickling again.

The two of them laughed and tussled on the bed, rolling around in a feigned wrestling match that crumpled the sheets until Garrick managed to pin Brenna's hands against the mattress and lay on top of her. They smiled at one another, suppressing laughter as they paused in their play, until Brenna whispered, "Kiss me!"

Very slowly, Garrick lowered his head, locking his gaze onto hers. He stopped less than a finger width from her mouth and ran the tip of his tongue very lightly across her lip. Brenna giggled and squirmed, wrapped her legs around his waist and twisted her body to the right. She pulled her left hand loose and used it to tickle under his arm until he released her and she managed to push him away.

In the midst of this, however, someone else opened the door. The head nurse, a broad shouldered, gray-haired woman, cleared her throat. When the young couple hurriedly parted from their entanglement and brushed their clothing straight, the old woman raised her eyebrows. "Fully recovered, I see!" she smirked.

"Uh, yes ma'am," Garrick replied. "I was just getting ready to leave."

"It's a hospital, soldier, not a cheap hotel!"

Garrick smoothed the sheets, picked up his backpack and gently guided his very embarrassed girl out of the room. "Yes ma'am. I'm really feeling much better now!"

The Long Journey: *Conversations and Introductions*

The nurse watched the two of them scurry down the hospital corridor, shaking her head as Brenna burst into open laughter again. "Foreign slut!" she muttered.

Garrick and Brenna escaped outside, where warm daylight filtered through a canopy of red maple trees planted on either side of the flagstone entrance walkway. Green lawns and flowers graced the hospital grounds. The scent of freshly mown grass permeated the still air, a welcome change from the antiseptic odor of the hospital ward.

They wandered hand-in-hand toward an arboretum, where a glass-enclosed atrium housed a collection of tropical plants, birds and amphibians. The day felt too pleasant to bother going inside, so Garrick paused on a shady bench and pulled a piece of paper out of his backpack. "Have a look at this," he offered.

Brenna stared at the portrait in astonishment. "That's me!" she exclaimed. "Who drew this?" A subtle quality in the artwork seemed unsettling; there was a longing in Brenna's eyes that didn't belong there.

"Astrid," Garrick replied. "That's how she remembered you. Algernon wouldn't let her give it to the police because he thought it sent them the wrong message. Before leaving this morning, he insisted that I take it."

Brenna sat down, stared at the paper for a moment longer, then returned the drawing to Garrick and crossed her arms. Another couple walking by gave them wide berth, and though Garrick heard the young man direct an epithet at Brenna, knowing she wouldn't approve of the response he really wanted to give, Garrick let the insult go.

"So if Kira was preferred by your mother, why did she get involved with Algernon's friend, Astrid?"

Though he didn't want to dwell on it, Garrick's mind occasionally wrestled with the same question. "I don't think my sister's conduct can be easily explained. Maybe she's acting this way to contrast herself with our mother's bizarre behavior, or perhaps this represents a different manifestation of the strong sensuality common among women from my mother's side of the family. I struggle to make sense of it."

Brenna thought this through. Though Garrick said his sister basked in her mother's obvious favor, Kira must have felt caught up in the strange cycle of acceptance and rejection from a mother whose fickle mercies prevented her children from developing confidence in her love. Perhaps the Ravenwood siblings longed for their mother's affection, not knowing whether she would offer it to them on any given

The Long Journey: *Conversations and Introductions*

day. Brenna shuddered, now understanding the sharp weapon that left its ugly scars on Garrick and his brother.

"Sometimes Mom pitted Kira against dad as a way of wounding him. She always said that Kira would grow up to become a seductress, with power over men. I heard her tell my sister that all men are weak, that we can be exploited and controlled. She boasted that my father would never be certain that a grandchild could trace his or her lineage back to him, but that he would always know that Kira's children were her grandchildren."

Brenna dropped her jaw and her eyes widened in disbelief. She knew that Garrick's pleasure-seeking cousin, Gudrun, came from his mother's side of the family, and well recalled how wickedly that girl had behaved. However, Brenna couldn't understand how a woman would do this to her husband. "My mother would never want to hurt my father!"

The well of deep, painful emotions within Garrick's soul had long run dry. "My mom is not a good woman in many ways," he admitted. "I don't understand how she loves him and why she's stayed with him. They would fight, then head off to the bedroom and make very loud, passionate love. Yet when my father began drinking and turned violent, she stood between his rage and us. She was our shield. Without her, we all would have been terribly abused."

"There's more than one way to abuse a child," Brenna murmured.

"Yes," Garrick agreed, falling silent for a moment. "I thought this would all end one day. I thought we could come together and be a real family for a change. But now my little sister's become an opium whore and run away to a war zone with some hairy, knuckle-dragging Kamerese who probably can't even read a sign, while my rancorous brother has gone to her rescue." Then, as if resigned to the situation, he shook his head. "I'm out of tears. I can't cry anymore."

Brenna felt sorry for Garrick and wished he could know the comfort, encouragement and support offered by a functional family life. She squeezed his hand in solidarity. "Let's go," she said, softly, arising. "Sometimes moving can make you feel better."

Garrick agreed. "I have to get back to the base pretty soon. TAC Vogel wants to talk to me again. I'll walk you up to your dorm."

They strolled through the hospital garden, down a long set of concrete stairs blackened with age and tinted green with moss and algae. At the bottom of the hill, the hospital grounds gave way to well-maintained residential bungalows clustered in semi circles around open

The Long Journey: *Conversations and Introductions*

space. Vegetable gardens, flowers and blossoming fruit trees flourished in the bright daylight. Cobblestone walkways connected the little houses to the neighborhood grocery store, a shoe and garment repair business, a dance studio and a bicycle shop whose marquee read: *Cranky Stefan's Bike Sales and Repairs*. It featured an image of a man pedaling a bicycle, and Brenna realized how far she'd come in comprehending Garrick's language when she smiled at the double meaning of the name.

Children raised their voices in play, boys running hither and thither in pursuit of a kicked ball, girls skipping rope as they chanted rhymes. Women gathered in small groups, drinking tea and talking on their covered porches, their work done for the morning.

A middle-aged man trimming his berry hedge scowled in disapproval as Garrick and Brenna walked by, refusing to honor a respectful greeting. A small, friendly dog wagged its tail and sniffed, then barked happily as the young couple passed its territory.

Garrick broke the long, comfortable silence as if their conversation had not stopped. "How much do you know about the trouble in Kameron?" he asked.

"Mariel told me that she stands a good chance of being recalled soon." Brenna paused, trying to match Garrick's long strides with her own. "I've been waiting for you to tell me that you're going to be deployed in the occupation force."

"Occupation force? Those are strong words, Brenna," he said, gently. "I haven't graduated yet, and I don't know what my orders are going to be, though I suspect I'll be sent south."

"Mariel thinks you're being groomed for operations among my people." She said this in a tone strangely devoid of emotion, as if she struggled to deny the unpleasant reality that the imminent, armed conflict might rend her heart in twain.

Garrick shook his head. "General Braun promised me it wouldn't be adversarial," he assured her. "If I go, my unit will liaise with whomever owns the property, whether it's your father's land, or someone else's. Our work there will entail defensive operations and community support. We're planning to contain the spread of Kameron's civil war and deter an Azgaril invasion, not to conquer territory."

Brenna cast her gaze to the cobbled pavement. "That's basically what Mariel thinks, but war has a strange way of bending the best intentions. Things that we accept as truth at the outset may not be so apparent once the killing begins."

The Long Journey: *Conversations and Introductions*

Brenna's opposition to the expeditionary deployment motivated Garrick to chose his words with great care. "There are no secrets in the army, Brenna. I have no real privacy. Everyone, all the way up the chain of command, knows about you and me. That's why Lieutenant Kohler warned me that being with you would put my career in jeopardy, despite your silver lions and outstanding record.

"It's ironic, however, that he couldn't have been more wrong. You've become the perfect person in exactly the right place at precisely the right time. You've attracted the attention of very important people who now have the power to save your family. Of all the warriors you could have met and loved, you chose me, the youngest soldier ever to have been nominated for officer's training. If I'm selected for service in Kameron, it's because I'm bilingual, and those people in the chain of command whom you've favorably impressed know that I love you.

"My life was a mess before I enlisted. My family rejected me as someone unworthy of their time and attention, and you know the army is my only hope for a decent future. It seems strangely coincidental that I just happen to be the perfect officer candidate, in exactly the right place at precisely the right time. It seems strangely coincidental that my training here and the success I've enjoyed as a platoon leader, creates a destiny for me that blends so harmoniously with yours.

"And you tell me that your God remains in control over the affairs of men, though he allows them free choice. You see problems related to my deployment, yet strangely deny any of your God's influence in this situation. I see how you strive to live in harmony with your understanding of God's will, while every decision that you and I have made has brought us together in the exact place, at precisely the right time. We're here now, preparing for action against forces that can destroy your loved ones. Whatever happens from this point forward depends on what we decide to do next. So what's it going to be? Will you stand against your own beliefs, or will you trust that everything's going to be ok?"

Brenna considered the words Garrick had spoken with wide-eyed wonder. "Sometimes," she replied, "I'm astonished to hear that your faith surpasses mine."

He didn't ridicule her statement, understanding that she intended her remarks as a compliment. "I don't believe in gods, but I believe in you," he said. "I believe you want to uphold truth and goodness. That's one of many things I love about you. But why have you become so cynical about this, Brenna? What happened to that brave and innocent girl who stole my heart in the Tualitin Valley last fall?"

She bit her lower lip. "I've been away from *believers* for too long," she admitted. "All of the violence I've witnessed, all the blood I've shed, the long isolation from my family and the grinding experience of walking in faith all alone has weakened me. I find it hard to stand strong when I don't hear anyone affirming me in their prayers, singing hymns with me, worshiping, sharing and acknowledging God's blessing. I'm worried that if you go to fight in Kameron, I'll have no one left to love when it's all over."

"Then maybe you need to go home," he replied. "Maybe you need to stand with your people in their hour of need. Maybe that's your destiny. Maybe that's what it will take to restore your heart."

*   *   *

Astrid did not speak to Algernon for a long time. The train sped along the sweeping, southeasterly turn of Fallen Moon Lake, past sleepy fishing villages nestled along its glistening beach. As the great lake narrowed toward its outlet, the opposite shore crept closer from the horizon until the patchwork of fertile fields and hedgerows beyond sharpened into focus. Fallen Moon Valley rose gently toward the Angelgate Highlands in the distance. Its verdant landscape, underlain with loess and glacial till, supported some of the most productive agriculture in all of Tamaria.

A cycle of exchanged air moderated the climate of this region. During the day, warm, moist air rising from the Bay of Kameron mingled with cooler, drier air descending from the highland plateaux and glacial scoured ridge lines. As the dry air from the mountains slipped beneath the humid on flow, moisture in the rising, warmer air condensed, resulting in abundant rainfall.

At night, a cool air inversion kept the spreading warmth from Fallen Moon Lake close to the ground, moderating the climate to such an extent that plants from further south thrived at a latitude and altitude whose normal temperature range should have damaged or destroyed them. Apart from this beneficent lake effect, the area would have sustained only a short growing season at the height of summer.

Two and a half hours after leveling out above Fallen Moon Lake, the train climbed westward to avoid the crumbling bluffs at Blind

The Long Journey: *Conversations and Introductions*

Beggar Bay, a shallow gem of bright blue contrasting markedly with the darker, deeper surrounding waters. Leaving the lovely lake behind, the rail line entered a sparsely populated area, passing lonely section houses sheltering isolated rail workers, the only man-made dwellings punctuating otherwise wild scenery. The train slithered among the pine-forested foothills where scattered hunters, loggers and trappers eked their meager living directly from the land, until the tireless machine entered a series of long tunnels cutting through a trio of ridge lines known locally as the Three Orphan Sisters. Beyond these snow-sprinkled peaks lay the big, hingeless arch trestle crossing the gorge over the Lost Maiden River.

The train clattered across this impressive engineering feat about an hour after leaving the lakeshore. Astrid stared past Algernon, out the window. "It looks like we're floating," she said. High above the steep canyon she could see clouds forming far away, somewhere over a rain forest that lay at the foot of the Angelgate Highlands.

Algernon, distracted by his own worries, wasn't paying attention and offered no reply.

On the south side of the Lost Maiden Gorge, the rail line made a hard turn toward the east and reached the western bank of the massive, Angry Bear River a little less than twenty minutes later. Turbulent waters swirled in chalky eddies, frothing in battle against ancient boulders whose hard facets gradually, imperceptibly yielded to the irresistible force of falling water on its restless journey to the sea.

Algernon felt hungry. He knew that the money pouch his brother had given to him contained sixteen sterlings, valuable silver coins struck by the Royal Tamarian Mint. This was more money than he'd ever carried in his life, but Algernon had a strong frugal streak and didn't want to squander his cash buying high-priced food on the train.

However, with at least two hours remaining until their first stop, he thought that offering Astrid something to eat might make her feel better and serve to mend their relationship. "Are you hungry?" he asked.

Astrid nodded, and though she said nothing, a look of hope lingered in her eyes. She followed Algernon to the crowded dining car, where the two of them were shocked to discover that a simple pan bread and lentil soup combination cost a whole quarter sterling!

Algernon bought the expensive meal without audible complaint, fully intending to let Astrid eat all of it herself. They found a clean table

The Long Journey: *Conversations and Introductions*

behind the galley, but neither of them touched the food. "Aren't you going to eat?" he asked.

"Not if you don't," she replied.

"Don't be ridiculous, Astrid, I bought the lunch for you. I'll find a shrine and get something to eat when we arrive in Desperado Falls."

Astrid shook her head. "It's not right for me to have food while you go hungry." She blessed the meal, broke off a piece of pan bread, scooped up a generous portion of lentil soup, then held it up to his mouth. She'd fallen into the habit of feeding him, a task that in Tamaria illustrated compassion and humility.

Algernon accepted the morsel from her fingers, and watched Astrid feed herself while he chewed on the coarse bread. Strong light pouring through the window brought out the vivid green of her eyes. Her narrow nose and small, pouty lips suggested that her family originated in the northern part of the country, where Tamarians and the tall, pale Vatherii clans often mingled.

"What do you know about your family?" Algernon inquired.

Astrid tore off another bit of bread, dipped it, and offered it to Algernon. "Nothing, really," she replied. "My earliest memories come from the Temple. It's always been home to me. Priestess Dorothea told me that giants killed my parents and relatives. An itinerant salesman found me crying all by myself, took pity and brought me to Marvic."

As Algernon chewed, his eyes swept across Astrid's slender face. "My brother says it's dangerous in Kameron. Why didn't you go back to the Temple with Dmitri when you had the chance?"

She stared at the thick, spicy soup. "You and I faced danger in Marvic, too." Astrid lifted her head and paused, misty-eyed. "I know you don't understand. Maybe you can't understand, but I can't let Kira go. She means the world to me."

Algernon nodded, and finished the rest of the meal in silence.

After they washed their hands and returned to their seats, Algernon and Astrid passed the time playing a word game. One of them would come up with an obscure term and a part of speech, then ask the other to combine them in a sentence. The object of the game involved stumping the other player. Algernon thought he'd trump Astrid easily in this contest, but she proved delightfully capable of holding her own.

"Minger," she said, "as a verb."

Algernon groaned. "Let's see ... Gertrude mingered thieves and scoundrels away from the house."

The Long Journey: *Conversations and Introductions*

"That doesn't illustrate the meaning of the word!" Astrid complained.

"Yes, it does!" he argued. "Gertrude is so hideous that even thieves and scoundrels dare not trespass on her property."

"But the word doesn't connote fright," she countered. "Minger means *ugly*, not inspiring fear!"

They bantered back and forth with this until the train crossed a long truss bridge over the Angry Bear River and pulled into Desperado Station, the main switching terminal for rail traffic heading east toward Burning Tree, and south to Red Claw on Tamaria's southern border. Given the political tension in Kameron, most of the trains scheduled for Red Claw carried freight, rather than passengers. From this point onward, the journey southward would be far less comfortable.

Desperado Falls, a town built upon a massive, rocky island in the midst of the Angry Bear River, sustained an unfairly applied reputation that suited its name. The Tamarian government built a criminal reeducation campus there, a place more conservative citizens complained only served to take in illiterate social deviants and turn them into ones who could read, write and effectively use mathematics. While many former inmates left the facility with marketable skills and a new lease on life, a handful of spectacular failures created the perception among many Tamarians that all inhabitants of Desperado Falls teetered on the brink of incorrigible criminality.

Thus, Astrid nervously followed Algernon to a baggage car where they waited among a large group of travelers for their bicycles to be unloaded. Teams of workmen checked each of the wheel-bearing packs while the locomotive took on fuel and water. Moments before the porters brought the bikes out, Algernon felt the weight of his pouch leave his pocket and whirled around just in time to see a small figure flee, weaving through the crowd gathered on the loading platform.

"Stop!" he yelled repeatedly, leaving Astrid, their bikes and backpacks, to pursue the thief.

Although the pickpocket moved with impressive agility, Algernon's longer legs propelled him far faster than the thief could run. He raced out of the train station, downhill along a street that ran toward the waterfront. The young monk could tell from the thief's flowing hair and shapely hips that she was female, from her stature that she was tiny as a child, and from her knowledge of the street layout that he'd most likely not been her first victim.

The Long Journey: *Conversations and Introductions*

When he followed her around a corner near the edge of town, he found himself in an alley lined with garbage cans and populated by a handful of dirty, ill-tempered street dogs. Algernon felt something small and very fast whisk by his head as he struggled to catch his breath, and heard the dangerous growl of canine rage echo across the cobbled pavement.

The girl seemed familiar to the dogs, who ignored her. She backed herself into the alley with a drawn and battered short sword in her left hand. Her right hand held a sling, and another stone already lay in its leather pocket. A grim, angry expression shone on her unusually-proportioned face as she whirled the sling overhead.

"Take it easy, little girl," Algernon warned. "I don't want to hurt you!" He didn't really mean it, but it seemed like the right thing to say.

She didn't reply, but strangely, Algernon heard the articulatory voice in his own head telling him that she was, in fact, older than he, and that if he didn't let her go, she fully intended to kill him and feed his flesh to the hungry dogs.

He smirked, raced forward, dove and rolled toward a garbage can. The thief anticipated his move. Algernon felt a stone smack hard off of his left hip as he reached for the trash bin. Hearing the dogs charge forward, Algernon grabbed the trash can and hurled it toward the thief and offending dogs as hard as he could. Litter flew and dogs scattered, but as the can noisily bounced across the alley, the girl deftly leaped over it, switched her sword into her right hand and slashed at him.

Algernon dropped and rolled to avoid the blow, but another came at him so fast he barely had time to react. The young monk grabbed the trash can's lid by its handle and used it to bash aside a thrust that would have slain him. With a presence of mind developed by years of martial training, he managed to hook his left leg behind his attacker's knee and slide his right leg in front of hers. As the girl swung at his body again, Algernon rolled to the left, smacking her weapon hard with the garbage can lid. He caught both of her legs between his own and twisted his body with all his strength.

This action flipped the lightweight girl to the pavement, where he pinned her weapon arm down with the garbage can lid, and grabbed her throat with his right hand. Her pitiful, unintelligible cry of pain stopped short as his strong hand squeezed her airway. He forced his body over hers, with his right knee holding her frail form down.

The Long Journey: *Conversations and Introductions*

"Your life is in my hands, little girl! Drop the blade! Now!"

A look of surprise–mixed with terror–flashed upon the thief's face, and though he sensed an overwhelming feeling that she'd not expected him to fight with such fury, she didn't let go of her weapon and desperately clawed at his arm with the dirty fingernails of her left hand. One heartbeat later, she felt his weight lift as one of the dogs leaped toward Algernon with slavering jaws open wide, and he turned to honor the threat.

Twisting to the left, Algernon brought the trash can lid up in a perfectly timed bash that crushed the half-wild canine's teeth and knocked it aside. Algernon leaped to his feet, adjusting his grip to hold the girl around the neck with his forearm, and lifted her completely off the ground. He tossed the trash can lid at the next dog and forced the girl's right hand up with his left hand, using her weapon to defend himself.

Though she resisted his command of her sword, Algernon was far bigger and stronger. The girl only managed to irritate him as he lunged forward, skewered an attacking dog in the chest, then slashed right and left to maim and kill the feral creatures. An unwilling blade cut canine flesh, leaving great gashes and gaping holes in its wake, while Algernon snapped bone crushing, left-footed front kicks that shattered jaws and rib cages. The injured yelped and retreated, their cries serving to warn the others that attacking this particular human quickly resulted in pain or death. Growling and snapping, the dogs retreated, disappearing down the street.

Breathing hard from exertion, his spent rage cooling, Algernon gripped the girl's forearm tendon with such force she dropped her sword and he kicked it out of reach. Then he patted her body looking for his pouch and stopped, startled for a moment, when he realized that she had breasts. He found his moneybag tucked beneath the elastic waist of her skirt, and as soon as he regained it, the boy pushed her away with less force than he might have if she'd not been so obviously feminine.

But she came after him again!

Though at this point he didn't really want to hurt her, Algernon felt little patience for someone who'd stolen his money and put his life in danger. He grabbed her right-footed kick in mid air and simply flung her leg aside, expecting that she'd land in a heap. However, her left foot flipped up toward his face in a perfectly executed helicopter kick that very nearly hit him. Algernon ducked and knocked her foot aside, slammed a hard hook punch into her thigh, then stepped back into a fighting stance as the persistent little thief landed awkwardly and slid into a fighting position of her own.

"What is with you?" he snapped. "Do you want me to kill you?"

She stopped, her wide brown eyes staring at the fierce young man. Then, as her badly bruised leg wobbled, she dropped her hands and with a quivering lower lip, sat on the ground and began to cry.

"Grief!" he groaned, relaxing. When she looked at him again, he heard the voice in his head tell her she'd been hurt and was hungry. A *Gottslena* verse flashed into his memory: "Let no one despise a thief who steals to sate his hunger."

Algernon felt no sympathetic regret and warily watched her as he moved from his stance. He picked up her sword and put the garbage can back in place. The girl looked at him and sniffed, but he glared at her. "Stealing from a monk is pretty low!" he muttered, turning to quickly scan the alley with his eyes.

"You have an awfully heavy coin bag for a poor monk!" she retorted, an accusing tone pervading her squeaky voice.

"Oh, so you can talk!" Algernon pointed the blade at her. "And my life is only worth a little silver?" Brenna had also given him a small, crystalline disc that she said would be important in proving his relationship to her, but he said nothing about this to the thief.

The girl crossed her arms, pouting. The tips of her soft, prehensile ears shifted rearward in a catlike display of irritation. In her mysterious, psionic manner, she reminded him that she was hungry. She complained that all she wanted was some food, and that she thought a holy monk wouldn't mind sharing with her.

"You went about it all wrong," he said. "Had you asked me, I would have helped you get something to eat. You might have found me more charitable if you hadn't stolen my money tried to kill me first."

The girl seethed in impotent frustration. She blasted his mind with laments that he'd used excessive force, and how she didn't appreciate being fondled by a pervert. She hoped he would meet a foul end soon, that his demise would be filled with suffering, and that in the end, his body would slowly rot in the hot summer, send up a foul stench and provide food for carrion birds, jackals and maggots. She dreamed that his mother might stumble across his decaying flesh and weep for the rest of her miserable days!

The Long Journey: *Conversations and Introductions*

Algernon lunged for her, grabbed a handful of her dirty hair, placed the blade at her throat and pulled her face nose to nose with his. She could smell the lentil soup on his breath, and he the hunger in hers. "Leave my mother out of this!" he warned. "If you want to hate me, that's fine, but any other thought of my family will be the last your pathetic, decrepit little mind can muster."

And she, reading his thoughts and searching through his memory, felt a powerful terror grip her soul. She realized that the clemency he extended toward her was a fragile restraint at best.

"You're hurting me!" she complained.

Those had been Astrid's words... Algernon dropped the girl and glared at her in deepening suspicion. "What kind of a creature are you?" he wondered aloud.

Though she said nothing, Algernon heard her voice in his mind warning that he could hide no secrets from her. Then, when he looked away, her control over the voice in his head vanished. When he returned his attention to the little thief, he picked up her train of thought without interruption. She wanted her sword back.

Algernon shook his head and looked her over. The girl stood about four feet tall, with matted, greasy blonde hair in spiky strands that draped across an old, moth-eaten cloak. Dressed in a stained, tattered blouse, a ragged skirt and well-worn boots, she looked like she'd been without a bath far too long. Strangely, though her garments could have been collected from a dumpster, she didn't stink. Her face didn't look quite human either, but Algernon couldn't figure out what is was about her that seemed out of place.

He looked away so that she couldn't interfere with his thoughts, strode toward a tall, heavy garbage bin and tossed her sword inside. Then, despite her virulent protests, he began walking away. Just before Algernon reached the street he turned, opened his money pouch and tossed the girl a silver coin. She caught it easily.

"Get yourself some food, a bath and decent clothes! You'd probably look better if you were clean," he said, believing he'd reached the absolute limit of his charity. Hoping to never again lay eyes on the tiny thief, Algernon trotted back toward the train station, not thinking that she might follow.

*   *   *

The Long Journey: *Conversations and Introductions*

"She's not stupid!" Mariel Hougen asserted. "She's already suspicious and it won't be long before she figures out the whole scenario."

Colonel Madeline Vines, an older woman with a stern demeanor and hair turning a lovely silver-grey, served as the highest-ranking female officer in the Tamarian armed forces. Her province consisted of evaluating the social context of planned operations. She was a very difficult woman to please, and as she sat across from Mariel, the officer crossed her arms. "Have you lost sight of our objectives, Dr. Hougen?"

Mariel didn't like Colonel Vines at all, and the two men sitting around a conference table in the stuffy room understood this from the way the two women snarled at one another. General Leo Braun wrinkled his lips and self-consciously wiped his bald head with an irritated hand. Ulrich Stassen, a three star general whose oversight of military intelligence had been critical in Tamaria's success against the Azgaril, stared at Dr. Hougen with a glare that warned even her startling beauty could not hold back his impatience much longer.

"My understanding of the mission remains clear, Colonel Vines!" Mariel retorted, struggling to remain calm. "I've reported my observations in excruciating detail, and you should know that people's motives are difficult to uncover. I've been telling you for better than a month now that Specialist Velez hasn't been sleeping properly, she's an emotional wreck, and I'm warning you that she thinks our operations in Northern Kameron will amount to an invasion of her family's territory. We understand the strategic importance of her father's land, and I'm fully aware of the investment our people have made in the Velez family textile factories, but she simply doesn't see the potential conflict through our world view. How much more matter-of-fact do you want me to be?"

General Stassen tapped the table with a pen. "Dr. Hougen, you claim that despite your best effort to explain the situation on the ground in Northern Kameron, the Velez girl believes we intend to fight against her father's army."

"That is correct," Mariel replied.

"As a veteran, I'm sure she is aware that we outclass her father's forces in numbers, weaponry and logistical support. Do you think she believes we're trying to manipulate her into arranging his surrender?"

Mariel nodded. "She's told me she worries about that."

"So she doesn't understand our intentions."

The Long Journey: *Conversations and Introductions*

"What do you expect her to think, sir? Until we come clean on this, she's operating on the basis of very limited information."

"She doesn't need to know any more than you've already told her!" Colonel Vines replied. "We didn't put you on this case to befriend the girl, or to confuse her, but to secure her cooperation. If she doesn't work with us, we will have no choice but to do the very thing she fears most."

Mariel breathed out an irritated sigh. "She can't be controlled. I know she already reads well enough to understand things not intended for her to see, and it's becoming more difficult to hide what I'm doing from her. One day she'll find my name on the graduate board and figure out that I'm not actually taking any classes, and that will be very difficult to explain. We're living in the same room. We have very little privacy."

"You said it would take her months to comprehend written language," Colonel Vines retorted. "Now you claim that she can figure out you're working for us after only a few weeks of study. Have we overestimated the quality of your judgment?"

"No, I told you. She's bright. How could I have known the depth of her intellect when you first outlined this operation?"

General Braun sighed deeply. "So what do you suggest, Dr. Hougen?"

"I think you should tell her the truth," Mariel replied. "She's more than worthy of our honesty. I've listened to this woman talk about her experience in combat, and I find it hard to believe that all of this secrecy is warranted."

Colonel Vines interjected. "It sounds to me like you've lost your objectivity, Dr. Hougen. It sounds to me like your friendship with this foreigner has adversely impacted your ability to function as a professional in this operation, and I warned you beforehand not to become emotionally involved!"

Lieutenant Hougen bristled, but she held her tongue. "Look in her file, colonel," she replied in a controlled manner that belied the anger she felt at that moment. "Everyone who gets to know this girl loves her, from the lowliest buck private up to the commanding officer at Dead Hand Ridge. The way that you've elected to go about this operation denies her the respect a woman of her caliber deserves."

The Long Journey: *Conversations and Introductions*

"She's a foreigner, lieutenant, a mercenary. Her loyalties can never be fully trusted." Colonel Vines tilted her head to the side and raised her eyebrows. "Do you think otherwise, Dr. Hougen?"

"What I understand," she began in reply, "is that you can trust Brenna Velez to do what is right and good. She won't fail you in that regard. But if you're really interested in using her to accomplish some nefarious end, you will be continually disappointed."

General Stassen interrupted the argument. "That is enough!" he demanded. "We have no evil intent, and it's clear from the content of your report that we must interview this Velez girl personally and secure her cooperation."

Mariel Hougen stood. "How do you intend to do that, sir?"

"By convincing her that working with us will enable her to do what is right and good," he replied.

*   *   *

Later that afternoon, as heat from the day radiated through the walls and into the dorm room, Brenna sat on her bed counting coins. She'd finished her meticulous combing ritual, her long locks woven into a singular braid in order to keep her neck as cool as possible. Dressed in her military parade uniform, Brenna's eyebrows knitted together in a puzzled expression. "Mariel?" she inquired. "Have you been putting money in my bag?"

Mariel shook her head. "Most people accuse their roommates of stealing, Brenna. You've got to be the only one alive who would suggest that someone else is contributing to your fortune, rather than taking away from it."

Brenna ignored Mariel's reply. "Look at this!" she admonished. "There were sixteen coins in this bag when we split the spoils from our battle with the giants. I paid two sterlings for my meal card, a quarter sterling for my dress, half a sterling for my shoes and I've spent the balance of my change on trolley fares. The train tickets cost me two sterlings each, so I should have only nine sterlings in my bag. But I still count sixteen."

Mariel's expression matched Brenna's. "That's strange," she responded. "I've not touched anything that belongs to you." The truth of that statement was reflected in the fact that Brenna was considerably less tidy than Mariel. The Lithian maiden, accustomed to having a

The Long Journey: *Conversations and Introductions*

servant look after her, generally did not pick up after herself. "Are you sure you counted right the first time?"

"Does the Great Eye shine in the summer?" Brenna queried. Her remark, delivered in a slightly sarcastic tone, ended that thread of conversation altogether. She removed a single coin to use in the event that she needed to buy something, tied the drawstring, then dropped the money bag into her drawer. Brenna paused as she walked toward the door. "Aren't you coming?" she asked.

Mariel pretended to be involved in a project. "No," she said. "General Stassen speaks vulgate fluently, and what he has to say to you is best said directly. Besides, I have work to do."

A look of terror crossed Brenna's face. She'd never felt comfortable meeting new people and suddenly experienced utter dread of encountering the Tamarian officer. "He wants to talk to me alone?"

Mariel nodded, and a long silence fell over the tiny room.

"You need to level with me now," Brenna murmured, looking at the floor.

"What do you mean?" Mariel inquired, feigning innocence.

Brenna hated confrontation with people she loved, and a mix of displeasure and sorrow resonated in her voice. "When we met you at Traitor's Pass you weren't there for rest and relaxation, were you? You were waiting for us to arrive."

Upon hearing this, Mariel realized that Brenna had finally unraveled a truth concealed for many weeks. "Yes, I was," she admitted. There was no point to continuing the charade. "I'd been ordered to join you at Deception Creek, but your ferry wasn't running. There was a weird, stalker guy who kept hitting on me at the station, so I took the afternoon train up to Mercenary Ridge and the morning run to Traitor's Pass to avoid him. Since nobody goes to Traitor's Pass unless they have to, I figured it would be a better place to wait. Besides, it's small and the trains don't run from there at night." Mariel paused, fearing Brenna's rightful indignation. "What else do you know about me?" she asked.

Brenna trembled. She walked over to Mariel's desk, moved some papers around and pointed to a tasking order buried beneath other documents and Mariel's diary. "I found this after our conversation this morning. I know the army is paying you to help me."

"You're looking through my papers now?" Mariel asked, more than a little hurt that Brenna had been snooping through her personal effects, when she'd been careful to respect Brenna's privacy, despite

The Long Journey: *Conversations and Introductions*

the Lithian maiden's habit of strewing her belongings all around the room.

"There've been too many things that don't add up, too many coincidences. You're far too well connected around here to be just a student. You've always been successful in clearing a path for me, making arrangements that perfectly suit what I need in every way. After listening to you talk about Kameron this morning, I realized that you hadn't been completely honest with me. I only looked through the things you left in plain sight. I don't know why you couldn't explain the truth to me. I thought we were friends."

Mariel shook her head, avoiding eye contact. "I'm sorry, Brenna. When I took on the job, I didn't expect things to turn out this way."

"Did they hire you to be my friend?" she asked, somewhat sadly.

"No," Mariel replied. "You've earned that right on your own merits."

Brenna felt betrayed, but she put her hand on Mariel's shoulder as a token gesture of forgiveness. "Thank you," she said. "What's General Stassen going to say to me?"

Mariel stood up. "He's going to tell you the truth."

"If that's the case, why have you been lying to me all this time?"

"I wasn't intentionally deceiving you," Mariel replied in a slightly irritated voice. "But I'd been ordered to be discreet and there are a lot of things going on behind the scenes that neither you nor I need to know about. Whether we like it or not, Tamarian forces are going to be deployed in Kameron. There is a lot of money invested in the region, and many wealthy people want to see their investments protected.

"While you and Garrick were fighting the Azgaril last winter, some analyst forwarded a copy of your file to Colonel Vines. She's responsible for evaluating how impending deployments impact the social domain, and after reading about you, she believed that your input would help us direct policy in Kameron with greater sensitivity. She wanted me to withhold information because you're a foreigner and she didn't think you could handle the hard reality of what our nation is facing because of the civil war in Kameron," Mariel admitted. "She doesn't trust you. She doesn't know you."

Brenna felt the familiar sensation inspired by unwarranted mistrust race up her spine and desperately wanted to change the subject. "So, in all honesty, have you been putting money in my bag?"

The Long Journey: *Conversations and Introductions*

Mariel smiled. "No, Brenna. Nobody has been in that bag other than you."

Brenna nodded, then turned wordlessly for the door. Mariel waited, watching through the window for her to leave the building and start down the path to the Dragon's Lair, then went to Brenna's messy drawer and pulled out the moneybag. She dumped its contents on Brenna's bed and to her astonishment, counted sixteen silver sterlings.

*   *   *

"Ten hut!" Sergeant Vidders announced.

The men stood on their feet when Garrick entered the room. A demure, dark-haired woman with a familiar form and face followed him, her blue eyes scanning the assembled crowd nervously to the left and right as they strode forward. Though his presence commanded the men's attention, her appearance distracted them. Reflected light gleamed from the quartet of lion figures pinned to her collar, an enigma to soldiers who had never seen the girl they called *ubermadchen* wearing a dress uniform.

Unaccustomed to such deference, the young officer candidate felt shocked and mildly bemused. His eyes swept over smiling faces, noting nods of approval and murmured greetings from the soldiers who'd marched with him through Hungry Valley and stood with him at Cutthroat Pass. Their clean fatigues, polished boots and shaven faces contrasted with his last memory of them, and likewise, they seemed pleased that his countenance no longer bore evidence of the beating he'd taken during the battle that day.

"You look much better, Mister Ravenwood," Sergeant Vidders remarked, nodding. "Welcome back!"

Garrick climbed the single stair of an elevated platform with Brenna at his side, stood behind a lectern, thanked Sergeant Vidders and asked the men to be seated. "Gentlemen," he began, "when TAC Vogel told me that you'd elected to delay your training until my recovery had been completed I found myself at a loss for what I should say in response. Our record in Hungry Valley testifies to your dedication, talent, hard work and cooperation. I'm proud to lead this team, and want to thank each of you for believing in me."

Replacements for the warriors slain in action against the giants stood around the perimeter in obvious unease. Having had no experience with their very young commander, hearing only rumors of his uncanny combat skill and noting that Garrick hadn't yet qualified as a fully commissioned officer, some of them silently questioned the esteem in which their fellow soldiers held him.

Oblivious to this dynamic and anxious to step back into command, Garrick launched into his prepared remarks. "The focus of our training has shifted away from its traditional emphasis on operations against giants because of changes in the threat environment. We have been selected, among a pool of other units, to train for a mission to stabilize our nation's border with Kameron."

A murmur swept through the assembled men, most of whom had engaged in speculation about a possible deployment for several weeks. Garrick reached toward a weapons rack to the side of the lectern and picked up a small caliber rifle, checked to make certain it was not loaded, then held it aloft for his men to see. "We will work with new weapons and utilize different tactics that will better suit the battle environment we expect to face." He brought the rifle down before continuing. "Each one of you will undertake cultural awareness training and learn selected phrases of the Northern Kamerese and Lithian languages. As part of our mission, we will serve as ambassadors that reflect the good will of our people, and I trust that all of you will approach this aspect of our commission with the same degree of enthusiastic professionalism I have come to expect from every member of this unit."

Garrick let that remark settle in before placing the rifle in its rack, turning around and offering Brenna his hand. "At this time I would like to introduce you to an important member of our team, Specialist Brenna Velez. She will be joining us at the conclusion of our training as part of the medical corps, in addition to her role as civilian liaison when our units deploy."

The shy girl in the autumn-colored dress uniform stood behind the lectern, cleared her throat and nervously scanned the assembled soldiers. Her voice quivered as she spoke, but the men extended her a respectful measure of grace as she addressed them. "I served with the honored men of the Fourth Platoon, Fifth Infantry Division in the Winter Saradon Campaign," she said, repeating a memorized phrase in curiously accented Tamarian. "It will be my honor to serve again with each of you." Then, her task completed, Brenna sat down, feeling hot embarrassment wash over her face.

The Long Journey: *Conversations and Introductions*

Garrick moved back to the lectern, overhearing stray remarks about being nursed by the *ubermadchen*, noting the smiles and suppressed lechery of some of his men. "Look all you like, guys," he said. "She's pretty, but she can fight, and she earned every one of those silver lions you see on her collar!"

* * *

Freight moved at a different, less urgent rhythm. Far fewer employees populated the train, and though the locomotive left Desperado Falls more than an hour late, its engineer maintained a leisurely, fuel-conserving speed that stretched what would have been a three-hour trip on a passenger line into a journey with an arrival time that soon slipped into the deepening twilight of farmland and forest.

Algernon, sitting in a nearly empty rail car, watched the landscape pass by in discomfort. A large bruise developed on his hip, where a stone from the thief's sling had struck him, but he dared not complain about it. Astrid had been less than happy to hear about his recent fight, his testimony confirming in her mind that little had changed with him since his inauguration into the priesthood.

She sat in silence, mostly because she felt tired and simply didn't want to talk anymore. An ache, a loneliness that she tried to ignore, grew within her soul with each passing mile. Astrid felt isolated and very far from home as darkness approached and the locomotive turned eastward–away from the river–and labored up a narrow, heavily forested ridge line known as The Serpent's Tail.

By the time the train climbed through Pit Viper Pass and began its long descent toward the Desolation River, Astrid grew weary and fell asleep. Flanked on the left by a series of cinder cone peaks called Thunder Ridge and The Serpent's Tail on its right, a broad grassland valley opened toward Tamaria's southern border. This area, far beyond the localized and moderating influence of the two large lakes that dominated weather patterns in well settled areas, had a dry, cool climate better suited for ranching than farming. Herds of scrawny, long-horned and wooly ungulates grazed on grasses only beginning to recover from winter's fading influence.

For three hours the train pushed southward. Algernon grew cold as a fog swelled from the Desolation River, and bored as Astrid slept. Part of him secretly wished for the comfort of feeling her body

The Long Journey: *Conversations and Introductions*

lean against his while she slumbered, but he didn't act on his desire. Instead, he reached into his money pouch and pulled out the crystalline disc Brenna had given him. It glimmered in the gloom, catching and reflecting light, revealing an unrecognizable pattern within.

She'd taken this device from the pommel end of her boot knife, held it up to him while speaking in her own language, then put the disc into his hand and warned him not to lose it. "When you get to Red Claw, find a boat named *Haililiah* owned by Lord Kerry Halvord." Algernon had written the name down because he knew he'd be unable to remember the Lithian word, nor how to accurately pronounce it. "Tell him I sent you and give him this disc. After he hears its message, he'll be confident that I sent you and will take you to see my parents."

Aside from Astrid's care and the love of his own sister, Algernon had not benefitted from the kindness of any other female in his experience. Though he longed for Marie, that girl sustained a confusing, conflicting attitude toward him. Marie loved talking to Algernon late at night, confiding the secrets of her soul to him when they managed to find time alone. Yet in mixed company, particularly in the presence of her friends, Marie treated him coldly.

And her selfishness hurt more than he would ever admit. One night, when she'd met him in the belfry, she'd worn nothing more than a thin nightgown. Though he did his best not to stare, though he restrained his desire, she moved close enough for him to touch her and lingered there. He gently laid his hands on her incredibly soft breasts, but she stormed off angrily, refusing to accept his sincere apology, and spreading the news of his misdeed among her friends.

Yet Brenna, though she'd spent very little time with him–and while he fantasized about trying, he didn't dare fondle her–never condemned or repudiated him. She didn't shrink from his defense when the police investigated the incident at Fang's Boutique. When he explained his quest to find Kira in Kameron, Brenna immediately offered aid without condition. The key to establishing a contact network in Kameron lay in his hands, and Brenna Velez had given it to him freely.

"Garrick's always been lucky," Algernon brooded, cursing a fate that condemned him to witness love at a distance, while never experiencing its warmth himself. Algernon hated the concept of celibacy, longing for intimate contact with a willing woman, someone beautiful like Brenna, someone soft like Marie. But he felt unlovable,

The Long Journey: *Conversations and Introductions*

and every time his thoughts drifted toward the girl who stirred his imagination, regret overflowed from the melancholy well of his soul.

By the time the train pulled into Red Claw, a thick fog dominated the dark landscape. Halos of gaslight demarcated the train station, where cold, damp air swallowed all comfort. Because the locomotive pulled freight for this journey, all passengers exited on the track itself and had to walk to their destinations. Algernon and Astrid spent the better part of a frustrating half hour trying to track down the whereabouts of their bicycles before leaving the sprawling train station and heading to the river.

Red Claw could be fully explored in less than an hour by a healthy person on foot. It stood on the western face of a rocky promontory that pushed well into the main channel of the Desolation River, creating a placid bay in its shadow. The town owed its existence to this unique geography. Because it served as the southwestern terminus of the Tamarian National Railway, most of the freight destined for Kameron City that originated in Marvic went through Red Claw, heading further south by barge on the Desolation River.

Three silent canneries rose out of the mist, and all along the quiet bay fishing boats lay still at their moorings. Algernon searched for the *Haililiah* along the docks, experiencing the uncomfortable sensation that he was being watched and followed the whole time. Male voices, speaking a strange, vowel-dominated language, echoed from somewhere across the water. Algernon increased his pace, with Astrid nearly running to keep up, then stopped suddenly and warned Astrid to remain silent with a single finger raised to his lips.

Footfalls approached from the rear, and through the fog a small figure emerged into the ghostly glow of a gaslight. It stopped at the fringe of visual range, waiting.

Algernon groaned. "What are you doing here?" he lamented.

A small, squeaky voice reached out through the gloom. "I'm hungry," she replied.

"I gave you enough money to feed you for a month!" he exclaimed. "Go away!"

Astrid seemed perplexed. "Who is that?" she asked, but as she peered into the mist and made eye contact with the little thief, an answer to that question whispered into her mind. Astrid looked at Algernon with a startled, frightened expression on her face, but he merely shook his head.

The Long Journey: *Conversations and Introductions*

"Don't look at her," he said. "She can't put a thought into your mind unless you look at her."

Astrid, however, couldn't resist. "She's so cute! How can you help but look at her?"

The girl smiled, walked up to the young priestess and gave her a hug. "You're much nicer than he is!"

"Everybody says that," Astrid replied, appreciating the warmth of the girl's body in the cool, damp air. "But he grows on you once you get to know him."

Algernon grew impatient. "What do you want? Why are you following me?"

The girl looked at him and answered with her eyes, spinning a story about being accosted by a bully for the coin Algernon had given her. Though she intended this revelation to inspire sympathy, it didn't work, and a hurt expression evolved on her countenance. Algernon simply ignored her and pushed his bicycle to the end of the pier.

Astrid followed with the little thief at her side. "What's your name?" she asked.

"Jhiran Vell," the girl replied.

The priestess noticed a hint of womanly shape that seemed out of place on someone who could stand as tall as possible and yet not have a single hair touch Astrid's breast. Her artist's eye scanned the delicate, V shape of the girl's jaw, her very narrow nose and eyes that seemed both disproportionately large and spaced further apart than eyes found on a human face. "What are you?" Astrid inquired.

"I'm gwynling," she replied. Then, sadly, she added: "There are very few of my kind left alive."

"Get lost!" Algernon warned, leaning his bike against the pier.

"I can help you find what you're looking for," she claimed. "I know the boat. I know Lord Master Kerry. He's my friend."

Algernon sighed and Astrid looked at him imploringly. She knew he could detect a lie better than she could. "Do you think she's telling the truth?"

He shrugged. "I don't know. I have to look at her to tell, but when I do, she keeps filling my head with so much nonsense I can't think straight!"

Astrid leaned her bike against his and bent down to meet Jhiran eye to eye. "Can you take us there?" she asked.

The Long Journey: *Conversations and Introductions*

Jhiran pleaded with Astrid to help sate her hunger, but Algernon, observing this from the side suddenly grabbed a fistful of the gwynling's hair, thrust his hand into her skirt and produced a Tamarian silver sterling that had been tucked into her belt.

"You stinking little liar!" he spat, pushing Jhiran so hard she nearly fell off the pier.

Astrid was shocked. "Algernon!" she stammered. "Get control of yourself!"

"You hurt me!" Jhiran accused. "You always hurt me! You felt me up, too! That's why nobody likes you! That's why all the girls stay away!"

Algernon hands clenched into fists as he struggled to restrain his rage. Astrid moved in front of him and gently placed her hands on his shoulders. "It's not true," she soothed. "Let it go, Algernon. She doesn't know you." Then, inexplicably, Astrid gently kissed him on the cheek. "Let it go," she repeated, leaning near, her slender body a fragile shield he could have easily discarded, had he chosen to do so.

Relaxing, Algernon stepped back and fingered the coin for a moment. Returning to the bicycles, he picked up Astrid's and wordlessly offered it to her, then turned his own around. He walked toward Jhiran, whose expression of terror shone dramatically in her big, brown eyes. The young monk held the coin out to her. "I gave you a gift, little girl!" he said in that dangerous tone of voice Astrid had heard many times before. "Use it!"

Jhiran slowly took the money from his fingers and slid it back beneath her belt. When he began pushing his bicycle away, she ran forward. "I'll show you where to find the *Haililiah*," Jhiran said. "I'll show you, and we can find some food."

True to her word, Jhiran led Algernon and Astrid through the cool, misty darkness around Red Claw Bay to another dock. Moored in a large slip near the end of the pier they found a refurbished steamer whose crew formed a chain to load crates from an electric truck parked on the dock. Work continued unabated as three visitors approached.

Algernon, who'd grown up on the shores of Broken Wing Lake, recognized the style of steamer as an outdated gunboat that had long plied many waterways. Roughly 100 feet in length, the shallow draft ship had been built for riverine service. Her twin, side mounted paddle wheels enabled her to operate in tight channels and shallow waters that

The Long Journey: *Conversations and Introductions*

would ground a more efficient, screw propeller design. Her twin stacks lay dormant, indicating that she would not be leaving soon.

The name on her bow had been rendered in a script Algernon could not read, so he wanted to make sure that Jhiran had brought him to the right boat. Approaching the crew, he excused himself for troubling them. "I'm looking for the *Haililiah*," he said, speaking Northern Kamerese, but pronouncing the name as a Tamarian would.

Laughter resounded from the men on the dock and deck who'd heard him, a good-natured kind of laugh that indicated he'd not been the first to mispronounce the name. The Lithians paused in their labor, as if listening for more amusement. One of the men, dressed only in breeches, with a sheen of sweat over his muscular torso, responded with a broad smile. "I know her," he said, referring to Jhiran. "But who might you be?"

With no priestly deference extended toward him, the young monk suddenly realized that his feet stood very far from home. "I am Algernon, first priest in the Holy Order of Ravenwood. This is Astrid, my sister in faith and service to the Great God. We're looking for Lord Kerry Halvord."

A sudden silence descended. The sound of a gun bolt sliding back drew Algernon's ear, and glancing at the boat, he saw at least two rifles pointed threateningly in his direction from the shadows beneath the deck awning. Jhiran fearlessly trotted over to the boat and leaped aboard, disappearing into the deckhouse. The crewman moved in front of Algernon to prevent him from following. "What business have you with Lord Halvord?"

Judging from Brenna's description of Lord Halvord's crew, Algernon had not expected such a cold reception. "Have I found the right boat?" he inquired fearlessly, ignoring the question. "I was told to expect Lithian hospitality."

"Who told you that?" the man replied in an unfriendly tone.

"Brenna, eldest daughter of Lynden and Alexina Velez."

A murmur flashed through the assembled men, the rifle barrels dropped down and immediately the expression of the deck hand brightened. "You've seen Lady Brenna? Is she alive? Is she well?" he inquired.

"Yes, on all three counts," Algernon replied. "She said farewell to us in Marvic this morning. I carry a letter for her loved ones."

The Long Journey: *Conversations and Introductions*

"Come aboard," he beckoned, reaching for Algernon's shoulder as if he'd known him for many years. "Tell us all about her!"

All work stopped. A flurry of unfamiliar names, firm handshakes, unfamiliar faces sporting wide smiles, and the sudden need for everyone aboard to touch the two Tamarians wrought an overwhelming sense that they'd stepped into a completely different, unfamiliar world. Confronted with too many names to remember, too many new faces that looked too similar, Algernon resorted to smiling and nodding in as friendly a manner as he could muster. Astrid stood a better chance of sorting the characters out and seemed far more at ease as she blessed the men who welcomed her aboard.

In a narrow passenger cabin that ran down the center of the boat, illuminated in the harsh glare of bright, electric lights, Algernon took a seat and did his best to field questions from the crew. In truth, however, he didn't know very much about his brother's girlfriend and really had no clue of her plans for the future. The crew seemed genuinely disappointed. Every man regarded Brenna with high esteem, as if, like a collective daughter, she belonged to each one of them.

Algernon produced the crystalline disc from his money pouch. "She said there would be a message for Lord Kerry on this," he claimed. "But I don't really know how it's supposed to work."

A flurry of discussion ensued until some junior crew member raced forward and one of the men explained that he'd been sent to bring down the light machine. It could, apparently, read the message encoded on the disc by virtue of some arcane Lithian technology unfamiliar to the northerners.

Jhiran returned, eating a bowl of spicy, fried potato slices, riding the shoulders of a muscular and handsome middle-aged man whose brown hair grew in loose curls on his head. The crew members parted respectfully as he approached. "That's him!" Jhiran said, pointing. In a flash, she twirled off of the man's shoulders and landed on the deck behind him, peering around his right side as if using him as a shield.

"Jhiran says you're looking for me," he said in a rather unfriendly tone. "From what I've heard thus far, you are not a welcome guest on my boat."

"Did the little cutthroat tell you that she tried to kill me?" Algernon inquired.

Lord Kerry's eyes narrowed. "Speak respectfully of my friends, or do not speak at all!" he warned.

The Long Journey: *Conversations and Introductions*

Algernon heard Jhiran's whining in his own head as he locked his gaze onto hers. Then, breaking eye contact, he looked back at the Lithian lord in his brazen and fearless manner. "Do you include Brenna Velez among your friends?"

Astrid drew in a long breath and gently placed her right hand on Algernon's back.

Kerry Halvord's expression changed to one of curiosity. "You know Brenna?"

Algernon produced the crystalline disc. "She gave me this as a message for Lord Kerry Halvord."

"I am he," the man replied, reaching for the object, recognizing it with such familiarity no surprise registered on his face. He used his shirt to wipe off all finger marks.

The crew hand returned, bearing a small box that had what looked like a rectangular piece of clear glass on its top. He handed the device to Lord Kerry, who removed the glass and gently laid the disc into a cut out that matched it perfectly. He then put the prism on top.

By sliding a lever on the side of the box, a blue light came on and shone through the disc. A ghostly, three-dimensional image of Brenna appeared and slowly rotated in the prism. Her voice, uttering words in her native language, emanated from within the image as if she were speaking in person.

Astrid gasped, her attention riveted, while Algernon immediately turned his head away. "Don't look!" he rasped in Tamarian, keeping his voice in a low whisper. "She's my brother's girl!"

Astrid could not resist, especially since everyone else's eyes remained fixed on Brenna's hologram. "Wow," Astrid whispered. "That outfit doesn't leave much to the imagination!" Then, a minute later, she turned Algernon around. "Look! It's you!"

Algernon's face momentarily appeared in the hologram, then the image stopped rotating and winked off, its message delivered.

Lord Kerry Halvord removed the prism and returned the disc to Algernon. "For Brenna's sake, I offer my service," he said in a serious tone. "You, however, have a relationship to mend with Jhiran. I leave that task in your hands." Then, he turned toward his foreman, gave orders in the Lithian language for several moments, then tilted his head in Algernon's direction. After this, Lord Kerry accepted Astrid's blessing, patted Algernon on the shoulder and bade them both a good night.

The Long Journey: *Conversations and Introductions*

The foreman, whose name Algernon remembered as Waldemar, invited the two Tamarians to visit the galley for some food and drink. When Algernon offered to help with the loading, Waldemar shook his head. "Guests of Lord Kerry do not work on his boat. Miss Jhiran will show you the way. We leave in the morning, as soon as the fog lifts. Do not be late, or we will leave you behind!"

Jhiran led them below deck and aft, toward the galley. There, a wiry, dark-skinned cook prepared a vegetable stir-fry with eggs and offered them a glass of wine. Algernon, who did not drink, asked for plain water instead, but Jhiran and Astrid each enjoyed a cup with their meal. The gwynling ate ravenously, as if she didn't expect to eat again for a very long time, while the Tamarians waited for their food to cool down. Their habit of feeding one another using their fingers drew a disapproving stare from the cook.

Algernon and Astrid left the boat after dinner with Jhiran in tow. They found an inn near the waterfront and arranged to sleep for free in the common area according to Tamarian custom. Algernon laid out his bedroll beside the hearth and fixed a place for Astrid to rest nearby, then read through Dmitri's medical textbook while she and Jhiran disappeared into the washroom.

Algernon, weary from a long day of travel, tired of conversation and introductions, lay on his bedroll with his money pouch securely hidden beneath his pillow. He fell asleep quickly, and dreamed unpleasantly of Marie.

Mirrors

Silent, swirling mist obscured the main street, its buildings veiled in amorphous grey that softened lines and swallowed shadows. Diffuse color, devoid of its daylight vividness, blended leaf and branch into dim singularities drifting into, then receding from view as riverine fog rose through gaps in the bluff overlooking the sleeping town.

Algernon paused from his early morning run, panting at the crest of a hill. Running had to rank as one of his least favorite activities, but he'd reasoned that many hours of passive travel, by rail or on a boat, would take the edge off of his fitness if he didn't strive to maintain strength and endurance. A sense of foreboding gripped him as he looked into the featureless, slate-colored fog obscuring the Desolation River. He thought he heard the whisper of wings in the air, but he saw no stirring in the veiled sky.

Kameron lay on the river's far bank. Somewhere, beyond the mist, he almost felt the heart of his twin sister beating, yet he worried that she would be less than pleased to see him when he finally found her. Marco Fang could not have lured Kira so far from home without her consent, and though he loved his sister, Algernon secretly knew in his heart that Marie aroused stronger, more urgent feelings. Maybe Kira felt the same way about Marco. He spat at the thought and let his mind drift toward Marie.

Thinking about his love interest aroused unwelcome desire. Algernon trotted down the hillside, following a path through the tall, green grass and tightly closed wildflower blossoms until he reached a rock-strewn shoreline where clean water gently rustled over polished gravel. A high wall of nearly pure iron, heavily oxidized into flaky, orange-colored palisades, loomed to his right. These cliffs looked like the scratching post of some giant cat, and streams coursing through their alluvial piles carried rusty, mineral-laden runoff into the Desolation River.

Moving westward along the river channel, he found a copse of oak trees whose roots lay exposed by recent flooding that had washed away part of the bank. Behind the trees he found a grassy area where only the cooing of mourning doves broke the daybreak silence.

He stretched for several minutes, concentrating on the task until he'd cleared his mind of all other thoughts. Soon, the sound of his own

The Long Journey: *Mirrors*

breathing and the comforting sensation of muscles beginning to relax wrought a sense of well-being and strength to his young, strong body.

Although the morning air felt cool against his flesh, Algernon's acetic lifestyle inured him somewhat against discomfort. Pulling a bar of soap out of his pocket, he stripped and walked into the river with sandals on to protect his feet against the rocks. He gasped as his thighs and abdomen sank into the cold water, wishing for a moment that he could bathe in the hot spring on Superstition Mesa, the place he now considered home.

When he finished, Algernon turned back toward the shore, intending to retrieve his garments and wash them as well. He stopped, made eye contact with Jhiran and sank back into the cold water. "How long have you been watching me?" he asked.

"Long enough," she replied, her lack of innocence an indication that she'd seen more of him than he really wished had been the case. The gwynling sat in the grass, snacking on a handful of berries. Her hands showed bluish-colored stains, and her mouth looked like she'd eaten a lot of fruit a little too quickly. She stood, picked up his money pouch, dumped its contents on the shore, then looked carefully inside before discarding the small, leather bag on top of the strewn coins.

"Why are you stalking me?" he demanded, exasperation rising in his voice. Having nearly killed her the day before, he didn't understand why she would purposefully seek him out. Alone, pitted against someone stronger, faster and far more aggressive, didn't she realize that he could easily tear her apart? He didn't really want to hurt the gwynling, but she couldn't have known that. Or, was she reading his mind at the moment? "Why can't you just leave me alone?"

She locked into his gaze and filled his mind with indiscreet chatter about his unrequited desire for Marie, seamlessly weaving in unspoken and lurid details about Astrid feeling the same way. Jhiran wondered why two people who held such fascination for the shapely Marie were bothering to look for Kira, who probably didn't want either of them to interfere with her new life anyway.

That line of thinking touched a tender nerve, revealing Algernon's most compelling worry. The young monk waded backwards, further into the river, dangerously near the swift current of its main channel. He covered his ears with his hands. "Leave me alone!" he shouted, his words echoing across the water.

The Long Journey: *Mirrors*

Jhiran splashed into the shallows, a curiously blank expression on her strange, little face. She seemed to think nothing of getting her boots and skirt wet.

Algernon stumbled in surprise, wary of the river's pull.

"You tried to kill me. Now you back away? Why are you afraid, holy man?"

Algernon didn't answer.

"I know you're afraid," she stated, stepping toward him. "You're afraid and that's why you're angry. I hear pain within your heart. What do you fear, holy man?"

"I don't know what you're talking about!" he replied. "Go away!"

Again, Jhiran filled his mind with the hidden worry that Kira would reject him. Her voice in his own head brought forth memories of Marie's inconsistent conduct, her public disdain, her obvious revulsion reflected in an expression of disgust when she pushed him away and stalked off to spread the tale of his misdeed among her friends. Jhiran reminded him that Astrid would neither return his affection, nor ever reflect his carefully concealed feelings of desire. Jhiran also knew about Algernon's mother. Her whispered thoughts revealed his every secret. "You know!" she said aloud in a childlike, matter-of-fact manner. "And I know, too! You can hide nothing from me, holy man."

"What do you want? Why are you following me? I warned you not to even think about my family!" Algernon felt the familiar rush of rage pumping through his flesh. He strode toward her, malevolence rising within his mind. His hands hardened in readiness for violence.

A look of terror flashed onto Jhiran's face. She turned with astounding alacrity and scrambled up a tall rock in the midst of the stream. At its summit, the gwynling raised her arms high and as her cloak fluttered behind, Algernon saw a pair of thin, jointed limbs stretch out like extra arms behind Jhiran's blouse. A strong membrane resembling the flesh between a thumb and forefinger unfurled, revealing wings! They'd been folded on her back, hidden from view by her cloak and explained how she'd moved around so quickly and silently.

Jhiran dove across the water, where her wings gave her just enough lift to keep her small body above the river's surface. She glided in an arc, turning toward the shore, until her form vanished in the fog.

Algernon heard a splash far away and struggled to restrain the rapid pounding of his heart. The gwynling could not fly very well because of her size, yet this unexpected skill served her well in making a quick escape. She could read his thoughts, understand his worry and put her own words into his head. But was she right about Kira, or were those ideas only a reflection of his own concern?

Shivering, partly from the cold, partly from his peculiar encounter with Jhiran, Algernon decided against washing his clothes. He dressed quickly, picked up Brenna's crystal disc and his money bag, counting and reinserting all the coins Jhiran had scattered among the rocks. Knowing that he'd spent money already, Algernon felt baffled to discover that sixteen sterlings still remained in his collection. Uneasily, he trotted back toward the inn. Cool air and the paranormality of his moneybag inspired jitters. The smell of wood smoke pressed close to the ground, indicating that the innkeeper had another fire going to take the morning chill out of the common room.

Astrid sat near the wood stove, attacking the short locks of her damp hair with a comb. The hint of a smile elevated each corner of her lips as Algernon walked in and she followed him with her gaze. "Have you seen Jhiran?" she inquired.

He nodded, though he didn't really want to explain. "She can fly," he told her.

"I figured. I saw her wings last night when we were getting cleaned up," Astrid explained. "I wanted to tell you, but you'd fallen asleep and were gone this morning when I woke up. Is she around?"

Algernon shook his head, moving near the warm stove. "No. The little thief dumped my moneybag on the riverbank. I think she's added a few coins because all of a sudden I've got sixteen sterlings again. She took off afterwards and I didn't talk to her." Though he'd taken a sacred vow to tell the truth, Algernon lied to conceal the details of his encounter with her.

Astrid returned to her combing. "It's strange that a thief would do such a thing, don't you think?"

Algernon turned his back to the fire, avoiding the view through the top of Astrid's blouse that bagged when she bent over, revealing more flesh than she intended for him to see, and more than he had a right to gaze upon. "What do you mean?" he asked.

"I talked to her for quite awhile last night. If you ask her what she's doing tomorrow, she can't tell you. If you ask her where she's going, she doesn't know. If you ask her why she's hanging around with us, she can't come up with a reason. But if you talk to her about what's happened in the past, she can remember in vivid detail. If you talk to her about things that are going on right now, she can be very engaging."

"Maybe she's just not very bright," Algernon scoffed. "I gave her a sterling for food and some clothes, but she stayed in those filthy, ratty rags of hers and always complains about feeling hungry."

Astrid tied her bedroll into the handmade, wooden frame of her backpack. "Where is she going to find anything to wear that will fit her? Not only is she tiny, she's the only person I've known to have wings. And if she's that different from us physically, maybe she thinks differently too. She can easily connect our thoughts and project them into the future, but doesn't seem to do that with her own."

Algernon helped Astrid to her feet. He lifted her backpack and waited for her to get into it, then reached for his own. "You have to be careful what you think around her," he said. "Sometimes she draws conclusions without understanding the entire situation."

The young priestess nodded. "It's like she can only respond to what you're thinking right now," Astrid replied. "She can't analyze anything, strikes no balance between competing ideas, and has no grasp of complex feelings. She blurted out to me that you think Kira doesn't want us to find her, then asked me why we we'd come all this way to look for someone who wants to be left alone."

Algernon seethed. "That little ferret-faced, button-eyed, microencephalon! My thoughts are none of her business!"

Astrid touched Algernon's forearm and let her fingers linger there. Her face revealed a sorrow that pained Algernon's heart to see. "It probably doesn't help to say this, but I'm very afraid that Kira will not want to see us, and that she won't want to come home," the young priestess murmured. "When Kira left the Temple, you weren't the only one she abandoned. I don't know how we're going to persuade her to come back." Astrid's eyes welled with tears, but she fought the feeling, and Algernon made no move to comfort her.

They retrieved their bicycles and walked out into the morning mist together. Algernon noticed that Astrid seemed unusually quiet as he led her to a simple, wood-framed shrine overlooking the water. He'd scouted the place earlier, during his morning run. On its altar, covered by a screen enclosure to keep insects out, they found jars of preserved fruit–including a bowl of berries that looked mostly eaten already–and a tin of smoked salmon. Using hands and fingers, they ate their fill of applesauce, peaches, pears and fish. After washing, they rinsed the jars

The Long Journey: *Mirrors*

and placed them behind the altar so that whoever had donated the fruit could pick them up again. A strong prohibition against stealing from a shrine ensured that only the poorest of Tamaria's citizens, who were given the privilege by long-standing custom, took food from the altar.

A nearby spring provided cold water for washing and a drink made brief because of the strong, unpleasant odor and flavor of iron bacteria that thrived in the local water. As the town awakened and businesses opened for the day, the young couple strolled among its citizens, offering their blessings and prayers to whomever they encountered. They had to stop at the Kamerese Customs Agency and register to enter that country, but ended up waiting outside for quite some time before it opened. When Algernon saw movement through the window, he began knocking persistently.

The clerk, a mean-looking woman who donned a perpetual scowl, expressed irritation as she opened her door for the young people. "Don't know why you're in such a hurry. I wouldn't be so quick to head south these days," she complained.

Algernon wrote his name in the register, then stopped as an idea struck him. "Does this register record everyone who enters Kameron from Red Claw?"

She stared, as if that had been the stupidest question she'd ever heard, then realized the monk remained dead serious. "You don't get a visa without it."

Hurriedly, Algernon scanned back through the ledger holding his breath in anticipation. He found "Averil"–his mother's maiden name–on the previous page. Right next it he saw Marco and Kira's first names, and recognized his sister's writing. Now he knew why the police hadn't found them! Why hadn't he thought to check the train records under "Averil?" Algernon groaned and cursed his folly. The date showed that Kira had stood in this office less than a week before, and the registry recorded her entry into Kameron on a vessel named *Beulah*, bound for Fair Haven Fortress on the Tualitin River.

Astrid saw this as well. She bit her lower lip and a hopeful expression danced in her eyes. After all the fruitless searching, they'd found Kira's trail again!

Algernon signed for his traveling visa and waited for Astrid to do the same. He felt restless, anxious to cross the Desolation River and search with renewed vigor before Kira's trail vanished like the rising mist. At that moment, however, the boy also felt a sense of uncertainty and vulnerability that he hadn't experienced in a long time.

As Algernon followed Astrid down the path that led toward the bay, he heard the rapid patter of footfalls approaching from behind, and already knew the sound of those feet. The young monk turned and let out a sigh as Jhiran reappeared out of the mist.

"Holy man, are you going to be nice to me now?" she asked.

"Stay out of my head, little girl!" he warned. "I'll be as nice as I can as long as you don't steal from me, try to kill me, or whisper into my head about my family."

Jhiran fell silent. Her lower lip pushed outward and her brows arched with sadness. "I let you be you," she said. "Why won't you let me be me?"

Astrid joined the conversation. "Come on, Jhiran. Just do what he says and he won't hurt you. There's good in him if you look for it."

Suddenly, strangely, the gwynling smiled. She looked rather adorable when she smiled, even with the berry stains smeared around her lips. "Ok," she replied, and quickly her smile vanished. "But promise you won't hurt me, like you promised you wouldn't hurt her!" Jhiran pointed at Astrid.

"Do as I ask and you'll be safe with me," Algernon stated, his heart softening.

Jhiran smiled, ran toward him and leapt into Algernon's stunned embrace. "I knew you were good, holy man!" she exclaimed. "I could tell, and I knew you would like me!"

Had she been the weight of a comparably-sized human being, she would have knocked him off the path. Algernon, though surprised, held onto his balance and carefully put the gwynling back down. She felt very light and fragile. "Ok, but that's enough now. You need to stay out of my personal space."

Jhiran looked bewildered as she backed away from him, toward Astrid. Her expressive eyes widened. "What's wrong? I thought you liked me. I thought you'd like being hugged. You need love, holy man. Don't you want Marie to hug you?"

"Yes, I need love and like being hugged, but you're not Marie," he replied.

Astrid giggled and poked him in the side. "There are no secrets with Jhiran!" she teased, accepting an embrace from the gwynling and smiling contentedly.

The Long Journey: *Mirrors*

Jhiran jumped down from Astrid's arms and darted along the path, leading their way back to the *Haililiah*. In the daylight, Algernon noticed that the boat had a three inch gun mounted on her bow deck, smaller guns on either side of the ship, and a four inch twin turret on elevated platform behind the pilot house. No smoke visibly billowed from the boat's two stacks, but the scent of burning wood and the presence of electric light in the pilot house revealed that the efficient, gasifying boiler in her hull lay at idle, awaiting its work. An armed guard stood beneath the boat's awning, but Jhiran ignored him as she hopped aboard, calling for Lord Kerry like an excited child.

Astrid had no experience with boats and deep water. She felt far less confident about leaving the dock, now that she could actually see the surrounding water, but the guard put his rifle aside and came to her aid. He then helped Algernon load the bikes on board and told the young monk where to store them in the ships hold, below.

"The second door aft will take you where you need to go."

Algernon thanked him, then led Astrid toward the stern. A broad staircase, illuminated by electric light, led to the shallow hold. There, Algernon saw crates stamped with the word *fragile* and caught a glimpse of a Tamarian customs document written in two languages that stated the shipment consisted of lenses and mirrors.

He thought nothing of this, but suddenly a shadow appeared in the doorway and Waldemar, the muscular foreman he'd met the night before, scurried downstairs. "You need to leave this area now," he said. "There is nothing here for you to see."

Wordlessly, Algernon and Astrid complied. They passed the very same guard who'd told them where to put their bikes, only this time, he'd leveled the rifle in their direction until Waldemar shut off the light and latched the door.

"Tell no one what you have seen," the foreman warned. "Do you understand?"

Algernon nodded, wondering if the crates had been properly labeled. Were they taking passage with smugglers or gun runners? Such a possibility seemed strange, given that Brenna had recommended this boat by name and spoke highly of its crew. She, of all the people he'd met in his life, qualified for sainthood as far as he was concerned. Why would Brenna befriend a band of border thieves?

Because the Desolation River presented many navigational hazards, the *Haililiah* could not leave Red Claw until visibility improved.

The Long Journey: *Mirrors*

The crew seemed anxious, but whether this stemmed from nervousness concerning their clandestine cargo, or the obvious fact that their destination at the nexus of the Tualitin River lay eight hours away Algernon could not ascertain. He and Astrid remained in the passengers' galley, passing time by solving impromptu word puzzles, asking and answering riddles, and playing number games. Jhiran, ever hungry, ate what seemed like an endless supply of sliced, fried potatoes and tartar sauce. She sipped daintily at a cup of juice, never making much progress in finishing it off, then left it for Astrid to consume.

Finally, as the Daystar burned through the low clouds at midmorning, the low frequency vibration of paddle wheel drive machinery rumbled through the hull. *Haililiah* backed out of her slip and gently maneuvered out of the bay, turning at a steep angle across the Desolation's powerful, main channel to the deepest water near the far bank.

The Desolation River, originating in Broken Wing Lake, did not carry as heavy a silt load as the much larger Angry Bear River that it drained into, even though the more massive waterway arose from a far deeper lake. Both rivers ran swiftly throughout the year. At its downstream junction with the Angry Bear, waters from these two rivers remained very distinct for two or three miles, forming a visible dividing line until the greater volume of the cream-colored Angry Bear eventually diluted the Desolation's clearer contribution.

In the spring, with runoff at or near its peak, the Desolation frequently shifted in her bed, creating new gravel bars, dragging drowned trees just beneath the surface, or depositing alluvium wherever the valley broadened and the water slowed. At the mouths of its many tributaries, sand deltas created shallow places where a heavily-laden river boat might become snagged. In general, streams draining from the Tamarian highlands tended to carry more silt than those draining from the mountains further south, so the pilot had to watch the river carefully to ensure that *Haililiah* moved through the water safely.

Lord Halvord did not pilot the boat, but constantly moved from one area to another, supervising the comfort of his three passengers, checking the paddle wheels, stopping in on the boiler and steam engine crew, visiting the galley and finally the pilot house. Although the morning air felt cool to Algernon, the Lithian captain wore a thin, button down shirt, short pants and rubber-soled deck shoes that seemed the standard attire for every Lithian onboard.

The Long Journey: *Mirrors*

The boat carried no women other than Astrid and Jhiran. Astrid, who could not swim with great confidence and seemed very nervous about traveling on the river, confined herself to the passengers' galley. She grew silent and moody as the boat glided upstream, an unspoken terror of swift water evident on her face.

Jhiran wandered about the entire boat with ease, familiarity and fearlessness, ever snacking on something grilled or sweet, brought out especially for her. Judging from the way crew members and Lord Halvord treated her, the gwynling elicited tremendous affection and provided welcome amusement onboard the *Haililiah*.

Algernon, standing on the starboard deck to get some fresh air, inquired about this when Kerry Halvord came by to greet him. "The little girl likes you a lot. How do you know her?" he asked.

Lord Kerry smiled, recalling his first encounter with the gwynling. "Jhiran's not a little girl. She has five daughters, all of whom are older than you are," he replied. "But in response to your question, she actually came with the boat.

"When I brought my family up to Kameron from Illithia, I took my son to the university in Kameron City so he could continue his studies there. On the way back, I intended to buy and refit a river boat to serve as the flagship of my personal fleet. Years ago, this vessel served as a patrol boat for the Kamerese Inland Navy, but had been retired. It was in good repair, yet I found it for sale at half the price of a comparable craft. Despite this, there were no interested buyers. When I inquired, I discovered that the owner believed an evil spirit haunted the boat. Knowing the nonsensical nature of Kamerese superstition, I bought the vessel anyway. It was haunted, but the evil spirit turned out to be Jhiran."

"So where does she come from?" Algernon inquired. "How did she end up on a gun boat in Kameron City?"

"I'm not sure. Her story isn't very clear, but she consistently claims that she's a widow," Lord Kerry stated. "The gwynling are nearly extinct now. Those that remain survive only in isolated settlements deep in secluded valleys where humans do not set foot. Their culture doesn't adapt well to changes in the outside world, so in many ways their customs seem ignorant and antiquated to us.

"Among her people, women play subservient roles and enjoy few rights beyond the protection of their husbands. Widows find little to no support in their community, unless their children take them in.

The Long Journey: *Mirrors*

Widows without family either beg, become prostitutes, or burn themselves to death because they simply can't survive."

Algernon wrinkled his face in disgust. "It's immoral to treat women that way!"

Lord Kerry shook his head, knowing that Tamarians valued their women highly and treated the weakest members of their society, including prisoners, with compassion. "That's how it is among the gwynling in Northern Kameron. Even among the human Kamerese, women do not share the rights of their sisters on the Tamarian side of the river.

"One winter, Jhiran's husband contracted influenza and died shortly thereafter. Had he perished in a hunt, or been slain in battle, she would have been welcomed into a son-in-law's home. However, the gwynling believe that illness results from the disfavor of their gods, so no family members would take her in. Left with no other recourse, Jhiran became a thief to support herself."

"How is it that she can read my mind?" Algernon inquired. "She can speak my language fluently and puts her own thoughts into my head."

"Many gwynling have some psionic ability," Lord Kerry replied. "Jhiran has likely developed a higher degree of psionic skill out of necessity, and she's smart enough to mimic the speech patterns she pulls out of your head, as long as what she has to say is relatively simple. I'm not sure why, but she stammers badly in her own language and prefers not to speak when she has something complex to relate. Jhiran tends to assimilate the thoughts and feelings you're projecting at the moment, then acts on them accordingly."

Algernon scoffed. "She stole my money pouch and tried to kill me."

Lord Kerry laughed. "You were thinking about your money when you got off the train in Desperado Falls, weren't you?"

Algernon paused, remembering, but then he nodded. "We'd just eaten an expensive lunch. What I've got has to last us until we get back."

"Well then," Lord Kerry continued, "she would have picked up on your worry. Jhiran went up there with Waldemar to check on our cargo, and probably figured that because you're a monk, you ought to be compassionate toward the poor. She felt hungry, like she always does, and likely took your pouch because she wanted money for food."

The Long Journey: *Mirrors*

"I'd have helped her, but she didn't ask for my assistance, wouldn't return my money, and even tried to kill me!" the young monk complained, defensively. "She hurled rocks with a sling, and hacked at me with a sword while I had to fight off a pack of feral dogs!"

A smile spread across Lord Kerry's ruddy face, and he snickered through his closed lips. "You didn't ask her to give you the money back," he countered. "Instead, you assumed that fighting was the only solution to the situation. She simply mirrored your aggression."

Algernon felt stunned. "So it's my fault that she tried to kill me?"

Lord Kerry nodded. "Jhiran would never think to harm you unless she picked up an intention to harm her, or someone she loves, first. She told me that you nearly killed her, and apparently, your threat against her life was not your first brush with death, either."

Suddenly Algernon felt ashamed and struggled to control his rising emotion. "I'm trying," he stammered. "I'm trying to see things differently and become slower to anger. But it's hard!"

"Indeed," Kerry Halvord replied, nodding. "To your credit, Jhiran admits that you restrained yourself when it was in your power to take her life. Given her fighting skill and quickness that is, in itself, a high compliment of your martial abilities. However, she says your anger is rooted in fear that you are not loved, and I say that you must confront this problem and accept yourself as valuable in Allfather God's sight before you can move your life forward."

This drew an irritated sigh. Algernon rolled his eyes and shook his head. "What does she know about me, anyway?"

Lord Kerry put his hand on Algernon's shoulder, the kind of affectionate gesture an older man reserved for a younger man under his care. "Jhiran doesn't understand where the path has come from, nor where it will lead. She only knows what is–right now–and will reflect your soul with complete integrity. Where your path extends from here is entirely up to you."

"Great!" Algernon sighed. "My thoughts are open to a mind-reading freak!"

"Don't be so quick to dismiss her. You will find Jhiran Vell a loyal and valuable friend," Lord Kerry replied, ignoring the younger man's insult. "She can see into your soul, but in doing so, she also bears witness to the goodness that lives within you. Had a wicked spirit held you in bond, not even Brenna's recommendation would have landed you a seat on my boat."

The Long Journey: *Mirrors*

The last remark, delivered in a warning tone, sank into Algernon's mind. He didn't know what to say in response. His eyes swept over the water's smooth surface, then to the far bank, the sky and the boat deck, but he couldn't look at Lord Kerry again. Old feelings of shame and repudiation welled to the surface of his consciousness, forcing the young monk to stare down the demons that mocked him.

"Wisdom is the fair daughter of pain," Lord Kerry continued. "I don't know what you've experienced, but I believe that wisdom grows within you. Last evening I noticed that you turned away from Brenna's hologram in a rather obvious manner. Among my people she appears as an innocent maiden, but your culture has given you a different set of values and you cannot see her through my eyes, nor those of my crew.

"It's better not to look and not to see, than to become blinded by temptation. You are wise to understand this. I recommend that when you arrive at the estate of Lord and Lady Velez, you treat their daughters as sisters, with unquestioned purity and greater discretion than you did with Brenna's hologram. Your companion should do the same."

"Astrid?" Algernon inquired, finally finding courage to look at Lord Kerry again.

"Yes, Jhiran told me all about her," the Lithian merchantman admitted, lifting his eyebrows. "Some people are born with your friend's propensity, and some are molded into this manner of behaving by the influence of others. The reasons are unimportant, but I warn you for her sake that Lord Velez tolerates no mistreatment of his children. You're traveling into a land torn by strife and fraught with innumerable dangers. I wouldn't wish such a journey on two who are so young and vulnerable. Yet if you must go, let your quest begin among allies, not enemies."

"Do I stand among friends now?" Algernon inquired, suspiciously.

"I think you know the answer to that question," Lord Kerry replied.

"Then why all the secrecy about the contents of your cargo?"

Lord Kerry paused, as if considering his words with care. "Mirrors and lenses are fragile. They require delicate treatment," he said. "That's all you really need to know. The less you know of this, the better off you'll be on the south side of the river."

Then, without another word, Lord Kerry smiled and patted Algernon on the shoulder. He trotted up to the pilothouse, leaving the

The Long Journey: *Mirrors*

younger man alone. Algernon watched the tireless, mesmerizing rotation of the starboard paddle wheel as it churned the *Haililiah's* wake into froth. All the confidence he'd felt in Marvic seemed like foolish bravado now. Algernon worried in solitude, brooding over what Brenna told him concerning courtesy among Lithians.

"Remain silent in my father's presence unless he speaks to you. Bow your head to my mother when you first meet her, until she lifts your face with her own hand. You will find that my sisters rival our mother in beauty," she'd said. "Remember their names. Because you're Garrick's brother, they will embrace you. It's considered appropriate and respectful for you to kiss them on the forehead when you meet them for the first time, or if you have not seen them for a while. Do not offer your hand to help them up, open doors for them, pull out their chairs or offer to assist them in any physical way, as you do for Astrid. I know you Tamarians think these things are polite, but women among my people find that kind of treatment insulting.

"Remember that my parents will be watching you carefully, even if it looks like they're leaving you alone. Their first impression will form an opinion about you and your brother that will be very hard to undo if it's not done well. So do it well, Algernon.

"When they invite you to eat with them, discretely pull my mother aside and ask her not to serve wine with your meal, as it is impolite to refuse anything that is set in front of you. She will be puzzled and want to know why, but if you tell her the truth, she will understand and respect your decision to abstain.

"Also, do not eat until my mother has eaten and never put food into your mouth using your fingers, as you and Astrid do. My people will find that detestable! Among Lithians, eating together is integral to relationship-building, and important conversations with non-family members most often occur with a meal. As a result, Lithians take much longer to eat than you Tamarians, so do not leave the table until my mother leaves the table.

"Servants in my parents' household are treated as members of the family. I know how sensitive you Tamarians are about slavery, and that Temple monks preach egalitarianism, but servanthood among Lithians differs from the way it's practiced among humans. You must allow the servants to care for you, as this is part of our hospitality. Treat each one with respect and they will serve you with gratitude."

The Long Journey: *Mirrors*

The conditioning of culture wrought revulsion in Algernon's mind, and as a poor monk, he'd only been served by others of equal status. While he understood that the Lithians actually indentured themselves to one another by mutual agreement for a set period of time, the thought that one person should own the rights to another's labor inspired disgust. In response, Brenna reminded him that many kinds of slavery exist. A *Gottslena* verse support her view: "Every man forges the chains of his own desire."

Kira, with whom he'd shared the best and worst of childhood memories, remained in bondage to her addiction. Perhaps the path to which Lord Kerry referred led her to the point where she simply couldn't make a rational choice about where she was going when Marco lured her to Kameron. As he turned the mirror of this analysis upon himself, Algernon realized that he had to deal with the consequences of his own poor decision-making, and that in some ways he had become enslaved by both fear and desire.

Yet, as Algernon thought through his line of reasoning, he remained free to make new choices. *Gottslena* writings promoted love as the ultimate goal in all human interaction. The young priest believed he could rescue his sister because he loved her, not with the ardor and passion inspired by Marie, but with a quieter, more rational love that did not bind Kira with conditions, nor insist that his love for her be requited in any way.

Algernon watched the shoreline of northernmost Kameron in silence, gazing at its sparsely populated fields and forested hills. Grasses once greened by gentle spring rains already transitioned to gold and brown beneath the warming sky. Several miles to the south, a sharp rise revealed the bluffs of a primeval river bank whose calcite and quartz outcrops caught gleams of the Daystar's light and fluoresced like an azure line of lighthouse beacons. To Lithian eyes, in particular, this area projected a haunting beauty. Yet even Algernon gazed upon this landscape in awe.

Marble quarries dotted the distant cliffs. Limestone from this area served Kameron's cement manufacturing and steel industries, and the calcite itself found use in specialty optics. Kameron regularly exported tons of this material into Tamaria, where it was utilized in manufacturing precision glass for spectacles, telescopes, gunsights and lighthouse lenses. Products of this kind would not warrant the security and secrecy Algernon witnessed concerning the contents within

The Long Journey: *Mirrors*

Haililiah's hold. Why was Lord Kerry so evasive about his cargo? Why was an armed steamboat taking lenses and mirrors to Lord Velez in Kameron?

Algernon kept these thoughts to himself and forced his mind to contemplate more benign matters whenever Jhiran drifted by. After lunch, he spent the balance of the afternoon in the passengers' galley playing a word game called "misfortune cookie" with Astrid. This involved coming up with clever, insulting snippets they wished certain people in the Temple community would one day receive, hidden within an almond cookie.

"Your incompetence will result in endless failure, and no one will be surprised," Astrid quipped.

Algernon nodded. "How about: You will meet many interesting and beautiful people, none of whom will ever like you."

"You will live in grinding poverty and disrespect."

"You will travel far seeking love, yet never find it."

"People dread your company!"

"Your secret desire to completely change your life will be ridiculed."

"Friends, family and neighbors speak badly about you behind your back."

As the afternoon wore on, a wind picked up and the river became rough with whitecaps. Their game slowed considerably as the *Haililiah* plowed through waves and turbulent water, until Astrid complained about discomfort and twice ran to the toilet because of motion-induced nausea.

Shortly before dusk, the *Haililiah* passed a huge waterfall where the Venom River, the main tributary of the Desolation that drained the northeastern side of Thunder Ridge and its heavily populated plateau complex, tumbled into its mother stream in a thunderous, misty display of raw power. Along its eastern shore, and climbing up the bench overlooking the Desolation River sprawled the gritty town of Vengeance, a regional government center, in whose industrial complexes the compressor wheels, gimbals, gyroscopes and fuel pumps for big Tamarian military rockets were designed and built. Hydroelectric power derived from the Venom River also fed sawmills, thread looms, breweries, fuel reformers, specialty machine lathes for engine building and weapons manufacture. Huge, hydrogen reduction smelters produced excellent steel from the abundant iron and nickel ores of this region. Copper wire, electric motors, nails and the glass within the *Haililiah's* hold came from this town.

Swirling vortexes that produced extreme turbulence, gravel bars and frequent log jams made a riverine approach to Vengeance impractical. Rail lines connected the town with Burning Tree to the east and Marvic through Desperado Falls to the west, so even though the important industrial center sat on the northern shore of the Desolation River, all of its thriving commerce moved to and fro by freight train.

Fifteen miles upstream, the gentler mouth of the Tualitin opened into the Desolation's southern bank. Slightly west of this important river junction, the crumbling, Kamerese town of Fair Haven Fortress stood in isolated solitude. Originally built to protect the northern frontier from raids by marauding giants who attacked from across the river, the citadel had long outlived its function. The town remained populated more out of habit than any compelling economic reason, but during the summer tourists interested in historical places traveled here to peruse the period architecture, high walls and discolored cannon.

Long beyond human memory, local residents built a stone causeway leading into the Desolation River. Centuries of silt deposition from the Tualitin's sand delta accumulated on its eastern edge and broadened this causeway until cottonwood, cypress and willow trees colonized the area. Eventually, it became a park where families gathered for picnics and children played in the shallow water along its western shore. Near the end of the causeway, Fair Haven Fortress maintained a small dock area and fuel supply depot.

The *Haililiah* turned out of the current and gently moved into a slip to take on fuel and moor for the night. Although the ship docked with its long axis facing the wind, turbulent air rocked it gently. Astrid, who'd felt hemmed in and ill on the boat, desperately wanted to stretch her legs and check around the town to learn if anyone had seen Kira. She pulled the well-worn portraits of Kira and Marco out of her backpack and urged Algernon to come with her.

Though he felt uneasy, Algernon told the boat foreman, Waldemar, where he and Astrid were headed, and that they expected to return before long.

"Go in Allfather's care, holy children!" the Lithian foreman said, partly in blessing, partly in warning. "Fair Haven is neither fair, nor a haven!"

The Long Journey: *Mirrors*

Through a lingering twilight the young Tamarians scurried along the boardwalk toward the town. Thick walls loomed against the darkening sky and few people milled through the litter strewn, cobblestone streets. Within its sheltered walls, the place smelled vaguely of beer and sewage, with the scent of burnt kerosene mixed into a decidedly unpleasant aroma.

Algernon and Astrid wandered through the dark streets looking for a rail depot. Whispering figures observed them from the shadows, and the occasional outbreak of nervous laughter warned that foreigners merited no warm welcome here. Near the edge of town, Algernon found a rickety sign swaying in the breeze that directed visitors to the railway station. Upon arriving there, however, deserted docks and locked doors greeted them. The one story brick building lay dark and unused, with only a single lamp shining through a grimy office window in the back.

Algernon found a door and pounded on it with increasing insistence until finally, an unshaven, grey-haired man unsteadily opened the latch and peered into the windy gloom through rectangular spectacles.

"Ain't no more trains," the old man said.

"Why not?" Algernon inquired, speaking fluent Northern Kamerese.

"Banditos, boy!" the old man replied. "Tore up the tracks just south of Indigo Bluff. Won't be trains here for some time, I'm afraid."

"When did this happen?"

"A couple of days ago. You can read it in the papers. Now go away!" The old man began closing the door but Algernon's foot stopped it cold.

"So there were trains out of here before then?"

"Yup."

"And you keep a record of the passengers?"

"Yup."

"Can I please have a look at the register?"

"No! I said go away, now!"

Algernon restrained his growing irritation. Astrid, who understood none of the interchange, watched with increasing apprehension until she saw Algernon fish into his moneybag and pull out an unfamiliar coin. It wasn't a silver Tamarian sterling, but rather, a Kamerese kroner, minted in gold and worth at least two months' wages to a field worker. Astrid wondered where it had come from.

The Long Journey: *Mirrors*

"Just a look, sir, and it's yours."

When the old man reached for the money, Algernon pulled it away. "You can have it when you show me the register for last week."

With a grunt, the Kamerese man opened the door to let the Tamarians inside. He picked up his kerosene lantern and led them down the hall into a room where tickets were sold. He pointed to the register, a large book on the counter, then held out his hand.

Algernon put the kroner into the man's greedy fingers in exchange for the lantern. Scanning through the pages the young monk found only Marco Fang's name at the head of the last passenger record from four days earlier, beneath which the words "slave girl" had been scrawled. This time, Kira's distinctive writing did not appear at all.

Astrid saw that familiar, predatory look rise upon Algernon's countenance and she knew something had gone dreadfully wrong. The young priestess unfolded her drawings and placed them on the counter. She motioned for the old man and pointed to the pictures, watching carefully and witnessing a flash of recognition in his eyes. A flurry of unpleasant sounding discussion followed, then Algernon picked up Astrid's art, took her by the hand and stalked out of the building, slamming the door behind them.

"That was rude!" she complained as they scuttled away from the train station.

"You didn't hear him call my sister an unhealthy whore not worthy of being fed pig slop, nor did you hear him tell me that Marco owned her now. You didn't hear him curse us for disturbing his work and wasting his time. You didn't hear his uncouth remarks about foreign barbarians like us defiling his country. Don't tell me that I'm acting rudely, Astrid!"

She fell silent as they walked hand in hand back through town, but Astrid's mind raced in hope and stumbled in fear as Algernon explained what had happened to the train tracks and what he'd read in the register. That dangerous anger she'd seen him try so hard to repress over the past several days returned with terrifying speed.

A bell tolled, calling the faithful to an evening worship service. "Maybe we should go to the church and pray," Astrid suggested, hoping this would cool Algernon's rage.

He stopped, considering her words for a moment, then looked directly into her face as the final traces of daylight faded from the sky. "All right," he replied. "I suppose I could use a little prayer right now."

The Long Journey: *Mirrors*

She sensed he was lying, but lacked the skill to be certain and felt afraid of confronting him at that moment. Astrid worked her fingers out of Algernon's hand and followed him toward a tall building illuminated by oil-burning torchiers. Four large doors opened into its vestibule, and eight priestesses sprinkled sacred oil on the heads of all who entered.

Astrid's artist's eye gazed upon lovely buttresses and graceful spires, but also upon the hideous, stone gargoyles intended to frighten away evil spirits. The Tamarian priestess felt a sense of horror as the figures flickered grotesquely in the orange light. "This is not a holy place," she whispered as they joined the swelling ranks of townsfolk pressing up the broad stairs and into the building.

Algernon felt the same way. Overhearing political talk in the crowd, he noted that much of it expressed dismay about the influence of foreigners and threats against the big landowners who owed their existence and allegiance to King Alejo and his oppressive army. A nervous energy hummed within his soul, and in reflexive response his hands automatically tightened into a pair of two-knuckled fists.

Candlelight cast deep shadows across the stone interior and the air smelled of sweat and wax. They took seats on a hard bench near the back of the sanctuary nave, listening to strange choral music composed in language so ancient, Algernon's ear struggled to extract even the most basic meaning. A procession of singing choirboys, bearing burning candles to represent the souls of the ancestors, followed. There were readings from a large red book, whose words, like those in the opening songs, sounded strange and incomprehensible.

Blue stone, quarried many hundreds of years earlier from the cliffs Algernon had seen onboard the *Haililiah*, lay in tightly-fitted courses that extended into arch work lofting high overhead. Windows oriented toward significant stars and the Daystar's position on important dates in the Kamerese calendar dotted the roof line. Among the silvered, cedar rafters the overtones of melodies mixed and lingered. Though Algernon recognized the style of music, it didn't match his taste and he couldn't understand enough of it to make sense of the worship.

On an elevated dais, three bronze cymbals suspended on velvet ropes hung from ivory crossbars. Three baldpated priests in white breeches came out and hammered these cymbals with cloth-covered mallets, while a fourth priest in full regalia, bearing a smoking thurible crafted from brilliant metal, entered from the side of the platform. This priest knelt at the main altar, set his censer on a horizontal mensa made of marble and prayed with a flourish of hands. Then, down the aisles came the eight priestesses, also bearing incense. The women chanted their unintelligible mantras in unison and gestured over the congregation in choreographed grace, praying as they moved forward.

At first, it all seemed terribly formal, as if these people had been frozen into the same liturgical cycle for thousands of years. As this part of the observance came to a close, however, the main priest stood and offered an elaborate prayer for ceremonial wine. The eight priestesses stood and passed great flagons down each aisle. Every person present, except Algernon, took a deep swig, turning the vessel ever so slightly so as not to place his or her lips on a spot used by someone else.

As the flagons reached the end of each aisle, the priestesses dipped a white cloth into pure ethanol and wiped the entire rim, then passed the containers down the next aisle. Choral music reverberated through the sanctuary while the intoxicant made its rounds.

Astrid blanched. "That wasn't just wine," she whispered to Algernon. "It's too strong, and it tastes like there's something else in there too!"

After this, the music stopped and the main priest introduced a guest speaker from the deep south, whom he said had endured many hardships in traveling to Fair Haven Fortress. This man claimed to be an itinerant prophet with a vital message from the dead.

That's when the trouble began.

The speaker, an attractive young man with flawless, milk-chocolate-colored skin and the chiseled features common among people originating in the far south, had a powerful, resonant voice. His speaking skills ranked among the best Algernon had ever heard, but the intolerant message he delivered fanned the simmering coals of widespread congregational discontent into a hot flame.

A restlessness moved through the assemblage as the orator decried the systemic oppression wrought by the evil minds of wealthy landowners and a corrupt regime in Kameron City. He claimed intimate knowledge of how foreigners meddled in Kamerese affairs: the Azgaril, the Islanders, the Nordans, the Tamarians and especially, the Lithians, for whom he reserved his most scathing reproach. Spoon feeding the swooning crowd with anecdotes of foreign complicity in the social order that enslaved masses and denied them basic human rights, he called for the decent, peace-loving citizens of Kameron to revolt and throw off the yoke of oppression and destroy the chains that bound them.

"Your ancestors call to you from beyond!" he cried. "Rise up my children! Take up arms against your tyrants! Burn their boats, their fine houses and plunder the luxuries they've stolen from the sweat of your labor! This land belongs to you. The soil of our great nation is a legacy that belongs to your children, not the foreign leeches who come here to pillage!" He paused, staring directly at the two Tamarians sitting in the back of the sanctuary.

For a moment, silence reigned and Algernon felt many eyes resting upon him. When the speaker resumed and the congregation's attention drifted away, Algernon pulled Astrid by her sleeve and tried to make a discreet exit. The four back doors, however, remained shut, locked, and eight strong men with truncheons stood guard before them.

"Let us out!" Algernon demanded. "We don't want any trouble."

"It's a little late for that, fair-haired foreign boy!" one of the men spat in a threatening manner. "You'll get what's coming to you right here and now."

Fearing the declining favor of the assembled crowd, Algernon had little time to think through a strategy. Reaching into his pouch, he pulled out a handful of kroners and showed them to the guards. Then, as they advanced to take his money, Algernon tossed the coins backwards, toward the sanctuary nave. The metallic tinkle of gold on marble drew the attention of many worshipers, and as a collective gasp spread among them, greed instantly narrowed the odds into Algernon's favor. All but two of the temple guards dashed forward in a scramble for the discarded currency.

One of the security men approached and swung his truncheon at Algernon's head. The boy slid his right foot backward, hooked the guard's legs with his front foot while seizing the weapon arm with his right hand. Algernon pulled on the man's arm, then pushed him forward by jabbing his left palm into the unlucky man's back, driving him toward the ground. Then, twisting in the opposite direction, he stepped his left foot down, slid it back, hammered the guard's weapon hand with a powerful fist and yanked the truncheon free. He pointed the stick at the remaining guard and spoke with all the menace he could muster. "Get out of my way or die!" he warned.

Seeing the nearly effortless manner in which the Tamarian had disarmed the other guard, the Kamerese man yielded. Unfortunately, the door had been locked from the outside and wouldn't open. Algernon grunted and gave the center door a fearsome side kick that buckled its latch and shook the lintel, yet the heavy oak did not give way. One heartbeat later, he'd spun and slammed his left heel into the exact same spot, and this time every screw holding the locking mechanism in place sheared off. Algernon pushed his left shoulder through the broken door, discarded the stick and dragged Astrid into the street beyond.

After seeing what he'd done to the door, the other guards became understandably reluctant to give chase and subdue the young couple. One of them leaned outside and called curses upon Algernon's head, a slow and vile death upon his mother, and warned that he could not escape the righteous judgment of the Kamerese people.

By this time, Astrid felt dizzy and struggled to stay on her feet. Unaccustomed to strong drink, with her stomach emptied from nausea onboard the boat, the full impact of consuming spiked wine hit her very hard. Terrified that they wouldn't live to see another day, Astrid staggered down the stone staircase, pushing Algernon forward. She noticed he'd begun limping, and prayed that she wouldn't have to fight to protect him.

The last blow against the door, a side kick delivered from a rotating position, landed at an odd angle that didn't distribute impact force through the long bones in Algernon's left leg, damaging his ankle. Yet terror proved a stronger motivator than pain an impediment and the boy struggled onward. Holding Astrid around the shoulder he urged her to walk in a rhythm that enabled the two of them to support one another.

Part of the crowd spilled out of the temple and into the dark street, shouting and pointing in confusion until someone saw shadows fleeing toward the river. A handful of stout men took off in pursuit, and for the first time in his life, Algernon uttered a sincere and desperate prayer to the Great God for deliverance.

Somehow they made it to the town entrance before the crowd caught them, but its gate had already been lowered and locked for the night. Trapped between the wall and a gathering mob, Algernon let go of Astrid, ordered her to find a way out, then turned and steeled himself to fight for his life. The boy slid into a martial stance and put his mind into an ugly state where mercy dared not venture.

Angry shouts drew near. Algernon saw male figures running toward him in the darkness and others spilled into the street from taverns and brothels along the way. He didn't want to fight, didn't want to die here, but if compelled, Algernon fully intended to exact a heavy toll for any attempt to wreak vengeance upon the innocent.

"Astrid, hurry!" he urged.

Just as the leading edges of the mob drew close enough for their individual features to appear clearly in the moonlight, Algernon heard a whooshing sound, followed by a forceful smack that sounded like bone being crushed. He watched in astonishment as the mob leader fell backward and screamed, as if struck in the head by an invisible club. Another did the same, then a third, and the mob slowed as a fourth man cried out and fell to the ground with blood gushing from his face. Smooth stones pattered to the pavement.

Astrid found the mechanism for raising the gate. She fumbled with the chain-driven pulley in drug-induced ineptitude but managed to lift the huge door just enough to slide beneath it. "Come on!" she called, sliding the locking mechanism into place. "Let's go!"

Algernon heard another townsman go down as he limped toward the gate and rolled his wounded body toward freedom. Astrid had already reached the tree line, running faster along the boardwalk toward safety than Algernon had ever seen her move, but as he retreated, something led him to look back at the wall. There, standing on the edge of the balustrade he saw the tiny, unmistakable figure of Jhiran Vell.

She turned and made eye contact with him, her face grim and intense. He heard her voice in his head warning him to flee as the gate opened fully and men began pouring onto the causeway. The gwynling twirled her sling twice and let fly a stone that struck one of the hapless Kamerese in the back of the head. Another rock sang from atop the wall and yet another townsman went down, allowing Algernon the chance to get into the trees where he couldn't be directly observed.

With his heart pounding, the boy paused in the shadows. He heard someone shout in recognition of the threat and point to the catwalk high above. Movement caught his eye on top of the wall as armed men raced forward to subdue the gwynling, but Jhiran stood her ground and flung stones that sent her adversaries scurrying for cover.

She could not defend herself from a gun, though. A rifle shot rang out. In horror, Algernon saw the gwynling turn and fall backward from the thirty-foot wall, as if stricken. He held his breath, watching her spin with uncanny agility and transform her motion into a graceful dive.

The Long Journey: *Mirrors*

As she neared the ground, Jhiran unfurled her wings and glided harmlessly across the water toward the *Haililiah*.

He could not run fast enough to get away from the mob because rising pain in his ankle impeded motion. But Algernon, who'd grown up along the shores of Broken Wing Lake, knew how to swim well. Just before the angry Kamerese reached him, Algernon hobbled across the boardwalk, dove into the wind rippled water behind the causeway and swam toward the Lithian boat as her crew pushed the vessel away from the pier.

The shock of enveloping cold inspired a gasp. Algernon forced his body into a steady, powerful rhythm, churning through the water with all the strength he could muster. With his goal firmly fixed and his attention focused, the young monk did not realize that men bearing rifles and scatterguns reached the shore and aimed their weapons to kill him.

Algernon heard bullet impacts strike the surrounding water. Taking in a big breath, he dove beneath the surface, knowing that two or three feet of water would protect him from any bullet fired from shore. A very bright light from the *Haililiah* illuminated the entire bay, suddenly stopping all gunfire from the causeway. Then, he heard the boat's hull shudder with machine gun fire and a dull thud reverberated through the water. A moment later, the whole cove thundered with an explosion whose shock waves shook Algernon's body violently and echoed painfully in his ears.

Gasping, he reached the surface. A loud voice coming from the boat sternly admonished the mob to stand down. In between the warnings, Algernon heard the onboard machine gun chattering and Astrid calling him from the boat deck, desperately urging him onward. He swam as fast as he could, but the cold water sapped his strength.

Astrid threw out a circular float attached to a rope. Algernon reached it and held on, as her arms pulled him toward safety. Though he tried grasping the boat edge and heaving himself up, the boy felt numb and kept slipping back into the water. Astrid held onto him for all she was worth and screamed for help. Waldemar came to her aid, and together, they pulled Algernon onto the deck.

Someone from the shore scored a direct hit on the spotlight, bursting it spectacularly and plunging the entire area into darkness.

Jhiran brought a blanket as bullet impacts bounced off the boat's armored hull and splintered into its deckhouse. The locals remained eager for a fight–moving down the tree line and advancing toward the

The Long Journey: *Mirrors*

boardwalk–hurling rocks and improvised fire bombs made from glass bottles filled with ethanol and stuffed with old rags. One landed on the fore deck and spread fire along the front of the boat.

Shouts from the *Haililiah's* crew, uttered in Lithian and therefore unintelligible to the Tamarians, rang from various places, and suddenly the boat began accelerating backward in eerie silence. A brief burst from one of the machine guns discouraged the Fair Haven rabble from approaching within throwing range, but soon fire bombs that had fallen short ignited the dock and flames spread rapidly along the shoreline. Meanwhile, crew men activated a pump and quickly subdued the onboard blaze with a water hose.

Waldemar dragged Algernon inside, then picked him up and carried him through the darkness to a warm place below. Algernon saw the comforting flicker of firelight as the strong foreman put the young monk down. "You're safe now," he soothed. "Get yourself out of those wet clothes."

Algernon complied and stripped to his underwear. Two men in shorts busily stoked the gasifier, throwing in hunks of dry wood. The steam engineer watched his gauges carefully, then called up to the pilothouse on the sound-powered phone, speaking words the young Tamarian could not understand.

Amid the noise and activity Algernon trembled uncontrollably, his body struggling to regain warmth. "We didn't do anything," he insisted, inching closer to the boat's boiler. "Yet they came after us like wolves!" Then, confused by the vessel's silent movement he inquired: "How can we be underway when the steam engine isn't running?"

The sound and recoil of *Haililiah's* 3-inch deck gun rocked the boat. Machine gun fire followed. Waldemar offered a brief prayer, then rose and explained to Algernon that the gunboat had been fitted with an electric drive motor and a battery bank for emergency use. "This means the war has finally begun for us," he said. "Everything changes now. Praise Allfather you two made it back safely!"

Gradually, Algernon's eyes adjusted to the gloom. He heard Astrid come down the stairs and saw her sit. "Are you ok?" she asked, fear lingering in her voice.

Shivering in his blanket, he ignored her question. "Thank you for saving me," he said. "That water is freezing! I don't think I could have done another stroke."

"Don't thank me," she replied, modestly. "Jhiran saved us."

The Long Journey: *Mirrors*

Lord Kerry's words flashed back into Algernon's mind. The gwynling had risked her life, and the boat crew fought for their protection as well. As he reflected on his recent experience, Algernon mulled over how often other people had come to his aid. Everyone from High Priest Volker, to Dmitri, Brenna, Garrick and even Lieutenant Streng, the police detective, helped him in his quest to find Kira.

Then he thought of Astrid. A few weeks ago, he'd despised her. Why had he never seen any value in this skinny, plain-looking girl when they'd lived within the Sacred Enclosure? Why was he so focused on Marie, that self-absorbed, traitorous vixen who cared for him only when they were alone? "I've been blind," he murmured. "I've been looking for love, but not recognizing when it's been given to me."

Somewhere within the core of his being a subtle shift took place. The young priest sat in thoughtful silence, considering Dmitri's counsel, remembering how the older monk told him that a purpose for his life would become clear. Algernon felt that the fog long obscuring the mirror of his soul began to fade somehow. He didn't know where this new line of thinking would lead, but now he realized how persistently he'd shut his ears to the counsel of people around him, people who loved him, people who recognized his value and patiently worked to build him into the man he would become.

He prayed in silence, thanking the Great God for mercy, expressing sincere gratitude for deliverance from certain death. Then, trembling, the young monk remembered every soul who had ever shown love in word and action, asking the Great God to honor each of those people.

And the fear that had long held sway over his heart began to melt away.

Gradually he began feeling warm again. The steam engineer wandered all over the big machine with an oil can, filling up various lubrication points while he waited for the brass gauge showing boiler pressure to rise. As it did, the draft feeding air into the firebox began to roar and the two men tossing hunks of hardwood into the flames perspired profusely. Because the entire boat had undergone an extensive refit, the steam valves did not leak, but the condenser lines soon began to sweat and drip.

Careful control over the fire box air flow ensured a clean burn. The *Haililiah's* boiler contained a secondary, ceramic chamber wherein superheated air created a turbulent vortex, ensuring that nearly all of the energy contained within fuel turned into heat, rather than smoke. Steam pressure rose, the water gauge moved backwards, and the engineer began working the feed water injector.

Because the boat had not been docked for very long, her boiler system still contained a lot of energy and the steam plant warmed up quickly. Getting underway in a steam-powered ship often took hours, but because *Haililiah* regained full power by the time her battery bank energy dipped to roughly 40% of its total. With the steam plant in operation, the whine of its electrical generator signaled that interior lights could shine once again.

Algernon did not remain in the boiler room very long after concluding his prayer, as its stifling air soon made him seek the evening cool. However, by the time he dressed into his dried clothing and limped to the upper deck, darkness lay across the landscape and the steam boat had long since departed the Desolation and pushed through the less strident flow of the Tualitin River. Interestingly, no lights graced the bow. The pilothouse remained only faintly illuminated by dim, blue-colored instrument panel displays.

A clear sky, swathed in beautiful starlight, stretched overhead and into the southeastern horizon, where the halo of the Great Eye Nebula crowned distant mountain ridge lines in a blue-green aura. Within an hour, the Great Eye would rise and begin its nightly circuit of the heavens. A fortnight hence, and it would become visible in the late afternoon again, a ghostly, stellar grave marker growing in prominence as it moved beyond the glare of the Daystar's corona.

The sight of Jhiran snacking on potato slices and tartar sauce in the deck house reminded Algernon that he hadn't eaten in some time. The boy sat on a bench and elevated his swelling foot, wishing he had some ice to reduce its inflammation. Astrid went down to the galley to get him some dinner, claiming that she'd already eaten her fill.

Lord Kerry entered the passengers' galley and inquired about Algernon's foot, then examined it with a careful eye. In questioning Algernon about the injury, he learned that the young monk could still use it to bear some weight. "Sometimes it's hard to tell the difference between a sprain and a fracture, but if you can still put some weight on it, I don't think it's broken."

He ordered Algernon to rest, keep the foot elevated, and made arrangements for ice to be brought up from the galley every few hours.

The Long Journey: *Mirrors*

"Jhiran can wrap your foot in a bandage. Don't keep the ice on for more than 20 minutes at a time, and rest it until we reach the Velez estate."

"How long will that take?" Algernon inquired.

"From Fair Haven, it's 150 miles to the mouth of the Virgin River," Lord Kerry replied. "From there, it's about 90 miles to the dock in Helena. At eight or nine knots going against the current, that's at least 24 hours of travel time. We'll also have to stop for fuel a couple of times along the way."

Algernon's heart sank. Having come so close to finding his sister, another day of delay seemed intolerable. Yet, though his facial expression showed a hint of disappointment, the young priest thanked Lord Kerry for his ministrations and said nothing of how he felt. By the time Astrid returned with a sandwich and some fruit, he'd already fallen fast asleep, and she didn't want to awaken him.

Steadily, the *Haililiah* moved up the Tualitin River through the night. Algernon did not rest well and could not rise before dawn, as was his habit. By midmorning, the riverboat stopped in the Tamarian village of Windstorm to take on more fuel. Though Algernon felt bored and anxious to help, Lord Kerry insisted that he rest and keep up the ice and pressure bandage treatment Jhiran had begun on him the night before.

Jhiran took her nursing role quite seriously. Algernon noticed that the gwynling projected a decidedly maternal character that he found both surprising and delightful. She doted on him as if he'd been her own son, cutting slices of apple and toast for his breakfast, bringing tea while Astrid lay sleeping, adjusting cushions for his comfort. In addition, Algernon learned that she could control her strange ability to project her thoughts into his head.

Astrid, however, seemed distant. She let him eat by himself. Throughout the morning she sat on the opposite side of the passengers' galley gazing out of the window, across the golden vistas of Northern Kameron, for long periods of time. All efforts on Algernon's part to stimulate discussion, or start the games they'd enjoyed playing resulted in single word, conversation-ending responses that quickly gave Algernon the impression that Astrid wanted to be left alone.

Shortly after the noon meal, the *Haililiah* turned southward, into a small, slow-moving river of turquoise-colored water whose heavily treed banks crowded into the channel. Through gaps in the tree cover, abandoned farmhouses–many of them burnt to their foundations–stood upon land overgrown with weeds and wildflowers, conditions that

The Long Journey: *Mirrors*

stretched into the western horizon. On the eastern shore, vineyards, fruit and nut orchards and small, market garden plots blended into a patchwork of connecting roads and small villages. Sheep grazed on hillsides alive with verdant grasses and dotted with oak trees. This contrast in the lovely landscape demarcated the vast estate of Lynden and Alexina Velez, on the eastern shore of the Virgin River, from the various land holdings of absentee lords on its western bank.

Astrid, weary of her solitude, at last came over and sat near Algernon. She watched Jhiran remove the pressure bandage around Algernon's ankle, noting that the swelling she'd seen earlier had gone down. "It looks better," she stated. "You'll be walking soon."

Jhiran turned. "Lord Kerry says one more day."

Algernon sighed. "It feels better. What does he know anyway?"

"He's a doctor," Jhiran replied. Then, staring into Algernon's eyes, she told him that Lord Kerry knew far more than he let on, warning Algernon not to make assumptions and underestimate the Lithians. "The tea helps, too." It had been steeped from the inner bark of the yew tree, a well known source of analgesic relief. Then, her task finished, the gwynling stood to her feet and vanished downstairs.

Astrid rested her chin on the back of a seat. Her stringy hair needed washing again, amplifying an expression that seemed troubled and sad. She kept looking at Algernon then looking away whenever he caught her green-eyed gaze with his own.

"What's wrong?" he inquired, softly.

She shook her head. "Nothing. We're just so far away from home. I don't understand why Kira would travel all this way. I keep trying to figure out why she left me. What did I say? What did I do? How could I have made her so unhappy?"

"Maybe you didn't do anything," Algernon replied. "Maybe she bought into an elaborate pack of lies. Maybe Marco got her mind so plastered on his opium that she simply didn't realize he was taking her away."

"She's not stupid!" Astrid said, defensively. "You shouldn't talk about your sister like she doesn't have a mind of her own."

"You'd rather believe that she hates you? You'd rather imagine that she was simply using you every time she crawled into your bed at night? Come on, Astrid. Does that scenario make any sense?"

Deep within, Astrid knew something she'd never admitted to Algernon. She'd been very careful not to look at Jhiran while she mulled the memories over in her mind, but one time Kira had asked her directly if she really wanted to be known as a lesbian for her entire life. The way Kira spoke implied that both girls had freedom to make a selection in the matter, as if they could choose to remain lovers or simply walk away from one another.

Astrid could not believe what she'd heard. Intelligent and beautiful Kira had captivated Astrid's attention. Those words sounded strange, distant and dissonant. The secret burden Astrid carried in her heart centered on a fear that Kira had already made up her mind to forever abandon their relationship. The incident on the road to Marvic, where she'd witnessed Algernon's arousal, stirred that prospect every time she looked at her lover's brother.

But she couldn't say anything. "Maybe you're right," she replied.

Algernon looked carefully into Astrid's face. "You're lying to me," he said. "Tell me the truth, Astrid. You don't believe Kira left you for the opium, do you?"

At this, Astrid's face reddened and anger flashed in her eyes. The young priestess put her hands up in shame and scurried out of the passengers' galley. Algernon watched her go, feeling powerless and frustrated. He never seemed to say the right things to her! Yet her response made him realize how thoroughly Astrid's sense of worth tied into her relationship with his sister. Astrid remained willing to risk her life by traveling into a war zone for Kira, but how would the woman feel if Kira no longer shared her devotion?

Several weeks earlier, he would have laughed at Astrid's misfortune. *Gottslena* writings taught that love changed everything, and true to these words, Algernon found that he could no longer cast aspersions upon the skinny priestess. He actually cared about her feelings, even though he didn't understand them, even though he felt repulsed by her love affair with his twin sister.

Twilight arrived many hours later, then faded into darkness again. Anxious to complete this part of his voyage, restless from inactivity, Algernon remained awake long after he normally went to sleep. Sometime during the early part of the evening, a sense of excitement and anticipation arose among the ship's crew. Algernon saw the glow of Helena's electric lights rise out of the darkness and limped painfully toward the river boat's burned bow in order to catch a better look.

The Long Journey: *Mirrors*

Astrid joined him. "Finally!" she breathed, implying forgiveness by her proximity.

Because the beacon light had been shot out, the *Haililiah's* pilot warned over the loud speaker that he was about to sound the steam whistle. Its resonant, mournful cry echoed off the hilltops. As the boat neared Maidenhair Creek a waving crowd, full of smiling faces and good cheer, began assembling at the dock, a welcome reception that contrasted greatly with the send-off the boat crew experienced at Fair Haven Fortress.

The overall joy expressed by the citizens of Helena and gathered members of Lord Lynden's personal army filled Algernon's heart with a sense of relief. Waldemar and another crew man came forward, bringing the hydraulic bicycles with them.

"We will send a message to Lord Velez concerning your arrival," the foreman said. "In the meantime, you must remain onboard. It would be helpful for the messenger to bear the disc and letter from Brenna, explaining your presence to her father."

"I thought this thing was for Lord Kerry," Algernon replied, removing the disc and placing it in Waldemar's hand. He retrieved the letter from his backpack and handed it over as well.

The Lithian foreman smiled. "Lady Brenna would not forget her family. There is, without doubt, a personal message for them on the disc, in addition to her letter."

Soldiers wearing armor and helmets that looked suspiciously like those used in the Tamarian army participated in and supervised the unloading process. Their uniforms had an uncanny ability to blend into whatever lay in the background, forcing Algernon to look very carefully in order to discern body shapes. The Lithian soldiers standing guard carried rifles, but never held them in an aggressive posture. Crates piled up on the dock before strong warriors lifted them onto horse-drawn carts that disappeared into the darkness, escorted by teams of armed men.

The need for such tight security unnerved Algernon. Nagging questions about the contents carried within *Haililiah's* hold moved to the forefront of his consciousness, and further, as the sight of gun-bearing soldiers blended into his memory of the angry mob at Fair Haven Fortress, Algernon questioned the wisdom of traveling through Kameron in the midst of a civil war.

The Long Journey: *Mirrors*

Pain forced the young priest to sit down. Perhaps Lord Kerry had been right in warning him that his injury needed more rest. Astrid noticed his expression and fetched another cup of analgesic tea. Well over two hours later, as the Tamarians leaned against their backpacks and struggled to stay awake, a tall, muscular man with very dark skin strode up the gangplank with a very dark-skinned woman in tow. They wore fine, brightly colored linen robes that draped loosely over their shoulders, garments of Abelscinnia, a great city in the east, that were better suited to the desert than a scrub forest.

The 'Scinnian man's irises, black and deep, looked like comforting portals beckoning from sclera as white as a cloud, and when he smiled, his perfect white teeth shone like friendly windows. He held his right arm aloft and open, and with the other, gestured broadly toward the shore.

"I am Jawara, son of Penda, third wife of Tegene, my beloved father. This is Farisa, daughter of Ngoni, first wife of Tegene, our beloved father. On behalf of Lord Lynden and Lady Alexina Velez, we bid you welcome." The man spoke in Azgaril Vulgate, the common tongue Astrid could understand, yet with the unusual accent of the Abelscinnians.

Algernon, who had never met a 'Scinnian nor ever seen skin so dark, liked him immediately. He arose in awkward discomfort and raised his own right hand to meet and clasp Jawara's in a common gesture of peace. "Are you a servant?" he inquired.

Jawara laughed. "In one sense, we serve the Holy God. But we are free. Tegene, our beloved father, has long commanded Lord Lynden's army. We are here to escort you to the villa. There you will meet the servants assigned to your personal comfort."

Farisa stepped forward, placed her hands together and bowed. "Blessings in the name of the Holy God and the honored Velez family." After the two monks offered their traditional supplications in reply, Farisa gave each of them a small piece of cloth. "Please accept these as gifts from the Velez family."

Algernon looked at the item, a diminutive tubular cloth woven in an angular shape with a hole in its center. An expression of befuddlement rose upon his face. "Forgive me, Farisa, but I don't know what this is."

She turned toward him with a patient expression in her dark eyes. "We understand that you have injured your foot. Slide it into the brace as you would a sock and you will very soon know what you have been given."

Algernon sat down and stretched the thin fabric over his sprained ankle. His toes poked through one end, and his heel through the center, while the cloth tube went around his lower leg like a sock. It conformed to his flesh as if it were a thing aware of its function. Instantly, the pain in his foot vanished, as if it was floating in water. He stood without further difficulty, gently putting weight on his left leg until he could lift his right foot completely off the ground. "Wow!" he exclaimed in disbelief. "That's remarkable! Thank you!"

Astrid looked at the tiny bit of cloth she'd been given. It looked like a camisole for a doll. "I'm sorry, but this will never fit me," she said.

Farisa exchanged a knowing look with her half brother. "You must try it on," the 'Scinnian woman urged, gesturing.

"Here?" Astrid inquired, astonished. "In public? In front of everyone?"

"You are not a virgin?" Farisa replied.

Jawara looked at Algernon in surprise, until the young priest remembered Lord Kerry's remarks concerning Brenna's hologram and realized that these dark-skinned people likely projected Lithian social etiquette onto the even lighter-skinned Tamarians. Responding quickly, he came to Astrid's rescue. "We differ from the Lithians in our social views," he explained. "Our people consider modesty a virtue, whether a person is married or not. Therefore, Tamarian women find it shameful to appear uncovered in front of any man to whom she is not espoused, and neither of us is married."

Jawara nodded, understanding, and Farisa smiled, reaching for Astrid's shoulder. "Then we will find her some privacy!"

The two women disappeared into the passengers' galley and Astrid went into the toilet room by herself. She emerged wearing a huge smile. Astrid said something to Farisa that inspired laugh.

"It fits?" Algernon inquired when Astrid returned.

"Like skin!" she exclaimed. "Oh, it's wonderful!"

That had to be a girl thing, Algernon mused. He helped her with her backpack, then shouldered his own as they pushed their bikes down the gangplank together. Astrid stopped him briefly when their feet hit dry land.

"It's no wonder Brenna looks so good!" Astrid whispered in Tamarian. "If you saw Marie wearing this, you'd have an even harder time keeping your hands to yourself. I need to get Kira one of these halter things!"

Mildly annoyed that Astrid kept referring to his humiliating experience with Marie, Algernon tried to change the subject by explaining his observation concerning the soldier's uniforms. "There's something magical about Lithian clothes," he replied. "Not spooky like my moneybag, but practical."

He wanted to talk about the suspicious cargo. He wanted to know what motivated the secrecy, including the need for Jawara and Farisa to welcome them to the Velez estate, rather than someone in Brenna's family. He felt uneasy, unaccustomed to receiving gifts. As the mystery swirled within his mind, Algernon felt grateful that Jhiran remained on the boat so that he did not have to conceal his thinking.

They walked on Maidenhair Avenue, alongside Helena's downtown, toward vineyards that rolled across gentle slopes laden with fruit-bearing vines. An electric truck arrived a few minutes later. The machine carried them up to a ridge that overlooked a small lake to the south. At the ridgeline stood a crumbling villa. Soldiers patrolling its perimeter and guarding its gate exchanged friendly words with Jawara as he led his entourage within the compound.

Two Lithians emerged, one a slender, dignified, elderly man and the other a middle-aged woman with an athletic build and strikingly beautiful, pale eyes. Jawara did not defer to them, but began a brief conversation in the Lithian language that resulted in expressions of understanding among the servants.

"I am Calvert," the old man said in introduction. "I have served the Velez family for more than forty years, and it is my honor to serve them by serving you."

"Bless you, sir," Algernon responded, nodding as Brenna had told him to do.

"And I am Tirra," said the woman. "I have served the Velez family for more than thirty years, and likewise, it is my honor to serve them by serving you."

Jawara and Farisa bade the young Tamarians a good night and promised to meet them again, before breakfast. They walked through the double door, into the main house, but Calvert and Tirra beckoned their guests to follow them toward a smaller building. Oil torchiers revealed cracked and yellowed plaster. Candle lamps, placed upon a table beneath the roof overhang, provided light for indoors.

The Long Journey: *Mirrors*

Tirra took Astrid upstairs, while Calvert led Algernon to a comfortable chamber on the lower floor. Calvert explained that this room belonged to Algernon as long as he remained a guest of the Velez family, but the young priest, so accustomed to ascetic living conditions, remained too distracted by the well-cushioned chairs, lamp stand and feather bed to listen. He felt strangely embarrassed by the obvious comfort surrounding him.

"Will you be needing anything else, Master Algernon?"

"No, thank you," he replied, anxious to be left alone. "I really need to sleep."

"Shall I awaken you in the morning?"

"That won't be necessary. I like to rise early."

"An excellent habit, young sir. I will bring fresh clothing for you in the morning before breakfast. When would you like me to arrange your bath?"

This might have been a polite way of informing Algernon that he actually needed a bath, but so unaccustomed to being served, the monk stared at Calvert for a moment before responding. Once the two of them had successfully negotiated a time for bathing, Calvert bade Algernon a good night, and Algernon collapsed on the soft bed.

He slept well. Early the next morning, just as daylight kissed the mountains, Calvert knocked on the door, interrupting Algernon's morning prayers. He followed the elderly man outside, where cool, fresh air consorted with the pleasant hint of wood smoke.

The bathhouse, a communal one, segregated genders on either side of a dividing wall. Excess humidity vented from screened windows along the top of its perimeter, a misty veil that rose and vanished into the scented morning sky. Algernon wanted to remove his ankle brace, but Calvert told him it could be immersed without damage. Several other men introduced themselves, but not all could speak vulgate, so they essentially left Algernon alone. The young priest, grateful to bathe in warm water, felt thoroughly clean and refreshed afterward.

He dressed in a silky, red robe with matching pants that Calvert provided. Unlike much of the clothing Algernon saw the Lithians wear, this outfit revealed very little of his physique and satisfied his need to remain modest. Tirra and Astrid met him in the courtyard outside. The priestess wore a similar gown, had washed her hair and looked well rested and happy. Together with Calvert, they went into the villa for breakfast.

The Long Journey: *Mirrors*

A large foyer opened into a spacious, vaulted room filled with people. The beauty of the building's interior belied its outward appearance, with redwood paneling, and hand-crafted furniture that lay arranged to stimulate small group conversation. Expensive hardwood floors lay beneath their feet and Lady Alexina's landscape paintings graced the walls. These attracted Astrid's attention immediately.

Lord Kerry and his crew, along with several dark-skinned Abelscinnians who looked remarkably similar to Jawara and Farisa, milled about in conversation. Jhiran, ever enthusiastic, jumped into Algernon's arms again, then did the same for Astrid. This was, apparently, the way she greeted people she liked.

Algernon felt uncomfortable amid all this luxury, but Jawara arrived with his disarming smile and offered to make introductions. First, the 'Scinnian warrior's son brought the Tamarians to a well-muscled Lithian named Jared, who looked no older than Algernon did. He wore the thin, diaphanous clothing that revealed his fit form and marked him as unmarried. Jared wore a pair of glasses on the bridge of his nose and exuded a confident, intelligent demeanor devoid of any snobbery. He greeted Algernon with an attitude of warm expectation.

"I understand you've become part of the Velez family," he said, smiling. "One day I hope to have the same pleasure."

Algernon struggled to stay afloat in the elite social waters and didn't fully think through the implication of Jared's remarks. He had to ponder for a moment before making the connection. "You know about my brother and Brenna?"

"We all do," Jared replied. "Woodwind carried a letter from Lady Brenna just before the spring rains came, and last night we watched the hologram you brought down from Tamaria. Let me extend an advance welcome!" Jared met Astrid with similar grace, then promised to find Acacia so that she could meet them.

Jawara moved among the crowd, bringing the Tamarians to his siblings, two of his father's three wives, and finally Tegene himself. Algernon had never seen such a big and powerful man, yet Tegene projected a gentle demeanor and embraced the Tamarians as if they were his own children. This remarkable acceptance made both Algernon and Astrid feel more comfortable among wealthy strangers.

Jared returned with a shy girl in tow. "This is Acacia, the eldest of Brenna's sisters. We call her Cassie."

The Long Journey: *Mirrors*

Algernon kept his attention riveted on the girl's dark eyes. She approached and put her arms around his back, drawing him close, then moved slightly away and raised her face toward his. He accurately interpreted this as the moment when he was supposed to kiss her forehead, and as he did, she smiled brightly. Acacia said nothing the entire time.

Astrid had been warned by Tirra not to expect the same treatment from the Velez family, and not to take offense, implying in a subtle way that Astrid should be careful in how she treated them. The priestess felt a little jealous though, as Brenna's lovely siblings came, one at a time, to receive a hug and kiss from Algernon. Astrid put on a brave face and blessed Acacia, then Cynthia, whose physique appeared generous and womanly when compared to her slender sisters, and Camille, the youngest and most extroverted of the children.

Just before the steward announced breakfast, Algernon felt a feminine hand gently touch his neck. He turned, catching a glimpse of Alexina's breathtaking countenance. Algernon stifled a gasp and immediately lowered his head, a respectful posture among the Lithians. With his eyes averted, he noticed Brenna's mother was pregnant, but a moment later felt her soft hand reach under his chin and lift his face.

"Welcome to my home, Master Algernon," Alexina said softly.

"Thank you," he replied, blushing. "I have seen the image of your face reflected in Brenna's smile, your kindness in her character, and I'm honored to meet you."

"Well said, young man!" Lynden, Brenna's father, appeared out of the crowd from Algernon's left side. The grey mixed into his hair gave the warlord an appearance of ennobled wisdom, yet his voice and dark blue eyes portrayed an unmistakable ferocity. He slipped his left arm around Xina's back and extended his right hand upward, palm out, to grasp Algernon's in the common gesture of peace. Though his demeanor initially intimidated Algernon, the power in Lynden's hand and the smile he returned when the warlord felt youthful vigor in Algernon's strong fingers seemed simultaneously confident and reassuring.

Having been spoken to, Algernon felt that he could introduce Astrid without offending his hosts. Alexina kissed Astrid on both cheeks, inspiring a blush that lingered as Lynden followed with a respectful kiss on her forehead.

The Long Journey: *Mirrors*

When the steward announced food service, Algernon discreetly explained that he'd taken a sacred vow to refrain from intoxicating beverages. Alexina seemed initially puzzled, but nodded, then asked Calvert to relay the message to the kitchen staff.

Seating followed a strict arrangement. Twelve chairs surrounded each table, neatly dividing the assembled people into three groups. At the first table, Lord Kerry occupied the seat of honor, with Lord Lynden and Lady Alexina to his right. Across from them sat Tegene and his first wife, Ngoni, with Cynthia and Camille occupying the spaces beside the commander's wife. Next to Alexina, Acacia and Jared took their places. Algernon sat to Jared's right, across from Astrid, with Jhiran seated on the far end.

Everyone else in the room, including the servants, took their assigned seats and silence fell as Lord Lynden arose and offered a blessing on the food. Servants brought in prepared plates for themselves, then everyone else who was seated, so the family's food was served hottest. Once everyone had been served, Lady Alexina picked up her fork and put a morsel into her mouth. Then everyone followed suit, and the room filled with conversation.

Eating with a fork proved a bit cumbersome for the Tamarians, but far worse than the awkwardness of using a utensil, the searing spices of Lithian cooking left Algernon's mouth and lips with a burning sensation that no amount of fresh water could sate. This aroused laughter from Camille, who found Algernon's facial expression comical as he tried to keep himself from spitting food back onto his plate. Calvert came to his rescue, bearing a bowl of tasteless yogurt. He advised the Tamarians that mixing the yogurt generously into the food would diminish their discomfort. Thankfully, this turned out to be true!

Well over an hour later, as the guests enjoyed tea or a glass of champagne, Algernon asked Jared about his relationship with Acacia. Jared–whom Algernon learned was a lawyer, and was, therefore, much older than he appeared–explained that he lived in the servants' quarters of the Velez household while courting Acacia. This custom enabled the girl's family to get to know a prospective suitor well, and he in turn, learned her household dynamic. Because many Lithians remained with the bride's parents for several years after marriage, the ritual live-in period served as a prerequisite to formal engagement, during which the groom's parents played host to the young couple.

"What about you and Astrid?" Jared inquired.

The Long Journey: *Mirrors*

Algernon sipped his tea. "There's nothing between us, we're just friends," he replied. "Astrid has come along to help me find my sister, who has run away from home."

"Algernon really likes her," Jhiran chimed in, "but Astrid's in love with his sister, Kira."

Jared stopped short, nearly dropping his glass. "Excuse me?" he responded.

Algernon filled his mind with warnings about discretion and tried to establish eye contact with the gwynling, but her attention remained focused on Jared.

"Astrid's a lesbian," Jhiran stated in a matter-of-fact manner, as casually as she'd mention that clouds brought rain and rivers flow to the sea. "She loves Kira, not him."

All conversation stalled. As silence settled upon the family and guests, Astrid stared at Jhiran in wide mouthed horror, then rose from the table and fled from the room.

Algernon looked at Alexina, pleading with his eyes. The Lithian woman saw his distress, arose and nodded in his direction. As Alexina stood, others began doing so as well. With the entire family and all their guests pausing from their meal, Algernon excused himself and scurried after the young priestess, following the sound of doors slamming against their jambs and sandaled feet rapidly ascending wooden stairs.

He could hear her weeping. He could sense her shame. Astrid locked herself into her room and wouldn't let him in. "Go away!" she demanded, sobbing.

With a sigh, Algernon placed his hands on the door. "Come on, Astrid," he replied, gently. "It's only me, and you know that I don't want to hurt you." He waited for several moments, then added: "When you're ready to talk, I'll be right here."

Several minutes later, Astrid opened the door. She'd drawn the shades to hide tear streaks and puffy eyes. She reached for him, pulled him into the dimly lit room and sobbed into his shoulder. "I've never been so embarrassed in my life!"

"Don't be," he replied. "You are what you are." He held her in a strong embrace, stroked her hair, patted her shoulder, then pulled away and looked directly into her eyes. "I'm not ashamed of you," he said. "If anyone in there thinks less of you for knowing that you love my sister, that's not your problem. Hold your head up, girl!"

She sniffed. "It's not just me," she replied, looking away. "Now they know I love Kira, and that will ruin everything for Brenna and your older brother."

"Garrick has broad shoulders. He can take care of himself," Algernon soothed. "Brenna has nothing to worry about among her own people. Stand up straight, put your shoulders back and hold your head high!" He held her face in his hands and very gently lifted her chin until their eyes met. "There's no need for you to feel ashamed."

"I can't go back in there," she whispered, shaking fearfully. "I just can't!"

Algernon remained firm. "Yes, you can," he responded. "I'm with you. Nobody is going to hurt you while I'm around. I promise."

Again she looked away. Astrid turned toward her bedside table where she found a handkerchief and dabbed her eyes dry. Then, after blowing her nose, the priestess steeled herself. She looked at Algernon's fearless face, so much a masculine mirror of his sister, Kira, and rising wordlessly, left the room with him.

Conversation stopped once more when they entered. Alexina rose from her seat, her noble face expressionless as the Tamarians walked in, and again, everyone else followed her lead. Algernon made a point not to pull out Astrid's chair.

"Thank you for rejoining us," Alexina said quietly.

Lynden whispered something to his wife, who smiled sweetly, then the warlord strode over to Astrid and placed his arm around her shoulder. "In my house," he breathed, "and among my family you remain an honored guest. Don't be afraid."

"Bless you sir," Astrid replied. "Bless this house and all your loved ones!"

Brenna's father kissed Astrid's forehead, the tension in the room evaporated, and conversations between family and guests gradually resumed as if nothing had happened.

Jhiran, for her part, seemed completely oblivious to her own social blunder and continued eating as if unaware that anyone might have been hurt by her remark. Astrid could not bring herself to look at the gwynling, but sipped her tea in silence, watching as Lynden moved over to where Algernon sat and said something into her companion's ear. She saw Algernon make eye contact with Alexina, who nodded demurely, then watched him stand and leave the room with Lynden.

Jared and Camille, Brenna's youngest sister, leaned over to

The Long Journey: *Mirrors*

Astrid and began asking a myriad of questions about Tamaria, the city of Marvic, the Temple Elsbireth, and Garrick. Initially, Astrid didn't feel like talking, but Jared handled the awkwardness with remarkable skill, and Camille's sweet demeanor broke down Astrid's resistance.

Algernon followed the Lithian warlord outside. He relished the strong daylight, noting that beyond the villa, hills covered with mixed forest climbed into taller, steeper slopes to the east. A strengthening warmth radiated from the courtyard flagstones and deteriorating, plastered walls. The air smelled of sweet blossoms, sap, the nutty aroma of acorns and the scent of pine needles.

Lynden Velez appraised his young guest, tightened his lips and breathed slowly through his nostrils. "I have learned of your quest," he began. "I know your brother is a fearsome warrior, and I've been told that like him, you fight with great skill."

Not knowing where this monologue was heading, Algernon remained silent.

"I expect to meet your brother very soon," the Lithian warlord continued. "He will come here with his army and bring my firstborn daughter safely home. He will help us defend this land from the insurrection. We will come to understand him; we will learn to love him as Brenna loves him." Lynden paused, as if considering his words carefully. "But if you leave my protection in search of your sister, we may never meet again. We may never know you and never grow to love you, as we will know and love your brother.

"Many people have perished where you intend to go. I fear that you will forfeit your life in a vain effort to save your sister from a fate that she has chosen for herself. The tragedy of her folly will only double if you do not return."

Algernon closed his eyes. He didn't appreciate being lectured by a stranger, but the gentle tone in which Lord Velez delivered his reprimand reminded the young monk of High Priest Volker, and something far deeper and stronger than the strident masque he'd worn for so many years prevailed in Algernon's response. "How can you speak of love and say these things to me? Brenna told me that when she found herself trapped and surrounded by armies, you sent one man to find her and ensure her safety."

Lynden nodded. "I sent a trained, well-equipped and experienced warrior, who understood the risk and volunteered for the task."

"Brenna said that you sent a man who loves her."

The Long Journey: *Mirrors*

Again, Lynden nodded.

Algernon pointed to his own chest. "My heart beats in aching sorrow for my twin sister. As long as I have lived, she has lived. I can't rest while she remains under threat. I can't breathe freely if she remains enslaved. I love her. I must go!"

"You have the heart of a warrior!" Lynden replied, not entirely surprised. "Yet you will take your girl companion with you?"

Shaking his head, Algernon admitted that he had no control over Astrid's decision to join in Kira's rescue. "What Jhiran said about her is true. I don't like it, and I don't understand it, but I know that Astrid's fidelity to my sister is as genuine as my own."

Lynden began walking, expecting Algernon to follow. "You carry no weapons and you wear no armor. How do you expect to survive in the midst of a civil war?"

Algernon, who'd long believed he could live by his wits alone, now understood how much he'd depended upon the aid of people around him. He knew that he couldn't survive independently and framed his response in light of recent thinking. "Wherever I go, I walk in the shadow of the Great God. In whatever peril I face, he is my armor. Against all enemies who confront me, he gives strength to my hand."

In his interactions with Tamarians, Lynden had yet to meet one who viewed the world through a paradigm of faith. Brenna mentioned in her letter that Algernon often behaved in a manner difficult to accept, but that the true excellence of his character would become clear in time. Lynden Velez struggled to determine the degree of sincerity expressed by the young monk, but seeing how much he cared for Astrid and listening to him express love for his wayward sister gave the warlord a strong impression that this boy meant every word that came out of his mouth. "You speak well," Lynden admitted. "May it be as you say."

Algernon's curiosity emerged. "You told me that my brother will come here soon. Garrick believes his unit will be deployed to Kameron, but how do you know he'll be sent here?"

Lynden paused, considering his response for a moment. "He will be deployed on my land. Allfather God speaks to my daughter, Cynthia, in dreams and visions. She received such a message several weeks ago and told me the Queen of the High Land will send Garrick and Brenna to us very soon. The other rationale is more mundane."

He stopped at the villa's gate and asked one of the soldiers there for his rifle. Lynden adroitly cleared its chamber. "This," he continued,

The Long Journey: *Mirrors*

holding the rifle with its barrel pointed downward, "is a redesigned version of the Tamarian rifle my servant Woodwind obtained while lending aid to your nation's army. We'd been working on firearms based on Abelscinnian designs before the Azgaril invaded our land. These were an improvement over the Azgaril trap-door conversions which which are basically muskets modified to fire cartridge ammunition. But Abelscinnian guns proved delicate and prone to jamming in combat. We've learned that the Tamarian rifle, though it fires too large a bullet, is more accurate and reliable.

"We have re-engineered several items that Woodwind brought with him, including this rifle. Rather than the single action bolt that manually ejects and inserts a new cartridge into its firing chamber, we have designed an automatic reloading system that uses a shortened bolt and rod cam system. This weapon fires a .312 gauge bullet, which is much lighter, faster and has a flatter trajectory than the .700 Giant Slayer cartridges used by your army. The automatic cycling system reloads the weapon for the soldier from this magazine inserted through the bottom of the gun, allowing a far more rapid rate of fire than is possible with any weapon other than your multi barrel cannon." Lynden removed the magazine, revealing a stack of spring loaded bullets, jammed it back into the weapon and returned the rifle to the soldier, who nodded respectfully.

"We have also redesigned the Tamarian military armor, incorporating many improvements into the fabric of our own uniforms. Though the Tamarian armored vest can stop a bullet from penetrating, it's heavy, bulky, and once damaged, must be repaired before re-use."

"I noticed last night that the soldier's uniforms blended into the background," Algernon remarked. "But that doesn't seem to be happening here, in the daylight."

Lynden smiled. "The magic you've witnessed is woven into the fabric," he replied. "The camouflage effect works whenever the soldier wants it to work. Here in the villa, it's important that my warriors be seen. In the field, however, concealment can mean the difference between life and death. Now, in addition to camouflage, the torso, thighs and upper arms of every uniform worn by my warriors contain lightweight armor we developed that protects them from small arms fire. Their helmets are lighter, yet significantly stronger than the ones worn in your nation's armed service."

"So how does all of this relate to my brother coming here?"

The Long Journey: *Mirrors*

"Follow me, and I'll explain."

They left the villa and walked uphill along a gravel path through the forest. Chattering squirrels and squawking jays warned of their approach, and the gentle whisper of wind in the tree tops carried the scent of smoke and warned of distant danger. Lynden set a brisk pace that Algernon struggled to match. They climbed for a long time.

"Success on the modern battlefield requires a high degree of mobility. Soldiers who are weighed down by heavy equipment tire more quickly. I command a small army, but we defend a very large estate. Therefore, I must provide my forces with an edge in firepower and maneuverability. Equipping and training my warriors costs money that I have to raise, somehow, but the growing civil unrest in Kameron complicates commerce and reduces revenue for every business venture in the country.

"After consulting with my family, I approached your industry and military leaders with the improvements we'd made in their equipment. I went to Vengeance and met with representatives of the Tamarian army, weapons and textile merchants to arrange investment and negotiate terms for manufacturing. I brought several samples along.

"The textile people expressed interest in our clothing, most particularly women's undergarments!" Lynden laughed and looked at Algernon, who remembered Astrid's response from the previous evening. "The army, however, seemed far less enthusiastic about our modifications of their equipment."

"They probably think they can't trust a foreigner," Algernon admitted. That seemed the most probable explanation.

Lynden shrugged. "Apparently, they already have a small caliber rifle that is used by the Queen's guard and their military police. A consortium of textile merchants, however, agreed to finance the construction of new light forges on my land. The agreement we reached specifies that I purchase material from their suppliers and give them a small royalty on my exclusive sales agreement in Tamaria, in lieu of interest on their investment money.

"This arrangement subverts the import duty because we will be using Tamarian flax as the base fiber for the hammer forge, just as we have done with your ankle brace. I hope to develop employment opportunities for local people, attract skilled labor and diversify the economy of Helena, weaning the town from dependence on bulk wine sales. By doing this, we will provide superior quality undergarments for

The Long Journey: *Mirrors*

the women of your nation, and those living further north. With the anticipated revenue I can fund education and infrastructure development projects, such as reforestation, effective flood and erosion control, cleaner water and electrical power. Some of my profits will also pay soldiers who have gone for months without drawing a salary."

"What's the catch to all this, and what's a light forge?" Algernon inquired, panting.

Lynden crested the hill, breathing easily, though he had done the bulk of the talking, while Algernon struggled to keep up. The warlord stopped and pointed a black, multihedronal structure built of steel and glass that stood upon a barren height. "That building is light forge, a small one. Its design is based upon the non-imaging optics found among insect eyes, and it's black because it's very efficient at absorbing light.

"The forge has three main parts. On the outside, each facet consists of specialized glass with impregnated microfunnels that channel and amplify the Daystar's energy. At its core, the light forge produces a high temperature flux that simulates temperatures within a star. In such an environment, we can manipulate matter to produce materials with specialized properties, like those within your ankle brace.

"The second part involves heat driven micro centrifuges, which separate gases from the air we breathe, and the third section uses cascading waste heat recovery to generate electrical power and drive the micro machinery, especially the hammer forge, in which our famed ceramic-metal tools are fashioned."

"I understand," Algernon replied, though he didn't. "And Lord Kerry is importing lenses and mirrors so you can build another one."

Lynden nodded. "Several, actually. Our agreement specifies that we import optics from Tamaria for this purpose. But my financiers, who've provided significant seed capital, have become very nervous about the civil war in this country. To address that concern, they're insisting that Tamarian soldiers come here to help provide security for their investment. I understand that your brother has already been selected for this duty at the conclusion of his officer training, hence I am confident that he his army will soon be here."

Algernon turned away, uncomfortable with the idea that Garrick and other Tamarian soldiers could serve their country by occupying another. The scenario Brenna's father described seemed subversive, especially in light of the sermon he'd heard at Fair Haven Fortress. Could the Lithian warlord actually do this without inspiring anger

The Long Journey: *Mirrors*

among the Kamerese? Would the king in Kameron City approve of these arrangements?

As the young monk admired the lovely view from this elevated spot, he noticed dark columns rising from the horizon. Among the brown lands that lay in the hazy distance beyond the shining Virgin River, these black and grey splotches lingered and drifted with the wind. "What's that smoke all about?" he asked.

Lynden Velez, who'd already lived 62 years and spent decades facing danger in combat, knew very well. The expression on his face darkened into worry. "Artillery fire," the warlord responded. "Every day it comes closer. I expect that we will engage hostile forces from across the river within a week or two."

Algernon's heart raced. "Not much time."

"No, it's not." Lynden took several steps back downhill, then stopped. "I want you to think about this with care," he said. "Examine your soul and motives with an honest mirror, and please reconsider your decision to leave my protection."

Then the Lithian warlord walked downhill, leaving Algernon to contemplate his words in solitude.

Three Little Words

Lengthening days, lingering twilights and the strengthening heat of oncoming summer inspired listless discontent, a longing to enjoy the blissful peace of solitude somewhere far beyond confining walls. As a gentle afternoon breeze rustled through countless, fluttering leaves and branches bent in a graceful glissade, Brenna struggled to focus on her textbook. Though her comprehension of required readings steadily improved, the long anticipated reunion with her family in Kameron stretched into intolerable waiting, that on this afternoon inspired feelings of vague dissatisfaction.

Seduced by sultry, early summer warmth, Brenna felt restless and disinterested in the content of her studies. The Lithian girl lay on a wide, quilted blanket that she and Mariel placed beneath the shade of a maple tree, twirling her pencil and staring at the fountain and reflection pool across the broad lawn. Her mind drifted toward memories of her family, recalling the comfort of their company, seasons of contentment and humorous situations among sisters that brought a smile to her face.

Mariel, whose skin blossomed with dark freckles as her exposure to daylight increased, looked up from her newspaper. "Are you going to get anything done today?" she asked. "You've got that far away look in your eyes again."

"I'm just thinking about home," Brenna replied. She didn't appreciate the tone in which that remark had been delivered, but didn't voice any displeasure. Having felt betrayed and manipulated by Mariel's role in her recent experience, Brenna guarded her responses to conceal any resentment welling up her reaction to Mariel's comments, wishing that she'd never been given reason for mistrust, rather than working through a difficult and honest confrontation that might have resolved their differences and repaired the broken relationship.

However, Mariel correctly interpreted Brenna's muted replies, body language and facial expressions. The Tamarian linguist, saddened by the decline in her friend's trust, hoped that time would heal the rift that rent the fine fabric of their friendship. Until that happened, she restrained any line of inquiry that might be interpreted as prying into the Lithian girl's personal life. But as the afternoon enveloped them in its languid arms, Mariel felt compelled to do something productive, preferably in Brenna's company, as she hoped that working together would reestablish cordial relations. Besides, reading news about the butchery and endless atrocities occurring in Kameron wearied her.

"Well, if you're just going to stare at the fountain all afternoon, I have three words for you: Combat Rifle Assessment. I have to qualify on the new guns being issued to the expeditionary units, and I'm sure that no one is scheduled on the firing range today. Come down to the base with me. I could use your help with scoring and since you're not studying anyway, now is as good a time as any to get it done."

Brenna's expression lightened. Going to the base meant that she might run into Garrick, and running into Garrick ranked high on her list of preferred activities. She had no idea how tough it was to qualify with a rifle in the Tamarian army, nor how long it would take for Mariel to fire the 500-odd rounds required of each qualification attempt. But the possibility that she might catch a glimpse of Garrick, or better yet, to bask for a moment in his pleasant company filled her with more motivation than she'd known in days.

The two women folded up their blanket and hurriedly returned to their dorm room. After dressing into their grey running sweats, Mariel donned a red beret while Brenna put her hair into a single braid, then the two of them headed downhill toward the base.

An increased police presence became obvious as they neared the section of Discovery Park that faced the Dragon's Lair compound, where a chanting crowd of marchers gathered, bearing protest signs. Most of the participants were beyond the prime age for military service, which meant that among the men, at least, many veterans stood among their ranks. Brenna now boasted sufficient skill in reading the Tamarian language to comprehend three word messages such as "Foreigners, Go Home," and "No Blood for Kameron," or "Defend OUR Homeland" written on the placards.

The signs attracted Mariel's attention and she paused for a few moments, listening to an orator who urged his fellow citizens to contact their senators and decry any admission of Kameron's refugees, as well as the imminent deployment of Tamarian troops to that country. A chill raced up her spine. How would the protesters have known about that? She urged Brenna onward. "This is not a good place for us to be seen right now," she said.

Someone threw a bottle. The glass shattered on the street a short distance to their left and angry shouts emanated from the crowd. Brenna glanced over her shoulder and saw police men restraining several unruly protesters, feeling strangely attracted to the scene. "Why are those people so upset?" the Lithian maiden inquired, her curiosity aroused by unfamiliar and unsettling social behavior.

Mariel increased her pace. "We've been fighting wars for a long time," the lieutenant replied. "Most Tamarians think foreigners are supporting and sustaining the giants to keep us from growing too powerful. We've also had low-level conflicts with the indigenous people on the Saradon, a big war against the Azgaril, a few skirmishes with the Vatherii, and an ongoing feud with the Peran Confederation on our northeastern border. Basically, I think people are just tired of sending their sons off to die."

"But without warriors, you could not defend yourselves, and maintaining an army is a legitimate function of your government. Shouldn't every Tamarian citizen support their elected leaders in an effort to preserve freedom?"

Though Mariel agreed with Brenna in this, she understood that the Lithian maiden viewed this issue through the lens of a warlord's daughter. "Part of that freedom includes the right to protest. If we can't tolerate the expression of ideas, especially ones we don't like, then we aren't free."

Brenna wrestled uneasily with this concept as they approached the Dragon's Lair gate. Lithians had never developed centralized governance, had no history of social protest, and Brenna preferred to shy away from conflict rather than voice her views aloud. In a surge of strong emotion, she'd been known to confront individuals with their misbehavior, but the idea that citizens should openly and publicly defy their government seemed fundamentally wrong. After all, wasn't the primary function of authority rooted in representing the needs of its people? Why would any government behave in a manner inconsistent with the higher good of its citizenry?

Two soldiers standing guard recognized the women and stiffened as Lieutenant Hougen approached. "Welcome back, ma'am," one of them said. Then tipping his beret toward Brenna, he smiled and greeted her with an informal: "Miss Velez."

As they passed, Brenna whispered to Mariel. "How does he know my name?"

Mariel, slowing as she entered the safety of a compound where armed warriors had standing orders to prevent unauthorized entry, repressed laughter. "Let's just say you're not exactly forgettable," she replied. "And trust me, guys always talk about girls like you."

Brenna wondered what that really meant, but said nothing.

The faint sounds of gunfire echoing off the walls in the distance, proof of yet another training exercise in progress, seemed strangely comforting. A familiar, predictable haven existed on the base that felt detached from the unrest overflowing in the outside world.

Mariel followed a path to the armory, where she scanned the posted schedule for the practice range. None of the active units had reserved time that afternoon for qualification, so Mariel checked out one of the new .255 rifles and a marksmanship note pad. Ammunition awaited her use at the rifle range. "I'll need your help and I think at some point you'll be required to do this too," she told Brenna, "but first we have to go over some basic rules."

With practiced efficiency, Mariel checked the chamber to make sure the weapon remained empty. "We always treat a gun as if it's loaded," she explained. "Never point at anything you don't intend to kill. Keep your finger straight and off the trigger until after you've taken aim on your target." She looked Brenna dead in the eye. "And we never pull the trigger unless we're absolutely sure that our target is what we want to hit. We can't make the bullet come back once it's left the gun."

Brenna nodded. The safety rules sounded similar to those for archery practice, and after her combat experience, the Lithian maiden had no illusions about the danger posed by firearms. Further, like archery, accurate shooting with a rifle required intense concentration, relaxation and control over breathing.

When Mariel approached the safety official at the qualifying range and explained what she intended to do, he looked at Brenna with less respect than he should have extended to her and shook his head. "This is not a place for fun and games with your friends, lieutenant," he said while he checked her rifle to ensure it had not been loaded and looked to be in good repair. "I'll be watching the two of you carefully, and officer or no, you'll not be permitted to jeopardize safety on my watch, especially with a civilian in your company."

"I expect nothing less, sergeant," Mariel replied.

He grunted, informing her that she'd have the opportunity to warm up and sight in the weapon before official scoring began. The sergeant gave each of the two women a pair of protective ear muffs,

The Long Journey: *Three Little Words*

wished Mariel good luck in a curt manner, then trotted over to the observation booth.

The Tamarian military helmet featured padded ear covers that muted the tremendous sound produced by the .700 Giant Slayer rounds. Even though the new rifle utilized a smaller bullet and generated much less noise and recoil, the range safety rules required that all participants on the practice range wear ear protection. Both women complied.

A rope demarcated two zones. The outer zone consisted of a safe area, where no weapon could remain loaded. Beyond the rope lay the live zone, where the guns were loaded and fired. Mariel put three rounds into the rifle's magazine and waited for a signal from the safety official before moving in front of the rope and inserting the magazine into her weapon. In order to properly zero in her rifle, she was permitted to fire nine shots.

Brenna, who stood behind the rope, took notes on Mariel's behalf. She recorded where Mariel had been aiming, where the round actually hit, along with data on wind speed and temperature. Mariel fired from a prone position, working the rifle's bolt action in between each shot. She studied her target groups and adjusted her rifle sights every three rounds to compensate for her own errors. The Tamarian lieutenant left the bolt open, then stepped behind the rope to examine what Brenna had written down, making minor adjustments that improved accuracy and consistency.

Once satisfied, Mariel watched for the signal to proceed and moved in front of the rope again. Qualification began with Mariel in a standing position. Her initial targets were set at a 50-yard range. Each hit in the center of the target earned Mariel two points, and each hit in the surrounding circle a single point. A threshold score of 16 points enabled the shooter to move into the next round. Mariel scored a 17.

"It's easier to shoot this gun than the big rifles used by the infantry boys," Mariel remarked. "I'll do this from a kneeling position, like I'm in a foxhole, and prone before moving up to the next level."

Brenna watched Mariel carefully, her appreciation of the Tamarian woman's skill growing as she noticed the degree of physical control and concentration Mariel exerted. Shooting a rifle required less exertion than firing arrows with a bow, but the focus needed to become proficient with either weapon seemed similar.

When the target papers came in, Brenna tallied a 16-point score and clipped the targets together. Mariel fired more accurately standing than she did kneeling, which was unusual, but in a prone position, the Tamarian lieutenant scored a more impressive 18.

"I'm nine in the hole," Mariel complained. "I have to do better than this!"

"But you're a linguist," Brenna replied. "You don't train with the infantry for combat. Why do you have to be so good with a rifle?"

Mariel reloaded the gun. "The Tamarian army is a small force. If headquarters ever needed defending, we couldn't count on the line boys coming to our rescue. Everybody in the army has to know how to shoot. Your turn will come."

While Mariel moved through the qualification process, Brenna caught a glimpse of the warrior spirit in Mariel, a quality she'd never seen in the woman before. Though the Tamarian lieutenant had been fiercely assertive in some situations, Brenna had never envisioned her wielding a weapon.

The minimum qualifying score was 192 out of 240. Mariel fired ten rounds at ranges of 50, 150, 300 and 500 yards in each of the three positions. Her final tally totaled 204 points, which gave her the *marksman* qualification. Although she'd improved on her score with the big .700 caliber Giant Slayer rifle, Mariel expressed disappointment.

"I've never been very good at shooting," she complained. "Words are my thing. Would you like to give it a try?"

Brenna, having secretly wished for this, nodded excitedly.

Mariel reloaded the weapon and selected the zeroing option of a single paper target at 100 yards. "The gun is set up for me, but it should be close enough for you," she said.

Brenna stood in a comfortable position, following Mariel's directions to focus on the front gun sight. Keeping the carbine barrel steady proved more difficult than she'd imagined, and the first time she touched the trigger, Brenna felt the weapon wobble just before it fired. Her shot skimmed the top of the target paper. She tried twice more before wrinkling her nose in disgust. Shooting a rifle wasn't as easy as it looked.

Mariel suppressed a laugh. "Why don't you clear the weapon, Brenna. Let's set you up on a bench rest."

The device to which Mariel referred consisted of a steel tripod base with a padded, U-shaped cradle that held the carbine's forestock. With the base firmly bolted to a flat, elevated bench, this device restricted movement and improved accuracy. Shooting competitions

The Long Journey: *Three Little Words*

held among experts at the firing range required the use of a bench rest, but it was not permitted during qualification.

Since the Lithian girl had never fired a gun before, Brenna found the weapon far easier to aim steadily with its forestock resting on a tripod. Listening carefully to Mariel's instructions, she chambered another round to fire again. Once she had the target lined up, she moved her index finger over the trigger, all the while maintaining concentration on the exact center of the dark circle printed on the target paper, 100 yards away.

This time, she felt mild surprise when the gun went off. Steadying the gentle recoil of the weapon, Brenna worked the bolt action, adjusted her aim and fired again as she was directed, repeating the procedure four additional times. With the gun suitably steadied, not only did she find the rifle easy to hold and shoot, Brenna liked the idea of not having to worry about a bow string banging into her left forearm.

Gently removing her right hand from the rifle's wooden grip, the Lithian girl checked the open bolt as she'd been taught to do and removed its ammunition magazine. She set its safety into the "lock" position before stepping back behind the rope.

Mariel examined the target after retrieving it with the electric pulley, her bright smile a genuine expression of delight. "That's a tight group!" she exclaimed.

Brenna looked carefully at the target paper and smiled in satisfaction. "I wanted to make a flower," she replied.

Four circles clustered around a hole in the exact center of the target, their scalloped edges overlapping like stylized petals. As she often did when surprised, Mariel put her hand on Brenna's arm. "You could see what you were doing? You did this deliberately?"

Brenna nodded, pleased with herself. "With that bench rest thingy, I'm sure I can put them all in the same hole if you'd like, but it would be a shame to waste a whole sheet of paper like that."

Mariel stifled an expletive for Brenna's sake, shaking her head in astonishment. "I'm really glad you're on my side."

Had Mariel seen Garrick's qualifying score on the practice range two days earlier, she would have felt completely deflated. Having honed his firing skills in actual combat, the young officer candidate attained "expert" qualification by scoring a 227.

That achievement availed no advantage in his current situation. Crouched behind a garden wall in a training area known by officer

The Long Journey: *Three Little Words*

candidates as "The Graveyard," Garrick, Sergeant Ringer and the eight men remaining in the sergeant's squad became trapped in a crossfire between three OpFor snipers.

Urban warfare training in the Tamarian army accurately depicted the brutal nature of combat in a city. The objectives for this exercise sounded simple during the pre-combat briefing: Garrick's platoon would secure access to a bridge over the Honeywater, so that follow on troops could assault the town center. Unlike open field exercises, where head to head engagements often resolved quickly, fire fights in the urban environment stretched into hours. Progress seemed painstakingly slow, they'd not met the majority of their deadlines, and the observers scoring Garrick's platoon had already ruled six of the men in Sergeant Ringer's squad either dead or wounded.

Struggling against his own impatience, Garrick willed his emotions under control. He felt powerless, huddled in the dirt behind the wall, where many boot prints and discarded shell casings spoke of previous assault leaders facing a similar situation. "Ok," he said to Sergeant Ringer. "We need smoke grenades and covering fire. After we secure the building on the northwest corner, we'll take out the snipers and cover you to storm the one across the street." Then, pointing at the individual men as he spoke, Garrick continued. "Skinner, Krieger, Bauer and Kellerlein, come with me!"

Sergeant Ringer stayed Garrick for a moment. "You're going to lead the assault?" he asked. When Garrick nodded, the sergeant shook his head. "Don't force anything, Mister Ravenwood. It's only an exercise. We don't need you getting hurt again."

Though Garrick nodded, he subconsciously dismissed Sergeant Ringer's advice. Smoke grenades landed in strategic locations across the open ground while the five men remaining behind the wall began firing to keep the snipers down. Garrick scrambled over the wall through a noisome cloud of stinging smoke, his heart racing, his lungs and eyes burning.

Poor visibility veiled the assault team as they dashed through a weedy garden, clambered over yet another wall and raced across a debris-strewn street. Since, for safety reasons, the training complex had no glass on any of the buildings, Garrick took care not to approach within a direct line of any window. These were hard to see in the swirling, blue-grey smoke, but the smoke also made his movements harder to detect.

The Long Journey: *Three Little Words*

The assault team's footfalls seemed enormously loud on the pavement as the covering fire died down. The men hunkered down against the plastered wall of a two-story building while Garrick oriented himself and evaluated his tactical options. Relying on hand signals, Garrick sent his men toward a verandah that would hide them from the OpFor snipers once the covering smoke dissipated. Private Otis Krieger leaped onto the patio and tossed a flash grenade into an open window, shielding his eyes as the ordnance detonated.

Brilliant light cast hard shadows and a concussive sound trembled through the verandah's supporting beams. Clutching his shotgun with its barrel pointed toward the street and scanning his surroundings for potential threats, Garrick urged his men onward.

Gunfire erupted from within. Private Krieger let out an exasperated, three word expletive as he felt a rubber bullet smack into his shoulder. Amid the noise and confusion, Garrick stood in front of the window, quickly selecting targets he saw entering the room against the dark background. He fired his shotgun over the heads of his own men, its rubber pellets striking two OpFor soldiers while narrowly avoiding an observer. The referees were always considered neutral "civilian" bystanders in combat exercises. Garrick's quick response cleared the room, allowing him to slink through the open window with less urgency than had been the case with the infantrymen who preceded him.

A staircase, angling up and to the left, led to the next level, but Garrick sent Skinner, Bauer and Kellerlein to check the rest of the lower floor while he reloaded his pump action shotgun. Garrick remained in the first room to ensure that no one came down the stairs or entered the building from behind them, wary that he had no clue how many OpFor warriors occupied the building. Dust lingered in the air, dirt covered the floor, and the two OpFor soldiers ruled down by the observer paused to light cigarettes.

Garrick eyed them, knowing that had this been a real encounter, each man would have been splattered against the far wall. He forced the unnerving thought out of his mind as a brief exchange of gunfire, followed by the sound of another door bursting open and more gunfire, captured his attention. After this, the OpFor soldiers rose and shuffled outside, glaring at Garrick as they slunk past him.

Just as the assault team returned to report they'd cleared the bottom floor, a grenade bounced down the stairs. Garrick pushed his warriors back from whence they'd come, and dove behind a wall just

The Long Journey: *Three Little Words*

before the grenade went off. His helmet banged against a table leg and he landed uncomfortably on top of his shotgun, but the sheer adrenaline rush inspired by combat action pushed all pain from his conscious mind.

The moment after the grenade went off, Garrick sprang to his feet and dragged Kellen Bauer off the floor, pushing him and Imre Kellerlein into the room where the explosive had detonated. Bauer subsequently tripped over the observer, whose senses had been shocked by the flash and noise of the grenade, and Kellerlein froze for a moment, not knowing what to do.

Annoyed, Garrick flipped the safety of his shotgun off and stormed up the stairs, his advance preceded by painted rubber pellets that caught an OpFor sniper by surprise. The observer upstairs wanted to rule Garrick killed by the flash grenade, but the officer candidate shook his head. "Verify below!" he said. Then, yelling for Kellerlein and Bauer, Garrick studied a dim, unpainted hallway scarred by many make-believe battles. The structure had been built oversized for training exercises involving giants, then remodeled to more human dimensions after the army's recent experience in the Winter Saradon Campaign.

Light spilled in from four rooms that overlooked the street on one side and the bridge crossing the Honeywater on the other. Garrick ordered Dietrich Skinner to eliminate a sniper whose perch in an adjacent building lay uncovered to them from this angle. "Make it count!" Garrick said. He left Dietrich to the task and followed Bauer and Kellerlein down the hall to ensure the floor had been cleared of all OpFor warriors. Silence dominated the gritty, empty spaces. No one else remained in the building.

Private Skinner took down the OpFor sniper with a single shot. Garrick borrowed Otis Krieger's rifle, climbed onto the roof of the building and used the gun to dispatch the third sniper, who'd hidden himself on a roof to the east. With one building secure and the snipers eliminated, he waved Sergeant Ringer and his men forward. They would gain control over the building to the south, giving Garrick's platoon command of the western access to the Honeywater Bridge, as they'd been tasked to do.

Garrick set up his surviving men in key positions overlooking the bridge, then paused to think through his actions thus far. He fingered a carefully folded slip of paper that contained a note he'd written for Brenna, letting his mind wander for a moment to its contents. After this, he went downstairs to straighten out the dispute

The Long Journey: *Three Little Words*

over the grenade attack with the observers. In the midst of their discussion, he heard small arms fire coming from the east. That meant trouble! Garrick ran back upstairs to see what was going on.

Before advancing to secure this position, Garrick had left Sergeant Vidders and his squadron behind to act as a rear guard, providing security. Just as Sergeant Ringer and his men reached the eastern building, a company of OpFor soldiers raced up the street behind the garden wall where Garrick's men had been pinned down a few minutes earlier.

Something had gone terribly wrong!

Calling for his team to abandon their positions overlooking the bridge, Garrick used Otis Krieger's rifle to fire upon the OpFor warriors and prevent them from pinning Sergeant Ringer and his men against the building. Cursing his luck, Garrick selected targets carefully and held off a direct assault for a few minutes, allowing Sergeant Ringer's men to get inside. Sounds of a fierce fight ensued from within, but soon afterward Garrick noticed that all the ordnance coming from that building focused on the OpFor unit, indicating that Sergeant Ringer had successfully gained control of his objective.

Privates Bauer, Skinner and Kellerlein left their positions and joined the battle. Garrick warned them to conserve ammunition, but the sheer volume of gunfire directed toward them, coupled with repeated attempts by the OpFor commander to maneuver under covering fire, militated against any real savings.

Though they could not defeat the much larger force arrayed against them, Garrick's warriors held the OpFor at bay for what felt like a very long time. In reality the firefight lasted a little more than five minutes. The main assault force they were expecting hadn't arrived to reinforce or relieve them, and with ammunition running low, the young commander realized that defeat would inevitably result from trying to hold this position. Reluctantly, Garrick ordered his men to abandon the building.

They hustled downstairs, departing through a back door. With the sound of gunfire muted by the structure they'd just deserted, the assault team slid down a grassy embankment near the steel bridge and into the warm, shallow edge of the Honeywater. Garrick sent Bauer and Skinner wading across the river to set up a defensive position, while he and Imre Kellerlein moved behind the battered building where Sergeant Ringer and his men had been holed up.

The Long Journey: *Three Little Words*

Imre Kellerlein scrambled up the bank, went in through a back door and appeared presently with Sergeant Ringer and the three surviving men in his group. Using the bridge as cover, they forded the Honeywater and retreated to the east.

Moments later the mournful sound of a siren rose over the training compound. An authoritative male voice repeated the three word command that ended the exercise through elevated loudspeakers mounted on steel posts: "All units disengage!"

Garrick's team had been beaten in a combat exercise again, and he wasn't happy. Though he tried not to stew, Garrick had never been good at concealing his emotions and the men responded to his demeanor in sullen silence. They trudged back toward their headquarters along a gravel road, where they met with Sergeant Vidders and four of the fourteen men in his squadron. All those who'd been "wounded" or "killed" in action had already returned to clean their weapons and prepare for the post exercise report.

"You survived!" the stocky sergeant exclaimed, seeming far happier to see Garrick than the grim situation warranted.

Garrick shook his head. "We got our butts kicked, sergeant!"

"Perhaps, but they tell me you actually took your objective. That's better than most have done today."

"We did, but we couldn't hold it, so I had to withdraw. I left you behind to secure our flank," he said, accusingly, "but we got attacked from there instead."

Sergeant Vidders smiled and nodded. "Yes, you did! The OpFor hit us with a battalion-sized force and we were overrun. They left a full company in our position and sent the other one after you."

Garrick shook his head. "Well that figures! I'm sure you did your best to hold them off, sergeant. Nonetheless, we got our shorts washed today."

"It's only an exercise, Mr. Ravenwood. That's how we learn. It's better to make mistakes here than on the battlefield."

Exasperated, Garrick let out a stream of invective. "Learn what? Had this been a real fight, we'd have lost better than half the men in my platoon. I didn't make any mistakes, yet we couldn't hold our objective! What was I supposed to do to make this work? Now I've lost two consecutive leadership exercises. What lesson is there in this for me?"

Sergeant Vidders took Garrick by the arm and forcefully led him away from the other men. He spoke quietly, but firmly. "Where do you

The Long Journey: *Three Little Words*

get the idea that you're already perfect, Mister Ravenwood? Where do you get off believing that you fully understand what's going on around here? You'd better toughen yourself up, and right quick, if you expect the men to keep following your lead."

Garrick, who often acquiesced quickly in confrontational situations, didn't back down this time. He twisted his arm away from Dagmar Vidders. "I'm not insisting this is all about me, sergeant. I'm thinking about all the men we would have lost had this been an actual combat engagement."

"That's not what you're saying, nor is it how you're acting. Nobody wins every fight, Mister Ravenwood. That's a fact of life for every commander. Son, you were outgunned and overwhelmed this afternoon. The brass did that deliberately, to every officer candidate participating in these exercises to find out if any of you've got what it takes to lead when all hell breaks loose.

"Now get your face off the floor and think, Mister Ravenwood. What did you learn today? You can't evaluate what went right and what went wrong if you believe there's no room to improve, or if you're feeling sorry for yourself. Yet that kind of cold analysis now will save the lives of your men in the future. If you can't put yourself into a learning frame of mind, you're simply not cut out to lead men in battle."

Garrick felt shocked that his sergeant had taken him to task. However, he knew that Sergeant Vidders once served in front line fighting and that his counsel carried the weight of hard experience. "Ok sergeant," he replied, more reluctantly that he should have responded. "I hear you."

Sergeant Vidders slapped the younger man on the back in a good-natured way. "That's good. You've got a knack for combat, son. You were smart enough to realize that you couldn't win, so you backed off to a defensive position. That kind of thinking makes you a dangerous enemy. Don't worry about your score, Mister Ravenwood. I daresay you fared better this afternoon than did most of your classmates. You've done well."

Though these words were intended to make Garrick feel better, and though he put on a brave face as he stepped back into his commanding role, Garrick couldn't ignore the hurt he'd felt in failing to hold his positions overlooking the bridge. He didn't like being told that legitimate frustration should be held in check, and that his sense of impotence somehow stemmed entirely from a selfish motive. In addition, Garrick dreaded the imminent After Action Review, where TAC Vogel, who seemed particularly merciless when it came to performing evaluations, would dissect his every move.

As a westerly wind picked up and mountain peaks beyond Superstition Mesa vanished behind dark, brooding clouds, Garrick and his men entered the armory's covered weapon cleaning pit. White colored steel lattice work, held up by steel columns painted red, supported a wooden planked roof that gave this place the appearance of a sunken elementary school lunch area. Tables and benches equipped with old newspapers, bore snakes, solvent, cleaning rags and gun oil lay arranged in neat rows. Members of the training squadrons assembled here to clean their weapons after live fire exercises.

A pervasive sense of defeat hovered over the four-dozen men working in the cleaning pit. Garrick walked toward Greg Schmidt, who sat along the outer edge. His gloomy expression indicated he'd not done very well in reaching his objectives either. The older man pulled a bore snake through his disassembled rifle with care, then used a pen light to check the weapon for any residual fouling. He frowned, ignoring Garrick completely, while he reinserted the brass weight of his bore snake back through the rifle and gently tugged it through again.

"Tough exercise, huh?" Garrick began.

"Nothing that a little heavy artillery wouldn't fix," Greg responded, keeping his attention riveted on the task of inspecting his weapon. "Seems to me the best way to take a city is to completely level it first. Any senior commander crazy enough to attack an urban environment outnumbered like we were today ought to be strung up and flogged."

Garrick nudged him. "Watch yourself. People are listening."

At this, Greg fell silent for a moment, carefully applying oil to the action of his rifle. "I suppose you and your guys tromped the OpFor," he muttered in disgust.

"No," Garrick replied. "We held the objective for less than fifteen minutes before an entire OpFor company counterattacked and pushed us out."

Greg reassembled his gun, then stared straight into Garrick's eye. "So you're not invincible after all, Mister Ravenwood. That's the best news I've heard all day!" Candidate Schmidt, who'd always treated Garrick with kindness, made no effort to hide the bitter edge to his

The Long Journey: *Three Little Words*

voice as he looked away in anger and frustration. "If they wiped you out, then none of the rest of us stood a chance."

Although that remark had been meant as a compliment, the words stung and left a lingering welt. Garrick took his shotgun apart in silence and only grunted in farewell when Greg Schmidt departed. Suddenly, he didn't feel like talking to anyone.

In the midst of oiling the shotgun's hammer action, a strong gust of wind whipped loose newspaper across the pit, and a swirl of dust billowed around his work. In an effort to restrain the fluttering paper, Garrick accidentally knocked over a jar of gun oil. Uttering three loud curses, Garrick reached for a clean rag to mop up the spill.

"Your *ubermadchen's* here," Talon Waldheim teased. "Watch your language, Overhead!"

Garrick caught a glimpse of grey cotton running sweats rippling in the wind across a familiar female form as he looked up, and heard Brenna's light laughter in response to a remark Mariel had made. Garrick let his eyes linger on his Lithian girlfriend, thinking about the words he'd written for her the night before. These remained in his breast pocket while he waited, with rising nervousness, for an opportunity to give them to her.

Brenna could tell, as she approached the pit with Mariel, that an ugly mood prevailed among the men assembled there. She met Garrick's grey eyes and noticed the strange mix of frustration and delight expressed therein as his glare softened and he shifted over to make room for her and Mariel on the bench. Brenna picked up a fresh rag and dabbed Garrick's soiled cheek with it. "You've been rolling in the dirt, but your face is still cleaner than your mouth," she teased.

He shook his head and tightened his lips. Though he wanted to embrace and kiss her, he did not. "I'm sorry, Brenna. I'm glad you're here, but I've just finished a really tough exercise and I'm not looking forward to my After Action Review."

Mariel began taking her rifle apart. "Urban combat can wreck anyone's day," she remarked. "It's nearly as humiliating as qualifying with one of these."

Talon Waldheim, sitting behind her, overheard the remark. "Is that weapon not big enough, lieutenant? You want a real man's gun?"

Mariel could have reprimanded the officer candidate for the discourtesy implied in the double meaning of his words, but instead of using her authority to shut him up, the lieutenant dealt with this issue in a different way. She turned and patted Talon's shoulder as if he were a child. "Nothing you've got would ever satisfy me, soldier," Mariel quipped, drawing laughter and applause from some of the other officer candidates nearby. Talon Waldheim flushed in embarrassment. He would not soon live that one down.

Brenna understood the remark and her eyes widened, but she looked down and said nothing in response. Tamarians, at least the secular ones it seemed, maintained a double standard concerning sexual morality. They fretted over external issues, such as the clothing a woman wore in public, yet never considered risque conversation an indicator of a deeper, spiritual problem within.

Mariel, who lamented that men only seemed interested in what she looked like, often used her slim shape to manipulate them. However, she never subjected this conduct, nor her own propensity to engage in innuendo, to the same scrutiny by which she measured the behavior of men. Her response, while effective in stopping further harassment, demanded that Mariel's highly sharpened wit exceed the intellect of her antagonist. She was smart, and in most instances the lieutenant easily outmaneuvered her adversaries. But Brenna found her friend's proclivity debasing, and genuinely wished Mariel could simply rise above the gutter talk that so easily sprang from her lips.

Although Brenna said nothing about this, Garrick accurately read her facial expression and knew that she felt bad for Mariel. He'd learned enough about the way his girl thought to understand how she linked underlying attitudes with behavior, yet he also believed that Mariel handled the situation in a far more effective manner than an authoritative tongue lashing, or filing a formal complaint would have achieved. Talon Waldheim could easily protest that his remark had been uttered in complete innocence, and though everyone would secretly know that such a claim was a complete lie, Mariel might emerge from a formal investigation looking like a feeble, whiny female. She'd just proven herself neither feeble, nor whiny, but rather, a smart woman fully capable of holding her own among soldiers.

Garrick remained silent, completing his cleaning task, enjoying his nearness to Brenna and building up the nerve to give her the note he'd written.

Gusting wind waxed in strength. Dark clouds rolled in from the mountains, their sullen spires flattening into high altitude, anvil-shaped crowns from whence thunder began rumbling. Branches bent with

The Long Journey: *Three Little Words*

increasing urgency, their quivering leaves rattling in machine gun rhythm as a cell of hard rain clattered on the weapon pit's roof.

Looking up at the metal lattice supporting the roof boards, Garrick imagined the structure a giant lighting magnet and frowned. "It wouldn't hurt us to get out of here," he said. "Are you done with that rifle, lieutenant?"

Mariel, who'd put more than 500 rounds through her gun rolled her lovely brown eyes at Garrick. "If you can clean it faster than I, have at it!" she quipped.

He hadn't intended to clean it for her. "Here," he offered. "Let me help you finish."

Working cooperatively, the two of them completed the cleaning just as a blinding flash illuminated their surroundings. Garrick counted the elapsed time between the lightning and subsequent thunder, divided by five, and in so doing calculated the distance of the strike from their location as a little less than two miles.

Rain pelted the trio and drenched them as they raced toward the armory. Upon reaching the shelter of its overhanging roof, the two Tamarians paused to catch their breath while thunder roared overhead and hailstones began hammering the ground behind them. Brenna smiled, unaffected by the short sprint, noting that the dirt she'd seen on Garrick earlier now ran in rivulets down his cheeks and smeared when he wiped his face on a sleeve. She repressed the urge to clean him up, because she knew Garrick didn't like to be mothered. In addition, she suspected he would shower before attending the After Action Report with TAC Vogel.

Mariel opened the airlock door and held it against the gusty wind before walking into the vestibule. She paused when Garrick and Brenna didn't follow. "Aren't you coming in?" she inquired.

"I'll be there in a minute," Garrick replied, his words a signal to both women that he wanted a moment alone with Brenna.

As the door closed and Mariel went inside to return her weapon, Garrick pulled out the slip of paper he'd been carrying in his breast pocket. "This is for you," he said. "But don't read it in front of me, and please don't let Lieutenant Hougen see it."

Brenna accepted the note with a sense of trepidation, wondering what Garrick had written on the paper. She winced as lightning flashed and a loud crash of thunder immediately rumbled over the city skyline.

The Long Journey: *Three Little Words*

The Lithian maiden raised her eyebrows and expressed just a hint of a pout as he opened the door to the airlock and held it for her.

"I'll wait here," she told him. Brenna watched him go, then quickly unfolded the note. It had been dampened in the rain, and moisture spread the ink into watercolor lines that mirrored the script in lighter shades around the letter margins, but he'd written the words neatly, and the message they conveyed in her native language inspired a tear and sniffles.

Brenna folded the paper again and slipped it into a pouch within her sweat pants, drying her eyes as she watched hailstones bounce among blades of grass. Wind roared across the landscape and the rain returned, its heavy drops falling at such a steep angle Brenna sought shelter in the vestibule to keep from getting soaked. When Mariel returned, she noticed the emotion brimming in Brenna's dark eyes. "Are you all right?" the Tamarian woman inquired.

"Yes," said Brenna, sniffing. "It's nothing."

The storm passed several minutes later. A break in the clouds flooded the landscape with brilliant, golden light. Garrick emerged from within, his face clean in response to an admonition from Mariel to consult with a mirror. He reached for Brenna's hand, judging correctly from the expression on her face that she'd read his note.

"I have to get ready for the After Action Review," he told her. "Say a prayer for me."

Brenna nodded, but remained silent. She held onto his hand as he began pulling away, drawing him back with a sense of urgency in her tightened fingers. As he neared, she stood on her toes, her lips parted, her face imploring.

He kissed her gently, pulling on her pliant mouth with his own. She trembled and returned his affection with fervor, wrapping her arms around his waist and falling into his strong embrace. Brenna pressed her face tightly against his chest. Garrick stroked her damp hair and shut his eyes, losing himself for a moment in the comforting warmth of Brenna's soft body pressing tightly against his own.

Mariel tapped her right foot. "Ahem!" she said, clearing her throat in a manner warning that they should immediately cease their public display of affection.

Garrick let go, his expression a blend of longing and sadness. Without speaking another word, he turned, opened the outer door and trotted off in the renewing rain toward the mens' barracks.

The Long Journey: *Three Little Words*

"Really!" Mariel stated in mock disgust, her hands on her hips. "You two should employ a little discretion when you're in public."

"Envious?" Brenna queried, the mischievous smile she donned on such occasions just hinting at the corner of her lips.

Mariel nodded. "Yes, a little." Then she laughed. "What girl wouldn't be?"

Rain accompanied their walk back to the university. The fierce, summer storm chased away the protesters and their three word signs. No policeman patrolled the silent, litter-strewn street. The two women did not speak as they walked up the long staircase that climbed Liberty Hill, each lost in her own thoughts.

Like the scent of the air after rain, Brenna felt refreshed within her soul. She re-visualized the affectionate words Garrick had written for her:

"There are three little words
> that are all too often said,
>> which can be spoken in a whisper, or
>>> written down and read.

And I've often longed to tell you
> as I've watched you from afar, that
>> you inspire in me three little words
>>> and you know what they are."

A Prayer for the Living

Vultures circled in the cloudless sky. The gradual, almost imperceptible decline of a landscape stretching toward the vast wetlands bordering the Bay of Kameron paralleled a like descent into the madness of civil war. Sweating in the afternoon heat, Algernon pedaled past a long line of refugees whose ghostly eyes appraised him with silent apathy. No one asked why he and his companions steadfastly headed into the wrong direction, and none of the Kamerese seemed more than momentarily interested in the two Tamarians, the armed Abelscinnian warrior on horseback, and the gwynling who rode behind him.

Their route had been empty when they first set out from the Velez estate the day before. Leaving pleasant vineyards and rolling hills behind, the four companions crossed a narrow, stone bridge that arched over the Virgin River and followed the Mistress of the Woods Road toward its origin at the river port of Magnolia Bend, nearly 180 miles away. Jhiran sat on the hindquarters of Jawara's horse, chewing on carrot sticks while two stray dogs trotted behind, their tongues lolling in the heat.

Although the Mistress of the Woods Road had once served as an important link in the transportation infrastructure of the Kamerese frontier, rail lines had largely supplanted its function. The blue slate flagstone paving that had once marked this road as an engineering marvel had long ago either fallen into disrepair, or succumbed to vandalism. Grasses flourished between the stones and grew in places where the freeze and thaw of bygone seasons cracked the lovely slate. Thieves had torn out long sections of the paving for sale on the thriving black market. Slate flagstones cloven into thinner sheets found functional and decorative use in private estates for roofing material, wall wainscots, and patio pavers. The distance from central authority in Kameron City assured that crimes of this nature were seldom investigated and most often remained unpunished.

A canopy of old maple trees shaded the Mistress Road for several miles. Along its flanks a pair of low walls demarcated lands long abandoned as wealth and settlement patterns drifted further west and south. A young forest thrived in soil that had not seen plow and harrow for generations, crowding out fruit trees whose branches desperately stretched, thin and leggy, toward light filtering through taller pines. Vine-tangled stone buildings with sagging roofs and empty doorways

The Long Journey: *A Prayer for the Living*

overgrown with ferns, mosses and epiphytes slowly crumbled to the ground. In places where men and women once worked, where their children laughed and played, song birds chittered and the occasional deer paused in its grazing to gaze in vigilant stillness at the travelers passing by.

The landscape inspired a strange mix of feelings within Algernon's heart. He felt drawn to the oldness of this place in the same manner he felt an attachment to Superstition Mesa. He imagined what life had been like here in the days of its glory, before the banditos reigned, before neglect and lawlessness plunged this once pleasant place into its current desolation. Beneath his longing for what might have been, Algernon felt sadness for what had happened here, and a strong foreboding for what lay ahead. The sensation haunted him as he pedaled forward in contemplative silence.

Broken gates, burn scars on ruined foundations and tree trunks, trash and damaged farm equipment littered vacant villages where peasants had fled the oppression of criminal gangs. The workers' pleadings for order, unheeded by absentee land lords, echoed like thin ghost voices among walls scarred by fire and bullet holes. No one had come to save the peasants. Once the banditos arrived, living here became very dangerous.

Perhaps some of those whose ancestors ran from the historical anarchy now swelled the ranks of refugees streaming from the southwest. After the pleasant maple canopy thinned and the Mistress Road led into the open landscape, its broken, weedy trail approached the junction of the better maintained Old Fair Haven Road, where a small inn and a general store provided the first evidence of contemporary civilization the travelers had seen since leaving the Velez estate. Here, as the Daystar climbed beyond its zenith, they stopped to rest Jawara's horse beneath the shade of an oak tree.

Jhiran gathered twigs to cook what promised to be a simple meal while the stray dogs ran off in search of something their noses found interesting. Accustomed to a rather bland mix of vegetables, fruits, grains and tasteless fish the monks ate in the Temple, Algernon found that spicy Lithian food served in the Velez household set his mouth on fire! After his first encounter with Lithian cuisine, small bowls of *zhi*–a thick, sweet Tamarian yogurt made from sheep milk–appeared whenever he and Astrid sat for their meals, providing welcome relief from the searing entrees he'd eaten in discomfort. Though he didn't like to cook

The Long Journey: *A Prayer for the Living*

and felt grateful that Jhiran took up this task, Algernon would've prepared every meal just to eat food that better suited his palate.

Jawara stayed with Jhiran. He laughed at her antics while he tended to his horse and sorted through food items retrieved from Algernon's bike trailer. Lady Alexina provided generously for their journey; they carried enough to feed five people for two weeks. After selecting the lunch menu, the big Abelscinnian lay his automatic rifle nearby while he struggled to start a fire in Algernon's tin can stove.

Algernon and Astrid walked down to the road and mingled among the refugees, inquiring if any of them had seen either Marco or Kira. Very few people acknowledged the foreigners with more than a glance, and Astrid grew increasingly frustrated with the lack of cooperation the Kamerese extended to her. As they moved further up the Old Fair Haven Road, a strange, putrid smell that had lingered in the air grew stronger, and soon they discovered one of many reasons why the refugees remained reluctant to speak with them.

The stray dogs who'd been following them found a human body that had been tied to a pole. The animals tore off large hunks of meat from the victim's legs and ran off to devour their meal as Algernon shooed them and scavenging crows away. People recoiled from the scene, sickened at the sight and smell of decaying flesh, but as Astrid approached her eyes widened in the added horror of recognition.

Flies and beetles fed within festering wounds. Dried blood and deep bruises covered the bloated body, yet despite the obvious disfigurement, Astrid matched the decaying face and clothing with that of the fiery speaker in Fair Haven Fortress whose sermon incited the mob several days earlier. She'd have retched, had there been any food in her belly.

Algernon held his breath. The body had been wrapped to the post with rusty barbed wire, his hands bound above his head. Judging from the dried bloodstains that formed enlongated ovals below each wound, the itinerant preacher had been alive when hung here. A placard, suspended by similar wire around his neck, contained a single word and warning: "Traitor," it read in Northern Kamerese.

Astrid turned away. "What kind of person would do such a thing?" she breathed.

The common revulsion of gazing upon an unburied body also struck Algernon, whose mind raced through the possible implications of the gruesome scene. Remembering the sermon, he concluded that

The Long Journey: *A Prayer for the Living*

whoever had slain the itinerant preacher strongly disagreed with his revolutionary message. "Someone loyal to King Alejo," he replied. "Or maybe someone interested in preserving the status quo."

"We shouldn't leave his body exposed," Astrid said, keeping her eyes averted. "It's not right."

Algernon nodded. "But we don't want to touch it either. I see fly eggs in his mouth so he's not been dead long enough for maggots, but I don't think we should handle his corpse. I've got an idea."

Gently placing his hand on Astrid's back, the Tamarian monk moved her away from the grisly site. They walked over to the general store, an establishment curiously lacking patronage, given the large number of people passing by on the road. Algernon bought a large container of lamp oil using a Kamerese kroner, rousing the suspicion of the clerk, who eyed him in mistrust.

"You don't have anything smaller than this?" the balding man inquired, his eyes narrowed. "Seems an awful lot of money for a holy man to carry around."

"I have only what I'm given," Algernon replied. Saying this wasn't precisely true and technically violated one of his vows, but no matter how much money he spent or gave away, 16 coins of the local currency remained in his moneybag. Since the pouch had been a gift from Garrick, Algernon's conscience didn't flinch. He had taken to wrapping each coin in cloth so they wouldn't clink together and arouse unwanted curiosity. However, using a golden kroner for a small purchase didn't fit the profile of a poor monk, and Algernon worried that revealing his treasure to the store keeper would stir more attention than he desired.

But he couldn't stomach the thought of leaving the preacher's body to rot on the pole and serve as food for wild animals.

Algernon returned to the oak tree and used a tiny bit of lamp oil to help Jawara light the tin can stove, explaining the situation to his Abelscinnian friend. Then, he found a long stick, dipped it into the lamp oil, ignited its end by sticking it into the hot cookstove and gave the firebrand to Astrid. She followed him back to the murder scene where they offered prayers for the soul of the dead man.

After this, as Algernon dumped lamp oil on the festering body, several armed riders on horseback approached. "Hey! What do you think you're doing?" one of them demanded.

The Long Journey: *A Prayer for the Living*

Algernon stepped away from the corpse and took the firebrand from Astrid's hand, touching it to the oil-soaked robe of the dead preacher. Sooty flames quickly engulfed the body as the oil, clothing and eventually the flesh itself, caught fire. A noisome reek arose that almost smelled worse than had the rotting remains. Algernon set the burning stick at the base of the pole and turned to face his accuser. He crossed his arms and moved his left foot slightly back, a subtle defensive posture, but said nothing.

"I'm talking to you!" the man said sternly. "Answer me, boy! What are you doing?"

Algernon didn't know how to respond. Standing on foreign soil and confronting half a dozen armed men on horseback, he realized that any action that might escalate the conflict would likely result in his own death, yet that's precisely how he'd always behaved in the past, and now he found himself at a loss to come up with a better strategy. He also worried that if the men killed him, they'd quickly and publicly have their way with Astrid. Algernon had grown fond of her and simply couldn't bear that thought. The young monk closed his eyes, breathed a brief prayer for wisdom, and the words of High Priest Volker flashed into his mind: "A wise man responds to anger with gentleness."

"Had this been your body, or that of someone you loved, wouldn't you or your family appreciate my courtesy? If you can't show kindness to the living, you can at least respect the dead."

A murmur swept through the assembled crowd. People began backing away, and Astrid's eyes flashed from Algernon to the armed men on horseback. They were puzzled by Algernon's carefully worded response and some of them suddenly seemed less intent on causing trouble. Light-skinned and bearded, these men most likely originated locally and might have been well known among the natives who now gave them a wide berth. Because they spoke Northern Kamerese, she understood none of the discourse, but accurately interpreted their postures and facial expressions.

"Answer my question, monkey boy," the rider demanded. "Who gave you permission to burn that body?" He could have sworn he'd seen this Tamarian monk before.

Algernon felt Astrid drawn close and heard her whisper words of caution into his ear. He reached for her hand and gave it a squeeze in response. "It's the universal right of every man to have his remains

The Long Journey: *A Prayer for the Living*

disposed of with dignity," Algernon replied, calmly. "No one deserves to be eaten by dogs."

The horseman pointed at the stinking conflagration. "That was not a man. That was a wild pig. His demise served as a warning to the insolent. Now you have removed that deterrent, and you should take his place."

Algernon had spoken at length with Jared concerning the legality of his sister's disposition in Kameron, and spent two evenings reading through law books the Lithian attorney had provided for him. So when Algernon replied to the horseman, he put his hands on his hips and adopted an accusatory tone. "Under whose authority do you make such a judgment? Do you speak for the king? Are you a land owner?"

The horseman dismounted. He stood taller and broader than Algernon, and thought–wrongly–that moving close would intimidate the young monk. "I'll speak for the king. I say that insurrectionists and all foreign swine should die."

Algernon remained calm. "You're a liar!" he replied. "You speak for no one other than yourself."

"You'd better watch your mouth, monkey boy! I've a good mind to string you up like him!" The man pointed to the burning body.

"Oh," Algernon replied, feigning interest. "Are you confessing to murder now, or merely threatening my life?"

The man stridently poked his finger into the younger man's chest. "You act like there's law and order in this country. The law won't help when there's no one around to protect you from me."

Algernon stood his ground. He could have easily knocked the man's hand away and sent him sprawling with a hard knee to the gut and an elbow to his face, but he chose not to up the ante. "You say I need someone to protect me, but you're the one holding a gun. Why are you afraid of a priest? I bear no weapons."

"I told you to watch your mouth, monkey boy!" The man's anger flashed into a backhanded slap across Algernon's face.

Astrid felt tension rising in Algernon's arms. She knew he could have killed the horseman, who left himself wide open for attack and had no clue of Algernon's fighting skill, but she saw his hands open as the young monk willed restraint upon himself.

Algernon wiped his face. Blood covered his hand. He stared into the dark eyes of his adversary and held up his palm for all to see. "Are

The Long Journey: *A Prayer for the Living*

you a man, now?" he inquired, struggling to suppress his rage. "Did hitting me make you feel better about yourself?"

Some of the other horsemen began to laugh. "Hey Iago, are you actually a man?" one of them teased.

"Maybe he's only dressing like a man!" remarked another in a quasi-serious tone.

"I've never seen him naked. Have we been following a woman this whole time?" inquired a third.

"Eew! A cross-dressing woman with a beard!"

"Just leave him alone, Iago!"

At that moment Jhiran dashed between the stirring horses. She ignored the Kamerese men and stood between Algernon and his adversary. Jhiran wiped blood from his face with her sleeve in a strangely childlike, yet tender and motherly way that Algernon would have found irritating had he not been so concerned for his life. "He's hurt you, holy man!" she said worriedly. "Why did you let him do that?"

Astrid tried to pull Jhiran away, but the gwynling did not wish to leave Algernon. She glared at Iago for a moment, then pulled her sling from the back of her belt and went after the horseman, using the leather weapon like a lash. "You bully!" she snapped, painfully thrashing any exposed flesh she could reach. Though Iago tried to restrain her, Jhiran proved far more nimble, and the one time he managed to get a hand on her, she bit him hard.

The other horsemen laughed. "Better quit while you're ahead, Iago," one of them said. "That girl is gonna give you a good beating!"

"Maybe that's what he wants!" responded another. "Look at her go! She's a master beater!"

"Oh, beat me too little girl!" chimed in a third, and the commentary among the other horsemen degraded from there.

When Algernon noticed Jawara standing on the roadside with his rifle readied for action, the young monk felt a surge of confidence that an experienced warrior would come to his aid. "Alright, that's enough now!" he warned, holding out his arm to keep Iago away from the gwynling. He picked up Jhiran as if she were a wayward child and shielded her from any potential retribution by holding her on his left hip while his right foot remained forward.

The gwynling's gaze burned into the horseman's eyes. She filled his mind with imagery of Algernon tearing apart the Kamerese merchant and his cronies in Marvic. She imprinted every bone crushing move into the man's consciousness, until Iago felt the blood drain from his face and his heart pound in fear.

"Where have I seen you before?" Iago inquired. "Why do I know your face?"

Jhiran searched through the horseman's memory, then looked at Algernon, whose eyes widened as he gently set the gwynling down. Jhiran turned to Astrid and silently spoke a message into her mind, and the priestess covered her mouth in hope and trepidation.

"Tell me the truth!" Algernon demanded, sniffing a trickle of blood that dripped from his nose. "You're no land owner. You're nothing more than a bounty hunter!"

Iago backed away with a leveled rifle, far more leery of Algernon than he'd been a few moments before. "What's it to you?" he asked.

"You've seen my sister!" Algernon accused, fearlessly approaching with a predatory look in his eye. "Where is she now?"

"I don't know what you're talking about! I've never seen your sister!" Iago hissed.

"Liar!" Algernon spat in reply. He asked Astrid for Kira's portrait, then strode to one of the horseman and held up the drawing.

"Isn't that Marco Fang's slave girl?" he replied, turning to one of his companions, who looked at the drawing and nodded. "She's that little opium whore who ran away after her master had his fill of her." Turning toward Algernon, he leaned forward. "We caught her not far from here a little over a week ago." Then grinning, he added: "She was a lot of fun!" Other men murmured in assent.

Algernon ignored the remark, though it pained him to hear the implied abuse done to his sister, and returned to Iago. "Where can I find her now?"

"What? You think you're going to save her, monkey boy? Within a week she'll be sold to some rich, old pervert who'll make good use of her skills. That's all she's good for anyway.

"And be warned! Marco Fang and his kin won't think twice about killing you once they know you're down here, snooping around and meddling in their affairs. Lord Fang's army is within two days' ride of this place and when they catch you, I promise they won't be as nice to you as I've been. If you're smart, monkey boy, you'll turn your tail and head right back home to mommy."

Astrid touched Algernon on the shoulder and spoke in Tamarian. Because she didn't understand what Iago had said, Astrid interpreted

The Long Journey: *A Prayer for the Living*

Algernon's fierce facial expression as an indication that the Kamerese horseman had uttered something unpleasant. "He sold Kira to a broker and collected his fee from Marco Fang," she whispered. "Jhiran says the broker met these guys at a place called *Cavidade Sonoliento*, which means *Sleepy Hollow* in our language. I've seen it on the map. We could probably make it there today."

Algernon glared at the Kamerese bounty hunter. "I want the name of the broker who bought my sister from you," he demanded.

"And you think I'm going to tell you?" Iago replied, not realizing that merely thinking about the transaction revealed his thoughts to Jhiran. "I'll soon spit on your dead carcass, monkey boy!" Iago turned back toward his horse and pulled himself into the saddle. He motioned with his head for his companions to move on, and they trotted northwest toward Fair Haven Fortress. The refugees along the road quickly moved aside to let them pass.

Algernon breathed a sigh of relief, noting that as the horsemen moved on, Jawara kept his eyes keenly focused on them, ready to respond to any threat. When the Tamarians passed him, the big 'Scinnian cleared the chamber of his weapon. "God be praised!" he said quietly. He slapped Algernon on the shoulder in a sign of solidarity and walked with his companions back to the oak tree.

Astrid put her arm around Algernon's waist and squeezed him, laying her head on his shoulder. "I'm proud of you!" she said.

"I let some thug smack me in the face, and you're proud of me?" Algernon shook his head. "That doesn't make any sense!"

As Astrid leaned against him, the sensation of her nearness felt pleasant. "It's not that," she replied. "You used your head. He may have given you a bloody nose, but you proved yourself much more of a real man than he did. It took courage to stand your ground and not retaliate instead of fighting a bully like him. I knew it was in you!"

Algernon rolled his eyes. That kind of thinking had to be a girl thing, he thought. He certainly didn't feel brave. As he often did when unhappy with a particular event, he let his imagination conjure a more typical outcome and meditated on the alternative course of action. Death loomed at the end of that path, and as he thought about this, Algernon remembered Astrid's counsel while they waited for Garrick in the university's security office. Feeding the rage he felt swelling inside would have cost him his life, and though Jawara might have fired quickly

The Long Journey: *A Prayer for the Living*

enough to prevent the bounty hunters from killing him, they carried six rifles to his one. There would have been a lot of death in any case.

She'd been right. Astrid had proven that she was a smart girl. Why hadn't he recognized her wisdom before? Why had he so ruthlessly dismissed her as unworthy of his time and attention? Her softness and proximity, the way her hip swayed while she walked and the warmth of her attention aroused him again. Algernon let her go to regain control, but she didn't seem bothered by his withdrawal.

Jawara had doused the cookstove fire with dirt, so it had to be emptied, stoked and relit before they could eat. Algernon and Astrid sparingly wet and carefully washed their hands with soap and rinsed, using as little water as possible. This technique testified to their experience in Marvic, and Jawara, whose family originated in the desert, washed with similar care.

Only Jhiran, who'd grown up near a river, used water with less concern for conservation. The gwynling remained strangely quiet. She puckered her lips and muttered something unintelligible as she heated up a slab of flat bread, flipping it with a dexterous flick of her wrist to warm the other side.

Algernon approached and sat down, cross-legged, in the grass. "Can you tell me the name of the slave broker who bought my sister?"

Jhiran nodded her head but didn't look at him. Emotion choked in her voice, and her large, brown eyes narrowed in anger. "Those are bad men!" she said. "They beat your sister and held her down. Then they all took turns..."

Her response seemed more empathetic than Algernon expected. Having vicariously witnessed the collective agonies of every mind she met, Jhiran's capacity to care about strangers faded with ongoing exposure to many tormented experiences. However, though she'd never met Kira, Jhiran genuinely recoiled at the brutality imposed upon Algernon's twin sister. This sympathetic response indicated that her affection for the Tamarian monk had grown since she'd first met him, but Algernon, who knew little about gwynlings and tolerated Jhiran as he would a bratty cousin, missed the implications of her response.

The Tamarian monk closed his eyes and sighed quietly. "That's what I thought."

"They should all die!" the gwynling rasped. "And it should hurt!"

"Now you know why we have to save my sister," Algernon replied. "But I need you to tell me the name of the slave broker."

The Long Journey: *A Prayer for the Living*

Jhiran finished heating the last of the flat bread and dumped a mixture of smoked fish and chopped vegetables into the pan. "Chale," she said, pronouncing the name as "CHA-lay," precisely the way a Northern Kamerese native would say it.

Algernon thanked her, electing not to share Jhiran's revelation with Astrid. He struggled to suppress his own emotions, feeling impotent, and wandered a few yards away so that he could pray in peace. Unaccustomed to sincere prayer, uncomfortable with the concept of talking to the Great God as if the remote, unknowable deity actually cared about Kira, Algernon's frustration smoldered and he soon gave up on what he considered a useless exercise after a few, feeble attempts at intercession. He felt desperate to move on, before someone abused Kira badly enough to kill her.

When Algernon returned to eat, Astrid sat and fed him, as was her custom. She accepted food from his hand as well, read the tension in his facial expression and understood that he didn't want to tell her something important. He seemed too upset to talk about whatever it was that bothered him, and Astrid felt too afraid to ask.

Witnessing the tender way in which the two Tamarians treated one another, Jawara shook his head. Although the thought of Astrid's relationship with Kira repulsed him and the holy writings of the Abelscinnians condemned homosexuality in strident terms, as he watched the girl care for Algernon the 'Scinnian warrior couldn't help feeling impressed by her humility and the servanthood she displayed. The Abelscinnians honored these traits among both genders and his culture's holy writings exalted servility, so Astrid's behavior presented a genuine paradox for his mind to consider.

It would have been easier to despise her, had she not been so likeable. Jawara might have treated her with minimal respect if she'd been haughty, brazen, or if Astrid had insisted on flaunting her immorality for all to see. Jawara struggled with these issues when Lynden Velez first charged him with protecting the Tamarians. He'd accepted that task willingly, but the 'Scinnian warrior had to admit that the task of watching over Astrid was made easier because her conduct remained liberally seasoned with gentle grace.

After everyone had eaten, Astrid pulled a map from among many papers she'd packed in the saddlebag. The town of Sleepy Hollow appeared near a low ridge where the Mistress Road angled slightly

The Long Journey: *A Prayer for the Living*

north of the hills. However, Astrid had been dreadfully wrong about its proximity.

Algernon examined the plat carefully. "That's nearly thirty miles away!" he exclaimed. Though Algernon believed he was in good enough shape to ride that distance by evening, he doubted that Jawara's horse could do so. He turned toward his Abelscinnian friend. "How far can your beast go in a single day?" he asked.

"She can get better than halfway there," Jawara replied. "We have at least seven hours of daylight remaining, but even if we didn't stop, she can't go fast enough to make it before nightfall. The water bladder is too heavy." The Abelscinnian warrior patted the flanks of his spotted mare. "She will need rest, and we'd be wise to rest as well."

Algernon reverted to his own language and cursed in a rather unholy fashion. In ancient times, he'd read, humans hunted horses by running them to exhaustion. The legendary horse clans of the Saradon were known to cover more than 100 miles in a day, but their warriors pushed the animals onward until their mounts dropped dead, then the men simply climbed upon another.

The four travelers could not afford to lose Jawara's horse, as she carried the 'Scinnian warrior and Jhiran, as well as most of their water. She would carry Kira whenever they found her, and at that time Jhiran would ride in the bicycle trailer behind Algernon, where most of their food had been packed.

During Algernon's brief stay at the Velez estate, Jared explained that the illegal slave markets most often met when the moons were new, a time considered sacred in the Kamerese religious calendar. Secular activities halted, and under normal circumstances the police and the national army returned to barracks to receive their monthly pay. Jared warned that finding the location of a clandestine slave auction would not be easy, especially now that the civil war had made many Kamerese suspicious of all foreigners.

The twin moons had been waning and would begin their orbital cycle again in about a week. To reach the big slave market at Magnolia Bend in that time frame, the travelers had to cover at least 14 miles per day, but they had no guarantee of actually finding Kira in the river port city once they arrived, if, in fact, she hadn't been sent even further away. And worse, the longer they took in locating her, the greater the chance that the fighting between rebel warlords, militias and the Kamerese National Army further south would overtake them.

The Long Journey: *A Prayer for the Living*

Frustrated, Algernon urged his companions to finish packing up and resume their journey. The burden on his heart increased in weight and sharpness as he pedaled for hours to narrow the distance between himself and his headstrong sister. An instinctive sense that something beyond control would impede all progress heightened as the travelers approached two separate check points and waited for uncaring soldiers to verify their documents and allow them to move forward.

Staffed by a twenty-four-man platoon of the Kamerese National Army, these makeshift stations served to harass refugees and screen for criminals. While Algernon and his friends waited at the second stop for an officer to check their papers, a commotion ensued. Three soldiers pulled an uncooperative young man out of the refugee line. He complained loudly and flailed to escape as the warriors beat him down with their rifle butts. An older woman protested with increasing agitation, but the soldiers knocked her away while they bound their prisoner's hands and forced him to kneel. A moment later, one of them coldly shot him in the back of the head with a pistol.

The woman screamed and wept in bitter anguish, lamenting the loss of her son. One of the soldiers warned her to be quiet, then cuffed her across the mouth when she didn't immediately obey. As the travelers watched, the Kamerese soldier grabbed her by the hair, dragged and shoved her beyond the checkpoint while one two of his companions picked up the corpse and threw it onto a stinking pile of slain bodies. The woman fell to the ground and wept inconsolably.

Anger burned in Algernon's heart. He didn't know why the young man deserved death, but compassion rose within his soul for the woman and he felt very upset about the hasty judgment and punishment he'd seen. Dispensing justice without trial, without hearing arguments concerning the condemned man's innocence nor allowing anyone to speak in his defense, these soldiers executed a fellow citizen simply because he matched the description of an accused criminal.

The crowd grew restless in response. Fearing the potential for a riot, the nervous platoon members fired warning shots into the air, then aimed their rifles directly at the refugees. At this threat, the civilians drew back, but the bitter seeds of revolution had been sown among many fertile minds.

Old struggles against authority and control simmered in Algernon's heart. The scene he'd witnessed stirred fantasies of heroic reprisal, of standing fast against the oppression of the powerful. Yet

The Long Journey: *A Prayer for the Living*

deep within, Algernon felt beaten down by the harsh reality that no one could stop the soldiers from killing. They exercised their authority with a ruthlessness Algernon had only imagined in his darkest mood, and for the first time since coming to Kameron, the Tamarian monk wished his brother had been here with his army to make things right. Some problems, Algernon reasoned, could only be solved by force. Some freedoms, he realized, were only bought in blood.

A long line of sullen refugees on the far side of the check point thickened in the waxing afternoon heat, and as the young monk wiped the sweat from his brow, he noticed vultures circling high in the bright sky. The carrion birds would soon eat their fill of flesh.

The officer who checked Algernon's guest visa saw his swollen nose and shook his head. "This is no place for the holy," he remarked.

Algernon nodded. "I can see that." He wanted to heap verbal abuse on the Kamerese officer for permitting what amounted to cold-blooded murder, but fear that the soldiers would think nothing of killing a foreign monk motivated restraint. Algernon uttered a prayer for the murdered man, but said nothing more as the officer checked through his companions' identity documents.

The Tamarian monk held his breath every time one of the soldiers looked at Jhiran's papers because the gwynling did not possess formal citizenship. Had the Kamerese officers known who and what she was, Jhiran could have been detained or forbidden from traveling further. Anticipating this problem, Astrid created identification on Jhiran's behalf with some assistance from Jared. Apparently, the priestess possessed sufficient artistic skill that Jhiran's forged papers consistently passed inspection without comment.

An hour after leaving the last checkpoint, the line of refugees thinned considerably and the travelers approached a low rise crowned by oak trees along the south side of the road. Here, where golden grasses stood as withered reminders of brief spring rains, an old homestead had fallen onto its foundation. A deep well on this property had been dug by the pioneering family many years ago. Jawara encouraged Algernon to pause for refreshment among the overgrown fruit trees that marked a long abandoned orchard, and though Algernon agreed to stop, he did so with clearly stated reluctance.

As they approached the well canopy, Algernon read a hand-painted sign warning that the water had been poisoned and relayed the message to his companions. While the sign might have been a ruse to increase the misery of refugees, drinking potentially poisoned water didn't seem worth the risk. Jawara led his horse beneath a stand of grapefruit trees and loosened the saddle. He draped the heavy saddlebag water bladder over his shoulders and cupped his hands while Astrid controlled the flow of warm, clean water with a valve. Working together in this manner, they gave Jawara's horse a well-deserved drink.

Jhiran climbed the trees to collect fruit while Algernon trotted past the homestead ruins and ascended the hill, intending to relieve himself among the oak trees. A path of trampled grasses led the way, and the glimmer of many spent shell casings flashed in the strong, afternoon light. He heard a multitude of bird voices as he approached, and peering through the oaks, a sickening sight met his eyes.

A refugee camp littered with torn, bullet-ridden tents and burned equipment lay just beyond the rise. Fallen bodies rotted on the ground, and among them, avian scavengers hopped, waddled and fought with one another over bits of flesh. Jackals and feral dogs roamed among the dead. As a gentle air current shifted, an overwhelming stench drifted into Algernon's nose and inspired a strong rush of nausea.

He could see that most of the casualties were civilian refugees, irregular militia forces and the camp followers who attended them. From their positions and injuries, it looked like many had been shot in the back while attempting to run away. This had not been a battle. This had been sheer butchery.

Several people wearing kerchiefs over their faces wandered among the slain, stripping shoes, watches and trinkets like reapers in a ripened field. Algernon caught his breath, thinking that the only harvest he'd seen thus far in Kameron involved human flesh. Poor Kira! He had to find her before she wound up in a place like this!

Algernon discreetly emptied his bladder, then scurried back down the hill to warn his friends and motivate them onward. Jawara sat near his horse in meditation with a holy book, his lips forming words while he read. Jhiran stuffed last year's oranges into her mouth as if she hadn't eaten in weeks, while Astrid lay on a blanket in the shade. Her face looked flushed and she had no intention of leaving right away.

"I'm tired!" she complained, deliberately speaking in vulgate so that everyone would understand. "We've been riding for hours! My butt hurts, I'm getting a skin burn and I want to rest in the shade for a while."

"Come on, Astrid!" Algernon urged. "We'll never find Kira if we don't get going!"

The Long Journey: *A Prayer for the Living*

At this point Jawara put down his book and intervened. "Stop for a moment and think, my friend," he said gently. "We are making good progress, but we can't sustain the pace you're setting. My horse needs a rest. In addition, both you and the priestess have fair skin that's turning red in the strong daylight, and she's warning you that she is tired. What good will moving forward do if she soon becomes exhausted? Will you leave her behind to fend for herself?"

Algernon seethed in frustration. "If we don't find Kira soon, we may not find her at all!" he exclaimed. "We went all the way to see Brenna's parents and wasted our time there. Now all of you are moaning about fatigue and want to slack off! I knew I should have done this on my own." He stormed away angrily, muttering curses.

Yet their time at the Velez estate had been productive for many reasons, and in a more rational frame of mind Algernon understood this clearly. In addition, the fortuitous timing of their encounter with Iago set them directly back on Kira's trail. Without Jhiran's ability to detect the bounty hunter's thoughts, or the map Astrid had copied during their stay in the Velez compound, Algernon would have wandered through Kameron aimlessly. Further, the protection of Jawara's automatic rifle restrained the responses of Iago's companions, who had to honor the threat he represented. Thus, each of his companions contributed to the ongoing success of his search for Kira. These facts didn't make him feel better, but as the monk swatted at trees in frustration he realized that he'd been wrong to criticize his trustworthy friends.

Jawara, who was several years older than Algernon, considered the manner in which every detail of their journey dovetailed together, underscoring his faith that they walked a path ordained by God. He *believed* they would find Kira soon. He had a strong sense that she remained alive, and with this in mind, the 'Scinnian warrior bowed his head and prayed briefly for her protection.

"What is with him?" Astrid inquired to nobody in particular. "Why can't he ever think of anyone other than himself?"

"He's young," Jawara said in Algernon's defense. "He will learn patience."

Jhiran shook her head. "He's afraid," she stated, chewing an orange. "The holy man only wants to save his sister."

"Well so do I!" Astrid snapped.

Jawara gently placed his hand on Astrid's shoulder, his calm demeanor like a shady tree on a hot afternoon. "Then pray," he

The Long Journey: *A Prayer for the Living*

commanded. "Help for your friend lies beyond our power, but the Holy God will honor our faith and protect her if we pray."

When Algernon returned and witnessed Jawara and Astrid interceding on behalf of Kira, his wrath cooled. Jhiran lingered in the tree branches, discarded a rind and bit into her fourth orange. Her face, fingers and elbows gleamed with orange juice as she slurped into the sticky, sweet fruit. When he looked up at her in disgust, Jhiran merely wiped her mouth on her blood-encrusted sleeve and silently informed the Tamarian monk that she was hungry, that she'd been married, had borne children, and thus she felt no need to impress anyone–especially him–with her appearance.

Jhiran acted as if she was perpetually hungry. As Algernon sat in the shade of a nearby grapefruit tree, watching hot air rise in ripples from the distant landscape, he counted 12 orange rinds on the ground by the time the gwynling climbed down from her perch. She remained perfectly content to leave the sticky remnants of citrus juice on her skin and clothes, raising the suspicion in Algernon's mind that something was very wrong with her. When she looked at him, Algernon turned away so that she couldn't read his thoughts.

Anxious and restless, the young monk picked and peeled a few oranges for himself, carefully separating the carpels and slowly chewing them as the afternoon wore on. Citrus trees, which did not grow anywhere in Tamaria, produced fruit considered a luxury food far beyond the means of impoverished monks. Algernon enjoyed oranges and couldn't understand why the Kamerese left perfectly good fruit hanging from healthy trees.

A cool breeze soon swept in from the Bay of Kameron, bringing welcome relief from the sweltering heat of late afternoon. The wind strengthened until dust and leaves began fluttering. Astrid, who'd drifted to sleep, stirred. Jawara put down his holy book and began preparing his horse for departure.

They all drank deeply before leaving. Algernon's bicycle seat felt uncomfortable, and as he ventured back into direct daylight, the sensation of heat on his reddened skin made him long for the cooler, cloudier climate of his homeland. He didn't complain, however, because he'd made such a fuss about stopping to rest. But his beloved Tamaria seemed very far away as the gently rolling topography of Northern Kameron stretched into the western horizon.

The Long Journey: *A Prayer for the Living*

By nightfall they'd become worried about finding shelter amid the desolation and sounds of artillery fire in the distance. Jhiran claimed that she could smell food and pointed down a rutted path that led to the northwest. Several hundred yards later, as her acute senses accurately indicated, they found an occupied farmhouse. A small adobe cottage with a white candle illuminating the front window beckoned like an old friend. The aroma of soup and bread wafted through open windows. Weary from their travels, the companions approached the covered porch and Algernon knocked on the door.

An elderly woman bearing an oil lamp answered his call. Rail thin, wearing a striped poncho and an embroidered, pleated skirt, she appraised the Tamarian monk with an expression of maternal concern, smiled and reached for his hand. "It looks like you've had a long day, friends. Please come in and rest."

"We don't want to trouble you," he replied. "All we ask is permission to camp overnight in your barn."

The woman dismissed Algernon's remarks as she gestured for his companions to enter. "Nonsense!" she replied, switching to vulgate so that all could understand. "You're children, not cattle! Shelter your horse in the barn, then come inside. I'll get you something to eat."

Jawara led his horse away while Algernon pulled the bicycles onto the porch and introduced Astrid and Jhiran. Fatigue and worry masked Astrid's usual demeanor. She wanted to express gratitude and bless the Kamerese woman, but the priestess felt so tired all she could think to do was bow her head and ask to lie down on a blanket-covered couch in the living room. Algernon followed her and plopped into a padded chair, displacing a skittish cat who darted from the room and vanished into a hallway.

The lady of the house bent down and put her hands on Jhiran's shoulders, staring into the gwynling's eyes for quite some time, willingly allowing Jhiran to search her mind. "You are a rare sight!" the woman said. "I haven't seen any of your people in many years."

No sooner had she uttered these words, than Jhiran embraced her and smiled, demonstrating acceptance and approval. In this manner Algernon confirmed that their hostess could be fully trusted.

Jhiran scurried to the bathroom to wash, repeating the words to a gwynling song. After this, she wandered into the kitchen and stirred the stew.

The Long Journey: *A Prayer for the Living*

A few minutes later Jawara returned, his friendly face showing little of the distress that marked his companions' expressions. The old woman smiled radiantly as he entered, strode toward him and offered a traditional blessing and welcome in the Abelscinnian language.

Jawara set his backpack and rifle case down, then introduced himself as the son of Penda, third wife of Tegene, his beloved father. "How do you know the tongue of my people?" he inquired.

Introducing herself as Maia, the only daughter of Benicia and Javier–the one time Kamerese ambassador to Abelscinnia–the woman explained that she'd grown up in the east. Many of the trinkets that adorned her plastered mantle, the tapestries and ceremonial wooden masks that decorated her walls had been gifts given to her late father by various tribal chieftains. Though most of these had come from the animist peoples living well beyond the big city, her description of Abelscinnia's vast sprawl across several islands in the midst of the Dagon River revealed an intimate knowledge of the place.

Maia had prepared a hearty supper in expectation of her adult daughter's imminent return from town, and the delay in her arrival inspired worry. Joining Algernon, Astrid and Jawara in the living room, she placed her wrinkled hands upon her lap and sighed. "These are difficult times," the old woman said. "The insurrection is growing and I worry for my daughter."

"Why don't you evacuate with the other refugees?" Algernon asked. "The lands north of here remain virtually empty."

When she turned her head, Maia's expression reflected a vigor the Tamarian monk had not expected to witness. "They remain empty for good reason," she replied. "I have lived 85 years in this world, I have seen my share of suffering and do not wish to endure more of it. My time to depart will come soon enough." Then she shook her head and the lovely, white curls of her thin hair repeated the motion with a half heartbeat delay. "When the rebels come they will take my land, even though it has been in my family for more than five generations." She glanced around the room, evaluating the memories of other places where she'd lived. Then, at Jhiran's call for assistance Maia stood. "I will not starve along the road and give my body to the ravens. I will die here, where I belong," she stated.

Algernon knew, from his study of agriculture and ecology, that Northeastern Kameron never produced the steady, abundant crop yields of the land further south. As the landscape rose toward the mountains

The Long Journey: *A Prayer for the Living*

in the east and Tamaria in the north, karst deposits underlying the topsoil effectively drained the water table. Any decline in total rainfall resulted in withered fields, food shortages and famine-induced disease.

Deep wells and irrigation canals became resources worth fighting over, but most of the land owners had long since given up their struggle against the elements and heavily-armed criminal gangs. For these reasons, much of Northeastern Kameron lay fallow, and the few remaining areas blessed with independent water supplies lay along the three rivers that formed Kameron's northern border, or close to the mountains, where thin, acidic soil supported marginal food production. Not coincidentally, the vast majority of Lithian refugees had settled in the areas that provided reliable access to water. This fact angered many native Kamerese, who believed that foreigners shouldn't have been permitted land ownership in these productive areas.

Algernon thought about this as Maia dished hot stew into bowls, laid out warm bread and poured olive oil for her guests. Where would the thousands of refugees he'd seen on the road go? Their journey northward had to stop at the border because Tamaria could not even support her own population without importing grain from Kameron, and the Tamarian government would not permit entry to a horde of refugees. Aside from the Velez estate and small animal herds scattered across lonely hillsides owned by the armed Lithian warlords who'd been driven out of their own homeland, he'd seen virtually no formal agriculture anywhere south of the Desolation and Tualitin Rivers. This meant that the refugees were moving into places that simply could not sustain them. The young monk had a feeling that this land would not see the end of mass killing and death by starvation for a long time.

Maia's daughter did not return. Algernon and Astrid helped with dishes while Jhiran disappeared in pursuit of the house cat and Jawara conversed with Maia in the living room. Drained by physical exhaustion, Algernon unpacked his bed roll and collapsed on the hard floor of the hallway, fell asleep quickly and dreamed of carrion birds, poisoned water and defenseless civilians marching toward their own demise.

He woke up an hour before dawn, strangely aware that Astrid lay next to him. Jawara snored loudly in the living room and Jhiran sat cross-legged in front of Maia's bedroom door, that curiously blank expression so often found on her strangely-proportioned face barely visible in the fading blue-green light of the Great Eye.

The Long Journey: *A Prayer for the Living*

Algernon vaguely remembered Astrid pressing her back against his in the middle of the night, as Kira had done whenever she'd had a nightmare. While the memory felt comforting, the way Astrid's hair fell over her slender shoulders, the outline of her spine pressing through her thin garment and the manner in which her nightgown gathered at her waist, revealing a hint of flesh on her thigh just above her blanket, inspired a different feeling. He wanted to embrace Astrid and hold her close, but he didn't because Jhiran was watching.

"Don't!" the gwynling said in a whisper.

When Algernon turned his attention toward her, Jhiran put her thoughts into his head. She told him that Astrid had been frightened by the death she'd witnessed, and only came to him because she'd been too afraid to fall asleep alone.

"I'm not going to do anything," he replied, quietly.

Jhiran's voice whispered "Liar!" into his mind and admonished him not to take advantage of the girl when she felt vulnerable. Something fiercely maternal and protective projected into Algernon's conscience, and he suddenly felt ashamed of his own selfishness.

"I have to go outside and relieve myself," he whispered. "Can you please turn around?"

The gwynling retained her blank expression and filled his mind with the memory of his bath in the Desolation River. She'd been watching him that morning and reminded the young monk that he possessed no physical attributes with which she was unfamiliar. Jhiran would not move, nor would she turn from her watch over the priestess.

Algernon waited for his arousal to subside, then rummaged through his backpack, found his soap and quietly crept down the hall. He avoided eye contact with the gwynling as he passed, then opened the door and stepped outside without stirring anyone else.

Jhiran ignored him and kept her gaze focused on Astrid. She filled the sleeping girl's mind with imagery of warm days, fragrant flowers, gently flowing water and delicious food. In response, the priestess smiled.

Mist obscured the stars, and only the lingering glow of the Great Eye, which had already vanished over the western horizon, bathed the tangled almond trees clinging to life in Maia's orchard with an eerie light. Algernon stretched for a long time, trying to rationalize the embarrassment he felt over his encounter with Jhiran. When he found that mulling the situation over didn't make him feel any better, he

The Long Journey: *A Prayer for the Living*

focused on planning the day while he prepared his body for another session of sustained exertion.

He ran downhill along the road that led northward from Maia's fallow fields until it narrowed into an immature pine forest and became a barely visible footpath frequented only by wild ungulates and their predators. Less than two miles later, the Tamarian monk passed into a ghost town where curiosity inspired him to explore for a few minutes. Young pines had invaded the main street. Tall weeds ran wild between teetering buildings tangled in vines. Peeling paint and the scent of dry, rotting wood testified that many years had passed since this settlement last experienced the care of human hands. Now it remained the domain of nesting birds, feral pets, wild mammals and burrowing reptiles awaiting the warmth of another summer day.

Even at its zenith, the population in this place must have remained small. A tiny, ramshackle train station fronted an abandoned spur line leading northeast, but the steel rails and wooden cross ties had long ago been stripped from the elevated bed. Sedges crowned the railway and cottonwood saplings grew on its northern border, where water trapped by the rail bed formed lingering pools whenever rain fell during the spring.

Algernon made a mental note to check this on Astrid's map, then turned back toward the farm and walked, rather than ran, back to have breakfast with his companions. First, however, he used a hand pump to draw water into a bucket from a deep well on the property. Then he walked around to the back side of the barn, stripped and washed using a minimal amount of water. After rinsing off his soapy flesh, Algernon doused his clothing and wrung out the robe to remove most of the moisture. He dressed, returning to the well where he laboriously filled the bucket again, then brought it to the front porch.

Maia puttered in the kitchen, a sorrowful expression etched into the lines on her lovely face as she boiled a pot of water on the wood stove for tea. She acknowledged Algernon's presence with a nod.

"Did your daughter come home last night?" he inquired.

Maia shook her head and blinked back tears, but didn't say anything in response.

Jhiran trotted in with fresh eggs from the chicken house. When she saw Algernon, she smiled and embraced him, nearly crushing the eggs she carried. "You're wet!" she exclaimed. She acted as if their earlier confrontation hadn't even happened.

The Long Journey: *A Prayer for the Living*

That had to be an gwynling thing, he thought.

Astrid entered the room, her nose, cheekbones, chin and arms reddened by a daylight burn she'd earned the day before. She looked like she'd slept well, but she needed to wash her hair, and when Algernon mentioned that he'd fetched her some water, she snapped at him irritably. "Mind your own hygiene!" she exclaimed in their native tongue. "I'm sick of you thinking that I need a bath!"

Algernon felt stunned. He couldn't recall a single instance when he'd said such a thing to her. "What did I do to deserve that kind of a response from you?" he inquired, the tension rising in his own voice. "I'm simply trying to be nice."

"That's not what you're thinking!" she replied.

"Oh, you can read my mind now? Don't be ridiculous, woman!"

And as the conflict between the two of them escalated, Jawara came in from tending his horse and intervened again. He stepped in front of Algernon and gently backed the Tamarian monk away. "This does not help," he said. "Just leave her be."

Algernon seethed as he retreated to the hallway and rolled up his bedding. He felt hurt by Astrid's repudiation. He wanted her to look her best and didn't understand why she got upset at him for caring about her appearance. The tension remained during breakfast, where she fed herself and refused to talk to, or even look at him.

After cleaning the breakfast dishes, the travelers bade Maia a grateful farewell and headed back toward the Mistress Road. The sounds of artillery that they'd heard the day before had fallen silent, but a line of Kamerese National Army troops trudged eastward. Many wounded walked among them, their mangled limbs and torsos wrapped in bloody cloth bandages. These men displayed a grim demeanor, as if they expected defeat. Even their officers looked unhappy.

Many times during the morning journey Algernon had to stop so that Astrid could catch up. She didn't complain about sore muscles or discomfort on the bicycle seat, but he knew that Astrid had never been among the most physically fit of young women from the Temple, and the way she kept falling behind indicated she could not match his pace to the same degree that she'd been able to sustain the day before.

He tried to be patient. Two hours later, as the mist began burning off and the road surface became increasingly littered with the detritus of warfare, Algernon's back tire hit a shard of shrapnel and blew out. He spent nearly thirty minutes with the repair kit, while Jawara let his horse graze in an adjacent field. Frustrated by yet another delay, Algernon got back on his bike and set an even faster pace in order to make up time. Astrid began to cry because she simply couldn't keep up, so Jawara put her on the horse, adjusted the bike seat and rode the hydraulic machine himself.

When Sleepy Hollow finally appeared on the hillside ahead, the rumble of artillery fire trembled through the ground. Abandoning the Mistress Road just before it crossed a narrow trestle bridge that arched over an arroyo, they climbed a rutted gravel trail that led toward a low ridge line. The town lay at the tail end of a long chain of hills, partially hidden among live oak trees that flourished within deep arroyos that drained the landscape, while the hilltops remained rocky refuges of chamise, sage, buckbrush and yucca.

The smoke they'd seen earlier still rose from a building overlooking the town. As the travelers approached, a distant crumping sound, followed by the thunder of explosions landing near an artillery position they'd passed, indicated rebel counterbattery fire. Jawara began to worry. He knew that they were moving into very dangerous territory, but getting caught amidst an artillery duel ranked high among risks he did not wish to take.

As they approached the outskirts of Sleepy Hollow, a military checkpoint blocked their entrance. Debris covered the streets and a pile of rotting corpses simmered in the midmorning heat. Murder and reprisal killings had become so commonplace here the Kamerese National Army moved in to restore order, yet their preferred method of restoring order also involved murder and reprisal killings. This irony caught and held Algernon's attention. He felt sorry for all the civilians who were fleeing this senseless conflict.

A scruffy sergeant waved the rifles of his squadron down as the Tamarian monk approached. "What's your business here?" he barked.

Algernon produced his travel documents and his companions followed suit. "We're looking for my sister," he replied.

The sergeant glared at Algernon with a lowered gaze that suggested incredulity at the Tamarian monk's stupidity. "Your sister ain't here," he responded, shaking his head. "No one comes in, and no one goes out without us knowing about it."

Algernon, who'd earlier witnessed the demoralized condition of Kamerese warriors on the road, dismissed the bravado as mere posturing. "I'm sure you take your job seriously," he began. "But with your permission, I'd like to look around myself."

The sergeant glanced at all the other travel documents. "Your sister, huh? You know, a blonde-haired foreign girl would really stand out in a small town like this. Around here, a blonde-haired girl with certain bad habits might not be worth looking for after awhile." He eyed Astrid in a threatening manner, but averted his eyes when he noticed that Jawara stepped closer to the Tamarian priestess in response. Returning his attention to Algernon, the sergeant offered the identity papers back and leaned forward to press his point home. "You know what I mean, holy man?"

Jhiran tugged on Astrid's sleeve. She made eye contact and flashed her thoughts into Astrid's mind. The priestess turned away, her heart pounding in disgust.

"She's my sister," the Tamarian monk replied, electing to avoid escalating a potential conflict. "I'm not looking for trouble. I just want to take her home."

"Then you've come to the wrong place, holy man. There's nothing but trouble for you in this town."

"I've come too far to worry about that," Algernon responded. "I promise I won't bother you or your men."

The sergeant turned toward his squad and gave them a knowing look, one that inspired laughter among the assembled soldiers. "You have money for entrance tax?" he inquired.

Algernon knew what he meant, but he'd not encountered a demand for bribery before. "A tax? How much tax do you intend to collect, sir?"

"One kroner," the sergeant replied. Then, with a smile he added: "One kroner for each of you."

Feigning astonishment, for a common laborer worked for two months to earn that kind of money and he was supposed to be poor, Algernon pretended that he'd been insulted. "A kroner each?" he reiterated. "That's robbery!"

"Think of it as the price of admission," the sergeant replied. "If you don't pay, you can't come in and look for your fair-haired sister."

"Excuse us for a moment," Algernon requested. He turned toward his companions and huddled together a few yards away. "He's a liar," the young monk told his friends. "He knows that Kira's here, and he wants us to pay four kroners before he'll let us in."

The Long Journey: *A Prayer for the Living*

"Pay it and move on," Jawara suggested. "He'll simply have us killed if you don't."

"But that's going to tip him off that I'm carrying a lot of money," the Tamarian monk replied. "Then when will the extortion end?"

"Give him one," Jhiran suggested. "You go. We'll wait for you."

Astrid shook her head. "I don't like the idea of you going in there by yourself."

He didn't intend to insult her, so Algernon chose his words carefully. "Judging from the way he looked at you, I'd say there's a far bigger threat to your personal safety than mine."

"They have guns, Algernon, and you're unarmed!"

"Just pay it!" insisted Jawara. "We should stay together. It will be harder for them to kill all of us than you by yourself. We'll put the gwynling on the back of my horse so she can face them as we go through. That way, she can warn us of any ill-intent and if I have to engage them, at least I won't be surprised.

"We stay close to the arroyo, and if they cause trouble, we go downhill and follow the gully out. The trees will screen us. There are less than ten of them, and none have automatic rifles, but any one of them could put a bullet into your head. I can't protect you if you go in there alone."

The 'Scinnian warrior made sense. They pretended they were pooling their money when in fact, Algernon produced the required bribe from his moneybag while Jawara quietly chambered a round into his rifle. Returning to the sergeant, the Tamarian monk discreetly put the coins into his hand. "There's your admission fee," he said.

The sergeant smiled, fingering the money. "I have a feeling you aren't exactly who you appear to be. Good luck, holy man." Then, as Algernon moved forward the sergeant stopped him again. "You'll want to visit *The Bloody Bucket* while you're in town. You might find someone there who knows a thing or two about fair-haired foreign girls."

Algernon nodded, holding his breath and carefully holding his tongue while the soldiers affronted him.

"I still taste your sister on my tongue!" one of them jeered.

"How much you want for that other girl?" inquired another.

"Don't take a wrong turn!" a third exhorted. "Bad boys like blonde boys!"

As the travelers moved into the town, Jhiran sat backwards on the horse's flanks and passively stared at the soldiers, occasionally flicking her eyes to Astrid, who followed behind her. The gwynling detected considerable lechery in the warrior's thoughts, but little more. She didn't reflect their lust back toward Astrid, who served as the warning trigger for Jawara and Algernon as she watched Jhiran for signs of trouble.

Wishing to get away from the soldiers and their insults, Algernon pushed his bicycle onward in silence, sweating from the rising heat and fear as he looked for an inn that might still be operating. He turned due west at the first major intersection, crossing a bridge over the arroyo. On the north side of the street he found several small bungalows leading back toward the Mistress of the Woods Road. A sign hanging from the covered porch of an adobe house offered weekly rentals, but no one answered the door when he knocked upon it.

Jawara eyed the place carefully. He liked the idea that they might find shelter close to the arroyo, as it offered a barrier between the connecting road and also might serve as an emergency escape route. With all the shutters closed, it proved impossible to discern what lay inside each cabin, but with no sign of occupation, Jhiran trotted over to the last two cabins without commentary, produced a tiny pick out of her pouch and very quickly defeated the locks on their doors.

She was a thief, after all . . .

"One room for you guys. One for us," she said.

The cabins consisted of a single room with two bunk beds, chamber pots, a bucket for collecting water and a wash basin. Stifling heat and stale air wafted from within, so they opened the shuttered windows to provide some ventilation. The outdoor toilet smelled unpleasant, as if it had been filled beyond capacity for too long. Worse yet, when Algernon checked the well, rust-colored water came out of the pump no matter how long he worked it, and the water stank. Nobody would be bathing in this place.

Jawara loosened the saddle on his horse and led her to the shady side of the last cabin, where a bit of green grass remained. He tied the beast to a small tree and gave her water from the saddle bladder that he poured into one of the buckets taken from a cabin. By the time he'd finished ministering to his horse, Algernon had vanished.

"Where did he go?" Jawara asked.

Astrid shook her head. "He went to find *The Bloody Bucket*," she replied.

Jawara looked puzzled. "What's that?"

The Long Journey: *A Prayer for the Living*

"It's a kind of bar that caters to a certain clientele," she began with a sigh. "There's one in every town, but no self-respecting person would ever go there."

Alarmed, Jawara reached for his rifle. "We shouldn't let him wander off by himself!"

Astrid stopped him. "No!" she replied. "He told me that this is something he has to do alone. If we go after him, no one will talk."

"He's just a boy!" Jawara exclaimed.

"That's why he has to go by himself. No one there will think him a threat."

This made no sense to the 'Scinnian warrior. "Without back-up he's bound to get hurt! Come on, girl. We've got to find him."

Astrid shook her head. "There are no guns allowed in the bar. Trust me when I tell you that Algernon can fend for himself. Just sit down. He'll be back soon enough. He always comes back."

Jawara felt uneasy about leaving Algernon alone in hostile territory, then realized that Jhiran's remarks at the military checkpoint probably reflected Algernon's thinking. Walking through the shade of his cabin's front porch, Jawara pressed the stock of his rifle against his forehead and whispered a prayer before departing. He had no intention of letting Algernon face danger alone.

Finding *The Bloody Bucket* proved simple enough. Algernon wandered through Sleepy Hollow until he found a street leading away from the main business district, where the marquees advertised bars, cabarets and low scale cathouses. At this point the road turned steeply uphill, toward the south, and led into an area of increasing squalor.

The Bloody Bucket occupied the lower floor of a flop house near the end of the road, beyond which the chaparral landscape rose to the ridge crest. An oaken cask, painted to look like blood had been poured from its lip, hung over the door. Traditional Kamerese folk music wafted from within, along with hoots, hollers and whistles advertising a stripper working the platform. Algernon breathed deeply, steeled himself, then pushed open the door and walked into the darkness.

It took a moment for his eyes to adjust. Lunch hour patrons lined the smoky bar and crowded around the protruding stage upon which a Kamerese girl wearing a ribbon skirt and covering her breasts with a pair of feather fans pranced a burlesque tease. Algernon caught a glimpse of her flesh, rolled his eyes and let out a sigh. She was somebody's daughter, somebody's sister, and while something primal within him found the sight of her provocative and alluring, he could tell by the sadness he glimpsed in her eyes that this had not been a future she'd dreamed for herself as a child.

He walked purposefully to the bar and drummed his fingers on the lacquered surface while he waited for the bartender's attention, but the slightly overweight man with heavy jowls and bleary eyes simply ignored him. A woman who waited tables came by with a tray of empty glasses. She bent down to put the tray on the bar and in doing so, noticed the young monk, who seemed conspicuously unwilling to look at the dancer.

"Whatcha doin', sweetie?" she inquired, her manner far more kindly than she usually extended to the establishment's regular clientele. The boy looked very out-of-place here.

Algernon reached for the inner pocket of his robe and removed Astrid's portrait of Kira. "I'm looking for someone. Have you seen this girl?" he inquired.

The sudden change in the woman's expression spoke volumes. She nodded, quickly folded the drawing and gave it back to Algernon. "How do you know her?"

"She's my sister. Is she around?"

Glancing over her shoulder, the woman paused, then gently put her hand on Algernon's thigh. "It's very dangerous here," she said in a voice barely audible over the lively music. "Do yourself a favor and get out while you can."

Algernon took hold of her arm and lifted it, his grip just firm enough to hint at far greater strength he could muster. "I've come a long way," he replied in a warning tone. "I didn't ask you for advice on my safety. I need to know where I can find my sister, and if you've seen her, I want to know where."

The woman tried to twist away, but Algernon proved stronger than she'd imagined. "I don't know! Let me go!" she demanded.

Algernon arose, tightening his grip. "If you don't know, then tell me where I can find a man named Chale."

Her face blanched as he let go and suddenly the bartender and a bouncer became very interested in the conversation. The bouncer grabbed Algernon by the shoulder and started to spin him around, intending to give the offending youngster a sound thrashing.

In a whirl, Algernon twisted his torso to the left, twirling on the ball of his left foot while his right foot stepped forward. He held his left

The Long Journey: *A Prayer for the Living*

hand up in a blocking motion that contacted the bouncer's forearm and knocked it cleanly away. At the same time, the Tamarian monk torqued a dangerously quick, right-handed, two-knuckled punch into the bouncer's throat. Immediately, Algernon grabbed the bouncer's left ear and a handful of his hair, pulling forward with a grunt while the boy's left knee rose and slammed into the grown man's groin. Simultaneously, Algernon's left elbow smashed into the weak skull bone behind the bouncer's right eye.

Pulling the bigger man's head toward the floor with his right hand, Algernon stepped his left foot down while sliding his right foot backward. As the bouncer crashed into a table, splintered a chair and rolled onto the ground with a painful thud, Algernon withdrew into a perfect martial stance, ready to defend himself again.

Silence prevailed as the music faltered and the dancing girl covered her open mouth with a gloved hand. The bouncer lay still on the sticky floor, groaning from three crushing blows delivered before he'd been able to take a breath, let alone respond. A palpable sense of fear arose among the bar patrons, none of whom had given a second glance to the Tamarian monk only moments before.

Algernon strode back toward the waitress and pointed at her. "Where can I find Chale?" he demanded.

She looked terrified, glancing toward a dark corner over her shoulder. From there a large, muscular man arose. Not a single hair grew on his heavily tattooed head, and his neck and arms likewise boasted the artistic stains earned by many hours beneath a tattoo needle. He sported a walrus-like moustache and a patch of trimmed beard on his chin that he groomed with the thumb and index finger of his right hand. Two other men stood up with him, but he gestured for them to stay put.

"What you want, monkey boy?" the man boomed, striding toward Algernon with a menacing expression on his face.

"Take it outside, Chale!" the bartender warned.

The slave broker's eyes narrowed, but his raised his chin in acknowledgment of the bartender's demand and turned toward one of the men who'd been sitting with him. As his attendant approached, Chale pointed at Algernon. "The boss says outside!"

Warily the Tamarian monk backed toward the exit, carefully appraising the man who followed him. He could see the attendant reach for a hand gun carried in his belt. Algernon quickly opened the door and then shut it again as he stepped onto the porch. He could hear laughter from inside. The young monk crouched directly in front of the door while his eyes adjusted to the strong daylight. As soon as the gunman emerged, Algernon charged into action.

Long ago, in a martial lesson with Dmitri, Algernon learned the simple truth that a firearm has to be pointed at its intended victim in order to do harm. He felt his heart rate increase as the moment of greatest danger neared, but he fully intended to utilize that lesson. In the temporary blindness that occurred before the gunman's eyes adjusted to the outdoor light, while his gun barrel projected high through the doorway, Algernon pushed the weapon away with his left hand while leaping upward. The gun went off with a terrifying, deafening report, but with its barrel angled away from his body Algernon remained unhurt.

With his left hand holding firmly onto his assailant's right arm, Algernon made a V shape with four fingers of his right hand and jabbed them forcefully into the Kamerese gunman's eyes. Reacting instinctively, the adversary reached up to protect his damaged vision. Algernon slipped his left hand to the other side of his enemy's right forearm, grabbed the wrist tightly, then twisted it inward so that the Kamerese man's elbow faced upward, his head went down and his back faced the Tamarian monk. Using his right hand, Algernon painfully pressed the man's wrist in the anterior direction and sent a strong front kick into his abdomen, knocking the wind out of him.

Now in full control of the situation, Algernon quickly backed the man away from the door. Pushing down on the gunman's wrist until the carpal and metacarpal bones snapped under the pressure, Algernon forced the stunned, gasping gunman to drop his weapon. The young monk kicked it out of reach.

A familiar sense of power and control pulsed into Algernon's mind. He raised his right knee and simultaneously thrust the heel of his right palm downward. As his knee and palm slammed into the gunman's forearm, Algernon felt the satisfying crunch of his assailant's radius and ulna splinter from the blow.

He flung aside the shattered arm, spun and smacked a left-footed, spinning side kick into the man's chest that struck with such ferocity, the Kamerese gunman lifted off the ground and flew backwards, into the door frame. Algernon took a moment to hurl the discarded pistol far into the chaparral scrub, then grabbed the stricken gunman by the hair and belt buckle, dragged him back inside and shoved the man into a nearby table, where he collapsed and did not move again.

Bar patrons scrambled for the back door. Musicians abandoned their ensemble and the dancing girl screamed, then scurried behind the curtain. Algernon's chest heaved from the exertion as he glared at Chale. "Where's my sister?" he demanded.

Chale stood his ground, tilting his head to the side in a peculiar way. He nodded and a slight smile rose for a moment, then vanished from his face. "You got spunk, monkey boy. I'll give you that."

"Answer my question!" Algernon replied, his tone of voice a solemn warning that patience had never been his favored virtue. "Where is she?"

"Your sister? You must mean Kira Fang," Chale said in response. He walked toward Algernon with a confident expression on his face that belied the terror he felt in his soul. "You come into my town looking for my slave girl, and you have the *huevos* to think I'm just going to give her up to you? Is that it, monkey boy?"

"Her name is Ravenwood, and she's not a slave!" Algernon retorted. "She's been brought here against her will, and you have no right to her."

Chale shook his head. "She has the mark, boy! I have the papers. She belongs to me."

"Is that the story you're going to tell the magistrate? Do you know the penalty for slave trafficking, Mister Chale, or do I need to enlighten you?"

"There is no law around here," the Kamerese slave broker retorted. "You're in the wrong place, monkey boy!"

"I passed a squad of soldiers on the way in here this morning. They've got a nice collection of lawbreakers like you piled alongside the road. I can prove that my sister has been brought here against her will, and if I must I'll press the charges in a martial court."

"Those men enjoyed your sister. They're not going to do anything to me!"

Algernon stepped forward and lowered his voice. "Those men wouldn't think twice about putting a bullet into the back of your head. I've seen them kill on a far weaker case than I can bring against you! Don't play bluffing games with me."

Chale tilted his head toward the left again and narrowed his eyes. A slight smile lingered for a moment on his lips, then passed into something closer to a sneer. This boy proved himself a bold and worthy adversary. In addition to his fear of the young man's martial skill, Chale knew that if the Tamarian took him to court, no judge would rule in the slave broker's favor, a fact he couldn't admit. "Alright monkey boy. What do you want?"

"I want my sister back. You give her to me, and you'll never hear from me again."

At this, Chale put his hands on his hips. "You think I'm going to just give you my valuable property? I paid a lot of money for that girl."

The bouncer, who still lay on the floor, moaned in agony as he tried to get up. Aside from this sound, *The Bloody Bucket* remained dangerously silent. That girl, Algernon's intelligent and talented twin sister, had been reduced from an acolyte priestess with a potentially bright future to a mere financial transaction. Her dreams, her beauty and value to society now boiled down to a bargaining process between a brother who loved her, and an uncaring slave broker seeking profit on a human soul. Algernon's heart ached for Kira, and he felt so close to saving her that he had to fight the strong emotion welling up from within his soul in order to continue bargaining without breaking down.

"How much do you want?" Algernon asked.

"Tell me what you got, and I'll let you know if that's enough."

"You give her to me, and I'll pay you everything I have." Algernon tapped his moneybag, and Chale could see that it was full.

"Show me!" the slave broker demanded.

Algernon reached inside and pulled out a single kroner. He held it up for Chale to see, then returned it to the pouch. "Now it's your turn!" he replied.

The slave broker motioned for his companion. "Alano, get Enrique out of here and bring the blonde girl!" he ordered. Then, turning back to Algernon, he continued. "When you leave this place, I don't ever want to see your ugly face again. You darken my door, and I will kill you."

He'd already tried that, but Algernon didn't think it prudent to remind him. "I told you. I just want my sister and her documents."

Alano nodded, and dragging Enrique's broken body, disappeared backstage. After what seemed like a long time Alano returned with his arm around a slim, blonde girl. He made a show of fondling her. Stripped of her clothing and staggering drunkenly, Kira Ravenwood clung to the Kamerese man because something was wrong with her feet and she couldn't maintain her own balance. Her once beautiful hair had been shorn. Algernon saw scratch marks and cuts on her shoulders and breasts, evidence of bleeding between her thighs, and in many places her body showed extensive bruising. In addition, her left forearm had been branded with a stylized mark that indicated her status as a slave.

Algernon struggled not to cry. He took off his robe as Kira careened forward, slipped it over her shoulders, tied its belt and welcomed her into his embrace. She stank of urine and sweat. Despite the darkness in the room, her pupils remained tightly constricted and her breath smelled like she hadn't eaten in a long time.

"Algernon," she whispered in her native tongue. "What are you doing here?"

"I've come to take you home," he replied.

Kira closed her eyes and shook her head. "They'll hurt you. They always hurt you..." She slumped and Algernon struggled to hold her up.

"How touching!" Chale sneered. "You got your slutty sister. Now let's see your money!"

"I want her slave papers," Algernon demanded, knowing that as long as Chale possessed them, he could claim that Kira belonged to him. Alano looked at Chale, who nodded, then the Kamerese crony handed the documents over.

Algernon read through them, then reached for his pouch and dumped its contents, unwrapping the coins so that all 16 kroners clattered noisily on a table. He kept the pouch upside down and shook it to show he had nothing left.

Chale's eyes widened. "You pay a lot for a cheap whore, monkey boy!"

Algernon backed toward the door. "She's worth all I have," he snapped. "She's my heart and soul."

Chale began counting the coins as Algernon lifted Kira and retreated. Once the monk had vanished outside and the door swung shut, he turned toward Alano and handed him a gun. "Kill him," he ordered, "and bring the girl back."

From his sheltered place across the street Jawara saw Algernon carry his sister out of *The Bloody Bucket.* Immediately afterward, a Kamerese thug burst outside with a drawn pistol. A single shot from the automatic rifle put an end to Alano's murderous aspirations, and Jawara kept his weapon trained on the door. "Over here!" he called in vulgate.

The Long Journey: *A Prayer for the Living*

Though he could hear the 'Scinnians' voice, Algernon couldn't see Jawara. Struggling to carry his sister across the street, Algernon headed for the horse and realized that Jawara's Lithian clothing was effectively blending the warrior into the shadows. As windows opened from the flop house in response to the gunshot, Jawara squeezed off three rounds to keep curious heads down and potential weapons from returning fire. "Come on!" he urged. "Get her out of here!"

But Kira, though she'd lost a lot of weight, proved too heavy for Algernon to lift onto Jawara's horse, and she felt too lethargic to assist him herself. In response, he crouched down and told his twin sister to lean onto his back. Algernon wrapped his arms under Kira's legs and with a grunt, heaved himself upright.

He carried her down the street this way. Though his muscles screamed in protest and his heart pounded after several minutes of this exertion, Algernon dashed through the town of Sleepy Hollow with Kira draped upon his back, drawing the astonished attention of various townsfolk along the way.

"Where are we going?" she murmured, repeatedly.

"Somewhere safe," he replied, panting from the strain. "They won't hurt you again!"

Gunfire reverberated among the building walls. It sounded like far more than could have come from Jawara's rifle alone. As Algernon approached the main road, several Kamerese National Army soldiers hustled toward the commotion, their rifles at the ready.

Worried for his friend's life, Algernon gritted his teeth and prayed for Jawara's safety. Adjusting the position of his twin sister by lifting her a little, he pressed onward. Expending energy on a hot day opened every pore on the young man's already sweating skin, and the resulting sheen that covered his bare back and forearms made his burden increasingly slippery.

By the time he reached the street where he'd found the cabins, mortar explosions began erupting within the town. Staggering forward, he willed his aching body onward and stumbled into the courtyard. "Astrid!" he cried. "Help me!"

The priestess came running, her eyes widened in an overwhelming mix of fear, relief and hope. "Algernon! Kira!" she screamed, desperation overflowing in her voice.

Algernon felt his sister raise her head, heard her sigh and utter a curse before her head flopped back down onto his shoulder. When

The Long Journey: *A Prayer for the Living*

Astrid came to his side, Kira turned her head away. "Take her feet," he said. "She can't walk."

The look in Astrid's eyes displayed the deep pain of obvious rejection, but she reached for Kira to relieve Algernon of his burden. Gently grasping Kira's legs, Astrid saw that the soles of Kira's feet had been brutally lashed with a studded leather whip to prevent her from being able to stand or walk on her own. Astrid gasped and struggled to not weep upon seeing the mistreatment Kira had experienced.

Algernon turned and cradled his sister under her arms. Working together, he and Astrid brought Kira to one of the cabins and carefully laid her down on a bunk bed. Algernon collapsed on the floor and closed his eyes, his strength spent for a spell. Astrid knelt next to Kira, held onto her hand and stroked her head gently.

"Leave me, Astrid!" Kira whispered, pushing Astrid's hand away and turning her head again. "Don't touch me. Just let me die!"

Something tender within Astrid's soul fell into an abyss and perished in that moment. She slumped to the floor, put her head in her hands and sobbed uncontrollably. She wept for the obvious abuse heaped upon someone she loved. She wept in exhaustion for the long journey down to Sleepy Hollow. She wept for joy because Algernon had finally found and rescued his sister, but she wept most bitterly as the fear she'd secretly held within her heart blossomed into the reality of brazen repudiation.

Algernon approached to offer comfort, but she pushed him away and fled to the other cabin. Anger boiled within his soul. It seemed he never did anything right. What did Astrid expect, anyway?

The sound approaching gunfire, of mortar explosions and the rhythmic hoof clopping of Jawara's horse brought Algernon back into the moment. He arose just as the 'Scinnian warrior dismounted. "You're safe!" he exclaimed in relief.

"Get the women and load up!" Jawara ordered tersely. "The rebels are here."

"Kira can't walk," Algernon protested. "Where are we going?"

"I said get the women!" Jawara exclaimed, picking up the saddle bladder and laying over his horse's flanks. "They will kill us all if we don't go now!"

Algernon obeyed, gathering Jhiran and Astrid, along with their belongings. Jawara gently lifted Kira from the bed and put her on the back of his horse while Algernon helped a reluctant Astrid slip into her backpack. The two men shouldered their own burdens, then Algernon and Astrid retrieved their bicycles. After this, they all followed Jawara as he led his horse by the bridle, down into the arroyo.

Beneath the shade of the oak tree canopy a thick layer of fallen leaves lay in a narrow stream bed. Finding their footing proved tricky, as rocks and roots hidden beneath the leaves made their path more challenging to navigate. Not only did the canopy hide their egress, it also remained far cooler than the air beyond its shelter, and walking downhill out of direct sight allowed them to clandestinely escape the battle in town.

Hours after passing under the bridge that marked the Mistress of the Woods Road, the sheltered arroyo widened onto the coastal plain of Northern Kameron, and they all stopped to rest before the shade petered out. The afternoon wind arose, so Algernon had to build a windbreak with several rocks in order to light his cookstove. He insisted on making some of Brenna's medicinal tea for Kira before Jhiran warmed up food for everyone else.

Kira sat cross-legged in a patch of cool, green grass. A sorrowful expression lingered on her gaunt face as Algernon approached with a cup of medicinal tea. She accepted the drink and sipped from the cup. "Why did you come after me?" she asked as he sat down.

Algernon shook his head. "What kind of question is that, Kira? How could I leave you? How could I abandon you to your fate? I don't understand why you ran away from home in the first place."

She looked off into the north, where their mountainous homeland lay, far beyond visual range. "Marco told me that you tried to kill him," she replied. "He said that you'd force me to go back to the Temple, so he had to save me from you. He had to take me away so that you couldn't find me."

Algernon seethed. "Marco's a liar."

"No!" Kira insisted. "Marco loves me."

Astonished, Algernon looked into his sister's constricted eyes. "Marco made you an addict, brought you to Kameron and turned you into a slave. He loved you so much he sold you to a bounty hunter, who sold you to a broker, who would have sold you to someone else had I not found you. Marco doesn't love you, Kira!"

"What do you know about love, Algernon?" she accused, a little cry in her voice. "You don't love anyone but yourself!"

The Long Journey: *A Prayer for the Living*

"How can you say that? I searched everywhere in Marvic for you. I've traveled all the way down here to find you. I've been interrogated, beaten, shot at, nearly drowned, attacked by a mob, threatened and humiliated all for your sake. I've heard the most disgusting things about what these lowlife Kamerese have done to you, and every word felt like a knife in my heart. I came here for you, Kira, for no other reason than I love you!"

Kira spat her tea in his face. "Well I hate you!" she screamed. "I hate you for your smug, arrogant attitude! I hate you for leaving me to the lesbians in the Temple! I hate you for threatening Marco, and I hate you hunting me down!"

Algernon trembled, but made no effort to stop tears from spilling down his cheek. He shook his head and took hold of Kira by the shoulders, looking directly into her familiar, grey eyes. "I don't care what you say, Kira. I love you!" He wrapped his arms around her and held her closely, sobbing. "I know I should have protected you in the Temple, and I was wrong. I was so wrong! But Kira, I need you to know that I love you! I would go anywhere, fight anyone, pay any price for your sake! Hate me if you must, but you will never stop me from loving you! You're the beat of my heart, the breath of my soul. I love you, Kira! As long as I live, I will always love you!"

As he held her Algernon broke down, weeping without shame. "Open your fist," he pleaded. "Open your heart and let me love you!"

A moment later, he felt Kira lean her face against his bare shoulder, drop her tea cup and wrap her arms around his back. Her tears fell upon his skin. The siblings held onto one another and wept until their frustrations, their anger, their years of pain and abuse faded like an ebbing tide.

Jhiran, watching this unfold, turned her head away in respect for their privacy.

Astrid, her eyes reddened, sniffled and looked toward Jawara.

The 'Scinnian warrior raised his head toward the sky, opening his arms and lifting his hands. According to the ancient custom of his people, the strong man sang a prayer for the living.

Hurry Up and Wait

A sense of excitement filled Brenna's heart, overflowed onto her facial expression and into her body language. She tapped her feet nervously, chewed on her lower lip and toyed with a strand of hair while she waited for her turn to look at the bulletin board where final grades had been posted. This anticipation stemmed from high marks she'd achieved on her last three papers, a string of successful quiz scores, and confidence that her final test mark demonstrated solid understanding of watershed management.

Though she possessed the innate ability to succeed in an academic environment, a combination of additional factors markedly improved her performance. These included a rapidly advancing grasp of the Tamarian language, thanks mostly to Mariel's expert guidance, encouraging letters she'd received from every member of her family, and the fear that Garrick might not complete officer's training. He'd been struggling as the imminent deployment to Kameron drew nigh, despite his obvious leadership talent. Brenna worked harder in the hope that Garrick would find her increased effort motivating and rise to overcome his own difficulty.

Once the crowd thinned, Brenna approached the board, found her name and smiled at her results. She ranked twenty-sixth in her class, a significant increase over her standing earlier in the semester. Though her final mark remained marginal, she'd achieved a passing grade without the conditions for additional work over the summer that marred the final scores of other, less capable foreign students.

Knowing that she couldn't have succeeded without Mariel's help, Brenna decided to find a special gift for Mariel as a token of her appreciation. Further, as she prayed about the breakdown in her relationship with the Tamarian linguist, Brenna felt Allfather's Spirit influencing her to forgive and reconcile. A peace offering would show her sincerity, but the present had to be something unique and valuable.

Having completed their exams earlier in the week, many students had already departed. With the early fruits like cherries, and cereals such as winter wheat and barley ready for harvest, the need for workers in the orchards and grain fields lured most of the students away to agricultural areas where they could earn a bit of money. Brenna enjoyed walking along the empty paths alone, basking in the pleasant sensations of warm daylight on her skin and a floral fragrance lingering

The Long Journey: *Hurry Up and Wait*

in the air. The now familiar geometric patterns of Marvic, its tall, angular buildings, broad avenues, green belts and the silvery curves of the River Honeywater, ascended a gentle slope toward the city gate and the great hill upon which the white-walled Temple Elsbireth overlooked the nation's capital.

Banners and signs protesting Tamarian involvement in the Kamerese Civil War remained near the university's entrance, planted like temporary crops on a stretch of lawn. Here, with the tacit permission of the administration, a few students lingered to gather signatures on a petition calling for an immediate halt to the logistical build up of military equipment along the border with Kameron.

Brenna demurely declined to sign the petition, even though she felt sympathetic toward the protester's position. Despite her time in Tamaria, where citizens retained a right to petition their government for redress, the Lithian maiden felt uncomfortable with the concept of formally expressing grievances against authority. As a guest, shouldn't she respect and honor the rulership of this country?

Yet as she crossed Victory Street and approached one of Marvic's famous covered shopping plazas, Brenna wondered how the Tamarian senators viewed the civil war in Kameron, and whether or not the men and women representing the Tamarian people genuinely considered these popular protests in their closed door deliberations.

To those who claimed that all rulership ultimately derived from God's authority, Brenna argued that the kings, prime ministers and legislative bodies among the nations often contravened God's stated will. Sacred Lithian writings overflowed with admonitions to care for the weak, to sustain justice and honor the principles of equality and humility. Lithians disdained formal governance because the framework supporting power tended to create the need to sustain that power, ultimately resulting in oppression of the very people the government was intended to protect.

Further, many Lithian scholars pointed to the tyrannous rulership of nearby nations as evidence of their spiritual depravity, believing that God's disfavor with cruel, dictatorial policies would naturally result in the fall of such governments. Yet the pagan Azgaril and the corrupt Kamerese survived, while many spiritual and devout Lithians no longer controlled their own territories.

King Alejo in Kameron was widely believed to be a deeply pious and kindly man. If this was true, why didn't he take responsibility for

The Long Journey: *Hurry Up and Wait*

the rebellion against him, rather than fighting against it? Why didn't the king listen to his subjects and address their concerns? If he truly cared about his people and ruled with the kind of integrity Allfather demanded of leadership, why did it seem so obvious that God abandoned him? Or, would Allfather use the Tamarians in Kameron as he had against the Azgaril several months earlier?

Having heard the justifications for military intervention that Mariel and General Stassen laid out, Brenna felt her heart torn between principle and emotion. She'd always believed that Allfather God gave people the inherent right to determine their own destinies. Standing with the Tamarians against the Azgaril incursion harmonized well with this view, and thus, Brenna initially believed that the Tamarians should stay on their own side of the border in the Kamerese Civil War.

With her family facing the dual threats of a rebel army determined to overthrow the established society, and the Kamerese National Army intent on preventing any alteration to the current social order–changes like those Lynden Velez had already begun to implement–Brenna realized that Tamarian troops on Kamerese soil represented the best way to protect her family. Thus, the foundation of her principled view began to tremble.

She felt easily drawn to the rationalization that some divine purpose existed in Garrick's imminent deployment with the Tamarian Expeditionary Force, but she resisted placing too much stock in this kind of thinking because vivid memories of the Azgaril overrunning her own homeland haunted her soul. Brenna once told Garrick that Allfather had withdrawn his protection of the Lithian nation because of corruption and wickedness among the people and their priesthood; yet many warlords whose piety she respected, including her own father, took up arms against the invaders.

If Allfather God ordained this punishment against Illithia, why had so many devout men resisted? Did the act of fighting against the Azgaril constitute disloyalty to Allfather? If so, why had her father's life and those of the warriors under his command been preserved? Could the desire she felt to rationalize a divine purpose for Tamaria establishing a buffer zone in Kameron mask a deeper, unconscious motivation lurking within her own soul?

It seemed that as she thought about these issues, Brenna's meditation uncovered complexities that defied simple explanations. In the end, compelled to defend her family out of devotion to the people she

The Long Journey: *Hurry Up and Wait*

loved, Brenna accepted her upcoming role in the Kamerese invasion as an act of faith. She prayed that Allfather would make the moral path clear, and give her the will and requisite courage to follow his leading.

This conclusion represented the only satisfactory resolution of the many conflicts stirring in Brenna's mind. She pushed through the double doors of the airlock vestibule and walked into a pleasant shopping area paved in brick and sheltered from the elements by a translucent roof, high overhead. Full-sized trees and trimmed shrubbery grew within circular garden plots surrounded by cut and fitted bluestone planters that stood roughly as high as Brenna's waist.

Seating benches, arranged in a manner that encouraged socializing, lay beneath the trees. Bright green leaves provided shade from the strong light filtering from lofty windows high overhead, and beneath these sheltering branches groups of old men huddled around board games. Buskers, jugglers and magicians performed on various stages strategically placed among the walkways between businesses ranging from financial services to apparel shops and various eateries. Some of the shoppers lingered to watch or listen, while others passed without a second glance.

The alluring aroma of baked goods and sweet things spread from a shop whose marquee read: *Isadora's Tummy Yummies*. Brenna smiled and waved to the sturdy blonde woman making chocolate bars in the window. The young Tamarian woman wiped sweat from her brow and returned pleasant greetings, her expression reflecting the muted joy of performing a task she simply loved to do. As Brenna watched, the young woman skillfully chopped nuts, which she subsequently mixed into a batch of molten chocolate.

Cakes and sweet tarts, carefully arranged on glass shelving, flanked fudge forms, marzipan bars, nut and honey treats wrapped in phyllo leaves and breakfast pastries. Soft cookies rolled in cinnamon sugar, oatmeal biscuits, cream puffs and brownies occupied their very own display case, atop of which several colorful jars of jelly beans, suckers and rock candy stood for inspection. It looked as if many of the baked items had already been sold earlier in the day.

"You all make?" Brenna inquired, stammering over the words.

Isadora Sweet stopped her work for a moment, appraising her customer and appreciating her difficulty with Tamarian language. "We make everything but the hard candy here," she replied, speaking vulgate in hope that the foreign peasant girl would understand.

The Long Journey: *Hurry Up and Wait*

Brenna's pretty face brightened. She felt much more comfortable conversing in vulgate than in Tamarian. "That's really impressive! What are you making now?"

"Oh these?" Isadora replied. "I've got a contract with the army to make chocolate bars. I pour the liquid into forms, then put them on trays to cool. Afterward they get wrapped in foil paper. The soldiers will use them to make friends with children."

Brenna nodded, her eyebrows raised in understanding. "That's an excellent idea," she mused, imagining that somebody in the Tamarian military had done a lot of thinking about the operating circumstances in which warriors like Garrick would soon be involved.

"Would you like to try one?" Isadora inquired.

"I don't really care for chocolate," the Lithian girl replied, remembering that her friend, Woodwind, adored it. She turned to the display case behind her. "Those cream puffs look really good, though. I'd like to pick up some of those for a friend."

Isadora smiled sweetly, her eyes alive with delight, her pale skin glistening in a sheen of perspiration. "An excellent choice!" she said, scurrying around the counter to retrieve half a dozen pastries. She moved with confidence and vigor, her blonde pony tail swishing to the rhythm of her stride. The Tamarian girl washed her hands, then reached into the display case with a pair of steel tongs and put her treats in a bag lined with wax paper. "I baked these this morning, so they're fresh. I hope you enjoy them."

"I'm sure I will," Brenna replied, returning the smile as she slid a sterling across the counter.

Isadora's eyes widened and she pursed her lips. She'd half expected to give the pastries away to the peasant girl. "Do you have anything smaller than that?"

"No, but you can keep the change. I can see you deserve it." Brenna turned away, leaving the puzzled Tamarian girl to contemplate how a foreigner who dressed like a poor farmer's daughter could afford to be so generous.

A long line nearby caught Brenna's attention. She wandered to a women's boutique called *Bare Essentials* and peered into the display window, noting that no one seemed the least bit interested in the silky camisoles, flannel nightgowns, corsets and rather utilitarian undergarments hanging on the racks. Every woman in line seemed intent on purchasing something available only at the counter.

The Long Journey: *Hurry Up and Wait*

Brenna's eyes caught a familiar sight and she held her breath when she recognized what kind of garment the women were after. She slipped into the back of the line and waited nearly half an hour for her turn with a salesclerk. During that time she listened carefully to the conversations of fashion conscious, wealthy women in front of her, as well as those who queued up behind, eventually realizing that the recent availability of this new style of underclothing inspired high interest and excitement.

At the counter, she heard other women express skepticism about the "one size fits all" nature of the apparel. The salesladies assured their customers that the unique garment would indeed fit, while the prim woman who seemed mildly annoyed to assist an impoverished foreigner expressed surprise that Brenna asked no questions.

"I'm afraid they only come in white," the saleslady lamented, somewhat disinterestedly.

Brenna shook her head, a smile flashing across her face as she checked the product label. She noticed that the fabric seemed thicker than normal and completely opaque, features likely designed into the garment to make it more acceptable to a target market concerned about modesty. "They any color be," she said falteringly, struggling to pronounce the Tamarian words and misplacing the verb, as was her habit.

The saleslady smiled in a condescending manner. Though she really didn't want to help the foreign girl, she had no reason to refuse her service and the manager might not approve of her being rude to a customer, even one who probably couldn't afford the merchandise. "I'm sorry, miss, they **only** come in white."

"I show," Brenna replied. She picked up the tiny halter and held it to her face. "Blue you like?" she queried, thinking about the color of her own eyes.

"Miss, I have other customers to serve and . . ." Astonished, the woman stopped in mid sentence. "How did you do that?" she asked, her eyes widened.

All conversation stopped as the women nearby stared at the ultramarine fabric.

"It do . . . to please you, only must touching skin be," Brenna replied, thinking about green, with a gradual change in the garment's color. She folded the halter with a single hand. "How much for two?"

"Uh, they're five sterlings each," the astounded woman replied.

The Long Journey: *Hurry Up and Wait*

Brenna lifted her eyebrows. That was expensive, but she knew that Tamarians did not barter, and that the durable cloth making up the halter would last for years. The Lithian girl counted ten silver coins from her moneybag and placed them on the counter, inspiring a suspicious expression in the pale eyes of the store clerk. As she waited for her receipt, Brenna haltingly answered questions from the women nearby, explaining that the garment would not bind or chafe, and demonstrating that the fabric could not be torn.

"How do you know all of this?" the saleslady inquired.

Brenna pulled out the label. It read: *Alexina's Underthings. Made in Kameron with native Tamarian fibers*. With her unique, mischievous smile Brenna folded the garment again. "Alexina mother mine be," she replied, touching her breastbone. "Father mine for her a light forge build!"

*   *   *

Tegene walked along the Virgin River with Lynden Velez, outlining the various defensive fortifications he and his men had completed. The verdant riverbank still supported its lush vegetation and small birds fluttered away as the two men approached. Many hours of careful planning and hard labor transformed the natural surroundings into one retaining the chamise, narrow leaf buckbrush, black sage and manzanita that thrived in and around the wild oak groves, yet far different in its purpose and completely lethal.

"Here in this area," the big man explained, "we're seeking to channel potential offensive thrusts into defined kill zones." Tegene pointed out the subtle contouring that gradually ascended toward xeric slopes, where Lynden's army planted many surprises amidst the dry vegetation. "The enemy will evaluate our defenses, and seek to exploit perceived weaknesses, driving forward through these lanes. As planned, we will progressively withdraw to higher ground as the tactical situation evolves.

"Even after they've established themselves on this side of the river, our positions along the ridge lines will give us a significant terrain advantage. We hope to confine the rebels to these open, lowland areas where artillery is most effective, but if a large enough force turns to face us, the best we can do is slow, not stop, their advance."

The Long Journey: *Hurry Up and Wait*

Lynden appraised the cleverly hidden barricades, trench works and machine gun nests, noting with satisfaction that the defenses had been set up in a multilayered fashion. He understood Tegene's point. "Mayor Meta has expressed dismay about our operational plans. He tells me that most of the citizens here agreed to evacuate, but did so in duress. They're afraid our defenses will become permanent features, and that their evacuation to more marginal land further north will effectively negate the land reforms we've negotiated."

Tegene shook his head. "They don't understand the reality of our situation. As far as your land settlement contracts are concerned, they should know that we're facing rebels whose idea of land reform involves atrocity, redistribution of resources among existing landlords and ethnic cleansing. No matter how well prepared we may be, the battle will begin when the rebel leadership elects to either finish off the NKA forces before they can be reinforced and then take us on at their leisure, or turn to fight us first.

"In either case, we have no choice than to stand against them, and we will be far more effective doing so from prepared positions. Sometimes a good leader must do what is in the best interest of his people, even when they can't comprehend why this is so."

Lynden looked across the rippled, glacial blue river waters, where fallow farmland would soon become a battlefield. Though he did not intend to goad the rebel armies to engage his own forces in combat, Lynden knew that Lord Nemesio Fang commanded seven thousand well-equipped troops who could be supplemented by many thousands more, should the warlord persuade others to join him in attacking the Velez estate.

Enmity festered between the Fang and Velez families. The Kamerese merchant and drug lord had once claimed Brenna for his wife as part of an ill-fated land purchase contract, then accused Lynden of swindling his daughter back in a Kamerese court. Last autumn, Lord Fang had also lost a huge contract to supply the Azgaril Northern Liberation Army with blankets and warm clothing, after his Maridom Trading Company barges mysteriously exploded and sank while docked near Helena. Lynden had no doubt that Lord Fang would return–leading his army–with ill-intent and vengeance on his mind.

At this point in the season, the Virgin River already lay very low in her bed. Warm temperatures melted most of a thin snow pack that fed her headwaters, and modest rainfall during the early spring limited

The Long Journey: *Hurry Up and Wait*

the volume of water draining down from the highlands. Light infantry could certainly ford the river on foot, and once in place, it would only be a matter of time before they could bridge the shallow river to bring artillery within range of his new light forges. Lord Fang would come, and likely very soon.

Three months earlier, when informal fighting further south congealed into full blown civil war, Lynden held a meeting with his subordinate commanders. He presented a detailed list of assets requiring defense, outlined various options for doing so, then listened carefully to the input of his men. Working together, they fleshed out a plan to deprive rebel forces any significant control of the Velez estate. The initial phase of their plan involved evacuating civilians, servants and family members northward, where pre-positioned food stores, temporary shelters and sanitary facilities awaited them.

After several weeks of devoting his energy and rapidly rebuilding wealth to assure the safety of the people under his care, Lynden Velez contacted and coordinated with Tamarian Special Forces units already in operation on the far side of the Virgin River. He sent a dozen of his best snipers, equipped with UV enhanced sighting scopes, to supplement the Tamarian units, and in return, received regular intelligence on the often fractious rebel forces, especially concerning force disposition, favored tactics and movements.

He'd learned about the rebel break out at Sleepy Hollow, knew that the KNA retreated to the northwest, and thus he expected to face the enemy within a few days. Lynden worried about Tegene's son, Jawara, and his three companions. If they hadn't found the Ravenwood girl yet, or if they didn't make a very rapid egress, the rebels would overtake and kill them as foreign conspirators. This problem had been the subject of many passionate prayers and much concern.

Work crews began building the layered defenses around the Mistress of the Woods Road, its bridge across the river, the Velez villa and the town of Helena shortly after the midwinter meeting, resulting in a complex labyrinth of protected positions linked by trenches and sheltered by berms that afforded protection from direct fire. Yet the vast expanse of land owned by the Velez family simply could not be effectively defended with the small number of troops in Lynden's army, at least until the Tamarians, with their famous and feared rocket artillery, arrived in sufficient numbers to blunt the enemy advance.

The Long Journey: *Hurry Up and Wait*

In the mean time, he could not permit his operating light forge and the others under construction to suffer damage or fall into enemy hands. Therefore, the most critical task his own forces had to accomplish involved protecting the fragile, glass and mirror factories located on an exposed ridge line to the northeast of his villa. To do this, the Velez army needed to stall the rebel advance while maintaining control over the two water resources flowing through his land. Although he'd positioned his small army with care, Lord Velez believed he would not be able to stop the rebel advance without significant help.

Lynden's troops intended to yield ground as necessary, but he'd warned his warriors to prepare for bitter fighting along Maidenhair Ridge. They could not retreat beyond that point. With their defenses in place and too few artillery and mortar tubes at their disposal, members of Lord Lynden's small army individually made peace with God before setting out to patrol the dusty roads of the Velez estate. Every soldier eyed the west uneasily while waiting for the enemy to mass and attack.

A swell of refugees arriving from further south compounded the civilian evacuation. Sherman Mason, Lord Lynden's chief engineer, explained that the facilities constructed to shelter families native to the Velez estate would prove adequate only for that small population. As many more hungry people sought entry, Lynden's army drew the unpleasant task of escorting new arrivals back across the Virgin River.

In an effort to assuage the legitimate complaints of the people over which they ruled, Lord Lynden and Lady Alexina allowed children, siblings, nieces and nephews directly related to a family member who permanently lived on their estate permission to stay in the temporary relocation camp, which lay about sixty miles further north near the Tualitin River. The Velez family permitted these people to remain with their loved ones until lands beyond the Virgin River became safe again, or until adequate employment and housing could be found for them.

Lady Alexina coordinated the relocation process, moving the people whose homes stood closest to the potential battle away from danger first. She arranged for long caravans laden with people and supplies to head north, escorted by armed citizens trained to look after security for their neighbors and families. Alexina did not travel toward safety, but remained behind with her husband.

All unmarried Lithians living within the estate worked closely with the refugees. Though the Velez siblings, especially Camille, complained loudly about having to dress like the Kamerese, each one assumed an active and obvious role in the evacuation and sustenance of local people. This public display of solidarity and support proved vital in assuring skittish citizenry that the Velez family remained committed to their welfare.

With the addition of extended family members to the ranks of local residents, the resulting population expansion compounded every task related to getting people out of the combat zone and adequately fed. Jared, with Acacia working silently at his side, led the effort to assuage complaints from civilians, solving a myriad of problems as they arose. The young couple received substantial help from the ever extroverted and multilingual Camille, who willingly spent all day walking through the refugee camp, stopping to visit with every family so that she could record their concerns and various requests.

Binta, Farisa and Lungile, three of Tegene's adult daughters, along with Helena's four temple priests followed up on any expressed spiritual needs and attended to stores of clothing, blankets and hygiene supplies. It became evident that Kamerese women preferred to interact with other women when requesting personal items for their families.

Tegene's eldest son, Muenda, served as physician in a medical clinic along with his younger sister, Sekai of Tegene's first wife, Ngoni. Cynthia and her adult cousin, Hansel, arranged schooling for children whose education had been interrupted by the civil war.

A few troublemakers among the recent arrivals attempted to stir dissension among fellow citizens who'd been relocated to safety further north. One young man, who lacked the profound charisma often associated with Kamerese clerics, advertised a community support rally one morning that was not only poorly attended, the majority of people who did show up made a concerted effort to heckle him.

"Look at how you've been herded into this concentration camp, like sheep prepared for slaughter. Where is the compassion of your landlord?" the young man shouted.

"Where's your brain?" someone replied. "Nobody forced you to come here, and I'll bet you haven't even met Lord Velez!"

Flustered, the young man responded with rhetoric that had worked well, elsewhere. "When the rich elites hide behind their high walls in their fine houses, where will they escape when the righteous wrath of the Kamerese people rises up against them?"

A middle-aged woman, whose deeply tanned skin had been darkened from long hours of outdoor labor, arose. "You're not from

The Long Journey: *Hurry Up and Wait*

around here," she said. "Hiding behind high walls? Whom do you think set up this camp for us, and who looks after our needs here? Whom do you think provides our food and shelter? You don't know what you're talking about and you'd better shut up before local folk throw you back across the river!"

Other voices rose in affirmation.

"The foreigners care nothing for you!" he continued. "They will melt like glass before the onslaught of the people! They will cower in the mountains or fall among the slain! They have grown fat on your land and heap on luxuries stolen from your labor. Rise up, my people! Let them bend their necks to our righteous judgment!"

"Idiot!" a man shouted. "Lord Lynden has already enacted reform! This is our land!"

"His words are like clouds without rain. He will not deliver on his promises! Wealthy foreigners drain the life from The Great Land, and your lord is no different!"

Of course, this was untrue and the people who actually lived on the Velez estate knew it. Shortly after their arrival well over a year ago, Lord Lynden and Lady Alexina began investing their own wealth and time into rebuilding the region. Aside from establishing order and driving out ravaging bands of banditos who terrorized the local people, the Velez family brought in erosion control, drip irrigation systems and most importantly, a land buy back system whereby local peasants actually gained ownership over their own property, something none of them had ever dreamed possible in the past. Proceeds from their payments went into financing the first light forge, a reestablished school and repairs to roads and public buildings, rather than supporting a lavish lifestyle or being siphoned off to other investments, elsewhere.

The mood of the small crowd turned uglier, but not in the expected manner. When the young man realized he could not stir the emotions of these people against their benevolent landlord, he raged at them, calling them simple-minded fools. He warned that they would also suffer when the rebel armies arrived.

Once the assembled refugees heard this, they began throwing dirt, dung and rocks at the young man until he fled for his life. Only the restraining influence of a local sheriff prevented the situation from escalating into bloodshed. The sheriff promised to escort the young man across the river, and afterward, no one saw or heard from that particular troublemaker again.

The Long Journey: *Hurry Up and Wait*

Yet as word of this episode spread through the refugee camp, several threats against the Velez family mysteriously emerged in the form of graffiti and intimidating letters addressed to Jared, Acacia and Camille. Some of these expressed intolerance of their religion, claimed that their slender, shapely bodies were produced by demonic influence, and warned vaguely that their virtue would soon be compromised and their exquisite beauty marred. Others referred to the Lithian family in vile, racist language and promised imminent, unspecific retribution against ill-defined crimes. Even Cynthia, whose porcelain skin and glacier-blue eyes alone hinted at her ancestry–for otherwise she looked very much like a human girl–had a rock thrown through the window of her classroom one afternoon. A palpable tension emerged from these incidents, illustrating that despite the best effort to help the people living in the camp, dissidents remained among the refugees.

Whenever Cynthia Velez felt the need for solitude, she'd wade across a shallow backwater of the Tualitin River and climb a favored oak tree that grew on an island in the river. As was her custom, she brought binoculars and scanned the far bank, noting that the mountains of military equipment she'd seen near the rail terminus had grown considerably in a single day.

Brenna and her Tamarian warrior remained somewhere on the north side of the river, where Cynthia's binoculars aided in the observation of several soldiers. Though she couldn't tell them apart from this distance, she'd seen Garrick's face in her dreams and secretly hoped that she might recognize him. If she saw the young Tamarian, Cynthia knew that Brenna would be near, and she couldn't wait to see her sister again!

*   *   *

The pace of Garrick's training regimen seemed increasingly frenetic. Three major tests in two days, a seemingly endless series of cross-country runs and marches, the final in-garrison leadership exercises and common core tasks blended into a hazy nightmare of experience from which he never seemed to awaken.

He craved sleep. Had it not been for the aid and encouragement he received from the older officer candidates, Garrick would have succumbed to fatigue and simply given up. The other men, however, were determined to pull Garrick through, and he owed his precarious

The Long Journey: *Hurry Up and Wait*

survival in the class to their efforts. Candidates Richard Marsten and Dr. Erich von Brecker, the two highest achievers in the course, spent most of their limited free time helping Garrick study and coaching him on how to write cohesive essays. A cadre of other aspiring officers kept Garrick running when he neared the limits of his endurance, while Greg Schmidt helped him organize and refine presentations on combat doctrine so that he didn't ramble nervously in front of senior officers.

Without all of this help, even Garrick's astonishing success during the field combat exercises wouldn't have ensured passing marks and a commission at the conclusion of the program. Only the Tamarian Special Forces candidates experienced more rigorous demands for physical fitness, yet that track did not exact as high an academic competence requirement as did officer training. The Tamarian army produced an elite leadership corps, and aside from the field exercises and related common core tasks, Garrick Ravenwood's name consistently fell to the bottom of his class list. He simply couldn't run fast enough and lacked the developmental maturity to successfully compete with older, more experienced candidates in the academic realm.

Though he wanted to do well, though he desired to prove TAC Vogel's initial assessment wrong, Garrick longed for the end of his training program and dreaded every exam. TAC Vogel remained relentlessly critical, and his evaluation of the recent Urban Combat Exercise illustrated the high standard to which Garrick and the other students had to aspire.

The TAC Officer's words echoed within Garrick's memory: "Candidate Ravenwood missed milestone times in several areas, and took his objective well behind schedule. He failed to establish proper communications within the internals of his unit, resulting in his being surprised by OpFor movements on his flank and the subsequent, forced withdrawal from the objective.

"As has often been the case, Candidate Ravenwood tends to abandon caution and charge in where even the gods fear to tread. Although this bravado is inspirational, it will likely get him killed in actual combat. No one disputes Mister Ravenwood's valor, but he would do well to remember that he can only serve his country while he is alive.

"Along these lines, the candidate often behaves like an ordinary line soldier, performing combat tasks for his men, such as borrowing their weapons and fighting for them, instead of letting them do their work. In addition, he often becomes so involved in the actual combat that he forgets to command his unit.

"To his credit, Mister Ravenwood was one of only three candidates who successfully captured their objectives, and of these, the only one who recognized withdrawal criteria and successfully moved into a defensive position."

He'd been recommended for a pass on that exercise and didn't have to repeat it, as nearly all of the other candidates were required to do. Nonetheless, the constant, public criticism Garrick experienced often left him feeling demoralized. Sergeant Vidders understood and told Garrick that effective field leaders were seldom ranked at the top of their OTS classes.

"Now is the best time to make all your mistakes," the sergeant concluded. "You've come too far to give up now. Just keep working hard, son."

But Garrick didn't think he could sustain the kind of effort required to maintain passing scores much longer. He squirmed in an uncomfortable chair, listening to Talon Waldheim deliver a briefing about the logistical problems likely to face the Tamarian Expeditionary Force when it deployed to Kameron. Numbed by the long list of potential supply concerns, Garrick let his imagination wander toward pleasant memories of time spent with Brenna. These thoughts held his attention as Talon Waldheim concluded.

Greg Schmidt nudged him. "Wake up, Ravenwood! It's your turn." The officer candidate smiled. "Show us what you've got!"

"Remember, Overhead," Darren Schultz called out as Garrick approached the platform. "A briefing is brief!" Mild laughter erupted among the men.

Garrick had been tasked to identify the challenges of coordinating operations with Lithians and native Kamerese. He'd trimmed a lot of material that concerned Lithian culture, even though he believed it was important, because Greg Schmidt insisted that he focus only on issues directly relevant to his topic.

Dividing his presentation into four parts, Garrick introduced the potential problems a Tamarian force might encounter with the Kamerese National Army, then the various units under the command of Lithian warlords. He outlined differences in weapons, tactical doctrine, language and contrasts in familiarity with terrain, explaining that the

The Long Journey: *Hurry Up and Wait*

influence of culture might compound the misalignments in each area. In his final segment, Garrick offered solutions to these issues.

"Above all," he concluded, "we must prosecute this campaign as professional soldiers. If our conduct remains above reproach, we will be respected. If our ears remain willing to listen, we will be consulted. If we behave like guests, we will be welcomed."

"Ten hut!" a sergeant at the doorway called.

Suddenly, a senior officer walked into the briefing room and every soldier rose to attention. Garrick recognized the dignified neatness of Colonel Weiss as he approached, and retained the presence of mind to quickly assemble his papers and yield the lectern.

Without indicating that he recognized Garrick from their meeting in Hungry Valley, Colonel Weiss stood behind the podium and ordered the men at ease. He paused, appraising them with pride.

"With due consideration for your hard work these past weeks, the senior officers of the Dragon's Lair Military Training Center would like to recognize and celebrate your achievements. Ordinarily, we schedule an officer's dance on the eve of your graduation ceremony, but our treaty commitment to the Kamerese government has prompted a Readiness Order, signed by Her Grace this afternoon. These events will preclude any celebration for candidates in this rotation.

"Final unit command assignments have been posted in the administration office. At eighteen-hundred hours those who have successfully completed their studies to date will attend a brief ceremony where each will receive his formal commission. All units designated for the expeditionary force will embark by rail for Kameron at oh four-hundred hours. Officer candidates assigned elsewhere must check at the administration office after oh eight-hundred hours for transportation arrangements. That is all, gentlemen."

Before leaving the lectern Colonel Weiss turned to Garrick. "Son, report to TAC Vogel right away. He's expecting you." Then, the colonel strode out of the room without speaking another word.

A murmur swept through the assembled men. Stunned and terrified, worried that he'd not made the final cut, Garrick trembled as he sat down. The boy put his head into his hands and pulled his short hair while the other officer candidates scrambled for the exits.

Not only had his battle injuries kept the young Tamarian from completing the field exercises in Hungry Valley, he'd not gone through the Combat Water Survival Training either. Garrick's well-known struggle in formal study often dragged his overall standing below the 80% minimum performance level. TAC Vogel had warned him several times to exert more effort, and now, the fact that Colonel Weiss singled him out inspired real concern.

The last two weeks of officer training involved specialization and administrative preparation, where candidates separated according to the particular discipline in which they would serve in the field. Garrick slogged through military management and professional ethics course work in a desperate attempt to raise his academic standing, but the class contents seemed bewildering. He floundered under the stress of scholastically demanding material and chronic fatigue.

Now, that final week–a time in which some claimed the most difficult studies were undertaken–had been cut from their schedule, and nobody had actually completed all of the required course work. Something had gone dreadfully wrong!

When Garrick nervously returned to TAC Vogel's office, the scene unfolded very much like his first encounter with the man. "You're simply too young for this program," Manfred Vogel told him. "I suspected that you were inappropriately recommended and most of my initial concerns have proven true."

As the TAC officer flipped open Garrick's dossier, he shook his head at a string of marginal scores. "Several times we have considered cutting you, and any objective examination of your classroom performance reveals that you are not ready to serve in the esteemed position to which you aspire. One day, perhaps, but not now."

Garrick felt strong emotion welling up within his soul. "I am doing my best, sir."

Manfred Vogel glared at the young officer candidate, a cold expression fixed upon his angular face. "Your best?" he queried. "I don't know how you pull it off, Mister Ravenwood, but you've managed to get nearly everyone else involved in helping you get through this experience. It's clear that your best simply doesn't make the grade in this army.

"The last three examinations you've completed have pulled your marks well below the passing line, and under normal circumstances I would be sending you back to Burning Tree." The TAC officer removed a letter from Garrick's folder and turned it toward him. "Initially, I'd suspected that your pretty, little girlfriend had something to do with your assignment here, so I made sure that she couldn't

The Long Journey: *Hurry Up and Wait*

influence the outcome of your program and tasked Lieutenant Hougen to watch the foreign girl carefully and keep her busy. At present, however, I'm confident that Miss Velez had nothing to do with this."

Garrick glanced through the letter, struggling to restrain an emotional outburst. The other officer candidates had petitioned Colonel Weiss on his behalf. Every candidate's name–even that of Darren Schultz, who'd abandoned him at Dysentery Ridge–appeared on the document. In essence, his classmates risked disqualification in requesting special consideration for Garrick because they believed in his obvious leadership ability, and he felt deeply moved by this testament of their commitment to him.

"Sir, I don't know what to say," Garrick replied. "I didn't ask them to do this."

TAC Vogel grunted, raising his eyebrows. "It's mildly insubordinate, as the decision concerning your disposition does not rest with any of them. And of course, in signing such a letter they've put themselves in jeopardy of disciplinary action. However, your current academic standing officially disqualifies you as an officer candidate, and no appeal from your classmates will change that fact."

Tears welled up in Garrick's eyes. "I'm very sorry to disappoint you, sir."

Manfred Vogel paused, watching Garrick regain his composure. "I am not disappointed, Mister Ravenwood," the TAC officer continued, his voice morphing into something far more gently paternal than Garrick had ever heard from him before. "I told you that these are not normal circumstances. The newly formed expeditionary units are deploying to Kameron tomorrow morning. In light of your outstanding combat leadership at Cutthroat Pass, Colonel Weiss has elected to give you a battlefield promotion."

TAC Vogel produced a small, yellow envelope that contained two brass bars, one for each shoulder. He handed the envelope to Garrick. "Congratulations, Lieutenant Ravenwood."

Garrick restrained his sense of shock and surprise. He stiffened and saluted. "Thank you, sir!"

TAC Vogel returned the salute and nodded. "You've earned it, son. Get yourself ready to go, see to your men and get your girl on that southbound train tomorrow morning. Though you are not receiving your commission at the ceremony this evening, in the spirit of solidarity with your classmates it would behoove you to attend."

The Long Journey: *Hurry Up and Wait*

"Yes sir!"

"One more thing, lieutenant," the TAC officer said. "When you go to Kameron, promise me that you'll be careful out there."

Garrick smiled. "Yes sir!"

"You're dismissed."

Retaining enough poise to avoid a very non-gentlemanly outburst required all of the self-control Garrick could muster as he put the officer's bars into his pocket and raced down the spiral stairs. Breathlessly he ran into the administration office, discovering that all the other officer candidates' names and their assignments were posted on a bulletin board, while his remained conspicuously absent.

Puzzled, Garrick moved beyond the various administrative clerks' desks and studied a huge chart pinned along the back wall that outlined the command structure of the 1st Tamarian Expeditionary Force. This chart detailed the officers responsible for each of the new units being sent to Kameron.

Forty thousand soldiers, an army larger than the one responsible for defeating the Azgaril's Northern Liberation Army in the Winter Saradon Campaign, were scheduled for recruitment or reassigned and specifically trained for service in Kameron. Coordinating this massive deployment on such short notice proved a logistical nightmare, but Garrick wouldn't appreciate the difficult task of organizing and equipping this fledgling army for some time.

Major General Leo Braun led the 7th Division, and below him Colonel Hans Adler served as one of three brigade commanders. Lieutenant Colonel Ulrich Innsmann was listed as Garrick's battalion commander, while Captain Meinrad Engels would be the leader of Company Alpha, to which Garrick's platoon had been assigned. Greg Schmidt and Talon Waldheim rounded out the platoon leadership for Company Alpha, and the OpOrd Garrick picked up specified that they would be the first unit to cross the Desolation River and deploy into Kamerese territory.

When Garrick returned to the officer candidate barracks with 2nd lieutenant bars pinned to his uniform, the men welcomed him warmly. Handshakes and smiles–the friendly camaraderie of the successful candidates–gave Garrick a sense of belonging that exceeded every other experience in his life, even his most positive moments in Lieutenant Kohler's platoon.

The Long Journey: *Hurry Up and Wait*

"You guys are the reason I'm wearing these," he said, pointing to the brass bars. "I couldn't have earned them without your help."

"Don't forget it!" Talon Waldheim warned. "We'll kick your butt if you swagger."

Though the others offered remarks in a similar vein, Garrick smiled, knowing that each one of them meant well. Yet, despite their encouragements, his thoughts began drifting away. Older, more complicated feelings replaced the ebbing joy as he picked up a clipboard that lay at the foot of his bed.

A release form and a document for contacting next-of-kin in the event of his demise had been neatly attached to the spring-loaded clip. The names of his siblings, Algernon and Kira, appeared on the lines designating beneficiaries for death benefits. If he met his end in battle, they would each receive a small stipend from Tamaria's treasury as long as they lived.

For a moment he paused. A maelstrom of strong emotion swept over his soul. What had happened to Kira? Where was Algernon? He longed to see his siblings again and enjoy their company, but if he died in combat, would either of them understand how much he loved them, or how much he'd been willing to sacrifice for their sakes? Pulling a pen from his breast pocket, Garrick signed the document and dropped the clipboard back onto his bed.

A letter would have to do, he decided.

With only a few hours remaining until the graduation ceremony, Garrick needed to verify that Sergeants Vidders and Ringer were fully aware of the impending deployment. He went to the enlisted barracks, where his platoon soldiers greeted him with the deeper respect and courtesy extended to officers throughout the Tamarian army.

"I want to thank you all for your hard work," Garrick said as the men informally assembled around him. "We've walked a tough and demanding trail in preparation for our deployment, but the lessons we've learned will serve us well. In Kameron we expect to fight battle-hardened rebels. I know from experience that some who are standing in this room today will not return. So tonight, prepare yourselves for the bigger test ahead. Find a way to tell your families that you love them, and get some rest. We'll assemble at the rail platform at 0330 hours."

Later, after taking a shower and changing into his dress uniform, Garrick left the barracks and went to the rifle range to find Brenna. She'd been scheduled for qualification that afternoon, having completed the classroom instruction segment and a significant amount of practice with the .255 caliber carbine over a period of several days.

The afternoon heat produced a flush of color on Brenna's cheeks and a sheen of glistening sweat on her brow. After firing 500 rounds during her Combat Rifle Assessment, she felt hot, tired and a little grumpy. A cadre of rifle range instructors hovered nearby, their mildly irritating presence contributing to her aggravation.

Brenna didn't like the way they stared at her, but as she tallied her score, she noticed them stiffen to attention as someone approached. Thinking Mariel had come to check on her, the Lithian girl paused and stood on her toes to get a better look.

"As you were, gentlemen," Garrick said. This automatic deference would take some getting used to, he thought. A bit of brass suddenly set him into an elite, celebrated group for whom lesser-ranked individuals made way. His new status forced older, more experienced people to take him seriously, but their respect seemed strangely undeserved. As the range instructors parted and Garrick saw Brenna's annoyed facial expression morph into one brimming with delight, he felt happy that he'd done something to make her proud.

Brenna's expression displayed sheer joy. This emotion sparkled in her dark eyes as she put her rifle down on a table and opened her arms to embrace him. "You've graduated!" she exclaimed, disbelieving only because she'd not expected to see him wearing a lieutenant's insignia for another several days. "How did you manage that?"

He drew her near and placed a very brief kiss on her damp forehead. Though she raised her face toward his expecting a full mouth meeting of lips, with the instructors watching him, Garrick restrained his behavior. "No," he replied. "I didn't graduate. The colonel gave me a battlefield promotion."

Because she felt sweaty and hot, and because her fingers were smeared with a coating of gun oil that she didn't want to get onto his clean uniform, Brenna stepped away. "Doesn't matter," she said, inspecting her handsome warrior with renewed appreciation.

He winced because it did matter, at least to him. "I guess I'll always know that I didn't make it through the course, but the guys were good about it. They really wanted me to graduate."

Brenna wished they were alone. She felt very proud of Garrick's accomplishment and wanted him to know this in a way better expressed between just the two of them. As she glanced toward the instructors, an aspect of disappointment that Garrick didn't understand appeared on her face for a fleeting moment, then faded as she returned her gaze toward him. "I thought you had another week to go," she said, an inflection of uncertainty lingering in her words.

Garrick felt his heart pound under the strong influence of her attention. He picked up her rifle, made sure its chamber was clear, then handed her the weapon. "There's been a change of plans," he told her, explaining how the Readiness Order essentially usurped everything. "You need to get this rifle cleaned and wash up for the graduation ceremony this evening."

A sense of excitement raced up Brenna's back. She closed her eyes and imagined what it would be like to introduce Garrick to her family. The brief and blissful thought of that encounter quickly tempered in the harsh light that any deployment to Kameron would likely mean battle and more bloodshed. When she looked at Garrick again, the image of his face from their first encounter several months earlier flashed into Brenna's consciousness. He'd been a warrior then, he remained one now, and she could not deny that this fact ranked high among many attractions she found in him.

The young couple walked over to the weapons pit, exchanging bits of unimportant news, letting their steps linger that they might enjoy a few moments together. After cleaning the rifle and handing it in, Garrick and Brenna stopped at the women's barracks where his new rank smoothed the effort to obtain a room for Brenna to rest in overnight. He thought it would be easier for her to stay on base, rather than having to come down from the university so early in the morning.

Another large scale antiwar protest at the Dragon's Lair gate prompted Garrick to lead Brenna along the cross-country endurance trail, which followed the River Honeywater's meanderings toward the city wall. The path ascended the northern side of Liberty Hill and joined the university's well-maintained running track. From there, the young couple climbed a long, steep set of concrete stairs toward the mathematics department, then crossed the campus toward the women's dorm.

This lengthy route gave them time to talk, but their conversation soon drifted into comfortable silence. Amid the manicured lawns, neatly trimmed trees, cobbled walkways and flower beds they strolled, hand-in-hand. Garrick wanted to savor the moments, preserve them in his memory somehow, but time slipped away and all too soon they arrived at the women's dormitory.

Because Garrick could not go upstairs with Brenna, she gave him a lingering kiss and left him in the lobby. The caress of her soft lips, the warmth of her imploring tongue, the strength of her embrace and the compression of yielding flesh reawakened his ardor. Garrick wandered over to a window and looked beyond the covered patio to a maple tree planted on the lawn, considering his good fortune, contemplating his future. Doing this helped calm his racing heart and drain away his desire.

A long time later Mariel Hougen came downstairs, looking more shapely than Garrick remembered her to be. The linguist's clean hair fell to slender shoulders and her trim dress uniform hugged her body in a delightfully feminine manner as she approached. She carried a duffel bag that she dropped on the lobby floor. Lieutenant Hougen smiled sweetly, straightened her blouse and held out her arms to embrace Garrick. "Congratulations, lieutenant!" she said. "Brenna gave me the good news!"

Her embrace lingered just a bit longer than it should have. Garrick, who'd already felt aroused by Brenna's farewell, gently backed away from Mariel in a manner he hoped would establish a respected boundary. "Thank you!" he replied.

Mariel picked up on the physical cue and tightened her lips in response. Nothing in her arsenal of charms successfully dislodged the firm grip of Brenna's affection on this boy's heart, and in moments of self-reflection, Mariel admitted that in addition to his handsome face and fit physique, that fierce loyalty formed a large part of the reason she found Garrick attractive. "So, we're all off to Kameron?" she more stated than asked.

Garrick shrugged. "I didn't see your name on the list. Are you going too?"

"I'll be translating for Colonel Adler and performing intelligence duties," Mariel replied. "The command roll doesn't detail all the support staff." She tilted her head to the side, brushing an imaginary bit of dust from Garrick's new insignia. "And you'll be leading infantry, I suppose?"

"That's the plan," Garrick responded. "It looks like we'll be the first to go in."

"Oh," she said, sounding either disappointed, fearful, or both. "That puts you in Captain Engel's Alpha Company. The full division won't be ready for a couple of weeks yet, but the Lithians need boots on the ground right now."

Garrick wrinkled his forehead. "What? You mean we're not going in full strength?"

Mariel shook her head, and in doing so, her lovely hair danced seductively. "No, Garrick. Most of the units haven't even been formed yet..." And once the words were spoken, Mariel immediately regretted saying them.

This information was the second indicator of an increasingly desperate situation in Northern Kameron. The fact that two dozen new officers received a Readiness Order without fully completing their training was one thing, but being sent to war without sufficient numbers to dominate the battlefield sounded a lot like what the Tamarian army had experienced against the Azgaril's Northern Liberation Army a few months earlier. This time, however, they wouldn't have the weather on their side. "So we're cannon fodder?" he asked.

"No," Mariel replied, her authoritative tone deliberately squelching his sarcasm. "We'll serve as a deterrent. The initial deployment involves a full brigade sent to aid in the defense of Brenna's family estate, where the threat to Tamarian interests is perceived as most critical right now. Five thousand soldiers, including me, you and your platoon, will supplement a Lithian force roughly the same size. We will represent a credible threat to the Kamerese rebels, and they should think twice about attacking us."

"Hmm," Garrick mused, correctly evaluating Mariel's bluster. "I've read that rebel troop strengths are estimated in the hundreds of thousands. An army that size would hardly consider a supplemented brigade formidable. In fact, an aggressive rebel commander might think our limited forces present the perfect opportunity to humiliate King Alejo's ally."

"Don't patronize me," Mariel replied. "Those figures represent the rebel armies nationwide. This is a very broad-based revolt, and I'm sure that even a reformed grunt like you understands that not all of the rebels roam the northeastern part of the country."

Though he had no right to push the issue, and knew Mariel had no obligation to tell him anything significant, Garrick pressed his luck. "But you have to admit that I have good reason for concern. We both

The Long Journey: *Hurry Up and Wait*

know that a single brigade can't defend territory as vast as the Velez estate, so why won't you tell me what we're up against?"

Mariel didn't like the direction this conversation had taken. "Captain Engels will brief you at the appropriate time."

As she turned to leave, Garrick stopped her with a firm hand on her upper arm. "You started this, lieutenant. Don't play innocent with me like you did when we first met. TAC Vogel admitted that you'd been assigned to watch Brenna and keep her away from me, but we're in a far more serious situation now and the time for secret spy games ended when I pinned the brass on this afternoon.

"My men and I are about to put our lives on the line in a foreign country, something none of us has ever done before. Now, I've long suspected you're more than just a linguist, and that you know more than you're letting on. It's only right that I know what kind of enemy we're going to face, and I suspect you're well aware of the numbers we'll be up against."

Mariel glared at him until he let go. "I liked you better before you got your promotion, Garrick. You did as you were told and didn't stick your nose into places where it doesn't belong."

"Well, the stakes are higher now," he replied. "I have a platoon to command, so this is not just about me anymore. We're supposed to be on the same side, so why the secrecy?"

"Decisions about what to do with you and your men are made well above your pay grade," she snapped. Mariel could play hardball when she needed to do so, and she had far more experience in this realm than he did. "Take your orders and do as you're told, and before you get your underwear in a wad, understand that no one can know how many rebel forces will array against us until we get there. But I promise that you'll have your hands full doing your own job, lieutenant. Focus on leading your men. Let the senior officers worry about the disposition of enemy forces."

"Point taken, ma'am," Garrick replied, his formal address both an indicator of his willingness to capitulate and an implied complaint that her informality led them both to the point where she essentially needed to pull rank in order to shut him up.

Mariel felt wounded by the manner in which he responded, but she didn't say anything about this directly. As someone deeply involved in the military analysis of the Kamerese Civil War, Mariel not only understood the complexity of the conflict and the overwhelming

The Long Journey: *Hurry Up and Wait*

numerical superiority enjoyed by the rebels, she also knew that their weapons were more modern than any yet employed against Tamarians. Further, Mariel believed that the quality of rebel military leadership surpassed that of the National Kamerese Army.

The upcoming fight, in which Garrick's unit represented the figurative tip of the Tamarian spear, would occur among forces more evenly matched than had been the case during the Winter Saradon Campaign. Mariel didn't have the heart to tell him that she expected higher casualties, difficult and persistent logistical problems, and a far longer conflict than had been the case against the Azgaril Northern Liberation Army. Because she liked him and didn't want to see him hurt, Mariel wished that she had the influence to assign him elsewhere.

Though she'd been right about senior officers making decisions about the order of battle, Garrick's superlative record in combat exercises and his knowledge of the Lithian culture singled him out as the type of platoon leader expected to be most effective in Kameron. Colonel Weiss deliberately promoted him, despite his academic difficulties, for these reasons. Whereas the uncanny leadership ability that Garrick consistently demonstrated illustrated his suitability as an officer, and his courage inspired the men under his command, his charisma made higher-ranking officers who knew him reluctant to commit the young man to battle. TAC Vogel and Mariel, had they ever discussed the issue, would both have preferred to defer Garrick's involvement in combat until he matured, until his judgment gave him the ability to think carefully and weigh options before responding.

Ironically however, Garrick's tendency to make the most tactically intelligent decisions quickly and consistently lay at the root of his success. Slowing that process down in an environment where decisiveness often made the difference between life and death would have made him a less capable combat leader.

For this reason Mariel appraised Garrick wistfully. She feared for his safety, not only because she liked him herself, but also knowing that her friend, Brenna, would be emotionally crushed if anything terrible happened to him.

"Take care of yourself," Mariel said softly. She shouldered her duffel bag without another word and hurried out of the dormitory, lest he witness the tears that welled up in her eyes spilling onto her cheeks.

While Garrick had no idea why Mariel felt so conflicted, he knew that he'd managed to hurt her somehow. As she scurried down the

The Long Journey: *Hurry Up and Wait*

outside stairs, Garrick opened the door and called after her, warning that she should take the back route to the base in order to avoid the protest at the Dragon's Lair gate. Mariel nodded, waved, then went on her way.

Brenna stood at the bottom of the stairs as he shut the door. She wore her dress uniform and polished boots, with her sword, bow and quiver strapped to her back. The girl held her backpack in her right hand, as if ready to hoist it over her shoulder. "What happened?" she inquired, evaluating Garrick's expression and correctly deducing that he'd been arguing with Mariel.

"It's nothing," he replied, lying.

Brenna knew he wasn't telling the truth, but didn't confront him. She hoisted her backpack, then grudgingly accepted his offer to carry it for her. Though she didn't like being treated as if too fragile to bear her own burdens, Brenna knew Garrick well enough to understand that small acts of service demonstrated love and affection among Tamarians. He could not escape the influence of his culture any more than she could her own. She smiled in resignation and reached for his hand. "Let's go" she said.

They had to hurry because the graduation ceremony would begin in less than 30 minutes. Since most of the route lay downhill of the women's dorm, their pace could quicken without either of them breaking into a sweat.

Garrick's contemplative silence differed from the comfortable kind of quietness they'd enjoyed on their way up to the women's dorm. Brenna didn't wish to pry, so she left him to his thoughts while she enjoyed the bird songs and pattering of a woodpecker hunting bugs on an old snag within the university research forest.

After dropping off Brenna's belongings in the women's barracks, the young couple attended the graduation ceremony and applauded each candidate as he received his commission. Though several new officers wanted to visit a local restaurant for a celebratory dinner and drinks, Garrick, knowing that he would soon have no time alone with Brenna, politely declined and elected to eat a quiet meal with her in the mess hall.

Twilight lingered beyond the snow-clad mountains, and in the Daystar's fading light they walked slowly along a gravel path near the Honeywater. As the Great Eye rose in the east Brenna's dark eyes brightened, and a world of colors invisible to her Tamarian boyfriend gradually emerged. She saw the familiar bulls-eye pattern of flowers

The Long Journey: *Hurry Up and Wait*

and the fluorescence of urine trails left by small animals scurrying through the underbrush. Quartz bearing rock glowed in jasper phosphorescence, and the beautiful and ghostly sheen of bird feathers fluttering across the darkening sky caught and held her attention.

Brenna stopped and took hold of Garrick's hands. Ultraviolet light penetrated the upper layers of their skin, revealing a similar network of tiny blood vessels and hair follicles. "There's something I need to talk to you about," she warned, dropping her gaze to the ground.

Garrick felt a sense of dread rising up within him, inspiring insecure worry that Brenna was about to deliver bad news. "I'm listening," he replied.

The Lithian girl bit on her lower lip, not really knowing how or where to begin. When she raised her head an expression that blended embarrassment with meekness melded onto her heart-shaped face. "Among my people there are certain expectations and limitations imposed on relationships between men and women of marriageable age. My family is rather . . . conservative, and they've developed a misunderstanding about us that's not going to be easily undone."

This prelude played in a different key than Garrick had been expecting, given her introduction to the topic. "Misunderstanding?" he questioned. "How can that be? They've never even met me!"

Brenna's expression morphed into something that fell somewhere between helplessness and despair. "I suspect they'll love you as I do, or at least, learn how to love you, but there's no guarantee that their acceptance will be immediate," she continued. "As it is, I have some relational mending to do, because when I left home I did so against my father's advice. My whole family worried that I'd get hurt or killed, and though they were relieved to learn that I'd survived the war, they were expecting me to come back home right away. When I didn't return with Woodwind, when he told them that he'd given up pursuit of me because of my love for you, it strengthened certain assumptions they'd made about our relationship."

"You're not being clear, Brenna. What are you trying to say?"

She closed her eyes and shook her head. "I'm telling you, but you have to bear with me because this is hard to explain. You know that I ran away from home because I didn't want to marry Nemesio Fang. I did that not only to save myself, but also because as long as I remain free, he can't have any of my sisters either. Our customs require that the eldest daughter marry first, so leaving home spared them of any potential union with Lord Fang in my absence. In effect, coming here saved my entire family–especially my siblings–from the wicked aspirations of a Kamerese war lord.

"But a few days ago I received a letter from my younger sister, Cassie. She has a boyfriend named Jared, a lawyer who comes from a respected, God-honoring family. They've been seeing one another for a long time, things are beginning to get serious between them, and now he's moved into my father's house as a prelude to formal engagement."

Perplexed, Garrick shrugged. "What's wrong with that?"

Brenna came quickly to the heart of her concern. "That's not ever done unless every older daughter is already married."

The realization of Brenna's problem dawned upon Garrick's mind, though he didn't appreciate the breadth of the issue, having never considered the impact of his relationship with Brenna on her family. "Have you told them something you haven't shared with me?"

A desperate expression deepened on Brenna's face. "No," she responded. "It's a misunderstanding. Thea, my clairvoyant sister, had a vision last fall in which she saw me wearing a Tamarian uniform. Because I wasn't dressed like a virgin, she assumed I'd married you and told this to the rest of the family." Brenna wrinkled her forehead, pursed her lips and widened her eyes. "So, they think we're already husband and wife."

Garrick laughed. "Well, just tell them we're not. How difficult can that be?"

"Clearly harder than you realize," she replied, not appreciating the fact that he took this issue so lightly. "A whole chain of events has been set in place because of this. I can explain to my parents that we're not married, but when I do, I'll also have to prove that I'm still a virgin, and that requires a rather humiliating examination."

"Won't they take your word for it?" he asked. "Don't they love you enough to trust you about something like this?"

Brenna sighed. "Of course they would, but the need to clarify my virtue is not an issue limited to my family," she said. "Among Lithians, virginity at marriage establishes clear lines of succession. In the event that something happens to you in battle, or should the two of us part ways for any reason, I'll have to prove my virginity to every potential suitor because my relationship with you hasn't been supervised by my parents, who can't vouch for what they haven't observed. That fact, along with the misconception of my younger sister, puts my virtue into question. This means that the humiliating exam to which I referred earlier has to be repeated every time anyone gets serious about me.

"And further, it means that Jared and Cassie shouldn't continue their courtship until the disposition of our relationship is resolved. This isn't fair to Cassie, who invited Jared to live with our family in sincere faith that there were no complications to their courting.

"For his part, Jared moved into our house with my father's blessing, believing that no impediments existed to his pursuit of my sister. Not only is the integrity and reputation of my own family at stake, Jared's loved ones have an interest in this issue as well, and we have no idea how Jared and his family will respond to the news that you and I aren't married. In essence, a host of expectations and misunderstandings will have to be unraveled when we get to Kameron."

Stunned by this revelation, Garrick felt momentarily at a loss for words. "We're going to be fighting a war," he replied. "When are we going to have time for all of this?" Then the worry in Brenna's eyes inspired an idea, and a smile spread upon his face in response. He pulled her close and spoke softly. "But we could resolve the whole problem if you'd marry me," he stated.

Brenna stiffened and caught her breath. "Now? Tonight?" she asked in alarm.

"If it would put an end to your family's trouble, why not? What do you have to lose?"

"No!" she said firmly. "It's too sudden, too soon. I'm not ready for that yet."

Garrick felt a stab in his heart, a wound that bled in silence for a moment. He paused as a geyser of strong feelings erupted from within his soul. "I don't understand you!" he said, more forcefully than he should have. "You tell me that virtue is an important principle in your life, but I'm the one who's always putting the brakes on the physical part of our relationship. I do that for no other reason than I love you!

"Then you say that we have a problem because your family thinks we're already married, and you explain all of the resulting complications as if we're caught in some kind of trap from which there is no escape. You make it sound like we've really created a mess when neither of us has done anything to establish, nor perpetuate, the misunderstanding.

"And you say that you love me, that you want to spend time with me, then without any hesitation you stridently reject blending your life with mine. So what am I to you anyway, Brenna? Where is this relationship headed? Are you just stringing me along, or can I hope to have you as my wife one day?"

"I wish you wouldn't make it sound like I'm repudiating you," she said, a tone of hurt tearing an edge on her voice. Brenna looked away, conflicted and confused. "It's not like that at all!"

"What else do you expect me to think?"

She looked up at him, wet-eyed and saddened. "Why the rush? What's your hurry? Don't you love me enough to wait?"

Knowing that she'd caught him with his own words, Garrick shut his eyes and breathed deeply. The evening air felt cool in his lungs, and as the hot passion that possessed him faded, Garrick regretted his impulsive request and subsequent rebuke. Yet he couldn't deny his desire for her. In the anomic mix of feelings he experienced at that moment, words fled away and he elected to say nothing in response.

Brenna looked at him in silence, her lower lip quivering. Her mind raced in fear that she might lose his honored affection, but she also withheld words that might have worsened their misunderstanding.

Unnerved by the silence and desperately afraid that she might simply walk away, Garrick left the wound in his soul open. "I can't deny my desire for you, Brenna," he said. "I need something tangible to affirm that you really love me in return."

As he held out his arms to her, the Lithian maiden melded into his embrace. She sniffed as she leaned her cheek against his chest. "I love you!" she whispered forcefully, the strength of her grasp underscoring the intensity of her emotion. "But I'm not ready for this!"

"Ok, Brenna," he soothed, stroking her hair. "I just don't know how long I can be patient." Though he remained willing to wait for her, part of him wanted to ask her if this waiting involved months or years. Something within his soul constrained him and wisely, Garrick didn't add to what he'd already told her.

Brenna shook her head, wishing that she could be alone to pray. An ache opened within her heart, and from this a tempest of contradictory feelings, regrets and dreams emerged. "I'm sorry, Garrick," she breathed. "I don't ever want to hurt you. It's all my fault that everything is such a mess!"

He didn't know why she consistently blamed herself for situations beyond her own control. Garrick didn't understand how his simple, innocent love for her could stir such a vortex. Tired of arguing

The Long Journey: *Hurry Up and Wait*

and afraid that her rebuff indicated some deeper displeasure, Garrick contented himself to hold Brenna close and savor her warmth as the twilight brought a cool wind down from the distant mountains. He kissed the top of her head and let her go.

"I have to write a letter to my brother and sister," he said. "And we both have to get up early tomorrow. We should get some rest."

"Please don't be upset at me," she implored. "Please don't walk away with anything but love for me in your heart."

He breathed a tiny laugh and gently held her face in his hands. "How can I possibly stay upset at you? I always hold you in my soul."

Brenna smiled, stood on her toes and kissed him gently. "And I will forever hold you in mine. Sleep in God's hands," she said.

And the two of them parted ways for the evening.

Garrick felt so distracted by his conversations with Mariel and Brenna, that composing a letter to his brother and sister kept him awake far longer than he'd intended. Mariel's admission that he'd be going into battle with a smaller than expected force and limited logistical support inspired worry that combat success might be difficult to sustain. Then he recalled that in every training exercise his platoon had been outnumbered and outgunned.

As he pondered this, Garrick realized that the senior officers knew that all Tamarian units deployed in Kameron would face similar circumstances. Sergeant Vidders had been right about the training exercises presenting the best opportunity to learn from mistakes, as from this point forward, errors would be fatal.

That thought brought him back to the letter. What could he possibly say to Algernon, upon whose shoulders his dream for a reunited family rested? How would Kira, whose life had taken such a radical turn, respond to his desire for reconnection? With the troubled deployment looming large in his consciousness, with his tumultuous love affair in flux, Garrick poured his soul into words that would only be read in the event that he would never speak to his siblings again.

By the time he finished his letter, other new officers began returning to barracks in various stages of inebria. Garrick closed the door to his sleeping cubicle, set his alarm, shut off his light and pulled a pillow over his head.

He dreamed that Kira came to see him, but his mind struggled to complete the picture of her as a young woman when in every memory

The Long Journey: *Hurry Up and Wait*

she appeared as a little girl. "Help me!" she pleaded. "Hurry, Garrick! I need you!"

And thus, when the alarm clock rang, he felt tense. Having not slept well, he arose by virtue of sheer willpower and forced himself to shower, shave and dress. Very little discussion occurred among the new lieutenants as each of them prepared for the day. Garrick made his bed, packed the last of his personal belongings and left his sleeping cubicle in perfect order.

He ate a light breakfast in the mess hall while waiting for Brenna to arrive. Nervously checking the time, he'd nearly finished his second cup of tea when the Lithian girl walked in with Mariel.

Brenna ran her fingers across his neck and shoulder, down his right arm and took hold of his hand as she sat down. "You look tired," she said, just before lifting a piece of toast to her lips.

Her touch felt gently reassuring. "I didn't sleep well," he admitted, "but the train ride will be long and maybe I can do some catching up on the way south."

"You think she's going to let you sleep?" teased Mariel with a wink. "From what I've seen I'll bet you two can't wait for the tunnels!"

Garrick felt too tired to contend with Mariel's wit, but her willingness to bait him indicated a measure of forgiveness that he accepted gratefully. As he shook his head and muttered an incoherent remark, Garrick let his eyes drift below Mariel's shoulders, noting again that she seemed shapelier than he remembered.

"It's the new bra," she remarked, quite pleased that his gaze lingered there. "Brenna bought it for me yesterday. Do you like it?"

Embarrassed, Garrick's face flushed. He swallowed the last of his tea and put his cup down. "Yes, ma'am, I do. You look exceptionally beautiful, lieutenant."

Brenna didn't appreciate his leering, so she leaned close, pressed her body against his and whispered in his ear. "Does that mean I have to try harder to keep your eyes on me?"

Garrick smiled, then deliberately dropped his gaze. "Hmm," he mused, overtly staring for the first time where his eyes had only dared steal an occasional glance before. He kissed her lightly on the mouth and slid his nose along her cheek. "I don't think you have anything to worry about," he murmured.

Mariel raised her eyebrows, knowing that the demonstration Garrick had just put on was intended as much for her benefit as it was

The Long Journey: *Hurry Up and Wait*

for Brenna's. They finished breakfast over small talk until Mariel arose. "Well, lovebirds, I think we all have a train to catch."

Running late, they hurried to the depot. Arriving there among hundreds of waiting soldiers, Garrick didn't feel at all surprised that the tracks lay empty. Mariel bade the young couple farewell, vanished among the warriors, and neither Garrick nor Brenna saw her until after they'd arrived in Kameron.

Garrick found his platoon, checked with his sergeants to make sure that all remained in order, then sat with his men on the loading platform where they waited for the locomotive to arrive. Though he tried to sleep, the combination of pre-deployment adrenaline and caffeine in his tea kept him awake. He and Brenna leaned back to back near a wall at the station, speaking very little to one another in the presence of Garrick's platoon. The affection that had come to characterize their interaction over the past few weeks vanished like the fading stars.

Tempers shortened as minutes stretched into hours. Some soldiers slept, but among those who stayed awake, everyone seemed grumpy and tired. Sergeant Ringer, in particular, meted out discipline with an edgy sternness normally reserved for serious misbehavior. Garrick felt a measure of relief that he didn't have to deal directly with crabby warriors annoyed at the delay in their transportation. He silently wished that he'd been able to sleep, when nearly two hours later, an old Model 11 engine backed into the station.

Dawn brightened the cloudless, eastern sky. A full battalion, consisting of slightly more than 700 soldiers and their officers, boarded the economy class coaches and headed south. As the train rumbled through the empty rail corridor, over stone bridges arching above the Honeywater and through the silent business and financial districts, vagrants, late shift and early morning workers hardly raised an eyebrow at its passing.

Brenna stared out a window at the very back of the last passengers' car, her heart filling with unexpected sadness. Memories of this lovely, pleasant city, its green belts, shopping plazas, clean air and unique skyline flooded through her mind, filling her soul with a wistful thought that her departure marked the closing of a crucial chapter in her life. Although she longed to see her family again, somehow Brenna didn't feel like she was heading home. She felt like she was leaving it.

The Long Journey: *Hurry Up and Wait*

The gentle, side-to-side sway of the train motion moved her shoulder into contact with Garrick's broad chest, and as she adjusted her position to move closer to him, she felt his strong left hand squeeze her left shoulder reassuringly. Brenna felt content, leaning against his body, her thoughts adrift.

Several minutes after the train passed under Marvic's heavily defended gate, the locomotive slowed and stopped on a siding. A collective groan arose from the men onboard as they waited for a Marvic-bound freight locomotive to pass. Curses and complaints abounded, but Brenna noticed that Garrick didn't grouse. He seemed distracted and nervous somehow.

When the train finally pulled back onto the main line and headed down the long, steep slope to Fallen Moon Lake, Brenna leaned her head against Garrick's shoulder and ran her fingers through the chest hair nestled in the V of his shirt. No sooner had their rail car entered the utter blackness of a long, spiral tunnel than she felt Garrick turn and pull her close.

For a moment they flirted with another physical escalation of their relationship. Brenna did not resist as his left hand slipped beneath her blouse and moved to her breast. She willed her undergarment loose because she wanted him, but then regretted doing so as something in her soul warned that this was not a path she should walk down. Her body shuddered as she struggled for control. He kissed her cheek, descended her neck with endearing strokes of lips and tongue, then nuzzled the junction of her neck and shoulder while his hand caressed her and the urgency of his arousal teased between her thighs.

Brenna pushed his hand down, kissed him passionately, then pulled away to her own seat. Garrick let her go without protest. Brenna's heart raced, her flesh tingled, and she desperately longed for more of that wonderful feeling, but this was not the way a pious Lithian girl was supposed to behave, and no one knew this more than she did.

Before the tunnel brightened, she smoothed her rumpled clothing. No one had witnessed their brief encounter, yet she felt nervous and guilty about consenting to his advance. As light crept into the coach, she looked at him with accusation in her eyes. "What was that all about?" she inquired softly.

The train passed into full daylight again. Garrick met her gaze fearlessly, unashamed. "Don't play with my heart, Brenna," he replied,

The Long Journey: *Hurry Up and Wait*

quietly. "I want you. I want all of you." Then he drew close and kissed her soft lips. "I know that you want me, too."

"I do," she responded, a little bit fearfully. "But the way we're going about this isn't right."

Garrick nodded, knowing her heart, but he wasn't about to let her off the hook so easily. When he spoke, he did so in a whisper. "Then be honest with me, Brenna. What's the matter? What do you want? Why do you always shrink back from committing to me?"

This question haunted Brenna's soul from the moment of their first meeting, a moment months before when he'd come to rescue her from freezing to death. He'd always been trustworthy, yet that question arose anew whenever she thought about where their relationship was heading. "Do you really want the truth?" she asked.

He nodded.

"Even if it hurts?"

Garrick's facial expression hardened. "You said you didn't want to hurt me. Are we living a lie, or is this relationship real?"

Brenna, who'd never been caressed before, who'd never known any desire as strong as the one she experienced for Garrick, felt stung by his remark. She sat back and sighed. "What do you think?"

He leaned over and whispered into her ear. "It's real for me, Brenna. But you're sending me mixed messages, and that's not fair."

She didn't respond right away, and soon the train plunged into darkness again. The moments dragged by in silence, yet Garrick did not touch her this time. When light flooded the passenger cabin, Brenna seemed fearful. "You ought to know how I feel," she pleaded. "Do you think I would offer the gift of my virtue if I didn't love you with all my heart?"

"You're still a virgin," he reminded her, though in Brenna's mind this had now become a matter of semantics. "You can walk away from me any time you wish."

"I would never do that!" she replied.

"Then what's constraining you, Brenna? Why do you pull me in, only to push me away? Why won't you tell me what's wrong?"

"Why are you pressuring me?" Brenna didn't like being compelled to do anything, and Garrick's urgency annoyed her.

"Because there's an invisible barrier between us, and I want to know what it is!"

The Long Journey: *Hurry Up and Wait*

Brenna dropped her face into her hands and shook her head. When she looked at him again, her eyes were brimming with tears. "You are not a man who honors Allfather," she admitted, her whispered voice rasping. "That bothers me!"

She'd been right. The truth hurt. "You're talking about something that's not going to change," he reminded her. "If you're waiting for me to accept your faith as my own, we're going to be cycling through guilt and suppressing desire as long we're together. Are you using your body as bait to provide me with an incentive to convert? Is that what you want? Is that what you're waiting for?"

"That's not fair!" she replied, the truth of his accusation exposing something within her that she refused to recognize. "You know that I want you. I'm not teasing you, or leading you on with the intention of breaking your heart, Garrick."

"Then what are you waiting for? Are you biding your time with me until someone more suitable comes along?"

She shook her head and reached for him. "No!" she pleaded, squeezing his hands. "It's not like that at all!" Brenna pulled his hands into her lap, dropping her gaze from his. "I just don't know what to do," she sniffed. "My mind is overwhelmed with all of these contradictory feelings. I want you, but I'm afraid to bind myself with someone who doesn't share my faith. I want you, so I know that I can't be objective about this. What about your family? What about mine? I want you, but I'm torn by doubt. I can't decide what is right, so I want you to meet my parents. I want to know what they think."

Garrick lifted his head until it contacted the wall behind him. "And what happens if I don't meet with their approval?" he inquired. "Will I have loved you in vain?"

"No," she replied. "Love is never for naught. I wish I could reassure you, but I honestly don't know what they'll say."

"Whose life are we talking about, Brenna? Your parents have already chosen their partners, and besides, they think we're married already. Ultimately, this is your decision to make, not theirs."

The truth of Garrick's words resonated within Brenna's heart. She had every right to choose her own destiny, just as she'd done in the past. On their way to Marvic many weeks ago, she'd pushed Garrick across a threshold from which neither of them could now retreat, and if she wanted to salvage her tattered virtue, Brenna understood she would

The Long Journey: *Hurry Up and Wait*

have to marry the boy she loved and bask in the fullness of his passion for her, or kill their relationship.

The young couple sat in brooding silence while the train completed its descent to the lakeshore. Two and a half hours later, beyond Blind Beggar Bay, the locomotive raced across a long, sweeping, eastbound turn that led toward Tamaria's longest suspension bridge. It took nearly eight minutes for the train to cross the narrow point where the Angry Bear River spilled from its origin at the mouth of Fallen Moon Lake. Here, the frothing waters leapt toward the tracks and a mist condensed on the outside windows that obscured vision until motion and rising temperatures washed the moisture away.

Ancient prose, poetry and wisdom literature flashed into Brenna's memory. She knew that among God's people there should be absolutely no immorality, yet Allfather established sexual expression in the context of marriage. God wanted married couples to rejoice in their intimacy and enjoy every benefit of a loving, committed relationship.

But she and Garrick were not married.

Brenna recalled advice to virgins, urging the passionate to find a suitable partner, settle down and have children. But how could Allfather approve of a relationship between a believing daughter and a non-believing man? Yet how could Garrick, who really loved her, be worse than a hypocrite like Nemesio Fang, who feigned faith to gain control over fools?

Perhaps Allfather, who judged knowing the motives of the heart, extended more grace and compassion toward those who lived by faith than the faithful themselves were often willing to offer one another. Such thinking had an appeal, but Brenna worried that these thoughts merely represented a rationalization of her own lust.

Whom was she deceiving with this? Brenna loved Garrick. She couldn't change how she felt about him. If she walked away from their relationship, other girls–including Mariel–would eagerly line up to take her place. Would any of them treat him with the kindness and respect he deserved? Would any of them appreciate his intelligence, his restraint and gentleness? Would any of them accept his broken family as she did?

Brenna prayed in silence, earnestly seeking wisdom. She prayed as the landscape swept beyond her window and early summer heat baked the aluminum rail car. The Lithian maiden prayed as the train tirelessly climbed into the foothills fronting the Angelgate Range, yet

The Long Journey: *Hurry Up and Wait*

Allfather did not speak directly to her. All she heard were Garrick's words echoing in the recesses of her memory. Indeed, this was her decision to make.

Finally, Brenna broke the silence between them. "Garrick," she said softly. Looking into his eyes, she took in a deep breath. "I've made up my mind. I want to marry you."

He didn't know whether to laugh or cry, but his heart leaped at the sound of her words. "Are you sure?" he inquired, suddenly afraid that he'd guilted her into making the decision.

Brenna nodded. "You may never be a believer," she said. "But I'm sure that you're the one for me."

Garrick wished they had some privacy. His pounding heart ached in anticipation of being alone with her. "When?" he inquired.

"I can't be certain," she replied. "It will take some time to arrange, and I want my family there. I want your family there, too."

"That's not possible," he replied, a sadness creeping into his voice that often accompanied their discussions of his loved ones. "My parents have disowned me, and I don't know when I'll see my brother and sister again, if ever."

She fell silent, desperately seeking words that would offer assurance to him. Brenna looked into grey eyes that filled with longing, knowing that hers reflected the same feeling. "Then we'll have to do the best we can."

Garrick stroked the curve of her cheek with the back of his index finger. "That's good enough for me," he said.

As he ran his finger down her neck, along the soft flesh that burgeoned beneath a plunging V on her combat uniform, Brenna caught his hand and faced him with her impish smile. "But until then, anything beneath my clothing is strictly off limits, Lieutenant Ravenwood!"

He smiled back at her. "Will you at least let me look?"

"Only if you'll stop leering at Mariel!" she replied with feigned indignation. "But if you want your hands under my blouse again, you're just going to have to wait!"

Deliverance

With the sounds of another artillery duel drawing near, the hammering of gun tubes and the explosions wrought by falling shells stirring dust and smoke into the air, Jawara led his companions on a bearing parallel to the Mistress of the Woods Road. Small arms fire erupting from the tree cover a few hundred yards to the south motivated the travelers to increase the pace of their egress, but Jawara didn't want to wander too far from the road and wind up lost in hostile territory.

Algernon, working hard to make progress across the rough ground with Jhiran's added weight in his bicycle trailer, glanced at his sister. Kira sat on the horse behind Jawara, her face flushed in the afternoon heat and awash in sweat. She sniffed constantly, gazing across the gently rolling landscape with a vacant stare, her grey eyes teary and unfocused. Blood seeped through the bandages Jhiran had wrapped around her feet, and dark stains appeared on Algernon's robe wherever its fabric soaked up blood and pus oozing from recent wounds on her back and shoulders. He simply didn't understand how Kira endured the suffering inflicted upon her body while remaining loyal to that ill-bred, knuckle-dragging, coprophagiac who'd deceived her.

Though he wished he could wrap his hands around Marco's skinny limbs and rend muscle from every bone, fear of the encroaching rebels and their well-known hatred of foreigners focused his energy on flight. Algernon relentlessly pushed himself onward.

Golden foxtail, flowering buckwheat, amaranth and ragweed grew in large, open patches called *potreros* that dotted the undulating topography. Clumps of serviceberry, stands of manzanita and the ubiquitous groves of live oak trees painted the hillsides and snuggled into arroyos that broadened as they reached toward the distant coastline. Algernon grimaced, knowing that as they moved through the dry, virgin grasses, they left behind a trail of flattened vegetation that even a child could follow.

"Holy man!" Jhiran called from the bike trailer between bites of jerky. "Stop!"

Algernon turned to see that Astrid had fallen behind again. With a sigh he shrugged off his backpack, called to Jawara, then dismounted and retraced his trail for a few dozen yards. Although he wanted to portray a sense of urgency, something weary and defeated in Astrid's face stirred compassion within him. "Come on, Astrid," he encouraged, more gently than he thought appropriate at the moment. "The rebels are coming. We can't stay here!"

Astrid straddled her bicycle, leaned her slender, lightburned arms on its handlebars and dropped her face down. "I can't go on!" she lamented. "I just can't!"

"Here," he offered, tugging at her backpack. "Let me carry this for you."

She let him pull the straps from her shoulders and modestly straightened her gown afterward. Saddened and fearful, Astrid looked into Algernon's eyes as if seeking solace there. "Kira hates me! Why am I even trying to escape? Just let them kill me!"

Gently, Algernon reached for Astrid's face. "Don't say that! She's not herself right now," he murmured in defense of his twin. "It's the drug talking. She doesn't realize what she's saying."

Astrid's eyes dampened. "I knew," she complained. "I knew that she didn't love me when she left the Temple."

Worriedly, Algernon glanced downhill, watching shadows emerge from the trees several hundred yards away. "Astrid, please! We have to keep moving!"

Blinking back tears, Astrid sat on the bicycle seat and pushed forward, riding unsteadily between clumps of sage toward Jawara, his horse, and the girl she loved.

Algernon hefted her backpack onto his shoulders and trotted behind. His legs felt leaden and his whole body ached from intense and sustained exertion. Years of discipline and martial training enabled him to push beyond the boundaries of normal endurance, but his strength had limits, and he worried that he simply couldn't continue at this pace.

"I'm sorry, little girl," he said to Jhiran as he approached, "but you'll have to sit on top of this." When the gwynling jumped out of his dusty bicycle trailer, Algernon set Astrid's backpack on top of their food stores, thinking that it might not be a bad thing for Jhiran to be separated from what they had left to eat.

Jhiran climbed back on, her blank expression moving from Algernon to Astrid, Jawara and finally Kira, whom she appraised carefully. The gwynling reached into her waistband for a carrot, then proceeded to chew on it without uttering a word.

Algernon strained against the added mass of Astrid's belongings in his bike trailer. Though he rested whenever their path led downhill, at the trough of every hillside lurked another crest to climb. His bare

The Long Journey: *Deliverance*

arms and shoulders reddened as the Daystar lingered in the cloudless sky, and only the late afternoon onshore flow of marine air from the distant Bay of Kameron brought relief from his sweltering labor.

A long time later, with the battle sounds fading, Jawara stopped beneath the shade of oak trees growing on a north-facing slope. He dismounted, checked Astrid's map and scanned the landscape to verify their location. "I think we're safe to rest here for a while," he said. Then, pointing in a westerly direction, he continued. "That's the road leading to Maia's house. If we're far enough ahead of the battle, maybe we can stay there tonight."

The thought of sleep filled Algernon's mind with rising anticipation. He helped his sister down from Jawara's horse and carefully, gently set her in the wild grass. "I wish Brenna was here," he said, fretting over Kira's feet. "She could help you."

Kira trembled, wiping her nose on the sleeve of Algernon's robe. Though she wondered who her brother was talking about, she said nothing as she watched Jhiran deftly prepare a fire in Algernon's cookstove, blowing start-up smoke away until the little gasifier began working so she could brew a cup of tea. When Astrid pulled up to help Jawara water his horse, Kira deliberately looked at Algernon instead, noting that he followed the priestess with his eyes. "I know you want her," she whispered. "I can see it."

Algernon shook his head. "It's you she came to find. It's you she cares about."

Kira put her sweaty hand on her brother's right shoulder. He winced in pain, his skin tender from the light burn, so she slid her fingers down to his forearm. Her body twitched involuntarily and her hand felt heavy and hot. "I can help you, if you'll help me."

"What are you saying?"

Kira glanced to the side, making sure that no one could overhear their conversation. "She's sweet as cream and sensitive, brother. Astrid's got a honey tongue. She can fill your mouth with a kiss that will set you on fire. Her thighs are soft as warm butter, and when you caress her, she responds like a mink in heat. Get her going, and she'll last for hours. She's passionate, willing to please, and once you've had a taste of her, you'll always hunger for more."

"I really don't need to hear this!" he replied, backing away.

The Long Journey: *Deliverance*

Kira held onto him, an unfamiliar and wicked expression in her watering eyes, a sense of urgency in her breath. "I know what you want, Algernon."

He leaned forward, his hot, angry look melting her brazen heart. "What I want is to have my sister back! I don't know who you are!"

Breathing through her nose in little pants, her fingers trembling in desperation, Kira pleaded with her brother. "Come on! She's a virgin! I can get her all warmed up and ready for you! I know what she likes, and trust me, she really is a wild filly! Don't tell me that you don't want her!"

Algernon shook his head. "You don't want her!" he snapped in a whisper. "Astrid offered her life for yours. All she wants to do is love you, but you want to give her away like she's some hand-me-down blanket. You make me sick!"

Kira gritted her teeth. "I don't want her! I don't need her! I need a fix, and you've got to help me!"

"No!" Algernon said, firmly. "Never again!"

She forcefully dug her fingernails into his arm, but he twisted out of her grip and knocked her hands away. When she tried to hit him, Algernon caught her fist in an iron grip. She kicked at him, but not only were her feet were so badly injured she couldn't bring herself to kick very hard, he was stronger and in her weakened condition, a far better fighter than she. He restrained her so that she couldn't hurt either of them. "I hate you!" she screamed. "I hate you and I hate her too!"

Once the ugly words had been uttered, Kira could not take them back. Astrid, who'd been watching the last part of the conflict, abandoned Jawara's horse and fled downhill. Algernon groaned in a rage, pushed Kira backward, and chased after the weeping priestess.

Jawara, who understood none of the exchange between the siblings, seemed bewildered.

Jhiran, however, picked up the gist of the entire conversation and her respect for Algernon deepened. She cautiously came to Kira's side with a cup of tea she'd just brewed and offered it to the wounded Tamarian girl.

"Get lost! I don't want your smelly drink," Kira snapped.

"I know what you thirst for," Jhiran replied in her strangely expressionless manner. "But what you want is bad for you. Drink this! You'll feel better."

The Long Journey: *Deliverance*

"You give me the creeps!" Kira said, trembling. "I hate the way you stare at me!"

"You hate your pain," Jhiran replied. She put down the cup and backed away, disturbed by images and words she pulled out of Kira's memory. The gwynling rummaged through Algernon's bike trailer until she found a bread stick, then wandered over to Jawara, with whom she sustained eye contact for several seconds. Understanding the gwynling's thoughts, Jawara shook his head and glanced over his shoulder at Kira, who sipped her tea with quivering hands.

"It's going to get worse before it gets better," he warned, speaking in vulgate.

Kira flashed a sullen glance at the 'Scinnian and switched languages with an ease that underscored her intelligence. "What's it to you?" she snarled. "Why couldn't you just leave me to die on my own?"

Jawara wiped the lather from his horse's neck with a towel he'd dipped in water. "Life is a gift of God," he replied. "You shouldn't throw yours away."

"What's it to you?" she repeated. "I'm just a whore. My life isn't worth anything!"

For a moment Jawara remained silent, appraising Kira's negative self-talk. Then he approached, squatted near her feet and spoke gently. "You are a daughter of the Holy One, the object of his tender care, and that makes you worth far more than you think."

"God doesn't give a rat's tail about me, and I don't give a rat's tail about God either!"

"Hmm," Jawara mused. "The Holy One seeks those who have lost their way. He cares enough that he sent your brother into a den of very wicked men to deliver you."

"My brother . . ." Kira mumbled. "My stupid brother shouldn't bother with me." Then her eyes reddened and two tears raced down her cheeks. She sniffed and turned her head away from the deep, compassionate eyes of the Abelscinnian warrior.

Kira gulped down the rest of her tea. She watched Algernon talking to Astrid, saw them embrace and after several moments, head back uphill. When they lived at the Temple, Algernon's contempt for Astrid and her whispered reputation led to several arguments between the siblings. He'd been ruthlessly critical of Kira spending so much time in Astrid's company, and the irony of his current tenderness toward her impressed Kira, even through the darkness of her withdrawal.

The Long Journey: *Deliverance*

As Astrid approached, she struggled to look at Algernon's twin sister. Deep sadness filled her heart, seeing the girl she loved so broken, so defeated, so angry. The brand burned onto Kira's left forearm, a double chain helix with shackles on each end, marked her as the property of some cruel master. Astrid believed Kira belonged to her, but she never would have subjected the girl to such bondage.

"What have I done to you?" the priestess pleaded. "Why do you hate me?"

Kira, shaking and looking increasingly pale, did not respond.

Algernon helped Jawara lift Kira back onto the horse. As soon as she'd straddled the creature, Kira felt an overwhelming rush of nausea and retched miserably. Algernon used a bit of water to clean her up and didn't complain, though he felt frustrated that his sister couldn't keep her medicinal tea down.

By the time the travelers reached Maia's house, Kira's condition had deteriorated even further. Bent over and moaning in pain, drenched in sweat and repeating a litany of paranoid fears, the Tamarian girl could hardly hold on to Jawara and remain on the horse.

Maia heard her guests returning and scurried onto her porch with a delighted expression reflected in the lines of her beautiful, elderly face. "You found her!" Maia exclaimed. "Bless the ancestors!" The gentle woman fussed over her visitors, insisting that they bring Kira inside right away. "Put her in Hermosa's room," said Maia, hinting that her daughter had not yet returned.

Jawara went to care for his horse while Algernon struggled to carry Kira inside. "Toilet!" the Tamarian girl exclaimed. "Now!"

They'd hardly made it to the multrum toilet when Kira's bowel loosened. "Leave me!" she demanded in humiliation. "Just leave me!"

Maia wrinkled her nose at the smell of her new guest and asked Algernon to draw water for a bath before she allowed Kira into her daughter's bed. "There's a daylight water heater on the south side of my house," she told him. "It warms a tank next to the bath, but after you've filled the tub, you'll have to pump in refill water for me."

Though the system seemed primitive compared to pressurized water heaters with passive, tracking heliostats he knew in Tamaria, Algernon figured out how to empty the water heater and refill it. This meant even more exertion with a hand-powered transfer pump. He already felt physically drained and couldn't touch the water because his light burn made him exceptionally sensitive to hot and cold.

The Long Journey: *Deliverance*

When Kira had finished on the toilet, Algernon carried her into the bath. Maia brought her a change of clothing, some fresh towels and soap, then shooed Algernon out when Kira shamelessly removed her robe. "This is no place for a young man!" she said.

"Grief!" he muttered, turning his back. "She's my sister! It's not like I want to look!"

All of them could have benefitted from a good scrubbing, but Astrid wanted Kira to finish first, and Jhiran simply didn't care to be clean. As she waited for her turn, Astrid whispered to Jhiran while washing Algernon's robe and Kira's bandages in the kitchen sink.

Algernon and Jawara had to content themselves with a cold water sponge bath drawn from the well outside. Afterward, the two young men relaxed on Maia's front porch. Algernon shivered from the cool sensation of evening wind blowing through his damp robe, but it felt better than the afternoon heat. Jawara sharpened his bayonet while they talked, and soon their conversation drifted toward spiritual matters.

The 'Scinnian warrior had been meditating on the relationship between the young women under his care. "What can you tell me about the morality of your sister's involvement with the young priestess? How do your sacred writings deal with this issue?"

Algernon paused, reluctant to continue, though he knew the answer without having to think. "*Gottslena* condemns many aspects of human behavior that secular people might construe as normal," he began. "Any form of selfishness, ranging from greed to negligence, is considered sin. Homosexuality is not permitted, but then, neither is fornication, nor adultery. The central tenet of *Gottslena* involves denial of self in service to the Great God."

"So your holy writings do not approve of their liaison either," Jawara responded with a nod. "Ours speak of seven abominations: the sins of lust, adultery, promiscuity, bestiality, homosexuality, incest and pedophilia. We believe that any sexual contact beyond the marriage vow between a man and woman violates the will of the Holy One."

Algernon shook his head. "Well, it's easy to call their relationship sinful and project my distaste for that behavior upon God. It's a simple matter to complain about a proclivity I don't like when it's practiced among strangers within the minority of people who engage in it, but what do I do when the sinner is someone I love?"

"You're speaking of your sister?" Jawara inquired.

The Long Journey: *Deliverance*

"And of Astrid, too," the Tamarian monk admitted. "Before I left the Temple in search of Kira, I couldn't stand her and thought myself superior because her kind of sin seemed so much worse than mine. Yet deep inside I always felt troubled, knowing that my sister loved the woman. Now I understand Kira's attraction. Now I know why she favored Astrid, and now I'm far less willing to judge either of them."

Jawara chose his words carefully. "Man's urge for gratification takes many forms. Some people decry the public sins of others because they also struggle with these things themselves, albeit secretly. Some who think themselves wise tolerate aberrant behavior because, aware of their own sins, they realize how everyone must struggle to overcome the evil that lives within. However, truth and purity do not bend to suit the will of mankind."

Algernon interrupted him. "I get that. But what I don't understand, is why do religions so universally condemn homosexuality when the relationship that Astrid maintained with Kira was far more harmonious with the intent of the Great God in creating love for humankind to enjoy, than was the case with Kira's heterosexual and abusive relationship with Marco?"

"You are comparing kindness with cruelty," Jawara responded. "You are contrasting a best case scenario with a worst case one. Therefore, your conclusion about harmony with God's will rings false. Now I believe that both of the relationships you describe are sinful, so you are simply comparing one that is obviously more destructive with another, instead of contrasting either or both of them with God's clearly stated ideal."

Frustration brimmed in Algernon's voice. "It just doesn't make any sense!" he stammered. "I can see that Astrid loves Kira. How can love be wrong?"

"The love is not wrong, my friend. How that love is manifest is where the problem arises. You love your sister enough to risk your own life for hers, yet you do not make her the object of your sexual desire."

"Of course not!" Algernon replied. "She's my sister; that would be disgusting!"

"Likewise, Astrid clings to you for comfort in her hour of distress, yet does not project feelings of sexuality upon you. Astrid clearly adores the gwynling, who is, I'm afraid, more pleasing to the eye than your sister at present. You and I know that Astrid could not conceal any lust from Jhiran–who I know wouldn't tolerate an

The Long Journey: *Deliverance*

inappropriate advance–and it's clear from observing the two of them that the gwynling treats Astrid as she would a daughter, and Astrid seeks counsel from Jhiran as though the gwynling was her mother."

"So you're saying that Jhiran loves Astrid in a maternal way, and Astrid responds in kind. Therefore, Astrid responds to love, right?"

"She does respond to love, my friend."

"Yet she doesn't respond to mine!" Algernon replied, revealing a deepening wound.

Jawara smiled. It was a kindly smile that radiated warmth and fellowship. "She is very sweet to you," he began. "She serves you and honors you. I know many men who would envy your friendship because they never receive such treatment from their wives."

"Yes, Astrid is nice," Algernon admitted. "But she doesn't like me in the way I want her to like me."

"Ah, then the true nature of the problem is revealed," Jawara said, triumphantly. "If you really loved the girl, would it matter if she requited your love in kind?"

Algernon's eyes widened. "You think I should extend charity, understanding and friendship to her without limit, and never expect anything in return?"

Again, Jawara smiled. "That depends on how you define love," he said. "I was once your age and I well recall experiencing a similar conflict. You need to learn the difference between love and desire. Judging from the courtesy you extend to the priestess and the way you seek to fulfill her needs, I can argue that you love her. Likewise, her deference and service to you indicate love as well. There are many benefits you enjoy from her.

"What you are seeking, however, has more to do with sexual release than love. In that case, you are no different from her, as she seeks the same thing from your sister. In that light, you are both guilty of sin. From that perspective, the tension that you feel in your religious belief, with its prohibition against immorality, condemns your behavior as well as hers. For this reason, you feel conflicted."

"So, as usual, the problem lies with me," Algernon complained, shaking his head. "God is perfect, and it's all my fault!"

"The nature of the human heart ensures that we are all in need of God's mercy."

The Long Journey: *Deliverance*

Algernon, however, hated admitting culpability in this matter. "If I am created by God, why then does this passion burn within me? What purpose does it serve, aside from driving me insane with desire?"

At this, Jawara let out the barest hint of a laugh. "When you are in public and your bladder fills, do you empty it immediately or do you seek privacy before relieving yourself?"

"What kind of a comparison is that?" Algernon snapped. "You're equating excretory function with desire. That's utterly absurd!"

"That is not so, my friend. Your desire is as much a bodily function as your need to urinate. My point in this exercise is to illustrate that you exhibit control over your bladder as a matter of fact, yet complain when you must exercise similar control over your libido."

Though he didn't really feel like arguing that point, Algernon vented more of his own frustration. "I see a fundamental difference between the need not to offend other people by exposing myself and peeing in public, and the natural arousal I experience in the presence of a girl. You're saying there's a similar moral connection between control over my sexual desire and the social norm of seeking privacy to relieve myself. I think your linkage is weak at best."

"The connection exists, without doubt!" Jawara continued. "All of the intelligent races perform their excretory functions in private. Likewise, sexual relations among humans are also performed in private. In contrast, this is not the case among the animals, even the great apes who are most like us. We alone have the capacity for moral judgment, and sometimes that judgment compels us to limit the expression of our instincts. Thus, we measure morality by the degree of moderation we impose upon our own desires.

"Your body obeys your mind in restraining the urge to urinate in public, and in a like manner will obey your mind in restraining the urge for sexual release. I've seen that this control already exists within you."

"Nonsense!" Algernon argued. "It's an automatic response. I can't help how I feel."

Jawara disagreed. "I've seen you turn your eyes away from the young woman when she inadvertently reveals her flesh. I see that you respect her privacy. Also, I noticed that you struggled not to let your gaze wander in the presence of Lord Lynden's daughters."

Algernon rolled his eyes. "That's another problem! Those Lithians project an air of holiness, like they're so devout, yet their young

The Long Journey: *Deliverance*

and nubile ones prance around in filmy clothes that leave very little to the imagination. Where's the morality in that?"

Jawara nodded with a smile, understanding. "The Lithians have a very different way of thinking about this issue than you and I do. To them, God created beauty to be appreciated. Their children wear no clothing at all until they reach puberty. At that time, the unmarried among them dress quite deliberately to display their flesh with the intent of attracting a suitable mate. They believe this pleases God."

"Well, it's easy to make that sort of claim about the young and beautiful. It's easy to appreciate a gorgeous girl who has no discernable flaws. It's easy for the girls to swoon over someone like Jared, who looks like the living statue of some ancient god incarnate, presenting himself as an object of worship for the benefit of all adoring females in the world. But what about the older ones who don't marry? What about the Lithians who are unattractive, who have bad skin, who are overweight, or too skinny?"

Jawara laughed. "Have you ever seen such a specimen? That's like saying there are ugly voices among songbirds!"

Incredulous, Algernon narrowed his eyes. "You're telling me that Lithians are uniformly attractive?"

"I'll say it this way. I've seen many thousands of Lithians in my life, and I have yet to encounter a single one who did not please my eye. This is why they never develop an individual sense of superiority concerning their appearance. They are all well formed and flawless."

"What about the elderly, then? Do they not wrinkle and sag as they age?"

"Not in the same manner that we do," Jawara replied. "They live a very long time and sustain vigor well into their advanced years. Consider Lady Alexina. Did you not see that she remains a slender, shapely and beautiful woman?"

"Well, yes. But that just means she must not be very old!" Algernon replied.

"She is 70, my friend, and expecting another child. Yet the ravages of time have not diminished her loveliness, and she will likely remain strong and fair for centuries to come."

"But she and Lord Lynden have grey in their hair already," Algernon countered.

The Long Journey: *Deliverance*

"Yes," Jawara agreed. "They have always had grey in their hair, as does their daughter, Camille. The indicators of ageing that we experience simply do not apply to the Lithians."

"So that gives them the right to show themselves off and inspire lust without restraint? I mean, have you ever looked at Cynthia?" He outlined an exaggeration of her buxom shape with his hands. "Where is the morality in dressing like she does?" Algernon shook his head, partly in disgust, partly in desire and partly in envy.

Jawara maintained his calm demeanor in the face of his friend's rising emotional intensity. "Holiness is a deeply personal matter to the Lithians. They do not seek to inspire sexual cravings in anyone. In truth, they're bewildered by this concept because arousing another person's desire does not enter their minds. This is a critical point. Sexual fantasy and lust exist only in the mind of a man who lacks self-control."

"Nonsense!" Algernon countered. "I can't help feeling aroused when I see all of those breasts and hips and thighs revealed like that!"

"So is the lust that you experience their problem, or yours?" Jawara asked.

"Well, it might be my lust, but they inspire it by dressing that way! How else am I supposed to respond?"

Jawara grunted. "You will find that after awhile the display of these attributes loses its erotic quality."

"I don't think so!" Algernon replied, ignorant of a truth Jawara understood from personal experience.

"Then let me drive my point home," Jawara continued. "You've admitted that you find Astrid attractive. Does she arouse you?"

"That's a rather personal question!" the Tamarian monk complained, his annoyance increasing.

"Have you ever seen her thighs revealed? Have you seen her breasts uncovered?"

"No!" Algernon spat. "Of course not!"

"Yet she's able to stir your imagination without being dressed like a Lithian, is that not so?"

"Not to the same extent!" Algernon protested.

Jawara looked away. "I think you are being less than completely honest," he said. "Think about this when you are alone and your thoughts are your own to measure. Lust is a perversion of the normal drive to reproduce and should not be confused with the decision to love. In the case of the Lithians, I can assure you that they do not intend to inspire lust with their manner of dress. It is purely a cultural expression of their love for beauty, and nothing more."

"That makes no sense to me!" the young Tamarian complained.

Jawara slapped him on the knee in a friendly way, then stood up and stretched. "Only because you are not Lithian," he replied. The 'Scinnian warrior sheathed his bayonet, opened Maia's screen door and went inside to get some food.

Algernon grew cold in the gathering gloom. Just before arising to go inside, he saw movement coming from the southeast, following a trail through the wild grasses that he and his companions trampled earlier that afternoon. "Jawara!" he called in alarm.

"What's wrong?" the dark-skinned man inquired.

"Bring your binoculars, I think we've got trouble!"

When he had to be quick, Jawara's large body moved with astonishing grace. Within moments he'd brought out his binoculars and began examining the figures Algernon had seen. "Get up!" he ordered, tersely. "Take the women deep into the orchard and don't come back unless I call for you."

Algernon suddenly forgot about feeling cold and fatigued. He leapt to his feet and raced inside, calling for Astrid and Jhiran. Down the hall he pounded on the bathroom door where Maia had was in the process of wrapping fresh bandages around Kira's wounded feet. "Get dressed!" he said urgently. "We've got company!"

Astrid dragged their knapsacks to the rear door, grateful they hadn't unpacked anything yet. An expression of terror flashed onto her face when she saw Jawara load a magazine into his automatic rifle and fix the bayonet to the front of its barrel.

"Go!" Jawara said sternly.

When Maia opened the door, Algernon beckoned her to come with them, but the old woman shook her head. "I will not run from thieving rebels!"

"Please, ma'am," Algernon replied, "if they find you've opened your home to us they will kill you."

"This is my home, and my land," she stated flatly. "I will entertain whomever I wish!"

Algernon shook his head. "Then I will pray for your safety." With a grunt he picked up Kira and carried her toward the back door, whispering a prayer to the Great God for deliverance.

The Long Journey: *Deliverance*

"They're coming," the Tamarian girl warned, her eyes wide in fear, her skin covered in goose bumps. "And they're going to kill us!"

Algernon turned sideways and pushed the back door open with his foot, emerging into the cool, evening air. "They've already tried," he told her in a soothing tone. "Don't worry, Kira. I'm not going to let anyone hurt you anymore!"

Whether Kira knew something about the men from whose company she'd been recovered, or her statement reflected the anxiety common among opium addicts withdrawing from their favored drug the young monk couldn't tell. But as he carried her through the irregular shadows beneath the ragged almond trees growing in Maia's orchard, he knew that he had to keep her away from the Kamerese, yet he could not take her very far without Jawara's horse. She was simply too heavy and he couldn't sustain the exertion.

As Astrid called, Algernon followed the sound of her voice until he arrived, out of breath, somewhere deep within the tree canopy. With great care, he put Kira down and turned to Jhiran. "Don't leave her," he ordered. "We've got to go back for our bikes."

Taking Astrid by the hand, Algernon hustled with her to the edge of the orchard. They stole across Maia's yard, retrieved their bicycles and pedaled soundlessly back among the long neglected trees. Jhiran held her hand over Kira's mouth as the Tamarian girl, experiencing a withdrawal episode, writhed on the ground in sweat-sheened agony. When Jhiran let go Kira rasped: "They're going to hurt me! They're coming to hurt me!"

Jawara understood the imminent danger, and though he urged his hostess to flee, Maia refused and remained on the front porch while he slunk into the shadows. Eight men on horseback, probably rebel scouts from the look of their weapons and uniforms, approached. Their leader dismounted. Jawara understood nothing of their terse conversation, but the demeanor he saw in the rebels spoke of ill intent. He quietly pulled the bolt back on his rifle.

Angry epithets and gesticulations quickly escalated into violence. Jawara watched in righteous rage as one of the men knocked Maia to the ground, pulled out a pistol and shot her in the head. Laughter ensued as the killer proceeded to urinate on Maia's body.

Jawara felt compelled to act, knowing that these men would hunt down his companions and kill them in a similar fashion. With a clear

The Long Journey: *Deliverance*

field of fire, knowing that his friends had fled into the orchard, Jawara lined up his targets and squeezed the trigger.

Bodies jerked toward the sound of the rifle, then away from it as Lithian bullets found their mark and ripped through flesh in heartless efficiency. In rapid succession the rebels went down, surprised and horrified that vengeance for their murder of the former Kamerese ambassador's widow occurred so quickly. The 'Scinnian warrior happened to be a very proficient marksman, and in the Great Eye's eerie light he didn't miss.

Warily, Jawara approached the grisly scene. Two of the men remained alive, so he thrust through their hearts with his bayonet to relieve their suffering, conserve rounds and ensure they could not threaten him. He stripped the dead of their weapons, collecting two rifles and a handgun, along with all the ammunition he could carry. He took five wide-brimmed hats from the soldiers, then hid their bodies and the rest of their rifles beneath Maia's front porch.

After this, Jawara picked up Maia's frail body and carefully laid her on her own bed where he prayed for her soul. Then he took one of the rebel mounts to use as a pack animal, retrieved and saddled his own horse from the barn and rode into the orchard to find his friends. He distributed the hats and weapons among them, somberly explaining what the rebels had done to Maia. In shock and sorrow, Algernon and Astrid paused to pray for her.

"When the scout party does not return, another will go out to find them," he warned. "I know that you're tired, but we're in grave danger as long as we stay here. If the rebels will murder a native Kamerese woman in cold blood, they will think nothing of doing the same to us. We must move."

Algernon remembered the derelict town alongside the abandoned rail line and recommended that they seek shelter there. "It's close," he told them. "And because we won't leave so obvious a trail getting there, we should be safe until morning."

Jawara agreed to go, but Kira suddenly experienced another bout of diarrhea and everyone turned away so that she could empty her hyperactive bowel unobserved. Astrid, her heart filled with pity, came to help her crippled former lover clean up.

But Kira found the experience utterly humiliating. She pushed Astrid away and cried in shame. "Just leave me here!" she demanded. "Let me die! It's me they want, and I'm only going to slow you down."

The Long Journey: *Deliverance*

Algernon brought a water bottle over for his sister and gently moved Astrid aside. Kira washed herself while the others milled about at a respectful distance. When she was done, he knelt beside her and spoke firmly, yet quietly. "I didn't come all the way down here to abandon you," he reminded her. "So shut up and cooperate!"

Kira, however, couldn't stop sobbing. Many demeaning and cruel memories swirled in her mind, experiences that her brother could not imagine. Although he didn't seem sympathetic, Algernon wiped away her tears and brought her to Jawara. The strong 'Scinnian warrior lifted the trembling Tamarian girl onto the back of his horse.

Astrid felt forlorn. Her heart slipped into a numb feeling somewhere between despair and regret. She seeped silent tears as she followed her companions into the gloom. The pain of aching muscles and the soreness wrought from sitting on a bicycle seat for three full days paled when compared to the sense of loss she experienced over Kira's ongoing rejection.

Soon the path became a trail, and the encroaching trees blocked the waxing light of the Great Eye. Long shadows intensified Astrid's darkening mood and she ached in lonely, bitter silence until her soul emptied of all emotion.

Jawara thought the train station would be the most appropriate place to stay. Though its floor lay covered in dust and leaf litter, it had bathrooms–though no running water–and separate areas in which they could sleep for privacy. In addition the station fronted the old spur line, providing an exit, should they need to escape by a different route.

Jhiran made another cup of tea for Kira, then cooked pan bread and a vegetable stir-fry while Jawara unsaddled and cared for the horses. Kira curled up in a corner near the bathroom door, close enough that she could drag herself to the toilet on her own.

Though he felt utterly exhausted and very hungry, Algernon tried to feed Kira before allowing Astrid to offer him food, but his sister wouldn't open her mouth. Astrid pulled apart strips of hot pan bread and scooped up vegetables for Algernon, while Kira watched the two of them in silence. He felt grateful to eat again, but noticed that Astrid served him stoically, ate without enthusiasm and didn't even thank him when he fed her.

Later, after Jawara had fallen asleep and Jhiran disappeared into the night, Algernon unpacked his bedroll on the loading platform and collapsed from sheer exhaustion. He'd nearly fallen asleep when he heard footsteps approaching.

Astrid sniffed and dropped her bedroll next to his. "Please don't take this the wrong way," she whispered, "but I need to be near you."

Too tired to feel excited, Algernon grunted. "Ok."

Astrid remained still and at a distance for a long time. She watched as Algernon's breathing become progressively more shallow, then drew near, nuzzled against his back and fell asleep.

He awoke the next morning to find Kira sitting at his feet, staring at him. She'd dragged herself across the floor to get into her current position, and she was rocking back and forth like an unloved orphan. Her eyes looked heavy. Her feet were bleeding again.

"How did you sleep?" he asked.

"Didn't," she replied. "I can't sleep."

Algernon sat up, and in doing so, Astrid rolled over and her arm fell limply across his thighs. Careful not to awaken her, the young monk slid away quietly.

"Was she as good as I told you?" Kira inquired.

"What do you mean?"

"You're hard as a rock. Was she good for you?"

Algernon rolled his eyes. "Good grief Kira! It's first thing in the morning and I've got to pee! Get your mind out of the gutter!" He stood and stomped off, looking for privacy.

A few minutes later, at the sound of raised female voices, Jawara stepped onto the platform. The girls were in the midst of a heated argument, and Kira was screaming at Astrid. "Stop!" he roared in vulgate. "Fighting solves nothing and we're still in grave danger. Settle your differences peacefully, or leave each other alone!"

Astrid sulked away, leaving Kira angry and abandoned on the platform. The priestess used the toilet, then found Algernon stretching outside. A cool mist swirled about him, smothering the landscape, obscuring sound and shadow. Doves cooed mournfully in the trees. Astrid sat down on the worn wooden steps, breathed deeply and watched in sullen silence.

Pain twisted his face into a scowl. Persistent stretching and relaxation eased the discomfort, but what his body really needed involved more rest than he could afford at present. "How did you sleep?" he asked.

"Ok," she replied. "But I'm really sore from all the bike riding."

The Long Journey: *Deliverance*

"It would help you to stretch," he advised. "If we can survive today, we'll probably still be alive the day after tomorrow."

Astrid yanked on a weed and began mutilating it, piece by piece. "What does that matter?" she muttered. "Dying might not be such a bad thing."

Algernon stopped, appraising her with measured incredulity. "Why do you talk like that?" he asked. "What happened to the spunky girl I knew in Marvic?"

"She's dead," Astrid replied. "She died of a broken heart."

He stared at her for a moment longer, then returned to his stretching. "I think you're judging my sister too harshly."

"Oh really? What do you know about real love? For guys its all about big tits, blow jobs and tight vaginas. Ten seconds of pleasure, and it's over for you!"

Algernon stood, his shirtless physique lean, well defined and vigorous. He walked over to her while looking at his powerful hands, opening and closing them to stretch ligaments that had too long clenched his bicycle handlebars. She realized how badly burned the skin on his shoulders and arms had become, and she felt a little sorry for him.

"What do I know? Let me tell you, what I know, Astrid. I know what it's like to look longingly at someone, day after day, without ever having the right to act on how I feel. I know what it's like to never be taken seriously, to never be reckoned worthy of consideration. I know all about unrequited affection."

Astrid shook her head. "You left Marie behind a long time ago!" she spat.

"I'm not talking about Marie," he responded accusingly. "I'm talking about you!"

As his words settled upon her soul, Astrid held her breath. "No!" she replied. "Not me! I'm not that kind of girl."

"See what I mean?" he smirked, palm extended. "You complain that Kira spurns your love and lament that you're suffering loss, yet we haven't even spent a full day in her company. You've kept me at arms length for weeks now, and I've never acted on my desire for you because I know that you're simply not interested. You believe I know nothing about a broken heart, but how do you think your rejection makes me feel?"

The Long Journey: *Deliverance*

Astrid looked at him with an expression that seemed as close to disgust as any he'd ever witnessed on her face. "But you're a . . . boy . . . What are you expecting from me?"

"Nothing, Astrid. But I'd like you to extend some grace to my sister. Dmitri's book says it can take as long as ten days to withdraw from opium, and after that, she's going to need a lot of time to work through all of the trauma she's experienced.

"Why are you so concerned with yourself all of a sudden? What happened to your love and compassion? Look at how those people brutalized her! If her body is wounded, how much more her soul? Do you really think she can shunt all of that aside in such a short time? You're not the only one she's trying to push away, here. I love her too!"

"It's not the same," Astrid complained. "You're related. She can't hate you forever. She has to live with you for the rest of her life!"

"We don't know how deeply her hatred is rooted, and that's all the more reason why it's worse for her to reject me than you. I have a history with Kira that goes back as far as the two of us can remember, and we'll be siblings as long as we live. While I don't want to make light of the love you offer, try to keep things in perspective, Astrid. Kira isn't the same girl you knew at the Temple. Don't expect her to feel the way she did back then."

Astrid realized this in a rational way, but logic had no impact in the affective realm where her devotion to Kira resided. The priestess put her head into her hands and struggled not to weep. "I know!" she cried. "I know she's been hurt. I know those men mistreated her. It breaks my heart, Algernon. It really hurts me!"

He didn't like seeing Astrid upset, but felt afraid to offer comfort, lest she misunderstand and think he was coming on to her again. Algernon drew near, knelt down and put his hand on her knee. "You're the bravest girl I know," he said softly. "You have to find the courage to carry on. I'd never have been able to do this without you."

She stood, pulled him into her embrace and held him, sobbing into his shoulder.

Jhiran appeared from the forest carrying a slain hare and two quail for breakfast. She held the beheaded animals by their feet, and from the look of the blood smeared around her mouth, Jhiran had used her teeth to decapitate them.

Either ignoring or not understanding the intimacy of the moment, she cheerfully stepped between the Tamarians, embraced

The Long Journey: *Deliverance*

Algernon, lingered in Astrid's arms, then dropped the hare and offered them a few strips of yew bark, projecting the concept of analgesic relief into their minds. Once her good deed was done, Jhiran retrieved the hare and bounded up the stairs to prepare breakfast. The gwynling possessed energy in inverse proportion to her social sensitivity.

Algernon heard his sister calling. He kissed the top of Astrid's head, wishing she would wash her hair, pulled on his robe and dashed upstairs to check on Kira. The girl lay in a tight ball on the loading platform, her face frozen in pain.

"Help me!" she cried. "I can't move!"

Suppressing his own sense of panic, Algernon remained calm, thinking that massaging might bring her some relief. Kira's legs felt tight as a loaded spring, and as he tried to stretch them out, her muscles went into ferocious and protracted spasms. Kira gritted her teeth and gasped for air. Her skin felt hot and became frighteningly pale. She retched until she began coughing, but didn't throw up because she hadn't eaten anything. This episode continued for a long time until his ministrations wrought comfort and Kira's body gradually began relaxing.

Algernon had read about this kind of thing in the medical textbook, but reading about episodes of this nature and witnessing the actual manifestation of withdrawal differed by an order of magnitude. Algernon felt frightened, but said nothing to Kira.

She reached for him, wrapping her arms around his neck. She trembled and wept silently. "It hurts!" she murmured. "I need a fix! Everything hurts!"

And Kira loathed herself. She hated being a whore. She hated being a slave. She hated being beaten. She hated her pain, and she hated the fact that her brother and his friends witnessed all of her suffering. But something very old in her soul clung to Algernon, a glimmer of hope, a candle in the distance. She knew he loved her, despite everything she hated about herself.

When Jawara came back Algernon laid his sister down on his own bedroll and rose to talk to his friend. "She's getting worse," he said, worriedly. "We might have to hunker down here and wait until she feels better."

Jawara let out a slow breath. "We'll get everything ready to leave and post a watch on the path. Then we pray for deliverance!"

And the long, difficult hours dragged on through the morning and afternoon. Kira wanted Algernon to stay close, so Astrid and Jawara split what would have been his turn on watch between the two of them. Boredom separated the increasingly frequent and intense incidents of cramping, nausea and diarrhea that Kira experienced. Though Brenna's tea reduced Kira's craving and the analgesic bark that Jhiran steeped into the blend dulled her pain, the Tamarian girl suffered through a terrible ordeal that day.

Between Kira's withdrawal pangs Algernon cleaned her feet and re-wrapped them with fresh bandages, noting redness and swelling that indicated an infection had begun taking hold. She needed medical attention soon, or she might never walk again. Unnerved, he talked to her about pleasant events from their shared childhood, hoping to get her attention away from the awful condition of her feet.

Kira asked about Garrick, learned of his military service and heard more about Brenna than she cared to know. They reminisced about their time in the Temple, but as their conversation continued Kira's focus shifted toward her brother's frequent misdeeds. She reminded him of the many times he'd neglected her, how he'd criticized her unrelentingly, belittled her achievements and constantly made her feel inferior to his supreme intellect and excellent physical condition.

"You were angry all the time!" she accused. "Marco made me feel wanted. I felt special whenever I was with him. The Temple never felt like home."

Algernon didn't want to remind her that she'd also played a role in the breakdown of their relationship. Though he resented her tone and found her accusal exaggerated, Algernon restrained his emotion, spoke gently and overlooked the invective she heaped on him. "If you had known that he'd turn you into a slave and sell you to a broker; if you had known that he'd offer you to men who would abuse you, beat you and ruin your feet so that you couldn't get away, would you have come down here with him?"

"It's my fault," she claimed. "I ran away from Marco after we got on the train in Fair Haven. He'd promised we would marry, then got me high and burned this brand on me." She pointed to the shackle helix on her left forearm, the ugly reminder of her social status. "He said it was for my protection. He said the brand would prevent the rebels from killing me when we crossed their lines. He said that it didn't matter to him, but it did. He changed after that. He started treating me like a dog, or a concubine worthy of little more than a fondle and a bit of food. Things were never the same with him again."

The Long Journey: *Deliverance*

"From what I've learned, his demeaning treatment began much earlier than that," Algernon accused in a low tone. "I heard about what you were doing in Marvic."

Kira shook her head. "It's not what you think. I needed to earn money for our southbound train fare. Marco said you'd hurt his cousins, that you were trying to kill him and that we needed cash right away. He was just a student, so money was tight."

That outright lie burned within Algernon's soul. He knew that Marco had been among the Kamerese operating a lucrative opium trade within the city, using his uncle's textile factory as a front for importing the narcotic. Marco owned an electric car, a luxury item so expensive that very few among the most affluent Tamarians could afford one. His enrollment at the university earned him a student visa to enter the country, but he hadn't come to study. Marco Fang was simply a criminal, a very wealthy criminal.

When Algernon wouldn't meet his sister's eyes, she shook her head. "There you go again! You're judging me! What I did at *The Bloody Bucket* in Marvic was no different from what I was already doing with Astrid, Bronwyn, and guys like Gunnar in the Temple, except I was getting paid for what I'd been giving away for free."

Anger rose rapidly in Algernon's eyes. "I'm not judging you!" he replied. "It's Marco Fang that I've got a problem with. He lied to gain your trust. He lied to make you think I would drag you back to the Temple, though we both know that the Supreme Council would never allow either one of us to return there. Everything he told you was a lie. He's a rich warlord's son, and his father's army and allies are the ones who are ruining Kameron right now.

"He didn't need your money. He debased you until you grew accustomed to the kind of treatment you'd receive from him and his kind. When he got tired of you, he simply sold you, Kira. He used you, abused you, then made money off you. What you choose to give away is your own business, but he compelled you to offer yourself for sale!"

"Shut up!" she snapped. "Marco loved me. He was a lot nicer to me than you are!"

Algernon shook his head, feeling helpless. "Look at you! How can you say that?"

Kira's looked away. She gave her brother a sideways glance, unable to meet his eyes, and tightened her lips. "Things didn't get really bad until the broker caught me," she murmured.

The Long Journey: *Deliverance*

"Iago?"

"Yeah, that's him." Kira grew quiet. She didn't tell her brother what happened that dreadful night, when Iago's men found her hiding and abused her with unspeakable brutality. "He'd heard that I'd run away from Marco, so he lashed my feet until I couldn't move." Tears soundlessly traced the outline of her cheek and fell from her face. Kira sniffed. "I've never felt pain like that in my whole life."

Algernon gently put his hand beneath his sister's chin. "And you'll never be mistreated again as long as I live," he promised.

Astrid came running into the train station. "They're coming!" she warned, breathlessly. "They've burned Maia's farmhouse and they're headed this way!"

Despair washed over Kira's face. Algernon picked her up and carried her to Jawara's horse. With great effort, he and Astrid pushed Kira onto the animal's back as the sound of small arms fire made the great beast nervous and eager to flee.

"Where's Jawara? Where's Jhiran?" Algernon asked in alarm.

"They're holding them off!" Astrid replied. "He said to take the horses and keep heading west along the rail bed until dark. He said they'd find us."

Algernon threw his hands up in exasperation. "Get up there!" he ordered. "Kira can't ride without someone to hold on to."

Astrid looked fearful, but she obeyed, holding onto the lead rope of the pack horse. Kira reluctantly put her arms around Astrid's slender waist to avoid falling off the horse's back.

Algernon dumped their knapsacks in his bicycle trailer, tied the lead of Jawara's horse to the trailer frame, then led the creature along the derelict rail bed toward the east. He kept looking over his shoulder as the noise of a gun battle increased, fearful that his friends might die, fearful also that his own life would end soon thereafter.

Jawara, a skilled and experienced warrior, bought time for his charges to escape. Knowing that they faced only a small number of men, he'd quickly planned an attack with Jhiran that used the forest and surprise to their advantage. While his Lithian clothing rendering him invisible among the trees, an eight-member squad of rebel militia filed past him on the trail. He studied them carefully. As they marched from his left to his right, Jawara took aim at the man acting as their leader and dropped him with a single shot.

The Long Journey: *Deliverance*

Panic erupted among the rebels. Not knowing where their enemy had hidden, the seven remaining militiamen fired blindly into the trees, wasting ammunition. Amidst their confusion, Jhiran, who'd hidden herself high in a mature pine on the opposite side of the path, opened fire behind them. Though she was not used to using a carbine and the recoil hurt her shoulder, the gwynling had excellent aim. The weapon's recoil nearly knocked her out of the tree, but Jhiran had an uncanny sense of balance. She worked the bolt, took aim and easily hit two rebel soldiers in the back, gleeful that merely squeezing the trigger had such devastating effect. She snickered and laughed to herself, creating a lot of noise and crossfire that pinned the others down, enabling Jawara to move.

As her gun went off the 'Scinnian used the distraction of her firing to cover the sound of his retreat deeper into the forest, allowing him to be less cautious about making noise as he stepped through the underbrush and dead fall. Jhiran promised to shoot the six rounds loaded into her weapon's magazine, then abandon the gun and fly to safety. If the enemy retreated, she'd alert him with a whistle.

Jawara set himself up again a short distance further down the trail, hiding within a thicket while his clothing blended itself into shadows. Long, golden shafts of daylight reached through the forest, illuminating the tangle of bower and branch in which the 'Scinnian steadied breathing, his rife, and waited in silence.

Fearfully, five militiamen crept down the trail, their weapons nervously pointed into the trees. Jawara couldn't understand why they continued instead of retreating, for if they'd gone back he'd have let them live. Lining his first target up, the 'Scinnian waited for the right moment, let out his breath and gently pulled his trigger, moved his weapon slightly to the left, squeezed on the trigger again, then repeated the process once more. Red splotches appeared on three separate chests. The men fell backward as high velocity rounds ripped into their unarmored flesh.

Jawara, with his Lithian rifle, simply outgunned the rebel Kamerese, and the two survivors fled back from whence they'd come in a flurry of wild counterfire that proved completely ineffective. Just to be safe–though he'd only fired four shots–Jawara swapped in a fresh magazine, then moved back toward his original position further east.

Once her initial combat task had been completed, Jhiran did not fly to safety as she'd promised. She noticed that one of the fallen soldiers

The Long Journey: *Deliverance*

carried a short sword. Her attention immediately riveted on the weapon–since Algernon had dumped the one she'd carried in Desperado Falls–and as soon as the surviving rebels marched farther down the trail, she glided silently down to the path to investigate.

Jhiran removed the blade from its sheath, and wide-eyed, took in a deep breath at her good fortune. Roughly three feet in length with a gentle curve, a single edge, and what amounted to a two-handed grip for a gwynling, the lightweight weapon suited her perfectly. She used the sword to cut its scabbard away from its former owner's belt, but before she'd finished, Jhiran heard gunfire and footsteps running toward her on the path. She was about to flee into the forest when the sword's owner clamped his hand around her ankle.

Her presence in the midst of the ambush site attracted the unwanted attention of two fleeing rebels, who skidded to a stop in momentary uncertainty. From a distance, Jhiran looked very much like a young girl who wouldn't represent a threat, but when the flash of a bright sword appeared in her right hand and she actually swung the blade to dismember one of their fallen comrades, the two men raised their rifles to cut her down.

Jhiran leaped into the underbrush, dashing through redtwig dogwood in a random path that made pinpointing her impossible. The zing of ill-aimed ammunition swept through low hanging branches, and bits of bark exploded above Jhiran's head. She fled into the forested gloom where her attackers were reluctant to follow, but in their zeal to kill the gwynling, the Kamerese rebels forgot about the enemy lurking behind them.

Jawara didn't have a clear field of fire, but fearing for Jhiran's life, he put four shots into the rebels and dropped them in their tracks. He raced deeper into the forest looking for his ally, crashing through aromatic laurel and coffee berry, not daring to call her name lest he attract any follow-up troops to their location. As he lumbered through the immature oak and conifer trees she stepped out of her hiding place, the blank expression that normally appeared on her strangely proportioned visage replaced by one that reflected complete innocense.

"That was a fool thing to do!" Jawara snapped.

When Jhiran filled his mind with imagery of Algernon dumping her own sword, when her contempt for being scolded and the reminder that she'd actually escaped without harm echoed within Jawara's consciousness, he stopped her with an uplifted hand. "It's not worth your life," he said. "We need you."

They headed back to the trail, discovering to his dismay that their firefight attracted attention from a larger group of rebel soldiers who scurried in their direction from Maia's farm. Jawara picked up Jhiran and held her facing backwards against his right shoulder before heading toward the abandoned village at a dead run.

Jhiran jumped off as Jawara leaped up the stairs leading into the derelict rail station. He dashed through the door and moved through the station to its loading platform, where he found Astrid's bike. Jawara adjusted its seat using its quick release mechanism, sat Jhiran backwards on its handlebars, with her feet on the frame and her hands on his shoulders, then pedaled eastward as fast as the hydraulic machine could take him.

The bike accelerated quickly, the torque multiplying effect of its gear system enabling him to reach top speed with a few yards. He worked the pedals through a slight northeasterly turn as Jhiran shouted excitedly about men on the station platform.

They'd covered nearly four hundred yards before Jawara heard bullets pinging off the trees and rocks nearby. To either side of the rail bed lay a long neglected mixed forest consisting mostly of live oak and madrona trees. Its thick undergrowth prevented him from considering a detour, so he focused his strength and energy into pedaling.

"Horses!" Jhiran cried.

"How many?" he asked, not wishing to break his rhythm and slow down by looking over his shoulder.

"Four," she replied.

Algernon had told him that a healthy man on a bike could outdistance any horse. Jawara, despite his considerable lead, knew that all the horsemen needed to do was stay within range of their rifles, and that a single lucky shot could kill him. But he did not intend to die easily. The 'Scinnian warrior called upon reserve stamina, pushed his body to the limits of exertion and prayed for the Holy One to deliver him.

However, one bullet bounced off a nearby rock and blew out his back tire. Jawara struggled for balance, eased the bike to the edge of the rail bed, then crashed into the sedges, bulrushes and cattails growing in a swampy area along its margin. Jhiran abandoned the handlebars and leapt upward, fluttering to safety, while Jawara suffered bruises from hitting the handlebars and several minor cuts from woody plants he smashed through on his way into the marsh.

Picking himself up and limbering his rifle, the 'Scinnian evaluated the terrain and elected to push a little bit further into the wetland. He warned Jhiran to remain still while he set up an ambush on a rise that paralleled the old rail line. Recovering from his exertion and releasing the fear he felt into God's hands, Jawara steadied his rifle against an oak tree and quietly, patiently waited.

Algernon heard four gunshots ring out from somewhere behind him, far closer than he believed possible, given the distance he'd just ridden. Weary from sustaining a sprint and worried for his friends, the Tamarian monk began searching for a place to hide.

Astrid felt Kira begin another of her contortions. "We have to stop!" she warned. "Kira's not doing well."

Though their surroundings seemed wild and uninhabited, Algernon felt exposed. To his left a low ridge rose above the muddy remnants of a rain-fed pond. He stopped and helped his sister off the horse, carrying her through muck that sucked at the soles of his sandaled feet. Algernon struggled uphill, fighting through the underbrush, desperate to lay his sister down somewhere safe, somewhere comfortable.

Algernon tried not to drop her, but his muddy sandals did not provide sufficient traction for the task and twice he slipped and nearly fell. It didn't help that Kira trembled and twitched involuntarily, though he knew she couldn't exert any control over this. Her groaning increased his sense of urgency, and the traitorous thought of simply dropping her and running off on his own dangled dangerously in his conscious mind.

On the reverse slope of the rise he'd climbed, Algernon paused among a grove of live oak trees. A canopy beneath their branches provided shade from the sweltering heat, and among their tangled roots a carpet of soft grass grew among brittle, brown leaves long shed by the evergreen oaks. It seemed like as good a place to hide as any. He brushed the leaves away, providing a more comfortable place for Kira to rest.

Astrid slipped when she tried to dismount, landing on her backside in a very unfeminine manner. She suppressed a cry of pain, but her lower back really hurt. Dusting herself off and trying to retain some dignity, she sat up and eyed the horse with suspicion. The beast turned its great head to the side as if observing the antics of a silly young woman playing in the dust, then backed up and nuzzled her, encouraging Astrid to stand.

She untied Jawara's horse from Algernon's trailer frame and tried to move the bicycle across the mud, but only succeeded in getting it stuck. Astrid dropped both horses' lead ropes, sat on the rail bed and began crying in frustration.

Algernon came to her rescue. He wordlessly pulled Astrid to her feet but offered her no comfort, lead the horses around the muck on a roundabout trail through drier ground, then went back and rescued his bicycle. When he'd finished, Algernon's legs and robe were spattered in mud, he'd fallen into a foul mood and felt readier to fight than run.

He didn't feel confident using a rifle, but he aimed the weapon when he heard the clatter of steel shod hooves approaching. Jawara and Jhiran rode a horse taken from the Kamerese rebel scouts and led two others in tow. Astrid's bike had been tied across the saddle of one of the extra horses, its blown out back tire spinning forlornly.

"An infant could find you!" Jawara called. "We've caused the rebels enough trouble to warrant alerted patrols actively looking for us, so we can't stop so close to where we camped last night."

Algernon complained that he felt too exhausted to move on, but Jawara did not back down. And thus, the two men moved everything onto the rail bed, secured Algernon's bike–with its trailer detached–to one of the extra horses, roped the trailer to the same beast, and rode until Kira experienced a withdrawal, then another, a third and a fourth.

The constant stopping and starting wearied everyone, but Algernon–in particular–felt increasingly impatient with his sister. At one point Jawara pulled the young monk aside and warned him to treat Kira with greater tenderness. "It doesn't help for you to be gruff and agitated," Jawara told him.

"I'm tired of getting her off the horse every ten minutes!" Algernon complained.

"Grow up and get used to it!" Jawara replied, tersely. "We still have a long way to go, and she's a very sick young lady."

Algernon resented the scolding, but he knew that Jawara spoke truthfully. With a deep breath he helped Kira back into the saddle and rode for another several minutes before she complained that she had to stop for a toilet break.

The Long Journey: *Deliverance*

They traveled this way until well after the Great Eye rose, the Daystar set, and just before the long twilight faded into darkness. With the landscape gently rising toward the distant mountains, plant life gradually thinned. A few scrub oaks survived the drier, sandier conditions, and sage soon dominated the biome. Scattered between the low bushes, withered grasses held offerings of spiny seed heads aloft toward the wind.

Leaving the woodland vastly improved horizontal visibility. Camping out in the open required the travelers to take greater care with Algernon's cookstove. Jhiran quickly prepared a meal, brewed Kira another cup of medicinal tea, then doused the fire. After eating, Algernon used a shovel he found in the saddle pack of a Kamerese rebel horse and dug a toilet for his sister. He felt so tired after this that he simply couldn't stay awake, collapsed into a deep sleep and remembered nothing.

The thunder of distant artillery awoke him in the hour between the Great Eye setting and the first light of dawn. Thick fog smothered the countryside, coating everything it touched with a film of moisture. Though his soreness persisted, a sense of purpose and drive returned to his soul and Algernon began the day eager to continue.

Kira sat nearby with her knees drawn close to her breast, yawning and rocking. She looked increasingly exhausted and frail. Dark circles beneath her grey eyes and an ashen tone to her complexion revealed chronic fatigue, and she smelled worse than she had when Algernon found her in Sleepy Hollow.

"Can't sleep?" he inquired.

Kira shook her head and willed her body to control a set of convulsions that rippled through her limbs. "I need a fix!" she said. "I can't go on like this."

"Give yourself time," he replied. "I read that once you start to sleep, you'll begin to feel better. I promise!"

She ignored him and went back to her rocking.

As Algernon stretched for the day, his companions stirred. Astrid arose last. She seemed distant and sullen, but she let him feed her breakfast and offered thanks after eating. Jhiran, whose face was now smudged in soot from operating the tin can stove, stared at Kira to read her thoughts. Thus inspired, the gwynling heated a thin slab of pan bread, slathered its browned crust in almond butter and lightly sprinkled cinnamon and brown sugar over the top of it. She gave this to

The Long Journey: *Deliverance*

Kira, along with medicinal tea, and for the first time in two days, the Tamarian girl smiled at Jhiran and allowed some food into her mouth.

Their journey began anew as the first light diffused through the fog and the birds began to stir. Brenna's tea finally worked to settle Kira's nausea, diarrhea and cramping, allowing excellent progress for nearly three hours before they had to stop for her again.

Within an hour, all the fog vanished and an oppressive, humid heat replaced the cool comfort the travelers had known to that point in the day. Refugees, camped in the open, watched them pass. A few approached to inquire news of loved ones left behind, but each time, Algernon apologized and responded that the only people they'd seen lately had been rebels.

The rail bed angled northward. Jawara considered leaving it and taking a bearing back toward the Mistress Road across country, but their progress had been so good he reckoned that when the derelict spur line met the main track coming down from Fair Haven, they could travel due east from that point and arrive at the Virgin River on the same day.

That decision turned out to be providential.

Another mixed forest that first appeared on the northwestern edge of the rail bed spilled across it within several miles, encroaching upon the elevated rail line until its form lost all distinction and became little more than a seldom used path through the trees. They rode in single file, with Jawara taking up the rear, until the 'Scinnian called for them to pause, eat lunch and rest.

By this point in their journey, stopping for anything longer than a few moments involved a well-established routine. Digging a toilet, watering horses, preparing food and tea had become automatic chores. However, the addition of extra pack animals drained their water resources quickly and dangerously. Jawara decided they should set the extra horses free, so Algernon went to work repairing the rear tire on Astrid's bicycle while Jhiran washed her grimy hands and began preparing lunch.

Astrid felt uneasy. She kept looking into the trees as if trying to find something there, and when questioned, couldn't identify the source of her fear. "I think somebody's watching us," she breathed. A flash of some kind caught her eye once, but the reflection occurred in her peripheral vision and she was unable to pinpoint its source.

Later, Jhiran noticed several figures on horseback heading southwest on the trail. They looked familiar, so she left her task of

The Long Journey: *Deliverance*

cleaning the cast iron pan undone and scurried over to Algernon with a worried expression on her dirty face. "The bad men are back," she said.

Jawara picked up Kira and set her down behind a large tree several yards from the trail. He told Astrid to hide as well, then prayed and prepared his rifle for its grim task.

Algernon pretended to be unconcerned as Iago and his henchmen approached, but Jhiran kept her gaze riveted on the bounty hunter and contempt overflowed from her large eyes.

"Well, if it ain't the monkey boy!" Iago teased. "Fixing a girl's bike, but there's no girl in sight, unless you want to call that little freak of yours a girl."

Algernon ignored him. Jhiran blasted his mind with foul curses, dismay and ill wishes.

Iago pointed his rifle in Jhiran's direction, trying to distract her and get the Tamarian monk's attention, but the gwynling picked up his intent and mentally encouraged the horse to rear. A single gunshot went high as the bounty hunter struggled to stay in the saddle.

The other men laughed.

"I'm talking to you!" Iago roared.

Algernon had flinched at the sound of the discharge, pausing in fear that Jhiran had been hurt. His heart pounded as he glared at the bounty hunter, but the young monk said nothing.

"Did someone cut out your tongue?" Iago asked. "I'll bet Chale was really happy to see you!" The bounty hunter settled his horse, put his gun into its saddle holster, dismounted and made a show of walking slowly closer, looking carefully at his surroundings. "Find your sister, monkey boy? See, my men and I haven't had a woman for a while. We were thinking you might want to share that little honey pot again, and if we can't find her, your little freak might have to do."

Though it took every bit of self control within him, Algernon held his tongue.

"Are you deaf now?" Iago inquired. "Deaf, or just plain stupid?"

Behind the tree, Kira began another withdrawal. She groaned and writhed in agony, and though Astrid covered Kira's mouth the sound of her voice attracted Iago's attention. He smiled and moved toward the tree. "Ah, I hear that someone's in the mood for love!"

Algernon stood, put his hands up and blocked the larger man's path. "Why don't you just move along," he warned, a menace pervading his gaze that exposed an unwillingness to exhibit mercy.

The Long Journey: *Deliverance*

Iago laughed. "Get out of my way, little boy!" He grabbed Algernon by the lapel of his robe and tried to shove him away. It was the last action the bounty hunter ever took of his own volition.

All the rage the young monk felt at the mistreatment of his sister erupted in a singular burst of martial energy. Sliding his arms between Iago's push, Algernon grabbed the man's jaw with his left hand and wrapped his right hand behind the bounty hunter's head, snatching a fistful of hair. In doing so, he pulled his enemy forward. Algernon curled his right knee onto his own chest, planting his foot on Iago's belly. Then the young monk rolled backwards, dragging his opponent down with him.

As his back hit the ground, Algernon pushed his left hand away while his right hand pulled in a clockwise rotation. With a grunt his leg shoved Iago's torso skyward and toward the left, twisting the bounty hunter's body in the opposite direction of his neck.

Cervical vertebrae snapped, Iago's spinal column ruptured, nervous activity below his shoulders forever ceased and he landed, unable to break his fall, in a rumpled heap amid a cloud of dust. Wide eyed, the bounty hunter gasped and slowly suffocated.

Rifles came out of holsters.

Astrid screamed.

Jawara opened fire at the men on horseback, hitting four of them and knocking them out of their saddles before his weapon jammed. "Holy God!" he cried, desperately trying to clear his gun. "Deliver us!"

Jhiran saw something moving very fast and fell to the ground, covering her ears.

Thunder erupted from among the trees. Iago's henchmen twisted from multiple bullet impacts, their limbs flailing as the involuntary twitch of extreme trauma overrode every individual's will to take aim and kill the Tamarian monk.

Horses reared and whinnied. Bodies fell and weapons clattered to the ground.

"Stay down!" Jawara shouted. "Don't move!"

Algernon obeyed, wondering what had happened. As the echoes of gunfire faded and the horses began to calm, an eerie silence settled upon the scene. Algernon peered up from the ground, but saw no one left alive. Every one of Iago's henchmen lay still and silent in the waxing heat.

The Long Journey: *Deliverance*

A strong, male voice called out from beyond the trail, speaking words in the Lithian tongue. "Jawara . . . Penda . . . Tegene . . . beloved father . . ." Algernon remembered hearing that introduction when he'd first met Jawara, but didn't understand anything else.

"Who knows my name?" Jawara replied, speaking in vulgate.

Algernon saw movement from within the trees across the trail. A man too tall and tanned to be Lithian, carrying a rifle like Jawara's over his shoulder and a large sword on his back, emerged. He wore the uniform of Lord Lynden's army, but he looked Kamerese. The man stopped just beyond the horses, laughed and held out his arms. "Tell me you don't know!" he exclaimed.

Jhiran stood up and ran toward him, calling his name and leaping into his embrace.

Jawara came out from his ambush position, weaponless and with a big smile brightening his dark face. He held his right arm aloft, gesturing to the man in the Lithian uniform with his left arm. "Woodwind!" he cried. "What are you doing here?"

As the two men greeted one another, Algernon stood and dusted himself off. He breathed deeply as he wiped the sweat from his brow, wishing that he could escape from the relentless heat and humidity of the Kamerese summer. As he put his hat back on, Algernon noticed other men stepping out of the tree line, and his eyes widened. These were Tamarians!

Garrick had talked about a deployment to Kameron, but the shoulder patches worn by these soldiers wore identified them as Special Forces, elite troops trained to effectively deploy in difficult situations where finesse and adaptability were more important virtues than brute firepower and large numbers.

As five rifle-toting Tamarians approached, Algernon sighed. "Am I ever glad to see you guys!"

They each offered the traditional Tamarian blessing, which Algernon returned in kind. It felt good to be respected again. One of them, however, lingered at Algernon's side. "You must be the young monk we're looking for. You're a long way from home, son. Kameron's not a place for the holy."

He'd heard that before. "You were looking for me?" Algernon inquired, skeptically.

The warrior nodded. "We learned about the breakout at Sleepy Hollow and our host, Lord Velez, asked us to find you. Since there are only two ways back from that direction, and the rebels are controlling the Mistress Road, we figured you'd come this way. Wearing that rebel hat didn't help," the soldier said in a sober tone. "We almost took you out first."

Algernon felt momentarily overwhelmed. Lord Lynden sent men to find him, just as he'd sent someone to find Brenna. Why had he done that? "How did you know it was me, then?" he inquired.

The Tamarian warrior smiled. "If I tell you, I'll have to kill you!" he replied. Then he shifted his weight and looked toward the edge of the forest, where Astrid stood, holding her hands to her mouth. "In truth," he continued, "Woodwind, our guide, recognized the little girl and your dark friend over there. The refugees are talking about a little run-in you'd had with the bounty hunters, and knowing their penchant for revenge, we tracked them to find you."

The man named Woodwind came over, appraising Algernon with a pleasant expression that indicated recognition and friendliness. "You must be a Ravenwood," he said. "You look like a scrawnier version of your brother!"

"You know my brother?"

Woodwind nodded. "I met him last fall on the Saradon. He's a good kid. Didn't he tell you about me?"

Algernon shook his head.

"What about Brenna Velez? Do you know her?"

This time Algernon nodded. "She's my brother's girl. Why do you ask?"

Woodwind pursed his lips, but he didn't answer the question. "She didn't say anything about me?"

"No! Why should she?"

Woodwind grunted and nodded in affirmation. He put his hand onto Algernon's lightburned shoulder. "Of course. You're right. She shouldn't." Then he turned away, leaving Algernon wondering what that encounter had really been about.

Astrid came up next, a worried expression lingering on her face. "They could have killed you!" she said. "You really need to be more careful, Algernon."

She had this way of expressing concern that melted his heart. "They'd already seen me and Jhiran," he replied. "If we'd gone into the woods to hide, they simply would have dismounted and come after us. As long as they stayed on horseback they were up high and it was easier

The Long Journey: *Deliverance*

for Jawara to hit them. After what Jhiran told me about Iago, I couldn't let him anywhere near Kira again. I promised that I wouldn't let anyone hurt her."

Astrid's green eyes, damp with well-suppressed tears, sparkled in the strong light. "I wish I had a brother like you," she said.

Though her words were meant as an affirmation, they hurt. All she needed to do was ask, and he'd have willingly given himself to her. Algernon looked down, noting that like his own, Astrid's sandaled feet suffered from light burn. "I wish I had you," he admitted.

"You shouldn't talk about me like that," she replied, softly.

"Why Astrid? What's wrong? Why are you so repulsed?" He looked at her with vulnerability seldom revealed to anyone.

She looked away. "You don't repulse me," she admitted. "It's just that every time I look at you, I see your sister." Astrid's eyes met his again. "Is that what you want, Algernon? Do you want a girl who is thinking about her every time she looks at you?"

Algernon sighed, tempering his frustration. He reached for her hands and she did not pull them away. "I just want you to be happy," he said. Then he kissed the top of each hand and turned, noticing that Kira had crawled over to Iago's body.

Breathing hard from the exertion, desperate in desire to relieve her suffering, Kira pawed through Iago's pockets. She turned his lifeless body over and found a small pouch with a familiar aroma dangling from a string around his neck. Kira yanked the string off, ripped open the pouch, unwrapped a cachet of dark, sticky sap and greedily stuffed its contents into her mouth.

"No!" Algernon shouted.

The sap tasted awful, but her anticipation of promised euphoria proved a powerful motivator and Kira tried to swallow the entire lump. She felt her brother's strong arms envelop her and repeatedly compress her belly with great vigor. Kira struggled against him, fighting to swallow and deliver her body from its affliction. She raged, twisting and thrashing to escape, until the overwhelming urge to vomit brought her modest lunch, the tea she'd consumed, and the offending lump of opium into her mouth.

Using his right hand Algernon squeezed her cheeks against his shoulder, causing Kira to spit all over his left arm. He thrust the heel of his left palm against her belly again and she coughed, spewing everything out. Then he pushed her down, clamped his fingers around her nose and forced her to open her mouth.

She began choking. Kira felt him jab his fingers between her teeth, so she bit him. That earned her a hard slap, then his fingers went right back into her mouth. She heard voices and suddenly felt her brother's weight lift off of her body.

"Easy there, buddy!" one of the soldiers said.

But Algernon was in no mood to be restrained. He twisted out of the warrior's grip, grabbed the soldier's arm, hooked his right foot behind the warrior's knees and flipped the surprised man onto his back. Then the young monk went directly after his sister again.

Laughter erupted among the other warriors, but Jawara stormed over and held his hand up to stop the offended Tamarian soldier from retaliating. "Wait!" he commanded.

Kira began weeping as Algernon overpowered her. She submitted, allowing him to wipe through her mouth, first with his fingers, then with a cloth that Astrid pulled out of her pack and handed to him. Afterward, he cleaned the residue from her fingers and gently pulled his sister close, whispering into her ear as his rage cooled. "Never again, Kira! I want you back!"

As Jawara explained the situation to the Tamarians, using the Azgaril Vulgate that everyone understood, he saw anger inspired by Kira's mistreatment rising within them. A sergeant named Erickson, noting the bloodstains on Kira's bandages, called for help.

Their medic turned out to be a very tall, willowy woman named Hilde von Huesen. She pointed to the lump of narcotic laying in a pool of vomit and gestured to no one in particular. "Destroy that," she ordered, having heard that her patient tried to swallow what would have been a lethal dose. Then appraising Kira with experienced eyes, sadness appeared on her pale, gentle face. "What have they done to you, sweetheart?" she asked.

Kira offered no reply. She sniffed and yawned, then worked at swallowing the bitter remnants of opium sap that lingered on her tongue, passively allowing the medic to do her work.

Hildegard unwrapped the bandages on Kira's feet and wrinkled her nose at the smell of decay. Kira's swollen flesh had reddened, flecks of white fungus grew around the wound margins and a viscous discharge seeped from the scars left by the bounty hunter's lash. "This

The Long Journey: *Deliverance*

girl needs serious medical attention right away. She will lose her feet, or worse, if she doesn't get help very soon."

Sergeant Erickson sent a messenger to the Tamarian forward base while Hilde cleaned Kira's wounds and wiped them with an antiseptic salve before wrapping them in fresh bandages. She turned toward Algernon because Jawara didn't speak Tamarian. "Keep her feet clean and off the ground," she warned. "And you need to stay in the shade, young man! That burn on your skin is looking terrible!"

Jhiran made Kira another cup of tea. With the gasifying stove very hot and his sister at a safe distance, Algernon burned the opium. He stared at the inferno raging in his tin can stove. "I've killed five people because of that junk!" he murmured. "And my sister almost killed herself with it."

"You saved her life," Astrid replied.

"Yeah," he complained, examining the teeth impressions on his finger. "And she bit me in gratitude for her deliverance!"

Within an hour an electric truck similar to the ones Algernon knew from Marvic, but painted a nondescript tan color, arrived. Kira, basking contentedly in a minor rebound high, had been resting on a litter in the shade. Two soldiers lifted her into the back of the truck, secured her to a rack designed for this purpose, then rolled its canvas cover over a curved, metal frame to protect her from the daylight. Algernon, Astrid and Jhiran rode in the back with Kira, while Jawara enjoyed a cab seat with the truck's driver.

After the soldiers loaded Algernon's bike trailer and the emptied water bladder into the back, they tied the two hydraulic bicycles to the rear bumper and bid the travelers a farewell. Jawara's horse stayed in Woodwind's care until he could find his way back to the Velez estate.

Initial progress seemed slow because the narrow trail did not allow the driver to accelerate up to cruising speed. As far as Astrid was concerned, sitting on the hard, metal floor in the shade while being carried to her destination ranked as far more comfortable than riding her bike another 15 miles to the Virgin River, and then another 30 uphill to the Velez villa.

Algernon brooded over Kira. Once the small amount of opium in her system metabolized, she'd have to start the withdrawal process all over again. Because she hadn't slept in two days he worried that her body might crash and simply shut down, but under the influence of her favorite drug she relaxed and seemed blissfully unconcerned.

The Long Journey: *Deliverance*

Jhiran rummaged through the bike trailer, found a jar of dates and began snacking noisily on them. Though she offered some to her companions with great insistence, neither Astrid nor Algernon felt particularly hungry after watching her eat. The gwynling chewed on dates until her fingers became thoroughly sticky, then she wiped them on the dirty hem of her skirt. A few minutes later she curled up near the bike trailer and fell asleep.

The truck crossed over the main rail line leading up to Fair Haven Fortress and a short time later, arrived at the Old Fair Haven Road. Where only a few days earlier a steady stream of refugees plodded northward, the road now lay curiously empty. As the truck quietly sped southward, the rumble of artillery returned, grew progressively louder and more terrifying until it seemed that some of the shells threatened to hit them.

Jhiran slumbered peacefully the entire time.

Through the open back of the vehicle, Algernon recognized the junction of the Old Fair Haven and Mistress of the Woods roads. He saw the charred, skeletal remains of the itinerant preacher, the general store, the nearby inn, and then as the driver turned sharply eastward on the Mistress Road, the sounds of battle faded like the dust kicked up by the truck's tires.

Within thirty minutes they'd crossed the old stone bridge over the Virgin River and turned north, toward the Velez villa. A sense of relief washed over Algernon's soul. He put his head into his hands and prayed in gratitude for deliverance, but he noticed that Astrid remained quiet. A wistful expression, mingled with exhaustion, lingered on her reddened face.

"We're safe now," he told her, squeezing her knee with affection. "Everything's going to be ok."

She didn't stop him from doing this, but Astrid shook her head. "I want to go home, Algernon," she said. "I just want to go home." The priestess tightened her fingers around his hand, then leaned against his shoulder. Several minutes later the heat, her fatigue and the gentle movement of the electric truck along the dusty road lulled her to sleep.

Algernon savored her nearness, feeling content for the first time in many days.

Kira watched her brother through dreamy eyes. She yawned and sniffed, relieved from the cramping and nausea that had tormented

The Long Journey: *Deliverance*

her since leaving Sleepy Hollow. "Where are you taking me?" she asked. "What are we going to do?"

"We'll stay with Brenna's parents until you feel better," he replied. "Jawara has a brother and a sister who are doctors. They live with the Velez family, and if Brenna's not around, one of them will be able to treat your wounds. Once you've recovered, we'll head for home."

Kira leaned on her elbow. "I'm not going back to the Temple!"

Algernon shook his head. "We both know that's not an option, but I found a place on Superstition Mesa we can fix up. When Garrick's done with his deployment, he'll come back to Marvic, and we'll be together as a family again."

"What about her?" Kira inquired suspiciously, pointing at Astrid.

"She's an adult. She can make her own plans."

Kira flopped back on her litter. "I don't want her living with us."

"I think you've made that quite clear already," Algernon replied. "But I can't figure out why you reject the people who love you, and love the people who mistreat you."

Kira sat up, rolled her eyes and shook her head. "What's gone on between me and Astrid was never about love," she replied. "Astrid took this way more seriously than I ever did. In the beginning I just wanted to do something that would prove to those pious hypocrites in the Temple that they couldn't control me. I had to find something that would really bug them, really prove the impotence of their philosophy.

"So I started kissing girls. It began with Bronwyn, just for fun, and a few of the adult priestesses either encouraged it, or simply looked the other way, until Astrid went to the Supreme Council and the leadership kicked them out. I didn't see the harm in a little bit of necking, and kissing girls is not really any different from kissing boys, except that girls don't give me beard burn. Everything was fine until Priestess Alba found out and started coming to my room at night.

"Astrid saved me from her. She kept that evil woman away, and by doing so I became Astrid's girl. What you never understood, was that as long as I lived in the cloister I had to choose between Astrid and Alba. The only freedom I had involved whether I stayed in my own bed until Alba arrived, or went to Astrid's room and slept with her.

"Now I admit that Astrid was a lot of fun at first. She's a lot less inhibited than Bronwyn, and I tell you honestly that no one kisses better than she does. No one responds to a touch like she can either, but a little bit of sex wasn't enough. She wanted me all to herself. Astrid started making demands on my time so that I lost my other friends. She complained if I talked to anyone else and threatened to take away my privileges when they found me with Bronwyn and Gunnar. Astrid manipulated my schedule so that I could work in the garden, where I loved to be, but under the condition that we'd sleep together every night. I had no life of my own. Marco delivered me from her."

"Astrid loves you, Kira. Why did you continue the relationship after the Supreme Council removed Priestess Alba? You didn't need her protection anymore. You could have ended it then."

Kira shook her head. "It wasn't that easy, Algernon. I'm not like Marie. I didn't cozy up to Astrid when we were alone and then ignore her when other people were around. I was her true friend, and I was grateful that she saved me, but Astrid doesn't want to be just friends. She wants me to be her lover for life, and I'm not a lesbian!"

Algernon listened like he never had before. He listened as he should have while living at the Temple. For weeks he'd only heard Astrid's side of the story, and now, listening to Kira's version, a more complicated picture emerged. While something within him felt relief that Kira wanted to renounce her lesbian love affair, Jawara's words returned from his memory and the young monk realized that in the realm of morality, a long path remained ahead for both of them.

Yet a strange sense of loss crept into his mind because he empathized with Astrid. Despite Kira's claim to the contrary, several parallels existed between her attitude toward Astrid and Marie's fickle treatment of him. The remonstrance of an unrequited love haunted his soul, and the genuine affection he felt for Astrid inspired a different response than Kira expected from her brother.

"There is no way that I could have found you without her," he began. "Astrid told me you had run away, and she figured out whom you'd run away with. She drew your portraits so we could question people concerning your whereabouts, and she stood in front of Marco when he fired a gun, intending to kill me."

Kira didn't want to hear this. "Marco would never have tried to hurt you!" she countered, angrily.

"How do you know, Kira?" he responded, an irritation with Marco's lying evident in his voice. "I was there when it happened, and so was she. When Astrid drew the scene for the police detective, she put Marco's face behind the weapon. She remembers everything she sees!"

Kira covered her ears. "Liar!" she accused.

The Long Journey: *Deliverance*

Algernon shook his head but didn't verbally respond until she'd dropped her hands. "I'm telling you the truth. It's Marco who's the liar. You owe your life to Astrid, and so do I. She helped me escape when a mob tried to kill us in Fair Haven Fortress. She drew the maps that let us navigate around a war zone to find you. She also forged an ID paper for Jhiran that looks so real nobody ever questioned it."

"But more important than anything else I've told you, Astrid inspired me to examine myself and deal with all the crap in my past, rather than lashing out in a rage at everything. She's done a lot for us. The least you could do is express some gratitude for her devotion."

"I left the Temple to get away from her," Kira reminded him. "And you brought her all the way down here to find me. Don't expect my thanks for that."

Algernon leaned his cheek against Astrid's head and put his arm around her soft shoulder. She murmured in her sleep. "It doesn't sound like we're talking about the same person," he replied. "She's never tried to manipulate me."

"You're a boy," Kira said, leaning back on the litter once more. "She'll never love you like you want her to. You're thinking with your prick and not your head." Kira crossed her arms, knowing she'd hurt her brother, but also thinking that if he'd listen to her for a change, he'd be spared a broken heart.

The siblings did not speak again for a long time.

Just before arriving in Helena, the truck driver made a right-hand turn onto a dirt road that led uphill through vast acreages covered in vineyards. Tiny grapes hung from beneath sheltering leaves, the unfulfilled promise of a harvest endangered by the approaching civil war. As the truck labored through rolling hill country, Kira glimpsed the contrast between lush, green vines neatly trimmed on their supporting wires, and the ruddy, volcanic soils in which they grew. She'd never beheld well-tended agriculture in Kameron, and the farm girl within her soul delighted in the beauty sweeping before her exhausted, opium-hazed eyes.

Aside from soldiers standing guard at the Velez compound, no one came out to greet the truck as it rolled into the cobbled courtyard and stopped in front of a dry, stone fountain. Amid ripples of rising heat, Algernon and Jawara untied the bikes, unloaded the trailer and the rest of their supplies, then carried Kira's litter into the guest compound.

The Long Journey: *Deliverance*

The truck immediately departed for a nearby recharging station, leaving Jhiran and Astrid behind. The gwynling vanished into the main house, while Astrid picked up her backpack and scurried over to the guest quarters, grateful that the air within its thick walls remained cool, despite the oppressive warmth outside. She went to the room where she'd previously slept, shut the door, set down her belongings and breathed a heavy sigh in solitude.

Astrid drifted into formal prayer. For many years the routines of the Temple liturgy had brought a sense of order and comfort to her life. Astrid had always been a willing, unquestioning participant in the Temple services, and her faith–though not fervent like Brenna's, nor doubt-ridden and self-disciplined like Algernon's–reflected a solid belief that societal institutions preserved the stability of her people.

Now, however, rejected by the girl she loved, far away from the only place she'd ever known as home, Astrid felt adrift and misplaced. The emotional void in her soul that she'd hoped could be sated by Kira's love deepened, and no anger, no resignation, no promise of new love rose to fill that emptiness. Her interminable sadness and regret found no cure beyond the fading dream of reconciliation.

Kira didn't want her.

She answered a soft knock on the door. A married Lithian woman, who introduced herself as Larissa–Lady Alexina's personal servant–offered to see to Astrid's comfort. "I'm afraid everyone else has evacuated already," she said apologetically.

"I need a bath," Astrid replied. "I have to wash my hair and my robe smells like the road. And also, how can I get home from here?"

*   *   *

Later that afternoon, Lord Lynden learned Jawara had returned safely with his charges, and that he'd been successful in locating and retrieving Algernon's wayward sister. Lynden breathed a prayer of gratitude for the search party's deliverance, but as he stared across the Virgin River through his binoculars, the Lithian warlord appraised an increasing number of rebel forces gathering in the empty fields beyond, and his prayer shifted in focus to the threat at hand.

He'd split his command with Tegene, taking charge of the southern approaches to his territory and giving his Abelscinnian friend control over more numerous units defending Helena. Reports from the

The Long Journey: *Deliverance*

Tamarian Special Forces and his own scouts attached to those teams suggested that Lord Fang and his ally, Lord Navarro–from whom Lynden originally purchased the title to the land now under his control–had split off from the main rebel army and turned eastward. Given that the Kamerese National Army had been falling back toward the capital in the west with the rebels in hot pursuit, Lynden correctly believed that Lord Fang and his ally were coming to wreak vengeance on the Velez family.

Just before twilight he received a hand written ultimatum. "You have twelve hours to stand your forces down and surrender without condition. You must cede all of your holdings to Lord Navarro, pay reparations for damage done to the Maridom Trading fleet and its cargo, and offer your eldest daughter to me in marriage.

"Failure to comply with these demands will be deemed an Act of Hostility toward the People of Kameron. Your occupied lands will be returned to their rightful owner by force. You and your family will be charged with crimes against the People and executed." The note had been signed in blood by Lord Nemesio Fang.

Lynden Velez didn't bother replying. The remark concerning the Maridom Trading Company and its ill-fated steamboats referred to an incident several months earlier. A flotilla of Lord Fang's steamboats attempted to supply the Azgaril's Northern Liberation Army with blankets and warm clothing while those forces were attacking the Republic of Tamaria on its bitterly cold, high elevation frontier along the Saradon Plateau.

Careful planning, along with Lady Alexina's judicious use of Allfather's power, enabled Lynden and his warriors to stop the resupply by sinking the Maridom steamboats, thus depriving the Azgaril of warm textiles necessary to survive the Tamarian winter. This time, however, with Lady Alexina expecting her fifth child, she could not intervene without endangering her baby. Any hope of stopping Lord Fang in their current predicament rested with more conventional means, supplemented by the promise of direct help from Tamarian Expeditionary Forces that had not yet arrived on the scene.

Earlier that morning, 538 fully armed men native to Lord Lynden's land approached his villa requesting permission to aid in the defense of their territory. "This is our home too!" they insisted. "Why should you bear the burden of fighting the rebels alone?"

That kind of loyalty moved Lynden's heart. These men, however, hadn't trained for combat and the Lithian warlord didn't consider them as reliable as his own, professional soldiers. He assigned them to Tegene's forces, thinking that the rebels would be less likely to attack from the north. Reasoning along similar lines, Tegene put the militia on Helena's northern frontier, where he believed they were less likely to encounter serious resistance.

Lord Velez sent orders alerting his men of imminent action and warned Tegene to prepare for an enemy incursion before daybreak. Then Lynden returned to his villa where he prayed alone in a private room until Alexina came to join him.

Intermittent artillery fire during the night escalated as morning approached. By the time the Great Eye set, a furious bombardment of Lithian positions on the southeastern bank of the Virgin River began in earnest. Heavy shelling continued until midmorning.

The first rebel infantry attack started at the one lane bridge leading over the Virgin River. Lynden could have had the bridge wired for demolition, but its small size actually presented a choke point for the delivery of troops and supplies, and its historic value militated against its destruction. Further, with the Virgin River near its summertime ebb, successful fording on foot could be achieved in many places anyway. Therefore, Lynden chose to preserve the ancient structure.

Lithian warriors allowed the rebels to establish a toehold on the eastern side of the bridge before opening fire with rifles and mortars. In the face of fierce resistance rebel troops struggled to form their skirmish lines and move forward. This initial foray turned into a slaughter that reddened the Virgin River and left corpses piled high on its eastern bank. Shortly after its onset, the faltering advance ended in ignominious retreat.

Two hours later another column charged across the bridge and fanned out on the eastern shore. These troops pushed into the prepared kill zones, where machine guns and overlapping infantry fire fields cut them down like ripened grain at harvest time. On this occasion the bottleneck of the river bridge prevented an orderly retreat, and several hundred rebels found themselves trapped between the most concerted defense they'd ever encountered and follow-up troops crossing the bridge behind them.

When Lithian artillery shells began dropping into the horde on the far side of the river bank, many of the rebel soldiers fled south, where dozens fell into leg pits featuring sharpened stakes that

The Long Journey: *Deliverance*

punctured their boot soles and rendered them lame. Those who survived faced small Lithian units with automatic rifles and mortar support deployed on the southern flank.

Lynden Velez appraised the battle, shaking his head at the senselessness of his enemy's action. Most of the men dying on this day had never even seen Northern Kameron and had no clue that their lives were sacrificed to suit the grandiose aspirations of a greedy drug lord.

As the rebel attack decayed into defeat, another heavy artillery bombardment followed. Ordnance fell for well over an hour, and then columns of rebel soldiers charged across the river in several different places. Some of the enemy warriors fell into channels dredged into the river bed, where they drowned under the burden of their equipment. But the vast majority climbed up the far bank and pressed forward, the sheer weight of their numbers overwhelming Lithian resistance.

The advance stalled as the Lithian warriors fell back into steeper terrain just beyond the range of the heaviest rebel artillery. Despite a vast superiority in numbers, the rebels faced a determined force with better weaponry and well-prepared defensive positions. Unlike the Kamerese National Army, the Lithians didn't run when the tide of battle turned against them. They held onto the high ground and forced their enemy to pay heavily for every inch of conquered real estate.

As the Daystar set, the rebels tried to consolidate their hold on the eastern bank of the Virgin River. In the evening when human eyes saw only darkness, the Lithian forces counterattacked from the flanks, pinning the rebels against unyielding defenses on higher ground until the invaders panicked and ran. Before midnight, forces loyal to Lord Velez had driven their enemy back across the river.

The success Lynden's army enjoyed came at a relatively modest cost in casualties. Of the 1280 soldiers deployed to defend the southern part of his estate, Lord Velez lost 39 men, most of these to small arms fire during the third enemy incursion. In a single day's combat, however, Lynden's forces depleted nearly 20% of their munitions.

Before dawn of the following day, rebel artillery tubes unleashed another barrage that by midmorning had transformed the east bank of the Virgin River into a moonscape for several hundred yards. During the night roughly 500 enemy soldiers marched five miles southward, crossed the river well upstream and tried a flanking maneuver as they moved northward.

The Long Journey: *Deliverance*

Lithian scouts, following this movement, reported news of the rebel attack. Four batteries of the much feared, 3-inch "mountain gun" Lynden bought from the Tamarians aimed their tubes southward and lobbed air bursting anti-personnel munitions with a wide sheaf above this concentrated enemy formation. The devastating attack utterly demoralized the invaders, whose few survivors fled across the river. Many of them simply continued running without looking back.

When Fang's army began another massed incursion from the west at daybreak, they lacked the expected support from the south, and the Lithians concentrated all of their firepower in blunting the advance. Three more times that day Lord Fang ordered frontal assaults against the entrenched Velez army, and every time, his forces were soundly defeated. After this, he sent messengers to other rebel warlords requesting aid to dislodge these particularly stubborn defenders.

To the north, however, Lord Navarro's much larger army enjoyed more success. After a protracted artillery duel, he began his initial assault on the second day of Lord Fang's humiliating failures, sending nearly five thousand infantry troops across the shallows just south of Helena. As had been the case further upstream, Lithian and Abelscinnian warriors in prepared defensive positions–using automatic rifles, machine guns, mortars and artillery–blunted, then crushed the attack before the enemy could mass his forces on the eastern shore of the Virgin River.

Unlike Lord Fang, Lord Navarro had once served as a Kamerese army officer and successfully used the failure of his frontal assault to mask troop movements further north and south. Understanding the futility of flailing at the Lithian / Abelscinnian strong points, Lord Navarro used his artillery to maintain pressure on the defenders while his cavalry troops raced northward, crossed the river and hooked south. As they encountered resistance, Navarro's troops dismounted, formed skirmish lines and probed for weaknesses in the defenses.

About two hours after noon, the invaders reached the outskirts of Helena and sent word back to their commander that they were encountering less disciplined militia forces and might succeed in breaking through the lines with additional support. At this point, Navarro reinforced the units attacking from the north and sent another frontal assault against Helena.

Tegene, fighting on flatter terrain than Lord Velez, realized that his forces were in danger of being encircled and ordered a tactical

The Long Journey: *Deliverance*

retreat. His men gave up Helena and fell back in an orderly manner, gradually withdrawing to progressively higher ground until they consolidated their defenses among the steep cliffs of Maidenhair Ridge. Everyone understood that the fate of Lord Lynden's territorial command hinged on access to water resources, and Maidenhair Ridge both overlooked and controlled the Virgin River's largest tributary stream.

Once Lord Navarro was able to move his heavy guns across the river, his biggest cannon could target Maidenhair Ridge and hit the fragile light forges high in the hills. If they got pushed off the ridge, the Lithians would be forced to abandon their territory and flee northward, through the mountain passes. Lord Navarro pressed his attack and his men fought ferociously, but the Lithians, Abelscinnians and surviving militia proved very resilient in denying territory to the rebel warlord.

This battle soon ranked as the bloodiest to date in the entire civil war. By mid-afternoon, some of Navarro's subordinate commanders reported casualty rates exceeding 30%, and though Tegene's forces fared better in their entrenched positions, Lithian and Abelscinnian losses mounted as the rebels pushed forward, quickly worsening the situation because the defenders had fewer fighting men to lose.

Tegene sent word to the Velez villa that Lady Alexina and her guests needed to prepare for evacuation on short notice. As Navarro's troops climbed toward the rocky heights, big Lithian guns and mortars located behind a series of debris dams pounded the reinforcements crossing flatter land in unrelenting fury. By late afternoon the strength of Navarro's attack faltered under crushing artillery and withering fire from the highlands.

However, the Kamerese warlord fully intended to win his land back by force and brought his big guns forward. Careful to avoid targeting the villa located on the southern reaches of the ridge line, Navarro's four inch field guns hammered defensive positions further north, allowing troops closing in from the flat lands to advance while the Lithians elevated their gun tubes and adjusted their own artillery to provide counterbattery fire.

Tegene, with his son Jawara at his side, watched these developments in dismay. The two men prayed earnestly, with hands held aloft, imploring the Holy One for deliverance.

A shrieking sound, loud as thunder, interrupted their prayers. When the Abelscinnian warriors opened their eyes dozens of fiery, cylindrical shapes arced downward from the sky in the north. Massive

The Long Journey: *Deliverance*

bursts of heat, flame and smoke blossomed along the riverbank, spreading across its breadth and onto the flat lands south of Helena. For well over a minute, huge, white hot fountains of fire concealed the Virgin River, and as the burning raged along its shores, oily clouds of smoke rose toward the heavens. In the aftermath of these great explosions the Kamerese heavy guns fell silent.

Deliverance had come. The Tamarians, with their long range rockets, had finally arrived.

Reunion

"Contact!" Garrick scribbled in shorthand on a notepad. "Small arms fire at 200 yards. Objective in sight and engaged!" The lieutenant tore off the note and handed it to a runner, a boy not much younger than himself. "Get this to Captain Engels." Scouting reports had accurately pinpointed the enemy's position, and now Garrick and his men had to dislodge them.

Engrossed in the multiple tasks of a platoon commander evaluating a target, Garrick studied a winery and its surroundings through his binoculars and didn't further acknowledge the boy who hopped on a bicycle and swiftly pedaled northward. An adrenaline rush replaced the fatigue and discomfort he'd felt after marching over 20 miles the previous day, and nearly seven more through the predawn darkness.

Sergeant Vidders, kneeling in a ditch next to Garrick, eyed his young commander in anticipation. "What'll it be, lieutenant?" he asked.

Garrick used a grease pencil and his knee board to sketch the surroundings. He circled a slump between two small drifts where tall, dry grasses grew. "Take your squad through there and set up a crossfire as close as you can get without being seen. You'll cover our advance as we swing left through those trees." He drew a line leading toward a path between vineyards, where mature, well-spaced live oaks served as a windbreak between two properties. "Once we're in position I'll signal you with the mirror before we move on the objective. I'll flash three times when we need you to attack.

"If we can't make it, we'll fall back here. I'll send word and we'll cover your withdrawal. Talon's men are on your right flank. Be careful, sergeant!" Garrick wiped the knee board clean.

The ruddy-complected sergeant mopped his sweaty forehead, nodded and signaled his squad to move out. Garrick sent another runner to advise both Talon Waldheim and Greg Schmidt of his platoon's advance.

"Suppressing fire!" Garrick ordered. "Make it count, men!"

He'd repeated the mantra of conserving ammunition so many times it seemed second nature for the members of Garrick's platoon not to fire their weapons without a compelling need to do so. Accuracy at a range of 200 yards favored the Tamarians, as whoever was shooting at them from the winery discharged vast volumes of ordnance in the hope of producing a positive effect; whereas Sergeant Ringer's squad kept the enemy down using limited and highly accurate rifle fire, while Sergeant Vidders and his men maneuvered into position.

One machine cannon crew and rocket launcher accompanied Sergeant Vidders, while Garrick set up the other at the intersection of the path and the road they currently occupied, so that he and Sergeant Ringer had some firepower back up in the event that they needed to withdraw. He checked lines of sight, breathed a heavy sigh and glanced at Brenna, who timidly hunkered in the ditch, watching with wide eyes.

Brenna, who had never witnessed Garrick leading men before, appraised him with a mix of trepidation and wonder. He'd become far more confident and decisive, indicating that the intensive officer training he'd undertaken refined and amplified his natural leadership talent. Brenna admired these traits and knew from experience that Garrick could fight with great courage, but sincerely hoped he wasn't leading them into a bloodbath. She thought the volume of fire being expended from the winery seemed disproportionate to the threat that a single platoon presented.

"How do you know those aren't friendly troops?" she asked.

It was a good question. "I don't know for certain," he replied, "but they're shooting at us. Scouting reports claim these are rebel positions, the forward Special Forces observer teams tell us the rebels need places like this because they're short of water, and messages from your father's Abelscinnian commander–flown to battalion headquarters by homing doves–indicate this was the first area Navarro's army overran."

He crouched and began moving forward, following his men. "Besides," he added, "Your father's troops wouldn't blow through ammunition like that. They don't have a lot, so they have to be careful. Whoever's shooting at us can't hit the broad side of a barn, they don't understand ordnance conservation, and that's typical of a militia."

Brenna hoped he was right. She glanced heavenward while chanting a brief prayer, hefted her backpack and scurried behind the line of men moving down the ditch on the far side of the road.

"What happens if you're wrong?" she inquired.

Garrick paused as his men scrambled across the road in single file intervals. "Then good people die and my butt ends up in a sling." He tightened his lips, gazing into her dark eyes with revealed longing, then turned and pressed onward.

The Long Journey: *Reunion*

Though only a few hours had transpired since dawn, the day already felt hot. Sweat and dust coated the tan-colored Tamarian uniforms. Some of the men had already rolled up their sleeves and loosened blouse buttons beneath their armored vests, but for the sake of modesty Brenna did not follow suit. She sweated uncomfortably, took a sip of water from her canteen and swished the warm liquid around in her mouth before swallowing, then dumped a bit beneath her armor and swabbed her neck to cool off.

A low ridge draped in oak trees, several hundred yards further east, dominated the rolling topography of this area. On its crest an old monastery overlooked vineyards on three sides. Greg Schmidt's platoon had been tasked to seize that ground, but they hadn't arrived yet. As had been the case during their training, Third Platoon–the unit Garrick commanded–represented the leading edge of the Tamarian forces.

Battle noise shifted westward, toward Sergeant Vidders' squad. Sergeant Ringer sent his men advancing from tree to tree in pairs, their movements masked by the firefight. Down the lane they crept until the entire group assembled on the far side of the path. "This is the real thing," Garrick said in a low voice. "Nagel and Krieger will stay here with me to cover the approach. The rest of you, get ready!"

Garrick crept toward an oak tree and pulled a small mirror out of his breast pocket. He angled it toward the position occupied by Sergeant Vidders, and once he saw a flash of recognition from the far side he put the mirror back and readied his rifle. "Go!" he ordered. Eight men advanced in unison at his command.

Normally, Tamarian soldiers moved across open ground in a leapfrog fashion, with pairs of men alternating a drop to cover with a brief sprint to progress. This time, because nobody fired at them from the winery, Sergeant Ringer urged them to quickly press through tended rows of fruiting vines.

Garrick watched the squad assemble on the winery's eastern wall. Sergeant Ringer used hand signals to direct his men into assault positions. Within moments Kellen Bauer destroyed a padlock with a shotgun blast and the men vanished inside a large double door. Small arms fire echoed through the stone building. Garrick longed to be in the midst of the fighting, directing his platoon from the front, but he'd been reprimanded for doing this so many times the new lieutenant constrained the urge to dash across the vineyard and lead the assault.

The Long Journey: *Reunion*

Soon afterward the doorway opened and Private Skinner appeared. He gestured with hand signals that indicated the assault team needed help, then pointed upward and made a circular motion. Garrick turned to Brenna and patted her on the backside. "Go!" he ordered. "And be careful!"

He adored watching the way she moved. Even with her lovely hair pinned into a bun beneath her helmet, laden with her bow, sword and a heavy pack strapped onto her shoulders, Brenna glided across the ground with facile, feminine grace. Garrick's appreciation was tempered by the fact that he was, for the first time, ordering her into danger. At present, he alone fully appreciated her value to the platoon, knowing that she was irreplaceable; but in addition, Garrick's love for the girl made his heart pound worriedly.

After signaling Sergeant Vidders to attack, Garrick watched and waited for the outcome of the battle. He listened to a ferocious firefight rise and fall as his men moved through the winery, his anxiety heightened, his desire to join them suppressed with great difficulty.

Brenna understood nothing Private Skinner said to her. An excited tone gushed from the young man's voice and he spoke too fast for her to make out the words. She followed him through the double door into the press room. A wide, V-shaped stainless steel trough with a perforated cylinder and rotating paddles served to de-stem and extract juice from the harvested grapes. Even though it had been several months since this equipment had last been used, the distinctive aroma of the grape crush lingered in the air.

Walking across the press room, Brenna stepped over three Kamerese bodies. Two bullet holes in each torso told the tale of their swift demise. She could tell they'd been shot from the front and bled out trying to crawl away. Their weapons, bolt action rifles, had been cleared and moved well out of reach.

Several gunshots startled her and Private Skinner. They both dropped to the floor and Brenna squirmed beneath the press as the sound of boots approached. Sergeant Ringer appeared in the portal and angrily reprimanded Private Skinner for some transgression Brenna didn't understand. The Lithian girl scuttled out from beneath the press and followed Sergeant Ringer as the sounds of gunfire, the enraged voices of fighting men, and the agonized cries of the wounded increased in tempo.

The Long Journey: *Reunion*

Tall, cylindrical fermenting vats and several casks lined the walls of the next room. At least two of these had been punctured by bullets and wine spilled into a spreading pool on the floor. Brenna slid out of her backpack when she found Ziggy Hoenzaer holding his hand against Erich Ulmann's right thigh. Erich cried out in pain and cursed, thrashing in a shallow pool of wine and blood. When Ziggy let go at Brenna's urging, a spurt of arterial blood sprayed across her neck. Brenna stopped the hemorrhage with her own hand, then urged Ziggy to press against the wound again.

She'd seen this kind of damage many times before and knew that it was most often fatal. If a bullet remained in Erich's body, especially wedged within the leg muscle of an active young man, he might suffer ongoing damage to his arterial network and bleed to death. The Lithian maiden wiped her hands with a rag and fumbled through her pack for a pressure dressing. She had Ziggy press the dressing down while she pulled out her boot knife and cut through Erich's pant leg.

Wine stained Erich's uniform and skin, making it very difficult for her to see an exit wound. Brenna felt around the back of Erich's thigh, but couldn't find another hole, which meant that in all likelihood the bullet remained lodged in the flesh, and she knew she couldn't leave it there. However, extracting the bullet was risky, and by doing so, she ran the risk of killing him.

Though she'd had nightmares over unsuccessful attempts at healing this kind of injury in the past, Brenna placed her hand over the pressure dressing and uttered a prayer. A sense of calm flooded her soul as she kissed her fingers and plunged them into the wound.

Erich screamed and thrashed.

"Hold!" Brenna demanded sternly, searching for the severed artery. If she could stop the bleeding he might survive, but it was very difficult to find a ruptured blood vessel without her patient moving, and more so whenever he did.

"Give him some morphine!" Ziggy urged.

Brenna understood the request for a pain killer but knowing that morphine depressed the cardiovascular system, she shook her head. This man had lost too much blood for her to risk using morphine. She glanced briefly at the young Tamarian soldier, her dark eyes stern and authoritative. "Me you trust!" she said, then returned to her task.

Ziggy's face reflected panic. He tried to soothe his friend with calm words while clamped onto Erich's leg. The wounded warrior cursed him and called Brenna every foul word in a soldier's lexicon, but something about the way the Lithian girl worked gave Ziggy hope as he tried to hold his friend's leg still.

"Yes!" Brenna exclaimed as the artery melded back together. She felt the bleeding stop and her heart raced in the thrill of Allfather's power flowing through her fingers. After pulling out of the wound, she wrote "NM" for "no morphine" in blood on Erich's forehead, then wiped her hands clean and washed the wound in warm water. After this, Brenna reached into her pack for a forceps, touched it with her lips and in her native tongue said: "Light."

A deep blue glow emanated from the tip of the instrument, and at the sight of this magic, Ziggy shuddered fearfully. He watched the Lithian girl carefully probe through the wound, examining intently as she manipulated the clamp. Her actions inspired Erich to scream, but a moment later she removed a flattened, Kamerese bullet from his thigh, kissed her fingers again, then began healing the permanent cavity from the inside out.

Erich settled. Ziggy appraised Brenna with dread and wonder, then helped her carry the wounded soldier back into the crush room. "Will he live?" Ziggy inquired.

Brenna, her apprehension of losing another patient easing, shrugged. "Allfather only know," she replied.

The firing stopped. Intense shouting ensued while Harmon Grossmann, the tallest and broadest member of Garrick's platoon, helped his buddy, Ritter Wagner, into the crush room. Ritter had his right hand clamped on a gunshot wound and he grimaced in shock and pain. The back of his uniform had been drenched in wine and his left arm dangled limply.

Harmon Grossmann grinned at Brenna. "Ritter was thirsty and wanted a drink!" he said. "We had to pick him up off the floor!"

"Shut up Grossman!" Ritter snapped. "It was wet and I slipped!"

Brenna ignored the banter. "I look," she said, examining the trauma to Ritter's left arm. A clean entry and exit wound traced the path of a bullet that had pierced his muscle. Bits of tattered fabric clung to coagulating blood that had already crusted on his skin, and spatter on Ritter's armored vest surrounded the spot where a rebel bullet lodged.

The armor had spared Ritter's life after a direct hit knocked him to the ground. Enduring pain and gasping for breath, this man had risen

The Long Journey: *Reunion*

to his feet again and kept fighting. The wet floor had nothing to do with his falling.

Brenna cleaned him up, kissed her fingers and healed his wounded flesh. As she finished with Ritter and sent him away Sergeant Ringer appeared, leading other men who dragged critically wounded Kamerese into the crush room. Brenna performed triage and became so engrossed in her task that she didn't see Garrick come inside.

"We've secured the water tanks," Sergeant Ringer explained to his young commander. "After Sergeant Vidders attacked the rebels fell apart, so we gained control pretty quickly, and they didn't have time to sabotage them. However, we found a little surprise when we reached the cellars. I'd like to know what you want to do."

Garrick followed Sergeant Ringer, mentally counting bodies as they moved further into the winery and down a set of stairs that led into the underlying karst. He'd counted seventeen dead rebels by the time they arrived in the cellar's cask filling room.

A light stick illuminated many rows of wine barrels, stacked and stored in the cool depths for ageing. Huddled in terror at the back of the room, guarded by Luther Sondheim and Otis Krieger, twenty-nine women–some clutching young children–awaited their fate. Most of these were foreigners: Azgaril, Vatherii and a strikingly beautiful teenaged girl with Nordan features. However, some were Kamerese, and of these several bore the double chain helix brand that identified them as slaves.

Sergeant Ringer pointed to a middle-aged woman. "Her name's Hermosa. She's the only one who speaks vulgate, and she says they were brought here to, uh . . . keep the men happy." Then he leaned over and whispered into Garrick's ear. "I think they're worried that we'll want them to keep us happy, too. It might be a good idea for you to reassure them."

Garrick approached the woman. "You were brought here against your will?"

She nodded, her eyes betraying uncertainty.

"But you're Kamerese." He glanced at her left arm. "And you're not a slave."

"My father was King Alejo's ambassador to the Abelscinnians. In honor of his service, the rebels used me for their pleasure." The woman's voice, once proud and strong, dripped with humiliation.

The Long Journey: *Reunion*

"There will be no more of that," Garrick promised. "Tell the others we won't harm them. I'll personally see about getting you to a safe place soon."

Garrick turned to Sergeant Ringer. "Leave them here for now," he began. "If we take them upstairs, some may try to get away, and we don't need a bunch of women running around on a battlefield. I'll request an MP escort and send them up to the refugee camp." He turned and began climbing the stairs. "And if anyone else lays a finger on any of these women, he answers to me."

"Yes sir!" Sergeant Ringer acknowledged.

Garrick's platoon killed a total of thirty-two rebels in taking the winery. Twenty-eight Kamerese fell into their hands as prisoners. After having the rebels disarmed, Garrick's men bound their POWs with belts and held them in the foyer until the military police arrived.

In the midst of organizing the prisoners, Sergeant Vidders approached with a map his men recovered from an office. Though he could not read Kamerese, the sergeant thought it might be important.

Garrick, who was not fluent in Kamerese either, recognized the word "water" in several places. The reason his platoon had been tasked to take the winery stemmed from the fact that it had a large artesian spring and storage tanks for irrigation. In the hot and dry environment, control over water resources ranked high among Tamarian priorities, and he felt proud that his men had successfully secured their first objective.

Just after he moved his machine cannon and rocket crews into strategic positions, Garrick sent the map and another message reporting his success at the winery to Captain Engels. As the messenger pedaled away, the shrieking sound of incoming artillery scattered the Tamarian soldiers assembled in the courtyard.

Bright flashes, flames and the concussive burst of four inch artillery shells bloomed above the vineyard. Shrapnel shards rained upon old vines renown for producing deep red wines. Sweeter varieties, inter-planted to make mixed field wine withered under the assault. Shattered stems, broken branches, shredded leaves, strings of hot wire and orange-red volcanic dust rent the hot, morning air.

After establishing range, the gunners walked their rounds into the winery courtyard and a hail of destruction ensued. Holger Faust, a member of Sergeant Vidders' squad, suffered a direct hit that literally burst his body into chunks of charred meat, and a grisly rain of flesh fell on the hot cobblestones.

The force of one explosion blew Volkard Wexler into the winery wall, killing him instantly. Kasch Nagel, the platoon's communications specialist, screamed in agony as shrapnel riddled his legs, arms and neck. He tried to crawl away, but overwhelmed by pain, Private Nagel couldn't even lift his own head.

Brenna heard his cry for help amid the din, took a deep breath, and dashed from within the relative safety of the crush room out into the courtyard to save him.

*   *   *

Algernon stood in the shade of an observatory that some nameless astronomer had built nearly a hundred years earlier. He gazed at the smoky landscape from the heights of Maidenhair Ridge, overlooking the gently undulating topography that opened toward the Virgin River valley and the small reservoir, *Lago Caliente,* further south. Trapped with his sister and Astrid at the Velez villa, he'd grown weary of arbitrating their ongoing quarrel and felt hemmed into a walled compound surrounded by Lithian women whose speech he didn't understand. With all the men tied up in battle, every warrior guarding the Velez residence came from the pool of able-bodied wives, widows and mothers of the Lithian men engaging rebel forces.

Astrid, who once thought of Kira as her true love and soul mate, spiraled into depression as she wrestled with Kira's rejection. Her obsession with reconciliation and the continual recounting of pleasant memories in Kira's company exhausted him, yet Astrid had to process her feelings and Algernon remained the only one available to hear her maudlin recollections. But he felt torn between his physical desire for her and resentment of her emotional fragility. Algernon wanted Astrid's attention on simpler, more favorable terms, and though he tried to support the priestess during her misery, he lacked the developmental depth to offer beneficial counsel.

As Kira pulled through her second withdrawal, she developed a bad headache and fever that continually demanded Algernon's care. He vacillated between gentle servility toward his sister and irritation of her neediness, quickly losing interest in providing basic care. At Kira's request, to protect her from Astrid's advances, Algernon allowed his twin to sleep in his bed from the first night they spent together at the Velez estate.

They'd slept together as children, but Algernon soon found his sister's proximity an impediment to adequate rest for several reasons. They weren't innocent siblings anymore, and Kira had quite obviously grown accustomed to sharing her bed with someone else. With the aid of Brenna's tea the withdrawal episodes and opium cravings declined, but Kira's fever caused her to sweat and moan. Though she'd gradually begun sleeping for longer periods of time each night, whenever she fell asleep Kira became restless, cried out in her dreams and frequently thrashed about in bed.

Algernon took a pillow, a blanket, and moved to the floor. He heard Astrid weeping upstairs and couldn't sleep because he really hated hearing her cry. The following evening he slept on the floor again, but this time–and every night thereafter–Astrid came in to lie down beside him. As artillery crumped and boomed in a relentless, inexorable approach, fear flourished in the darkness. Astrid trembled, Kira quivered and despite their differences, the three Tamarians huddled together for comfort until exhaustion overtook them.

During lucid moments, Kira brooded about her experience. She moved from devotion to Marco into absolute contempt for him like the pendulum clock swinging slowly from the ceiling in the observatory. Algernon wished she would hurry up and process all of her mixed feelings, but Kira had become a twisted, frayed bundle of knotted emotions, and chief among these, she often lamented the loss of her identity to opium addiction.

Dealing with the two young women proved depressing. Algernon sought refuge in meditation, prayer and his stretching routines, yet found rituals of this nature powerless to cope with the intense emotional pressures he faced. Climbing high up Maidenhair Ridge to the observatory and the light forges beyond provided a welcome distraction from the harsh, twin realities that Astrid didn't love him as he wished she would, and that Kira had become a tormented and sulking stranger whose physical infirmity exhausted him.

Tegene, though preoccupied with the ongoing battle, sensed that Algernon needed something to do. He tasked the young monk with decoding and translating messages received from the Tamarian battalion commander via homing dove. Algernon understood the way Tamarians thought, and Tegene found his cultural insight invaluable.

The Long Journey: *Reunion*

Algernon read a message from a colonel named Hans Adler that Lieutenant Mariel Hougen had transcribed. The young monk turned toward Tegene and translated the document. "He says that his lead elements are engaged north of Helena and suggests you may have to hold out for as long as two days before those forces can clear the town. He strongly suggests that you cut off the water supply if you can."

Tegene grunted, looking across the battlefield through his binoculars. The Tamarians seemed very conservative about committing to a time schedule, but then, the Abelscinnian commander understood that his ally was projecting power from a considerable distance. Tegene suspected that logistical problems complicated the Tamarian deployment, yet he couldn't hide the hint of frustration in his voice when he addressed Algernon again. "Tell him we have ammunition for a day, perhaps two if we're careful and the rebels turn to face his forces. Artillery munitions are critically low. Ask if he can supply ammunition for our 3 inch guns. They're Tamarian in origin, so their shells will work in our guns. I will arrange to cut the water supply."

Algernon wrote as Tegene turned toward a messenger and said something in the Abelscinnian language he didn't understand. Then, after keying the contents into a Tamarian military encoder, Algernon included a separate message for Mariel Hougen, hoping she could forward it to Garrick, somehow. After doing this, he rolled the fragile paper messages into a tiny scroll case that clipped to the right foot of a homing dove. When released, the bird circled twice, then headed toward the northwest.

Soon afterward, a strange lull descended upon the battlefield. Where Lord Navarro's forces had been pressing hard against the highlands, they fell back upon defensive revetments overrun two days earlier. In the relative calm that followed, Algernon gazed across the ruined vineyards with a sense of loss overflowing from within his soul. Having grown up tending to an orchard, his heart ached in witnessing the reckless destruction of fragile soil and fruitful vines. Trying to cover the growing despair he felt, Algernon revealed a primal worry to Tegene. "What will happen when your men run out of ammunition?"

The tall, broad-shouldered Abelscinnian appraised his young companion gently. "That will not happen," he replied.

Algernon shook his head. "I don't understand how you can be so confident. If Colonel Adler says he can't get his forces down here for two days and you're running low on munitions, it's only a matter of time before the rebels push you right off this ridge."

Tegene raised his eyebrows. "You're a priest, a man of faith, and yet you talk this way? I'm surprised!"

Taken aback by this response, Algernon clarified his position. "Are you expecting the heavens to part and the armies of the Great God to come to our rescue?"

"If that is what the Holy One wills, then it shall be so. However, he often uses the most mundane and ordinary circumstances to attain his ends. In this manner, people of faith recognize his work and ascribe him the honor he is due."

Cynically, Algernon wrinkled his lips. "So if my brother and his army wipe out Lord Navarro, you'll give God the credit?"

"If God intends them to defeat Lord Navarro that will be so. There is no resisting the Holy One," Tegene said. "He will use whatever means necessary to reveal his power and glory, so that we who believe in his name experience our faith affirmed. You, of all people, should understand this."

Algernon shook his head. "That's circular reasoning. It doesn't make sense!"

"Only to a man who lacks faith!" Tegene replied. "Think of your own experience. How many times has your life been preserved when it should have ended?"

Algernon refused to acknowledge Tegene's point. He shook his head, deflecting the direction of the conversation. "That's illogical," he claimed. "In the first place, how can I really know that my life should have ended, were it not for some divine intervention? And secondly, if I ascribe every incident in which someone else has come to my rescue as the Great God's working, then all of us are merely puppets tugged on celestial strings, and no deliverance has any real meaning. How is there any glory in that?"

Tegene nodded. "I comprehend your thinking, but you fundamentally misunderstand the Holy One. He needs nothing from you, but he deserves your honor because he is God. Consider the rebels," he said, gesturing across the valley. "They've come here on their own volition to destroy all hope of prosperity in this land. They care nothing for the people who live here, but aggrandize themselves as liberators. Therefore, they do not see ruined vineyards, destruction of valuable property and the senseless killing of innocents who have not harmed them as evil.

"This proves that the Holy One permits free will in the minds of men. Lord Navarro and Lord Fang have chosen to attack here, though the Kamerese National Army has retreated to the west. Lord Velez did not provoke the rebels. They are violating the Holy One's clearly stated will for peace within his creation."

Algernon shrugged. "But if you consign the rebels' defeat to some Act of God, how can you be sure that he didn't put them up to attacking here for some other purpose?"

Tegene shook his head. "That is another thing you misunderstand," he replied. "You are ascribing evil intent to the One who is Holy. There is no wickedness in him."

"I don't doubt the integrity of God. But how can you know his will?" Algernon insisted, using the vulgate term for knowledge that referred to external, verifiable evidence that might be objectively examined.

"We know by what the Holy One has revealed about himself through the writings of the ancients. We also know through experience that stands the test of time. The arrow of our faith does not fly forward unless it is first drawn back in the bow of remembrance."

Algernon considered this remark, quietly thinking over Tegene's wisdom. As the gentle Abelscinnian commander called for a subordinate to report on the break in fighting, Algernon excused himself and returned to the observatory seeking solitude.

* * *

Many miles further south Lynden Velez faced a desperate situation. The men under his direct command fought with undeniable ferocity, and their valor repulsed repeated frontal assaults. After four days of unrelenting battle, ammunition stocks had fallen so low he believed his men should have run out of bullets already. In addition, as the intensity of nearly continual artillery bombardment pounded his defenses, 143 wounded warriors and 87 of their slain comrades had been depleted from his ranks.

Losses of this nature might have rendered a less motivated combat force ineffective, yet devotion to their warlord, their success in blunting Lord Fang's attacks, and the cause of fighting for their own land kept the plucky defenders viable beyond Lynden's expectations. He

The Long Journey: *Reunion*

earnestly petitioned Allfather to do something about their situation, for without some form of resupply, he and his men would have to abandon their strategic southern boundary, with its vital control over fresh water, and retreat northward.

Denying water to the rebels had been a key feature of his defense plan. With Tamarian Special Forces disseminating disinformation about poisoned wells across the river, disrupting the rebel supply chain with carefully planned demolitions and small scale attacks, the rebel armies simply had to seize a local water supply. Lynden correctly assumed that Lord Fang would initiate his attack where he could dominate the headwaters of the Virgin River, but in this area the topography favored the defenders. Further, Lynden and Sherman Mason, his chief engineer, had a plan in place to completely deprive Lord Fang's forces access to any sizeable quantity of water.

Lynden felt hot, sweaty and filthy. Personal misery increased with a corresponding rise in daytime temperatures, yet as he studied the battlefield from a sheltered bunker, the Lithian warlord wondered how Lord Fang managed to inspire rebel soldiers to repeatedly and unsuccessfully flail themselves against his defenses. With not a single tree surviving the constant shelling, and no shade under which rebel warriors could seek solace, they baked beneath the Daystar and suffered the demoralizing impact of long range sniper fire while the Great Eye dominated the darkness.

A courier ducked under the concrete roof, bearing three messages. "I got here as fast as I could, sir," he said, apologetically.

Lynden thanked him, offered the man a drink, then unrolled the first communique while the courier refreshed himself. This one had come from Woodwind, his trusted former servant who'd been operating with a Tamarian Special Forces unit in Northern Kameron, and had been dated the previous afternoon.

"Many deserters fleeing west. Captured rebels report Fang offered unit commanders your daughters as slaves for battlefield success. Water critically short. Morale declining." Woodwind's familiar signature ended the note.

The second message came from Tegene, who wrote: "Tamarian allies engaged. Navarro advance stalled at Maidenhair Ridge. Ammunition low. Casualties high. Reinforcements needed. Water cut to Helena and Maidenhair dam spillways closed. May God be praised!"

The Long Journey: *Reunion*

Lynden and Tegene had been close friends for many years and the two men trusted one another. However, as long as the forces under his direct leadership remained in contact with those of Lord Fang, Lynden could not march northward to support Tegene in his defense of Maidenhair Ridge. But he hoped that with the Tamarian Expeditionary Units finally attacking, Lord Navarro would be forced to turn his army around and in doing so, relieve pressure on the ridge defenders.

He wrote a message in response, informing his Abelscinnian commander that as long as Fang's army threatened the southern water supplies he could not quit the field and come to Tegene's aid. "Be strong and have faith," he wrote in conclusion.

The third and final note came from Sherman Mason. On it he'd written only four words: "Operation *Virgen Privada* completed."

This reference to a "bereaved virgin" referred to Sherman's use of explosives to create a rock dam at *Lago Nacimiento*, the headwater source for the Virgin River, located about 40 miles to the southeast. With the lake level already declining due to a regional drought, blocking the river's flow would deprive rebel forces of the only major water source they could currently access. Within hours, the Virgin River would ebb into a collection of rocks and very shallow pools.

That left *Lago Caliente*, the tiny, shallow reservoir visible from the Velez villa, as the singular source supplying the Virgin River. Since Lynden's forces on both fronts were already drawing from that body of water, it could not support the vast number of men gathered for battle on Lynden's land, and he expected the whole focus of the rebel campaign to shift in response. Control over *Lago Caliente* would be an important key to victory.

*   *   *

"The hand of Allfather preserves and protects me," Brenna whispered, repeating a memorized psalm. "I am sheltered beneath his mighty shield. He is my strong fortress. He is my powerful defender!"

Bursting artillery shells rained shrapnel across the courtyard. Cries of pain and rage mingled with the clatter of falling debris and fleeing boots. Through the smoke and deadly downpour Brenna scurried toward Kasch Nagel, her attention riveted on his broken body despite the blinding flashes and the stench of burning flesh. All shadows vanished as a very close explosion knocked the girl to the cobblestones, a wave of heat washed over her body, and she heard a deluge of sharp metal shards rattling against the pavement.

Breathing hard to suppress her own terror, *believing* that the comforting poetry invoked Allfather's protection, the Lithian maiden crawled toward Private Nagel. When she reached him, Brenna spoke soothingly while she flicked shards of hot metal out of his neck with her left hand, kissed the fingers of her right hand and pressed them against his wounds. Flesh melded into place at her touch, but the private's entire back had been riddled with flechette and it took her a long time to stop the serious bleeding from his injuries.

Sergeant Ringer yelled something unintelligible from the doorway. A moment later Harmon Grossman raced across the courtyard, lifted Kasch Nagel and carried him into the crush room. Brenna followed, fully intending to continue with her ministrations, but Sergeant Ringer grabbed her arm and spun her behind the doorway.

His face was enraged. He yelled at her, shouting words so rapidly she could only make out the Tamarian terms for "hell, stupid, valuable, dead" and an assortment of swear words she'd learned by listening to the soldiers talk. No one had ever treated Brenna this way. She didn't understand why the sergeant was so angry with her, and the hurt welling up from within her soul inspired her lip to quiver and a pair of tears to race down her dirt-stained cheeks. All she wanted to do was help. What had she done wrong?

Sergeant Ringer flung her arm aside and stalked off in disgust. He paused several feet away and pointed at her again, speaking slowly enough for her to understand. "Never do that again!" he warned.

Brenna sniffed, wiped away her tears and ducked under the sturdy crushing machine, where Harmon had found a resting place for Private Nagel. It took every bit of self-control for her not to break down and weep. Brenna tried to focus on her task, systematically evaluating Nagel's injuries so that she could deal with the most serious of them first. She opened a morphine ampule, held it under the wounded soldier's nose and said: "Sniff!"

Harmon Grossman knelt down next to her. He patted Brenna on the back to get her attention. "Little sister," he said, using the same term of endearment she'd earned in action on the Saradon Plateau the previous winter. "Don't worry about the sergeant. We can see that you're a lioness."

The Long Journey: *Reunion*

Brenna nodded and went back to her work. The artillery bombardment rattled the crush room equipment and knocked dust off the rafters, but the air-bursting fragmentation munitions were designed to kill unprotected people, and as long as the shells did not hit the winery directly, its strong roof and walls withstood the punishment.

Brenna heard Garrick enter the room with Sergeant Vidders, but she remained too busy to pay attention to him. A tone of incredulity hardened in his voice. "You caught him doing what?"

"His pants were down, but if you asked me, the girl was a willing participant," Sergeant Vidders replied. "It's not like she hadn't done this kind of thing before."

"He didn't hear me say that no one was to lay a hand on any of those women? What's wrong with him?"

"Don't overreact, lieutenant."

"Overreact?" Garrick had already moved far beyond that point. He liked Luther Sondheim, but he expected professional behavior from the men under his command. "Come on, sergeant! What do you think I should do?"

Sergeant Vidders shook his head. "Let Ringer deal with it, and stay away from Sondheim until the sergeant talks to you."

Garrick felt exasperated but he got himself back under control. "Look, don't ask me to pretend nothing's happened. I expect a consequence of some kind. I gave a direct order!" In frustration, he glanced outside at the ongoing bombardment that laid waste the lovely vineyard and swore profoundly. "Where's that counterbattery fire?"

By the time Tamarian rockets responded to Garrick's request and silenced the Kamerese artillery firing at them from the monastery, Brenna had nearly plucked all of the shrapnel from Kasch Nagel's right leg. She glanced at Garrick, displaying distress with a timid expression normally reserved for overbearing strangers.

Of all the strains relating to his leadership role, seeing that look on Brenna's face pained him the most. "How's he doing?" Garrick inquired, calming under the influence of her gaze.

Brenna kept her damp eyes riveted on him. "Ok," she responded.

Though he could see she'd not been physically hurt, he knew something was wrong. Garrick knelt beside her and spoke gently. "What happened?"

The Long Journey: *Reunion*

She looked away, rubbing her eyes in the elbow of her uniform. "I went outside to save Nagel during the artillery barrage, and Sergeant Ringer yelled at me."

Garrick sat down, shut his eyes and let out an exhausted sigh. He was trying to formulate a response to this when Brenna interrupted his thoughts again.

"Why didn't you stop him?" she asked, accusation brimming in her voice. "Why did you let him treat me that way?"

When Garrick looked into Brenna's eyes again, she saw something cold therein–a ruthlessness that had grown under the care of Tamarian military ethic–and she felt saddened for innocence lost. "You put yourself at risk when shells were falling right on top of us, and you wonder why he got upset? I'd have personally chewed both of you out if he hadn't."

Her mouth dropped open in shock. "My only job in this platoon involves saving life, Garrick. Would you have preferred me to leave Nagel out there?"

Garrick shook his head. "I know your job, but you're misunderstanding the whole point. Suppose one of those shells had fallen on you. Then what would we do? Who'd be left to care for Sergeant Ringer's wounded?"

"Udo Barth," she replied, her lips tightening because she knew Garrick wouldn't understand–wouldn't *believe*–that Allfather always protected her.

Garrick rolled his eyes. "He's got his hands full with Sergeant Vidders' men, and we both know that he doesn't have the skills you do. I'm not being selfish here. You belong to everyone in this platoon. Every soldier under my command needs you, and now they finally understand you're much too valuable to risk.

"Besides," he said, dropping his voice to a whisper, "I don't want to live without you."

"What about Private Nagel?" she inquired, avoiding eye contact.

Knowing that Kasch Nagel didn't understand vulgate, Garrick answered in a manner that struck Brenna as insensitive. "Soldiering is a risky business, and frankly he's worth less than you are. Next time, leave him out there or send someone else to get him."

Brenna shook her head. "What happened to you?" she inquired. "What happened to that sweet, compassionate boy I knew?"

The Long Journey: *Reunion*

Garrick realized she had a point, but he didn't want to argue with her. "My job is full of ethical compromise," he replied softly. "I have to make choices that are not about my own integrity because I have a bigger picture to consider. While I can't let my love for you impact the platoon, minimizing risk to you is in everyone's best interest. Please be more careful!"

"What if that had been you?" she asked, the emotion brimming on her face. "Do you think I could leave you out there to die?"

Garrick wanted to kiss her, grateful for the love she willingly lavished on him and feeling strangely unworthy of her devotion. He sighed, resisting the urge, and stood. "Treasure me in your heart and know that I love you," he replied. "But when it's my turn to die, don't risk your life for mine. I told you that I don't want to live without you, and I meant every word."

Turning away from her proved difficult, but if he'd stayed a moment longer, she would have seen tears. Garrick didn't want to be perceived as weak, so he went outside to examine the carnage.

The courtyard paving had been blackened by the bombardment, but in the midst of the grit and soot something strange caught his eye. He stopped in wonder at the sight of a negative image imprinted on the ground. Flash burns on the cobblestones marked the outline of a small female figure. Shrapnel fragments had pelted and penetrated the ground surrounding the ghostly facsimile where she had fallen, yet Brenna hadn't been touched by any flechette from the shell that exploded directly above her head.

A deep and dreadful fear made Garrick tremble. He glanced toward Brenna, then looked away and muttered muted curses upon himself for doubting her faith. A few moments later he found Faust's metal name tag and bits of burnt uniform, then examined Volkard Wexler's crumpled body near the winery wall and shook his head. Blinking back tears and sniffing to control strong emotion, Garrick removed Volkard's name tag and walked away.

Later, an EPT stirred a moving cloud of red dust as it raced down the road. A messenger hopped out, sought Garrick and expressed surprised at the obvious youth of a successful second lieutenant. "Captain Engels wants to see you," he said.

Garrick left his platoon in the capable hands of his sergeants and hopped into the back seat, where Talon Waldheim already waited. Garrick had never ridden in a car before, and a smile spread across his face as the machine smoothly and quietly accelerated eastward to pick up Greg Schmidt, and then headed north to Company Alpha's headquarters.

Despite the apparent chaos surrounding him, Captain Engels maintained a serene demeanor. The man seemed completely unflustered by the noise and movement flowing through his command tent, and like a gentle priest herding a host of unruly children, the captain exerted control with a soft, yet insistent voice. "Congratulations on jobs well done, gentlemen," he began. The captain gestured to a map on a table and pointed at various features as he spoke. "With our allies running low on munitions, we are tasked to secure the town of Helena and cut off potential rebel reinforcement of their positions below Maidenhair Ridge.

"Company Beta will deploy eastward along Maidenhair Creek to guard your flank and provide limited artillery support. We expect more serious resistance from the rebels than you received this morning, but part of our objective involves forcing them to face us as a means of relieving pressure on the Abelscinnians and Lithians on the ridge line.

"Lieutenant Schmidt will seize the temple on the town's eastern edge and control access to the road leading to Maidenhair Ridge. Lieutenant Ravenwood will secure the center of town and the city hall, which is currently serving as the command center for Lord Navarro's forces. Lieutenant Waldheim will proceed south along the waterfront and block any attempt to reinforce rebel units from across the river.

"Make sure your men have adequate water before you depart. We expect our allies to shut down the supply mains and close the creek today, so don't go into Helena thinking you'll find the taps running."

Captain Engels appraised his lieutenants with a hint of sadness, knowing he'd tasked them with a difficult set of objectives. "Any questions?" he asked.

"Yes sir," said Talon Waldheim. "When do we attack?"

"Immediately," the captain replied. "The rebels have consolidated their defenses, but we don't have the luxury to build force against them. Battalion reserves will occupy and secure your current locations, reinforcing your units as necessary. I've sent resupply wagons out to your platoons, and MP units to escort your prisoners and the women you captured at the winery."

Garrick didn't protest his assignment, but he already felt weary and the thought of another march in the midday heat wrought protest from every aching muscle. On the way back he struggled to stay awake as the EPT raced along the winding, undulating road.

"Tough luck on your assignment, Overhead," Talon Waldheim said, more sincerely than usual.

"That's what happens when you're the shining star in the company command," Greg Schmidt replied.

Garrick shook his head. "I think Captain Engels has it out for us. It's seven miles from the winery to Helena, and after walking that distance my guys will have to fight through fortified positions on two sides. I can hear their grousing already!"

Greg laughed cynically. "You'll be the monkey wrench in the midst of a meat grinder. They want you in the middle of town so that when Lord Navarro turns his army around and wipes me out, you'll have had a day preparing to make his life miserable, if there's anything left of your platoon by then."

"We didn't come here to die," the younger officer responded. "We came to restore this land to its rightful owners."

Talon smiled and smacked Garrick on the knee. "You're the poster child for Alpha Company! I can already see your face on an Expeditionary Force recruitment flyer!"

Garrick found no humor in that remark, though Talon and Greg thought it funny. He tolerated their teasing because they were his friends, but as Garrick hopped off the EPT at the winery he resolved to prove that his platoon could seize Helena's city hall on schedule. "Don't make me wait for you!" he warned.

*   *   *

Jhiran Vell scampered uphill as fast as her bantam legs could carry her. She arrived at the observatory, crept inside and found Algernon reading through an astronomy text in the cool and quiet planetarium hall. "Holy man!" she called, startling him, "Come quickly!"

Algernon let her put imagery into his mind. His heart pounded and immediately, he put down the book to follow her across the tiled floor. "How long has she been this way?" he asked.

Jhiran didn't know. She flitted around the observatory's pendulum clock, dashed into the oppressive heat outside, spread her wings and glided effortlessly downslope.

The Long Journey: *Reunion*

He raced down the long path, through the aromatic pine forest and into the Velez compound, sweating in exertion and fear. Panting to regain his breath, Algernon burst into his room without knocking. Lady Alexina, who'd heard his approach and thus was not at all surprised to see him, sat in a chair next to his bed, dabbing at Kira's forehead with a damp cloth. The girl looked flushed and delirious as she slept.

Immediately, he averted his eyes and waited for Alexina to acknowledge him.

"Your sister has developed a high fever," the Lithian woman explained in vulgate. "Her body is weakened from drug abuse, and the injuries to her feet have become seriously infected. I've treated her wounds with iodine, but at this point, there is little more I can do."

Algernon worriedly approached his twin. Her feet, now elevated by a stack of pillows, and her soles, stained a dark brown by the iodine, showed evidence of ulceration. He cursed himself, knowing that his preoccupation with avoiding the ongoing conflict between Astrid and Kira made him less diligent about keeping his sister's feet clean than he should have been. "She'll get better, won't she?" he asked.

Alexina stared at him, her dark eyes and flawless face reflecting more doubt than hope. "She's dying, Algernon. You should have told me about this when the two of you first arrived. I've done what I can, but now she's in Allfather's hands. You need to pray."

Algernon's heart ached. The cruel irony of having rescued Kira from those who mistreated her, only to have her succumb to wounds they'd inflicted tore through his soul like a massive, seismic tremor. He knelt and prayed over her, the psittacism of long memorized words rolling reflexively off his tongue. As he prayed, his thoughts wandered through a dark forest of feelings and fears, and hatred for Marco Fang blossomed from a root that reached down into the blackest abyss of his subconscious mind.

Astrid entered the room and joined him, quietly kneeling down. She clasped her hands with his and united with him in the formal prayer, but to Astrid, their entreaty to the Great God carried deep meaning. The ritual of speaking spiritual words in unison carried her soul to an orderly and peaceful mountaintop community where the memory of choral prayers uttered among the faithful wrought sanctuary, far from the reach of warfare.

* * *

The Long Journey: *Reunion*

"Therefore, the only viable options remaining for the rebel forces involve either retreat across the river, or regrouping to seize *Lago Caliente*." Mariel Hougen concluded the formal part of her briefing with Colonel Adler and his staff, waiting to answer their inevitable questions and respond to the colonel's expected criticism.

Sergeant Major Dylan Seller always listened attentively but never said anything during the question period. Mariel wondered what the sergeant major would learn from noncommissioned officers actually serving in the field, as he made the rounds of combat units and interviewed their NCO's in the upcoming days. His information, coming from experienced men actually engaged in battle, likely had a quality to it that differed substantially from her own.

Lieutenant Colonel Stefan Ernst, the battalion Executive Officer and the man responsible for day-to-day operations of the unit, always stared at Mariel. She liked attention, but there was something about the way he stared at her that made her very careful with her words. His demeanor exuded confidence that bordered on arrogance, and he sat like a vulture waiting his turn to pick at a carcass.

Colonel Adler didn't look like a typical Tamarian. A stubble shadow across his shaven face, his dark eyebrows and receding, black hair all hinted of a southern ancestry. Famous for his foul temper, and well known for raging at ineptitude whenever he uncovered less than complete competence, Mariel suspected she'd been assigned to the colonel's staff because of his gentlemanly deference to women.

While he behaved in a courteous manner toward her, Mariel could not rely on her charm and beauty in dealing with him. She knew that he respected sharp analysis, and found the challenge of rising to his high standards very appealing. He didn't care that she was pretty. He wanted her mind, and that fact gave Mariel an electric feeling inside.

"So what makes you think that Navarro will now turn eastward, rather than retreating, or turning to face our forces like you predicted would happen in yesterday's briefing?" he asked in a gravelly voice that seemed more distorted than tonal.

Mariel, already self-conscious of how sweaty she'd become, felt a hot breeze linger for a delicious moment in the stifling command tent. "With our allies successful in cutting off the water supply and our seizure of the large storage facilities this morning, it makes more tactical sense for them to focus on pushing the Abelscinnians off the heights.

The Long Journey: *Reunion*

That's the only force against which they've had any success since crossing the river, and in this heat they'll desperately need water."

Colonel Adler narrowed his eyes and began speaking so rapidly Mariel had no hope of interjecting a comment until he'd completed his critique. "You recommended that we engage before fully consolidating our supply lines in order to relieve pressure on our allies, who are running out of ammunition. We've got men marching to attack Helena with only marginal artillery support, and now you're saying that this is all for nought because Fang is dead in the water and Navarro will press his advantage toward the ridge lines anyway.

"You'd pumped up Navarro as a smart guy with military training. Only a fool would not turn to honor the threat we represent, and he's supposed to be a professional soldier. That was the gist of your presentation yesterday afternoon and I bought your argument because it made good sense. But now, 20 hours later, you've fed me a different line altogether.

"So let me tell you why this briefing of yours smells like a manure pile. If Navarro leaves his flank open there will be nothing stopping us from marching right over his back. Have you suddenly come down with a bad case of stupid, lieutenant?"

"I have not, sir," Mariel replied, unflustered by the attack on her analysis, "nor am I suggesting that Navarro is anything other than a clever and dangerous enemy. I think he'll make a tactical retreat in the hope that we're stretched too thin to pursue him. He's got to know that we're on the ragged edge of our capability to project power at the present time, so if he's going to make a move to seize water resources, he's got to do it now.

"I base my judgment on recent message traffic from our allies and the intelligence our own combat units provided from their engagements this morning." She produced the map that Sergeant Vidders had given Garrick and pointed to the Kamerese word for "water" underscored in various locations, all of which were now out of reach for Navarro's army. "The rebels have a large force in the field, we all know it's hot, and those men have to drink. They have a lot of wine in Helena, but if they drink wine they'll be in no shape to fight. Control over water resources is the singular reason Lord Fang keeps hammering at the Lithians in the south.

"Navarro knows we have a long supply tail and I think he'll gamble that an attack against battle-weary forces protecting the reservoir will be less risky than committing to a two-front scenario with our increasingly capable troops pressing from the north."

Lieutenant Colonel Ernst stopped her by holding out his hand in a manner that looked like he was either pushing something, or trying to constrain her physically. "But in harmony with your analysis from yesterday, the water resources we've just wrested from the rebels this morning would be easier for them to take back, would they not?"

Mariel had been prepared for that kind of remark. "That's not correct for two reasons. The bulk of Navarro's forces are committed against Maidenhair Ridge. Moving men from there to attack us here in sufficient numbers to guarantee success would take at least a day, and our numbers are growing by the hour. Also, we're not yet facing a critical ammunition shortage. It's true that our forward units are moving beyond the limits of heavy rocket support, but if Navarro's army turns toward us and tries to recapture what we've already taken from him, we can pound his forces with artillery in a manner that our allies have never been able to sustain, and the rebels have never experienced. It's more likely that he'll establish supply lanes to the south of our effective artillery range and execute a tactical retreat.

"Once he gains control over *Lago Caliente*, he can use overwhelming force to crush Lord Velez in the south and gain access to an even larger and more reliable water supply before we can consolidate our own logistical lines. As long as Fang stays put, Velez has to keep his forces engaged and Navarro can roll down his northern flank. Once he's done with Lord Velez, Navarro can turn his army around to deal with us."

Mariel watched the lieutenant colonel nod and reach for a glass of water. She then continued with her argument. "Should he elect to retreat across the river, he'll have to re-invade territory he's already conquered at a time when we've had the opportunity to build our forces and resupply our Lithian and Abelscinnian allies. That's going to be a lot harder to do, and he knows it."

Colonel Adler wiped sweat from his brow and frowned, his demeanor reflecting concentration and worry. "What about all the other rebel armies, and that El Caudillo guy?"

"Our Special Forces units report that main rebel army groups are still engaged with the nationals. Once we begin airship operations, we'll be able to keep a close eye on them. But even if they began marching eastward today, it would take them four days to get here. We are the only players in this game, other than Navarro, Fang and Velez. Of that group, our position is, by far, the strongest."

"You'd better be right, lieutenant," the colonel warned. "You'd better be right!"

*   *   *

Brenna accurately read Garrick's facial expression and began re-packing her medical supplies before he announced their departure. She watched him talk to the sergeants, consulting with a map he unfolded from his breast pocket, then he caught her gaze and struggled to control a smile. She always liked that endearing look of his.

"We're leaving?" she inquired.

Garrick nodded. "As soon as the backup troops get here. We're going to take Helena from the rebels."

That meant that her father's forces were in trouble. As a list of potential problems flashed through her mind, the emotions she felt were mirrored in her face. Brenna glanced away to prevent Garrick from seeing her troubled expression. She kept her thoughts unspoken and went to the cistern to pray and refill her nearly empty canteen.

Garrick intended to ask forgiveness for criticizing her bravery in saving Private Nagel, but the words he wanted to form never made it beyond his lips. Something rational in his thinking could not admit wrongdoing when his motivation for chastising her had come from a sincere desire to preserve her life.

He walked back out to the courtyard and stared at her image on the cobblestones. Something unnatural had happened here. Garrick justified Brenna's ability to heal wounds as some kind of innate talent, like her skill as a musician. She'd become more proficient with experience, as if every injury she treated served as practice for the next incident, and this kind of growth made it easier to understand her healing power as a normal–if unusual and exceedingly helpful–facility she naturally possessed.

But the outline of her figure on the pavement defied logic.

He felt Brenna's nearness without hearing her approach. When he looked at her, she was staring at the image on the ground with eyes widened. A shudder raced up her spine as the words to the psalm she'd been repeating flashed into her memory again, but she said nothing, and the magic of that moment vanished as the noise of arriving troops and supplies filled the courtyard.

A collective groan spread among the men as they learned of their new assignment. Odell Unruh complained that midday heat melted all of the chocolate treats he carried to pass out to children along the way. Although supplied to the warriors as a means of easing relations with the Kamerese people, after marching through the refugee camp, no Tamarian soldier had seen a Kamerese child. Odell had eaten most of his provision, but now the inner lining of his backpack had been slimed with chocolate and the other soldiers ribbed him for depriving children of their candy, only to discover the heat had done the same to their own.

Not knowing when they would be re-supplied, each soldier carried as much water and ammunition as possible. The machine cannon crews took turns carrying their weapons, grousing loudly about dragging heavy guns around at the height of the day's heat. They were all tired of marching, and several warriors voiced complaints that they had to chase the Kamerese all over the countryside, rather than waiting for the enemy to engage them on prepared ground.

Oak trees lined long sections of the road leading toward Helena. White scars lingered where bits of bark had been blown off in a running firefight between rebel attackers and the militia forces initially stationed north of the town. Broken branches, scattered leaves, gaps from damage to the tree canopy, burn marks and craters in the road testified to a futile, though valiant, defense. As Third Platoon marched onward, they passed scores of dead men. Bloated, festering bodies stank in the intense heat, attracted flies, scavenging birds and inspired disgust among the Tamarians.

Garrick put Luther Sondheim on point. By now everyone in the platoon, even Brenna, knew about his transgression with the attractive Nordan teenager in the wine cellar, and Luther endured a constant stream of badgering from other soldiers about his indiscretion. While there was nothing mean spirited in this banter, Garrick quietly imagined ways to punish Luther as he listened to their talk.

An hour later, as the weary platoon approached a fruit packing plant on the outskirts of Helena, the distinctive sound of incoming mortars snapped the soldiers into action. Both sergeants yelled for their men to disperse, and as had been planned before leaving the winery, Sergeant Vidders' group went left while Sergeant Ringer's group went right.

The Long Journey: *Reunion*

Four mortar shells landed better than twenty yards away, exploding on the road and among the battle-scarred oaks, creating a haze of red dust and a shower of tree fragments mingled with deadly shrapnel. The next set fell closer, and in the moment between salvos while the Kamerese adjusted their mortar tubes, Garrick's voice rose over the echoing thunder. "Move forward! Go! Go!"

Through the lane between the road and an olive orchard several yards to its west a machine gun and a cadre of riflemen opened fire, spitting a torrent of antimony-hardened lead rounds into Sergeant Ringer's squad. Luther Sondheim went down. Dietrich Skinner went down, and a stray mortar landed near enough to Neville Halvronson to kill him instantly. Eruptions of smoke and fire, hot shards of sharp metal, the screaming whine of flying bullets, a sense of panic and the cries of afflicted soldiers filled the air.

Sergeant Ringer told Kellen Bauer to silence the Kamerese machine gun. The young soldier loaded his rocket launcher and raced down the line of trees on the western side of the road to get a good shot.

As he crouched behind an oak for shelter Garrick evaluated the rebel positions, noting that the ambush had been carefully planned, well-executed, and in all likelihood, the Kamerese significantly outnumbered Third Platoon. They'd fired mortars to drive his troops toward shelter in the orchard, which lay across a drainage ditch, with the machine gun set up to slaughter them as they fled. Rebel riflemen, hidden among the olive trees, would slay any survivors moving in their direction.

But he had no intention of letting that happen. He scribbled a note and sent a messenger back to the winery, then shouted for his men to move further down the road, get out from under the mortar attack, and honor the threat of enemies hidden in the orchard who moved through the trees to flank them. As the messenger pedaled northward Tamarian rifles thundered a response to the rebel violence. Sergeant Ringer's squad took up defensive positions and their lethal fire blunted, stalled, then pushed back the Kamerese advance from the west.

Brenna, waiting anxiously, watched the unfolding carnage with increasing urgency. She wanted to help the stricken Tamarians, but Garrick held her back, not willing to send her into the midst of an ongoing firefight. She wrestled her arm out of his grasp with an irritated expression. "Let me do my job!" she pleaded.

"Wait!" he insisted. "Let me take out that machine gunner first!"

The Long Journey: *Reunion*

But she didn't think Dietrich Skinner had time for that and dashed off to help him.

Bullets swept through the tall, dry grass growing in the drainage ditch and sang through the trees, splintering bark as the machine gunner tracked Brenna's movement. Garrick chambered a round, took careful aim, let out his breath and ever so gently applied pressure to his trigger finger. Nearly one hundred and twenty yards passed almost instantly, as his Tamarian bullet found its mark in the machine gunner's head. A puff of misty blood followed the exit path of his bullet, the gun barrel tilted wildly upward and its feed mechanism jammed, buying a few moments for Brenna to reach the injured soldiers lying in the drainage ditch. Garrick then turned his rifle toward the orchard and fired repeatedly to protect the girl he loved.

Dietrich Skinner had been hit in the neck, his skin was spattered with gore and a huge blood pool warned of his imminent demise. His jaw flexed open and his blue eyes were wide in terror when Brenna kneeled next to him.

"You strong be!" she said to him. "You brave are!" The girl prayed while she kissed her fingers and began her work. A bullet had burst through his submandibular gland, shattered his larynx and ripped through his carotid artery. Despite her best effort, extensive damage and excessive blood loss proved too great for her words and ministrations to save him. Dietrich died with his head slumped against Brenna's right thigh, leaving his young, pregnant wife in Burning Tree to live a lonely, widow's existence.

Sadness washed over Brenna's soul, an old ache that often haunted her dreams and left her feeling broken. She was about to offer a prayer for Dietrich when a Kamerese bullet slammed into her chest, knocking the diminutive girl backward with such force that her feet tumbled over her head as she hit the ground. Brenna cried out as intense pain hammered just below her right collarbone and panicked for a moment when she felt she couldn't inhale. Fumbling in a search for the wound, her fingers found a hot round lodged in her vest. When she tugged on her armor and looked down her blouse, she saw that while the bullet hadn't penetrated, its energy had likely broken a rib.

Brenna rolled over, dropped her head back and mouthed a prayer of gratitude, thankful to remain alive. As she gasped for air, her eyes took in the intense, blue sky, the golden grass heads, green tree tops and the brief vapor trails of speeding bullets whisking above her.

The Long Journey: *Reunion*

For a moment she considered how so much life existed amid so much death, then let her mind drift toward the sound of rifles firing, men shouting and the whoosh of a rocket motor's ignition.

Garrick's voice called her name. She heard his footsteps trampling through the grass and a moment later his shadow fell across her face. "Brenna!" he repeated, his voice brimming with panic. "You're hit! Are you ok?"

Her lungs began working again and she nodded rapidly. She felt his right hand press against her vest, searching for the wound as he knelt beside her. His eyes reflected deep concern, but his worry faded when he realized she'd not been seriously hurt. Brenna saw him sigh in relief and shake his head. He bent to kiss her lips, gave her a stern, visual reprimand, then Garrick flopped down on the inside edge of the ditch and methodically found targets, fired and worked his rifle's bolt action by crossing over the barrel in a left-handed fashion. With the Kamerese machine gun out of action he fired into the orchard with impunity, killing every rebel who dared attempt an advance.

The Lithian girl grunted as she struggled against pain, rolled onto her belly, then crawled toward Luther Sondheim's voice. It took her a while to find where he'd fallen because the dry grass had grown tall and she needed to keep her head down to avoid getting hit.

Kellen Bauer's rocket exploded against the sandbagged machine gun nest, and immediately thereafter Sergeant Ringer's squad advanced into the ditch, forcing the rebels back with devastatingly effective small arms fire. To the Kamerese, who'd never seen surprised troops recover and press their attack, the Tamarians seemed utterly fearless, and a sense of terror spread rapidly among men who'd been confident of an easy victory only moments beforehand.

Sergeant Vidders moved his squad down the road quickly and set up positions among the oak trees adjacent to the fruit packing plant. Thorsten Lehman, operating a shoulder-fired rocket, placed a shot directly into a group of men who were organizing for a counterattack against Sergeant Ringer's troops. The exploding warhead obliterated four rebels, wounded three more, and several others, stunned by Tamarian firepower, began to run. Axel Jung and Lens Mehler, who'd just finished setting up Sergeant Vidders' machine cannon, shot the fleeing rebels and cut every one of them down.

Pointing at Bachman, Hirsch and Decker, Sergeant Vidders motioned them across the road. The four men established positions in the drainage ditch and began firing on rebel snipers shooting from opened windows at the front of the red brick packing plant. Screams emanated from within and soon the enemy guns fell silent.

Another mortar volley landed, but this time significantly behind both Tamarian positions. When Kellen Bauer noticed where the rebel mortar crews had been hiding, he scurried further south along the road–adjacent to Sergeant Vidders and his men–then yelled for Thorsten Lehman, motioned with hand signals toward the location of the enemy mortars, and indicated his desire for the other man's rocket to hit the group on the left. The two warriors loaded their weapons and took aim at the unsuspecting mortar teams.

Garrick met no more resistance as the rebels retreated. In watching how the Kamerese responded, he believed that the battle now hung on what he decided to do next. With perhaps twenty rebels remaining in the orchard, that area seemed key to controlling the battlefield. Noting that Sergeant Vidders' men were now in position to attack the processing plant, he crawled over and called for Sergeant Ringer's attention.

"Form a skirmish line and wheel to the left, through the trees. At the southern edge, set up suppressing fire for Vidders' men!"

Then Garrick grabbed Odell Unruh by the sleeve just as Kellen and Thorsten fired their rockets. "Tell Sergeant Vidders not to attack until we're in position to cover him. I'll give him a signal, and he makes the call on the building. Go!"

Two spectacular explosions ended all Kamerese mortar fire, and from Sergeant Vidders' squad, Tamarian mortars began falling on enemy troops setting up a reinforcement line at the southern edge of the orchard.

After Brenna washed the blood from her hands, she tried to calm Luther's angry outbursts while she untied his helmet strap. Grunting in exertion, wincing in pain, she rolled his body over to examine a bloody spot on the back of his head. Luther grabbed a handful of grass with one hand and slammed the other on the ground, cursing that he hadn't even managed to fire a single shot, behavior Brenna interpreted as indicating he'd not been seriously hurt. She washed the wound with water from her canteen, grateful that Luther kept his hair cut short.

"No move!" she warned, pulling out her boot knife. Quickly and dextrously, Brenna feathered back Luther's hair and examined the place where a bullet had grazed, but not penetrated, his skull. She felt

The Long Journey: *Reunion*

relieved as she prayed, kissed her fingers and healed his flesh. Rolling him over again she searched and found two bullets lodged in his vest, then loosened his armor, unbuttoned his shirt and pressed on his chest to check sensitivity. "Hurt?" she inquired.

Though somewhat embarrassed by her attention and a little surprised that she examined him so thoroughly, Brenna's clinical battlefield demeanor inspired trust in her healing skill. He winced and nodded as she evaluated the damage.

Brenna kissed her fingers, touched his ribs and pulled her hand away. She cinched up his armor again, determining that the soldier's thicker bone mass had not suffered any fractures from blunt trauma. The Tamarian combat vests were tough and saved many lives.

Luther patted the wetness at the back of his head, examined the watery, crimson liquid on his fingers, then rolled onto his side and stared at Brenna fearfully. All the pain he'd felt began fading. Who was this foreign, mercenary girl? Where had the lieutenant found her?

Brenna crawled over to Dietrich Skinner, pulled off his helmet and held it out. "On hat put!" she ordered in her halting fashion, tapping her own head. "You now fight! Brave be!"

Luther grinned, disarmed by the way she spoke. "Thank you, little sister," he said, reaching for the helmet and blowing her a kiss before rejoining the battle.

Garrick, preoccupied with orchestrating his platoon's attack, heard none of this. He saw Luther appear at his side and quickly shoved him toward Sergeant Ringer. On Garrick's signal, the sergeant motioned for pairs of men to form a staggered line and wheel through the orchard to clear out all remaining Kamerese. As the squad fought their way through the trees, he sent Zumwald and Kellerlein toward the western edge of the fruit packing plant to set up their machine cannon.

Odell Unruh arrived at the ditch, out of breath. "Ok... Sergeant ... will wait... for signal!" he managed to say.

Garrick kept Unruh nearby and together they crept down the ditch, following the progress of Sergeant Ringer's squad until the two warriors arrived at the shattered machine gun nest. The firefight among the trees turned into a rout from which the Tamarians emerged unscathed, while many rebels fleeing from the orchard ran into a hailstorm of Tamarian mortar flechette that riddled their unarmored bodies with hot shrapnel.

The Long Journey: *Reunion*

Recognizing the danger of potential fratricide, Garrick spat curses. "Tell the mortar crew to cease fire!" he yelled at Odell Unruh. Sergeant Ringer had to wait until Garrick's message had been delivered and the mortar crew stopped lobbing shells at the Kamerese before the Tamarians could move forward in safety.

Stopping the mortars took a long time, and Garrick swore fiercely because of the delay. But once the shells stopped falling and his men were in position, he ordered suppressing fire, then flashed his pocket mirror toward Sergeant Vidders' location further down the road. Immediately, Bachman, Hurst and Decker charged across the open ground and skidded to a stop at the packing plant's wall. Schiffer, Nussbaum and Lang followed, with Sergeant Vidders bringing up the rear while a flurry of Tamarian gunfire kept rebel heads down.

Private Hurst hurled a grenade into a window. A plinking sound, a momentary delay, and a flash followed by a fountain of shattered glass and a billow of black smoke erupted from within the building. Tamarian soldiers burst through the front door with rifles readied.

Brenna sat back in the ditch and prayed for her own healing. She loosened her armor and slid her left hand beneath her sweaty, cotton combat uniform and melded bone back into place. After re-tightening her vest, she scurried to Garrick's side, reading an increasingly familiar expression of utter ruthlessness and intense concentration on his dirty, sweaty face. She felt like wiping his brow with a cloth, but knew that he disliked motherly attention and further, she didn't want to distract him. Contenting herself with discreet physical contact, she put her hand on his left thigh while he watched the battle. He responded with a quick smile, then clasped his hand around her fingers.

Odell Unruh returned, saw this subtle exchange of affection–the first he'd ever witnessed between his platoon leader and the Lithian girl–and shook his head, annoyed that Lieutenant Ravenwood was fraternizing with the woman he'd secretly dreamed about, himself.

The whir of Zumwald's machine cannon on the far side of the orchard caught Garrick's attention. He turned toward Private Unruh. "Get down there and find out what's going on!"

Odell rolled his eyes, annoyed that he had to play messenger boy when he really wanted to get in on the fight, but he obeyed.

Oswin Schiffer, an intensely thin member of Sergeant Vidders' squad, came to the front door and signaled for Udo Barth, the squad's medic. He then turned toward Garrick and gave the hand signals that meant: "First floor secured. Engaging for control of second floor. Standby."

Garrick acknowledged and warned Sergeant Ringer to get his men ready. With Sergeant Vidders in control over the assault, Ringer's squad served as their back up and needed to respond quickly to any request for help.

The sounds of gunfire faded and a protracted silence ensued. Odell returned and squatted next to his platoon commander, speaking only after he'd regained control of his breathing. "Zumwald took down a whole pile of rebels who tried to escape. He doesn't know..."

At that moment the men from Sergeant Vidders' squad began running out of the packing plant, yelling for everyone to clear out. Brenna heard the words for "wired, blow" and "run," but Garrick had already evaluated the situation and drawn his own conclusion.

The young lieutenant shouldered his rifle, took hold of Brenna with his left hand, slapped Odell on the back and shouted toward Sergeant Ringer while he pulled the Lithian girl away. "Fall back now! Go! Go!"

A deep rumble shook the ground, stirring dust. Bright flashes, fire, glass and smoke belched from the packing plant windows, followed by an enormous concussion and a tempest of sounds that ranged from the thunder of rapidly expanding gases to the twisting of metal, the shattering of brick, the groan of collapsing walls and the whistle of high velocity debris whisking through the air.

Moments later, the ground where a fruit packing plant had once stood became a smouldering graveyard where flames flashed through dark swirls of smoke, ash and dust. Although all the Tamarians made it out safely, an unknown number of Kamerese perished and remained buried in the rubble.

Silence fell upon the scene after all the dust settled. With the surrounding area firmly in Tamarian control, Garrick sent Sergeant Vidders and a handful of his squad to scout the approach to Helena, and had a team of able-bodied men gather the fallen rebels and collect their weapons and ammunition. Company Alpha's Third Platoon–of which only 26 men remained fit for action–had slain 83 Kamerese and wounded 12 others in taking the ruined packing plant.

Garrick listened as Kurt Nussbaum, who was fluent in Southern Kamerese, interviewed and translated for the survivors. The young lieutenant became astonished at the arrogance of several prisoners, who cursed and threatened the Tamarians for intervening in Kameron's affairs. When asked to provide information on the number and disposition of troops defending Helena, no rebel prisoner offered anything substantive.

"They will kill you all!" one of them sneered. "May your corpses bloat in broad daylight! They will rape your Lithian whore before your impotent eyes!"

"You will never defeat the people of Kameron!" cried another. "We rise like the sea and you will be drowned in our merciless tide."

"I will taste your flesh!" said a third. "And I will dine in front of your mother!"

These responses filled Garrick's heart with loathing. Though he didn't think it was right to hate anyone, Dietrich Skinner, Neville Halvronson, Holger Faust and Volkard Wexler had been good men slain to save the decent people of Kameron from bottom feeders like these.

"Get them patched up," he ordered, walking away. "And give them food and water."

Kurt Nussbaum stared at Garrick. "Are you kidding me, LT?" he responded, incredulously.

Garrick paused and turned, speaking with a calm demeanor that belied the rage he felt inside. "I said medical attention, food and water. Don't ask for a third explanation." The young lieutenant strode purposely over to the messenger he'd previously sent back to the winery, who'd returned with a response that required his immediate attention.

The prisoners reserved a very intense contempt for Brenna, jeering and spitting in her direction when she approached to administer aid, until Harmon Grossman intervened, gently pulled her away and threatened to slowly kill every one of the rebels with the dull fork in his rucksack if they didn't settle down. Udo Barth came over to tend their wounds, performing his task wordlessly.

Brenna didn't understand the contempt directed at her, and it hurt because she would have cared for the Kamerese wounded with the same degree of tenderness she offered the Tamarians, had they allowed her to minister to them.

The Lithian girl put aside her own pain and returned to the Tamarians, healing several minor injuries–mostly cuts from flying glass–knowing that some of the men who approached her for care were more interested in attention than treatment. She'd seen this behavior many times in the past. After experiencing intense combat, men who initially shunned her as a foreigner or leered at her beauty would wait patiently in line while she ministered to others, just for the opportunity to feel her touch or linger for awhile in her company.

The most important difference between these warriors and the ones she'd come to know while fighting the Azgaril last winter centered upon Garrick's role as their commander. Because every man respected his leadership, they initially offered greater respect for her, and that made the transition from being a foreigner with awkward speech to an integral member of the unit easier than had been the case in the past.

Just after Garrick read the note given to him by the runner, he seemed anxious and nervous, though he didn't share the contents of the message with anyone. Sergeant Vidders returned from scouting Helena and Sergeant Ringer joined him. "The place is a fortress," the sweating non-com reported. "The sewage treatment plant is overflowing and it reeks. We saw a few rebels standing guard near the school, but the main street is blocked with barricades and swarming with Kamerese.

"Lieutenant Schmidt and his men are hunkering down in a vineyard across the road from the school, just beyond a mine field. They've got com lines established with Company Beta on the left flank for artillery support. Lieutenant Waldheim has his men in place on the far side of the sewage lagoon. So everyone's waiting for us."

"I take it they encountered no resistance then," Garrick muttered. "Very well. Tell the men to load up. We've got a support unit heading our direction who can take care of the prisoners. Leave Sondheim and Wagner here to guard them."

And thus, Third Platoon ended up being the last unit in place before the Tamarian attack on Helena commenced.

* * *

Algernon left his room so that Alexina and Astrid could wipe Kira's overheated, sweating body down with wet, cool towels. He sat cross-legged in the hall, with his head in his hands, tears in his eyes and an ache for Kira throbbing through every nerve. A debilitating maelstrom of raw feeling, driven by the guilt of long neglecting his twin sister stirred a tempest of disturbing, nameless fears that swept through his consciousness and beat down his swollen pride. Through this storm of strong emotions Algernon felt helpless and utterly

The Long Journey: *Reunion*

humiliated, weeping in shame on the hard tile floor of a stranger's guest house, in a foreign land, far from home.

The thought of Kira dying in this place inspired a cascade of regrets that flooded from the farthest reaches of his memory. He'd been so focused on his own wants and needs, so driven to prove himself worthy of love, he hadn't taken the time to show Kira how much he cared for her. Instead he subjected her to interminable criticism, ordered her around as if she were his personal servant, then ignored her whenever she expressed a need for him. At the Temple, he'd been so focused on his lust for Marie that he hadn't even heard Kira pleading for his time and protection.

Though she'd been the object of their mother's favor, this maternal affection came at the cost of domination and unending, emotionally manipulative demands. The sense of relief Kira felt in their flight from Deception Creek covered a void in her soul, a desperate need for love without conditions that Algernon well understood, but had been too self-absorbed to fill. As the girl transformed into a young woman she became ripe for a predator's picking, and Algernon, who could have defended his sister at the Temple and saved her from evil men like Marco by simply listening and caring about her concerns, hadn't even known about her disappearance until Astrid begged for his help.

Jhiran Vell trotted in, clutching a wooden bowl filled with cherries. She sat next to Algernon and ate in a rather noisy fashion, sloppily forcing more fruit into her mouth than was reasonable, given her size. She spat cherry pits into the same bowl without thought. Red juice stained her fingertips and dribbled down her chin. The gwynling held the bowl out to Algernon, offering him fruit as if oblivious to his sorrow.

Algernon wished to wallow in his misery alone, but Jhiran had wormed her way into his heart and he found it impossible to remain upset at her. He accepted the bowl, and in the moment he looked into her large, brown eyes she read his thoughts and filled his mind with a sense of understanding and kindness.

"Be the holy man!" she said.

The young monk looked at her with a quizzical expression on his face. "You know what I am," he replied, confused and a little bit hurt by her words.

The Long Journey: *Reunion*

Jhiran stood and stared intensely. "Be the holy man," she repeated. "You know what I mean!" Then she turned away, opened the door and went back outside, leaving the fruit bowl on the floor.

Indeed, he knew. High Priest Volker once told him that the essence of priesthood centered upon selflessness and service, but Algernon had rejected his counsel. Jhiran had been calling him "holy man" since they first met, but only now did he realize that she'd done this as a kind of invocation, a call to action that he'd not understood because he'd assumed she was only marginally intelligent. How often had he done this? Perhaps he'd been rejecting advice simply because he didn't like hearing what more experienced people–from High Priest Volker, to Astrid and Jawara–told him.

"Your path will become clear in time," Dmitri had said, and now, weeks later with his sister's life hanging in the balance, he understood the older monk's wisdom.

Astrid appeared at the door, her face reflecting a now familiar sadness. "She's asking for you," the priestess told him.

Algernon rose and dried his face on his sleeve. He gently lifted Astrid's chin and looked into her worried eyes, wishing he could offer some kind of reassurance. In a moment measured by a single breath he thought she might lean into his embrace, but instead, Astrid slid past him and scurried upstairs, the sound of her sandaled feet slapping first against ceramic tile, then clomping on lumber as she retreated upstairs.

Alexina rose as he entered. She strode toward him and brought her hand to his cheek, lifting his respectfully averted eyes to her own. "Have faith and pray," she said. "Allfather is compassionate. I'll be in my house if you need me." As the diminutive, pregnant Lithian woman walked out of the building Algernon watched the grace of her motion and found it hard to believe that she was 70 years old.

Kira reached for him weakly. "Be with me, brother!" she said.

Algernon came to her side, occupying the chair Alexina had been sitting in. Its leather felt warm. "How are you feeling?" he asked.

Though her face reflected the effects of her fever, Kira quivered. "I'm cold," she replied. "I'm so cold!"

He placed his hand on her forehead, sensing her elevated temperature, but he didn't want to say anything obvious about her condition. "Be strong, sister! Pull through this so we can go home."

"Where's home?" she replied. "I have no home."

The Long Journey: *Reunion*

Algernon drew closer. "That's not true," he said. "You're home is in my heart. We belong together. Garrick is coming soon, and when he does, we'll be reunited as a family."

"Garrick," she breathed, almost prayerfully. "Garrick won't come. Once he learns what's happened to me, once he knows what I've become, he won't love me anymore!"

"That's not true!" Algernon responded. "Nothing will ever change the undeniable fact that you are and always will be his little sister, the object of his concern and fondest affection.

"He's coming with an army, Kira. They're going to put an end to the fighting, and we'll be together soon. Be strong and hold on!"

She looked at him with tired eyes and squeezed his hand. Something in her expression changed as she appraised her twin brother, and the sparkle of her intelligence returned for a moment. "I'd given up on living," she said softly. "I thought I'd fallen between the cracks, into a secret prison of my own making, a place of high walls, torture and pain, from which I could never escape. I thought that nobody would care if I lived or died, so I let myself go and took comfort in the bliss of every opium high.

"But when I saw you again, something in my heart beat a little faster. When you came for me, that fear of unworthiness I felt faded in the expression I saw on your face. You searched for me, found me and took me out of my prison. You rescued me from people who always reminded me that I was worth nothing, that I'd become a cheap whore." Kira's grey eyes welled with tears that she didn't bother to stop. "Thank you, brother. Thank you for loving me! I'm so sorry for causing you all this trouble."

Algernon lifted her into his embrace, wrapping his strong arms around her gaunt shoulders. His mind drifted into a brief and sincere prayer, imploring the Great God to somehow preserve his twin sister's life and give them the chance to start over again.

*   *   *

"I don't understand what they're doing," Lynden replied, ducking beneath the beam that led outside. Though the underground bunker baked under the Daystar's heat, the air beyond it felt like the inside of a kiln. "They've been sitting there for hours now, and even their artillery has fallen silent."

The Long Journey: *Reunion*

Aril, one of Lynden's adult nephews, shook his head. "Perhaps Allfather has granted them the sense to quit after their failed assault this morning."

Lynden gazed through his binoculars, unable to tell whether or not Lord Fang's army actually remained in place. He could see movement behind their hastily erected barricades, and the banners that marked their positions remained aloft on their poles, but limp in the unmoving air. Several teams of men were digging for water near the riverbank, occasionally shooing away seagulls and ravens congregating nearby. "This is all along the front?" he inquired.

Aril nodded this time. "We thought they might move north to reinforce Lord Navarro's forces, but they're either sitting in their trenches–doing nothing–or they're sort of melting away to the west."

"Who told you that the river is dry?" Lord Velez inquired.

"I checked with Gowyr's men before coming up here. They sent a scouting party south this morning and returned a short time ago. The water level has been dropping all day, and by an hour or so after noon all of the remaining pools had pretty well dried up. Gowyr said there are dead fish everywhere."

That explained the birds. "What's our ammunition status?"

"That's another enigma, uncle. I've been keeping track and we should have distributed the last cases already, but every time I go up to the ammo dump, there's always one more crate waiting there."

Lynden lifted his eyebrows, not quite surprised. "How many times have you checked?"

Aril gave an impish smile that made his dark blue eyes sparkle. "Twice, but Cedric, Govannan and Evan told me the same thing. It's utterly inexplicable."

Lynden put his hand on Aril's shoulder. "Well then!" he said heartily. "May Allfather be praised!"

*   *   *

Pain returned as Brenna strung her bow. She might not have been thorough enough when healing the damage to her ribs, or maybe her collarbone had also been cracked by the bullet impact. Whatever the reason, she had no time to worry about discomfort now. Brenna placed two steel-tipped arrows in her sweaty fingers and tried to screen

The Long Journey: *Reunion*

out the distraction of Tamarian warriors watching while she mentally calculated the distance to her targets.

Garrick came up with the idea for her to take out the sentries standing guard in front of Helena's school gymnasium. She'd seen Sergeant Vidders shake his head and Sergeant Ringer roll his eyes, but neither man had ever seen her fire a bow. Garrick's unorthodox attack plan required the platoon to cross the school grounds and get into a treed green belt without being noticed. Brenna couldn't afford to miss.

She didn't.

Though the Lithian maiden had slain her enemies many times before, she never liked doing so and only agreed use her bow on this occasion because the battered, outnumbered platoon desperately needed to accomplish its mission quickly, with minimal casualties. Garrick believed that stealth favorably inclined the odds for success, and using her bow, Brenna skillfully dispatched two sentries in near silence.

Sergeant Ringer cursed quietly. "You're full of surprises, girl!" he whispered.

The platoon members scuttled across an open area in five groups of four, with Garrick and Brenna following, and assembled on the gymnasium's northern wall. Brenna dropped her backpack, climbed onto Harmon Grossman's shoulders and hoisted herself onto the roof carrying only her bow and quiver, with Odell Unruh–the soldier who secretly admired her–following with a rope and his rifle.

Odell watched Brenna peer over the western edge of the roof. She turned back to him holding up three fingers, then made a motion over her eyes as if looking through binoculars. She swept her hand over her face, indicating that she saw three rebels outside, but none were visible through the windows. Odell relayed this message to Garrick below, and immediately, Sergeant Ringer's squad crept to the northeast corner of the building, their rifles ready for action while they waited.

Sergeant Vidders served as the rear guard, ensuring that the platoon didn't get an unwelcome surprise from the trees behind them, or from Dry Leaf Street–the main road through the center of town–several dozen yards to their west. He also had men watching the gymnasium door, in case someone unexpectedly emerged from inside.

Brenna felt miserable and sweaty as intense heat rose from the clay tiles beneath her feet. She picked four arrows out, holding two in her right hand and laying the others on the hot roof. She aimed, fired twice, and as she picked up her second set of arrows, Odell gave Garrick the signal for his platoon to advance.

Ziggy Hoenzaer turned the corner and crouched with his rifle pointed to the south and his finger resting slightly to the right of his trigger. Otis Krieger stood over him, the tension of imminent danger manifest in rapid, shallow breaths that he struggled to control. Harmon Grossman and Imre Zumwald dashed across the walkway and leaned up against the old school building just as Brenna's swift and silent arrow took out the third sentry.

The squad advanced in a state of hair trigger tension, and as they moved forward, Sergeant Vidders moved his men into position to cover them. They'd practiced this carefully orchestrated maneuvering many times in training, and moving this way enabled Third Platoon to wind their way through the school without a single word spoken.

Odell tied his rope around the gymnasium's chimney, then tested it against his own weight before offering it to Brenna. She descended, waited for Odell to follow, then he threw the rope back onto the roof so that no one else could use it. The two of them scurried through the school compound with Sergeant Vidders' squad following.

When Sergeant Nathan Ringer saw the accuracy of Brenna's firing, he paused, astonished that she'd hit every rebel precisely in the throat, preventing any of them from crying out. While the waify girl didn't look like a fighter, the way she handled that weapon deepened the sergeant's respect and appreciation of her skill.

Between the buildings that lined Dry Leaf Street to the west and Zinfandel Avenue to the east, the Township of Helena maintained a pleasant parkland forest filled with live oak and sycamore trees. Just before Third Platoon began crossing the school's ill-maintained athletic field, sporadic small arms fire rattled from positions behind them and the shriek of artillery shells arced overhead–rising from the south and falling toward the north–as rebel guns pounded the Tamarian positions.

A series of deep and powerful explosions shattered the air, rattling windows and frightening birds into flight. Between the crash and roar of exploding ordnance, the distinctive whir of Tamarian machine cannon and the voluminous clatter of Kamerese rifle fire testified to a fierce gun battle developing several dozen yards to the north.

Sergeant Ringer looked at Garrick, waiting for him to make a decision. "What's it gonna be, lieutenant?" he asked.

The Long Journey: *Reunion*

Garrick pondered for a moment. Greg Schmidt's men were taking that fire and a simple change of direction could bring Third Platoon to their aid, perhaps saving lives in the process. On the other hand, he'd been specifically ordered to take Helena's City Hall and had fought two engagements against the rebels without the benefit of anyone's assistance. Further, he believed that sudden, overwhelming action against the enemy's command center would save far more life than Lieutenant Schmidt's platoon represented. Even though Greg was his friend and likely would have appreciated the help, Garrick made a cold-hearted, rational decision and pointed south. "Go!" he ordered.

Sergeant Ringer nodded and sent his men running in spread pairs across the field, with several seconds between each group and waiting soldiers covering the advance with readied rifles. This was the most dangerous movement the platoon had undertaken thus far, but because of the rebels remained preoccupied with heavy fighting to their north, no one fired at Garrick's men and every one of them made it safely into the central grove without being detected.

After catching his breath, Garrick moved among the trees for three hundred yards, carefully examining several houses and the back of the city library to the west, as well as a community center and museum to the east, before pausing in the overgrown shrubbery behind the city hall. The building had four porticos, one facing each direction, with a paved courtyard and small garden at the bottom of marble steps. Nearly every double-hung window had been opened to provide ventilation and relief from the stifling, afternoon heat.

Brenna examined her new targets while Sergeant Vidders pointed to various windows and doorways within line-of-sight that his squad would have to cover. They set up their machine cannons and loaded their rocket launchers for action. Sergeant Ringer had his assault team ready when Brenna let her arrows fly.

After a brief, whispered flight, one arrow found its mark in the throat of a rebel warrior sheltered beneath the rear portico. He gasped, knelt on the marble and tumbled down the back stairs, attracting the attention of another who met his demise half a heartbeat later. Two more rebel soldiers emerged from the glass doors to find out what was going on, and Brenna took both of them out too.

Sergeant Ringer shook his head in astonishment. "Who needs us?" he grunted toward Garrick. "She's a one girl army!"

The Long Journey: *Reunion*

"Are you leading the assault, sergeant, or do I have to do it for you?" Garrick replied.

Sergeant Ringer muttered something under his breath, then slapped Harmon Grossman and Imre Zumwald on the back to initiate their advance. Once the men reached the portico, Ziggy Hoenzaer and Otis Krieger followed. The Tamarians took up positions covering the entrance, pointing their rifles into the building. As Kellen Bauer and Odell Unruh raced upstairs, Grossman and Krieger opened the double doors and Tamarians charged inside to begin wresting control of the city hall from the enemy.

Gunfire erupted from within. As the rest of the squad pushed into the building, a crescendo of violence rattled windows. Shouts, screams and the noise of battle attracted the attention of rebels occupying the nearby library and museum.

Suddenly, pandemonium erupted.

A large group of enemy reserve troops, camped in a staging area north of Maidenhair Avenue three hundred yards to the south, quickly alerted, formed a skirmish line, and moved toward the Tamarian positions at 108 steps per minute. Kamerese mortars began falling within the oak grove, preceding their advance.

Sergeant Vidders' men opened fire and a ferocious gun battle ensued. Rebel troops occupying the library and museum dashed outside to counterattack, where their intentions were stymied by devastating machine cannon discharge that utterly destroyed three separate attempts to engage Garrick's battered unit. As rebel bodies piled up outside the building, follow-on troops retreated inside to seek shelter.

The rebel skirmish line moved into range and opened fire. Within moments, the warriors of Third Platoon found themselves cut off from contact with other Tamarians, surrounded by a much larger–if rather disorganized–force, and utterly consumed by the desperate task of trying to stay alive. The engagement disintegrated into a confused melee of flying bullets, exploding ordnance, dust, fire and smoke, and the moans of wounded and dying men.

Sergeant Vidders cursed, hoping that his lieutenant's luck would hold, and that they'd brought enough ammunition along to fight the rebels off. Despite the overwhelming number of enemy troops rallied against them, the Tamarian soldiers kept their nerve and held on, firing steadily, reloading and firing again.

The Long Journey: *Reunion*

Garrick picked his targets quickly, worried that the swelling, multidirectional Kamerese counterattack moved the momentum of the engagement dangerously in the enemy's favor. He screamed at his men to make every round count. The machine cannon sang its high-pitched dirge, precision rifle fire cracked, the whisk of rocket motors and the crump of Tamarian mortars rose in a deadly chorus that cut down great swaths of advancing rebels, destroyed their organization and sapped the will of follow-on troops to continue. Survivors soon began running in the opposite direction.

Heavy Kamerese artillery shells fell on buildings at the northern edge of town, crashing into the school, the community center and many of the houses lining Zinfandel Avenue. Smoke belched into the sky and fire spread through the dry grasses and fallen leaves near the buildings. What began as the enemy's tactical retreat changed rapidly into a rout as Greg Schmidt's First Platoon captured the community center south of the school that Garrick's men had passed through earlier. A few moments later, scores of enemy soldiers began running through an open area adjacent to the oak grove, their faces fixed in terror.

Axel Jung and Lens Meller whirled their machine cannon northward and slaughtered dozens of rebels who were racing toward them. The spinning barrels spat .70 caliber Giant Slayer rounds that lifted men off the ground and tossed them backwards on impact. Outgunned, the terrified Kamerese turned and fled westward, toward Dry Leaf Street and the commercial sector that lay on its western edge, only to find themselves facing the flank of Talon Waldheim's Second Platoon and more well-armed, well-trained Tamarians.

Sergeant Vidders' men kept steady pressure on the library, the upper floors of the city hall, the museum to their west, and the fire station to the southwest. Garrick lost track of time, but soon realized that fighting inside the city hall died down. Sergeant Ringer's men were now firing at the rebels from the upper floors of the building, Otis Krieger appeared at the back door, screamed for Garrick and indicated with hand signals they'd gained control of their objective. He motioned for the lieutenant to come quickly.

Brenna followed, not knowing what else to do, as Garrick scampered up the marble steps leading to the back entrance. Inside she saw a group of disarmed rebels–some of whom had been wounded–laying face down on the floor, their wrists bound with their belts, and Kellen Bauer standing over them with his rifle at the ready.

The Long Journey: *Reunion*

Twelve dead Kamerese lay near the staircase leading up to the second floor. Pools of blood coagulated on the dark tile.

Garrick walked toward the mayor's office, a large room lined with book cases and a map of the region, where Sergeant Ringer, Ziggy and Harmon stood guard over four nervous men. Papers littered the mayor's desk, as if the men occupying the office had been planning something and were taken by surprise when the Tamarians attacked. The youngest of the prisoners seemed to recognize Garrick and quivered fearfully, while the other men appraised the young lieutenant with a mix of fear and disgust.

Outside, the waxing sounds of heavy artillery, small arms and machine cannon fire added a sense of urgency to the proceedings. The nearby explosion of a Tamarian rocket warhead cracked the window glass and jarred everyone's nerves. Most of the language being shouted outside was Tamarian, and the voices sounded angry, rather than desperate. Sergeant Vidders had established firm control of the surroundings.

"Who are they?" Garrick asked, regaining his composure.

"They're not talking, but we think one of them is Navarro," Sergeant Ringer replied.

Garrick turned to Otis Krieger. "Get Nussbaum up here."

As Otis retreated, Brenna stood on her tiptoes to get a look over Garrick's shoulder. Her eyes widened. "That's Nemesio Fang," she whispered in his ear. "The younger man's his son, Marco."

Garrick turned his eyes onto the young man. "You're sure?"

"I saw him in the cafeteria at the university. That's him."

Rage boiled from within Garrick's soul and it took every bit of self-control he could muster to avoid beating the drug-dealing fop to a pulp with the butt end of his rifle. He slowly, deliberately moved closer. "You're Marco Fang, aren't you?" he inquired, speaking Tamarian in the hope that the other Kamerese wouldn't understand.

The young man said nothing in response, but he trembled like a tree shaken in a great wind.

"You're afraid of me," Garrick observed. "You're afraid because I look like my little sister. You know my sister, don't you?"

Marco nodded slowly.

"I'll deal with you shortly, but in the meantime you're going to cooperate with me, and rest assured, your pathetic life absolutely depends on doing exactly as I say."

The Long Journey: *Reunion*

Marco fell to the floor, begging for mercy. "Please spare my life!" he cried. "Please don't hurt me!"

"You don't deserve the spit from my mouth!" Garrick replied, stepping close enough to the young man that he could have ground Marco's face into the tile by moving a single foot.

Marco couldn't lift his eyes from the floor. "Anything!" he breathed. "I'll tell you anything you want!"

"Get up!" Garrick ordered.

Marco slowly lifted himself from the ground. His pants were soaking wet and his face reflected shame.

"Point to Lord Navarro!" Garrick spat.

Trembling, yet reluctantly, Marco pointed at one of the other men seated near a bookcase.

"Tell him to kneel in front of the desk."

Marco complied, and the older man's eyes burned at the betrayal. "What do you want of me?" Lord Navarro asked, speaking vulgate so that Garrick could understand him directly. Contempt lingered in the warlord's tone.

Garrick motioned to Sergeant Ringer, who moved over to the desk, pushed aside a map and some other documents, then pulled out several sheets of paper and a pen. "Surrender. Order your men to lay down their arms at the front of this building. Make three copies, and place your seal on each of them."

"I will not surrender to a mere boy!" the older man snapped.

Garrick chambered a round, willing to put a bullet through the man's head right then and there had the principles of conduct he'd learned in officer's training not constrained him. "I have orders to kill you if you don't cooperate. At my signal, this town will be laid waste with a sustained rocket bombardment if I don't report back with proof of your surrender." This was a lie, but Navarro didn't know that, and Garrick told the story with such a straight face the Kamerese warlord believed him.

"If you kill me, my men will continue to fight," Navarro replied. "They will kill you before you get your message out."

"Your men are wetting their pants and running in terror!" Garrick replied with an icy stare. "We have the upper hand, and you're in a rather weak position to make threats. You and I both know this is not your land anyway, so why not spare yourself and your men certain death? Write and sign the order now."

Lord Navarro paused, then reached for the pen. "Very well," he said. "But this is dishonorable, and not the way that gentlemen conduct their affairs."

Garrick thought of the displaced citizens huddling in the refugee camp along the Tualitin River. He thought of innumerable atrocities, broken lives, ruined vineyards, damaged orchards, the destroyed packing plant and imagined the homes and businesses flattened by Kamerese artillery. He thought of the men from his platoon who'd given their lives to stop the rebels' invasion. He thought of their widows and grieving mothers. And finally, glaring at Marco, he thought of his own sister, Kira, before returning his attention to Lord Navarro. "You're no gentleman," he retorted.

Brenna held her breath. That dangerous demeanor she'd seen carefully cultivated in Garrick's heart simmered beneath the calm surface of his controlled conduct. Had Lord Navarro refused the order to surrender, she worried that Garrick would have slain him coldly.

Lord Fang stared at her, and Marco wept uncontrollably while the thunder of Kamerese and Tamarian artillery crashed dangerously closer. Though Third Platoon had captured its objective, Garrick's hold on victory depended on how well the Kamerese believed his threat. Brenna backed into the hall and breathed deeply to quell her fear, praying that Garrick's plan would stop the fighting.

Kurt Nussbaum dashed inside, out of breath, inquiring about where he was needed. Brenna motioned him into the mayor's office.

Garrick held out one of the surrender documents signed by Lord Navarro. "Please check this," he said.

Kurt read through Navarro's orders and nodded. "It looks real. It will do," he replied.

Garrick motioned for him to come down the hallway. He pointed at one of the prisoners and ordered Kellen to unbind him. Speaking through Kurt Nussbaum, Garrick gave the prisoner instructions.

"Remember your friends, here," he warned. "Take this document to every artillery battery and every rebel unit to the east and south of this place. Tell them that if they don't comply, Tamarian forces will unleash a sustained, heavy rocket attack that will annihilate every rebel unit within a fifteen-mile radius of this place. And further, if those big guns aren't silent within five minutes, I will report to my commander, the rocket attack will commence immediately, and you and all your friends will die in it. Do you understand?"

The Long Journey: *Reunion*

The prisoner nodded in terror, then departed in haste to do the Tamarian officer's bidding.

Three minutes later, Garrick did the same with the second set of orders, this time telling the prisoner to take the orders along Dry Leaf Street and Water Lane, along the bank of the Virgin River. "I want all the barricades cleared and emptied. I want to see rebel troops laying down their weapons at the front of this building within five minutes, or every one of you will die."

Sergeant Vidders brought several slain enemy soldiers to the city hall and placed their bodies in strategic places. Ziggy forced Navarro to sit in a chair on the front portico and guarded the warlord with his rifle loaded and ready. Several minutes later, the Kamerese rebels began lining up at Helena's city hall. Kurt Nussbaum, using a megaphone he'd found inside, repeated disarmament instructions. Sergeant Ringer had Zumwald and Kellerlein man a machine cannon on the portico to make certain the rebel soldiers complied.

After dropping off their weapons and ammunition, Sergeant Ringer had the rebel troops herded into the theater on Zinfandel Avenue. Sergeant Vidders' men watched over the prisoners uneasily, worried that if the Kamerese figured out how thin the margin of victory had been, a concerted effort on the part of surrendering rebels might have turned the tables. However, the Tamarians learned later that the rebels–who had never faced a professional fighting force in the past and dreaded the threat of heavy rocket warheads falling on them again–feared the northern warriors intensely, and not a single enemy soldier in the immediate area resisted the call to yield his arms.

Within four minutes, the Kamerese artillery fell silent, the Tamarian guns followed, and shortly thereafter a sense of calm settled upon the township. Many of the rebels seemed relieved that the fighting had ended.

Afterward, Garrick sent Odell Unruh back to the winery on a bicycle with one of the surrender documents and a message for Captain Engels, then Karsten Bachman to contact Greg Schmidt's platoon and Meinhard Hurst to look for Talon Waldheim's men.

About half an hour later, Karsten returned with a troubled expression on his face and found Garrick studying a map in the mayor's office. "I'm sorry to tell you this, LT," Karsten began. "I know he was your buddy. Lieutenant Schmidt got hit by an artillery shell and died during the assault. His platoon took a real beating from those Kamerese guns."

Shock washed over Garrick's weary soul. Greg Schmidt had always treated him with kindness, and for the second time in less than a year, Garrick faced the loss of a good friend in combat. The young lieutenant struggled to control the involuntary tears brimming in his eyes and had to retreat upstairs for solitude, where he wept alone.

Tamarian troops from Company Beta, after hearing news of the rebel surrender, marched into Helena to supplement the Company Alpha warriors who'd successfully taken the town. Within two hours Tamarian soldiers consolidated their hold and disarmed over 500 rebels. An hour later, more troops from the battalion reserves entered the soldier-swollen village and the surrender process hastened.

Brenna kept herself busy treating wounded warriors from other units. Late in the afternoon, after Captain Engels arrived to take command of the situation, Garrick found Brenna and pulled her aside. She washed away bloodstains on her hands and wiped them dry on a towel she'd used several times for that purpose.

"How far is it to your parents' house from here?" he asked.

"It's a few miles east of here," she replied. "Why?"

Garrick pulled out the note from Mariel Hougen he'd been carrying since they left the packing plant. "My siblings staying are there," he said. "Algernon says Kira really needs your help."

"Can you leave?" she inquired.

"I've explained the situation to Captain Engels," Garrick responded. "He gave me orders to go and contact the commander of your father's forces with news of the surrender–and to see my brother and sister–under the condition that I must be back within three hours. Sergeant Vidders told me that a friend of his in Company Beta owes him a favor. He said he could arrange to get us up there in an EPT."

"That sounds reasonable. When shall we go?"

He seemed anxious. "Right now. The EPT's waiting for us at the temple, just up Maidenhair Avenue."

As they walked eastward, through the oak grove, Brenna sensed his troubled spirit and felt him reach for her hand. They turned south, toward Maidenhair Road and the promised EPT awaited them at the entrance to a small temple on the southeastern edge of town. This was the building Greg Schmidt's platoon had been tasked to control, but it now lay in the hands of a unit from Company Beta.

The Long Journey: *Reunion*

Their driver, a warrant officer who chewed gum incessantly, seemed quite laconic about driving through territory still controlled by the enemy. "We've already sent patrols up the road," he said. "The rebels have no fight left, now that we've got Navarro."

Brenna felt the exhilarating sense of acceleration press her into the back seat, and the wind created by the EPT's motion felt refreshing on her sweaty skin. Loosened strands of her hair drifted in the mechanically-induced breeze, and the thrill of moving quickly along the dirt road overwhelmed any fear she might have felt about traveling through rebel-held territory. She took off her armor and loosened the two uppermost buttons of her blouse, while Garrick, weary and emotionally drained, simply fell asleep.

As the landscape ascended toward Maidenhair Ridge, the impact of heavy shelling and the deep scars of defensive trenches marred the gently rolling hills. Most of the vineyards that once graced this area had been utterly destroyed, and the red soil, cratered and torn, lay barren beneath the hot sky. Disarmed Kamerese soldiers, under the watchful eyes of victorious Tamarians, stared as they passed by.

The electric vehicle crested a hill and turned toward the south. On the last rise–a finger of ridge line still covered in conifer and hardwood trees–stood an old, walled villa. Several dozen yards in front of its gate, a roadblock had been erected. Four Lithian women with automatic rifles appeared. Garrick awakened when he felt the EPT's motion stop.

Brenna removed her helmet, and let down her hair. A wave of surprise washed over these women, whose delight transcended the language barrier. Their joy and laughter echoed across the valley, and suddenly, Garrick became the object of their admiration.

He smiled a lot, accepted their kisses on his cheeks and forehead with more than minor embarrassment, but had no idea what they said because the women spoke so quickly and excitedly. When the EPT entered the Velez compound, other Lithian women poured into the courtyard and pulled Garrick and Brenna out of the vehicle.

In the midst of their celebrating, the double door to the main house opened and Lady Alexina Velez emerged. She held her arms wide, smiled, and scurried toward her daughter. "Blynn!" she cried, barely restraining tears. "My beloved Blynn! You're safe! You're back!"

The Long Journey: *Reunion*

"*Umma!*" Brenna exclaimed, using the Lithian term for "mother," spoken with deep respect and affection. "Blessed *Umma*! You're with child again!"

Though Garrick had always thought of Brenna as petite, she towered over her mother. The two women embraced and wept in the joy of their reunion, holding on to each other and rocking side to side for a long time. Alexina said something gentle that Garrick didn't understand, kissed her daughter on the lips, gave her a final hug, and turned toward the young Tamarian lieutenant.

He bowed his head, following Brenna's instructions, waiting for Alexina to acknowledge him. Garrick felt a soft hand raise his chin and beautiful, blue eyes–bright and vibrant in the late afternoon light–appraised him.

"You are my son," she said. "Welcome home!" Then she stood on her toes and kissed his cheek.

Garrick smiled, basking in the light of Alexina's attention. "Thank you, honored mother," he replied, speaking slowly, careful to pronounce the Lithian words exactly as Mariel Hougen had taught him. "I am delighted to finally meet you." He didn't think the moment to announce that he and Brenna were not actually married had arrived.

Alexina kept her right hand against Garrick's cheek for a moment longer. "We will speak at length as time allows. But now, you must come to see your brother and sister." She turned toward Brenna and beckoned. "Come, loving daughter. Allfather has work that only you can do!"

Brenna followed her mother, and Garrick, anxious to see his siblings again, trailed close behind. Alexina entered the guest quarters, a two-story structure with thick walls and a tiled roof, turned toward the left and stopped to knock on a door. A discarded bowl of cherries lay next to the door frame. Curtains, drawn against the window, allowed only a sliver of light to reflect off the wall. The odor of sweat, infection and blood tainted the air.

Algernon, whose skin had begun peeling after a bad light burn, looked skinnier than Garrick last remembered. He arose from his seat next to the bed with relief brightening his worried countenance. "Garrick! Brenna! I knew you'd come!"

While the brothers embraced, Brenna glanced at the gaunt figure of Garrick's younger sister lying on the bed. Even in the dim light the Tamarian girl looked pale, her lips were cracked, her skin damp with sweat and despite the heat, she shivered incessantly. Brenna gasped, held her hand to her mouth, then looked at her mother in horror.

Kira, barely able to acknowledge her brother's presence, whispered his name. As Garrick approached, he kissed Kira's forehead, holding his breath in shock at the sight of her terrible, emaciated condition. "My sweet sister," he said softly, worriedly. "I'm so glad to see you!" Garrick took her hand, but she couldn't muster the strength to squeeze it.

When Brenna saw this, she urged Garrick away. "Everybody out!" she ordered. "There isn't much time!"

Algernon, *believing* that Brenna could heal his sister, pulled Garrick into the hall outside. The two of them began an intense conversation, speaking their native tongue in low voices edged in strong emotion. Garrick seemed very upset. Alexina watched the brothers closely, observing how Algernon reasoned with his warrior brother and calmed his anger. It was, in her mind, an impressive display of maturity from such a young man.

Brenna approached Kira and spoke gently to her. "I your sister be," she said, stroking Kira's sweaty forehead. "In God trust." Then, not knowing how to correctly form the sentence she wanted to say, Brenna fell silent.

The Lithian girl prayed for insight and power, then feeling Allfather's Spirit moving through her soul she arose and pulled back the sheet that covered Kira. "Merciful God!" she whispered, stunned at the extensive damage covering Kira's thin body.

A long time later, Alexina heard her eldest daughter's voice calling from behind the door. "*Umma!* I need a wet towel, a dry towel and a robe for Kira. Then I need your help."

Alexina spoke rapidly to one of her servants, then went into her own house. She returned shortly thereafter with the requested items and opened the door to Algernon's room just enough to slide through it.

Brenna had healed every cut, every bruise and all evidence of physical abuse from Kira's body, save for the double helix burned onto her arm, which Kira insisted she leave intact. Brenna prayed with her mother for Kira's soul and her addiction–which she'd never done before and felt more comfortable attempting in the company of her mother–then kissed the Tamarian girl on the forehead.

Kira felt her fever fade away. All the pain in her body vanished like a bad dream. Her mind cleared, and she felt the self-made walls of

The Long Journey: *Reunion*

her misery crumble to fine dust, swept away by a divine wind. A sense of delight and hope filled her soul. She sat up, feeling light and young, then smiled and reached for Brenna as if embracing a friend.

"I'm alive again!" Kira exclaimed. "Thank you!"

"God you must thank," Brenna replied. "I for him work."

A few minutes later, Garrick and Algernon heard the women talking. Alexina opened the door, Brenna drew back the curtain, and light poured into the room. Kira stood on her feet without support, wearing a new robe and a pretty smile.

Algernon raced for his twin sister, strong emotion unashamedly evident on his face. Garrick joined them a moment later, and the three siblings rejoiced in their reunion.

Home

Writing letters home to new widows ranked as the most unpleasant non-combat task Garrick needed to perform as an officer. He'd put the writing off for nearly two days until he'd developed a kind of formula, starting with a statement that expressed his sincere regret for the loss of the soldier, then outlining qualities of the deceased that had made the man an integral part of the platoon, a brief and factual description of his demise, followed by a somewhat romanticized conclusion concerning valor in service to the Republic.

The letter writing bothered Garrick because something about the process underscored the senseless nature of many combat deaths. A soldier whose body had been vaporized by an artillery shell because he happened to be standing in the wrong place at the wrong time hardly seemed worthy of accolades for bravery. However, as Garrick struggled to reduce the measure of someone he'd known personally to a few dozen handwritten words on a piece of paper, attributing honor to the man's service softened the news of his death and offered his widow, mother or sister a measure of comfort.

Yet Garrick felt that his concluding remarks sounded hollow, especially in light of the fact that Holger Faust left behind four boys whose memory of their father would remain forever frozen in disconnected recollections that left an incomplete picture of the man. These children would grow up never knowing their father's witty sense of humor, remembering his preference for oat cakes with raspberries instead of apple sauce, nor would they ever benefit from his guidance and wisdom. Holger's wife would never again hear an endearing word spoken into her ear, know her husband's embrace, or prosper from his strong work ethic on their farm; all because he happened to be standing in the courtyard of a foreign winery when a Kamerese artillery shell exploded directly above his head, forever ending any contribution he might make to his family's welfare.

The man who'd fired that rebel gun would never know how much pain and grief he caused a Tamarian family far away. The man who fired the shell that killed Greg Schmidt had been simply doing his job, unaware of the hurt Garrick felt in losing a good friend. Yet as he thought about this, Garrick realized that the same argument could be leveled against him.

The Long Journey: *Home*

Every command that resulted in an enemy death, and his own actions in the orchard adjacent to the packing plant, and the successful attack on Helena also created a set of widows and grieving mothers. None of those women would understand the need that compelled him to exterminate men whose names he would never know, as they advanced with similar intent toward his platoon.

Although he rationalized the need to stop aggression and to restore this land to its rightful owners, something about the conflict escalating to the extent that taking life ended up being the only means of solving the problem bothered Garrick on an emotional level. He'd brooded openly about this until Captain Engels realized what was going on and pulled him aside.

"If you don't feel regret for killing other men," the captain told him, "I don't want you under my command."

Captain Engels knew the conflicts raging within his young lieutenant's soul from personal experience. Writing the "widow letters" and sending them home could be cathartic, a means by which combat leaders processed their own losses, and doing so encouraged every officer in the chain of command to evaluate his responsibility in the conduct of warfare. In Captain Engel's mind, this served to restrain unprofessional behavior and limit the escalation of conflict.

The captain looked up from a collection of papers that lay on the mayor's desk when Brenna walked in. He'd read Garrick's after-action report, but found it hard to believe that this waify Lithian girl had been key in getting Third Platoon past the sentries guarding Helena. Her conduct in combat contrasted with the shy demeanor radiating from her pretty face. "Ah, Miss Velez!" he said, greeting her in vulgate.

"You summoned me, sir?" she inquired, nervously sitting in the chair he offered.

"Yes," he replied. "I understand you've been rather busy."

Brenna nodded. "I've been working in the field hospital for the past couple of days. We're still getting casualties from units fighting rebels who refuse to honor the surrender. We've also been receiving wounded men from among the Abelscinnians, allied militia and my own people who were defending Maidenhair Ridge. They suffered terribly."

Captain Engels made a point of touring the field hospital and encouraging the wounded warriors from his own company every morning it had been possible for him to do so. He'd seen Brenna's handiwork preserve life among men who would otherwise have perished, and knew that her reputation as a healer had already spread among high-ranking officers in the Tamarian Expeditionary Force.

"So I understand," he replied. "In light of your work there I am formally relieving you of your position in Third Platoon. You are too skilled and too valuable an asset to risk in combat."

Brenna felt shocked and her jaw dropped open. She covered her mouth politely, then looked away in an effort to formulate her thoughts. "I'd just begun getting comfortable with the men," she stated, her softly-spoken words reflecting a mind adrift in a sea of unexpected possibilities. "They won't be happy to hear this."

"The men answer to me," Captain Engels said, dismissing her remark. "My decision is in the best interest of Alpha Company, and the men—especially your favorite lieutenant—will understand."

"Further, I've just received a directive from General Braun concerning the disposition of high-ranking rebel prisoners we've been holding in the city jail. The general would like to clarify jurisdictional issues with your father, and also wishes to congratulate him personally on a tenacious and successful defense against the rebel incursion. Since you are serving as the company liaison, I would like you to arrange a meeting between them."

"My father's forces remain engaged with Lord Fang's army," she replied. "How do you propose that I set up such a meeting, and where should it take place?"

"The time and venue will be determined at your father's pleasure," Captain Engels stated. "Given that the process of disarming Lord Navarro's forces has moved well ahead of schedule, I can offer an escort and an EPT to you."

Brenna, a little afraid of facing her father again after ignoring his counsel and running off to Tamaria, bit her lower lip and hedged for a moment. "Would it be possible to send Lieutenant Ravenwood with me?" she inquired.

"I'm afraid not," the captain replied. "Even though the cease-fire is holding and most of the rebels have thus far willingly given up their weapons, we still face a potential threat from other warlords allied with Navarro and Fang. Right now Lieutenant Ravenwood has many responsibilities requiring his attention. Perhaps Sergeant Ringer might escort you?"

The Long Journey: *Home*

"No! Not him!" Brenna responded, perhaps more stridently than necessary. She stood up in preparation to leave the office. "And not Odell Unruh, either. What about Harmon Grossman?"

Meinrad Engels, knowing that Brenna could take care of herself, found it somewhat amusing that she agreed to any escort at all. "I'll check with Sergeant Ringer," he promised. "And one more thing..."

Brenna paused, listening, but didn't reply.

Captain Engels smiled, having saved the best news for last. "Sergeant Ringer has recommended you for another combat lion."

"For what reason?" she inquired, hoping that it didn't involve the killing she'd done to get the platoon past the sentries at the school. She steeled herself, intending to refuse the award in that case.

When the captain stood the top of Brenna's head barely reached his chest. However, over the past few weeks she'd interacted with the captain several times. She always found his conduct docile and respectful, and as a result, didn't fear his proximity. He leaned on the desk to put his eyes on the same level as hers. "I heard about the episode at the winery," he began, his voice softened and fatherly. "The sergeant told me you risked your life during an artillery barrage to save Kasch Nagel. If the general hears about that, you'll be getting more than just another combat lion."

Brenna blushed and averted her eyes, her characteristically reticent demeanor inspiring an embarrassed response. Why would the sergeant recommend a citation for something he'd yelled at her for doing? "It's not customary for the company commander to comment on a platoon sergeant's recommendations," she replied.

The captain nodded, fingering a small envelope. "This is true," he said. "However, everyone in the command hierarchy understands that your platoon leader is hopelessly in love with you. He recused himself from pinning this on your collar because he thought it would be perceived as favoritism. I, however, have no such compunction. Would you grant me the honor in the ceremony this morning?"

Brenna held her breath. She'd not wanted to gain notoriety and understood more than anyone that Allfather had preserved her life at that moment in the winery courtyard. While the thought of standing in front of the assembled men and being recognized for valor wrought a tremble through her spine, the Tamarian military took these kinds of things seriously, and she didn't want to offend anyone. "It would be my honor, sir," she replied.

The Long Journey: *Home*

The captain smiled, thinking for a moment of his own daughter. This Velez girl was lovely to look at, but her genuine humility impressed him to a greater degree. Though he'd never met Lord Velez, Captain Engels imagined that he must have been an attentive and wise father. "Please return here in an hour," he said.

*   *   *

Kira sat on a porch swing behind the guest house, rocking back and forth as she looked through Astrid's sketchbook. "You've done a lot of work on this," she commented.

Astrid pursed her lips, afraid to say the wrong thing, afraid that speaking truthfully would drive Kira far away, forever. Her heart beat fast and her fingers trembled nervously as she looked away from her favorite girl and gazed at *Lago Caliente* in the distance. Just being near Kira filled her heart with hope. "I started it while we were still in Marvic," she replied. "I had a lot of time on my hands for a while. I haven't had much opportunity for drawing since we went across the river to find you because we've been traveling so much."

That was a lie and Kira sensed it, but she didn't say anything. Algernon had been urging her to deal with Astrid honestly, to speak her mind, set boundaries and stand up to the priestess, and though she'd agreed with him, following through had proven more difficult than she imagined. Kira didn't want Astrid as a lover, but she genuinely liked the girl and wished, somewhat wistfully, that she'd never known the pleasure of Astrid's caress.

With her sickness cured, her body healed and spirit restored, the lingering effects of decisions she'd made still rippled through her soul, and Kira fearfully faced the prospect of dealing with conflicts long avoided. She'd been rescued from her mother's domination by Garrick, from Priestess Alba's unwelcome advances by Astrid, from Astrid and her smothering, exclusivity by Marco, and Marco's abuse by Algernon. Kira really didn't know where to begin, or what to do, in making things right with the people she'd hurt, and hadn't processed the knotted mass of sentiments she felt for those who'd hurt her.

Astrid, in particular, posed a vexing problem. Kira felt conflicted because she couldn't deny the physical delight she'd experienced with the priestess, and more importantly, had long felt that Astrid listened with compassion and provided comfort to assuage Kira's personal pain.

The Long Journey: *Home*

At the same time, however, Kira believed that Astrid used her as a means to validate lesbianism, and further, that Astrid had taken advantage of a young girl's naivete in fully introducing her to intimacies for which she might have been ready physically, but certainly not emotionally or spiritually.

Now that the impact of illness and addiction no longer dominated her thinking, Kira struggled against an irrational fear that Astrid could somehow seduce her back into a lifestyle that she associated with shame and guilt. Now that her libido had returned to its normal level, her imagination often wandered toward memories of intimate moments in Astrid's company, and the intensity of that lure frightened her. For this reason she'd been reluctant to spend any time alone with Astrid, yet Kira desperately needed a friend–another girl–with whom she could share her feelings.

Kira had no history with Brenna, and though she seemed like a genuinely sweet girl, the language barrier between them made communication difficult. Brenna spoke Tamarian like a cripple walks when deprived of crutches, and Kira knew very little vulgate. In addition, the Lithian girl's healing skills had been in such high demand she'd come back to the villa only once in the past two days and, while there, spent every moment with her mother.

The Lithian women guarding the Velez household were uniformly older and, though polite, maintained an attitude that Kira interpreted as sanctimonious. Everyone knew she'd been a drug whore. Everyone knew that Astrid had been her lover. An attitude of moral superiority, though subtle, pervaded every interaction among the Lithian women. Kira found no comfort in their company, yet she longed for a female friend to whom she could relate and verbally process her frayed emotions.

That left Astrid as the only girl with whom she had a shared history, a common language and a spiritual frame of reference. Astrid always extended a sympathetic ear and never judged Kira for her drug problem, for her immorality or distaste for formal religious authority; yet in Astrid's eyes Kira saw a longing for intimacy that she was afraid to rekindle.

As her weakened self-esteem confronted this dilemma, Kira began to wonder whether or not she simply deserved nothing better than the relationship Astrid offered. She recognized this vulnerability as the same feeling she'd experienced when Priestess Alba first cornered, kissed, fondled and molested her in the dormitory. Back then, Astrid stood fiercely in Kira's defense and used every means available to subvert the older woman's unwanted advances.

Then Kira recalled how proficiently Astrid manipulated her, persuading Kira that her body's response to pleasure proved they'd been destined as partners. Kira remembered Astrid's need for control, how she skillfully used threat and tears to get her way, and anger trembled through Kira's soul.

Algernon had listened to all of this on a recent walk with Kira, and persuaded his sister to confront the issue directly. "It's not fair that you avoid expressing yourself clearly," he'd argued. "Astrid holds out hope for the restoration of your relationship because you keep sending her mixed signals. Make up your mind, Kira, one way or the other."

That had to be a boy thing, she thought. Algernon oversimplified everything, and boys never understood the complexity of relationships. For them, a few seconds of intense pleasure provided all the motivation needed to wander through the maze of messy and often contradictory feelings, but to his credit, Algernon hadn't condemned her for sympathizing with and longing for Astrid. He seemed to have grown up a lot over the past three months.

Kira returned her attention to Astrid's sketchbook, lingering for a while at the charcoal images of the Fang Family Fine Clothiers store Astrid had composed. Though she said nothing about this, Kira had been strung out upstairs that day. She remembered the screams, the gunshot, and how Marco had come into her room with a terrified look on his face. Now Kira saw his vague but recognizable countenance behind the gun he'd aimed at her twin brother. Algernon had told her the truth, and Marco's deception about that incident made Kira realize she'd been betrayed.

"That stinking liar!" she breathed, angrily.

Astrid turned her attention back to Kira, realizing the source of her lover's rage. "He is," Astrid agreed, struggling not to reach out and toy with Kira's platinum hair. "All men are liars, baby doll. They just want to seduce you."

Kira felt annoyed that Astrid referred to her using their favored term of endearment. "Is that a problem limited to men?" she inquired, her tone of voice an unsheathed weapon.

A look of horror widened in Astrid's green eyes and her heart bled from Kira's attack. "You should know me better than that by now!"

The Long Journey: *Home*

Kira looked away. "It doesn't feel any different to me, Astrid. The end result is the same. I'm your little toy, your pleasure doll with no will of my own. You play with me until you've had your fill, and then lock me away when you're done."

Astrid shook her head. "You've taken this all wrong, Kira. I've protected you so that others who had more power couldn't take advantage of you. I kept them away for your sake because I love you, and had you stayed with me, you'd have never been hurt!"

A fierce expression flashed upon Kira's face, one that Astrid had seen in Algernon many times, but never before upon the gentler countenance of his twin sister. "You chained me in a cage!" Kira protested. "I became your property, a creature on display that everyone could see, but the bars and the moat of your making kept them all at a distance. There is no real difference in the outcome of my relationship with you and my slave status here in Kameron."

"That's not true!" Astrid argued, feeling wounded by the analogy. "You were always free to come and go as you wished. I never forced myself on you, never branded you with a mark of ownership. I never judged you for publically fooling around with the other girls–especially that little slut, Bronwyn–and even though it hurt me to watch you getting exploited by the boys in the Temple, I never stopped you."

"There are many ways to judge and many ways to control," said Kira defensively. "You're so skilled at this you don't even recognize what you're doing."

Astrid bristled angrily at Kira's accusation. "How can you say that? How can you contend that I'm controlling you when I've never done a thing to stop your self-destructive behavior?"

Kira remained firm. "I'll give you the same example I gave my brother. Because you were the one in charge of the work schedule, you manipulated things in my favor under the condition that I sleep with you. If I didn't do what you wanted, I got punished by having to wash dishes, clean toilets or change diapers in the nursery for days on end.

"If I didn't come to you at night, you pouted and whined. You threatened Bronwyn too–though she's been my friend ever since my brother and I first arrived at the Temple, and she never did anything to you–then penalized her without mercy at every opportunity. You kept us apart and made me feel guilty for being with her. The same is true of Helga, who never laid her lips on me. I had no will of my own. It was all about you."

The Long Journey: *Home*

"I gave you work in the garden, Kira! I did that because you love plants, because it was your favorite place. Of course I wanted you to be with me, why wouldn't I? You're my soul mate, and doing a favor for my best friend is not proof that I controlled you!"

"There is no difference!" Kira sighed with resignation. "You're just playing with words."

"Yes, there is! The difference is that I love you!" Astrid insisted.

Kira stared at Astrid and spoke slowly. "If you really love me, stop making sex a requirement of our friendship!" she argued. "If you really love me, stop trying to seduce me with your eyes. I'm not like you, and I've had enough!"

Astrid struggled to contain her own heartache. Kira took everything the wrong way! She ascribed nefarious motive to actions undertaken with the intent of providing for her happiness. "How can you ask this of me?" she inquired. "Why are you being so selfish?"

"There you go again!" Kira complained. "You're making this all about you. I've been letting other people dominate me for too long now. It's time that I stood up for what is right, rather than running away from it, and the whole process has to start here and now!"

Kira turned away for a moment, letting her words sink in. Then, as her passion cooled, she returned her gaze to Astrid. "Stop being so desperate for my body, and just be my friend. Be the girl who listens and understands. Be someone whom I can trust. Be the girl who saved my brother from his bad temper and brought him down to rescue me." She paused again and crossed her arms, a familiar vulnerability etched upon her face.

Astrid drew closer. "I'm here, Kira. I'm right here! I'm that girl. I'm your girl."

For a moment, the tension of their proximity heightened. Kira let her eyes wander down Astrid's neck, toward the deep, V-shaped fold of her robe that concealed soft, sensitive and familiar flesh, then further to her tanned arm and the delicate hand resting in her lap. When she looked up, Astrid drew near to kiss her lips and Kira's heart pounded. She turned her head away and Astrid paused, asserting self-control.

"Ok, baby doll," the priestess whispered, her voice quivering as she suppressed the rise of choking emotions in her throat. "Have it your way."

Kira stared for a moment, torn between the desire to embrace Astrid and fear that if she did, Astrid would misconstrue her motives.

The Long Journey: *Home*

Yet a small sense of triumph blossomed within her soul. She'd faced down her fear and could now hold her head a little higher.

Astrid leaned back on the porch swing, a genuine desire to spare Kira of any more suffering the motivation behind relinquishing her dream of reconciliation. She truly loved the girl, and for this reason, though it broke her own heart, chose to give her up. "What are you going to do now?" she asked, her familiar voice now strangely distant.

"I want to go home," Kira replied.

"You think your parents will take you in?"

Kira shook her head. "Not back to Deception Creek," she stated. "I don't ever want to see that place again. I belong in Marvic, with my brother."

Astrid blinked back a tear. "The Supreme Council won't let you back in the Temple," she said. "Algernon has a place on Superstition Mesa, but it needs a lot of work."

"He told me," Kira replied. "We grew up on a farm and we're not afraid of working, but when we're settled, once we can sustain ourselves, I have to change what's happening in Marvic. I want to save the girls who come to the city full of dreams for a better future, but end up drug-addicted *strichmadchen* because they find no way to survive."

Having never heard Kira express a hope like this, Astrid seemed a little bit surprised. "How will you do that?" she inquired.

"My years in the Temple give me the right to visit schools and speak to the students. I'll meet with the girls and tell them my story." Kira pulled back the sleeve covering her arm, revealing the ugly, double helix chain that had been branded there. "I'll show them what happened and warn them about the evil men who will fill their heads with soft words and empty promises. I'll warn them about the seduction of getting high. I'll tell them what it did to me, and they'll listen because of this," she said, fingering her brand.

"Algernon told me that High Priest Volker has a sister who lives in the city. He says the woman has a big, empty house and a heart to help young people. He thinks she'd be willing to board stray girls who need a safe place to stay."

Astrid raised her eyebrows. "Freda Bergen hates your brother," she said. "She kicked him out of her house. He'll never talk her into doing anything."

"Never underestimate my brother!" Kira replied. "Algernon is really smart and can be very persuasive. Thanks to you he's not the arrogant, angry and tortured soul who abandoned me in the Temple. I think he'll make a better priest than most of the men who live there!"

"I don't doubt that," Astrid responded. "But won't you find it shameful to talk about everything that's happened? Aren't you worried about your reputation? People in town will talk about you, and you'll have no support in the community."

Kira shook her head. "I can't concern myself with that. You were my lesbian lover, and I'm not ashamed of you. I was a whore and I'm a drug-addict. I've been starved, beaten and gang-raped twice, but all of this makes my story more compelling, and no one can torment me with words that cause more pain than I've already been through.

"This is not about me, Astrid. I have to take the second chance I've been given and live my life in service to others, as the Great God intended. I can't waste my days being controlled by fear of what other people think."

"I've been worried about you for a long time," Astrid replied, quietly. "It lightens my heart to hear you talk this way." Yet in saying this, Astrid did not feel certain that the words coming out of her mouth reflected the truth of her own feelings.

She arose, desperate to change the subject. "I have a gift for you, a token of love for my best friend. It's something that responds to your control." The priestess promised to be right back, vanished inside the guest house and cried bitterly. When she came out a few minutes later, bearing a gift box that she gave to Kira, her eyes remained damp and reddened.

"What's this?" Kira inquired, seeing the emotion on Astrid's face.

"It was given to me, but I've been saving it for you. I only wore it once."

Kira took out the tiny halter and glanced at Astrid suspiciously. There was something doll-like about the garment, and she didn't appreciate the connotation its size implied when linked to Astrid's favorite term of endearment. "You expect me to wear this?"

Astrid nodded, sniffing and wiping her eyes. "Brenna and the other Lithian women have them too, but theirs are sheer. Trust me. You'll never put on anything more comfortable."

An expression of curiosity blossomed on Kira's face. "You said I can control it. How does that work?"

When Astrid explained, Kira spent a long time holding the fabric and making it change color. She learned that by using her imagination, she could make the garment wrap around her fingers without actually moving it, and this inspired an altogether different train of thought...

Kira smiled, offered thanks, then went inside to try it on.

*   *   *

Mariel Hougen stared at Garrick with incredulity slathered generously over her expression. "You actually bluffed Lord Navarro into surrendering?"

"Yes," he replied. "My orders were to take the town hall. I did, but I wasn't expecting Navarro and Fang to actually be there. Second Platoon was getting hammered by rebel artillery, so I had to do something to stop the shooting."

"How come he didn't realize that you only had 24 people left in your unit, and that First and Second Platoons were bogged down in heavy action at the north end of town? You're lucky they didn't figure that out and squash you like a bug!"

Garrick put a padlock on the steel bin where the fourteenth set of 50 surrendered Kamerese rifles awaited transport back home to Tamaria. He initialed the seal, indicating that he'd counted every weapon and certified the contents of the bin. "There was a lot of noise, lieutenant. We had both machine cannon holding off rebel infantry and a dozen rifles blasting away at the surrounding buildings. Artillery leveled the northern part of town, there were fires, smoke and dust, and in the midst of all that, Thorsten Lehman lit off a rocket that knocked out a bunch of rebels assembling to counterattack the town hall.

"Navarro and Fang must have thought we had a larger force because of all the shooting. We caught them there because we sneaked in the back way, took the building quickly, and they had no time to escape. Had we been more conventional about our attack, they'd have been long gone by the time we arrived. Kurt Nussbaum told me that he gave you a whole set of maps and plans for Navarro's forces, and that kind of thing wouldn't have been left laying around had they known we were coming. Navarro didn't know we had only a handful of men in the building and probably figured that we had overwhelming force outside."

Mariel put her hands on her hips. Her freckles blended into a tan from the strong daylight, and the contrast between her molasses tea complexion and her light-bleached, copper-colored hair accentuated her exotic beauty. "From what I gathered in my interviews with rebel officers, their forces outnumbered Company Alpha by a margin of 7:1. Now, these were mostly irregular troops, but for the life of me I can't figure out why they didn't realize you were commanding a platoon on the ragged edge of combat viability when they came in to give up their weapons."

"Well, Sergeant Vidders thought we'd up the ante a bit. He and his squad brought a bunch of dead rebels from the green belt area that we'd killed with the machine cannon and laid them around the steps. We took twelve bodies from inside the building and tossed them on the porches so that it looked like we'd wiped out an entire battalion just taking the city hall." Garrick grinned, a little embarrassed. "I've never seen guys so happy to give up their weapons before!"

Lieutenant Mariel Hougen rolled her dark brown eyes. "Remind me to never play poker with you!" she smirked. "I'd be sure to lose all my clothes!"

Garrick's face flushed, embarrassed at the thought of playing strip poker with Mariel, while knowing that was exactly the reaction she intended to inspire.

Sergeant Vidders arrived. Noting that Garrick's face looked like a glass of blush wine and figuring the saucy, scarlet-haired intelligence analyst had something to do with it, he elected to come to his lieutenant's rescue. "Sorry to interrupt, he said. "But you remember our little problem from the winery?"

Garrick nodded.

"Well sir, she came back."

"Luther's Nordan girl?"

"That's the one," Sergeant Vidders replied.

Garrick let out a groan. "How did she get here, and what does she want now, sergeant?"

"She came down in a truck with some other, uh, important people who've arrived from the refugee camp. They're all looking for you. I'm just giving you a heads up, lieutenant. Sergeant Ringer has the girl cutting bandages for Miss Velez and Udo Barth."

"Where's Sondheim?"

Sergeant Vidders struggled to keep a straight face. "He's cleaning out the clogged discharge pipe on the sewage lagoon, sir. It was Sergeant Ringer's idea. Luther smells like the collective behind of the rebel army. Let's say that he's not going to have any friends until the stench wears off, and I'll bet he'll think twice before being insubordinate to you again."

Garrick turned away, laughing. He composed himself and returned his attention to Sergeant Vidders. "I don't suppose the Nordan girl has seen him at work, has she?"

"Don't be cruel, lieutenant!"

"Luther's going to wear that perfume for a while, sergeant. There's no water in Helena. Make sure that girl doesn't get a whiff of Luther until he's had a bath!"

"Consider it done," Sergeant Vidders replied. "And lieutenant, you need to see the captain right away."

When Sergeant Vidders left, Garrick turned back to Mariel. "Do you suppose I'm in trouble?"

Mariel tightened her lips and shook her head. He thought she looked better with her hair down, but the summer heat and a desire to look professional inspired the lieutenant to pin it up. "You're the last person who'd be in trouble right now," she replied. "Single-handedly stopping a full-scale battle is an impressive task for anyone to achieve, let alone a green lieutenant on his first day as a combat leader."

But when Garrick walked into Captain Engels' office, the company commander seemed less than pleased to see him. "You have visitors," the captain said, not bothering to look up from his paperwork. "I know that these people are locally important, but you have a job to do and I expect your full devotion to it.

"You would do well to remind the Velez family that we're in a war zone, with pockets of active resistance remaining, and several thousand rebel troops still holding ground to the south of our position. This is not a place for fraternizing."

"I understand, sir!" Garrick responded, nervously.

Captain Engels sighed, placing his hands down on the top of the mayor's desk. He looked at Garrick intently. "But theirs is a very different way of thinking, right lieutenant?"

Garrick seemed puzzled. "What are you getting at, sir?"

The captain glanced past Garrick's shoulder to see if anyone happened to be standing nearby. He lowered his voice. "Your Lithian girl dresses decently, but if her sisters were my daughters, I wouldn't let any of them out of the bathroom looking like that!"

"Oh yes," Garrick replied, looking down and suppressing a smile. "I understand."

The Long Journey: *Home*

"So get them out of here before the entire battalion shows up to have a look, and I'd rather not see them around my soldiers again. Put it delicately, but firmly, to their family, and make certain that I don't have to speak to you about this a second time.

"While you're up there, I need you to find the Abelscinnian commander, speak to him face-to-face, and ask him to turn the damned water back on. Either he's not getting our messages, or something else is wrong. Find out what it is, fix it, and be quick about it!"

"Yes sir!"

"Your girlfriend's sisters and their 'Scinnian escorts are upstairs. There's a truck behind the building. Get them out of here quickly and be discreet about it!"

Once dismissed from the captain's presence, Garrick slipped into the bathroom to consult with a mirror and noted with dismay that his reddened skin was smeared in dirt. He found a bit of water in an upper toilet tank and rinsed his face as best he could, yet after going several days without shaving, he'd finally accumulated enough stubble to warrant some time with a razor. Brenna would have given him a hard time about this, had she actually seen him in the days following the cease-fire, but now he had to make a good impression on his future sisters-in-law looking like he'd been rolling around in the dust.

With a deep breath he ascended the stairs, taking care to step over the dried blood pools that remained where rebel soldiers had fallen. The air felt hotter and his heart beat fast in an irrational mix of curiosity and trepidation as he climbed. He could hear men talking and girls laughing, until his heavy, booted footfalls inspired silence at the top of the staircase.

Two Abelscinnian men–black-skinned, tall, well-muscled, handsome and dressed in Lithian combat uniforms–had been conversing near the back window. They seemed surprised at the obvious youth of the Tamarian officer, but both men smiled, clasped their hands as if praying and bowed in greeting. Garrick recognized the family resemblance with Tegene, the commander of forces defending Maidenhair Ridge, with whom he'd already conversed.

Just as Garrick was about to approach them and introduce himself, he heard a shriek from the opposite end of the hall. One girl, who'd been holding a canteen, dropped it onto the floor, covered her open mouth with both hands and stared, wide-eyed. She looked husky and tall when compared to her sisters. but would have passed for a particularly well-proportioned, teenaged human girl in Azgaril City or Marioch, save for her porcelain skin. That meant she had to be Cynthia, whom Brenna referred to as "Thea."

Her older, shorter and more slender sister rivaled the flawless beauty of their mother. The girl looked very Lithian, with deeply slanted eyes, low cheekbones, a slender jaw and narrow chin that gave her face its distinctive, heart shape. Acacia, whom everyone called "Cassie," moved behind Cynthia and whispered something into her sibling's ear that made her laugh.

The youngest one, Camille, had green eyes and the unusual, naturally dual-colored hair characteristic among Lithians of mixed parentage. Two locks of white hair framed her pretty face and hung to her waist, while the rest of her hair–dark and thick as Brenna's own tresses–lay tightly pulled against her scalp and flowed down her back in a braid. Garrick recalled Brenna comparing Camille to Algernon and Kira, but he had a hard time equating her age with that of his siblings because her Lithian ethnicity made her look younger than the twins.

All of the sisters wore clothing typical of fashionable and wealthy Kamerese. Their expensive, custom-tailored dresses, though more form-fitting and revealing of flesh on the shoulders and back than was considered polite in Tamaria, would have roused no attention among the social elite in Kameron City. Garrick was certain that if Captain Engels had seen Cassie and Thea dressed in the same manner as Brenna when he first met her in the Saradon foothills, the captain would have burst a blood vessel!

Camille scurried toward him wearing a big smile on her face. She reached for his hand and pulled him toward her sisters, an action that inspired laughter among the Abelscinnians. "Come!" she beckoned, assuming he understood her language.

Cassie stepped out from behind her sister, opened her arms and embraced Garrick. Then she backed away, lifted her face toward him and waited for the expected kiss. The girl smiled, but said nothing.

Thea managed to speak in vulgate after stepping into Garrick's strong arms. "You are my brother!" she whispered.

"Soon," he replied, gently kissing her forehead, "but not yet."

Thea's face reflected bewilderment. "Blynn loves you," she stated, using the blended form of Brenna Lynn's first and middle names that Garrick had also heard from Alexina. "And I've seen the two of you in vision."

The Long Journey: *Home*

"What you've seen is that among my people, all women dress as the married among your people dress."

Thea bent her head slightly to the side and spoke slowly, as if deliberating every word. "Like the Kamerese?" she inquired.

Garrick nodded. "Our customs are even more strict than theirs."

"I see," said Thea, who then backed away as if afraid.

"You needn't be fearful," he assured her. "I love Brenna, and I respect her faith."

"I'm not afraid of you!" Camille interrupted, throwing her arms around the Tamarian warrior. After he'd kissed her forehead, Camille jumped up and kissed his cheek, then held her hand to her lips in surprise. "Your face is rough!" she exclaimed.

Cassie pulled her away and whispered something stern to her sister that Garrick didn't understand. Thea simply giggled.

Garrick felt embarrassment wash over his lightburned skin. "There is no water here," he admitted. "So I can't shave. I need to see about getting the supply opened up again before we have a riot among our prisoners."

The two Abelscinnians, Kimoni and Xola, came over and introduced themselves as sons of Penda, third wife of Tegene, their beloved father. They clasped raised hands with Garrick in the universal gesture of peace. Xola listened to Garrick's concern, then promised to have him meet with Tegene and reactivate Helena's water supply.

Less than an hour later, the gates controlling runoff for Maidenhair Creek opened, and fresh water flowed into Helena's pipes. When Garrick reported to his commander, Captain Engels seemed pleased that the lieutenant handled his assignment so quickly and efficiently, thanked him, then sent him back to oversee Third Platoon.

*   *   *

During the long, hot ride up the Virgin River valley Brenna brooded over the prospect of meeting with her father. Nearly a year had transpired since she saw him last, and many times when she'd faced fear or meditated in solitude, regret for defying his wishes welled up within her mind. Though she'd rehearsed what she'd wanted to say, every word seemed trite, every rationalization shallow and every method she'd conceived to express genuine sorrow fell flat against the last words he'd spoken to her.

The Long Journey: *Home*

"You know what is right, what is good and what is honorable. Choose your path according to these things and you will walk in Allfather's favor."

As the EPT speed quietly toward its destination, the desolation of a denuded landscape spread across the barren hills. Canyons once crowned in an evergreen canopy of conifer and live oak trees–through which seasonal creeks flowed in the autumn, winter and spring–lay naked and shamefully exposed beneath the hot sky. Blackened craters, pits, trenches and the gleam of brass shell casings caught Brenna's attention. Burn scars on the red soil baked silently as ripples of heat radiated into the brilliant daylight of high summer. Carrion birds feasted on fallen flesh, but the sight of living rebel soldiers remained elusive for a long time.

Harmon Grossman first caught a glimpse of the enemy just as the EPT turned eastward and began ascending very steep terrain leading to the fortified Lithian positions on the high ground. Hundreds of unarmed men had lined up behind horse-drawn carriages. Lithian warriors with rifles supervised the procession as rebel soldiers waited for their turn to drink from water bladders brought down from *Lago Caliente*.

"What are they doing?" Harmon asked in vulgate.

To Brenna, the scene seemed so ordinary she hadn't given it a second thought. "They're giving water to enemy soldiers."

"Are they nuts?" the Tamarian warrior exclaimed. "They should be gunning them all down while they have the chance!"

Brenna raised her eyebrows. "My family lives among the Kamerese," she replied. "What better way to fight your enemy than to give him water when he's thirsty? Do you think that men will take up arms against people who saved them from dying in this heat?"

She had a point, he conceded, silently.

"And aren't you Tamarians letting the rebels depart for home after they've turned in their weapons?"

"We don't have provision to house all the prisoners," Harmon replied. "We're keeping the officers under guard, but we don't have the manpower or facilities to care for thousands of captured men."

Brenna crossed her arms. "The motivating principle may differ, but the outcome is the same. Besides, hasn't there been enough killing already?"

The Long Journey: *Home*

"Well, I wouldn't trust any of them!" Harmon countered, a small measure of contempt in his voice. "We've been hearing about pockets of resistance along Maidenhair Ridge manned by fanatics who will never surrender. We've sent troops in to root them out, and more good men have died. What makes you think the same isn't true down here?"

"I'm sure fanatics exist among these men as well," she replied. "That's why my father's men have guns, but the rebels have to lay theirs down before coming up to drink. Just because he's compassionate doesn't mean my father's a fool."

Harmon was taken aback by her remark, and a little surprised that the girl could be so straightforward, given his experience listening to her struggle with the Tamarian language. "That's not what I meant, Miss Velez. I'm sure your father is both honorable and intelligent, but I wouldn't want to put myself into a position where some lunatic might give me and my friends a nasty surprise."

Brenna didn't think Harmon would understand an issue she viewed through the lens of her faith, and she didn't know how much she ought to reveal concerning Mariel's analysis of the social problems in the country, so she chose her words carefully. "My father has already enacted reforms within the territory he controls," she explained. "He's invested in this land so that those who live here will have a better future. The men leading this rebellion are not interested in the welfare of their fellow citizens, nor do they care about justice and integrity. Powerful, slave-owning warlords with drug empires subverted the revolt within weeks of its beginning as a means to pursue power and gain additional wealth.

"But many of the men who are doing the fighting and dying believe in a noble cause. They dream that this revolution will put an end to their misery, allow them to own their own land and give them direct access to markets for Kamerese agriculture and manufactured goods. Many hope that this conflict will end slavery and crush the power structures of the elites who hold them down.

"I'm convinced that the warlords leading this conflict intend to kill off most of the discontented population in senseless fighting, so that they can return to the status quo ante and keep the survivors under their collective thumbs for another generation. That's why they're content to march all over the countryside, chasing the National Army without ever defeating them in a decisive battle."

"You sound terribly cynical," Harmon observed.

Brenna shook her head. "It's the way of evil men," she replied. "Allfather sent you here to stop them, and that is one thing they could never have foreseen."

Harmon shrugged at her spiritual explanation. He believed his nation's forces were active in Kameron simply to protect the Tamarian people from suffering the effects of a nearby conflict. "Whether or not the gods care about anything that happens among the affairs of men, the Kamerese aren't stupid," he said with a shrug. "If your explanation rings true, the warlords will fall once the common people figure out what they've done."

"Now who's being cynical?" she inquired, smiling. Brenna turned her head toward the rebel troops below. "These men will have to fight against their warlord masters in order to bring about real change. They need the kind of reform that's already taken place here, on my family's estate. The lies that men like Fang and Navarro have fed the Kamerese people will be revealed, and King Alejo will have to adapt or abdicate. That's when fighting men will flock to leaders with integrity, leaders like my own father."

Harmon smiled while listening to Brenna articulate her position, even though he viewed the conflict through eyes that were less concerned for the welfare of local people than her own. The lieutenant's girl, full of mysterious power and intellectual complexity, stirred his interest in a different way than her beauty alone could inspire. "And you think that giving water to the rebels will convince them that your father is worthy of being supported?"

Brenna laughed as the driver stopped to consult his map. "You've never been thirsty enough to know!" she smirked, hopping to the road, leaving Harmon to think and sweat with the machine cannon that had been mounted behind the back seat.

Though it had been marked in code on the map, the EPT's driver did not have to search for the Lord Lynden's command bunker. Once Brenna emerged from the vehicle and pulled off her helmet, warriors poured out of their prepared positions to greet her. Within moments, a sea of smiling and laughing soldiers embraced her one by one, tousled her hair, peppered her with many questions, praises, and smothered her forehead in kisses.

Watching this, Harmon Grossman felt like an outsider observing a community to which he didn't belong. He smiled, seeing the joy on Brenna's face as she shrieked in delight to reunite with men from her

The Long Journey: *Home*

father's army, many of whom had known her since childhood. This glimpse of Brenna's world, a place where her worth did not hinge on physical appeal, or her mystical healing ability, wrought a sense of longing for home in Harmon's heart.

As the adoring crowd of Lithian warriors swelled to several dozen, two of them lifted Brenna onto their shoulders and the whole group followed as they bore her up the narrow path to see her father.

Lynden Velez didn't wait for the procession to arrive. He'd just returned from reviewing his forces and raced down the path with his arms held wide, calling Brenna's name. The soldiers set her down and raised a loud and joyful shout as she leapt into her father's embrace.

* * *

Algernon peeled burnt skin from his forearms, feeling restless. In the shade of the observatory he stared toward the north, thinking of his high elevation homeland where long summer days with lingering twilights never smothered the landscape in the oppressive heat he experienced in Kameron. He dreamed of clouds, rain and the familiar sight of high, snow-clad mountains kissing the sky.

Superstition Mesa and the work that needed to be done there awaited his attention. Algernon mulled through a list of tasks he had to complete before winter arrived, examining potential problems and imagining how he could solve them on his limited budget.

He had to build a more permanent and well-insulated residence, with separate sleeping quarters for Kira because it had become clear to him after sharing a room with her that they both needed privacy. He'd construct a massive heating stove from brick, something he understood how to make, but had never actually done before. Algernon knew that he should have already begun gathering, splitting and stacking firewood to keep them warm during the long, cold and dreary months that lay ahead.

Food collection and storage would occupy much time, at least initially, since they'd been unable to plant a garden. An elevated storage cache with a removable ladder, built close enough to their residence to allow easy access during the winter, would serve to keep scavenging animals away from their food stash. They would catch anadromous fish in the north fork of the Lost Maiden River, or in Augury Creek, and preserve the flesh with smoking and drying. Kira would collect berries, nuts and edible mushrooms in the forest.

Surviving the winter meant a need for warmer clothes, boots, mittens and snowshoes. Blankets and basic furnishings would improve their quality of life, but where would the money come from to buy what they couldn't make? The magical moneybag Garrick had given to him remained empty after he'd dumped its contents to buy Kira back from Chale. She'd been worth everything, but now he had nothing.

Wealthy people in Marvic would be willing to support their basic needs, and they could spend their days in the city if their situation became untenable. Algernon wasn't worried about starving because both he and Kira had a right to eat from the shrines, but having grown up on a farm where the values of hard work and discipline were indelibly imprinted on his consciousness, he scorned any thought of living on charity.

Part of the anxiety he felt stemmed from no longer having a purpose to his visit with the Velez family, and having no one with whom he could really engage in conversation. Tegene, remembering his own youth, made a fatherly effort to keep Algernon active, but some of the tasks he assigned for the young monk felt like they'd been designed merely to keep him busy. Jawara had been a wise and trustworthy companion during their foray across the Virgin River, but now he'd become preoccupied with the rebel disarmament, and expected to remain engaged in restoration of the landscape for a long time to come.

"You should stay here," Jawara had urged. "With your farm experience you'd be a valued asset to the Velez family, and remaining as our guest would keep you close to your brother."

Yet as much as Algernon loved and esteemed Garrick, the many changes in their respective lives strained relations between the brothers. Aside from contrasts resulting from his more advanced education at the Temple and the many formative experiences there, Algernon also fretted over the way that Garrick's role as a platoon leader consumed his attention. Command responsibilities kept him very busy, leaving the brothers with little opportunity to talk. Worse, everything that Algernon told Garrick seemed trite when compared to the crushing workload of an officer struggling to cope with bewildering demands in the aftermath of combat operations. Complicating everything, Garrick had been deeply wounded by the loss of a friend, a pain for which Algernon could offer nothing more than prayers.

The Long Journey: *Home*

But Garrick didn't believe in prayers. Though he extended grace to Brenna for her religious view, Algernon concluded that his brother's love for the girl made her beliefs easier to handle. Besides, Brenna projected confidence in her faith and piety beyond anything the young monk could muster. Algernon worried about his spiritual shortcomings and felt too afraid to admit this to his older brother.

Yet the cynicism to which he'd ascribed for so long began crumbling in the light of recent experience. In the midst of a profound spiritual change, Algernon needed someone who could help him process his convoluted thinking, but Garrick had neither the time nor the inclination to do so.

The mentor Algernon needed did not exist in his own family. He found the deeply personal religion of the Lithians too informal and dependent on emotion for his taste. He liked the Abelscinnians individually, but didn't approve of their polygamous social structure and thought their holy writings were too rigid and restrictive. So he simply didn't fit-in a spiritual sense-within the Velez household, and didn't think he could tolerate staying as a guest for much longer.

Besides, Algernon found it nearly impossible to exist in close proximity to Cynthia Velez without leering at her all day. He couldn't talk to her without stumbling over his words, dropping something, drooling or otherwise making a complete fool of himself. She was too pretty, too shapely, and he simply didn't feel comfortable with her.

It took every bit of self-control for him not to let his gaze linger at her reflection in a window, or steal a glance when he thought nobody would notice, and the fact that she seemed oblivious to all of this indicated a degree of naivete that Algernon didn't want to spoil. He knew he couldn't sustain a relationship with her. He just wanted her in a raw, physical way that had nothing to do with love. His conscience warned that lusting after Brenna's younger sister would bring trouble, and he didn't want his own libido complicating things for Garrick.

Astrid, though skinny and fragile, had become the girl he wanted for all the right reasons. Intelligent, engaging and kindly, she'd grown into a friend he could trust. During the time they'd spent together his feelings for her evolved into appreciation, admiration, love and eventually, desire. Even Kira could see this.

But Astrid was a lesbian, and Kira was right in saying he could never have her.

The Long Journey: *Home*

Brimming with frustrations, Algernon tossed a rock toward the trunk of a tree. He needed a purpose, a goal, a reason to live. All of the energy invested in his quest to find Kira had made him feel vibrant and alive. Now that she'd been fully restored to him, he found that reading astronomy books in the observatory didn't capture his imagination anymore. What good did knowledge of the stars and planets do for him if studying wrought no practical meaning to his life?

Tamaria, the land of mountains, glaciers, huge trees and falling water was the place where he belonged. Everything he loved about life could be found there. Tamaria was home. Tamaria was where Marie lived . . .

Where had that thought come from? Did he even care about her anymore?

* * *

The lingering and distasteful aroma of sewage gradually faded after Luther Sondheim repeatedly scrubbed his body and clothes with soap and water. Nonetheless, he'd become the butt of many jokes among other members of Third Platoon, some of whom continued to talk to him with their noses plugged long after the stench for which he'd become infamous had worn off.

"The Kamerese prisoners need to change their underwear," Kellen Bauer teased. "Captain Diego will change with Corporal Hernandez, who will change with Lieutenant Sanchez, but nobody wants to change with you because everyone knows that your underwear smells like . . ."

"Sondheim!" Sergeant Ringer roared, stalking into the community center that his squad had been tasked to clean up. The sergeant held a piece of paper in his hand and stomped over to the window frame where Luther Sondheim was carefully removing broken glass. "What is this?"

Luther looked embarrassed and lowered his voice in an effort to deflect everyone else's attention away. "It's a request form, sergeant. You know what it is!"

"Have you lost your mind, boy? Have you stopped to think?"

A pained expression crossed Luther's face while Sergeant Ringer pulled him aside so that no one else could hear their conversation. "So I want to make her an honest woman. What's wrong with that?"

The Long Journey: *Home*

Sergeant Ringer came directly to the point. "Since you've swapped your grey matter for granite, let me make this very clear. This girl from the winery is no innocent thing you met at the Temple one day. She took one look at you and realized you'd be her free pass out of Kameron."

"But sarge, you don't even know her!"

"Ha!" he replied. "I don't even know her? Do you? She had your pants down within ten minutes of seeing your face! Convince me that she loves you for your mind and work ethic, soldier! Go on!"

Luther felt like he'd been backed into a corner. Something in the sergeant's testimony rang true, and Luther really hadn't thought about it that way. "Getting married was my idea," he admitted. "I just figured it was the right thing to do."

Sergeant Ringer sighed, letting his wrath cool. He put his arm on Luther's shoulder in a fatherly way. "I was born in the morning," he began, "but not this morning. You want to marry this girl because you've had a little fun with her, what she did for you was exciting, and you figure you'd like more of that sweetness; but your conscience has been bothering you, right?"

Luther nodded.

"That's 'cause you're a decent kid." Sergeant Ringer moved his hand and glanced at the men who'd been pretending to work while straining to listen. "If you want to marry this girl, that's really your business. But I want you to think about this for a couple of days. She's a foreigner. You really don't know who she is, or what got her into the mess she was in when we found her. You've never met her family, either. Think about that, boy! You don't know what you're getting into.

"Somewhere back home, there's a nice Tamarian girl who'd just love to have a handsome soldier for a husband. Why don't you stick to your own kind?"

"What about Lieutenant Ravenwood?" Luther asked. "He's got a foreign girl. Have you given him the same advice?"

That remark bordered on insubordination, but Sergeant Ringer let it go. "You find someone like her, and I'll give you my blessing! I'll even be the best man at your wedding!" Sergeant Ringer gave the request back to Luther. "Think about it, son. Don't do something you'll regret later on. If you still want to marry this girl in a couple of days, I'll talk to the lieutenant and we'll get the paperwork started."

Luther suddenly looked hopeful. "You think he'll let me do this?"

The Long Journey: *Home*

Sergeant Ringer shook his head. "If you'd kept your trousers buttoned back at the winery, we'd be having a very different conversation right now!"

*   *   *

After Mariel collected all the data from Alpha Company's successful attack on Helena, she spent most of the afternoon analyzing everything in order to give Colonel Adler an after-action briefing. Although she knew better than to examine the evidence with preconceived ideas about what conclusions should be drawn, the facts fit perfectly into the scenario she'd laid out three days earlier.

A conference room on the upper floor of the city hall served as the meeting place for the battalion intelligence briefing. Far more spacious and comfortable than the command tent, the room boasted tall casement windows on its eastern wall, a high ceiling, and though cooler air from below wafted through its open door, the air inside still felt hot and sweat-inspiring. It had an odor faintly reminiscent of a classroom, tainted by the aroma of old leather and lingering cigar smoke.

Lieutenant Hougen stood in front of a large wall map to present an overview of the battalion's current status, then launched into a post battle analysis of the Tamarian success against Lord Navarro's rebel army. She reported her findings on the crumbling resistance to the cease-fire and the burgeoning collection of captured Kamerese small arms and artillery tubes.

"You seem a little smug, lieutenant," Colonel Adler remarked.

Mariel tightened her lips, wondering if she'd ever manage to impress this man. "Only because all of the data I've collected indicate that Lord Navarro commenced his force relocation three days ago. He'd been moving his troops toward *Lago Caliente* before we engaged any of the units guarding his rear flank. Either he had poor intelligence concerning where we were, or he vastly underestimated our ability to project power."

"I'm not clear about this," Colonel Adler stated. "Are you claiming that we took Helena because it had been abandoned?"

"No sir," Mariel replied, shaking her head. "Alpha Company fought hard to take the town and suffered heavy losses. It was strongly defended."

The Long Journey: *Home*

"That makes no sense, lieutenant. You say the battle was over less than 30 minutes after its inception. I realize this place is very small, but how can you say the rebels fought fiercely when a single, outnumbered company captured all of its objectives so quickly?"

"There are two main factors involved here," she replied. "The first comes from the testimony of several front line sergeants who were engaged in the actual combat. They tell me that the Kamerese response to our attack was poorly coordinated. In particular, when Third Platoon took the city hall rebel units responding to their assault were unable to determine where they'd come from and could not mount an effective counterattack.

"I spoke to four rebel commanders who said they'd called artillery strikes down on the school and along the northern end of Zinfandel Avenue in the hope of blunting our advance. First Platoon took a real beating along the eastern edge of this shelling.

"But Third Platoon had already moved 400 yards south of that position, so much of the rebel artillery barrage ended up being fratricidal. Kamerese units attempting to flank First Platoon on the west did not coordinate their movements, and thus were caught beneath their own salvo. Survivors retreated south, only to run into a squad from Third Platoon. These enemy soldiers simply had nowhere to go, didn't realize how few troops we had on the ground, and their confusion contributed significantly to our success." Mariel used the wall map of Helena with a pointer to illustrate as she spoke.

Lieutenant Colonel Ernst, the battalion Executive Officer, wrinkled his forehead and pointed at the map with his thick finger. "What was Third Platoon doing out there all by itself?"

Mariel suppressed a grin. "That's the second point, sir. Taking the city hall had been their objective," she replied. "They infiltrated the town using stealth, then stormed the building and took its defenders by surprise. That's how they captured Lord Navarro, Lord Fang and forced the cease-fire."

Colonel Adler tilted his head to the side and pointed at Mariel. "Third Platoon, huh? That's the one led up by that young kid... What's his name?"

"Lieutenant Ravenwood," Mariel responded.

"Yeah, that's him!" The fact that Mariel knew his name favorably impressed the colonel. "General Braun told me to keep an eye on that boy."

The Long Journey: *Home*

"He's got a good head for combat," Mariel said with restrained, yet evident, pride. "Navarro thought he was safely out of our reach. Neither he nor Fang believed they'd be attacked here without warning."

"Did Navarro admit this to you?" Lieutenant Colonel Ernst asked, wondering how the pretty analyst had come up with this idea.

"Lord Navarro isn't talking right now," she replied. "But I've interviewed his subordinates and they were all shocked to see our forces in town so quickly. We captured signed battle orders, three maps detailing troop movements and an outline of their logistical plans when we took the city hall. After studying these, it's clear that Navarro intended to retreat toward *Lago Caliente* once his forces had taken the reservoir, and then push south to isolate the Velez Lithians and crush them against Lord Fang's army in a classic hammer and anvil."

Colonel Adler nodded. "But we took the hammer out of Navarro's hand."

"Exactly," Mariel replied. "Prior to their contact with us, the rebels had never faced a disciplined, motivated and professional force before encountering Alpha Company. Our people did a remarkable job."

Lieutenant Colonel Ernst nodded, understanding. "You report losses for Alpha Company that approach 25%. If our tactics and firepower were so effective, how do you explain the high casualties?" He asked the question seeking to improve Tamarian training.

Mariel took a deep breath. "The casualty counts were disproportionate across all three platoons. Second platoon lost only 15% of its force, mostly in the heavy street fighting required to secure their objective here in Helena. In general, they encountered less opposition on the way into town than either First or Third Platoon; hence they were also the healthiest group going in.

"First Platoon met substantial resistance when taking a monastery located about seven miles north of here, and entered the fight for Helena with a 12% casualty rate. Unfortunately, the rebels planted a mine field in a vineyard to the east of Zinfandel Avenue in an effort to channel any attack by our forces into a direct approach against their prepared positions along the street. Therefore, Lieutenant Schmidt's advance was slowed by the need to navigate around the mine field.

"Further, First Platoon got caught out in the open during the initial stages of the assault and suffered most of their losses during the

The Long Journey: *Home*

Kamerese artillery barrage. By the time the cease-fire went into effect, 13 of 33 men, including their lieutenant, had been killed or wounded."

Sergeant Major Dylan Seller let out a low whistle, his brow knitted in concern, but as was his custom, he didn't say anything.

Mariel glanced at him and nodded. "Third Platoon had already hit a 24% casualty rate before beginning their final attack on Helena."

Colonel Adler stopped her. "They initiated their assault in that condition? Was Captain Engels aware of their disposition?"

"Not initially sir," Mariel replied. "The rebels had set up an ambush near a packing plant a mile or so north of town. Third Platoon walked right into it and that's the engagement that pushed them close to the edge."

"Were those losses reported to Captain Engels?"

Mariel nodded. "Yes sir. I checked into that personally. Captain Engels ordered Third Platoon recalled and sent battalion reserves relieve them, but Lieutenant Ravenwood acted on earlier orders and moved forward with to capture his objective. By the time the revised orders arrived, he had already taken Navarro prisoner and secured the cease-fire."

Colonel Adler felt his blood pressure rising. He shook his head in incredulity and stopped short of saying the rude remark that nearly spilled from his lips. "The gods must be smiling down on that kid!"

"Lucky for us!" she replied, thinking about Brenna and the strong possibility that the colonel's words carried more truth than he realized.

"Tell me about our current threats," the colonel ordered. "What are we facing right now."

Mariel felt relief that she didn't have to discuss Garrick anymore. "The most imminent danger exists among isolated rebel units occupying territory on the Velez estate. These consist of more experienced troops who've not acknowledged the cease-fire orders."

"You talked about this yesterday," Lieutenant Colonel Ernst reminded her. "What kind of success have we enjoyed in dislodging these forces?"

"As of noon today we had only one hot spot remaining in our area," she replied. "Two platoon-sized enemy units remained in separate locations on the northern heights of Maidenhair Ridge. They were part of a larger force that occupied a strong position overlooking

The Long Journey: *Home*

the flood control dams on Maidenhair Creek and prevented the Abelscinnians from turning the water for Helena back on."

Colonel Adler had tasked Gamma Company to clear that area the day before. "I take it you've heard nothing definitive concerning their surrender?"

"It's only a matter of time, sir. We now enjoy a significant advantage in troop strength and firepower. The rebel units are cut off, have no artillery support, and there's no reason to expect they can hold out for the balance of the afternoon."

"I would like that resistance crushed before General Braun arrives tomorrow morning," Colonel Adler said. "What about other rebel warlords allied with Fang and Navarro?"

Mariel had just read a dispatch from a Special Forces unit watching critical road and rail lines. "Thus far we have no indication that any additional rebel units have detached from their main, combined force in pursuit of the KNA and turned toward us. The army we should be most concerned with is lead by a man the rebels call *El Caudillo*. He's ruthless, and he commands the largest and most capable force"

"How long do we have to wait before the airships arrive?"

"We should have overflight capability within three days, if the weather holds," Mariel replied. "We'll be able to keep a close eye on large scale rebel movements. They won't be able to surprise us."

"Very well!" The colonel turned to his Executive Officer. "Let's give the boys from Alpha Company a couple of days to rest. It sounds like they could use it."

*   *   *

Lynden Velez arrived home at twilight, just after the Daystar set. He took a bath, shaved and changed into clean clothes before coming into his house to meet with Alexina. Though they'd been married for 35 years, the sight of her still stirred Lynden's heart, and as she beckoned to him from the upstairs balcony, the Lithian warlord felt the familiar, comforting sensation of her nearness envelop his soul with quiet joy.

He could tell from the subtle expression lingering on her gentle face that she'd been worried for his safety. Alexina reached for her husband and lightly caressed his cheek, offering her lips for a warm, welcoming kiss.

The Long Journey: *Home*

"I've missed you!" she breathed, shutting her eyes and melding into his strong embrace. The hard bulge of their child, growing steadily within her womb, pressed against his loins in contrast with the yielding of her swollen breast. Alexina nuzzled her head against his right shoulder and thanked Allfather for preserving her husband's life.

Her hair smelled fragrant. On her fingers Lynden could see smears of oil pigment. She'd been working on a long unfinished painting, a peaceful landscape along the Sea of Tranquility that neither of them were ever likely to see again. "You've occupied the cherished places of my secret thoughts," he admitted.

Alexina smiled. "That's my home. That's where I belong."

They retreated to their room and shut the door, sitting close together on their bed so they could talk. Knowing that Brenna had visited with him and understanding her husband's mind, Alexina let him initiate the conversation when he was ready.

"Blynn came to see me," he said. "Her Tamarian commander asked that she arrange a meeting between me and their Division commander, General Leo Braun. I've invited him to come for dinner tomorrow evening."

"Most of our servants are not here," she reminded her husband. "This will have to be a simple affair."

"Blynn told me that the Tamarians are sensitive on the issue of servanthood. They will prefer it that way."

The faintest hint of a smile moved on Alexina's lips. "Did she introduce you to Garrick?" she inquired.

"No, he was detained with command responsibilities and could not make the trip."

"Then I am thrice blessed!" Alexina teased. "Blynn has come to see me twice, and the first time she brought the boy with her."

"Are you impressed?" Lynden inquired.

"He is handsome and even better mannered than his brother," she replied.

Lynden tightened his lips and narrowed his eyes. "I'd like to meet and spend time with this boy who has captured my daughter's heart." He paused, thinking, then turned toward his wife again. "Are you impressed with him?"

"Hmm," Alexina breathed. "He's hardly old enough to shave, yet seems wise beyond his years. I watched him treat his wayward sister with gentleness and compassion. He is a great warrior, and Tegene, whom we both trust, regards him highly."

Lynden raised his eyebrows. "Dear wife," he said with a hint of warning in his voice, "don't play with me. Are you impressed?"

Alexina laughed lightly. "What I think is less important than what Blynn thinks, don't you agree?"

"I agree that you are being evasive, and that tells me much of what I need to know." Lynden sat back and crossed his arms.

"Do you oppose their union?" she inquired.

Lynden moved his eyes toward her, then stared at the wall across the room. "Blynn admitted to me that they are not married."

"They might as well be," Alexina replied. "They are promised to one another."

"Yet she insists that despite their devotion, they both remain chaste," he stated. "That fact speaks well of his self-control. I admit that initially, I felt concern he would be much like his younger brother."

"Algernon struggles, but not in vain," she countered. "Among his people the unmarried do not display their beauty as we do, and I see that he is trying to avert his eyes, especially when Thea is nearby.

"Now, do you honestly think our Blynn would bind her heart to someone lacking discipline? She knows what is right and good."

Lynden nodded slowly, contemplatively. "Of course," he agreed. "But I would have much preferred that she select a mate from among our own community."

Alexina laughed out loud. "My father said the same thing of you!" she teased.

"I am referring to a man of our own faith, dear wife. Blynn has also admitted that her boy is not a *believer*." Lynden's gaze reflected worry that would have seemed irrational to anyone who did not share his belief in Allfather God.

"Why do I find myself defending him to you?" Alexina asked. "Have you no confidence in your daughter's judgment?"

"I trust in Allfather alone," Lynden replied. "Blynn has to live with her choices, but I do fear that in this matter she is allowing her feelings to interfere with good judgment. We know very little of this boy's family, and most of what we have learned thus far has not been complimentary. While we realize that the path of a man is not determined by his upbringing, the binding of two lives is not an act that should be undertaken lightly.

"Besides, my beloved, you will outlive me and all of our children. This has been an issue of contention with your parents and older relatives since we first met. Should Blynn marry this boy the same will be true of her, provided their union is a fruitful one."

"Oh, he's a warrior," Alexina teased, running her index finger along her husband's jaw. "I wouldn't worry about that!"

Lynden acknowledged the running joke about their fertility difficulties with a low murmur, an affectionate nuzzling and a gentle kiss on Alexina's ear.

"And isn't this the same choice I faced in marrying you?" she inquired. "If I found you the most noble of all men, and knowing you would perish before my time, elected to lavish my love upon you until your heart beats its last, why should I expect my own daughter to think otherwise?

"Shouldn't we support her decision and offer the counsel she needs to make this love of hers endure? Shouldn't we live according to our faith and accept this boy into our family with the same embrace that Allfather magnanimously extends to us?"

"We should take care," he cautioned, "that we do not discard restraint and wisdom. These are also gifts of Allfather, given for the benefit of all people. Perhaps we would be wiser to defer judgment in this matter until we know more of the boy's character."

"Then what of Cassie and Jared?" Alexina inquired. "Shall we ask him to leave our home and return to his loved ones until we're satisfied with Blynn's future husband?"

This remark cut at Lynden's appeal to wisdom, as he had given his approval of the relationship and formal courting between Acacia and Jared to the young attorney's family. Alexina had every right to bring this up, but Lynden didn't appreciate how quickly she'd found the flaw in his line of reasoning.

"We do not live vicariously through our children," he countered. "I'm not suggesting that we deny Brenna's love, nor reject the one she has chosen as her mate. We have always respected her independence, and we will learn to love the Tamarian boy in time. Yet she asked for my blessing with fear in her eyes. How can I see this and bless their union without knowing the full measure of the man she has chosen?

"Now, as far as Cassie and Jared are concerned, given the circumstances and information available to me at the time, I offered my consent for him to live with us and court Cassie. He's here now, we have come to love him, and we are witnessing the birth of real commitment between them. I would feel more confident in the long-term prospects for Brenna and her Garrick if I could see similar evidence of their fidelity."

"Blynn fears that you will not approve," Alexina responded. "I see an ocean of sorrow in her soul, and beneath a hardened veneer she remains frail. Blynn believes her love for Garrick is a gift from Allfather, but she is torn because though the boy respects her faith, he cannot accept what he does not personally perceive."

Lynden realized his firstborn daughter had changed, knowing from experience how witnessing death on a large scale and personally taking life left scars that could never fully heal. Brenna, though she could boast proficiency with a sword and bow that rivaled any man, now felt the bitter wounds of broken bodies, cruelty and suffering that accompanied combat experience.

"Blynn's emotional vulnerability underscores the wisdom of not rushing forward," Lynden said at length. "If their love is true, we will see evidence in time."

Alexina had been dreading this moment. "I'm not certain she can wait, my love." Once she'd uttered these words, Xina paused, holding her breath. "She has spoken to me of intimate things that a daughter can discuss with her mother, but not her father. She feels a measure of guilt for a strong, physical attraction to this boy, and has pushed him to the point where he feels compelled to marry her."

"So she lied to me?" Lynden asked, anger rising in his voice.

Xina shook her head and constrained her husband with gentle hands. "No love, she did not. The boy has exerted commendable self-control because he loves her. But if Blynn is ready to give up her virtue for him, how much longer can we reasonably expect him to rein in his desire? Blynn is lovely. What man wouldn't want her?

"Garrick is handsome, and truly a gentleman. He's already become an officer, an achievement not attained without strong effort. We know he comes from a troubled home, yet I have seen the redemptive power of Allfather at work among his younger siblings. How do we know that the boy will not, at some time in the future, come to an understanding of Allfather's love when he experiences a full measure of acceptance and grace in our relations with him?"

"You hem me in on all sides, loving wife. How do you expect me to respond?" Lynden, clearly troubled, let out a long sigh.

The Long Journey: *Home*

Alexina straddled his legs and held his face in her soft hands. "With good will," she whispered, her bright eyes alive in the evening light. She kissed him lightly. "With love, honor and understanding."

Lynden pushed his hand through Xina's thick, soft hair and shut his eyes, enjoying the sensation of her silken locks slipping between his fingers. "I share a serious problem with the Tamarian boy," he admitted.

"What is that, my love?"

"We are both utterly bewitched by beautiful Lithian women!"

Alexina giggled. "I am only encouraging you to righteousness," she teased.

Lynden responded by tickling her. "I think you just want to plan a wedding!"

*   *   *

Many hours later, long after the Lithians had gone to bed, Jhiran crept into the room where Kira, Algernon and Astrid lay sleeping. She tapped Kira on the shoulder and put her finger to the girl's lips, encouraging her to rise quietly.

Kira slipped into her robe and stepped over her brother. He lay with his back to Astrid, but the priestess had fallen asleep with her arm draped over his chest. They seemed peaceful together, and for a fleeting moment, Kira recalled the comfort of having Astrid hold her that way.

Jhiran motioned from the doorway. Kira tiptoed outside and followed the gwynling into the courtyard. Getting past the guards keeping watch involved sneaking into the main house kitchen and outside through a window over the sink. Jhiran moved quickly and quietly, while Kira struggled to duplicate the nearly silent path undertaken by her co-conspirator. A narrow blind spot between two of the lookout positions enabled Jhiran and Kira to slip into the shadowy, surrounding woods without being seen.

Light from the twin moons, though they were full, was overpowered by the dominating and eerie illumination of the Great Eye Nebula nearing its high summer periapsis. Jhiran warned Kira that she and the Lithians could see very well in these conditions, but to Kira, the forest growing beyond the Velez villa seemed forbidding and swathed in darkness.

She'd hidden Astrid's bicycle near a foot path. Having checked a map and after scouting the area in the late afternoon, while her brother was studying in the observatory and Astrid remained preoccupied with prayers, Kira saw that by following the trail she'd eventually wind up on the Mistress of the Woods Road near Helena.

As recently as two days ago, the last three miles of this route led through rebel controlled territory, where the double chain helix brand on her left arm would have earned her many kinds of mistreatment. Now, however, the disarmed rebels had gone home en-masse, their positions abandoned, and their pickets disbanded.

Initially, she'd thought to do this alone. Algernon had once described Jhiran as a thief and a skilled fighter who had nearly killed him when they first met, and that inspired an idea in Kira's mind. Anyone who could give her brother trouble in personal combat deserved respect and Kira reconsidered the wisdom of going on this errand alone. She decided that taking someone else along, especially someone with strong martial skills, was a wiser course of action. Though Kira knew how to fight very well, unlike her brother, she remained less willing to risk a violent encounter by herself.

For her part, Jhiran expressed mischievous delight when Kira first approached her about engaging in this clandestine plan. The gwynling could hardly contain her excitement at the prospect of sneaking through the villa at night, right beneath the watchful eyes of Lord Lynden's guard. But Kira didn't know that Jhiran had her own motives when she agreed to accompany the Tamarian girl that night.

Their path seemed uncertain in the darkness. Kira struggled to navigate the bike downhill with Jhiran sitting on its handlebars, and on more than one occasion responded with an emergency correction when Jhiran shrieked for her to turn!

The path vanished in the bleak landscape where Kamerese artillery had shattered the vineyards and flattened pockets of forest. Covering the four-mile route to the Mistress Road took nearly an hour, and for the last twenty minutes or so, Kira pedaled hard across open country, around broken barricades and past the ruins of stone houses destroyed in the conflict.

Maidenhair Creek, the largest tributary of the Virgin River, contributed so much water to her mother stream that beyond its nexus the Virgin River became safely navigable to boat traffic. This was the only reason Helena existed at all, yet the town remained so remote it had never grown beyond a few hundred residents. As she crossed over

The Long Journey: *Home*

the arched bridge leading into the village, Kira found it hard to imagine why anyone would bother sending an invading army to this place.

After stashing the bike beneath the bridge, Kira and Jhiran stole quietly along the northern bank of Maidenhair Creek, then followed a path along the Virgin River for about 200 yards. Remembering the map of Helena she'd studied in the Velez family library, Kira knew that the police station lay adjacent to the port authority building, slightly east of Helena's boat dock. Kira waited near a garbage bin behind the port authority while Jhiran scurried off to scout the police station.

Jhiran didn't come back for a long time. When she returned, the gwynling put an image of the station's back door into Kira's mind, then led her to the place and deftly picked its lock. Jhiran nodded to the Tamarian girl, then pulled out her sling and loaded it with a stone, waiting outside for her turn in the drama.

Kira felt her heart pounding as she ascended the steps and crept into the darkened jail at the back of the police station. She removed her sandals before entering in order to dampen the sound of her feet on the tiled floor, then nervously moved from cell to cell until she found the man she'd been seeking.

"Marco!" she whispered. "Marco! It's me!"

Marco Fang stirred, startled to hear Kira's voice. He sat up and whispered raspily. "Oh baby! I'd been looking all over for you! What are you doing here?"

Kira bristled at his lie, but in the darkness he could not see the telltale signs of anger rising in her face. "I've brought something for you," she said, quietly. "Come here!"

Marco became suspicious and didn't move from his cot. "Why are you here?" he asked. "Are you looking for a fix?"

"No honey, I'm just looking for you."

"How did you get in here? You have a weapon?" he inquired.

"The back door was unlocked, and I have no weapons," she replied, lying.

"Take off your clothes," he ordered. "I want to see you."

Kira shamelessly obeyed, as she'd always done before. Though she'd lost a lot of weight and her womanly curves had diminished, all of the scars from her abuse had vanished. The Tamarian girl looked beautiful in the dim light. She touched her halter top and willed it into her left hand. "Come to me," she called. "I want to kiss you."

The Long Journey: *Home*

Marco felt aroused and filled with a sense of power. He'd always controlled her, and she'd willingly submitted. Maybe Kira could help him escape from this place! Maybe he wouldn't face the wrath of her brother after all ... He came near and gazed at the girl he'd lured away from the Temple in Marvic. What a stupid girl! She'd come back to him like a stray dog, so he felt no remorse for disposing of her. Kira pressed her face next to the bars of his cell, opened her mouth and extended her tongue. When he kissed her, Marco felt electrified and alive.

But then something rapidly wrapped around his neck three times, something strong and tightly wound that instantly deprived him of breath. Marco couldn't even gasp, and though he clutched and tore at the fabric that choked him, its insistent, unyielding stranglehold around his throat sapped his strength. His eyes, widened in horror, saw that Kira gripped one end of a halter top in her left hand, while its other extended around his neck as if responding to her will. On her arm he saw the brand that marked her as his own, but her eyes were otherworldly cold, and vengeance hardened on her lovely face.

Marco felt his life slipping away. He gazed at Kira in horror, astonished at her treachery, desperate and terrified for his life. Just before he blacked out, the cloth released its grip and he slumped to the concrete floor, coughing and gasping for breath.

Kira spat on him. "I had your miserable life in my hand," she said aloud. "I want you to remember that I didn't take it! You disgust me, Marco! When you die, the Great God will make you will lie down in torment!"

She slipped her halter on as other prisoners stirred, pulled her robe over her shoulders and stalked outside, into the darkness.

Jhiran raced in from the shadows, her small form an unexpected apparition that drew Marco's fearful attention. She had her own purpose for accompanying Kira, and had he seen her expression, Marco would have witnessed the rare sight of an angry gwynling, her eyes narrowed and ears pinned back like a vengeful, wild cat. Every memory of pain and abuse Jhiran had pulled from Kira's mind blasted into Marco's consciousness. Vivid, violent images educed a sympathetic nervous response at the cellular level, until he actually felt every bit of pain Kira had experienced under his domination.

Marco tried to scream, but his throat felt constricted, as if he were being choked. Agony pulsed through his body. Endless waves of torment washed over his stricken flesh as every nerve burned hot. He wept, he bled and writhed on the hard floor, desperate to make the affliction end. Jhiran forced the gruesome details of gang rapes, repeated beatings and cruel torture into Marco's memory as if they were his own, until the intense scourging made him long for death.

The other prisoners heard his violent thrashing, but they only saw someone who looked like a child standing in the hall, staring into Marco's cell. A guard stirred, opened the door and turned on the electric lights. He saw what he swore was a little girl vanish into the night through the open back door, and when he heard Marco, opened the cell and tried fruitlessly to help, eventually giving up and heading off to call for a doctor.

By the time he returned, he found Marco suspended from the top of his cell bars, a belt wrapped around his neck, a fresh slave brand burned into the flesh of his left forearm, his body covered in weeping wounds, and a pool of blood beneath his badly torn feet.

* * *

Garrick woke up several times in the darkness, drifting back into a restless sleep filled with anxious dreaming. Later, when he heard the sounds of other men milling around outside his tent he nearly panicked at the thought that he'd slept in, until he remembered that he'd been given a two-day liberty. Though he flopped back onto his cot, work details tasked to clean up Helena and prepare for the return of its citizens created an ongoing, unending opera of loud noises. As an unwilling audience member, he gave up on dreams of additional sleep.

Every muscle in his body felt sore. Shortly after Garrick dressed and relieved himself, Brenna arrived. She wore her wonderfully form-fitting dress uniform with its top buttons loosened and its sleeves rolled up, revealing the impact of a darkening tan and the hint of lighter flesh around the margins of her clothing. She'd washed, combed and carefully braided her hair, and as she approached, the morning light glinted off the gold and silver lions pinned to her collar. Brenna smiled and her dark eyes gleamed in a unique way when she saw him, an expression he'd never seen her extend to anyone else.

The Lithian maiden reached for his hand and stood to whisper in his ear. "My father wants to meet you!"

Garrick desperately felt like kissing her, but did not. "I can't leave unless I report my whereabouts to Captain Engels, and I don't want to meet with your family looking like this!" He gestured toward his appearance for emphasis. "I haven't had a bath, my uniform needs washing and I'm in desperate need of a shave."

"Bring your dress uniform," she said. "You can clean up at my parents' house when we get there. Hurry! They're expecting us!"

Somehow, Brenna had arranged for an EPT to transport them. Given her limited skill in speaking Tamarian and her lack of command authority, Garrick wondered how she'd managed this. The driver, waiting in front of Helena's courthouse, didn't flinch when she and Garrick climbed into the vehicle. He calmly sped off toward the Velez villa as if he'd known their destination all along.

Brenna snuggled close, her excitement palpable. "Many of Tegene's family have already come down from the refugee camp," she told him, illustrating that the Abelscinnians had long been an integral part of the Velez household. "Our servants will arrive tomorrow, and the house will be full again!"

Yet when they reached the villa, it already seemed alive with people. Garrick retreated to the bath house and felt better after a hot scrub. Algernon came in while he was shaving and though the brothers sustained an unimportant conversation while Garrick put on his dress uniform, Algernon seemed distant and mentally preoccupied.

Many members of the Velez household were gathered in the great room as the brothers walked inside, and Garrick wondered how anyone would have been able to move had everyone come down from the refugee camp. Among those present, Brenna introduced Acacia's boyfriend, Jared, and Tegene's second wife, Ubequenisha. The heavyset woman possessed a beautiful smile and a disarming laugh that rang among the rafters. Garrick imagined that her lovely and powerful voice could fill the room with song. She presented her youngest daughter, Chanecia, who apologized that her elder brother and sister were still serving as physicians in the refugee camp and were unable to attend.

Confronted with so many new names and faces, Garrick had no hope of remembering more than a handful of them. He listened patiently as Brenna explained the complicated familial relationships. He greeted strangers warmly, following his girl around as if she were a guide leading him through a collection of rare treasures. Yet among the Lithians and Abelscinnians who lived in the Velez household, Garrick experienced a broad acceptance that made him feel welcome, adopted and at home.

The Long Journey: *Home*

As he concluded a conversation with Jawara, whom Algernon had introduced, Garrick felt Brenna take hold of his hand and pull him away. "Come and meet my father," she said, her face alive with delight. "I've told him all about you!"

In truth, Lynden had been watching carefully. He observed that the Tamarian lieutenant exuded a confident and friendly demeanor, handling people of different languages, culture and religious faith with genuine respect and courtesy. But the kindness Garrick extended toward Brenna, the gentle way the boy dealt with her, the softness of his voice when they spoke, and the way his attention inspired a smile on her face impressed the Lithian warlord more than any singular action he'd witnessed thus far.

"You are my true son," Lynden offered in greeting, extending a welcoming embrace.

Garrick replied in Lithian. "As your God wills, honored father."

Lynden smiled. Brenna had chosen well.

*   *   *

Breakfast lingered among the Lithians. Eating gradually blended into extended conversations lubricated with tea and wine, in which clustered family members and friends exchanged news or discussed issues that concerned them. Jhiran and several of the men rose to clear tables and wash dishes.

When Algernon left the table to help, Astrid and Kira followed. Xola, second son of Penda, Tegene's third wife, asked them to let others serve, but Algernon politely declined. "My brother has joined this family," the monk replied. "We're more than mere guests now."

Alexina, overhearing this, nodded to Xola.

Soon afterward, Brenna excused herself, left Garrick discussing the Velez family history with her parents, and followed Camille, Cassie and Thea back into the great room. As the siblings talked, Brenna sensed that a profound shift had taken place among her sisters, and she felt strangely excluded from the new dynamic that existed among them. They did not deliberately isolate her, but as Brenna listened to the conversation she realized that leadership among the siblings had passed into Cassie's hands. While she accepted the inevitable change with grace, a pang of hurt tingled in her heart.

The Long Journey: *Home*

Realizing this, Acacia picked up her lute and sat with Brenna on the piano bench. Fingers caressed keys and strings, gently and quietly at first, then rising in passion and volume. The young women began a slow improvisation in a major key that soon drew others into the room. Hand drums and stringed instruments, played with a bow, plucked or strummed, joined in until the entire house swelled with sweet, harmonious sound.

And then the voices rose. Camille, Cynthia and Chanecia heard Brenna modulate into a well-known 'Scinnian spiritual song and began picking out harmonies. The men finished their cleaning and joined in. Jawara and Tegene sang a call in rich baritone and bass, while Kimoni in a strong tenor and deeper-voiced Xola sang back their responses.

They sang to honor God's strength and power. They played to praise the one credited with their deliverance and sought to glorify the source of unfathomable love, whose protection shielded them in their troubles. All of the *believers*, though they differed in the manner of their expression and the extent to which their bodies and faces mirrored the joy of their souls, reflected on their lives with gratitude, irrespective of the cultural contrasts in the origins of the songs they sang.

Garrick, listening to this and understanding a fair amount of what was being sung, pondered how these people could credit an abstraction–if God existed at all–with the flesh and blood sacrifice that warriors, like the fallen under his own command, offered for their freedom. He thought about the greed of warlords like Fang and Navarro, who acted out of their own ambition to inflict suffering. Why would a loving God permit such evil men to impose cruelty upon his own people?

Yet something tugged on his heart strings. This wasn't just the result of Brenna's fingers fluttering rapidly and skillfully over the keys, nor the beautiful harmonies lingering in the rafters as song after song rose toward the heavens. Garrick felt an inexplicable force stir memories within his mind. Images of Brenna's valor in combat, and of her vulnerability at Traitor's Pass moved through his consciousness. He thought her form outlined on the winery courtyard cobblestones, of how the very lips that healed deadly wounds now sang offerings of praise in honor of the power flowing though her soul.

He looked at Algernon, whose courage rivaled any warrior he'd ever known, and beautiful Kira, his beloved sister. Now reunited, restored to health, and reconciled to one another–their survival linked

The Long Journey: *Home*

to Brenna and her remarkable family–Garrick felt strong emotion surging from somewhere within and struggled to blink back tears.

Could he attribute their gathering in this place to coincidence? He would have never imagined the scene playing out before his eyes, never dreamed of the awe-inspiring sound reaching his ears. A knot of conflicting feelings gathered in his throat. It all seemed so irrational, and he felt so tired he couldn't make sense of the swelling tide of disconnected feelings washing on the shore of his consciousness.

Brenna smiled blissfully, her peaceful expression reflecting the comfort of familiar melodies whose lyric meanings deepened in light of her recent experience. Garrick watched Brenna turn her head at the sound of Ubequenisha's soaring voice and adjust the improvised line played in her right hand in response. The Lithian girl lost herself in the music, enraptured by the sound of blended voices as the instruments faded and a final chorus echoed in the rafters, a capella.

Garrick clapped his hands together as the last song ended. He didn't realize that Lithians didn't applaud the performance of worship music, but everyone understood he'd meant well and they joined him.

"Hey little brother, why don't you sing for us?" he suggested. "Let's hear a Temple song!"

Algernon, ever the extrovert and appreciating a moment as the center of everyone's attention, shrugged and stood, pulling Astrid to her feet and beckoning for Kira to join them. After a quick discussion, he turned to Brenna and asked her to play a triad in the key of A minor. Tamarian music, stemming from a tradition of overcoming hardship and oppression, moved through sad, moody modulations. Singing a favored tune from the Temple Elsbireth, the three Tamarians quieted the crowd with a hauntingly beautiful, yet restrained trio that contrasted with the energy and exuberance of the Lithian hymns and 'Scinnian spiritual songs.

Listening to his siblings sing with Astrid, hearing the angelic sound of Temple music and thinking of lyrics that testified of their mysterious God, Garrick felt so moved that he had to leave in order to compose himself. It wouldn't do to break down in front of everyone.

In the shade behind the guest house Garrick found a porch swing. To the south, a sweeping vista of hills swathed in hardwood forest drifted into the hazy distance. Several miles away, nestled between the hills like a glistening and precious jewel, *Lago Caliente* shimmered in the heat. Had Lord Navarro gained control over that body of water, it seemed unlikely that a Tamarian officer would now be looking at it without a rifle in hand.

How could Brenna, her family and their friends possibly credit God for the work he and his men had done? Garrick rejected the bitter envy teasing at the fringe of his consciousness. He didn't want to begrudge the *believers* for their faith, yet they overlooked the obvious fact that Tamarian soldiers, well-trained, equipped with modern firepower and led by an experienced senior officer corps, had been the ones who snatched a military victory out of what would have been certain defeat for Lord Velez.

He'd marched 35 miles in two days, carrying his share of the platoon's equipment in the heat of high summer, to reach Helena and stop Lord Navarro. His body ached from the experience, so where was the miracle in that? If God actually existed, why did Third Platoon have to go through so much trouble to get the job done?

In the midst of his thinking, Garrick heard Brenna approach. She'd taken off her boots inside the house, and the milky white of her feet contrasted with the darker flesh of her arms and face. An expression that bordered on worry lingered in her eyes and on her brow. She sat down on the other end of the swing, a distance intended to show respect for Garrick's privacy.

"I know you've never experienced worship," she began. "I know you don't understand what this means to me, but at the core of my being, what you heard and saw in there is central to who I am. I'm a *believer*, Garrick. The words to the songs, the melodies, the act of praising God in the presence of other people honestly reflects the content of my soul. It's as much a part of me as the way I comb my hair, and I've missed the fellowship of others who share my faith since I've been away from home."

When Garrick spoke a sense of determination edged his voice. "Why would I wish to deprive you the joy you experience in singing with your friends and family? I see the rapture on your face, and I hear it in your voice. I watch you play the piano as if the happiness of some angelic host hinged on every note. How could I say that I love you and seek to take that experience away?"

Brenna turned her head and stared at the lake in the distance. "Then why did you get up and leave?"

"This is your home," he replied. "These are your people and this is where you belong. I come from a very different world. I don't ascribe divine providence to the mundane matters of life the way you and your family strive to do."

Garrick shook his head and gestured with his left hand, as if seeking to pull words out of the air. "There's something in you that displays evidence of logic-defying power. It's power that you describe as God's working, but that force simply isn't at work in me."

"How can you say that?" she replied.

"There's nothing supernatural about what I do, Brenna! With me, everything has a rational explanation."

She laughed. "You saved my entire family and stopped a war! Yet you don't think Allfather moves in you?"

"Oh, come on!" he said, dismissively. "I led a combat team into Helena and we captured Lord Navarro. That was flesh, blood and bullets at work."

Brenna rolled her eyes and shook her head. Her hair danced in response. "Your platoon was on the ragged edge of combat viability when we went in there. Where do you think the brilliant idea to sneak through the green belt and capture the town hall came from?"

"Out of my head," he replied.

"And what made you think it was possible to get past the Kamerese like that?"

"I don't know," he answered. "The idea just came to me and I figured we could pull it off."

"Has it ever occurred to you that my healing ability works exactly the same way? You *believed* you could stop the fighting in a way no one else thought was possible. Allfather God honored your faith, and the prayers of many others who were not in a position to impact the outcome, as you were. It started as an idea–an abstract concept, as you are so fond of saying–and you used the tools you had available and the experience you've gained to complete the plan.

"I do exactly the same thing. I *believe* I can heal wounds because Allfather has given me that gift. I use the lips and fingers he gave me, and whenever I'm in a position to help, I can restore wounded flesh according to his will. You and the men in Third Platoon think it's spooky that Allfather's power moves through me, but no more so than the ridiculous thought that a young platoon leader, on his first day of combat, could convince a vengeful warlord to surrender.

"Life itself is a miracle. Day after day God's providence is renewed. We who *believe* see this because we recognize that Allfather sustains all things. This is not an impossible concept to grasp. Even a child can understand."

Garrick shook his head. "It's just the impact of circumstances, and the power of choice," he replied, knowing that there was no sense in arguing with her. Brenna would never see the world as he did. "I simply don't get what seems so obvious to you. So how can I take you away from all of this when worship of Allfather is such an integral part of your identity?" he asked. "How can I ask you to bind your life with mine, when your home is here, with your family?"

Brenna moved closer, shaking her head. She reached for his hand, held it within her own, and paused as tension rose between them. When she spoke, Brenna breathed the words prayerfully. "My home," she replied, "is wherever you are."

The Lithian girl drew near, turned her head slightly, and gently met his lips with her own.

*   *   *

Later that afternoon, Algernon lifted the bicycles that he and Astrid had ridden all the way to Sleepy Hollow into the back of a military truck. Kira bade her eldest brother and Brenna's family a tearful good-bye, then hopped into the passenger's seat.

Algernon embraced Garrick. "Thanks for all your help!" he said, regretting that nothing more profound came to mind. "You hold the key to my heart!"

"And you to mine, little brother!" Garrick replied. "My arrangements will get you to Vengeance, but from there you'll have to buy commercial rail passes. Write to me when you arrive in Marvic. If you need more money, I'll send it along."

"Everyone here has been very generous. Our needs are few and I'm sure we won't need more help." Algernon patted his burgeoning money pouch. The entire Velez household had taken up an offering to get the three Tamarians back home in style, and Algernon now carried more than enough to see himself and his sister through the winter.

The brothers tarried together for a while, searching for words that eluded them. The Velez family and all of Tegene's clan gathered to wish them well. Jhiran folded herself into Algernon's arms and gave him a lingering embrace. Then she did the same for Astrid, but said nothing in farewell.

The Long Journey: *Home*

After receiving a kiss on the cheek from Brenna, Algernon helped Astrid into the back of the truck and climbed aboard. As the machine accelerated through the compound's gate and downhill toward Helena, Algernon saw Garrick and Brenna race to the estate entrance and wave. The gwynling appeared at Brenna's side, and for a moment, Algernon heard her words in his mind: "Find peace in your mountain home, holy man."

Algernon and Astrid traveled in silence, their thoughts occupied by a similar energy, a desire urging them back to familiar places. Following the winding road downhill, over battlefields and through Helena, neither Algernon nor Astrid spoke. The sweat-inducing and lethargy-inspiring heat smothered any thought of conversation, yet Algernon, who knew his moments with Astrid were numbered, cherished her company despite her silence.

Within an hour they'd left the visible scars of warfare behind. Small groups of local people trudged toward home, having left the refugee camp upon hearing the news of a Tamarian victory. Occasionally the truck had to yield so that traffic supplying the Expeditionary Force could pass along the narrow road. As the landscape climbed away from the river, changing from orchard and vineyard country into high, rolling hills covered in golden grasses, a breeze blew into the open back of the canvas-sided truck, carrying the promise of a cooler climate further north.

Somewhere in the midst of Lord Lynden's land, the truck stopped at a military depot. Many hundreds of soldiers and literally tons of equipment waited transport further south. Here, the three Tamarians disembarked so that the truck that had carried them thus far could recharge its batteries.

Algernon found the Resource Integration and Allocation Center, or RIAC, as the army boys called it, and presented the paperwork his brother had prepared for him that arranged transport back to Vengeance, the industrial town on the Desolation River. The officer coordinating the movement of equipment offered transport up to the refugee camp with crates of captured Kamerese weaponry, but warned Algernon that he'd have to wait for an hour or so before the truck was fully loaded for departure.

That hour turned into 90 minutes. Algernon, Astrid and Kira sat beneath an oak tree and played memory games to occupy their time. Kira began by calling out two numbers. Algernon added these two and

The Long Journey: *Home*

gave her the sum. Then Astrid gave him another number, to which Algernon calculated the absolute value difference with the second number Kira had given him. Then Kira gave him a third number, to which Algernon multiplied with the previous number Astrid had given him and stated the product. He cycled through addition, subtraction and multiplication in order, with the two girls checking his accuracy.

This tricky exercise continued until he made an error, then Kira took her turn, and after her, Astrid followed. When they tired of doing this, they played "Misfortune Cookie" for a while. By the time their transport further north was ready, the Great Eye had risen and the Daystar was well on its way over the western horizon.

They arrived at the Tualitin River well after dark, and because the cable ferry was not running until morning, they camped near the riverbank. The snowy, southern peaks of the Angelgate Mountains loomed in the distance, and Algernon's heart beat faster upon seeing the high ridge lines of his homeland.

Overhead, an aurora veiled the heavens in a shifting, diaphanous curtain of green and pink light. Through this iridescent glow Algernon pointed out the various stars and planets in the darkening sky, while Astrid and Kira competed to see who would first locate one of the many meteors streaking across the heavens.

Later, after eating, Algernon and Kira shared funny stories of their childhood in Deception Creek as they sat around Algernon's tin can cookstove. Though Astrid listened attentively, all of her memories came out of the Temple Elsbireth, and knowing Kira's sensitivity to that place, she didn't want to talk about growing up there.

When they grew tired and lay down, Algernon stared into the heavens until Astrid's breathing became shallow and rhythmic. He slid his arm around her waist and felt her fingers link with his own. The young monk held his breath and restrained his desire until he grew accustomed to her nearness and fell asleep.

* * *

He arose as the Great Eye disappeared beyond the western horizon, its fading eerie, blue-green halo lingering in the distance. Astrid and Kira remained asleep as he crept away to walk along the riverbank. He found a discreet place where the swirling, clear waters of the Tualitin invited a bath, stripped and waded in. Though he didn't

The Long Journey: *Home*

feel a need to wash, cold water quenched his ardor, and as he shivered in the shallows he wondered what had prompted Astrid to allow him so close the night before.

He dressed, then prayed and stretched. When he returned, both girls were drinking tea and chatting. Astrid offered him a cup as he sat down. After drinking, he washed their mugs in the river and helped the girls pack up for the day. He longed to talk to Astrid alone, but Kira stayed close and her nearness deprived him of any opportunity for private conversation.

Two steel cables, anchored to opposite shore lines and stretched across the river, served as guides for the ferry. Vanes affixed to the bottom of the ferry boat channeled the water one way or the other, allowing the current to power the boat to each side. Though not large, this ferry crossed quickly. Every Tamarian soldier and piece of equipment now located in Kameron owed its presence on foreign soil to this ingenious, yet remarkably simple engineering marvel.

The Tamarians ate fruit and bread for breakfast while waiting for the ferry to start for the day. With the expeditionary deployment in full swing, the boat would have gone to the Tamarian shoreline carrying only sealed crates of confiscated Kamerese weaponry, were it not for the three travelers heading home. Astrid feared the river and gripped Algernon's arm the entire time, relaxing only after they'd safely landed on Tamarian soil.

They boarded a bus that had just offloaded a group of soldiers, and followed a dusty road leading into the Angelgate foothills. The vehicle climbed laboriously toward a small firebase overlooking the river. Grey and angular concrete walls rose from the heights, and far below the golden fields of Northern Kameron baked under the heat of another summer morning.

All firebases were connected by rail. What would have been a 105 mile, two and a half hour trip up to the Desolation River, had they been able to travel in a straight line, instead required nearly four hours of travel in an empty passenger car. As the train wound through the forested hills of Southeastern Tamaria, Algernon pondered the isolation of an area where small clusters of homesteads huddled in narrow valleys that drained toward the southwest. Because no large settlements existed here, the families living in this area formed tightly knit communities largely independent of other regions.

The Long Journey: *Home*

A long grade swept down to the shore of the Desolation River. The train crossed a high trestle over the river gorge shortly before noon, then stopped on the far bank to take on fuel and water. Rail workers attached several cars containing raw materials and metals for recycling to the locomotive, and the many crates of Kamerese weapons that had accompanied the travelers on their journey were offloaded onto the dock, destined for Burning Tree.

Directly north lay a series of broad and fertile valleys where most of the Tamarian population lived. Fast flowing rivers spilled from high peaks, creating a natural transportation network and a means to generate power for manufacturing. Weary of talking and playing games, the travelers fell into silence, each one lost in thoughts of how the past led into the future.

Four and a half hours later, the military train pulled into Vengeance. The thundering of the Venom River rumbled through the ground as Algernon bought civilian rail passes for the last leg of their journey. Since the train bound for Marvic did not depart until the next morning, the travelers found an inn for the night. Astrid fed Algernon while Kira ate on her own, eyeing the way her brother interacted with her former lover and wondering where their kindness toward one another would lead.

They each took separate rooms that evening. Alone with many troubled thoughts, Astrid lit a votive candle and prayed. She interceded for Algernon, knowing that leading him on in the hope that something might develop between them was fundamentally wrong. Though she needed his comfort, cared about him and could see that he genuinely loved her, Astrid didn't feel any physical attraction toward him. She wanted Kira, and knew without question that if she couldn't have the girl, no one else would do. Lost in fervent prayer, Astrid struggled with the core of her sexual identity and felt an urge to do what Priestess Dorothea had counseled long ago.

Astrid decided to close the door on her love affair and take a sacred vow of celibacy. Once she'd uttered the words, though no one bore witness to her deed, Astrid felt peace flooding her soul. When she blew out the candle and went to sleep, the priestess fell into deep and satisfying rest.

Algernon hoped that Astrid would come to him that night, but when she did not he lay awake for hours, struggling with strong desire. He dreamed of her in the darkness, and when he awoke at dawn,

The Long Journey: *Home*

Algernon felt tired. He arose experiencing a sense of profound loss, knowing that this was the last day he'd ever spend in Astrid's company, and not knowing how he would handle another night without her.

Kira noticed her brother's moodiness, understood his motivation, but found no words to encourage him. On their final train ride north, Kira spent a lot of time thinking about the events leading to her escape from the Temple. She wanted to forgive Astrid and ask forgiveness for hurting the priestess, but whenever she made eye contact, lingering pain in her soul clutched at every word the rational part of her mind sought to utter.

The uneventful train ride to Marvic took well over seven hours. Though the afternoon felt warm in the city, the air retained its familiar freshness. The travelers moved through a crowd of people who deferred respectfully and offered grateful thanks for the blessings received from the young priest and his two companions. Algernon and Astrid picked up their bikes and turned toward the walled heights of the sacred mountain, where the Temple Elsbireth stood.

At the base of the forty-seven hundred stairs, Astrid turned to Kira. "I want you to have my bike," she said. "I won't be needing it anymore."

Desperate to savor a few more minutes in Astrid's company, Algernon offered to climb the stairs with her. Leaving the bikes below, the travelers joined dozens of pilgrims ascending the broad stone steps where many generations of the faithful had climbed to utter prayers in the lofty monastery. A healthy person required the better part of an hour to complete the journey, but there were prayer stops along the way that sometimes extended this time considerably.

Astrid struggled toward the top, stopping frequently to regain her breath and gaze out over the blue roofs and green belts winding through the city. Her countenance brightened in anticipation as she neared the summit. Her stringy hair and a multitude of fraying prayer banners danced in the wind, the rippling of fabric a familiar and comforting sound.

At the Sacred Gate Astrid stopped, knowing that Kira and Algernon could go no further. Marie, the well-endowed girl who'd once occupied a revered place in Algernon's thinking, and Dietrich, the boy whom he'd knocked to the mat many weeks ago, stood at the Temple entrance to welcome its visitors. Both acolytes ignored the blessings of entering pilgrims in their astonishment at seeing Algernon, Kira and Astrid together again.

Dietrich's face reddened in shame and anger, while Marie smiled coquettishly, but Algernon's eyes remained riveted on Astrid and he paid no attention to her. Marie had finally lost the right of relevance to Algernon's experience.

Astrid embraced Kira. They held one another for a long time, exchanging tears. Somehow Kira found the emotional courage to whisper into Astrid's ear. "I'm sorry for hurting you!" she said, sniffing. "Please forgive me!"

Astrid let her go, though their fingertips lingered, and nodded. "I do," she replied.

"Thank you for everything. Thank you for saving me. Thank you for saving my brother and giving him back to me again!"

"He loves you, Kira. Hold on to him!"

Then, turning to Algernon, Astrid tilted her head and gave him a soft, lingering kiss on the lips. "Goodbye, my friend!" she said.

"I love you!" he whispered, embracing her, his grey eyes brimming with tears. "I will never forget you!"

She nodded knowingly. The priestess wiped her eyes as she let go, turned toward the Sacred Enclosure, and walked inside without looking back.

Algernon held onto his sister outside the Sacred Gate until their feelings passed. Then, looking into the reddened, wet eyes of his twin, Algernon squeezed her hand. "Come on, Kira," he said. "Let's go home."

robert luis rabello
13:44
27 July 2006

A Lexicon of Uncommon Words

ablated: removed by abrasion or evaporation
alluvium: sediments deposited by flowing water
anadromous: fish that migrate up rivers from the sea to breed in fresh water
antiphonal: an array of organ pipes upon which responding melodies are played
arêtes: sharp-crested ridges in rugged mountains
arroyo: a deep gully cut by an intermittent stream
atlatl: a device for throwing a spear or dart that consists of a rod or board with a projection (as a hook) at the rear end to hold the weapon in place until released
chaparral: a biome characterized by hot dry summers and cool moist winters and dominated by a dense growth of mostly small-leaved evergreen shrubs
concupiscent: devoted to sexual love
coprophagiac: one who suffers from a mental disorder characterized by the consumption of excrement
cryosphere: a region of frozen water and permanently frozen ground
drumlin: an elongated hill or ridge of glacial drift
cerebral edema: potentially lethal swelling of the brain
encephalic: of or relating to the brain
epiphytes: plants, such as a tropical orchid or a staghorn fern, that grow on another plant upon which it depends for mechanical support but not for nutrients
esker: a long narrow ridge or mound of sand, gravel, and boulders deposited by a stream flowing on, within, or beneath a stagnant glacier
flechette: small, sharp anti-personnel fragments delivered by an artillery shell
fuller: a blood groove in a longsword made by a blacksmith's hammer
gas retort: a device that partially burns solid fuel to create heat and combustible gas
glissade: a gliding step in ballet, used to describe the bending of branches in the wind
heliostat: a device that tracks the path of a sun across the sky
jackleg: a drill with an air leg used in building tunnels through rock
jingoism: extreme nationalism
lapilli gravel: volcanic ashes, consisting of small, angular, stony fragments

loess: windblown deposits of fine-grained, calcareous silt or clay
maudlin: effusively sentimental
mensa: the flat, upper surface of an altar
microencephalon: small-brained, and therefore, not very smart!
oculus: a circular opening at the top of a dome
onager: a heavy catapult
ostinato: a short melodic pattern repeated continually, usually in the same part at the same pitch
periapsis: the point of nearest distance in the orbit of a celestial body relative to a gravitational center
psionic: an attenuated exosynapse enabling physical control beyond the body
psittacism: rote, repetitive recitation of words without consideration of their meaning
pyroclastic: composed chiefly of rock fragments of volcanic origin
ricasso: an unsharpened and unbeveled section just above the guard or handle of a sword
sacrosanct: regarded as sacred and inviolable
sanctimonious: feigning piety or righteousness
stoss: facing the direction of glacial movement
talus: a slope formed by an accumulation of rock debris
tarn: a small steep-banked mountain lake or pool
thurible: a censer used in certain ecclesiastical ceremonies or liturgies
vicariously: living as though one were taking part in the experience or feelings of another

Proof

4305412

Made in the USA
Charleston, SC
28 December 2009